原　文

魯　濱　孫　飄　流　記

附　譯　文　註　釋

THE LIFE AND ADVENTURES OF

ROBINSON CRUSOE

BY

DANIEL DEFOE

WITH CHINESE NOTES AND

TRANSLATIONS

BY

U.Y.CHANG. AND P.S.CHENG.

EDITED BY

RICHARD S. C. HSI.

1

凡　　例

（一）本公司所輯譯加註之標準英文文學讀本凡十餘種，均歐美名
　　　家之傑作，適用於中等學校，為時已久，可供中等學校教科及
　　　學者自修參考之用。

（一）此類英文文學讀本，學生欲明瞭其深意，細加翻檢，每以功課
　　　繁重，常恐時間不足；故譯成中文，置於原文之旁，以省讀者
　　　翻檢之勞，俾收心領神會之益。

（一）本書原文意義深奧，恐讀者難於明瞭，故於譯文之外，再加詳
　　　註，以1—2—3—4……等號碼，置於斜體字之左上角，作為標
　　　記，易於參照查閱。

（一）凡譯文之中有「　」記號者，其括號內之文字，乃補充文意不
　　　足之處，惟恐依照原文直譯，不能令讀者明瞭本義，故用括號
　　　內之文字補充之。

（一）本書原文用意深刻，謬為譯註，不免為大雅所譏。如蒙隨時賜
　　　教改善，則感甚幸甚！

狄 孚 旦 尼 爾 小 傳

—— 生 於 1 6 6 1 年 ——

—— 死 於 1 7 3 9 年 ——

　　狄孚生於1661年，他是一個倫敦的屠夫的兒子。他的生活是由貧而富，再由小康而變成造磚的，隨後他又變成祗求飯喫的新聞記者，又從犯人而變爲許多人所崇拜的人物。這種生活過程眞是難以盡述了。不過有四點可以使讀者明瞭他的作品的風格：第一期他是個商人，同時又是個作者，他對於勞工階級有極大的興趣；他很想敎導平民，那時候的作品祗可供給下等階級的人物讀。第二期他是一個熱誠的敎徒，他極力的傳敎。第三期他是個新聞記者，同是又是個小品作家，用記者的眼光，作有趣和美麗故事，他寫了許多的詩文，小品，和短篇故事。因爲他的健於寫文章，很受英國的兩個政黨所重視和借重。第四期是他知道犯人生活的時期。他把牢獄生活寫成文章在報上發表，在倫敦地方是傳誦一時的。他出獄以後充當公家便探，或者可說是專任偵探祕密的事情。

　　當狄孚差不多六十歲的時候，他致力於幻想的說部，他寫了一本永久被人傳誦的 "Robinson Crusoe" 就是這本〔魯濱孫飄流記〕。他在這本書上賺了許多金錢。從此就得很安逸的度着晚年的光陰。但是他並不因此就怠惰起來了，在1720年他著下了 "Coptain Singleton, Puncan Campbell" 和 "Memoirs of a Cavalier;" 在1722年他著下了 "Colonel Jack, Moll Flanders" 等書。後來因爲有人攻擊他，他逃到倫敦去，很模糊的在1731年過世了。

CONTENTS

ii   CONTENTS

PREFACE

THE story of Robinson Crusoe is founded on fact. It was written by an Englishman, Daniel Defoe, who lived from 1661 to 1731. During his lifetime reports were common in England of castaways on the newly settled continent of America and its outlying islands, and marvelous stories were told of the shifts such men had made to live. We have accounts of two men who, at different times, lived alone for years on the island of Juan Fernandez, off the coast of Chile. One was an Indian who was left there from 1681 to 1684, and whose adventures were described by Captain Dampier, the buccaneer, in his "New Voyage Round the World." The other was the celebrated Alexander Selkirk a Scotchman, who was rescued in February, 1709, after a stay of four years and four months according to Captain Woodes Rogers. Defoe's work shows some striking resemblances to both these accounts; and there is even a legend that our author once visited Selkirk at Bath.

The island which Defoe describes cannot, however, be in any way identified with Juan Fernandez. He himself says that it is near the mouth of the Orinoco. In this wise it answers to the island now called Tobago, as well as in such particulars as its distance from the mainland its relation to the island of Trinidad, and the indraft or current of the sea, of which Defoe makes mention. This island is also not wanting in a legend of a castaway. for there is an account of the finding of a solitary Frenchman who said he had lived there alone twenty-one years.

The storm which is described as striking Crusoe's ship was a characteristic West Indian hurricane, the like of which still sweep over those seas. Defoe had a large and exact geographical knowledge of all the lands which at his time had been explored and settled. He know not only the position and extent of each, but also the climate, the nature of the soil, the products and their commercial values.

While the story of Robinson Crusoe is thus based on actual events, it is none the less a product of Defoe's creative genius. His imagination seized a few experiences of Selkirk, or other castaways, and from them constructed this narrative of the struggles made by an active, energetic man forced to a lonely life. In writing of Crusoe's zeal, Crusoe's religious fervor, and Crusoe's untiring industry, Defoe wrote of himself and what he himself would have been upon Crusoe's island and in his solitude. It is such vigor, pluck, perseverance, and will as Crusoe's that have carried the English nation and English tongue to every part of the earth and given them practically the conquest of the world.

序　言

英文在今日的中國，有成爲「第二語言」的趨勢，成爲治學者所必需之工具，而英文之在學校課程中，佔--僅次於國文的重要地位，是不能否認的一種事實。

然而全國各學校中，英文敎學的效率，似乎不能令我們滿意。以中學畢業生而論，平均每個中學生，習英文至六七年之久，然而畢業之後，除了師長曾經講授過的課本以外，不能閱讀原文書籍的，是佔着絕對的大多數。

這是一個很可惋惜的現象，梁任公先生曾說，「通一種外國語，等於發現一處新殖民地。」(大意如此) 修習英文的目的，正在發現一個學問上的新大陸，從而獲取其中的各種寶藏。假使我們習英文而不至於「通」，除師長講授以外而不能自行閱讀，這彷彿我們雖在旅程中跋涉了一番，終還不能達到新大陸，獲得殖民地。則我們又何貴乎此旅程的跋涉，換一句話，何貴乎此六七年英文的修習？

學校中英文敎學的效率所以不高的最大原因，是在學生除師長指定的課本以外，不肯多閱讀。而學生之所以不肯多閱讀，則英文自修書籍之缺乏，應該負最大的責任。

在這點上我們覺得，奚君的譯註校閱英文學名著的這種工作，是值得鼓勵，值得讚美的。各校學生得到了這些英漢對照的書籍，可以無師自通，揣摩研究，用以識英文學之迷津，入英文學之堂奧。這種工作，這種貢獻，在全國各學校的英文敎學上，將證實其爲一個絕大的幫助。

我們希望奚君在這方面的努力能夠繼續下去，也希望他的努力能引起別人的相同的努力，以佳惠於全國的青年學子！

三十一，十二月，十日，

夏晉麟

THE LIFE AND ADVENTURES

OF

ROBINSON CRUSOE

CHAPTER I

I was born in the year 1632, in the city of [1]*York*. Being the third son of the [2]*family*, and [3]*not bred to any trade*, my [4]*head* began to be [5]*filled* very early [6]*with rambling thoughts*. My father, who was very old, had given me a [7]*competent share of learning*, [8]*as far as* [9]*house education* and a country [10]*free school* [11]*generally go*, and [12]*designed me for the law*; but I would be [13]*satisfied* with nothing but going to sea. My [14]*inclination* to this led me so strongly against the will, nay, the [15]*commands* of my father, and against all the [16]*entreaties* and [17]*persuasions* of my mother and other friends, that there seemed to be something [18]*fatal* in that [19]*propensity of nature*, [20]*tending* directly to the life of [21]*misery* which was to [22]*befall* me.

My father, a wise and grave man, gave me [23]*serious* and [24]*excellent* [25]*counsel* against what he [26]*foresaw* was my [27]*design*. He called me one morning into his [28]*chamber*, where he was [29]*confined by the gout*, and [30]*expostulated* very [31]*warmly* with me upon this [32]*subject*. He asked me what reasons, more than a mere wandering inclination, I had for leaving my father's house and my native country, where I might be well [33]*introduced*, and had a [34]*prospect of raising my fortune* [35]*by application and industry*, with a life of [36]*ease and pleasure*.

10

魯 濱 孫 飄 流 記

第 一 章

　　我是在一六三二年生在約克城中的。在全家之中我是排行第三，因爲從沒有做過事情，所以我的腦海之中充滿了遊歷的思想。我的極老的父親教過我許多關于出世的才學，至於普通的家庭教育和鄉村義務教育亦無所不至，並且還要我去學法律。但是我，除出航海以外，什麼事都不能使我滿足。我要去的心非常急切，至使我違反着父親的命令和母親與朋友的勸告，這個好像是我的不幸的天性催逼我去過那禍患的生涯。

　　我的父親是聰明而莊重，他預見着我的計畫，所以着實貼切地和暢快地開導我一番。他有一天早晨叫我到他房間中去，房間是他因脚瘋病而久居的，當時他激烈的和我談到這個問題。他問我爲何理由，那個理由不過是一種飄渺的意思，竟能使我離開祖屋家鄉，在家鄉我大有引荐發展的希望，倘使我肯專心從事職業，如此大可享福快樂地過生活。

1.英國北部大城名.2.家.3.未嘗從事於商業.4.心，頭腦.5. 充滿.6.游蕩之思想.7.商用之學問；足以問世之才學.8. 祇就……而言.9.家庭教育.10.公學，義學.11.普通.12.命余肆業法政；命予學律.13. 心滿意足.14.癖嗜，偏愛.15.囑咐.16.勸戒，懇求.17.勤勉.18. 凶；不幸.19.天性.20.傾向.21.禍患.22.降臨.23.摯誠.24.優越.25.勸教之言.26.預知.27.計畫.28.臥房.29.爲脚瘋病所罹聚.30.規勸.31.懇切.32.問題.33.介紹職業.34.致富之希望.35.專心勤勉而得之.36.安樂。

After this he ¹*pressed* me earnestly, and in the most
²*affectionate* manner, ³*not to play the young man*, nor to
hasten to ⁴*miseries* which nature, and ⁵*the station of life* I was
born in, seemed to have ⁶*provided against*. He told me
that I was ⁷*under no necessity of* ⁸*seeking my bread*, that he
⁹*would do well for me*, and that if I was not very easy and
happy in the world, it must be my mere ¹⁰*fate* or ¹¹*fault* that
must ¹²*hinder* it, and that he should have ¹³*nothing to answer
for*, having thus ¹⁴*discharged his duty* in ¹⁵*warning* me against
¹⁶*measures* which he knew would be to my ¹⁷*hurt* ; ¹⁸*in a word*,
that as he would do very kind things for me if I would stay
and ¹⁹*settle* at home as he ²⁰*directed*, so ²¹*he would not have so
much hand in my misfortunes* as to give me any ²²*encouragement* to go away ; and he would ²³*venture* to say that if I did
take this foolish ²⁴*step*, God would not ²⁵*bless* me, and I should
have ²⁶*leisure* hereafter to ²⁷*reflect upon* having ²⁸*neglected* his
²⁹*counsel*, when there might be none ³⁰*to assist* in my ³¹*recovery*.

I ³²*observed* in this last part of his ³³*discourse*, which was
truly ³⁴*prophetic*, though I ³⁵*suppose* my father did not know
it to be so himself — I say, I observed the tears run down
his face very ³⁶*plentifully*, and that when he spoke of my
³⁷*having leisure to repent*, and none to assist me, he was so
³⁸*moved* that he ³⁹*broke off the discourse*, and told me ⁴⁰*his heart
was so full* he could say no more to me.

I ⁴¹*was sincerely affected* with this discourse, and, indeed,
⁴²*who could be otherwise?* and I ⁴³*resolved* not to think of going
⁴⁴*abroad* any more, but to settle at home according to my
father's desire. But alas! a few days ⁴⁵*wore it all off* ; and,
⁴⁶*in short*, to ⁴⁷*prevent* any of my father's further ⁴⁸*importuni-
ties*, in a few weeks after I resolved ⁴⁹*to run quite away from
him*. However, I did not act quite so ⁵⁰*hastily* as the first

嗣後，他用極親密的口吻諄諄勸戒着我，不可效仿兒童的舉動，也不可急急於天然和環境所注定的禍患之事。他告訴我說我不必要自謀生計，因爲他極能替我做的，假使我不能在此世上安逸快樂，這是我的命運和誤事所致，他旣已盡職的對于我的計劃警戒于前，自不當負責于後了；總而言之，一切他都可以代我籌刷，假使我肯依他的指教住在家中，所以他對于我將來的不幸遭過，他完全不負責任，因爲他沒有鼓勵我出去。末了，他敢預斷，倘使我從事這種愚笨的行爲，上帝也不願保佑我；將來一定會有時光回想到輕忽着他的勸告的，當我達到了無挽回的地步。

我找到他最後的一句警告果眞是預言了，雖然，我想他自己當初亦沒有想到會這樣．當他說的時候，淚很多的滴下來，當他說到我必有反悔之時，而那時誰也不能助我這句話的時候，他大大的感動了，他欲說而不能說了，他告訴我他實因滿懷愁緒，不能再和我多說了。

我被他這一番的勸導，極受感動．實在，誰能夠不如此的感動呢？所以我決計不再想出洋去了，依照我父親的心願住在家中，可是，幾天以後，我又把這個決意打消了．因爲要免掉父親更進一步的嚕蘇，在幾星期內我決定靜悄悄地私奔．不過，我沒有卽刻依着我第一個念頭所決定的那樣快的去實行。

1.諄諄勸戒。2.親切。3.毋效兒童之舉動。4.禍患。5.處世之境況。6.防備。7.不必。8.自謀生計。9.必能善爲我謀。10.命運。11.過錯。12.阻礙。13.不任其咎。14.克盡其職。15.警戒。16.方法。17.有害。18.總而言之。19.安居。20.指定。21.如余遇難，咎非在彼。22.鼓勵。23.敢爲預斷。24.進行方法。25.保佑。26.閒暇。27.反省。28.輕忽。29.勸戒。30.助。31.補救，復元。32.認淸。33.勸言。34.預言。35.猜想。36.多。37.必有反悔之時。38.感動。39.欲言突然中止。40.滿懷情緒。41.大爲感動。42.熟能不若是。43.決定。44.出洋。45.全然消滅。46.總而言之。47.免除。48.嚕蘇。49.遠而避之。50.性急

heat of my ¹*resolution* ²*prompted*; but I took my mother at
a time when I thought her ³*a little more yielding than
ordinary*, and told her that ⁴*my thoughts were so entirely bent
upon seeing the world* that I should never ⁵*settle* to anything
with resolution enough ⁶*to go through with it*, and my father
⁷*had better give me his consent* than force me ⁸*to go without* it;
that I was now eighteen years old, which was too late ⁹*to go
apprentice to a trade* or ¹⁰*clerk* to an ¹¹*attorney*; that I was sure
if I did I should never ¹²*serve out my time*, but I should
certainly run away form my master before my time was
out, and ¹³*go to sea*; and if she would speak to my father to
let me go one ¹⁴*voyage* abroad, if I came home again, and did
not like it, I would go no more; and I would ¹⁵*promise*, by
a double ¹⁶*diligence*, to recover the time that I had lost.

Though my mother ¹⁷*refused* to speak thus to my father,
yet I heard afterwards that she ¹⁸*reported* all the discourse to
him, and that my father, after showing a great ¹⁹*concern* at
it, said to her, with a ²⁰*sigh*: "That boy might be happy if
he would stay at home; but, if he goes abroad, he will be
the most ²¹*miserable* ²²*wretch* that ever was born; I can give
no ²³*consent* to it."

It was not till almost a year after this that I ²⁴*broke loose*,
though, in the mean time, I ²⁵*continued* ²⁶*obstinately* ²⁷*deaf to*
all ²⁸*proposals* of ²⁹*settling* to business. But being one day at
³⁰*Hull*, where I went without any ³¹*purpose* of making an
³²*elopement* at that time —I say, being there, and one of my
³³*companions* being ³⁴*about to* sail to London in his father's
ship, and ³⁵*prompting* me to go with them with the common
³⁶*allurement* of ³⁷*seafaring men*, that it should ³⁸*cost me nothing*
for my ³⁹*passage*, I ⁴⁰*consulted* neither father nor mother any
more, nor ⁴¹*so much as sent them word* of it; but leaving them

但是我去和我的母親去商量，因爲我想她較爲遷就些．所以我告訴她，我的思想完全注重於去觀光世界，所以我决不能安心於不論何事用着足以實行的决心，所以我的父親還是准我去比威逼我不去要好得多；況且我現已十八歲了，不能去當商家的學徒或律師的書記，我可以决定，縱使辦得到的話，我决不會卒業的，我决定會在沒有卒業之前就要離開主人而奔向航海去的．倘使她能夠替我向父親說，許我只去一次，那時我再回來的時候，我以爲不合我意，以後誓不再去，我决允許對於事業將要加倍的努力，以期償還虛度着的光陰．

雖然我的母親反對着這樣去向我父親說，我後來聽得她把我的說話統統告訴他的．所以我的父親經過十分的考量以後，嘆着氣向她說道：“咳，這個孩子住在家中，正可過着舒服的日子，如果出洋的話，他將要變成最可憐的苦命人哩；我决不准他出去的．”

這樣不到一年以後，我就走了，在這一年之中，我對于他們所介紹給我的職業，我都堅决地置之不理．有一天我走到了(黑耳)地方，我到那地方去時完全沒有趁在那時，想從家中逃走的思想，——我在那裏，有一位我的同伴將要在他父親的船中駛往倫敦去，他引誘我去和他們一處當當水手，這樣，據他說乘船可不用出錢，我也不去同父親商量，也不和我母親商量，並且也不去通知他們，讓他們

1.主意．2.授意．3.較爲遷就．4.余於游覽世界之心，甚爲急切．5.安定．6.實行其事．7. 不如允我所求． 8.捨棄．9.投師學業．10.書記；文案．11. 律師，訟師．12.畢業．13、去航海．14.航行．15.誓允．16.勤奮． 17.不允．18.傳述．19.談話．20.嘆息．21。不幸：22.苦命人；窮厄無告者．23.允納．24.逃走．25.繼，仍舊． 26．強硬．27.悶悶．28.建議．29.固定．30.地名(在英國約君)31．宗旨．32.奔逃．33.友倪．34.卽將．35.激勵．36.引誘．37.水手．38.毫不取費．39.旅行．4．商量．41．甚至於致語於從

to hear of it as they might, without asking God's ¹*blessing* or my father's, without any ²*consideration* of ³*circumstances* or ⁴*consequences*, and in an ⁵*ill hour*, God knows, on the 1st. of September, 1651, I ⁶*went on board a ship* ⁷*bound for* London. Never any young ⁸*adventurer's* ⁹*misfortunes*, I belive, began sooner, or continued longer, than mine. The ship was no sooner out of the ¹⁰*Humber* than the wind began to ¹¹*blow* and ¹²*the sea to rise* in a most ¹³*frightful* manner ; and, as I had never been at sea before, I was most ¹⁴*inexpressibly* sick in body, and ¹⁵*terrified* in mind. I began now ¹⁶*seriously* to ¹⁷*reflect* upon what I had done, and how justly I ¹⁸*was overtaken by the judgment of Heaven* for my ¹⁹*wicked* leaving my father's house, and ²⁰*abandoning my duty*. All the good ²¹*counsels* of my ²²*parents*, my father's tears and my mother's ²³*entreaties*, came now ²⁴*fresh* into my mind ; and my ²⁵*conscience*, which was not yet come to the ²⁶*pith* of ²⁷*hardness* to which it has since ²⁸*reproached* me with the ²⁹*contempt* of advice, and the ³⁰*breach of my duty* to God and my father.

All this while the ³¹*storm* ³²*increased*, and the sea went very high, though nothing like what I have seen many times since ; no, nor what I saw a few days after. But it was enough to ³³*affect* me then, who was but a young ³⁴*sailor*, and had never known ³⁵*anything of the matter*. I ³⁶*expected* every ³⁷*wave* would ³⁸*swallow* us *up*, and that every time the ship fell down, as I thought, in the ³⁹*trough* or ⁴⁰*hollow* of the sea, we ⁴¹*should never rise more*. In this ⁴²*agony of mind* I made many ⁴³*vaws* and ⁴⁴*resolutions* that if it would please God to ⁴⁵*spare* my life in this one voyage, if ever I got once my foot upon dry land again, I would go ⁴⁶*directly* home to my father and never set it into a ship again while I lived ; that I

自己去探消息罷，也沒有去求上帝的保佑，也沒有去求父親的祝福，更沒有工夫去考慮到我的環境或結果如何，於是，上帝是知道的；在一六五一年九月一日一個不幸時辰之中，我就上船出發向倫敦駛去。我相信不論那一個少年冒險家的危險時期的光臨比我會來的這樣的迅速和這樣的長久。我們的船剛跨出（享勃）港口，可怕的風。因爲我以前從未經過航海的，此時我的全身都感覺着不可言狀的痛苦，心中非常的恐怖。此時我貼切地囘想到我以前所做的事情。如何我是極公正的被天所遣責，因爲我如此惡劣的離開我父親的家和放棄我的責任。我父母的一切的勸言，父親的熱淚，和母親的哀懇，一幕一幕的在我的腦海中活現着。我的良心，雖然還沒達到極點，却從此開始，責罰着我藐視忠告，不安本分，和輕忽我的父親。

　　正在此時，風浪的凶勢愈趨愈緊了，海浪湧躍得非常的高，雖然，同我已經多次見過的和我幾天以後見到的比較起來是算不得什麼。然而，已經足夠使我（恐怖），因爲我不過是個年輕的水手，一些沒有航海的經驗，每一個波浪的起伏，我總以爲要把我們吞下去了，每一個時候我以爲船要翻沉了，我以爲在此海濤凶湧的海中，我們必不能再生於世上了。
　　正在這個焦急的時候，我立着許多誓和決心；就是倘使上帝允許救我在這一次的航海的生命，那麼倘使我有一次脚踏到岸地上去，我就當立刻奔囘家去。我活着的時候，永不思投入航海的生涯；我要

would take his advice, and never run myself into such
[1]*miseries* as these any more.

These wise and [2]*sober thoughts* continued all the while the
storm [3]*lasted*, and indeed some time after. But the next
day [4]*the wind was abated,* [5]*and the sea calmer*, and I began to
be a little [6]*inured* to it, although I was very [7]*grave* for all
that day, being also a little [8]*seasick* still. Towards night
[9]*the weather cleared up*, the wind was [10]*quite over*, and a
[11]*charming* fine evening followed, The sun went down
[12]*perfectly* clear, and rose so the next morning ; and having
little or no wind, and a [13]*smooth sea*, the sun shining upon
it, the sight was, as I thought, the most delightful that
ever I saw.

I had slept well in the night, and was now no more
seasick, but very [14]*cheerful*, looking with wonder upon the
sea that was so [15]*rough* and [16]*terrible* the day before, and could
be so calm and so [17]*pleasant* in so little a time after. And
now, lest my good resolutions should continue, my companion, who had [18]*enticed* me away, comes to me : " Well,
Bob, " says he, [19]*clapping me upon the shoulder*, " how do
you do after it ? I [20]*warrant* you were [21]*frighted*, [22]*wer'n't* you,
last night, when it [23]*blew* [24]*but a capful of wind*?" " A
capful d'you call it ? " said I ; " [25]*t'was* a [26]*terrible* storm. "
" A storm. you fool you, " replies he ; " do you call that a
storm ? why, it was nothing at all ; give us but [27]*a good ship*
and [28]*sea room*, and we think nothing of such [29]*a squall of wind*
as that ; but you're but a [30]*fresh-water sailor*, Bod. Come,
let us [31]*make* a [32]*bowl* of [33]*Punch*, and we'll [34]*forget* all that ; d'ye
see what [35]*charming weather* ' tis now ? "

To make short this sad part of my story, we went the
way of all sailors ; the punch was made, and I was made

順從我父親的勸告，並且此後再不如此更甚的自尋煩惱。

　這類機巧的清醒的意念，跟着波浪起伏不已，的確繼續了好一會的時候。但是第二天風減小了，海浪也平靜了，我方始覺得有點慣常了，雖然我終日因暈船而非常不高興。到了夜快，天氣轉晴了，風亦靜止了，相繼着一個可愛而清朗的夕陽？太陽很清朗的落着：到第二天早上也很清明的升着；有一些微風或者可說是沒有風，陽光照在那平靜的海面之上，這個景緻依我想簡直是一幅極美麗的風景，爲我生平所未曾見到過的：

　我夜間很安靜的睡着，再也不覺得暈船了，我只是感到愉快。很奇怪地看着茫茫大洋，在前夜海是如此狂暴和可怕，却在一個如此短促的時間之中能夠變成如此平靜而有趣了。我正在繼續着我的有趣的幻想，我的同伴到我這兒來了，他是引誘我出走的人，他輕拍着我的肩膀說道，"好，擺佈，經過風浪以後，你覺得怎樣？我確信，你昨晚受了驚嚇了罷，但是這樣的吹風，僅僅一陣微風而已！"我說，"你說一陣風麼？那是可怕的狂風呢！""狂風，你這呆子；"他答着，"你呼麼？這算不得甚麼；不過給我們一個好地位駛船罷了。我們對牠爲狂風于一陣風並不在意。至於你呢，因爲是一個新水手。所以怕，擺佈，來，讓我們喝一杯酒罷，好使一切都忘懷。你瞧，天氣多麼高爽呀？

　將我這段悲愁的事情簡括的說說，我們學着水手的貫俗；盛好了酒，我是。

half ¹*drunk* with it, and in that one night's ²*wickedness* I
³*drowned all my repentance*, all my ⁴*reflections* upon my
past ⁵*conduct*, all my resolutions for the ⁶*future*. ⁷*In a word*,
as the sea was returned to its smoothness of ⁸*surface* and
⁹*settled* ¹⁰*calmness* by the ¹¹*abatement* of that storm, so the
¹²*hurry* of my thoughts being over, my fears and ¹³*apprehen-*
sions of being swallowed up by the sea being ¹⁴*forgotten*, and
¹⁵*the current of my former desires returned*, I ¹⁶*entirely* forgot
the vows and ¹⁷*promises* that I made ¹⁸*in my distress*.

CHAPTER II

THE sixth day of our being at sea we came into ¹⁹*Yarmouth*
Roads; the wind having been ²⁰*contrary* and the weather
calm, we had ²¹*made but little way* since the storm. Here
we were ²²*obliged* ²³*to come to an anchor*, and here we lay,
the wind continuing contrary — namely at ²⁴*southwest* — for
seven or eight days, during which time a great many ships
from ²⁵*Newcastle* came into the same Roads, as the common
²⁶*harbour* where the ships might wait for a wind for
the river.

²⁷*The wind blew fresh* and, after we had ²⁸*lain* four or five
days, blew very hard. However, the Roads being ²⁹*reckoned*
as good as a harbour, the ³⁰*anchorage* good, and our ³¹*ground*
tackle very strong, our men were ³²*unconcerned*, and ³³*not in*
the least apprehensive of danger, but ³⁴*spent* the time in rest
and ³⁵*mirth*, after the manner of the sea. But the eighth day,
in the morning, the wind ³⁶*increased*, and we had all ³⁷*hands*
at work ³⁸*to strike our topmasts*, and make everything ³⁹*snug*
and close, ⁴⁰*that the ship might ride as easy as possible*. By
noon the sea went very high indeed, and we ⁴¹*shipped several*
seas, and thought once or twice our ⁴²*anchor had come home*;

喝得半醉；這一晚上的惡劣行爲，使我把前夜的悔恨，以及我過去的行爲的回想和我對於將來的决心，都全然消滅。總而言之，當海洋囘復牠的平靜的海面，風浪減少而使牠歸於平靜；就使我的胡思亂想景遍情遷，我的恐怕和恐被海水溺死的恐怖都忘記去了，而我以前的思想又恢復過來了，我完全將在苦難中所立的誓言和許願都忘却了。

第　二　章

　　在海上的第六天，我們從遇到風浪行駛不多路，我們就到了(耶摩斯路)地方，風是迎面而至，氣候非常平靜。我們在此地必須停舶着，在我們停在此的時候，風依舊是繼續吹逆風，換句話說，就是西南風，我們停舶了七八天，正在這個時候，有許多由(牛宮)來的船碇泊於同一個路線上，因爲這是普通的港口；在這個地方，船必須都等候着順風，才可向海內一直駛行。

　　風又吹起，我們停泊四五天以後，風吹得愈加利害了。幸虧碇泊的地方有像港口那麼安隱，同時我們船上的錨具完好，轆轤纜篷等物都很堅固，所以同伴們可以處之泰然，並不知有一些危險。我們過着海上所通行的嬉戲生活，有時或者休息着；但是在第八天的早晨，風突然轉劇了。我們大家忙于收下第二節椗干，把一切佈置得安安隱隱，使船得以安泊無事。到了午刻，風濤大作，波浪屢次打入船中，我記得我們的船錨已經脫離了。

upon which our [1]*master* ordered out the [2]*sheet anchor*, so that we [3]*rode* with two anchors ahead, and [4]*the cables veered out to the better end.*

By this time it blew a terrible storm indeed ; and now I began to see [5]*terror* and [6]*amazement* in the faces even of the seamen themselves, The master, though [7]*vigilant* in the business of [8]*preserving* the ship, yet as he went in and out of his [9]*cabin* by me, I could hear him softly to himself say, several times, "Lord, be [10]*merciful* to us! we shall be all lost ; we shall be all [11]*undone* ! " and the like. During these first [12]*hurries* I was [13]*stupid*, lying still in my cabin, which was in the [14]*steerage*, and cannot [15]*describe* my [16]*state of mind.* I could ill [17]*resume* the first [18]*penitence* which I had so [19]*apparently* [20]*trampled* upon, and [21]*hardened* myself against. I thought the [22]*bitterness* of death had been past, and that this would be nothing like the first ; but when the master himself came by me, as I said just now, and said we should be all lost, I was [23]*dreadfully* [24]*frighted.* I got up out of my cabin and looked out ; but such a [25]*dismal sight* I never saw. The sea ran [26]*mountains* high, and broke upon us every three or four minutes ; when I could look about [27]*I could see nothing but distress round us,* Two ships that [28]*rode* near us, we found, had cut their [29]*masts* by the board, being [30]*deep laden* ; and our men cried out that a ship which rode about a mile ahead of us was [31]*foundered,* Two more ships, being [32]*driven from their anchors*, were run out of the Roads to sea, [33]*at all adventures*, and that not with a mast standing. The light ships [34]*fared the best*, as not so much [35]*labouring* in the sea ; but two or three of them [36]*drove*, and came close by us, running away with only their [37]*spritsail* out before the wind.

因此，我們的船主吩咐拋下大錨，於是我們在前面拋下兩只錨，盡其所長的伸在海內，

這個時候狂風愈吹愈加劇烈。到了此刻我鏠瞧見船上人他們自己面上都現着驚駭恐怖之色了，船主雖然已經盡心竭力的保護那只船，可是當他徘徊于他的臥房我的旁邊之時，我可聽出他囁嚅的自己向自己說道，"上帝，可憐我們罷！我們要全部失散了；我們將要滅亡了，"以及其他類似的話。擾亂的起初，我是糊裏糊塗睡在我自己的房間裏，房間是在船頭的艙裏，我實在不能描寫我這時的心境如何。我很可恥的收囘我第一次的悔罪，這個悔罪，我已經如此顯明的輕忽着，並且我自己堅持的反對着，我想悲慘的死神已經過去，這一囘的狂風亦不會過於像那第一次的情形；但是，當船主來至我身邊，像我適然所說的，我們都要散失了的話，不覺大起恐慌。我走出房間，望外面看看，但見那種悽慘的景象，我自來所未曾見過的。似山那麼高的波浪隔三四分鐘撞上我們的船來；環顧四圍，都是悽涼的情景。我們發覺靠近我們的兩只船，滿載貨物，帆柱是已被割斷；只聽得我們的同伴大聲喊着說在我們前一里路有一只船是沉沒了。還瞧見兩只脫錨的船，爲大風所趕出海港，冒着險逐波亂撞，船上沒有桅桿了。凡輕飄的船，駛行最爲便捷，用不着多大的苦力；但是有兩三只船搖着，向我們這邊近過來，只剩下斜扛帆顚簸于狂風之中。

1.船主．2.大錨．3.碇泊．4.盡錨索之長而拋之于海．5.怕懼之色．6.驚駭之色．7.細心竭力．8.保護．9.船上臥室．10.可憐；救．11.倉忙．12.滅亡．13.糊塗．14.船頭艙．15.描寫．16.心境．17.取囘．18.悔罪．19.明析．20.輕忽；21.苦楚．22.悲慘．23.可怕．24.受驚．25.慘悽之景象．26.山．27.目所能見者，惟有悽慘之景象耳．28.帆柱．29.重載．30.沉沒．31.脫錨．32.冒萬險．33.駛行最爲便捷．34.用力．35.搖船．36.斜扛帆．

Towards evening the [1]*mate* and [2]*boatswain* begged the master of our ship to let them cut away the [3]*foremast*, which he [4]*was very unwilling* to do. But the [5]*boatswain* [6]*protesting* to him that if he did not the ship would [7]*founder*, he [8]*consented*; and when they had cut away the [9]*foremast*, the [10]*mainmast* [11]*stood loose*, and [12]*shook* the ship so much they were [13]*obliged* to cut that away also, and make a [14]*clear deck*.

Any one may [15]*judge* what a [16]*condition* I must have been in at all this, who was but a young sailor, and who had been in such a [17]*fright* before at but a little, But I was in [18]*tenfold* more horror of mind [19]*upon account of* my [20]*former* [21]*convictions*, and the having [22]*returned* from them to the [23]*resolutions* I had [24]*wickedly* taken at first, than I was at death itself; but the [25]*worst* was not come yet. The storm continued with such [26]*fury* that the seamen themselves [27]*acknowledged* they [28]*had never seen a worse*. We had a good ship, but she was deep [29]*laden*, and [30]*wallowed in the sea*, so that the seamen [31]*every now and then* cried out she would [32]*founder*. It was my advantage [33]*in one respect* that I did not know what they [34]*meant* by "founder," till I [35]*inquired*. However, the storm was so [36]*violent* that I saw, what is not often seen, the master, the [37]*boatswain*, and some others more [38]*sensible* than the rest, at their prayers, and [39]*expecting* every [40]*moment* when the ship [41]*would go to the bottom*. In the [42]*middle of the night*, and under all the rest of our [43]*distresses*, one of the men that had been down to see, cried out we had [44]*sprung a leak*; another said there were four feet of water in the [45]*hold*. Then all hands were called to the [46]*pump*. At that word, [47]*my heart*, as I thought, [48]*died within me*, and I fell [49]*backwards* upon the side of my bed where I sat. However, the men [50]*roused* me, and told me that I that was

將近黃昏的時候，大副和船老大要求船主讓他們把前桅割去，這個船主極不願意做着。但是經過船老大的抗議說着，倘使他不允許，船要沉下了，如此他方始允許。當他們割去桅干時，中桅站立不隱，牽動全船震搖，他們只得也把牠去掉。於是使船面上空無一物。

誰都能猜定我在這個情形之中的狀況，我祇是一個初航海的人，並且我是經過小危險而已經恐怖萬狀了。我的畏懼之心是十倍于前，因為我同憶起我先前的惡劣的那種反覆無常的痛悔罪，因此我也就聽其自然了，但是極險的惡神尚沒有降臨。狂風巨濤不斷地向我們進攻，甚至于水手們亦承認從未見有甚于這一次的壞現象了，我們的船在海洋中顛簸不止；雖然船身是堅固，可是裝載過重，所以水手們時常喊着要船沉了的話。幸虧我那時不懂"沉"是怎麼一囘事，直至我問了以後才知道。但是我見到，風濤凶湧的時候，這個不是常見的。當時，船主，水手們，以及比較有智識的人們都祈禱着；當他們覺察每分鐘內這船有沉沒的可能。到了夜半大家都是紛紜不安，有一人走下船去，忽而喊道船有裂孔而漏了。另有一人說着船艙內已有四尺水了。隨後，大家忙着幫同水抽。聽了這類呼喊之聲，我感覺萬念俱灰，懶洋洋向後倒在我坐的牀邊。然而，他們把我喚醒，對我說道。

1.副船主．2.船老大．3.前桅．4.殊不願．5.船老大．6.辨明．7.沉沒．8.允許．9.前桅．10.中桅．11.站不隱．12.震搖．13.受迫．14.空船面．15.觀察．16.景象；情形．17.驚駭．18.十倍．19.因．20.先前．21.罪．22.同．23.決意．24.無理．25.極險．26.劇烈．27.承認．28.從未見有甚于此者．29.載貨．30.旋轉於海中．31.時常．32.沉．33.於一方面．34.意義．35.詢問；36.狂暴．37.船老大．38.關心．39.覺察．40.一分鐘．41.將沉于海底．42.半夜．43.困難．44.船有裂罅而漏．45.船艙．46.抽水器．47.我心．48.灰喪．49.向後．50.喚醒。

able to do nothing before, was as well able to ¹*pump* as another; at which I ²*stirred up,* and went to the pump, and worked very ³*heartily.* While this was doing, the master seeing some ⁴*light colliers,* who, not able ⁵*to ride out the storm,* were ⁶*obliged to slip,* and run away to the sea, and would come near us, ordered to fire a gun ⁷*as a signal of distress.* I, who knew nothing what they meant, thought the ship had ⁸*broken,* or some ⁹*dreadful* thing happened. In a word, I was so ¹⁰*surprised* that I ¹¹*fell down in a swoon.* As this was a time when everybody had his own life to think of, nobody ¹²*minded* me, or ¹³*what was become of* me ; but another man ¹⁴*stepped up* to the pump, and ¹⁵*thrusting* me aside with his foot, let me lie, thinking I was dead ; and ¹⁶*it was a great while before I came to myself.*

We ¹⁷*worked on* ; but the water ¹⁸*increasing* in the hold, it was ¹⁹*apparent* that the ship would ²⁰*founder.* It was not possible she could swim till we might run into any port. The master continued ²¹*firing guns* for help ; and a ²²*light ship,* that had ²³*ridden* it out just ²⁴*ahead of* us, ²⁵*ventured a boad out to help us.* It was ²⁶*with the utmost hazard* the boat came near us ; but it was ²⁷*impossible* for us to get ²⁸*on board,* or for the boat to ²⁹*lie* near the ship's side. At last the men ³⁰*rowing very heartily,* and ³¹*venturing their lives* to save ours, our men ³²*cast them a rope* over the ³³*stern* with a ³⁴*buoy* to it, and then ³⁵*veered it out* a great length, which they, ³⁶*after much labour* and ³⁷*hazard took hold of,* and we ³⁸*hauled* them close under our ³⁹*stern,* and got all into their boat. It was ⁴⁰*to no purpose* for them or us, after we were in the boat, to think of ⁴¹*reaching* their own ship. All agreed ⁴²*to let her drive,* and only to pull her in towards shore as much as we could ; and our master promised them that if the boat was

雖然我以前不會做其他的事，自當幫助他們抽水這件事，對于這個我就提起了精神，跑至抽水機那裏，就極力的去工作着，正在抽水的時候，船主遠望到有幾只小煤船，不能戰勝波浪，只得任其漂流，在海中亂飄，而且將要駛近我們，他連忙吩咐放礮，以示事之危急。我不知道他們什麼意思，以爲我們的船破裂了，或者遇有什麼可怕的不測。總而言之，我因爲受驚太重，立刻暈到於地。此時因爲人人忙着救護自己，沒有人來顧問着我，也不注意我究竟怎樣了；但是有一個人走到抽水處，用脚把我踢開一些，任我躺在地上，以爲我是已死的人了，我呢，經過了許久時候才得蘇醒過來。

我們繼續不斷地抽水，但是水愈增愈多，船將沉下，這是很明顯的事。這只船快要沉下去了。這船再不能駛行到甚何埠頭去了。船主只得接連着放礮求援；有一只飄流在我們前面的輕船。冒險着放艇過來援求我們。但是我們不能上船，並且小船也難以靠近我們的船，最後水手們極力搖划；拚着他的命來救我們，於是我們的人在船尾上投繩給他們。繩上總着浮飄，於是將繩盡量長的放着，他們用了極大的氣力和困難纔把牠握住，於是我們把那艇迫近在船尾下，然後我們都走進艇上，但是，我們登上船以後，他們和我們都沒有方法使他們的船靠近他們的大船。只好聽其漂流，祇不過用力推牠靠岸而已，我們的船主允許他們，如果艇

¹*staved upon shore*, he would ²*make it good* to their master. So partly ³*rowing*, and partly ⁴*driving*, our boat went away to the ⁵*northward* ⁶*sloping towards* the shore almost as far as Winterton Ness.

We were not much more than a ⁷*quarter of an hour* out of our ship till we saw her ⁸*sink*, and then I understood for the first time what was meant by a ship ⁹*foundering* in the sea. I must ¹⁰*acknowledge* I had ¹¹*hardly* eyes to look up when the seamen told me she was sinking; for from the moment that they rather put me into the boat, then that I might be said to go in, my heart was, as it were, dead within me, partly with ¹²*fright*, partly with horror of mind and the thoughts of what was yet before me.

While we were in this ¹³*condition*—the men yet ¹⁴*labouring at the oar* to bring the boat near the shore—we could see (when, our boat ¹⁵*mounting the waves*, we were able to see the shore,) a great many people running along the ¹⁶*strand*, to ¹⁷*assist* us when we should come near; but we made but ¹⁸*slow way*. At last we got in, and, though not without much ¹⁹*difficulty*, got all safe on shore, and walked afterwards on foot to Yarmouth, where, as ²⁰*unfortunate* men, we ²¹*were used with great humanity*, as well by the ²²*magistrates of the town*, who ²³*assigned us good quarters*, as by ²⁴*particular* merchants and ²⁵*owners* of ships, and had money given us ²⁶*sufficient* to carry us either to London or back to Hull, as we thought ²⁷*fit*.

Had I now had the sense to go back to Hull, and had gone home, I had been happy, and my father, as in our blessed ²⁸*Savior's parable*, had even ²⁹*killed the fatted calf for me*; for, hearing the ship I went away in was ³⁰*cast away* in Yarmouth Roads, it was a great while before he had any ³¹*assurance* that I was not ³²*drowned*,

能夠到岸，他决意酬謝他們的船主，如此我們一面划一面離我們的船斜向北岸而推，將近(偉脫登尼水)地方。

我們離船不到一刻鐘，就見到我們的船沉下去了。從此我才明白船沉入海中的意思。我承認水手們對我說船在沉沒的當兒，我簡直不敢抬頭睺望，因爲我記起當時他們要我走進艇內去。如果我不顧離船的話，我的心似乎已經死去了，一半是爲着恐怕，一半是爲着心上的驚惶，想着一切的事情將要降臨於我了。

當我們在這種情形之下……人們仍舊用力鼓槳前進使船靠近岸去……我們可以看見當我們的船衝澳而去的時候，我們已能見到岸了，許多百姓奔跑在海邊之上來救助我們，當時以爲我們的船一定會近岸的，可惜我們前進得很慢。最後我們經過許多困難，方得平安到岸，後來我們步行到(耶門)地方，在那個地方，我們都是遭不幸的人，却受着衆人殷勤欸待。並且也受到城中官吏的優待；他指定我們好的地位，待我們像高尙的商人船上的主人一般，並且送錢與我們，藉資使我們可以隨意到倫敦去或者回到(黑耳)，

假使我有意欲同(黑耳)，回到家中去，那是我何等的快樂，至於我的父親，眞像救主耶穌在他的譬喻內所說的一般，聽得我所搭的船隻已沉沒在(姚馬河的四航綫)，他一定要爲我而殺牛羊，當他聽到我沒有溺死的消息，

But my [1]*ill fate* [2]*pushed* me on now with an [3]*obstinacy* that nothing could [4]*resist*; and though I had several times loud [5]*calls* from my [6]*reason* and my more [7]*composed judgment* to go home, yet I had no power to do it. Certainly, nothing but [8]*some decreed unavoidable misery*, which it was [9]*impossible* for me to [10]*escape*, could have pushed me forward against the calm [11]*reasonings* and [12]*persuasions* of my most [13]*retired* thoughts.

Having some money in my pocket, I traveled to London by land; and there, as well as on the road, had many [14]*struggles* with myself what [15]*course of life* I should take, and whether I should go home or go to sea.

As to going home, it [16]*immediately* [17]*occurred* to me how I should be [18]*laughed at* among the [19]*neighbours*, and should be [20]*ashamed* to see, not my father and mother only, but even everybody else. I [21]*remained* some time, [22]*uncertain what measures to take*, and [23]*what course of life to lead*. An [24]*irresistible reluctance* continued to going home; and as I staid awhile, the [25]*remembrance* of the [26]*distress* I had been in [27]*wore off*. As that [28]*abated*, the little notion I had in my desires to return wore off with it, till I quite [29]*laid aside* the thoughts of it, and [30]*looked out for* a voyage; and at last I went on board a [31]*vessel* [32]*bound to* the [33]*coast* of Africa; or, as our sailors [34]*vulgarly called* it, a "voyage to [35]*Guinea*."

CHAPTER III

It was my [36]*lot* [37]*first of all* to fall into [38]*pretty* good company in London, which does not always happen to such [39]*loose* and [40]*misguided* young [41]*fellows* as I then was. I first got [42]*acquainted* with the master of a ship who had been on the coast of Guinea, and who, having had very good

但是我的蹇滯的命運催促着我固守我的頑固的思想，這種固執的性質什麼都不能和牠相敵；雖然當我有幾次理智清醒的時候，我能明白斷定應該回家去，但是我沒有勇氣去做。那是當然的，別的都沒有，都是因爲不能避免的劣根性始終催迫着我去反抗我的有理的性，以及久已存心的思想和自覺。

還有幾個錢在我的袋裏，我就得由陸地一路行到(敦倫)。在那個地方，在路上也是如此，有着許多的思想在互相爭鬥，我還是取如何的一種生活方法好，我還是回家呢，還是航海。

至於回家，我就立刻想起我將如何被隣人譏笑我，而且我是不僅不好意思去見我的父親和母親並且也不好意去見其他的人。停了一囘，我沒有決定應該採取那一種方法，也不知道適從何種生計。我的不願囘家的思想依舊繼續着下去；當我休息一會，我把我所經歷的危險的事情全然忘懷。災難和可怕既已在我腦中消滅，囘家的一些印象亦隨之消滅，直待這類思想完全擯棄於外，同時我就留心訪問航海的消息，到後來我就走上一只開往非洲的船，就是那些水手俗稱的"航行到(尼奶)"去。

1. 蹇滯的命運. 2. 催促. 3. 固執. 4. 對敵. 5. 警醒. 6. 理論. 7. 明斷之心. 8. 方不能免之苦難. 9. 不可能. 10. 避. 11. 理論. 12. 勸服. 13. 囘去. 14. 躊躇. 15. 活命之方. 16. 立刻. 17. 觸念. 18. 譏笑. 19. 隣人. 20. 慚愧. 21. 停止. 22. 不知採取何法. 23. 不知採取何種生計. 24. 殊不願. 25. 記憶. 26. 困苦. 27. 漸漸消滅. 28. 消滅. 29. 擯棄. 30. 留心探求. 31. 船. 32. 起程；開往. 33. 岸. 34. 俗. 35. 非洲西部諸地之總稱. 36. 命運. 37. 首先. 38. 非常. 39. 放蕩不羈. 40. 誤入邪途. 41. 人. 42. 認識.

第 三 章

這是我的命運了，我首先在倫敦得到了很好的陶伴，祇有我放蕩不羈誤入邪途的人是會遇到的。我起先認識一個船主，他在(尾奶)海口是熟識的，他在那裏已有很好的成功的佳績

[1]*success* there, was [2]*resolved* to go again. This captain [3]*taking a fancy to my conversation*, which was [4]*not at all disagreeable* at that time, and hearing me say I had a mind to see the world, told me if I would go the voyage with him I should be at [5]*no expense*; I should be his [6]*messmate* and his companion; and if I could carry anything with me, I should have all the [7]*advantage* of it that the [8]*trade* would [9]*admit*; and perhaps I might [10]*meet with* some [11]*encouragement*.

I [12]*embraced the offer*; and [13]*entering into a strict friendship with* this captain, who was an honest, [14]*plain-dealing* man, I went the voyage with him, and carried a small [15]*adventure* with me, which, by the [16]*disinterested* honesty of my friend the captain, I [17]*increased* very [18]*considerably*; for I carried about forty pounds in such toys and [19]*trifles* as the captain directed me to buy. These forty pounds I had [20]*mustered* together by the [21]*assistance* of some of my [22]*relations* whom I [23]*corresponded with*; and who, I [24]*believe*, got my father, or at least my mother, to [25]*contribute* so much as that to my first adventure.

This was the only voyage which I may say was [26]*successful* in all my [27]*adventures*. This I [28]*owed* to the [29]*integrity* and [30]*honesty* of my friend the captain; under whom also I got a [31]*competent knowledge* of the [32]*mathematics* and the [33]*rules of navigation*, learned how to [34]*keep an account of* the [35]*ship's course*, [36]*take an observation*, and, in short, to understand some things that were [37]*needful* to be understood by a sailor. As he [38]*took delight to* [39]*instruct* me, I took [40]*delight* to learn; and, in a word, this voyage made me both a sailor and a merchant. I brought home five pounds nine [41]*ounces* of [42]*gold dust* for my adventure, which [43]*yielded me* in London, at my return, almost three hundred [44]*pounds*; and this [45]*filled me*

於是決定再要動身航海去。船主頗能納受我的意見，因爲那個並不是一件不悅耳的事情，等到他德我說着有意遊歷世界；他告訴我說如果我肯隨他航海；我不必化錢；我可作他的食伴和伴侶；假使我要攜帶貨物，務須先探明那地方的商務情形，於該物的銷場怎樣，也許可以遇機賺錢。

我接受他的盛意；我同船主訂下生死之約；他是一個誠實而有信用的人，我就照他的吩咐帶些貨物和他一路去航行；靠了他的淸廉無私，我賺錢不少；因爲我依他所說的買了四十磅玩物和其他的細小的物件，這四十磅錢是由我通信的親戚們絡繼送我的，我把他積聚了起來。我想他們送我的錢是從我父親或母親那邊來的，藉以助我第一次的冒險事業，

這次航行可以說是我冒險事業中唯一的成功。這個我自當歸功於我那誠實敦厚的好朋友船主人。倚着他我獲得了許多智識，如航海中的算學，航海規則，以及如何計算船之行程。如何從事觀測，簡而言之，我已懂得許多關於一個水手應有的常識。他高高興興的教導我，我則樂于學習；換言之，這一回航行把我造成了一個水手，也（可說把我造成）一個商人。此次的冒險結果我帶回家去五磅九兩金沙，後來在（倫敦）賺三百磅，這次的勝利令我

1.成就。2.決定。3.悅納余言。4.並非不悅耳。5.不須費用。6.食伴。7.利益。8.商務情形。9.適合。10.獲得。11.利。12.領其厚意。13.與……訂生死之交。14.誠實。15.冒險之商務。16.淸廉。17.增加。18.多。19.細小之物。20.積聚。21.資助。22.親戚。23.與之通信。24.深信。25.捐助。26.勝利27.險冒事業。28.賴。29.敦厚。30.誠實3.1.全備之智識。32.算學。33.航海規則。34.登記。35.船之行程。36.從事觀測（指天文）。37.必需。38.樂於。39.教導。40.喜悅。41.兩；。42.金沙。43.爲我生利。44.英磅。45.令予異想天開。

with those aspiring thoughts which have since so [1]*completed* my ruin.

Yet even in this voyage I had my misfortunes too; particularly, that I was continually sick, [2]*being thrown* into a [3]*violent fever* by [4]*the excessive heat* of the [5]*climate* ; our [6]*principal* [7]*trading* being upon the coast, from the [8]*latitude of fifteen degrees north* even to the [9]*line* (equator) itself.

I was now [10]*set up for* a Guinea trader. My friend, [11]*to my great misfortune*, dying soon after his [12]*arrival*, I resolved to go the same voyage again, and I [13]*embarked* in the same vessel with one who was his [14]*mate* in the former voyage, and had now got the [15]*command* of the ship. This was the [16]*unhappiest* voyage that ever man made. Though I did not carry quite one hundred pounds of my [17]*new-gained* wealth, so that I had two hundred pounds left, which I had [18]*lodged with* my friend's [19]*widow*, who was very just to me, yet I fell into [20]*terrible* [21]*misfortun*es.

The first was this ; our ship [22]*making her course towards* the Canary Islands, or rather between those islands and the African shore, was [23]*surprised* [24]*in the gray of the morning* by a [25]*Turkish rover* of [26]*Sallee*, who [27]*gave chase to us with all the sail she could make*. We [28]*crowded* also as much [29]*canvas* as our [30]*yards* would [31]*spread*, or our [32]*masts carry to get clear*; but [33]*finding* the [34]*pirate* [35]*gained upon* us, and would certainly [36]*come up with* us in a few hours, we [37]*prepared* to fight,—our ship having twelve guns and the rogue eighteen, About three in the afternoon he came up with us, and [38]*bringing to*, by [39]*mistake*, just [40]*athwart* our [41]*quarter*, instead of [42]*athwart* our [43]*stern*, as he intended, we [44]*brought* eight of our guns [45]*to bear on* that side, and [46]*poured in a broadside upon* him, which made him [47]*sheer off* again, after [48]*returning our fire,*

異想天開，嗣後的(命運)破產亦因於此點。

　　就是在這次的航海，我也碰着了不幸的事情，特別的是繼續着生病，酷熱的天氣使我大發瘧症；我們的重要貿易是在海岸，自北緯線五十度直到赤道的線故。

　　我現在成爲一個(金尼)的商人了。我的朋友抵埠後就死了，這個於我是大大的不幸。我決定再走原路並且仍搭那船，現在長船的人是前次我朋友的副手。這是一次人生最不幸的航行，雖然我祇帶了不到一百磅我所新復得的財產，其餘的我把牠存在我朋友的孀婦家中，她也待我很公正，但是我竟碰着意外的不幸了。

　　起初是這樣；我們的船駛向(芙容島)進發，就是在海島和非洲海岸的中央，一天黎明，我們惶恐莫名，因爲有一隻(土耳其)海賊盡着他們的速力迴追着我們。我們儘量扯足帆杠，但是覺察海盜在一路緊追，必定會在幾點鐘內卽可追到我們，我們準備和他開戰——我們船上有十二尊礮，靶子有十五具。大約在下午三時牠果然趕上吾們。牠意欲收下我們船尾的帆，可是牠誤把我們後半船側上面的帆鷥收下，我們氣八尊礮對準一邊，向牠射擊，這使他一面駛退，一面還擊，

1.成就。2.染着。3.瘧疾。4.酷熱。5.天氣。6.首要。7.貿易。8.北緯線十五度。9.赤道。10.營。11.於我大不利。12.抵。13.乘船。14.副船主。15.管理之權。16.極不樂。17.新得之財。18.寄存於。19.孤孀。20.可怕。21.不幸。22.駛向芙蓉島進發。23.驚奇。24.黎明之時。25.土耳其海賊。26.鎮名。(當時爲海盜聚居之處)。27.極力而追。28.扯足。29.帆。30.帆杠。31.伸張。32.盡其桅檣之力所能容，俾可逃免。33覺。34.海賊。35.逼近。36.追及。37.準。38.收帆止駛。39.誤。40.橫止。41.後半船側之上面部。43.船尾。44.拿。45.對準。46.專從一面發不駭蟲煩。47.駛開以避之。48.發礮還擊。

and [1]*pouring* in also his [2]*small shot* from near two hundred men whom he had on board. However, we had not a man [3]*touched*, all our men [4]*keeping close*. He [5]*prepared* to [6]*attack* us again, and we to [7]*defend* ourselves. But laying us on board the next time upon our other [8]*quarter*, he entered sixty men upon our [9]*decks*, who [10]*immediately* fell to cutting and [11]*hacking* the sails and [12]*rigging*. [13]*We plied them with* small shot, [14]*half-pikes*, [15]*powder chests*, and such like, and [16]*cleared our deck of them twice*. However, to cut short this [17]*melancholy* part of our story, our ship being [18]*disabled*, and three of our men killed and eight [19]*wounded*, we were [20]*obliged to yield*, and were carried all [21]*prisoners* into Sallee, a [22]*port* [23]*belonging* to the [24]*Moors*.

The [25]*usage* I had there was not so [36]*dreadful* as at first I [27]*apprehended*; nor was I carried up the country to the [28]*emperor's court*, as [29]*the rest* of our men were, but was kept by the captain of the [30]*rover* as his proper [31]*prize* and made his [32]*slave*, being young and [33]*nimble* and fit for his [34]*business*. At this [85]*surprising* change of my [36]*circumstances*, from a merchant to a [37]*miserable* slave, I was [38]*perfectly* [39]*overwhelmed*. Now I [40]*looked back upon* my father's [41]*prophetic* [42]*discourse* to me, that I should be [43]*miserable* and have none to [44]*relieve* me, which I thought was so [45]*effectually* [46]*brought to pass* that I could not be [47]*worse*; for now [48]*the hand of Heaven had overtaken me*, and [49]*I was undone without redemption*. But, alas! this was but a [50]*taste* of the misery I was to [51]*go through*, as will appear in the [52]*sequel* of this story.

As my new [53]*patron*, or master, had [54]*taken me home to his house*, so I was in hopes that he would take me with him when he went to sea again, [55]*believing* that it would [56]*some time or other* be his fate to be taken by a [57]*Spanish* or [58]*Portugal*

同時在船上面的二百人也一齊射發鎗彈。但是，我們一人也沒有受傷，我們都在戒防之中。他準備再來襲擊吾們，而我們也防備守候。然而，第二次當我們埋服在後半船側之另一部，敵方來了六十個人一轟而上艙面。他們立刻劃去篷和繩。我們用細彈丸，短鎗，火藥等反擊，二次却退敵人，無論如何，把這件悲慘的事情簡單的說，我們的船已被撞破，三人死亡，八人受傷，我們都被逼迫屈服，合船的人全被促往（撒利）那個地方是，（摩耳）人的一個埠頭。

我的待遇並不是像我猜度的那麼恐怖，我也不像其他的人被送往皇宮，但是我作了海賊的專利品，做他的奴隸，因爲我是年輕，又敏捷，巧合他的生意，在這種奇突的變遷的遭遇之下，就由商人而降至奴隸，我是完全被征服了。現在我追念我父親的預言，說我應受苦難而無人救我，我想他的預言果然的應驗了，因爲事無更劣於此了；以爲此刻天降的禍已經臨到我身上了，我必泯滅於此而不可挽救了。但是，咳！這不過是我該受的困難的起頭，以後的危險在下文分解。

我新的主人或者說是東家帶我到他家裏，於是我希望着有和他一同出洋的機會，當他再去海洋之時也許會有一個時期他會被西班牙或葡萄牙的

[1]man-of-war, and that then I should be [2]set at liberty.　But this hope of mine was soon taken away ; for when he went to sea, he left me on [3]shore to look after his little [4]garden, and do the common [5]drudgery of [6]slaves about his house; and when he came home again from his [7]cruise, he ordered me to lie in the cabin to [8]look after the ship.

Here I [9]meditated nothing but my [10]escape, and what [11]method I might take to [12]effect it, but found no way that had the least [13]probability in it. [14]Nothing presented to make the supposition of it rational ; for I had nobody ro [15]communicate it to that would [16]embark with me,—no [17]fellow-slave, no Englishman, Irishman, or Scotchman, there but myself. [18]So for two years, though I often pleased myself with the [19]imagination, yet I never had the least [20]encouraging prospect of [21]putting it in practice.

After about two years, an odd circumstance [22]presented itself, which put the old thought of making some [23]attempt for my [24]liberty again in my head.　My [35]patron lying at home longer than usual without [26]fititng out his ship, which, as I heard, was for want of money, he used, [27]constantly, once or twice a week, sometimes [28]oftener, if the weather was fair, to take the ship's [29]pinnace, and go out into the [30]road a-fish ing.　As he always took me and young Maresco with him [31]to row the boat, we made him very merry, and I proved very [32]dexterous in [33]catching fish ; [34]insomuch that sometimes he would send me with a Moor, one of his [35]kinsmen, and the youth, — the Maresco, as they called him, — to catch a [36]dish of fish for him.

It happened one time that, going [37]a-fishing in a calm morning, a fog rose so [28]thick that though we were not half a [39]league from the shore, we [40]lost sight of it ; and rowing we

兵艦拿獲，那時可以被釋自由了．但是我的這種期望不久成了泡影；因爲當他去航海的時候，就留我在岸上看守他的花園，在他家中當通常僕人的苦工；等他從海上巡邏回家的時候，他又命令我躺在船上去看顧他的船。

在此，我唯一的希望就是設計脫逃，用什麼方法能夠成全其事，但是這是萬不可辦到的．我眼前的情形使我不能實行我的理想遁逃；因爲我沒有人和我商量此事，俾可從事此意——沒有同儕的奴僕，沒有(英國)人，沒有(阿列希)人，沒有(蘇格蘭)人，只有我自己，這樣的生活過了兩年，雖則我時常以妄想作爲自娛之法，但是總不能有勇氣去實行，

大約兩年以後，有著奇事自然的暴發了，因此我又與奮起我試逃的念頭。我的主人住在家中比通常的時期要長些，好久沒有裝置船具以待出發，而按平時他總是一星期出外一兩次，依我所聽見的是去賺錢，如果天氣清朗，他就坐大舢版去捕魚。他常常帶我和一年輕的(馬爾斯哥)同去，幫他划船，我們很可使他快樂，同時我一顯我捕魚技能的高妙；所以有時他要我同他一個(摩爾)親戚，還有年輕的人——他們叫他(摩爾斯哥)的——一陶去替他捉一盆子的魚。

有一次是這樣遇到了，在一個很清靜的早晨去捕魚，霧突然升降過密，甚至離岸只有半里路，我們就瞧不見岸邊了，我們划著

1．兵艦．2．釋放．3．岸上．4．花園．5．苦工．6．僕人．7．海上巡邏．8．看守．9．沉思．10．逃．11．方法．12．使成事．13．可能性．14．眼前各事無有能使我遁逃之意想顯爲合理者．15．商酌．16．從事．17．同爲奴隸者．18．如是者二年．19．幻想．20．勇氣．21．施諸實行之希望．22．發現．23．嘗試．24．自由．25．主人．26．裝置船具預備行駛．27．時常．28．多些．29．雙帆有槳船．30．碇泊所．31．划．32．巧手．33．捕．34．故所以．35．親戚．36．盆．37．捕魚．38．密厚．39．三英里．40．不能見岸．

knew not [1]*whither* or which way, we [2]*labored* all day, and all the next night. When the morning came, we found we had [3]*pulled off* to sea instead of pulling in for the shore; and that we were at least two leagues from the shore. However, we [4]*got well in* again, though with a [5]*great deal* of labor and some [6]*danger*; for the wind began to blow pretty fresh in the morning. But we were all very [7]*hungry*.

Our [8]*patron*, warned by this [9]*disaster*, resolved to take more care of himself for the future; and having lying by him the [10]*longboat* of our English ship that he had taken, he resolved he would not go a-fishing any more without a [11]*compass* and some [12]*provision*. · So he ordered the [13]*carpenter* of his ship, who also was an English slave, [14]*to build* a little [15]*state-oom*, or cabin, in the middle of the [16]*lonfboat*, like that of a [17]*barge*, with a place to [18]*stand behind it* to [19]*steer* and [20]*haul home* the [21]*mainsheet*; and room before for a hand or two to stand and work the sails. She sailed with what we call a [22]"*shoulder-of-mutton*" [23]*sail*; and [24]*the boom gibed over the top of the cabin*, which lay very [25]*suug* and [26]*low*, and had in it room for him to [37]*lie*, with a slave or two, and a table to eat on, with some small [28]*lockers* to put in some [29]*bottles* of such [30]*liquor* as he thought fit to drink; and his bread, rice, and [31]*coffee*. We went [32]*frequently* out with this boat a-fishing; and as I was most [33]*dexterous* to catch fish for him, he never went without me.

It happened one day that he had [34]*appointed* to go out in this boat, either for pleasure or for fish, with two or three Moors [35]*of some distinction* in that place, and for whom he had [36]*provided* [37]*extraordinarily*, and had therefore sent on board the boat [38]*over night* a larger store of [39]*provisions* than ordinary. And he had ordered me to get ready three [40]*fusees*

完全不知道方向和路程；我們工作了一天和一夜；等到第二天早晨到的時候，我們纔發見我們沒有向海岸前進，反划到外海去了；至少吾們離岸有二海里。無論如何，我們終於再划到岸邊了；雖則費許多氣力吃不少的苦；因爲早晨的風吹得很強，當時我們的肚子都很餓了，

我們的主人；受到這次災禍的警告；遂決定以後更宜謹愼保護自己；他有一只從英國船上搶奪來的大艇；他決定再不去捕魚了；除非有了一只領路的羅盤和充分的糧食。於是；他吩咐他船上的木匠；那木匠亦是個英國奴隸，在他的大艇中間造一個小房艙；像花艇的模樣兒；在房艙的後面留個地方可以把舵和拉轉大帆索；房艙前面留個空位足夠二三人站立駕駛的地位。牠是一只我們所謂的"三角篷艇"；牠的帆檣橫倒在船艙的上面，船艙是極寬暢且堅密，裏面有他和一二個奴隸所住的休息間；有一只膳桌，有存幾只抽屜，裏面放置他所歡喜的酒，和麵包，米和咖啡。我們時常乘大著艇去捉魚，因爲我善于替他捉魚，所以他沒有不帶我同去的。

有一天是這樣；他決定坐這只艇去遊玩或捕魚；帶同二三個在該地稍有望聲的摩爾人；因爲款待他們；他加倍的設備設備。所以隔夜他就遣人送糧食到船上，同時他叫我預備三把

(small [1]*muskets*) with [2]*powder and shot*, which were on board his ship, for that they [3]*designed* some sport of [4]*fowling* as well as fishing.

I got all things [5]*ready* as he had [6]*directed*, and waited the next morning, with the boat [7]*washed clean*, her [8]*flag and pendants out*, and everything [9]*to accommodate* his [10]*guests*. When by and by my [11]*patron* came on board alone, he told me his [12]*guests* had [13]*put off* going from some [14]*business* that [15]*fell out*, and ordered me, with the man and boy, as usual, to go out with the boat and [16]*catch* them some fish, for that his friends were [17]*to sup* at his house. And he [18]*commanded* that as soon as I got some fish I should bring it home to his house. All which I [19]*prepared* to do.

This moment, [20]*my former notions of deliverance darted into my thoughts*, for now I found I was likely to have a little ship at my command. My master being gone, I prepared to [21]*furnish* myself, not for [22]*fishing business*, but for a voyage, though I knew not, neither did I so much as [23]*consider*, whither I should steer—anywhere to get out of that place was my [24]*desire*.

CHAPTER IV

My first [25]*contrivance* was [26]*to make a pretense* to speak to this Moor, to get something for our [27]*subsistence* on board; for I told him [28]*we must not presume to eat of our patron's bread*. He said that was true; so he [29]*brought* a large [30]*basket* of [31]*rusk* or [32]*biscuit*, and three jars of fresh water, into the boat. I knew where my [33]*patron's* case of [34]*bottles* stood, which it was [35]*evident* [36]*by the mark*, were taken out of some English prize, and I [37]*conveyed* them into the boat while the Moor was on shore, as if they had been there before for our

亦短鎗裝滿火藥和彈子，這軍火是裝在他的船上，因爲這是他們預備着用以打獵和捕魚的。

我依照他的指揮一齊準備妥當，等候着明天的早晨，艇已洗滌一清，張旗掛幟，一切都備好以供應他的客人。不多時我的主人獨自一人到來，告訴我們，他的客人爲着事業失敗不去玩了，他叫我同那個男子和男孩子可照常坐艇去捕魚，因爲他的朋友約好在他家晚膳。他吩咐我捉得了魚，立刻拿到他的屋子裏去。這些事情我都去預備安排。

此時，我從前求救的心突然射入我的思想之中，因爲現在我發覺我有主使一隻小船的可能。我的主人去後，我就自己預備具裝，並非想去捕魚。但是想出去航行，雖然不知何往，又沒有考慮到目的地——不論何地只要離開這個地方，即可達到我的慾望。

第 四 章

吾第一個計策，是假作對摩爾人說，我們該去招尋艇上必需的我們的糧食；因爲我告訴他我們不可擅自取食主人的食物，他說這個不錯，所以他拿了一大籃的麵包，餅乾，和三缸清水進船。我知道我的主人放缸的櫃子，看缸的式樣就知道是他從英國人那裏拿來的，摩爾上岸時，我把這缸安置艇內，好似早已放在那裏等候我們的

master. I [1]*conveyed* also a great [2]*lump* of [3]*beeswax* into the
boat which [4]*weighed* above half a [5]*hundredweight*, with a
[6]*parcel* of [7]*twine* or thread, a [8]*hatchet*, a [9]*saw*, and a [10]*hammer*,
all of which were of great use to us afterwards, [11]*especially*
the [12]*wax* to make [13]*candles*.

Another [14]*trick* I tried upon him, which he [15]*innocently*
[16]*came into* also. His name was Ismael, which they call
"Muley," or "Moely;" so I called to him: "Moely,"
said I, "our [17]*patron's* guns are on board the boat; can you
not get a little [18]*powder* and [19]*shot*? It may be we may kill
some [20]*alcamis* (a fowl like our [21]*curlews*) for ourselves, for I
know he keeps the gunner's stores in the ship." "Yes,"
says he, "(I'll bring some;" and [22]*accordingly* he [23]*brought*
a great [24]*leather pouch*, which [25]*held* a pound and a half of
powder, or rather more; and another with [26]*shot*, that had
five or six pounds, with some [37]*bullets*, and put all into the
boat. At the same time I had found some powder of my
master's in the [28]*great cabin*, with which I filled one of the
large bottles in the [29]*case*, which was almost [30]*empty*, pouring
what was in it into another. Thus [31]*furnished* with
everything needful, we sailed out of the port to fish. The
[32]*castle*, which is at the [33]*entrance* of the port, knew who
we were, and [34]*took no notice of* us; and we were not above
a mile out of the port before we [35]*hauled* [36]*in our sail*, and
set us down to fish. The wind [37]*blew* from the [38]*north-
northeast* which was [39]*contrary* to my desire, for, had it
blown [40]*southerly* I had been sure to have [41]*made the coast
of* Spain, and at least [42]*reached* to the [43]*Bay of Cadiz*.
But my resolutions were, [44]*blow* which way it would, I
would be gone from that [45]*horrid place* where I was, and
[46]*leave the rest to fate*.

主人，我又帶了一大塊密蠟在船內，密蠟重六十磅，還有一小包麻綫，一把斧頭，一把鋸子，和一把鏈子，這些東西對于我們將來有極大的用處，尤其是可以做燃燭的密蠟。

在他的身上我另外再有一個詐計，他不知不覺的也墜入我計，他的名字叫(伊士馬兒)，人家叫他"墓利"或者叫"(馬利)"，所以我叫他"(馬利)"，當時我說道我們主人的礮都在艇中，你何不去取一點火藥與彈丸？或者我們可以爲自己殺幾只水鳥(似鷿鷈等的禽獸類)，因爲我知道他的軍藥都藏在他的船上"是啊"他說，"我要去拿點"．於是他取了一只大皮袋，裏面裝着一磅牛火藥，或不至一磅牛，另外還有槍還有五六磅彈子，他都放在船內．同時我在大艙內看見我主人的一些火藥，我把那火藥裝在櫃內的一只大瓶中，那只瓶差不多是空的，所有一些東西給我倒在另一個瓶內．如此，我所要的都預備好了，我們就得駛出海口去捕魚．海口出入處的堡壘那個是佈置在進口的地方的，他們都認識我們，並不留意我們；出口不到一里，我們把蓬拿下，開始促魚，風是北偏東北吹着，適和我的目的相反，因爲設若風自南吹，我定可行抵(西班牙)的海邊．至少可到(加低士海灣) 但是我的意志堅決，不管風怎麼吹，我總得離開這驚駭之地，其餘的則聽天由命了。

After we had [1]*fished* some time and [2]*caught* nothing, for when I had fish on my [3]*hook*, I would not pull them up, that he might not see them, I said to the Moor, "[4]*This will not do*; [5]*our master will not be thus served*; we must [6]*stand arther off*." He' thinking no [7]*harm*, agreed, and, being in the head of the boat, [8]*set the sails.* As I [9]*had the helm*, I [10]*ran the boat out* near a [11]*league* farther, and then [12]*brought her to*, as if I would fish. Then, giving the boy the [13]*helm*, I [14]*stepped* forward to where the Moor was, and making as if I [15]*stooped* for something behind him, I [16]*took him by surprise* with my arm under his [17]*waist*, and [18]*tossed him clear overboard into the sea.* He rose [19]*immediately*, for he [20]*swam* like a [21]*cork*, and called to me, begging to be taken in, telling me he would go all over the world with me. He swam so strong after the boat that he would have reached me very quickly, there being but little wind. Upon this I [22]*stepped* into the cabin, and [23]*fetching* one of the [24]*fowling pieces*, I [25]*presented it at him*, and told him I had done him no [26]*hurt*, and if he would be [27]*quiet* I would do him none. "But, " said I, " you [28]*swim* well enough to reach to the shore, and the sea is calm. [29]*Make the best of your way* to shore, and I will do you no harm; but if you come near the boat I'll shoot you through the head, for I am resolved to have my [30]*liberty*." So he [31]*turned himself about*, and swam for the shore, and I make no doubt but he reached it with [32]*ease*, for he was an [33]*excellent* [34]*swimmer*.

I could have been [35]*content* to take this Moor with me, and have [36]*drowned* the boy, but there was [37]*no venturing* to [38]*trust* him When he was gone I turned to the boy, whom they called Xury, and said to him, "Xury, if you will be [39]*faithful* to me, I'll make you a great man; but if you

我們捉了好些時候一點也促不到，因爲我鈎子上有魚之時；我故意不拖出水；使他不能見我已經得魚了，我向（馬爾）說：“這是不行的；我們那裏可以如此的（空手）去侍奉主人；我們必須略行駛遠”。他想沒有害處，就表同情于我，他在船頭上揚帆開駛；我就掌舵，我將船駛出相近一里之遠，那末我再停駛，像要去促魚的樣子。然後我以舵給孩子，再走到（馬爾）立的地方，傴腰裝着到他後面拾東西的形狀，乘他不備，我伸臂抱住他的腰部，將他拋入海中。他卽刻升起，因爲他游水能夠輕如輭木，他叫我，懇求我讓他上船，允許我他願同我遍遊世界。他游的如此快跟在船後，決定會很快的跟到我的船，因爲當時吹着極小的風，因此我走進艙內，取出一把烏鎗對他瞄準，對他說我決不傷害他；如果他肯安靜不擾，我決不加害於他。“不過”，我說，“你儘可以泅水到前上岸去，因爲海面很平靜，好好的自己游上岸去，我可以不害你；但是如果你走近艇邊，我要射中你的頭腦，因爲我決意要恢復我的自由。”所以，他反身游向岸邊。我可擔保他可很容易到岸，因爲他是個超人的游泳者。

我可以心滿意足的和馬爾住在一起，而溺死那個男孩，可是我不可冒險信任他。他離開後。我對這孩子說，他們叫他“柴萊”，假使你忠心對我，我要將你造成一個偉大的人物；但是假使你

1.捕魚．2.捉得．3.鈎．4.此必不可．5.必不可如此侍奉主人．6.略行駛遠．7.害．8.揚帆開駛．9.掌舵．10.將船駛出．11.三英里．12.使船停駛．13.舵．14.走．15.傴腰．16.乘其不備．17.腰部．18.投入海中．19.卽刻．20.游泳．21.輭木．22.走．23.取．24.烏鎗．25.舉以對之．26.傷害．27.安靜．28.泅．29.好自爲之．30.自由．31.反身．32.容易．33.超絕．34.游泳者．35.心滿意足．36.溺死．37.不可冒險．38.信任．39.忠心

will not [1]*stroke your face to be true to me*," that is, swear by Mahomet and his father's beard, "I must [2]*throw* you into the sea too." The boy [3]*smiled* in my face, and spoke so innocently that I could not [4]*distrust* him. He swore to be faithful to me, and go all over the world with me.

While I was [5]*in view of* the Moor that was swimming, I [6]*stood out directly to sea* with the boat, rather [7]*stretching to windward*, that they might think me gone towards the [8]*Strait's* mouth (as indeed any one that had been [9]*in their wits* must have been [10]*supposed* to do). For who would have supposed we were sailed on to the southward, to the truly [11]*barbarian coast*, where whole nations of [12]*negroes* were sure to surround us with their [13]*canoes*, and destroy us; where we could not go on shore but we should be [14]*devoured* by [15]*savage beasts*, or more [16]*merciless* savages of human kind!

But as soon as it grew [17]*dusk* in the evening, I [18]*changed my course*, and [19]*steered* directly [20]*south and by east*, [21]*bending my course a little towards the east*, that I might [22]*keep in with* the shore. Having a fair, fresh [23]*gale of wind*, and a smooth, quiet sea, I [24]*made such sail* that I believe by the next day at three o'clock in the afternoon, when I [25]*first made the land*, I could not be less than one hundred and fifty miles south of Sallee; quite [26]*beyond* the Emperor of Morocco's [27]*dominions* or indeed of any other king [28]*thereabouts*, for we saw no people.

Yet such was the [29]*fright* I had taken of the Moors, and the dreadful [30]*apprehensions* I had of [31]*falling into* their hands, that I would not stop, or go on shore, or come to an anchor. The wind continued [32]*fair* till I had sailed in that manner five days; and then the wind [33]*shifting* to the southward, I [34]*concluded* also that if any of our [35]*vessels* were

不願誓忠于我，"這就是以(馬海末脫)與其父的鬍立誓的意思；"我也將你拋于海中。"這孩子向我笑嘻嘻，他說話時的那副天眞爛漫的態度使我不得不信任他。他誓着忠心於我，且願隨我走遍世界，

當我看着(馬爾)泅水，我直向大海駛行；我沒有迎風而駛；因爲要避開他們的猜度我向海狹而駛(確實的，大凡人在着急之時，必會像他們所猜度的而進行)。因爲誰會料想我們向南駛行達到眞眞的野蠻人民居住的海岸，在那海岸上全國的黑人要划着小艇圍困我們，殺死我們，在那個地方使我們不能上岸，祇將我們給野獸吞吃或者給殘酷的野人吞食。

但是天光一黑我們轉易方向，直朝南偏東駛，略斜向車進發，俾可靠邊。倚靠和順的風，平靜的海面，我們得以張帆疾駛，到第二天下午三點鐘，剛見陸地時我想我們已在 (撒利)南面一百五十里，遠離(馬爾哥)領土了，或已走進了近段的國度，因爲吾們不見有人影，

我從(馬爾)人那裏所受到的驚愕，猶恐，再陷於他們的手中，因此我不敢停駛，或到岸上去或停泊一下子。風還是和順的吹着，我們如此駛行五天；隨後，風轉向南了，我亦推斷，倘使我們的船在

1.誓忠于我。2.拋。3.微笑。4.不信任。5.看見。6.直向大海駛行。7.迎風而駛。8.海灣。9.着急之時。10.推想。11.野蠻。12.黑人。13.小艇。14.吞。15.野獸。16.殘酷。17.暗。18.轉易方向。19.駛。20.南徧東。21.略斜向東進發。22.近……而駛。23.微風。24.張滿帆而疾駛。25.初見陸地。26.遠去。27.領土。28.左近。29.驚愕。30.惶恐。31.陷於。32.和順。33.變方向。34.推斷。35.船。

[1]*in chase of* me, they also would now [2]*give over.* So I [3]*ventured* to [4]*make to the coast,* and [5]*came to an anchor* in the mouth of a little river, I know not what, nor where, neither what [6]*latitude,* what country, what nation, or what river. I neither saw, nor desired to see any people; the [7]*principal* thing I wanted was [8]*fresh* water.

We came into this [9]*creek* in the evening, resolvnig to [10]*swim* on shore as soon as it was dark, and discover the country; but as soon as it was quite dark, we heard such dreadful [11]*noises* of the [12]*barking,* [13]*roaring,* and [14]*howling* of wild [15]*creatures,* of we knew not what kinds, that the poor boy was ready [16]*to die with fear,* and [17]*begged* of me not to go on shore till day. "Well, Xury," said I, "then I won't; but it may be that we may see men by day, who will be as bad to us as those [18]*lions.*" "Then we give them the [19]*shoot gun,*" says Xury, laughing, "make them run way." Such English Xury spoke by [20]*conversing* among us slaves. However, I was glad to see the boy so [21]*cheerful.*

[22]*After all,* Xury's advice was good, and I [23]*took it.* We [24]*dropped* our little anchor, and lay still all night. I say still' for we slept none. In two or three hours we saw [25]*vast* great creatures (we knew not what to call them) of many sorts come down to the [26]*seashore,* and run into the water, [27]*wallowing* and washing themselves for the [28]*pleasure* of cooling themselves; and they made such [29]*hideous* [30]*howlings* and [31]*yellings* that I never indeed heard the like.

Xury was dreadfully frighted, and indeed so was I too; but we were both more frighted when we heard one of these mighty creatures come swimming towards our boat. We could not see him, but we might hear him by his [32]*blowing* to be a [33]*monstrous huge* and [34]*furious* beast. Xury said it

追我,他們現在也該不追了。所以我冒險駛至海岸邊,在河口拋錨,我不知道怎樣辦法,也不知道在什麼地方，也不知道在緯線的那一度,也不知道在什麼省分,什麼國家和什麼河流,我不見一人,我也不願意看見什麼人；我所要的第一件東西便是清水。

我們在黃昏時候到這小灣,決定天一黑就泅到岸上.去觀察這個地方;但是天暗時,我們就聽到荒野動物的可怕的咆哮虓嘷之聲,我們不知是什麼野物,(這種震天動地的叫聲)嚇得男孩魂飛魄散,他哀求我不要上岸,待至天明再說'好,柴萊',我說,"那末我不去了,但是也許會白天裏我們可以看見人,人類或者同獅獸同樣的凶橫","那末我們射鎗"(柴萊)笑着說:"趕他們走是了".這類英語口吻是(柴萊)在我們奴隸中對說的。無論如何,我見他喜悅的模樣我自己也覺得愉快了。

到底(柴萊)的見解不錯;我就聽從他的勸告,我們拋下我們的小錨,靜守一夜。我說的靜,因為我們沒有睡覺。在兩三個鐘頭裏,我們看見各種極大的動物(我們不知怎麼呼他)走下海岸,撞入水中,在水中旋轉着,洗濯全身,使牠冷而舒暢,牠們發出那種可怕的大聲,疾呼的聲音,我從沒有聽到過。

(柴萊)驚愕非常,當然我也是如此;但是我們倆格外的恐怕了,當我們聽那兇猛的動物中的一個游向我們船來,我們看不見牠,但是我們從他的噴氣中可認定牠是一只麗大無比的兇猛的野獸.(柴萊)說牠

1.追.2.捨棄.3冒險.4.駛至岸邊.5.拋錨.6.緯度.7.第一,主要.8.清.9.小灣.10.泅,11.聲音.12.咆哮.13.呼叫.14.咆哮.15.動物.16.魂飛魄散.17.求.18.獅子.19.射.20.談.21.愉快.22.到底,究竟.23聽其言.24.拖.25.極大.26.海邊.27.旋轉.28.舒暢.29.可怕.30.大聲疾呼.31.呼嘯之聲.32.噴氣.33.麗大無比.34.兇猛.

was a lion, and it [1]*might be so for aught I know*; but poor Xury cried to me [2]*to weigh the anchor and row away.* " No," say I, " Xury; we can [3]*slip our cable*, with the [4]*buoy* to it, and go off to sea: they cannot follow us far." I had no sooner said so, but I [5]*perceived* the creature (whatever it was) [6]*within two cars' length*, which something [7]*surprised* me. However, I immediately [8]*stepped* to the cabin door, and taking up my gun, fired at him; upon which he immediately [9]*turned about*, and swam towards the shore again.

But it is impossible to [10]*describe* the [11]*horrid noises and hideous cries and howlings* that were raised, as well upon the edge of the shore as high within the country, upon the noise or [12]*report of the gun*,—a thing I have some reason to believe those creatures had never heard before. This [13]*convinced* me that there was [14]*no going on shore* for us in the night on that coast, and how to [15]*venture on shore* in the day was another question, too; for to have fallen into the hands of any of the [16]*savages* had been as bad as to have fallen into the hands of the [17]*lions* and [18]*tigers*. At least we were [19]*equally apprehensive of the danger of it.*

[20]*Be that as it would*, we were [21]*obliged* to go on shore [22]*somewhere or other* for water, for we had not a [23]*pint* left in the boat. When and where to go to it was the [24]*point*. Xury said if I would let him go on shore with one of the jars, he would find if there was any water, and bring some to me. I asked him why he would go? Why I should not go, and he [25]*stay* in the boat? The boy [26]*answered* with so much [27]*affection*, as made me love him ever after. Says he, "If wild mans come, they eat me, you go wey' " "Well, Xury," said I, "we will both go, and if the 'wild mans' come, we will kill them; they shall eat neither of

是一只獅子，照我的見解，也許會是的；但是可憐的（柴萊）喊我起錨擊槳而駛逃。"不"我說，"（柴萊），我們可以拋放錨索，且有浮筒接着，然後再進海去，他們不能殼那麼遠的追逐我們"。話還沒說完，我看見這個動物（不論他是什麼動物）相距不過二槳之遙，使我不覺驚愕。但是何論如何，我立刻走進艙門，把我的艙拿出，向牠射發，這一艙打過去，牠立刻轉身，游回岸去了。

但是，當鎗聲發出之時，從岸邊與遣地內所發出來的那種狂呼怒吼的聲浪，實在非筆墨所能描寫，鎗聲一物我想這類動物是從未聽得過的。這使我確信我們不可夜晚在那邊登岸；至於白天怎樣冒險登岸，那是另一問題；因為陷入壁人的手中，與落入獅虎的獸掌中是一樣的不幸，最低限度，我們知道所遇到的危險是不相上下的。

無論如何，我們須得到某處去取水，因為我們在船內所剩下的水，一磅也不到了。什麼時候以及什麼地方去取水是一個問題；（柴萊）說如果我准他拿一只水瓶上岸，他會去尋點清水，我問他為什麼他要去？為何我不要去，而留在艇上？他答覆我的話那麼親熱，使我以後更加愛護他，他說，"假使野人來了，他們喫我，你可避去。""好，柴萊，"我說，"我們兩人去，如果野人來，我們可殺死牠們，誰都不給牠們喫了"。

1.照予所見，或亦誠然。2.起錨擊槳而駛行。3.拋放錨索。4.浮筒。5.看見。6.相距不過二槳之遙。7.驚愕。8.走。9.轉身。10.描寫。11.狂呼怒吼。12.鎗聲。13.確信。14.不能登岸。15.冒險登岸。16.野人。17.獅。18.虎。19.恐怖其危險之心相等。20.無論如何。21.逼迫。22.此處或彼處。23.水磅。24.問題。25.留在。26.答。27.親熱。

us. '' We ¹*hauled* the boat in as near the shore as we thought was proper, and so ²*waded* on shore, carrying nothing but our ³*arms*, and two ⁴*jars* for water.

I did not care to go out of sight of the boat, fearing the coming of ⁵*canoes* with savages down the river; but the boy, seeing a low place about a mile up the country, ⁶*rambled* to it, and by and by I saw him come running towards me. I thought he was ⁷*purused* by some savage, or frighted with some wild beast, and I ran forward towards him to help him. When I came nearer to him, I saw something ⁸*hanging over* his ⁹*shoulders*, which was a creature that he had shot, like a hare, but different in colour, and longer legs; however, we were very glad of it, and it was very good meat. But the great joy that poor Xury came with, was to tell me he had found good water, and seen no '' wild mans. ''

But we found ¹⁰*afterwards* that we ¹¹*need not take such pains* for water, for a little high up the ¹²*creek* where we were we found the water fresh ¹³*when the tide was out*, which ¹⁴*flowed* but a little way up. So we filled our jars, and ¹⁵*feasted on* the hare we had killed, and prepared to go on our way, having seen no ¹⁶*footsteps of any human creature* in that part of the country.

CHAPTER V

As I had been one voyage to this coast before, I knew very well that the ¹⁷*islands* of the Canaries, and the ¹⁸*Cape Verd Island* also, ¹⁹*lay not far off from the coast*. But as I had no ²⁰*instruments* to take an ²¹*observation* to know what ²²*latitude* we were in, and not ²³*exactly* knowing, or at least ²⁴*remembering*, what latitude they were in, I knew not

我們將艇拖近岸邊，照我們視爲合適的地點，隨後我們涉水上岸，祇帶我們的軍器與兩只盛水的缸。

我不敢離開太遠怕不見船；惶恐野人乘小艇下水；却是這孩子見了離城一里地方，有一凹處，他跋涉過去，轉瞬之間我見他奔向我來了。我以爲他爲野人所追逐，或者他見了野獸而恐怖了，所以我跑過去援助他。等我走近他時我見有一物掛在他的肩上，那是被他射死的一只動物，像一只野兔子，就是顏色不同，與脚長點；然而我們很快樂着此物，這是很好的食物。但是這是更好的消息了，可憐的(柴萊)告訴我他找到了清潔的水了，那裏並沒有見到"野人"，

但是後來我們覺察得我們不必如此費力去取水，因爲在我們停的小灣上去一點，朝退時，我們看見清水流着，流的地方在上面祇有一點路。所以我們把瓶盛滿了水；歡宴着我們所殺的野兔，再預備出發前進，因爲見到在那方的一部份杳無人蹤。

第五章

因爲我到這海邊來過一次的，所以我得熟悉(加納拉)羣島，以及(浮特島)岬，這些島離岸不很遠。但是爲了我沒有觀測的器械，我們目今在什麼緯度因此不得而知，亦不能確實明瞭，或至少能夠記憶，這些島是在什麼緯度，我不知道。

where to look for them, or when to ¹*stand off to sea* towards them ; ²*otherwise* I might now ³*easily* have found some of these islands. But my hope was that if I ⁴*stood along this coast* till I came to that part where the English ⁵*traded*, I should find some of their ⁶*vessels* upon their usual ⁷*design of trade*, that would ⁸*relieve* and take us in.

⁹*By the best of my calculation*, that place where I now was must be that country which, lying between the Emperor of Morocco's ¹⁰*dominions* and ¹¹*negroes*, lies ¹²*waste* and ¹³*uninhabited*, except by wild beasts, the negroes having ¹⁴*abandoned* it, and gone ¹⁵*farther south*, for fear of the Moors, and the Moors not thinking it worth ¹⁶*inhabiting*, ¹⁷*by reason of its barrenness*; and, indeed, both ¹⁸*forsaking* it because of the ¹⁹*prodigious number* of tigers, lions ²⁰*leopards* and other ²¹*furious creatures* which ²²*harbor* there. So that the Moors use it for their hunting only, where they go like an army, two or three thousand men at a time ; and, indeed, for near a hundred miles together upon this coast we saw nothing but a ²³*waste*, uninhabited country by day, and heard nothing but ²⁴*howlings* and ²⁵*roaring* of wild beasts by night.

Once or twice in the ²⁶*daytime*, I thought I saw the peak of Teneriffe, being the high top of the mountain Teneriffe in the Canaries, and had a great mind to ²⁷*venture* out ,²⁸*in hopes of reaching thither*. But having tried twice, I was ²⁹*forced* in again by ³⁰*contrary winds*, the sea also going too high for my little ³¹*vessel*. So I resoleved ³²*to pursue my first design*, and keep along the shore.

Several times I was obliged to land for ³³*fresh water*, after we had left this place ; and ³⁴*once in particular*, being early in the morning, we came to an ³⁵*anchor* under ³⁶*a little point of land*, which was pretty high, and the tide beginnign to

在什麼地方可以望見那些島，或者什麼時候可以離岸入海向島直駛；否則，我可以不難找到那島。但是我希望如果我們沿岸駛行，直到英國貿易的部分：我該看見幾只他們做賣買的船隻，那船定會拯救我們，帶我們入港。

依我所算，我目前所在的地方一定是在（馬路哥）領土與黑人國的中央，這是一片荒野，沒有人住，祇見野獸；黑人捨去此地而遠朝南去。因為他們怕（馬兒）人，同時（馬兒）人覺得此地無殖居的價值，因為不事生產之故；還有一點兩者捨棄此地的緣故都是因為這個地方產生虎獅豹以及其他兇猛的野獸牠們都棲宿在那裏。因此，（馬利）人祇作牠為打獵的場所，他們去打獵時像一隊軍人，二三千人一次；這是真的，因為沿岸近一百里路，我們不見什麼，不過荒蕪之地，白天也無居人，夜晚祇聽得野獸的狂吼咆哮的嘈雜聲。

在白天有一兩次我好像看見（灘納利夫）山峯；是在（加納垃）的（灘納利夫）山上的高頂，我很想冒險到那邊去，可是試過一兩次，均被逆風趕回，海水漲得太高致不合我小船的駛行。所以我決行我的初意，就是沿岸而行。

有幾次我必須停泊取清水，我們離開此地以後：特有一次很早的早晨，我們停泊在一個小地角下面，那個地角很高，潮水起始。

1. 離岸駛行入海。 2. 不然。 3. 不難。 4. 沿岸駛行。 5. 貿易。 6. 船。 7. 為商業起見。 8. 救。 9. 按予所算。 10. 領土。 11. 黑人。 12. 荒。 13. 無人居住。 14. 捨去。 15. 遠。 16. 殖居；17. 蓋為不事生產。 18. 棄。 19. 眾多。 20. 豹。 21. 兇猛動物。 22. 棲宿。 23. 荒蕪。 24. 狂吼。 25. 咆哮。 26. 白天。 27. 冒險。 28. 冀達彼境。 29. 受逼。 30. 逆風。 31. 船。 32. 行余之初意。 33. 清水。 34. 特有一次。 35. 碇泊。 36. 小地角。

[1]*flow*, we lay still to go [2]*farther* in. Xury, *whose eyes were more about him* than it [4]*seems mine* were, calls [5]*softly* to me, and tells me that we [6]*had best go farther off the shore*; "for," says he, "look, [7]*yonder* lies a dreadful [8]*monster* on the side of that [9]*hillock*, [10]*fast asleep.*" I looked where he [11]*pointed*, and saw a dreadful monster indeed, for it was a [12]*terrible* great lion that lay on the side of the shore, under the shade of a piece of the hill that [13]*hung as it were a little over him.* "Xury," says I, "you shall go on shore and kill him." Xury looked frighted, and said, "Me kill! he eat me [14]*at one mouth*!" one [15]*mouthful* he meant. However, I said no more to the boy, but bade him lie still, and I took our [16]*biggest* gun, which was almost [17]*musket bore*, and [18]*loaded* it with [19]*a good charge of powder* and with two [20]*slugs*, and laid it down; then I loaded another gun with two [21]*bullets*; and the third (for we had three pieces) I loaded with five smaller bullets. I [22]*took the best aim* I could with the first piece to have shot him in the head, but he lay so with his leg [23]*raised* a little above his nose that the [24]*slugs* hit his leg about the knee, and broke the bone. He [25]*started* [26]*up, growling* at first, but, finding his leg broken, fell down again, and then got up upon three legs, and gave the most [27]*hideous* roar that ever I heard. I was a little surprised that I had not [28]*hit* him on the head; however, I took up the second piece immediately, and though he began to move off, fired again, and shot him in the head, and had the pleasure to see him [29]*drop* and make but little noise, but lie [30]*struggling for life.* Then Xury [31]*took heart*, and would have me let him go on shore. "Well, go," said I. So the boy [32]*jumped into* the water, and taking a little gun in one hand, [33]*swam* to shore with the other hand, and coming

流動着，我們依然更行遠進。(柴萊)低聲叫我，因他的目光比我的來得留心注意，告訴我說我們不如遠離海岸；"因為，"他說，"看呀，那邊橫着一只兇猛的怪物，在小山旳旁邊酣睡。,,我跟他所指的方向一望，果然看見一只兇猛的怪物：牠是一只龐大的獅子，橫臥在河邊的一片山影底下，山影略遮在牠上面。"柴萊"我說，"你何不上岸去把牠殺死"(柴萊)帶着懼色道，"我去殺！牠一嘴把我吞下去了，"他的意思是一口，然而我不再和這孩子說話，不過叫他靜待，我取了我們最大的鎗，有點像短手鎗，裝了多量的火藥，又取了兩枝長方形的鎗彈，將牠放下；於是又裝兩粒彈丸於另一鎗內；以及第三把鎗(因為我們有三把)我裝入五粿小彈子。我對準第一把鎗射進牠的頭上，但牠橫臥時把腿稍為伸在牠的鼻子上面，因此那粿長方形的鎗彈落在牠的膀上，將近膝部，打碎了牠的腿骨。牠猝然驚起，先是狂叫，等待覺察腿骨已斷，又跌倒在地，再用三足站起，極叫一聲，那種可怕的慘呼聲音我從未聞到過。我覺得有點奇怪，怎麼沒有擊中牠的頭部因此，我立刻拿第二把，雖然牠動起來，我再射擊，射中他的頭部；我很高興地看牠跌下，牠呼喊的聲音很微細了，但是他極力撑扎，以圖免死。其時(柴萊)壯着膽，要我准他上岸。"好，去罷"我說。於是，這孩子跳在水中，一手拿了一把小鎗，另一手划到岸上，他走

1.流動。2.愈遠。3.彼尤留心注重。4.似我。5.輕微；低聲。6.不如遠離邊岸。7.彼處。8.怪物。9.小山。10.酣睡。11.指示。12.可怕。13.猶略俯臨于其上14.一嘴。15.一口。16.極大。17.短手鎗。18.裝。19.多量火藥。20.長方形之鎗彈。21.鎗彈。22.對準。23.伸上。25.猝然驚起。26.咆哮。27.可怖。28.射中。29.跌到。30.極力撑扎。以圖免死引壯膽。32.跳。33.游

close to the ¹*creature*, put the ²*muzzle of the piece* to his ear, and ³*shot* him in the head again, which ⁴*dispatched him quite.*

This was game indeed to us, but ⁵*it was no food*; and I was very ⁶*sorry* to lose three ⁷*charges* of ⁸*powder* and shot upon a ⁹*creature* that was ¹⁰*good for nothing to us*. However, Xury said he would have some of him; so he came on ¹¹*board*, and asked me to give him the ¹²*hatchet*. "For what, Xury?" said I. "Me ¹³*cut off* his head," said he. However, Xury could not cut off his head, but he cut off a ¹⁴*foot*, and ¹⁵*brought* it with him, and it was a ¹⁶*monstrous* great one.

I ¹⁷*bethought myself*, however, that perhaps the ¹⁸*skin* of him might, ¹⁹*one way or other*, be of some ²⁰*value* to us; and I ²¹*resolved* to ²²*take off* his skin if I could. So Xury and I went to work with him; but Xury was much the better workman at it, for I knew ²³*very ill* how to do it. Indeed, it took us both the whole day, but at last we ²⁴*got the hide* ²⁶*off*, and ²⁵*spreading* it on the top of our cabin, the sun ²⁷*effectually* dried it in two days' time, and it afterwards *served me to lie upon.*

After this stop, ²⁸*we made on to the southward continually* for ten or twelve days, ²⁹*living very sparingly on our provisions*, which began to ³⁰*abate* very much, and going on oftener to the shore than we were obliged to for fresh water. My design in this was to ³¹*make* the River ³²*Gambia* or ³³*Senegal*, that is to say, anywhere about Cape Verde, where I was in hopes ³⁴*to meet with* some European ship. If I did not I ³⁵*knew not what course* ³⁶*I had to take* but to seek for the islands, or ³⁷*perish* there among the ³⁸*negroes*. I knew that all the ships from Europe which ³⁹*sailed* either to the coast of Guinea, or to ⁴⁰*Brazil*, or to the ⁴¹*East Indies*, made

近這個動物，把槍口放在牠的耳邊，又射入牠的頭部，這一來就結果了牠的生命。

這個對於我們眞是一種嬉戲，可惜不能用作食品；我很懊惱，因爲射掉三次火藥的代價，而射死的動物於我們毫無用處。不論如何，(柴萊)說他定要在牠的身上取得一些；所以他到岸上，要求我給他一把斧頭，"有什麼用，柴萊"，我說，"我要割去牠的頭"他說。但是(柴萊)割不掉牠的頭，他僅割去了一腿，他取了來，那是一只怪大的脚。

我自己忖着，也許牠的皮總可以對我有點價值，我決意在我能力範圍之內剝下牠的皮，於是(柴萊) 和我去割掉牠的皮；(柴萊對於這方面是個靈巧的工人，而我不善其術，的確我們費掉整天的工夫，但是到底我們把皮割脫，把皮鋪在我們的艙上，那太陽在兩天內把牠完全曬乾，以後牠使我當牠寢臥之用。

此事完畢以後，我們仍然向南進行有十一二天，對於我們的糧食水量非常節省，因爲糧食減少得很快，此時我們不時常須上岸去取清水 。我的計策乃是要駛到(克皮) 河或(散呢)河去，就是說，只須相近(浮特)地角地方，在此我希望遇見幾只歐洲人的船。否則我不知道該向那條路進駛，唯有去尋那羣島，否則必滅亡于黑人中間了。我明白凡由歐洲到(辭尼)或(巴西國)或(東印度)羣島的船隻必逥

1.動物。2.鎗口。3.射擊。4.結果其生命。5.不能用作食品。6.愁；懊惱。7.代價。8.火藥。9.動物。10. 於我等毫無用處。11.船上。12.斧頭。13.割去。14.脚。15.攜。16.怪大。17.我自怪。18.皮。19.用此法或彼法。20.價值。21.決意22.剝去。23.不善。24. 脫去其皮。25.鋪張26.得力，着勁。27.供我寢臥之用。28仍向南進行29.節飲縮食30.減少31.駛至。32.河名 (在非洲西部)。33.河名(在非洲西部)。34.遇見。35.不知何路。36. 我該進駛。37.死亡。38.黑人。39.駛。40.巴西國(南美洲大國)。41.東印度羣島。

this cape, or those islands. In a word, I put the whole of my ¹*fortune* ²*upon this single point*, either that I must meet with some ship, or must perish.

When I had ³*pursued* this resolution about ten days longer, as I have said, I began to see that the land was ⁴*inhabited*, and in two or three ⁵*places*, as we ⁶*sailed by*, we saw people stand upon the shore to look at us. We could also ⁷*perceive* they were quite black, and ⁸*naked*. I was once ⁹*inclined* [*to go on shore* to them; but Xury was my better ¹⁰*counsellor* and said to me, "No go, no go." However, I ¹¹*hauled* in nearer the shore that I might talk to them, and I found they ¹²*ran* along the shore by me a good way. I ¹³*observed* they had no ¹⁴*weapons* in their hands, except one who had a long ¹⁵*slender* ¹⁶*stick*, which Xury said was a ¹⁷*lance*, and that they could throw them ¹⁸*a great way* with good aim. So I ¹⁹*kept at a distance*, but talked with them ²⁰*by signs* as well as I could, and ²¹*particularly* made signs for something to eat. They ²²*beckoned to me* to stop my boat, and they would ²³*fetch* me some meat. ²⁴*Upon this* I ²⁵*lowered the top of my sail and lay by*, and two of them ran up into the country, and in less than half an hour came back, and brought with them two pieces of ²⁶*dried* flesh and some corn, ²⁷*such as* is the ²⁸*produce* of their cnuntry, but we neither knew what the one or the other was. However, we were willing ²⁹*to accept* it, but ³⁰*how to come at it* was our next ³¹*dispute*, for I would not ³²*venture* on shore to them and they were as much afraid of us. But they took a safe way for us all, for they brought it to the shore and laid it down, and went and stood a great way off till we ³³*fetched it on board*, and then came close to us again.

We made signs of thanks to them, for we had nothing ³⁴*to make them amends*. But an ³⁵*opportunity* offered that very

置地角或邪羣島.換句話講,我將我完全的幸運兒都在此一舉了.或者我必須碰着幾只船;不然只有滅亡了.

當我如是支持着我的意想約將十天之久,如上所逃,我開始看見地上有人居住了,有二三個地方我們船過的時候,我們看見百姓站在岸上望着我.我們亦能看出他們很黑的皮色,並且赤身露體.我一時亟要登岸,但是(柴萊),我的好顧問,對我說,"不去".不論如何,我划近湃邊一些,以便我可以同他們談話,我見他們遠趨避我.我窺見他們手中沒有軍火,除去其中一個人是拿了一細長底棒那個棒(柴萊)說是鎗;告訴我那個鎗可以射得很遠而且必發必準的,我故遠而遠之.不過,盡我所能夠對他們演手勢表意,特別表明我要東西喫.他們以手招我停泊,允許取食物與我,於是我下帆停船;他們中有兩人奔進城去,不到半點鐘他們回來了;拿着兩塊乾肉與幾件穀物,這些食物是他們的特產,可惜我們不懂是什麼東西.不論怎樣我們願意接受.但是如何取那物,倒是個待解的問題,因為我決不敢冒險上岸到他們這去,他們也同樣地見我們畏懼.但是他們用了個兩全的方法,因為他們把食物放在岸上之後,他們遠離站定看着,直待我們取之上船,他們才再走近我們.

我們演手勢表示謝恉;因為我們沒有酬報他們的東西.但是,恰好來了一個機會,使

instant to [1]*oblige* them [2]*wonderfully*; for while we were lying by the shore came two mighty creatures, one [3]*pursuing* the other (as we [4]*took* it) with great [5]*fury* from the mountains towards the sea. Whether they were [6]*in sport or in rage*, we could not tell, any more than we could tell whether it was [7]*usual* or [8]*strange*; but I believe it was the latter, because, in the first place, those [9]*ravenous* creatures [10]*seldom* [11]*appear* but in the night; and, in the second place, we found the people [12]*terribly frighted*, especially the women. The man that had the lance or [13]*dart* did not fly from them, but all the rest did. However, as the two [14]*creatures* ran [15]*directly* into the water, they [16]*did not offer to fall upon* any of the [17]*negroes*, but [18]*plunged themselves into the sea*, and [19]*swam* about, as if they had [20]*come for their diversion*. At last one of them began to come nearer our boat than at first I [21]*expected*; but I lay ready for him, for I had loaded my gun [22]*with all possible expedition*, and bade Xury load both the others. As soon as he came [23]*fairly within my reach*, I fired, and shot him [24]*directly* in the head. [25]*Immediately* he sank down into the water, but rose [26]*instantly* and [27]*plunged up and down*, as if he was [28]*struggling for life*; and [29]*so indeed he was*. He immediately made to the shore; but between the wound, which was his [30]*mortal hurt*, and the [31]*strangling of the water*, he died just before he reached the shore.

It is impossible to [32]*express* the [33]*astonishment* of these poor [34]*creatures* at the [35]*noise* and fire of my gun. Some of them were even ready to die for fear and [36]*fell down as dead with the very terror*; but when they saw the creature dead, and sunk in the water, and that I made [37]*signs* to them to come to the shore, they took heart and came, and began *to* [38]*search for* the [39]*creature*. [40]*I found him by* his blood [41]*staining*

我們立刻得以很奇怪的答謝他們了，因爲我們在海邊休息之時，來了兩只龐大的動物，一只在追逐另一只，(按我們的觀察)帶着怒色從山上直追向海裏去。牠們是眞游戲還是眞的發怒我們不能斷定，我們也不能斷定這是常有的事或是奇異的；不過我相信後者是對的，因爲第一方面，那種貪食的動物除非在夜晚是不常出現的，第二方面，我們看見百姓異常驚惶，尤其是婦女們。有長槍的男人們沒有奔走，其餘的都逃去了。但是當這兩只動物直跳入水中，牠們並不襲擊那些異人，就是突自投入海中，游泳着，好像爲娛樂而來。到了後來其中的一只開始游近我們的帆船，這是出我意料之外；但是我已準備好等待牠，因爲我已經很快底把我的鎗裝好彈子，然後叫柴萊裝另兩把。等牠游近我力所能達的地位，我開鎗射準牠的頭，牠立刻沉下水裏，但是立刻浮上，載沉載浮；似乎拼命地要保存生命；果然不出所料。牠立刻游到海岸；但是牠貪的是致命之傷。以至被水窒息了牠的呼吸使牠沒有抵前便死了。

那輩可憐的動物聽到鎗聲所現的驚奇的狀貌是不易說出的。有幾個嚇得要死，有的驚仆如死；但是當他們看見這動物已死而沉沒水中，以及我所演的手勢招他們到海岸邊來；他們就壯膽而來，他們開始尋覓這條動物。我在近段尋見牠的血染污了水。

1。答謝。2。驚人。3。追逐。4。視作。5。怒色。6。或眞或假。7。常有。8。少見。9。貪食。10。不常。11。出現。12。異常驚恐。13。投槍。14。動物。15。直。16。並不襲擊。17。黑人。18。突自投入海中。19。游泳。20。爲娛樂計而來。21。意料。22。至爲迅來。23。我力所能達。24。直。25。立刻。26。立刻。27。載沉載浮。28。出力以保存生命。29。不出所料。30。致命之傷。31。受水力之過制。32。說出。33。驚奇。34。動物。35。聲音。36。驚仆如死。37。暗示。38。尋覓。39。動物。40。予在近處得之。41。染污。

the water. By the help of a rope, which I *slung round him*, and gave the *negroes* to haul, they *dragged* him on shore, and found that it was a most *curious* *leopard*, *spotted*, and *fine to an admirable degree*; and the negroes *held up their hands with admiration*, to think what it was I had killed him with.

The other *creature*, frighted with the *flash of fire* and the noise of the gun, swam on shore, and ran up *directly* to the *mountains* from whence they came nor could I, at that distance, know what it was. I found *quickly* the negroes wished to eat the *flesh* of this creature, so I was willing to have them take it as a *favor* from me. When I made *signs* to them that they might take him, they were very *thankful*. Immediately they fell to work with him; and though they had no *knife*, yet, with a *sharpened* piece of wood, they took off his skin as *readily*, and much more *readily*, than we could have done with a *knife*. They offered me some of the *flesh*, which I *declined*, pointing out that I would give it to them; but I made signs for the *skin*, which they gave me *very freely*, and brought me a great deal more of their *provisions*, which, though I did not understand, yet I *accepted*. I then made signs to them for some water, and *held out* one of my jars to them, *turning it bottom upward*, to show that it was *empty*, and that I wanted to have it *filled*. They called *immediately* to some of their friends, and there came two women, and brought a great *vessel* made of earth, and *burnt*, as I supposed, *in the sun*. This they set down to me, as before, and I sent Xury on shore with my *jars*, and filled them all three.

有了一根繩，我就投繩而縛住牠的身體，呌黑人拖走，他們拖牠到岸上；瞧見那是隻奇特的豹；斑點累累，甚為可愛；黑人額手以示驚奇；當他們想到我殺死牠的東西。

其他一只動物受了閃光與鎗聲的驚醒游上岸去，直向他們來的山上奔，牠離去迢遠，我是看不見牠是隻何物。我即刻看出黑人要吃牠的肉的樣子，所以我願意任他們拏去，作我的賜贈物。待我表示他們可以拿去，他們是非常感謝。他們就著手工作；雖然他們沒有刀，但用尖利的木塊，他們很快把皮脫去，比我們用刀敏捷得多，他們送些肉與我，而我不受這肉並表示我決意送給他們；不過我暗示我要皮，他竟毫不吝嗇送皮與我，並且又送我許多他們的出產物，雖然我不怖他們的產物為何，我依舊接受，然後我表示要水，取出我的一只瓶，把瓶底向天顯出空無滴水，俾他們明瞭我要水盛滿此瓶；他們便叫他們幾個朋友，來了兩個女人拿著一只盛物之器具，器具是用泥做成的，其後在太陽光裏曬乾了的我想，他們也照以前把器具放在岸上，隨後我命(柴萊)攜帶我的瓶到岸上去，盛滿三瓶。

1. 擲而縛之。 2. 黑人。 3. 拖。 4. 奇特。 5. 豹。 6. 有斑點。 7. 甚為可愛。 8. 額手以以示驚奇之狀。 9. 動物。 10. 火之閃光。 11. 直。 12. 山。 13. 立刻。 14. 肉。 15. 賜贈品。 16. 暗號。 17. 感謝。 18. 刀。 19. 尖利。 20. 敏捷。 21. 不受。 22. 皮。 23. 毫不吝嗇。 24. 糧食。 25. 接受。 26. 取出。 27. 倒覆。 28. 空。 29. 盛滿。 30. 曝。 31. 於日中。 32. 水瓶

CHAPTER VI

I was now [1]*furnished* with [2]*roots and corn*, such as it was, and water; and leaving my friendly negroes, I made [3]*forward* for about eleven days more, without offering to go near the [4]*shore,* till I saw the land [5]*run out* a great length into the sea, at about the distance of four or five [6]*leagues* before me. The sea being very calm, [7]*I kept a large offing to make* this point. At length, [8]*doubling the point*, at about two leagues from the land, I saw [9]*plainly* land on the other side, to [10]*seaward.* Then I [11]*concluded*, as it was most certain indeed, that this was Cape Verde, and those the islands, called, from thence , Cape Verde Islands. However, they were at a great distance, and I could not well tell what I had best do ; for if I should be [12]*taken with* a [13]*fresh* wind I might neither reach one or other.

[14]*In this dilemma*, as I was very [15]*pensive*, I [16]*stepped* into the [17]*cabin,* and sat down, Xury having the helm ; when' [18]*on a sudden*, the boy cried out, "Master, master, a ship with a sail!" The foolish boy was [19]*frighted out of his wits*, thinking it must needs be some of his master's ships sent to [20]*pursue* us ; but I knew we were [21]*far enough out of their reach.* I [22]*jumped out* of the cabin, and immediately saw, not only the ship, but that it was a [23]*Portuguese ship* ; and, as I thought, was [24]*bound to* the coast of Guinea, for negroes. But, when I observed the course she [25]*steered*, [26]*I was soon convinced* they were bound some other way and did not [27]*design* to come any nearer the shore ; upon which I [28]*stretched out to sea* as much as I could, [29]*resolving* to speak with them if possible.

第六章

　　我現在已備辦了各種糧食和飲水；離別了我知已的黑人，我再向前進行了十一天；不想薄岸，直等到我瞧見了一塊伸入海中的長地，凸出在我之前約有五六里路之遙.當時海水平靜，我離岸甚遠，因為我要駛過這塊長地。後來就繞角而行，離地二里，我看清楚海的對面有岸地.因此我知道，其實可以確定無疑，這地是(綠峯)地角，那海島就是(綠峯)羣島.然而，羣島遙遙甚遠，我不知道應該怎麼辦，因為要是遇著一陣風，兩岸我也許都不能逾到了，

　　正在遞退維谷之際，我是很憂悶，我便進艙坐著，(柴萊)把舵；這孩子突自嚷著道，"主人，主人，一只船扯了篷"，這愚蠢的孩子嚇得魂飛魄散了，因為他以為這一定是他主人的一只船派來追趕我們的了，但是我明白我們相隔已遠.我跳出房艙，非但立刻看出那隻船，並且看出是一只葡萄牙的船，照我看來牠必須向(幾內亞)海邊，因為駛去的他們是黑人.但是，當我注視牠們駛行的路向，我旋卽確知他們必往別處，不會駛近海岸；因此照我能力所及，便駛至海中，如果可能的話，我决定同他們說話。

¹*With all the sail* I could make, I found I should not be able ²*to come in their way*, but that they would ³*be gone by* before I could ⁴*make any signal* to them. But after I had ⁵*crowded to the utmost*, and began to ⁶*despair*, they, it seems, saw, ⁷*by the help of their glasses*, that it was some European boat, which they ⁸*supposed* must belong to some ship that was lost; so they ⁹*shortened sail* to let me come up. I was ¹⁰*encouraged* with this, and as I had my ¹¹*patron's flag* on board, I ¹²*made a waft of it* to them, for a ¹³*signal of distress*, and fired a gun, both which they saw; for they told me they saw the ¹⁴*smoke*, though they did not hear the gun. Upon these ¹⁵*signals* they very kindly ¹⁶*brought to*, and ¹⁷*lay by for* me; and in about three hours' time I ¹⁸*came up with* them.

They asked me what I was, in Portuguese, and in Spanish, and in French, but I ¹⁹*understood* none of them. At last, a Scotch sailor, who was on board, ²⁰*called to* me; and I ²¹*answered* him, and told him I was an Englishman, and that I had ²²*made my escape out of slavery* from the Moors, at Sallee. They then bade me come on board, and very kindly took me in, and all my goods.

It was an ²³*inexpressible joy* to me, which any one will believe, that I was thus ²⁴*delivered*, as I ²⁵*esteemed* it, from such a ²⁶*miserable* and almost hopeless ²⁷*condition* as I was in. I *immediately* ²⁸*offered* all I had to the ²⁹*captain* of the ship, ³⁰*as a return for my deliverance*. He ³¹*generously* told me he would take nothing from me, but that all I had should ³²*be delivered safe to me* when I came to Brazil. "For," says he, "I have ³³*saved* your life ³⁴*on no other terms than I* would be glad to be saved myself; and it may, ³⁵*one time or other*, be my lot to be taken up in the same ³⁶*condition*. Besides," said he, "when I carry you to Brazil, so great

　　我雖則極力張帆行駛，我覺察我不能駛近他們，而且等我可以示他信號之時，他們已經駛過了；但是我竭力滿帆前駛之後，我慢慢兒的感覺到絕望，而他們似乎藉了望遠鏡之助力，遙見着這是歐洲的帆船，他們料想這艇是屬於某失事的船的，所以他們收帆讓我們追過去。這使我壯瞻了，我有我主人的旗在船上，我就對他們搖旗以示信號，一種危急的信號，並且放了一槍，兩者他們都可見到；因爲他們對我說，他們看見烟霧，雖然他們沒有聽見槍聲。見了這些信號，他們很表同情停船等待我們；在三個點鐘以內我才得追及他們。

　　他們用(葡萄牙)語，(西班牙)語，(法蘭西)語問我是什麼，但是我一些不懂。後來船上的一(蘇革蘭)水手高聲疾呼我；我答覆他告訴他我是個(英國)人，以及我是在(撒利)從(馬利)人奴隸之羈縛中逃出來的，他們總叫我上船。他們很仁慈底讓我進船，和我的貨物進船。

　　這對我是件樂不可言的事，這個誰都會像我那麼鄭重，因爲我得從這種苦難絕望的境況之中遇救。我就把我所有的奉獻船主，以報拯救之恩。我慷慨地告訴他我決不會拿我一毫的東西，但是他說到巴西國的時候，我的東西終儘可完璧歸趙。"因爲"，他說，"我救你生命莫非爲我自已被救而已；也許有時我亦要如是被人救起。此外"，他說，"當我帶你到(巴西)

a way from your own country, if I should take from you what you have, you will be [1]*starved* there. and then I only take away that life I have given. No, no," says he " [2]*Seignior* Inglese (Mr. Englishman), I will carry you thither [3]*in charity*, and those things will help to buy your [4]*subsistence* there, and your [5]*passage* home again. "

As he was [6]*charitable* in this [7]*Proposal*, so he [8]*was just in the performance to a little* ; for he ordered the seamen that none should touch anything that I had ; then he [9]*took every-thing into his own possession*, and gave me [10]*back* an [11]*exact* [12]*inventory* of them, that I might have them, even to my three [13]*earthen jars*.

As to my boat, it was a very good one ; and that he saw, and told me he would buy it of me for his ship's use, and [14]*asked* me what I would have for it. I told him he had been [15]*so generous* to me in everything that I could not offer to make any [16]*price* of the [17]*boat*, but left it [18]*entirely* to him. Upon this he told me he would give me a [19]*note of hand* to pay me eighty pieces of [20]*eight* for it at Brazil ; and when it came there, if any one [21]*offered* to give more, he would [22]*make it' up*. He offered me also sixty [23]*pieces* of eight more for my boy Xury, which I was [24]*loath* to take. Not that I was [25]*unwilling* to let the captain have him, but I was very loath to sell the poor boy's [26]*liberty*, who had [27]*assisted* me so faith-fully in [28]*procuring my own*. However, when I let him know my reason, he [29]*owned it to be just*, and offered me this [30]*medium*, that he would give the boy an [31]*obligation* to set him free in ten years, if he [32]*turned* Christian. Upon this, and Xury saying he was willing to go to him, I let the [33]*captain* have him.

離你自已的家鄉很遠，要是我拿你所有的佔爲已有，那麼你將餓死，這樣我只是取去我所賜與的生命了。"不"不，他說，"英國先生，我爲慈善起見送你到那邊去，那些東西可以給你在那兒買你的伙食，與作你的川資"。

他的建議懇切，並且他實踐其約，一絲不苟；他又囑咐船員不准動我所有的東西；然後他收管各物，一面給我一張詳細的品物單子，使牠仍爲我物，連我的三只瓶也寫在物單上。

至於我的艇，那是只很好的；他看見牠，他告訴我，他願意買牠，作爲船上的使用，他問我要多少錢。我告訴他說他各方面如此厚優我，我不能出價，全憑他是了。於是他說他須給我一紙借票，到(巴西)付我八十個銀幣；他又說到了那邊要是有人願出較高的價錢，他必補足其數。他又出了六十個銀幣賣我的童子(柴萊)，這個我殊不願受。並不是我不願給船主佔有，乃是我不願賣去這孩子的自由權之故，因爲他始終忠誠助我得到我的自由。但是，待我說明我理由以後，船主認爲公道，他位一個中庸之法，就是他寫給他一紙盟書，立着誓過了十年准予釋放他，不過他須變爲基督敎徒。於是，(柴萊)說他願意隨他，我便准許船主有他。

We had a very good voyage to Brazil, and I ¹*arrived* in the ²*Bay de Todas los Santos, or All Saints' Bay*, in about twenty-two days after. And now I was once more ³*delivered* from the most ⁴*miserable* of all ⁵*conditions* of life; and what to do next with my self I was to ⁶*consider*.

The ⁷*generous* ⁸*treatment* the captain gave me I can ⁹*never enough remember*. He would take nothing of me for my ¹⁰*passage*, gave me twenty ¹¹*ducats* for the leopard's skin, and forty for the lion's skin, which I had in my boat, and ¹²*caused everything I had in the ship to be punctually delivered to me*. And what I was willing to sell, he ¹³*bought* of me, such as the case of ¹⁴*bottles*, two of my guns, and a piece of the lump of ¹⁵*beeswax*,—for I had made ¹⁶*candles* of the rest. In a word, I made about two hundred and twenty pieces of eight of all my ¹⁷*cargo*; and with this ¹⁸*stock*, I went on shore in Brazil.

I had not been long here before I was ¹⁹*recommended* to the house of a good, honest man, like himself, who had an ²⁰"*ingenio*," as they call it; that is, a ²¹*plantaion* and a ²²*sugarhouse*. I lived with him some time, and ²³*acquainted* myself, by that means, with the manner of ²⁴*planting* and making of ²⁵*sugar*. Seeing how well the ²⁶*planters* lived, and how they got rich ³⁷*suddenly*, I ²⁸*resolved*, if I could get a ²⁹*license* to ³⁰*settle* there, I would turn ³¹*planter* among them; resolving ³²*in the meantime,* to find out some way to get my money, which I had left in London, ³³*remitted* to me. ³⁴*To this purpose*, getting a kind of ³⁵*letter of naturalization*, I ³⁶*purchased* as much land that was ³⁷*uncultivated* as my money would reach, and formed a plan for my ³⁸*plantation* and ³⁹*settlement*; such a one as might be ⁴⁰*suitable* to the stock which I ⁴¹*proposed to myself* to receive from England.

我們一路平安到了（巴西）；我約在廿天之後到（聖公灣）去，我現在又從我生命中最困難的情境內釋放了出來；我以後怎樣辦呢，我須得考慮一下。

這船主款待我的仁慈我是記不勝記。他不肯要我一點川資，給我二十個（錢名）賣豹皮，四十個賣獅皮，這些皮是在我的船內，以及按期將我所有各物，悉數歸我。凡我所願意出售的，他向我買，如瓶箱和兩把槍；一塊蜜蠟，因為其餘的蠟被成做了燃燭。簡言之，我把我所有的船貨買得二百二十塊銀幣；有了這點資本，我就出發到（巴西）去了。

我在此沒有好久，我就被介紹給一個忠誠的人家去，那家有一栽植地和製糖廠，依他們叫牠；那就是，一個栽種甘蔗的田園和一個製糖的廠，我和他住着好些時光，這樣我得以熟悉種植和製糖的方法。看到這栽植者所居住的優越，以及他們致富的迅速，我決意如果我能得到一張照會居留，我必將轉成他們中間的一個栽植者；同時設法將我寄留在倫敦的銀錢匯寄與我。因為要達到這種目的，獲得一種入籍證書，於是我儘我的錢購買未經開墾的田地，計劃着我的種植和居住的步驟，這個辦法，也許可以適合我意欲從英國匯來的資本的用處；

1. 海灣名．2. 到．3. 釋放．4. 困難．5. 情境．6. 考慮．7. 仁慈．8. 待遇．9. 記不勝記．10. 川資．11. 德國金幣或銀幣名，每約值英洋一元．12. 立刻將予名下所有各物，悉數歸我．10. 售．14. 瓶．15. 蜜蠟．16. 燃燭．17. 船貨．18. 資本、19. 介紹．20. 栽植地及製糖廠．21. 田園．22. 製糖廠．23. 熟悉．24. 種植．25. 糖．26. 有栽植地者．27. 迅速．28. 決意．29. 執照．30. 居留．31. 栽植者．32. 同時．33. 匯寄．34. 為欲達此目的起見．35. 入籍證書．36. 購買．27. 未開墾．38. 栽植．39. 居住．40適合．41. 我意欲．

I had a ¹*neighbor*, a Portuguese of ²*Lisbon*, but born of English parents, whose name was Wells, and ³*in much such circumstances as I was*. I call him my neighbor, because his ⁴*Plantation* lay next to mine, and ⁵*we went on very sociably together*. ⁶*My stock was but low*, as well as his; and we rather planted for food than for anything else, for about two years. However, we began to ⁷*increase*; and our land began to ⁸*come into order*; so that the third year we planted some ⁹*tobacco*, and made each of us a large piece of ground ready for planting ¹⁰*canes in the year to come*. But we both wanted help; and now I found, more than before, I had done ¹¹*wrong* in ¹²*parting with* my boy Xury.

But, alas! for me to do wrong that never did right, was no great wonder. I had ¹³*no remedy* but to go on. ¹⁴*I had got into an employment quite remote to my genius, and directly contrary to the life I delighted in*, and for which I ¹⁵*forsook* my father's house and ¹⁶*broke through* all his good advice. If ¹⁷*I resolved* to go on, I might as well have ¹⁸*stayed* at home, and never have ¹⁹*fatigued myself* in the world as I had done. And I ²⁰*used often to say to myself*, I could have done this as well in England, among my friends, as have gone five thousand miles off to do it among ²¹*strangers* and savages, in a ²²*wilderness*, and at such a distance as never to hear from any part of the world that had the least knowledge of me.

In this manner I ²³*used to look upon my condition with the utmost regret*. I had nobody to ²⁴*converse wtih*, but now and then this neighbor; no work to be done, but by the labor of my hands; and I used to say I lived just like a ²⁵*man cast away* upon some ²⁶*desolate* island, that had nobody there but himself. But how just has it been, and how should all

我有一個隣人,(里斯朋)京城的(葡萄牙)人,(英國)籍的父母,他的名字叫(彎耳),他與我的境遇相若,我呼他爲我的鄰人,因爲他的栽植場所在我的隣邊,彼此往返很密切的緣故,我的資本薄弱,他也是如此。我們只能栽植夠吃而已,約有二年。不論如何,我們逐漸擴充,我們的田園亦漸漸整頓有條;因此在第三年我們種些煙草。我們每人準備一塊大地,爲來年栽植甘蔗之用。但是我們都須要助手;現在我感覺到,較前尤甚,我不該捨去我的童子(柴萊)。

但是,我做錯的事永不會再對了,這原不是稀罕的事。在無法可施之時我只得敷衍下去。我可寄身於營業場中,然此項營業與我的天性才能大相矛盾,且與我所喜的生計,亦全然相反,我爲了這些才離別了父親家中,違逆他良好的勸告,假若我照這樣做去,我不如安居在家,決不會如是自受勞苦。我自己時常說我在(英國)的友朋中也可以這樣做的,何必跋踄五千里路到陌生人,野人,與荒山野地中間,而且如此遙遠,不聞世事而世界也不知復有我這人的地方來呢。

處此境地,目擊心傷,我沒有人和我交談,有時就是這隣人,沒事可做,只用手術的工作;並且我時常說我是同一個因遭遇失事而被棄於荒島的人,沒有他人,祇我自己一人,但是怎麼爲如此的,以及人們怎樣應該

1.隣人。2．葡萄牙之京城。3．與余境遇相同。4.栽植。5.彼此往還頗密。6．予之資本薄弱。7.增加擴充。8．整頓有條。9.烟草。10．甘蔗於來年。11.鎽。12.捨。13.無法可施。14．予巳寄身於營業場中。然此項營業,與予之天性才能大相矛盾,且與予所喜之生計,亦全然相反也。15．捨去。16.違逆。17.決意。18.居留。19.自受勞苦。20.常自語曰。21.陌生人。22.荒野。23.處此境地,我心憂傷。24.交談。25.因船遇難。而被抛棄。26．荒蕪。

men [1]*reflect* that when they [2]*compare* their present [3]*conditions* with others that are worse, Heaven may [4]*oblige* them to make the [5]*exchange*, and [6]*be convinced of their former felicity by their experience* !

I was, [7]*in some degree*, settled [8]*in my measures* for [9]*carrying on* the plantation, before my kind friend, the captain of the ship that took me up at sea, went back; for the ship [10]*remained* there, [11]*in providing his lading*, and [12]*preparing* for his voyage, nearly three months. When I told him what little [13]*stock* I had left behind me in London, he gave me this friendly and [14]*sincere advice*: "Seignior Inglese," said he (for so he always called me), "if you will give me letters and [15]*orders* to the person who has your money in London, to send your [16]*effects* to Lisbon, I will bring you the [17]*produce* of them, [18]*God willing*, at my return; but, since [19]*human affairs* are all [20]*subject to* changes and [21]*disasters*, I would have you give orders but for [22]*one hundred pounds sterling*, which, you say, is half your stock, and [23]*let the hazard be run for the first*; so that, if it come safe, you may order the rest the same way; and, if it [24]*miscarry*, you may have the other half to [25]*have recourse to* for your [26]*supply.*"

This was so [27]*wholesome* advice, and looked so friendly, that I did as he desired; and accordingly the [28]*gentlewoman* with whom I had left my money [29]*delivered* a hundred pounds to a [30]*merchant* at London. The merchant, [31]*vesting* this money in English goods, such as the captain had written for, sent them [32]*directly* to him at Lisbon, and he brought them all safe to me to Brazil; among which, without my [33]*direction* (for I was too young in my business to think of them), he had taken care to have all sorts of tools, [34]*ironwork*, and [25]*utensils* [36]*necessary* for my plantation, all which were of great use to me.

反省自己比別人的環境較好的時候，上帝也許勉強他們有這種互易，俾撫今思昔而知往昔之幸福。

我稍爲得以從我計劃繼辦錢植，在我的好友，就是從海內帶我上船的船主，回去以前；因爲這船停留在那邊豫備裝載貨物，預備出發他約有三個月的航海生涯。當我告訴他我在倫敦寄留的一些錢，他發表這一番視切底誠懇低意見："英國先生"他說，(因爲他常是這樣叫我) "如果你交給我信或支票分付在倫敦你寄存錢的人把你的動產寄到(里斯朋)來，我可以在回來時把你的生產物帶來，若得天助一路平安；但是，人有旦夕之禍患，我以爲你不如先寫一百念磅支票這依你所說的是你財產的半數，所以不妨一爲冒險；因爲，若使穩當的話，你儘可照辦；万一失事，你還有其餘一半可以賴以生活。

這是良善的忠告，看他知己的模樣我便照辦了，果然我寄錢的寡婦遞交一百念磅與倫敦商人，這商人把錢投資於英國貨物，依船主所寫的，直接運到(里斯朋)一手交他，他平安地寄到(巴西)給我，在這什物內，我並未指示 (因爲我在商業上的智識還幼稚得很)他却已處置各種貨物，鐵器，載種必須的器具，這些東西對我均有莫大的用處。

1.反省.2.比較.3.環境.4.勉強.5.互易.6.撫今思昔,方知前之幸福.7.稍.8.從予計畫.9.繼辦.10.留.11.豫備裝載貨物.12.準備.13.資本.14.誠懇意見.15.支票.16.動產.17.生產物.18.若得天助.19.人事.20.難免.21.不測之災難.22.一百金磅.23.不妨一爲冒險.25.失事.25.賴.26.供給.27.良善.28.寡婦.29.遞出.30.商人.31.投資本.32.直接.33.指示.34.鐵器.35.器具.36.必鎮.

79

When this ¹*cargo* arrived I thought ²*my fortunes made*, for I was ³*surprised* with the joy of it; and my good ⁴*steward*, the captain. had ⁵*laid out* five pounds to ⁶*purchase* and ⁷*bring me over* a ⁸*servant*, ⁹*under bond* for six years' service, and ¹⁰*would not accept of any consideration* except a little ¹¹*tobacco* which I would have him ¹²*accept*, being of my own produce

¹³*Neither was this all*; for my goods being all English ¹⁴*manufacture*, such as cloths, ¹⁵*stuffs*, ¹⁶*baize*, and things ¹⁷*particularly* ¹⁸*valuable* and ¹⁹*desirable* in the country, I found means to sell them ²⁰*to a very great advantage*; so that I might say I had more than four times the value of my first cargo, and was now ²¹*infinitely beyond* my poor neighbor,— I mean in the ²²*advancement* of my plantation; for the first thing I did I bought me a negro slave, and a European servant also,—I mean another besides that which the captain ²³*brought* me from Lisbon.

CHAPTER VII

You may suppose that after having lived almost four years in Brazil, and beginning to ²⁴*thrive and prosper* very well upon my plantation, I had not only learned the language, but had ²⁵*contracted acquaintance and friendship* among my fellow ²⁶*planters*, as well as among the merchants at San Salvador, which was our port. In my ²⁷*discourses* among them I had ²⁸*frequently* given them ²⁹*an account of my* two voyages to the coast of Guinea the manner of trading with the negroes there, and how easy it was to ³⁰*purchase* upon the coast for trifles—such as ³¹*beads*, toys, knives, ³²*scissors*, ³³*hatchets*, ³⁴*bits of glass*, and the like—not only ³⁵*gold dust*, Guinea grains, elephants, teeth, etc., but negroes. for the ³⁶*service* of Brazil, in great numbers.

當這一船貨物抵埠，我想我已獲得厚利，我簡直是驚喜欲絕；我其好的管家，船主，費了五磅替我賣來一個僕人，契據上註明六年工作，約上並無他求，除一點煙外，這煙我可以給他，因為那是我的出產品。

不特這樣；因為我的貨物是(英國)人手造的，譬如布，布呢，粗呢，以及種種在這個地方視為特別貴重與需要的貨物，我招到出售的方法，藉獲厚利；因此我可以說我有了第一次船貨四倍以上的價值，於是現在我的境況超勝我的隣人——我指我栽植的進步而言；因為第一件事我做的乃是買一個黑奴與一歐洲僕人——我指船主從(里斯朋)帶亦的另外的一個。

你們也許會想像住在(巴西國)四年之後，栽植上確已蒸蒸日上，我不久將學會了土語，在我栽植中結交朋友，以及和(聖薩耳伐)，我們的海上，地方人商人來往。我和他們的談話中，我屢次詳述我二次到(幾內亞)海岸航海的經歷，和黑人貿易的種種，以及怎麼易於在那海邊購買細小物品，如小珠，玩物，洋刀，翦刀，土穀，象牙等，但是黑人，要他們到(巴西)來做工，這類人的數目很多、

1.抵埠.2. 予已獲厚利.3.驚喜.4.管家.5.費.6.購買.7. 攜來給我.8.僕人.9.有契據.10.約中並無他求.11.烟草.12.愛.13.不特此也.14.手製.15.布呢.16.粗呢.17.特別.18.貴重.19.需要.20.獲厚利.21.極.22.進步.23.帶.24.蒸蒸日上.25.交結友朋.26.栽植者.7.談話.28.屢次.29.細則.20.購.31.小珠.32.剪刀.33.斧頭.34.小塊玻璃.35.金沙.36.工作.

They ^{1}*listened* always very ^{2}*attentively* to my ^{3}*discourses* on these ^{4}*heads*, but ^{5}*especially* to that part which ^{6}*related* to the ^{7}*buying* negroes, which was a trade, at that time, not only ^{8}*not far entered into*, but so far as it was, had been ^{9}*carried on by permission of the kings of* Spain and Portugal, so that few negroes were ^{10}*brought*, and those ^{11}*excessively dear*.

It happened, being ^{12}*in company with* some ^{13}*merchants* and planters of my ^{14}*acquaintance*, and talking of those things very ^{15}*earnestly*, three of them came to me next morning, and told me they had been ^{16}*musing* very much upon what I had ^{17}*discoursed* with them of the last night, and they came ^{18}*to make a secret proposal* to me. After ^{19}*enjoining secrecy*, they told me that they had a mind ^{20}*to fit out* a ship to go to Guinea; that they all had ^{21}*plantations* as well as I, and ^{22}*were straitened for* nothing so much as ^{23}*servants*; that as it was a trade that could not be carried on, because they could not ^{24}*publicly* sell the ^{25}*negroes* when they came home, so they ^{26}*desired* to make but one voyage, to bring the negroes on shore ^{27}*privately*, and ^{28}*divide* them among their own plantations. In a word, the question was whether I would go as their ^{29}*supercargo* in the ship, ^{30}*to manage the trading part* upon the coast of Guinea. They ^{31}*offered* me that I should have my ^{32}*equal* share of the negroes, without ^{33}*providing* any part of the ^{34}*stock*.

This was a fair ^{35}*proposal*, it must be ^{36}*confessed*, had it been made to any one that had not had a ^{37}*settlement* and a plantation of his own ^{38}*to look after* which was ^{39}*in a fair way* of ^{40}*coming to be very considerable*, and with a good ^{41}*stock* upon it. But for me, that was thus entered and ^{42}*established*, and had nothing to do but to go on as I had begun,

他們時常很注意着聽我談這個問題，尤其是注意着談到購買黑奴的一節，至若賣買黑奴的一種生意是不甚盛行着，而且須有(西班牙)和(葡萄牙)國王的許可才行，因爲那些帶來的黑奴很少，所以價值很昂貴，

因爲我恰好和幾個商人與所認識的栽植者，時相往來。大家很起勁的講這些事情，第二天的早晨有三人來訪我，告訴我他們已將我昨天晚上同他們談的話再四思維，並且來陳述他們的來意。警戒着各人勿要聲張洩漏此事以後，他們說着有意裝備一船到（幾內亞）去；還說他們像我一樣地有栽植場所，祇爲用人問題頗感困難；至於賣買人口不能實辦的原因，因爲他們同家時不可公然販黑奴，所以他們意欲航行，不過是一次，私帶黑人，然後在他們中間自己分配黑人簡言之，這個問題乃是我允否做他們商船中管理貨物的人，至(幾內亞)海岸督理賣買事務，他們准我享受同樣分配黑奴的權利，雖然我可不必投下資本。

這是件公道的提議．應該承認牠的．要是向一個他自己沒有住所沒有田園可照料的人說的話，那倒有獲厚利的希望，因爲資本是已有好的了。可是臨到我，想到當時怎樣來的與怎樣去建立事業的初衷，不必想做甚別的事，祇須像開始那麼再繼續下去，

1．聽．2．注意．3．談．4．題目．5．尤其的．6．論及．7．購買．8．不甚盛行．9．從事國王之旨准而得實行．10．帶來．11．昂貴．12．相……交游．13．商人．14．識認．15．起勁．16．密四思維．17．談．18．再陳意見．19．戒勿聲張．20．裝備．21．田園．22．爲……所磨難．23．僕人．24．公然．25．黑人．26．須求．27．私人．28．分配．29．商船中管貨物者．30．督理買賣事務．31．准奉．32．平均．33．投下．34．資本．35．提議．36．承認．37．居所．38．照料．39．頗有後望．40．將獲厚利．41．資本．42．創立事業．

for three or four years more, and to have sent for the other hundred [1]*pounds* from England, and who in that time, and with that little [2]*addition*, could [3]*scarce* have failed of being worth three or four thousand pounds [4]*sterling*, and that [5]*increasing* too,—for me to think of such a voyage was the most [6]*preposterous* thing that ever man in such [7]*circumstances* could [8]*be guilty of*.

But I, that was [9]*born to be my own destroyer*, [10]*could no more resist the offer* than I could [11]*restrain* my first [12]*rambling* [13]*designs* when my father's good [14]*counsel* was lost upon me. In a word, I told them I would go [15]*with all my heart*, if they would [16]*undertake* to look after my plantation [17]*in my absence*, and would [18]*dispose of it to* such as I should direct, if I [19]*miscarried*. This they all [20]*engaged* to do, and [21]*entered into writings or covenants* to do so. I [22]*made a formal will*, [23]*disposing* of my nlantation and effects [24]*in case of* my death, making the [25]*captain* of the ship that had saved my life, as before, my [26]*universal heir*, but [27]*obliging* him to [28]*dispose of* my [29]*effects* as I had [30]*directed* in my will; one half of the produce being to himself, and the other to be [31]*shipped* to England.

In short, I [32]*took all possible caution to* [33]*preserve* my [34]*effects*, and [35]*to keep up* my plantation. Had I used half as much [36]*prudence* to have [37]*looked into my own interest*, and have made a [38]*judgment* of what I ought to have done and not to have done, I had certainly never gone away from so [39]*prosperous* an [40]*undertaking*, leaving all the [41]*probable views of a thriving circumstance*, and gone upon a voyage to sea, [42]*attended with all its common hazards, to say nothing of* the reasons I had to expect particular [43]*misfortunes* to myself.

三四年，把那一百金鎊從英國匯來，這錢到那時可增值三四千鎊英國制幣，這個同時亦增——像我這樣的人要想去這次航行，眞是件最荒謬的事，豈一人在此環境之內所能犯的。

但是我生而爲自害自者，不能却其所請，正像我第一次游蕩的計畫定奪後之不可遏制一樣，甚至我父親的勸告亦不生效力。總之，我告訴他們我極願去，不過當我出外之時他們須得看守我的田園，萬一失事。他們須准我把黑人賣給我所指定的人。這個他們都應承可做，當時大家依此訂立盟約。我立一正式遺囑，處置我的田園產業，設若我死亡，救我生命的船主作爲承繼完全產業之後嗣，但他須照我的遺囑上所囑咐的處置；一半送他本人，其餘的運到（英國）

總之，我非常小心保全我的財產，與維持我的田園。如果我只稍有一半的智慧覺察着我利益攸關的事業與決斷我該做與不該做的事，我當然不會離去如是興隆的事業，與繁盛的前途；而向隨有尋常危險的船航海去，此時姑且不論我**自己尋求不幸的理由。**

But I was ¹*hurried on,* and ²*obeyed blindly the dictates of my fancy* rather than my reason. ³*Accordingly,* the ship being fitted out and the ⁴*cargo* furnished, and all things done, ⁵*as by agreement,* by my ⁶*partners* in the voyage, I ⁷*went on board* in ⁸*an evil hour,* the first of September, 1659, being the same day eight years that I went from my father and mother at Hull ⁹*in order to act the rebel to their authority,* ¹⁰*and the fool to my own interests.*

Our ship was about one hundred and twenty ¹¹*tons burden,* and carried six guns and fourteen men, besides the ¹²*master,* his boy, and myself. We had on board no ¹³*large cargo of goods,* except of such toys as were fit for our ¹⁴*trade with the* negroes, such as beads, bits of glass, ¹⁵*shells,* and other ¹⁶*trifles,* especially little ¹⁷*looking-glasses,* knives, scissors, ¹⁸*hatchets,* ¹⁹*and the like.*

The same day I went on board we ²⁰*set sail,* ²¹*standing away to the* northward upon our own coast, ²²*with design to stretch over* for the African coast when we had ²³*reached* about ten or twelve ²⁴*degrees* of ²⁵*northern latitude,* which, it seems, was the ²⁶*manner of course* in those days. We had very good weather, only ²⁷*excessively hot,* all the way upon our own coast, till we came to the ²⁸*height* of ²⁹*Cape St. Augustine;* from whence, keeping further off at sea, we ³⁰*lost sight* of land, and steered as if we ³¹*were bound for* the isle ³²*Fernando de Noronha, holding our coast northeast by north,* and leaving those isles on the east. In this ³³*course* we ³⁴*passed the line* in about twelve days' time, and were, by our last ³⁵*observation,* in seven degrees twenty-two minutes northern latitude, when a ³⁶*violent* ³⁷*tornado or hurricane took us quite out of our knowledge.* It began from the southeast, ³⁸*came about to the northwest,* and then ³⁹*settled* in the northeast,

但是我急于前進,就妄從着思想置理智於不顧,於是船與船貨就預備妥當了,一切均為我的航海同事按約辦定。我在一千六百五十九年九月一日的凶時登船,恰巧是五年前我在(黑耳)離開我父親的一天,因為要違叛他們的權限而盜賊我一已之利益。

我們的船載了一百二十噸重的貨物,帶了六把槍。十四個人,除去船主,他的孩子和我自已以外。我們船上沒有大件貨物,祗有我們和黑人貿易的玩物,如珍珠,小塊玻璃,貝殼以及其他零星雜物,尤其是眼鏡,小刀霸刀,斧頭等。

我在開船那天登舟,我們沿岸向北駛行,意欲駛到非洲海岸去,直待我們到了約有北緯線十或十二度,這好似常行慣了的。我們一路沿岸而駛,天氣尚佳,就是酷熱而已,迨至我們到了(聖奧客斯汀)角;從那邊,漸深入海,我們不見岸地。我們似乎駛向(非稜多拳龍哈)島去着,沿岸東北偏北駛行,羣島後在東邊。在此航海我們用了二十天的工夫駛過赤道,依最後一次的觀測,當是在北緯線七度二十二分,忽降颶風,致使吾儕昏暈不知所措。暴風起自東南,後變為西北,然後轉定東北,

1.逼進.3.茫然不知所從而妄行已意.3於是.3.船貨.5.按約.6.同事.7.登船.8.不吉之事.9.即以叛逆予父母之權限.10.盜賊予一已之利益.11.船載貨噸量.12.船主.13.大件貨物.14.貿易.15.殼.16.零星雜物.17.眼鏡.18.斧頭.19.諸如此類之物.20.開船.21.向北駛行.22.意欲駛至.23.伸至.24.度.25.北緯線.26.行程常例.27.酷熱.28.高處.29.角名.30.不見.31.駛向.32.島名(在大西洋中,屬巴西國),沿岸而駛.33.航路.34.駛過赤道.35.觀測.36.兇暴.37.颶風致吾儕昏暈不知所措.38.變為西北.39.轉止。

from whence it blew in such a ¹*terrible* manner that for twelve days together we could do nothing but drive, and, ²*scudding away before it*, let it carry us ³*whither ever* fate and the ⁴*fury* of the winds ⁵*directed*. During these twelve days I need not say that I ⁶*expected* every day ⁷*to be swallowed up*; nor, indeed, did any in the ship ⁸*expect* to save their lives.

In this ⁹*distress* we had, besides the ¹⁰*terror* of the storm, one of our men died of ¹¹*fever*, and one man and the boy ¹²*washed overboard*. About the twelfth day, ¹³*the weather abating a little*, the master made an ¹⁴*observation* as well as he could, and found that he was in about eleven degrees north latitude, but that he was twenty-two ¹⁵*degrees* of ¹⁶*longitude* farther west from Cape St. Augustine; so that he found he was upon the coast of Guiana, on the north part of Brazil, beyond the ¹⁷*river Amazon*, towards that of the ¹⁸*river Orinoco*, commonly called the Great River, and began ¹⁹*to consult with me* what course he should take, for the ship was ²⁰*leaky*, and very much ²¹*disabled*, and he was going directly back to the coast of Brazil.

I ²²*was positively against* that; and looking over the ²³*charts* of the ²⁴*seacoast* of America with him, we ²⁵*concluded* there was no ²⁶*inhabited* country for us ²⁷*to have recourse to* till we came within the circle of the ²⁸*Caribbee Islands*, and we therefore resolved ²⁹*to stand away for Barbadoes*; which, by ³⁰*keeping off at sea*, to avoid the ³¹*indraft* of the ³²*Bay or Gulf of Mexico*, we might easily ³³*perform*, as we hoped, in about fifteen day's sail; whereas we could not ³⁴*possibly* make our voyage to the coast of Africa without some ³⁵*assistance* both to our ship and to ourselves.

由此颶風狂吹的凶勢延長至十二天之久，**使我們不能做什麼事情**，祇是逐波猛衝，乘風飛駛，不拘何過，一任我們的命運和狂風所支配，在這十二天內那是不待說了，我每天只待波濤覆覆沒；誠然沒有一人在船上有得救的希望。

在這危險時期，除了這可怖的暴風以外，我們中有一人得了寒熱症而死去，同時又有一男人與這孩子爲波浪打入海中。約在第十二天風浪稍殺的時候，主人盡力觀測，查得他是約在十一度緯線，但他在二十二度的經線，離(開奧客斯汀)的西面很遠的於是他知道他是在(圭亞那)的海邊，(巴西國)的北部，(亞馬孫河)的遠處，對着(潴勒諾哥河)，俗稱(大河)，他始與我商酌，當向何路進駛，因爲船已漏了，損壞頗多，他想駛囘(巴西國)海岸去。

我極力反對這個，我和他看美國沿岸的航海圖，我們斷定此時船正向着無人居住的地方駛去，向着(加勒比羣島)中間駛去，我們因此決定駛向(巴巴特島)駛去；如此仍在海中駛行，避着(墨西哥海灣)內流的海水，我們希望約有十五天的駛行可以達到目的；另一方面，我們決不能行至非洲海岸，倘使無人與無船的互相援助。

With this [1]*design* we changed ous course, and [2]*steered* away [3]*northwest by west*, in order to reach some of our English islands, where I hoped for [4]*relief*. But our voyage was [5]*otherwise determined*; for, being in the [6]*latitude* of twelve degrees eighteen miuntes, a second storm came upon us, which carried us away with the same [7]*impetuasity* [8]*westward*, and drove us so [9]*out of the way of all human commerce* that, had all our lives been saved as to the sea, we were rather in danger of being [10]*devoured* by savages than ever [11]*returning* to our own country.

In this [12]*distress*, the wind still [13]*blowing* very hard, one of our men early in the morning [14]*cried out*, "Land!" We had no sooner run out of the [15]*cabin* to look out, in hopes of seeing [16]*whereabouts in the world we were*, than the ship [17]*stuck upon sand*, and in a moment, her [18]*motion* being so stopped, [19]*the sea broke over her* in such a manner that we [20]*expected* we should all have [21]*perished* immediately, and we were immediately [22]*driven* into our [23]*close quarters*, to [24]*shelter* us from [25]*the very foam and spray of the sea*.

It is not easy for any one who has not been in the like [26]*condition* to [27]*describe* or [28]*conceive* the [29]*consternation* of men in such [30]*circumstances*. We knew nothing where we were, or upon what land it was we were [31]*driven*,—whether an island of the [32]*main*, whether [33]*inhabited* or not inhabited. As the [34]*rage* of the wind was still great, though rather less than at first, we could not so much as hope to have the ship [35]*hold* many minutes without [36]*breaking* into pieces, unless the winds, by a kind of [37]*miracle*, should [38]*turn* immediately [39]*about*. In a word, we sat looking upon one another, and [40]*expecting* death every moment, and every man, accordingly, [41]*preparing for another world*; for there

　　有了這個計畫，我們改變我們的路向而駛去西北偏西，爲欲到英國的幾個島上去，以冀遇救。但是我們的航路另定方向；因爲在十二度十八公緯線內二次颶風臨到我們了，猛吹着我們向西，把我們撞出人類貿易的區域外。在這種情境之下，卽使我們的生命得從海內獲救，我們祇少也要被野物吞食而永不能囘本國去、

　　在這危險時候，狂風依舊猛烈的吹着，我們中有一人在很早的黎明喊着道，"岸地"，我們方才跨出艙向外觀望，希望看見我們的所在地，其實這只船突然的觸礁了，瞬時船的動力卽止，波濤撞擊上來的情形使我們感覺我們立刻就要滅亡了，我們迅速地趕進內艙密室以避海上的淈花濺沫。

　　要一個從未經歷此情此境的人去描寫或感覺人類在此環境內的驚惶失措實是件不易的事。我們不知道在什麼地方，亦無從知道我們被趕到的是什麼"岸地"——是大洲的一個海島呢，還是有人居住的或無人居住的地方。因爲狂暴的風淈依舊猛烈的吹着，雖然較起初時消滅了些；但我們不能希望船能支持數分鐘而不致碎成零片，除非這颶風得奇異的恩賜立變方向，簡言之，我們互相對視着，每分鐘期待着死的光臨，各人都是預備着死亡；因爲。

was little or nothing more for us to do in this.　That which was our present [1]*comfort*, and all the [2]*comfort* we had was that, [3]*contrary to our expectation*, the ship did not break yet and that the master said the wind began to [4]*abate*.

Now, though we thought that the wind did a little abate, yet the ship having thus [5]*struck* upon the sand, and [6]*sticking* too fast for us to expect her [7]*getting off*, we were in a [8]*dreadful* condition indeed, and had nothing to do but to think of [9]*saving* our lives as well as we could.　We had a boat at our [10]*stern* just before the storm, but she was first [11]*staved* by [12]*dashing against* the ship's [13]*rudder,* and [14]*in the next place* she [15]*broke away*, and either [16]*sunk* or was driven off to sea ; so there was no hope from her.　We had another boat [17]*on board*, but how to [18]*get her off into the sea* was a [19]*doubtful* thing.　However, [20]*there was no time to debate*, for we fancied the ship would break in pieces every minute, and some told us she was [21]*actually* broken already.

In this distress, the [22]*mate* of our vessel [23]*laid hold of* the boat, and with the help of the rest of the men [24]*got her slung over the ship's side*.　Then, getting all into her, we [25]*let go*, and [26]*committed ourselves*, being eleven in number, [27]*to God's mercy* and the wild sea ; for though [28]*the storm was abated* [29]*considerably*, yet the sea run dreadfully high upon the shore, and might be well called " [30]*den wild zee*, " as the Dutch call the sea in a [31]*storm*.

And now our case was very [32]*dismal* indeed ; for we all saw [33]*plainly* that the sea went so high that the boat [34]*could not live*, and that we should be [35]*inevitably* drowned.　As to [36]*making sail*, we had none, nor, if we had, could we have done anything with it.　So we [37]*worked at the oar* towards the land, though [38]*with heavy hearts*, like men going to

我們只有一線的希望或竟一線也沒有、我們現在的安慰,我們所有的唯一的安慰就是出乎我們的意料之外的,這船沒有裂開,而且船主說風勢亦漸減了。

現在,雖然我們覺得風在徐下, 然而船旣觸礁,冲入過堅,難有脫險的希望,我們的確是在一可怖的情境之內, 在無法可施時祗得儘力救我們的生命。颶風之前我們有一只小艇拖在船尾,但是那艇當觸礁時和船相碰,已經擊碎,繼則脫船,也許已沉或撞出海外;此點我們是絕望了。我們還有一艇在船上,但是怎樣取之放入海內倒是個疑問.不論如何,此時是無暇討論的,因爲我們幻想着每分鐘船要裂碎了,有的人說船確已裂開了。

在此千鈞一髮之際我們船上的船副執住此艇, 以及其他的人同來幫忙,將艇拖放於大海之旁。然後我們一共十一人都走進艇去開駛,聽天由命,和隨狂風的支配;因爲雖則風力大減,但是海水向岸上高衝的可怖,好像(荷蘭人)所稱"洪濤巨浸之海。"

現在我們的情境的確是悽慘;因爲我們看得很清楚,海水如此高聳,我們的艇難以抵抗了,我們決不能逃免溺死。至於張篷我們是沒有的,卽使有了篷,我們也沒有辦法,所以我們向岸划進時,已是心灰膽喪,好似人們往

1.安慰.2.安逸.3.出於予等希望之外.4.減.5.觸進.6.冲擊.7.脫離.8.可怖.9.救10.船尾.11.擊碎.12.相碰.13.舵.14.繼則.15.脫離.16.沉.17.船上.18.取而放諸海19.疑.20.無時討論.21.確然.22.大副.23.執住.24.抛放于大船之旁.25.開駛.26.就己.27.聽天由命.28.風勢大減.29.相當.30.洪濤巨浸之海.31.颶風.32.懷惻.33.清楚.34.難保無險.35.必不能免.36.張篷.37.鼓棹.38.心灰膽喪.

¹*execution*; for we all knew that when the boat came nearer the shore, she would be ²*dashed* in a thousand pieces by the ³*breach of the sea.* However, we ⁴*committed our souls to God in the most earnest manner*; and the wind ⁵*driving* us towards the shore, we ⁶*hastened our destruction* with our own hands, ⁷*pulling* as well as we could towards land.

What the shore was,—whether rock or sand, ⁸*whether steep or shoal*,—we knew not. The only hope that could ⁹*rationally* give us ¹⁰*the least shadow of expectation* was if we might find some bay or ¹¹*gulf*, or the mouth of some river, where ¹²*by great chance* we might ¹³*run our boat in*, or ¹⁴*get under the lee of the land*, and perhaps ¹⁵*make smooth water.* But there was nothing like this ¹⁶*appeared*, but as we made nearer and nearer the shore' the land looked more ¹⁷*frightful* than the sea.

After we had rowed or rather driven, about a league and a half, as we ¹⁸*reckoned* it, a ¹⁹*raging wave*, ²⁰*mountainlike*, ²¹*came rolling astern of* us, and plainly bade us expect the ²²*coup de grace*. In a word, it took us with such a ²³*fury* that it ²⁴*overset* the boat at once; and, ²⁵*separating* us as well from the boat as from one another, gave us not time to say, "O God!" for we ²⁶*were all swallowed up in a moment.*

CHAPTER VIII

²⁷*Nothing can describe the confusion of thought* which I felt when I sank into the water. Though I swam very well, yet I could not ²⁸*deliver* myself from the waves so as ²⁹*to draw breath*, till that wave having driven me, or rather carried me, a vast way on towards the shore, ³⁰*having spent itself*, went back, and left me upon the land, almost dry but half dead with the water I took in. I had so much ³¹*presence of*

處決塲去了；因爲我們都明白等艇駛近岸時，牠必被海波撞成千片。雖然我們極懇切地將我們的靈魂將託諸上帝；風却依舊趕着我們向岸去，我們將我們的手舉起，緊促着我們的滅亡，用力的向海灘推進。

這岸灘是什麼——是石子的或沙泥的或陸峭有的或是淺沙的——我們不得而知。唯一的希望我們可以得到的乃發見海灣或河口，籍以將船駛入避風，也許會駛抵風平浪靜之區。但是這種希望一無形蹤，不過我們漸漸駛向岸灘，岸地的情境較海尤爲恐怖，

我們搖船，其實是趕船，約有一里半路，依我們的計算，一陣洪波，像山那樣高的向船尾滾逐，這顯然是致命的一擊。簡言之，怒濤來勢猛烈，立刻有傾船之勢；將我們彼此分散，似同我們離開船一般，也不給我們一點辰光說句 "上帝啊！，" 因爲我們轉瞬已爲洪濤覆沒了。

第 八 章

我沉入水內的時候，神魂的昏亂，難以言語形容，雖則我很會游泳，然我不能在波浪裏呼吸，直等波濤將我趕到，可說帶我，向着極大的海岸衝去，用盡了他的力，那波浪於是折了囘去拋我在將乾的岸上，但我喝飽了水此時已是半死了，我是泰然自若，

1.處決.2.撞.3.波濤.4.將吾等靈魂托著上帝.5.趕.6.促我等之滅亡.7.拖.8.或陸峭之所.9.或淺沙之灘.10.一線之望.11.灣.12.僥倖.13.將船駛入.14.避湮.15.駛抵風平浪靜之區.16.蹤跡.17.可怖.18.計算.19.洪波.20.似山.21.向船尾滾逐.22.致命之一擊.23.猛擊.24.傾翻.25.分離.26.轉瞬已爲洪濤覆沒.27.此時神魂之昏亂，難以言語形容.28.救援.29.呼吸.30.用盡.31.泰然自若

[1]*mind* as well as [2]*breath left*, that, seeing myself nearer the [3]*mainland* than I expected, I [4]*got upon my feet* and [5]*endeavored to make on towards* the land as fast as I could, before another wave should return and [6]*take me up again*. But I soon found it was [7]*impossible* to [8]*avoid* it; for I saw the sea [9]*come after me* as high as a great [10]*hill*, and as [11]*furious* as an [12]*enemy*, which I [13]*had no means or strenght to contend with*. My business was to [14]*hold my breath*, and raise myself upon the water, if I could; and so, by [15]*swimming*, to [16]*preserve* my breathing and [17]*pilot myself towards the shore*, if possible, [18]*my greatest concern* now being that the sea, as it would carry me a great way towards the shore when it came on, might not carry me back again with it when it gave back towards the [S]ea.

The wave that [19]*came upon* me again [20]*buried* me at once twenty or thirty feet deep in its own body, and I could feel myself carried with a mighty force and [21]*swiftness* towards the shore a very great way; but I held my breath, and [22]*assisted* myself to [23]*swim* still forward [24]*with all my might*. I was ready to [25]*burst with holding my breath*, when, as I felt myself [26]*rising up*, so, [27]*to my immediate relif*, I found my head and hands [28]*shoot out* above the [29]*surface* of the water. It was not [30]*two seconds of time* that I could keep myself so; yet it [31]*relieved me greatly*, gave me [32]*breath* and new [33]*courage*. I was [34]*covered* again with water [35]*a good while*, but not so long but I [36]*held it out*; and, finding the water had [37]*spent* itself and begun to return, I [38]*struck forward* against the return of the waves and [39]*felt ground again with my feet*.● I stood still a few moments [40]*to recover breath* and till the waters went from me, and then [41]*took to my heels* and ran, with what [42]*strength* I had, [43]*further* towards the shore. But neither would this

正為還沒有斷氣，看看自已，出乎意料之外，近在大陸，在又一波湧回來衝擊我之前。我起來奮力迅速向內狂奔，但是我立刻看出這是不能避免的；因為我看見海水追隨在我後方像山那麼高像敵人那麼凶惡，這一來我無力抗拒了。我的事務祇有保守我的呼吸和將我的身體昇起於水面，要是我能夠辦到，那麼，泅泳可以維持呼吸力，同時可以將我泅至海岸，如果可能的話，我現在最關心的一件事便是這海水湧上的時候，可以把我帶進岸去，但波淚退時務須不使他能帶我同去。

　波淚又撞擊了，立刻將我埋沒在水底二三十尺之深，我可以感到我自己被猛大的迅速的濤勢一直衝進海灘很遠；但我屏着我氣息竭力再遊向前進。我幾乎呼吸窒塞，當我覺得自己升降時，為卽刻之救助，我的頭手伸出水面。我如是浮在水面不滿二分鐘但已經大減去我之痛苦了，給我呼吸與新起的膽力。我又為水遮沒。不過沒有先前那麼長久，但是我盡力支持着，覺水已用竭了牠的力而開始退回去了，我奮力直向退潮逆衝，我的脚此時得踏地上。我靜立了片刻，以恢復氣息，等水退去了已後，用我的殘餘之力奔進海灘，但這也不能

deliver me from the fury of the sea, which came *¹pouring* in after me again; and *²twice* more I was *³lifted up* by the waves and carried forward as before, the shore being very flat.

The last time of these two had *⁴well-nigh* been *⁵fatal* to me, for the sea, having *⁶hurried* me along as before, landed me, or rather *⁷dashed* me, against a piece of a rock, and that with such force that it left me *⁸senseless*, and indeed helpless as to my own *⁹deliverance*, *¹⁰The blow taking my side and breast, beat the breath, as it were, quite out of my body*: and had it returned again immediately. I must have been *¹¹strangled in the water*. But I *¹²recovered* a little before the return of the waves, and seeing I should be covered again with the water, I resolved to *¹³hold fast* by a piece of the *¹⁴rock*, and so to hold my breath, if possible, till the wave went back. Now, as the waves were not so high as at first, being nearer land, I *¹⁵held my hold* till the wave *¹⁶abated*, and then *¹⁷fetched another run*, which brought me so near the *¹⁸shore* that the next wave, though it went over me, yet did not so *¹⁹swallow* me up as to carry me away, The next run I took, I got to the *²⁰mainland*, where, *²¹to my great comfort*, I *²²clambered up the cliffs of the shore*, and sat me down upon the grass, free from drnger and *²³quite out of* the reach of the water.

I was now landed, and *²⁴safe* on shore, and began to look up and thank God that my life was saved, in a *²⁵case* wherein there was, some minutes before, *²⁶scarce any room to hope*. I believe it is *²⁷impossible to express*, to the life, what the *²⁸ecstasies and transports* of the soul are when it is so *²⁹saved,* as I may say, out of the very *³⁰grave.*

救我脫離怒海，波浪又跟我湧上；我又遭遇兩次波浪的打擊而又如前那麼被衝進去，直到平岸。

　　最後的兩次幾乎完結了我的生命，因為這海似前一般的激烈地衝我向前，放我，其實是衝我在一塊石上，衝力過猛至使我的知覺頓失，誠然我自己無力再救自己了，這一擊，正中我的胸部，而我的氣息飄飄然離身外；要是海水立刻再回頭，那麼我定會溺斃。但是波浪轉回以前，我稍為有點回覆知覺了，看到我將要再為水所撞沒之時，我決意堅握這塊石頭，同時停止我的呼吸，如果可能，我必須直待水折回了去。現在，因為波濤沒有先前那麼高，而且我是更近地了，我堅握我所把持之物，然後再跑，這一跑使我越發近岸了，所以後來的波濤，雖然衝過我，但是不能似前那樣把我吞滅而帶我去了。我下次的奔跑，我得抵大陸，方才心安慰，我攀登岸上的峭壁，坐在草上，危險已脫，因為離水尚遠了。

　　我現在登陸，平安抵岸了，我開始向上望着，感謝上帝救我的生命，從一個情境之內，在此境內幾分鐘之前，幾無一線的希望。我相信這是難以向生命用言語形容精神上的喜不自勝，當這個生命，我可以說，從墳墓中救出之時。

1・撞・2・兩次・3・舉起・4・幾乎・5・死・6・急・7・撞・8・如覺頓失・9・拯救・10・這一擊，正中我的胸脅，而我的氣息飄飄然離於身外・11・溺斃12・回復・13・堅握・14・石・15・緊握我所把握之物・16・滅・17・再跑・18・岸・19・吞・20・大陸・21・我的心安慰・22・攀登岸上的峭壁・23・尚遠・24・平安・25・情境・26 幾無一線之希望・27・難以言語形容・28・喜不自勝・29・救・30 墳墓・

I walked about on the shore [1]*lifting up* my hands, and [2]*my whole being* as I may say, [3]*wrapt up* in a [4]*contemplation of my deliverance*; making a thousand [5]*gestures* and motions, which I cannot [6]*describe*; [7]*reflecting* upon all my [8]*comrades* that were drowned, and that [9]*there should not be one soul saved but myself*. For, as for them, I never saw them afterwards, or any sign of them, [10]*except* three of their [11]*hats*, one cap, and two [12]*shoes* that were not [13]*fellows*,

[14]*I cast my eyes to the stranded vessel,* when, [15]*the breach and froth of the sea being so big*, I could [16]*hardly* see it, it lay so [17]*far off*; and I considered, Lord! how was it possible I could get on shore.

After I had [18]*solaced my mind* with the [19]*comfortable* part of my [20]*condition*, I began to look round me, to see what kind of place I was in, and what was next to be done. I soon found my comforts [21]*abate*, and that, in a word, I had a dreadful [22]*deliverance*. I was wet, had no clothes to [23]*shift* me, nor anything either to eat or drink to comfort me; [24]*neither did I see any prospect before me* but that of [25]*perishing* with hunger or being [26]*devoured* by wild [27]*beasts*. And that [28]*which was particularly afflicting to me* was that I had no [29]*weapon*, either to hunt and kill any creature [30]*for my sustenance*, or to [31]*defend* myself against any other [32]*creatures* that might desire to kill me [33]*for theirs*. In a word, I [34]*had nothing about me* but a knife, a [35]*tobacco* [36]*pipe*, and a little tobacco in a box. This was all my [37]*provision*; and this [38]*threw me into terrible agonies of mind*, that for a while I ran about like a [39]*madman*. Night coming upon me, I began, [40]*with a heavy heart*, to consider with would be my lot if there were any [41]*ravenous* beasts in that country, as at night they always [42]*come abroad for their prey*.

　　我在海邊散步舉起着我的手，全副的精神，我可以說，貫注於我的得救情形；我做了一千個手勢和動作，但是我不能把他們描寫出來；回憶我的溺死的同伴，他們都死了，只存我一人。因爲，講到他們，我以後永不能再見他們，或再見一些形跡了，除出了他們的三只禮帽，一只小帽，以及兩只不成對的鞋子。

　　我注視着擱淺的船。當時海波洶湧，我看不清楚這船，這船離岸很遠；我想，上帝啊！我怎麼能夠抵岸的呢。

　　我看到我的愉快的情形之處我覺得極可慰藉我的胸懷之後，我又開始注視着我的週圍了，觀察我現在的地方是如何，以及以後如何進行，我立刻看出我的愉快減少了，換言之，我到了可怕的出險的地步，我的全身潮溼，沒有更換的衣服，也沒有吃的或喝的東西可以撫慰我；一無可望的光景，祇有餓死或被野獸吞滅的路，就中最使我傷心的一件事，就是我沒軍器，去打獵與殺死野物使我會有食糧，或保護我自已抵抗野物，以免他們來吞吃我；簡言之；除了一刀一烟管和一匣內一點烟草以外，我並無長物，烟管就是我所有的食糧；這個令我心神懊喪，甚至我一刻之間好像瘋癡一般了。夜來了，我想到要是這地方有狼吞虎噬的野獸，我將怎麼辦呢，因爲夜晚牠們必定時常出外覓食，不覺憂心悄悄了。

All the [1]*remedy* that offered to my thoughts at that time was to get up into [2]*a thick,* [3]*bushy tree* like a fir, but [4]*thorny,* which grew near me, and where I [5]*resolved* to sit all night, and consider the next day what [6]*death* I should die, for as yet I saw [7]*no prospect of life.* I walked about a [8]*furlong* from the shore, to see if I could find any fresh water to drink, which I did, [9]*to my great joy*; and having drank, and put a little tobacco in my mouth to [10]*prevent* hunger, I went to the tree, and [11]*getting up* into it, endeavored to place myself so that if I should sleep I might not fall. And having cut me a short [12]*stick* like a [13]*truncheon,* [14]*for my defence,* [15]*I took my lodging*; and being [16]*excessively* [17]*fatig ed*; I [18]*fell fast asleep,* and slept as [19]*comfortably* as, I believe, few could have done in my condition.

CHAPTER IX

WHEN I waked it was [20]*brood day,* the weather clear, and the storm abated, so that [21]*the sea did not rage and swell* as before. But that which surprised me most was, that the ship was lifted off in the night from the sand where she lay by the [22]*swelling of the tide,* and was driven up almost as far as the [23]*rock* which I at first [24]*mentioned,* where I had been so [25]*bruised* by the wave [26]*dashing* me against it. This being within about a [27]*mile* from the shore where I was, and the ship [28]*seeming to stand upright* still, I [29]*wished* myself on [30]*board,* that at least I might save some [31]*necessary* things for my use.

When I came down from my [32]*apartment* in the tree, I [33]*looked about me* again, and the first thing I found was the boat, which lay, as the wind and the sea had [34]*tossed* her up, upon the land, about two [35]*miles* on my right hand. I

　　我現在腦筋中所有的計劃就是爬上一叢密之樹，這樹像一棵松樹，但是多刺的，此樹靠近在我旁邊，我決意全夜坐在樹上，同時考慮我明天死亡的事情，因為到了現在我還沒有生存的希望。我從海灘走進英里八分之一的路，去尋點清水湯，這個我已找到，所以不勝欣喜之至；喝了水，就放些烟在口內藉免飢餓，我走到樹邊爬在樹中，努力設法睡安，以免墜下，折了一根樹枝，類似一短根杖，以資防禦，我便歇宿在那裏了；因為非常疲倦，我睡得很熱，我相信很少的人在我情境之下會像我那麼安睡的。

第九章

　　等我醒來時已是白晝，天氣清朗，颶風滅殺，所以水波沒有先前的洶涌。但是使我最覺驚奇的乃是這船從泥土中在夜潮漲時所浮起，而被冲到將近我起初撞及的那塊石頭，這塊石頭就是我當時被潮水撞着受傷的，這石離我所在的海灘不到一里路遠，此船彷彿直立，我希望上船，在此我也許可以得到我所必須的東西。

　　當我在我樹內的宿所走下，我環顧四週，第一件東西我見到的便是這艇停在岸地，因為被風與海波所冲起，約離我右邊有二里路之遙。

walked as far as I could upon the shore [1]*to get to her*; but found [2]*a neck or inlet of water* between me and the boat, which was about half a mile broad. So I came back [3]*for the present*, [4]*being more intent upon getting at the ship*, where I hoped to find something [5]*for my present subsistence.*

A little after noon I found the sea very [6]*calm* and [7]*the tide ebbed* so far [8]*out* that I could come within a [9]*quarter of a mile* of the ship. And here I [10]*found a fresh renewing of my grief*; for I saw [11]*evidently* that if we had kept on board we had been all [12]*safe*,—that is to say, we had all got safe on shore, and I had not been so [13]*miserable* as to be [14]*left entirely destitute of all comfort and company* as I now was. This forced tears to my eyes again; but as [15]*there was little relief in that*, I resolved, if possible, to get to the ship; so I [16]*pulled off* my clothes—for the weather was [17]*hot to extremity* —and [18]*took the water.* But when I came to the ship my difficulty was still greater to know how to get on board; for, as she [19]*lay aground*, and high out of the water, there was nothing within my reach [20]*to lay hold of.* I [21]*swam* round her twice, and the second time I [22]*spied* a small piece of rope, which I wondered I did not see at first, hung down by the [23]*fore chains* so low as that with great [24]*difficulty* I got hold of it, and by the help of that rope I [25]*got up into the forecastle of the ship.* Here I found that the ship was [26]*bulged*, and had a great deal of water in her [27]*hold*, but that she lay so on the side of a bank of hard sand, or rather earth, that her [28]*stern* lay lifted up upon the bank, and her head low, almost to the water. [29]*By this means all her quarter was free*, and all that was in that part was dry; for you may be sure my first work was to [30]*search*, and to see [31]*what was spoiled and what was free.* And, first, I found that all

就岸上依路的走去走進艇去；但是看見有着狹流之水阻隔在我與這艇之間，河水約有里半寬。所以我暫時折回，但是我極欲趨到船中，希望得爲我目前養生之物，

　　在正午略過之時我發現海水平靜，潮已退去，我可以趨近這船相隔一里路四分之一時。到了這個地步，愁緒復萌；因爲我顯然看出如果我們留在船上，我們都可平安——這就是說，我們大家可平安抵岸，不致剩我這樣受苦，如我現在這樣零丁孤苦，全無樂趣，想到這裏我又流淚了；但是此無濟於事，我決定如果可能的到船上，我把衣服脫去——因爲天氣酷熱——而下水，待我走近船邊，我的困難更大了，爲了不知怎麼上去，因爲船擱淺，高聳水面，在我可伸到的範圍內，沒有東西可握住，我在船旁環遊兩遍，第二次我窺見一根繩，這個我覺得希奇何以第一次沒有瞧見，此繩掛在船頭錨鏈下面，所以我費了好些心力才把握住，有了這繩的助手，而得攀登我上船頭。在此我窺見船是漏水，船內有很多的水，不過這船停在硬的土地的岸旁，因此船尾舉起在岸灘而船頭朝下，幾近水面。因此船的艙面均保無恙，全部極乾；你們可以決斷我的第一步工作乃是巡查何物毀壞何物尚未損壞。第一我查得金

1．至彼船中．2．狹流之水．3．暫時．4．更欲趨至船中．5．爲予目前養生之物．6．平靜．7．潮退．8．出．9．一里的四分之一．10．愁緒復萌．11．顯然．12．平安．13．受苦．14．零丁孤苦，全無樂趣．15．但此無濟於事．16．脫．17．酷熱．18．下水．19．擱淺．20．握持．21．游．22．窺見．23．船頭錨鏈．24．困難攀緣．25．而上船頭．26．漏水．27．船艙．28．船尾．29．是故船的艙面均保無恙3．0．巡查．31．何者毀何者存

the ship's [1]*provisions* were dry and [2]*untouched* by the water,
and being [3]*very well disposed to eat*, I went to the [4]*bread-
room* and filled my [5]*pockets* with [6]*biscuit*, and ate it as I
went about other things, for I [8]*had no time to lose*. Now
I wanted nothing but a boat to [9]*furnish* myself with many
things which I [10]*foresaw* would be very [11]*necessary* to me.

It was [12]*in vain to sit still* and wish for what was not
to be had; and [13]*this extremity roused my application*. We
had several [14]*spare yards*, and two or three large [15]*spars of
wood*, and a [16]*spare* [17]*topmast* or two in the ship. I resolved
to [18]*fall to work* with these, and I [19]*flung* as many of them
[20]*overboard* as I [21]*could manage* for their weight, [22]*tying* every
one with a [23]*rope*, that they might not drive away. When
this was done I went down the ship's side, and pulling
them to me, I tied four of them together at both ends, as
well as I could, [24]*in the form of a raft*, and laying two or
three short pieces of [25]*plank* upon them [26]*crossways*, I found I
could walk upon it very well, but that it was not able [27]*to
bear any great weight*, the pieces being too light. So I
went to work, and with a [28]*carpenter's saw* I cut a spare [29]*topmast* into three lengths, and added them to my [30]*raft*, with
a great deal of [31]*labor* and [32]*pains*; but the hope of furnishing
myself with [33]*necessaries* [34]*encouraged* me to go beyond what
I should have been able to do [35]*upon another occasion*.

My raft was now strong enough [36]*to bear* any [37]*reasonable
weight*. My next care was what to [38]*load* it with, and how
to preserve what I laid upon it from [49]*the surf of the sea*.
But I was not long considering this. I first laid all the
[40]*plank* or [41]*boards* upon it that I could get, and having
considered well what I most wanted, I first got three of the
seamen's [42]*chests*, which I had broken open and [43]*emptied*, and

船的糧食是乾的，沒有浸過水，很屬可口，我走到麵包間，把我的袋盛滿了餅乾，一面着手搜尋，一路喫餅，因爲時不可失。現在我不須要什麼，祇要一只艇能供我裝我預見我所必須的物件。

這樣靜坐着妄想得不到的東西是無益的；這樣的思念振起我的勞動的精神了．我們有幾個餘下無用的船杠；二三根用以作帆杆的木棒，以及其餘無用的第二接檣在船上．我決定從事工作這些木頭，凡我力氣所能做到的我把這些木頭—— 放出船外，每根用繩縛住使不致漂流失散．這個完畢了以後，我便走下船邊，將木頭拖近我旁，其中的四根兩頭用繩縛住得很好，形若木排，放二三片薄版在木頭上面作卜字形，我看見我很可以在上面走走，不過不能載重量，因爲那幾片版太薄．因此我又去工作．有了木匠用的鋸，我把餘下無用的第二檣分割三條，用了許多的勞力和苦痛才把他安放在木排上；但是供我必需之物的希望激勵着我下次再去盡吾能力的能力範圍以外的去裝東西去。

我的木排現在是堅固了，足以裝載合度的重量．我第二件須注意的就是木排上裝些什麼東西，同時怎樣保留他不爲海浪所吞滅．但是這事我沒有考慮好久．我起初把我所招得到的板都放在木排上，既把我所最要的考慮定奪以後，我第一就先拿水手的箱子，箱子我已打開倒空，

¹*lowered* them down upon my raft; the first of these I filled
with ²*Provision*; namely, bread, rice, three Dutch ³*cheeses,*

five pieces of dried ⁴*goat's flesh* (which we ⁵*lived much upon*),
and a little ⁶*remainder* of European corn, which had been ⁷*laid*

把牠們放在木排上；第一只箱子我盛滿了糧食如饅頭，米，三匣荷蘭牛乳餅，五塊乾的山羊肉（這就是我們藉以養生的），一點殘餘的歐洲稻麥，稻麥儲藏着

1·放下·2·糧食·3·牛乳餅·4·內·5·藉以養生·6·殘餘·7·儲藏以備……必需之用·

by for some ¹fowls which we brought to sea with us. There had been some ²barley and wheat together ; but, ³to my great ⁴disappointment, I found afterwards that the rats had eaten or ⁵spoiled it all. As for ⁶liquors, I found several ⁷cases of bottles belonging to our ⁸skipper, in which were some ⁹cordial waters, and ¹⁰in all, about five or six ¹¹gallons of ¹²rack. These I ¹³stowed by themselves, there being no need to put them into the ¹⁴chests, nor any room for them, While I was doing this, I found the ¹⁵tide began to ¹⁶flow, though very calm ; and I had the ¹⁷mortification to see my ¹⁸coat, ¹⁹shirt, and ²⁰waistcoat, which I had left on the shore upon the sand, swim away. As for my ²¹breeches, which were only ²²linen, and ²³open-kneed, I swam on board in them and my ²⁴stockings. However, this ²⁵set me on rummaging for clothes, of which I found enough, but took no more than I wanted for present use, for I had other things which ²⁶my eye was more upon,— as, first, tools ²⁷to work with on shore. And it was after long ²⁸searching that I found out the ²⁹carpenter's ³⁰chest, which was, indeed, a very useful ³¹prize to me, and much more valuable than a ³²shipload of gold would have been at that time. I got it down to my raft, whole as it was, ³³without losing time to look into it, for I knew ³⁴in general what it ³⁵contained.

My next care was for some ³⁶ammunition and arms. There were two very good fowling pieces in the great ³⁷cabin, and two ³⁸pistols. These I ³⁹secured first, with some ⁴⁰powder horns and a small bag of shot, and two old ⁴¹rusty ⁴²swords. I knew there were three ⁴³barrels of powder in the ship, but knew not where our ⁴⁴gunner had ⁴⁵stowed them ; but with much search I found them, two of them dry and good ; the third had ⁴⁶taken water. Those two I got to my raft, with

以備我們所帶到海上的家禽所用。有些大麥和小麥在一起；但是：大失所望，我後來尋見都給老鼠吃壞了。至於酒，我招到屬於我們船主的幾箱酒瓶；其中有幾瓶是與奮藥酒；總共約有五六咖喻馬乳酒；這些酒我另置一處，因爲不必放在箱內，而且箱子亦沒有空位可盛。我在如是工作的時候，我看見海潮開始流動，雖則很平；然而我看見我留在泥土岸上的外衣，短衣，背心漂去了，使我且擊心傷。至於我的細廳布短袴和襪子我穿着游到海上的。不論如何，這激勵我搜尋衣服之心，這個我尋夠了，但是我祗拿我現在所須要的比，我有別的事務必須更注意，——如，第一，用以在海灘上工作的傢伙。招了好久，我方才尋着木匠的箱子，這箱誠爲我的無價之寶，比較一箱子的金子在當時尤其貴重，我把牠放下木排上完全一只，不容稍緩去察看；因爲我知道其中大概裝載的貨物，

　　其次我注意的乃是軍器。在大船艙內有二把很好的鳥鎗，和兩把手鎗。這個我就先拿了，還有幾個火藥角，一小袋，彈子兩把且舊上銹的刀。我知道船裏有三大罷罷桶的火藥可是我不知道管理鎗礮者把牠收藏在什麼地方；但是招了好久竟招到了，兩只是乾而完好；第三只已浸濕。這兩個吾放在木排之上，還有。

1.家禽。2.大麥。3.我之。4.失望。5.壞。6.酒。7.箱。8.船主。9.與奮藥酒。10.總共。11.咖喻。12.馬乳酒。13.另遺一處。14.箱。15.潮。16.流。17.傷心。18.衣。19.短衣。20.背心。21.袴。22.細廳布。23.襪。24.襪。25.激勵我搜尋衣服之心。26.更爲注意。27.用以工作。28.尋。29.木匠。30.箱。31.槳。32.一船之載。33.不容稍緩檢查。34.大概。35.容納。36.軍器。37.船艙。38.手鎗。39.獲得。40.火藥角。(中古之人多有以獸角製成器皿安置火藥者，故有此名)。41.生銹。42.刀。43.大罷罷桶。44.管理鎗礮者。45.收藏。46.浸濕。

the arms.　And now I thought myself [1]*pretty well freighted,* and began to think how I should get to shore with them, having neither sail, [2]*oar,* nor [3]*rudder* ; and [4]*the least capful of wind* would have [5]*overset* all my [6]*navigation.*

I had three [7]*encouragements* : a [8]*smooth,* calm sea ; the tide rising, and [9]*setting in to the shore* ; and what little wind there was [10]*blew* me towards the land.　And thus, having found two or three broken oars belonging to the boat, and, besides the tools which were in the chest, two [11]*saws,* an ax, and a [12]*hammer,* with this cargo I [13]*put to sea.* For a mile, or [14]*thereabouts,* my raft went very well, only that I found it drive a little distant from the place where I had landed before : by which I [15]*perceived* that there was some [16]*indraft* of the water, and [17]*consequently* I hope to find some creek or river there, which I might [18]*make use of* as a [19]*port to get to land with my cargo.*

[20]*As I imagined, so it was.*　There [21]*appeared* before me a little opening of the land, and I found a strong [22]*current of the tide setting into it* : so I [23]*guided* my [24]*raft,* as well as I could, to keep in the [25]*middle of the stream.*

But here I had like to have [26]*suffered* a second [27]*shipwreck,* which, if I had, I think, [28]*verily,* would have broken my heart.　Knowing nothing of the coast, my raft [29]*ran aground* at one end of it upon a [30]*shoal,* and not being aground at the other end, it wanted but a little that all my cargo had [31]*slipped off* towards the end that was afloat, and so fallen into the water.　I [32]*did my utmost,* by setting my back against the chests, [33]*to keep them in their places,* but could not [34]*thrust off* the raft with all my strength ; neither durst I stir from the [35]*posture* I was in ; but [36]*holding up* the chests [37]*with all my might,* I stood in that manner near half an

112

軍器;現在我想我自己裝載完備;始想我如何可抵岸,因為船上旣沒有篷,槳,又沒有舵;最微的風也可傾覆我的航行。

我有三件可以成功的希望:平靜的海,潮來向岸流去的水;還有微風吹我向岸去。如此外以,又尋着了屬於艇的兩三個舊壞的槳;除了箱子內的軍器;二把鋸子,一把斧頭,和一只鐵撬;有帶了這些貨物,我便開駛了,大約有一里路,我的木排安然駛行,不過我看出我現在到的地步就是離我先前停駛處不遠,在此我曉得有內流的水;因此我希望可以尋見內河,如此我可以使用海口運貨上岸。

事實正和我所幻想的相同。在我的前面發見一小塊的空地了,我見着有急潮流入彼處;所以我努力指揮我的木排,如此可以使牠在河的中心。

但是這裏我好像又要遭第二次的難了,如果真的成為事實的話;那麼我定要受極大的刺激。不知海岸的所在,此時我的木排的一頭在沙灘上擱淺,因為其他一頭沒有擱淺,所以祇消一動我全船的貨物;就要瀉落於浮在水面的一頭,致於落在水內。我竭力將背推住箱子使勿移動,但是用盡了全力仍不能推開擱淺的一頭;我也不能移動我佔立的地位,不過盡我的全力支持這箱;我如此立着半個

1.裝載完備.2.槳.3.舵.4.最微之風.5.傾覆.6.航行.7.有成功之望.8.平.9.向岸流.10.吹.11.鋸子.12.拋.13.開駛.14.大約.15.知曉.16.內流.17.因此.18.使用.19.運貨上岸.20.如願以償.21.發見.22.潮流入彼處.23.指揮.24.木排.25.河中心.26.受苦.27.船之遭難.28.果然.29.擱淺.30.沙灘.21.瀉落.32.竭力.33.使勿移動.34.推去.35.地位.36.支持.37.竭盡我全身之力,

hour, in which time the rising of the water brought me a little more upon a [1]*level*. A little after, the water still rising, my raft [2]*floated* again, and I [3]*thrust* her off with the oar I had into the [4]*channel*, and then driving up higher, I at length found myself in the mouth of a little river, with land on both sides, and a [5]*strong current,* or tide, [6]*running up*. I looked on both sides for a proper place to get to shore, for I was not willing to be driven too high up the river; hoping, in time, to see some ship at sea, and therefore resolved to place myself as near the coast as I could.

At length I [7]*spied* a little [8]*cove* on the right shore of the [9]*creek*, to which, with great pain and [10]*difficutly*, I [11]*guided* my raft, and at last got so near that, reaching ground with my oar, I could [12]*thrust her directly in*. But here I had like to have [13]*dipped* all my [14]*cargo* into the sea again; for that shore lying pretty [15]*steep*—that is to say [16]*sloping*—there was no place to land but where one end of my [17]*float*, if it [18]*ran on shore*, would lie so high, and the other [19]*sink* so low, as before, that it would [20]*endanger* my cargo again. All that I could do was to wait till the tide was at the highest, keeping the raft with my oar like an anchor. to hold the side of it fast to the shore near a flat piece of ground, which I [21]*expected* the water would flow over. And so it did. As soon as I found water enough — for my raft drew about a foot of water—I thrust her upon that [22]*flat* piece of ground, and there [23]*fastened* or [24]*moored* her, by [25]*sticking* my two broken oars into the ground, one on one side, near one end, and one on the other side, near the other end. And thus I lay till the water [26]*ebbed* away, and left my raft and all my cargo safe on shore.

鹽點：此時簡着水的升起，得與水面成一平線。不多幾時，水依舊繼續浮起，我的木排才得漂流，我用划槳把木排驅進水道，然後向上推駛；我終究看見我自已在一條小河口了，兩邊有地；急潮正在澎漲。我看看兩旁或者有適當的地方可上岸；因爲我不願遠駛進河；希望此時得見幾只在海內的船，因此我決定奮力駛近岸邊，

後來我窺見一個小灣在小河的右岸，於是我耗了許多麻煩的手續掌住我的槳，到了末來很近這灣了，我的划槳可以碰着的時候我方得推進直入。但是這一次我的船貨又像要傾倒於海了，因爲海岸橫得好尖——這就是說傾斜——沒有地方可以上岸，但是如果駛至岸上，木排的一頭必定橫着很高，另一頭很底，如同以前一樣，如此辦法又要置我船貨與危險的地步，唯一的辦法，祇有等潮升到最高點時，一方面以槳作錨，停止木排前進，排的邊緊貼着海岸的一塊平地，等待潮漲上這塊地。理想成爲事實了；待我看出水已充足——因爲我的木排被水浮高一尺了，——我立將本排推在這塊平地上，將兩只破壞的划槳插入地中，作爲停泊之用，一槳一邊，一槳近頭，一槳在另一邊，近另一頭，如是我停着直待水下潮，我的木排與貨物均很平安的留在岸上。

CHAPTER X

My next work was to [1]*view* the country, and seek a proper place for my [2]*habitation* and where to [3]*stow* my goods to [4]*secure* them from whatever [5]*might happen*, Where I was, I yet knew not; whether on the [6]*continent* or on an island, whether [7]*inhabited* or not [8]*inhabited*, whether in [9]*danger* of wild [10]*beasts* or not. There was a [11]*hill* not above a mile from me, which rose up very steep and high, and which seemed to [12]*overtop some other hills* which lay as in a [13]*ridge* from it northward. I took out one of the [14]*fowling* pieces, and one of the [15]*pistols*, and a horn of powder; and thus [16]*armed*, I traveled for [17]*discovery* up to the top of that hill where, after I had with great labor and difficulty got to the top, I saw my fate, [18]*to my great affliction*; namely, that I was in an island [19]*environed* every way with the sea. No land was to be seen except some rocks, which [20]*lay a great way off*, and two small islands, [21]*less than* this, which lay about three [22]*leagues* to the west.

I found also that the island I was in was [23]*barren*, and, as I saw good reason to believe, [24]*uninhabited* except by wild beasts, of which, however, I saw none. Yet I saw [25]*abundance of fowls*, but knew not their kinds; neither when I had killed them could I tell what was [26]*fit* for food and what not. At my coming back, I shot at a great bird which I saw sitting upon a tree on the side of a great wood. I believe it was the first gun that had been fired there [27]*since the creation of the world*. I had no sooner fired than from all parts of the wood there arose an [28]*innumerable* number of fowls, [29]*of many sorts*, making a [30]*confused screaming* and cry-ing, and every one [31]*according* to his [32]*usual note*, but not one

第　十　章

　　我其次的工作乃是察看這個地方，招一處適當的地方寄宿和收藏我的貨物，由此可以不致發生以外，我所在的是什麼地方，我還沒有知道，或者是在大洲上，或者是在島上，或者有人居住的或者是無人居住的，或者在野獸的危險中或者是沒有．那邊有一小山，離我不到一里路遠，這小山是尖而高，似乎高出他山就是在牠北面的山脈．我取出一把鳥鎗，一把手鎗，一只軍樂角；備了軍器，我旅行到山頂上去尋查一下，費了不少的氣力與困難繞到小山頂上，我看到我的前途殊覺悽楚；就是，我所在的島四周圍繞．沒有看見地祇有幾塊大石，大石坐落極遠，以及兩個小於這個的海島，朝西三英里路。

　　我又看出我所在的海島是不事生產，我有充足的理由相信沒有人居住，祇有野獸，而野獸我一只沒有看見．不過我看見許多禽類，但是不知道他們的類別；我把牠們殺了之後，我不知那個可食和那個不可食；轉同時我射死了一只烏，此烏當時坐在一桿樹上的一根大木頭的旁邊，我相信這是在此地自開天闢地以來的空前的第一次的鎗聲．我發了鎗不多時；從樹林的各部份飛來不勝其數的鳥禽；種類甚為復雜，呼號交作；每隻呼號都是依牠尋常的腔調；但是牠

1．察視．2．寄宿處．3°收藏．4．穩妥．5．遇6．大洲．7．有人居住．8．危險．9．野獸．10．小山．11．高越他山．12．山脈．13．鳥．14．手鎗．15．軍備．16．尋查．17．殊覺悽楚．18．四周為海所圍繞．19．坐落甚遠．20．小於．21．英里．22．不事生產．23．無人居住．24．禽類甚為豐富．25．適合．26．天地開闢之始．27．不勝其數．28．種類甚為複雜．29．呼號交作．30．依．31．尋常腔調

of them of any kind that I knew. As for the [1]*creature* I killed, I [2]*took it to be a kind of hawk*, its color and [3]*beak* resembling it, but it had no [4]*talons or claws* more than common. [5]*Its flesh was carrion, and fit for nothing.*

[6]*Contented* with this [7]*discovery*, I came back to my raft, and fell to work to bring my cargo on shore, which took me the rest of that day. What to do with myself at night I knew not, nor indeed where to rest, for I was afraid to lie down on the ground, not knowing but some wild beast might [8]*devour* me, though, as I afterwards found, there was really no need for those fears.

However, as well as I could, I [9]*barricaded* myself round with the [10]*chests* and [11]*boards* that I had brought on shore, and made a kind of [12]*hut* for that night's [13]*lodging*. As for food, I yet saw not which way to supply myself, except that I had seen two or three creatures, like [14]*hares*, run out of the wood where I [15]*shot* the [16]*fowl*.

I now began to consider that I might yet get a great many things out of the ship which would be useful to me, and [17]*particularly* some of the [18]*rigging* and sails, and such other things as might come to land; and I [19]*resolved* to make another voyage on board the [20]*vessel*, if possible. And as I knew the first storm that blew must necessarily [21]*break* her all in pieces, I resolved to set all other things [22]*apart* till I had got everything out of the ship that I could get. Then [23]*I called a council*—that is to say, in my thoughts—whether I should take back the raft; but [24]*this appeared impracticable*, so I resolved to go, as before, when the [24]*tide* was down. I did so, only that I [26]*stripped* before I went from my hut, [27]*having nothing on* but a [28]*checkered shirt*, a pair of [29]*linen drawers*, and a pair of [30]*pumps* on my feet.

們的種類我一隻也不知道；至於我所殺死的動物，我以其爲廳的一種；牠的顏色和嘴似廳一般，但是牠的爪是沒有的，所以與尋常的不同；牠的肉巴腐敗得不可食而又毫無所用。

尋視的好奇心滿足了，我就回到我的木排上去，從事把我的船貨搬在岸上，整個費了我這天餘下的時間。我不知道在夜晚我應該怎麼樣，也不知道在什麼地方休息，因爲我怕睡在地下，雖然不確實，可是也許有野獸來把我吞喫，但是這個我後來得知我不必怎麼害怕，

不論如何，儘我所能，保衞我自巳，方法便是把我帶上岸的箱子木版環繞我的周圍，做成一種草棚作爲夜晚寄宿處。講到食物，我還沒有尋出方法來供給我自巳，除了我見有二三只類似兔子的動物從我射死這鳥的樹林裏奔出來，

我現在開始考慮到我還可以到船上去拿些對于我有用的東西，尤其是幾根繩索和蓬張，以及其他類似之物可以攜到岸地上的；我決意再駛到船上，要是辦得到的。因爲我知道第一次的大風定巳把她打成碎片，我決意分匿其他的東西直待我能夠把船內的各件都搬出。然後我開了個會議——卽自行斟酌——我應否攜回木排；但此似不能行，因此我決定待潮一退，我便像先前一樣去。我就此實行：不過離草屋前，我脫盡了衣服，身無長物，就是一所有棋盤格紋的襯衫，一對細麻布褲，以及脚上的一雙薄底鞋。

1.動物. 2. 以其爲廳之一種. 3. 嘴類似. 4. 爪. 5. 其肉腐敗不可食而又毫無所用. 6. 滿足. 7. 尋視. 8. 吞喫. 9. 保衞. 10. 箱. 11. 木板. 12. 草棚. 13. 寄宿處. 14. 兔子. 15. 射死. 16. 鳥. 17. 尤其是. 18. 繩索. 19. 決意. 20. 舟. 21. 打破. 22. 分開. 23. 我則自行斟酌. 24. 此似不能行. 25. 潮. 26. 除盡衣服. 27. 身無長物. 28. 所有棋盤格紋之襯衫. 29. 細麻布褲. 30. 薄底鞋

I ¹*got on board* the ship as before, and prepared a second raft; and, having had ²*experience* of the first, I neither made this so ³*unwieldy.* ⁴*nor loaded it so hard*, but yet I brought away several things very useful to me. In the carpenter's ⁵*stores* I found two or three ⁶*bags* full of ⁷*nails* and ⁸*spikes*, a great ⁹*screw jack*, a dozen or two of ¹⁰*hatchets*, and, ¹¹*above all*, that most useful thing called ¹²*grindstone.* All these I secured, together with several things belonging to the ¹³*gunner*, particularly two or three iron ¹⁴*crows*, and two ¹⁵*barrels* of ¹⁶*musket bullets.* seven muskets, another ¹⁷*fowling piece*, with some small ¹⁸*quantity* of powder more, a large ¹⁹*bagful* of small shot, and ²⁰*a great roll of sheet lead.* But this last was so heavy I could not ²¹*hoist it up* to get it over the ship's side.

Besides these things, I took all the men's clothes that I could find, and a ²²*spare* ²³*fore-topsail*, a ²⁴*hammock*, and some ²⁵*bedding.* With this I loaded my second raft, and brought them all safe on shore, to my very great comfort.

I was ²⁶*under some apprehension*, during my ²⁷*absence* from the land, that at least my ²⁸*provisions* might be ²⁹*devoured* on shore. But when I came back I found ³⁰*no sign of any visitor*; only there sat a creature like a wild cat upon one of the chests, which, when I came towards it, ran away a little distance, and then ³¹*stood still.* She sat very ³²*composed* and ³³*unconcerned*, and ³³*looked full in my face*, as if she had a mind to be ³⁵*acquainted* with me. I presented my gun at her, but, as she did not understand it, she was ³⁶*perfectly* ³⁷*unconcerned* at it, nor did she offer to stir away; upon which. I ³⁸*tossed her a bit of biscuit*, though, ³⁹*by the way.* I was ³⁰*not very free of it*, for my store was not great. However, I spared her a bit, I say, and she went to it, smelled at it, and ate it, and ⁴¹*looked* (as if pleased) ⁴²*for more*; but I thanked her, and ⁴³*could spare no more*, so she ⁴⁴*marched off.*

我如前上船，準備第二次的木排；第一次既有了經驗，這一囘我又不裝得太輕又不加重其載，不過我再帶了幾件對我非常有用的東西。在木匠的貯藏所內我招到了二三袋的釘，一只大的起重的螺旋機，一兩打的斧頭，尤要的就是最有用的東西叫磨石。這些我都拿好了，又加上幾件屬於掌礮員的物件，尤其事兩三只鐵起貨鈎，兩桶短鎗用的小彈；七個毛瑟鎗，另外一把鳥鎗；再加上一點火藥，一大袋的小彈子，以及一大捲船片，但是最後的一件過重甚至我不能舉起以攜過船上，

除了這些物件以外，我取各人的衣服盡我所能招到的，一只餘下無用的船頭上的第一度接帆，一只吊牀，以及幾個被舖。有了這些我得裝成第二次的木排，平平安安地帶岸上去，這很可撫慰我的心，

我深茲疑慮在我離岸的當兒，至少我的糧食也許被在上岸的動物吞喫去，但是當我囘來時我看到毫無來客的蹤跡；不過在一只箱上坐着一只動物，類似野猫，當我走過去，牠跑得消爲遠點然後立定。牠坐着的態度從容不迫，注祇吾面而毫無懼色，好像牠有意要同我相熟一樣。我向他對準我的鎗，但是，因爲牠不懂是什麼一囘事，牠對之完全漠不關心，她也不動；因此我投以餅乾小塊，雖然，且說及，我的手段並不寬鬆，因爲我的貯物不多。不論如何，我給她一點兒，我說，同時牠走近食物，嗅一下纔喫，意欲再得；我祇得謝絕牠，不能再分讓，於是牠去了，

1.船上。2.經驗。3.不甚輕便。4.又不加重其載。5.貯藏的。6.袋。7.釘。8.大釘。9.起重的螺旋機。10.斧頭。11.尤重者。12.磨石。12.掌礮者。14.起貨鈎。15.桶。19.短鎗用之小彈。17.鳥鎗。18.量。19.一袋。29.一大捲船片。21.舉起。22.餘下無用。23.船頭梘上之第一度接帆。24.吊牀（多以帆製，亦有以繩結製之者）。25.牀舖。26.深茲疑慮。27.離。28.糧食。29.吞。30.毫無來客之蹤跡（來客者指鳥獸言）。31.立定。32.從容。33.不遍。34.注視吾面而毫無懼色。35.相熟。36.完全。37.漠不關心。39.投以餅乾小塊。39.且說及。40.手段並不寬鬆。41.意。42.欲略多得之。43.無可再加。44.離去

Having got my second cargo on shore,—though I [1]*was fain to* open the [2]*barrels* of powder, and bring them [3]*by parcels*; for they were too heavy, being large [4]*casks*,—I went to work to make me a little [5]*tent* with the sail and some [6]*poles* which I cut *for that* [7]*purpose.* Into this tent I brought everything that I knew would spoil either with rain or sun; and I [8]*piled* all the [9]*empty* chests and casks up in a [10]*circle* round the tent [11]*to fortify it from any sudden attempt,* either from man or beast.

When I had done this, I [12]*blocked up* the door of the tent with some boards within, and an empty chest [13]*set up on end* without; and [4]*spreading* one of the beds upon the ground, laying my two pistols just at my head, and my gun at length by me. I went to bed for the first time, and slept very quietly all night, for I was [5]*very weary and heavy,* for the night before I had slept little, and had labored very hard all day to [16]*fetch* all those things from the ship, and to get them on shore.

I had the biggest [17]*magazine* of all kinds now that ever was [18]*laid up,* I believe, for one man; but I was not [19]*satisfied* still, for while the ship sat [20]*upright* in that [21]*posture,* I thought I ought to get everything out of her that I could. So every day at low water I went on board, and brought away [22]*something or other;* but [23]*particularly* the third time I went I brought away as much of the [24]*rigging* as I could, also all the small ropes and [25]*rope twine* I could get, with a piece of spare [26]*canvas,* which was to [27]*mend* the sails [28]*upon occasion,* and the barrel of wet gunpowder. In a word, I brought away all the sails, [29]*first and last;* only that I was [30]*fain* to cut them in pieces, and bring as much at a time as I could, for they were no more useful to be sails, but as mere [31]*canvas* only.

已將我第二批的船貨載上岸：———　雖則我甚欲打開火藥桶，把牠們分成小包，因爲大的桶十分重；———我用蓬和我特爲此用而割留着的柱去從事做一個小的帳篷。凡在雨內或太陽中易於受損的物件都把牠們放在帳篷內；把空箱和空桶放在帳篷的周圍作一圓形，鞏固之以防不測，或是避人或人避野獸。

當我這些事情做完畢之後，帳篷的門口裏我用幾個木版塞住，一只空箱豎立在門外，鋪張其中的一只牀在地上，放我的兩把手鎗在我頭邊，以及最後安放我的鎗礮於我身旁，我第一次上牀而全夜酣睡，因爲我疲倦已極；因爲前晚我睡得狠少，而且整日的辛勞工作取船上的貨物搬到岸上。

我現在有一個最大的火藥室，我想從未有人像我收藏各種軍藥類別之多；但是我依舊不能心滿意足，因爲看到這船直立着的態度，我想我應該照我所能夠的把船內的東西件件都拿出。所以每天水低下時我便上船，取此物或彼物；特別是第三次我去帶出狠多的索具，還有我所能尋獲的小繩和數繩組合而成之粗索；隨有一條餘下無用的帆布，此帆布是用以修補篷布的，在必需之時；以及一桶溼軍火。總之，我把所有的篷布全數取出；不過我甚欲把牠剪成零條，而每次儘量的攜帶，因爲牠們再不能當作駕駛的船篷用，祇可視作帆布而已。

1.甚欲2.木桶、3.分成小包。4.桶。5.帳篷。6.柱。7.特爲彼用故。8.疊。9.空。10.圓。11.鞏固之以防不測。12.塞住。13.直立。14.鋪張。15.疲倦已極。16.取。17.火藥房。18.收藏。19.心滿意足。20.直立。21.狀態。22.此物或彼物。23.特別。24.索具。25.數繩組合而成之粗索，26.帆布。27.修補。28.必需之時。29.全數。30°甚欲。31.帆布

But that which [1]*comforted* me more still was, that last of all, after I had made five or six such voyages as these, and thought I had nothing more to expect from the ship that was [2]*worth my meddling with,*—I say, after all this, I found a great [3]*hogshead* of bread, three large [4]*casks* of [5]*rum*, or [6]*spirits*, a box of [7]*sugar*, and a barrel of fine [8]*flour*. This was [9]*surprising* to me, because I [10]*had given over* expecting any more [11]*provisions*, except what was [12]*spoiled* by the water. I soon [13]*emptied* the [14]*hogshead* of the bread, and [15]*wrapped it up*, [16]*parcel* by parcel, in pieces, of the sails, which I cut out ; and, in a word, I got all this safe on shore also.

The next day I made another voyage, and now, [17]*having plundered the ship of what was portable and fit to hand out*, I began with the [18]*cables*. Cutting the great cable into pieces such as I could move, I got two cables and a [19]*hawser* on shore, with all the [20]*ironwork* I could get : and having cut down the [21]*spritsail* yard, and the [22]*mizzen yard*, and everything I could, to make a large raft, I [23]*loaded* it with all these heavy goods, and came away. But my good luck began now to leave me ; for this raft was so [24]*unwieldy* and so [25]*overladen* that, after I had entered the little cove where I had landed the rest of my goods, not being able to guide it so [26]*handily* as I did the other, it [27]*overset* and threw me and all my cargo into the water. [28]*As for* myself it was no great harm, for I was near the shore ; [29]*but as to* my cargo, it was a great part of it lost, [30]*especially* the iron, which I expected would have been of great use to me. However, when the [31]*tide* was out, I got most of the pieces of the cable ashore, and some of the iron, though [32]*with infinite labor* ; for I was fain [33]*to dip for it into the water*, a work which [34]*fatigued* me very much. After this I went every day on board, and brought away what I could get.

更使我安慰的乃是最後一次的來回航駛，因爲如是來回了五六次我想我不能再希望從船上得些值得往返的東西了，——我說，這幾次以後，我招到一大桶的麵包，三大桶的糖酒或酒，一匣子的糖和一桶完好的麵粉，這個使我驚喜，因爲我絕到不想再得糧食，除了被水浸壞的以外。我卽刻倒空麵包桶，把麵包拿我所剪開的篷札成一個個包裹，簡而言之，我也很平安的將這些東西拿到岸上。

第二天我再駛去，現在，船中所有便攜帶而又易於搬運者，盡取一空，我開始工作錨鐼。剪這大錨鐼成條使我易取我獲得兩個錨纜和一大纜到岸，並有我能尋獲的鐵具；我把斜杠帆和後帆杠都剪下，做成一個大木排，我裝載許多重的貨物而行駛去。但是我的好運開始離我；因爲這木排很難運用，負載過重，當我駛進小灣，此小灣卽我卸其他貨物之處，爲了不能似同別的排那麼易於駕駛，木排傾覆，我和貨物都落水。至於我自己沒有什麼大損傷，因爲我是近岸；但是論及我的貨物，大部遺失，尤其是這鐵具，這鐵具的期望對我有莫大的用處。不論如何，潮水退後，大牛的錨纜我得拿到岸上，以及鐵具，雖然費無窮之工力；因爲我潛水去提取的，這是一種狠費我力的工作。此後我每天上船，盡我所能的帶回來。

1.安慰。2.值得干與其事（意卽到船覓物，不爲徒勢也）。3.大桶。4.木桶。5.糖酒。6.酒。7.糖。8.麵粉。9.驚喜。10.絕望。11.糧食。12.毀壞。13.倒空。14.大桶。15.包裹。16.包。17.船中所有便攜帶而又易於搬運者，盡取一空。18.錨鐼。19.大纜。20.鐵具。21.斜杠帆。22.後帆杠。23.裝載。24.難運用。25.負載過重。26.小灣。27.巧便。28.傾覆。29.至於。30.尤其。31.潮。32費無窮之力。33.潛水以提取。34.疲乏

I had been now thirteen days on shore, and had been eleven times on board the ship, in which time I had brought away all that one [1]*pair* of hands could well be supposed capable to bring; though I believe [2]*verily*, had the calm weather [3]*held*, I should have brought away the whole ship, piece by piece. But [4]*preparing* the [5]*twelfth* time to go on board, I found the wind began to rise. However, at low water I went on board, and though I thought I had [6]*rummaged* the cabin so [7]*effectually* that nothing more could be found, yet I discovered a [8]*locker with drawers in it*, in one of which I found two or three [9]*razors* and one pair of large [10]*scissors*, with some ten or a [11]*dozen* of good [12]*knives and forks*. In another I found about [13]*thirty-six pounds value in money*,—some European [14]*coin*, some Brazil, some pieces of eight, some gold, and some silver.

I [15]*smiled* to myself at the sight of this money. "[16]*O drug!*" said I, aloud, "what art thou good for? Thou art not worth to me—no, [17]*not the taking off the ground*. One of those [18]*knives* is worth all this [19]*heap*. I have no manner of use for thee; e'en [20]*remain* where thou art, and go to the [21]*bottom*, as a creature whose life is not worth saving." However, upon second thoughts, I took it away; and [22]*wrapping* all this in a piece of [23]*canvas*, I began to think of making another raft. But while I was preparing this, I found [24]*the sky overcast*, and the wind began to rise, and in a quarter of an hour it [25]*blew* a fresh [26]*gale* from the shore. It [27]*presently* occurred to me that it was in vain to pretend to make a raft with the wind off shore, and that it was my business to be gone before the flood of tide began, otherwise I might not be able to reach the shore [28]*at all*. Accordingly I let myself down into the water, and [29]*swam* across

我現在在岸上巳有十三天，到船上去過十一次，在此時期內我儘我兩手可拿的都把牠們帶來；雖則我確實相信如果天公繼續作美，我可以把全船一塊一塊帶去。但是正在準備第十二次的出發上船，我看見風開始吹起了。不論如何，低水的時候我去上船，雖然我想我巳經竭力搜羅一空，艙內再也招不到什麼了，可是我發見一有抽屜而又有鎖之櫃，其中藏着二三把剃鬚刀，一對大剪刀，以及十把或十二把刀與叉。在另一個抽屜中我招見約值三十六鎊價之銀幣，—— 幾個歐洲銀幣，幾個巴西的，幾個八分的幾個金的與幾個銀的。

我見了這些錢不覺暗自好笑。"廢物啊！"我喊道，汝今有何用啊？你于我是沒有用——沒有，棄如糞土。其中的一把刀便值這一堆錢的。我實在無可用你的地方；就是如此留着，或埋入地下去像一個動物，牠的生命沒有救活的價值，然而，第二個念頭轉來，我便拿了走；都包在帆布內，我開始想再做個木排。但是我正在佈置木排的時候，我看見黑雲蔽天，風起始吹了，在一刻中暴風從海岸吹過來。有了這麼大的風做排亦沒有用，我現在的事務乃是趁此地在潮水漲上的以前，否則我也許全然不得抵岸。於是我走下水去，游過

the [1]*channel* which lay between the ship and the [2]*sands*, and even that with difficulty enough, partly with the [3]*weight* of the things I had about me, and partly the [4]*roughness* of the water; for the wind rose very [5]*hastily*, and before it was quite high water it blew a storm.

But I had [6]*got home to* my little tent, where I lay, with all my wealth about me, [7]*very secure*. It blew very hard all night, and in the morning, when I looked out, [8]*behold* no more ship was to be seen! I was a little surprised, but [9]*recovered* myself with the [10]*satisfactory* [11]*reflection* that I had lost no time, nor [12]*abated* any [13]*diligence*, to get everything out of her that could be useful to me; and that, indeed, there was little left in her that I was able to bring away, if I had had more time.

I now gave over any more thoughts of the ship, or of anything out of her, except what might drive on shore from her [14]*wreck*; as, indeed, [15]*divers* pieces of her afterwards did. But those things were of small use to me.

CHAPTER XI

My thoughts were now wholly [16]*employed* about [17]*securing* myself against either savages, if any should appear, or wild beasts, if any were in the island. I had many thoughts of the [18]*method* how to do this, and what kind of [19]*dwelling* to make,—whether I should make me a cave in the earth, or a tent upon the earth; and, in short, I resolved upon both, the manner and [20]*description* of which it may not be [21]*improper* to give an account of.

I soon found the place I was in was [22]*not fit for my settlement*, because it was upon a low, [23]*moorish* ground, near the sea, and I believed it would not be [24]*wholesome*, and more

海峽。這海峽在船與沙濱的中央，就是這樣已經非常的困難於游泳了，一半是爲着在我上面的重量，一半爲着水的不平；因爲風吹得很快，水還沒有升得十分高，風浪就光臨了，

但我回到我的帳幕以後，我將我所有的財產頗安隱的放在裏面，全夜狂風劇烈地吹着，到了早晨我向外望時，看見船不知去向了！我覺得有些驚奇，但想到我沒有失掉時讒和智慧的知足，我的智覺又復原了，因爲有用的東西都已取出；不過，的確，船內還有好些東西我可把他們取出要是我有機會，

我現在把船或取出船內物件的思想完全拋棄，除去破船有什麼什物也許會被水冲到岸來；的確，各種的碎片後來是發見的，但是這些貨物於我沒有多大的用處，

第十一章

我的念頭現在完全充滿着如何從野人的手中拯救我自己，如果有得出現，或者抵抗野獸，如果島上有的，我有許多的思想作爲對付的方法，以及做怎樣的寓所，——我應否在泥土中做一個洞，或者在地上築一帳幕；總之，我決意兩者並做，把做寓所的方法描寫出來並不見得是一件不合宜的事，

我立刻看出我現在的地方不合我寓居，因爲這地低溼，近海，我相信這是不宜於衞生，

1.海峽。2.沙濱。3.重量。4.不平。5.疾快。6.同。7.頗安隱。8.看。9.復原。10.滿意。11.回想。12.減。13.智慧。14.破船。15.各種。16.充滿。17.救。18.方法。19.寓所。20.描寫。21.不合宜。22.不合爲我寓居之地。23.低溼。24.宜於衞生。

particularly because there was no ¹*fresh water* near it.　So
I resolved to find a more healthy and more ²*convenient spot*
of ground.

I ³*consulted* several things in my ⁴*situation* which I found
would be proper for me : ⁵*health* and fresh water, I just now
mentioned ; ⁶*shelter* from the heat of the sun ; ⁷*security* from
⁸*ravenous* creatures, whether man or beast ; and ⁹*a view to
the sea*, that if God sent any ship in sight, I ¹⁰*might not lose
any advantage* for my ¹¹*deliverance*, of which ¹²*I was not willing to banish all my expectation yet.*

In search of a place proper for this, I found a little plain
on the side of a ¹³*rising hill*, whose front towards this little
plain was steep as a house side, so that nothing could come
down upon me from the top. On the side of the rock there
was a ¹⁴*hollow* place, ¹⁵*worn a little way in*, like the ¹⁶*entrance*
or door of a cave ; but there was not really any cave, or
way into the rock at all.

On the ¹⁷*flat* of the ¹⁸*green*, just before this hollow place, I
resolved to ¹⁹*pitch my tent*. This plain was not above a
hundred yards broad, and about twice as long, and lay
like a green before my door ; and, at the end of it,
²⁰*descended* ²¹*irregularly* every way down into the low ground by
the ²²*seaside*, It was on the ²³*north-northwest* side of the hill,
so that it was ²⁴*sheltered* from the heat every day, till it
came to a ²⁵*west and by south* sun, or ²⁶*thereabouts*, which, in
those countries, is near the ²⁷*setting*.

Before I set up my tent I drew a half-circle before the
hollow place, which took in about ten yards in its ²⁸*semi-
diameter*, from the rock, and twenty yards in its ²⁹*diameter*,
from its beginning and ending.

尤其是因爲沒有清水，因此我決定去招一塊更衞生的，更便利的地方，

　　我顧念到幾件事情在我的地位我覺得可適宜於我的：衞生和清水就是我方才所提起的；避去太陽的熱光，無凶猛野物之危，人或獸；並且住着要可以見海的地方，這個如果上帝使我看見一只船，我可不致失去機會求救，求救之心我還不願絕棄，

　　在招尋一個適合這些條件的地方，我尋得在山的高低處的旁邊有一塊小平原，山的一面似同房屋的尖頂般地向着這個平原；因此沒有東西可由山頂下來，石的旁邊有一個洞，略向內灣入，類似一穴的出入處或門口；但是並不是眞的有個洞或者有路可進石洞，

　　在這青草平地上，適前于穴處，我決定張我的幕在那裏，這平地的寬不在一百碼之上，約有兩倍之長，好似一草地在我的門前；草地的盡處則四面參差斜下，直至海旁的低地，草地在北偏西北，因此每日得避去熱暑，直待陽光西偏南或者相近該處，如是則在這些地方已近夕陽西下，

　　我未曾安置我的帳篷之前，先在穴的前面劃了一個半圓形，圓形的半徑是十碼；從那石起，直徑二十碼，自始至終，

1.清水。2.便利。3.顧念。4.地位。5.衞生。6.避去。7.無危。8.凶猛。9.可以見海。10.不失機會。11.求援。12.不願絕予希望。13.斜山。14.穴。15.略向內灣入。16.出入處。17.平。18.草地。19.張予之幕。20.斜下。21.參差。22.海旁。23.北偏西南。24.避去。25.西偏南。26.近處。27.夕陽西下。

In this half-circle I pitched two [1]*rows* of strong [2]*stakes*, *driving them into the ground* till they stood [3]*firm like piles*, the biggest end being out of the ground [4]*above* five feet and a half, and [5]*sharpened* on the top. The two [6]*rows* did not stand above six inches from one another.

Then I took the pieces of [7]*cable* which I had cut in the ship, and laid them in [8]*rows*, one upon another, within the [9]*circle*, between these two rows of [10]*stakes*, [11]*up to the top*, placing other stakes in the inside, leaning against them, about two feet and a half high, [12]*like a spur to a post*. This [13]*fence* was so strong that neither man nor beast could get inth it or over it. This cost me a great deal of time and labor, [14]*especially* to cut the [15]*piles* in the woods, bring them to the place, and drive them into the earth.

The entrance into this place I made to be, not by a door, but by a short [16]*ladder to go over the top*. This ladder, when I was in, I [17]*lifted over after me*, and so I was completely fenced in, and [18]*consequently* slept [19]*secure* in the night, which [20]*otherwise* I could not have done; though, as it appeared afterwards, there was no need of all this [21]*caution* from the [22]*enemies* that I [23]*apprehended* danger from.

Into this fence, or [24]*fortress*, with infinite labor I carried all my [25]*riches*, all my [26]*provisions*, [27]*ammunition*, and [28]*stores*, of which you have the account above. And I made a large tent, which, to [29]*preserve* me from the [30]*rains* that in one part of the year are very [31]*violent* there, I made double, one smaller tent within, and one larger tent above it, and covered the [32]*uppermost* with a large [33]*tarpaulin*, which I had saved among the sails.

在這半圓形內我豎起兩排堅固的短尖木，插入地中直待牠們豎着牢固如椿，大的一端出地五尺半有餘，尖端在頂上，這兩排的距離不過六寸；

然後我取了幾張我在船上剪下的錨纜；把牠們疊成，在圈內，兩排短尖木的中央，直至其巔，放其他的尖木在裏邊，斜靠錨纜，約有兩尺半高，如柱上之橫枝，這圍籬非常的堅，無論人或獸誰都不能走入或越過離芭，這個工作費了我好多時間和苦力，尤其是到樹林中去伐椿帶牠們過來，打入土中，

我造的出入處不是門而是用一小梯越頂而過，這梯一俟我走進，我便隨着取去，如是我得完全包圍在內；俾得全夜安隱睡眠，否則，我全不得安逸；雖然，照以後的情境看起來，我用不到這樣的小心輒慮仇敵的危險，

我費了無限的苦力把我一切的財產，全部的糧食，軍器，伙食都搬進這個圍籬或堡壘，至於這些物件的細目已如上述無容多贅，同時我做了一個大的帳篷以防禦淋雨，因為在一年中的某時常有狂風暴雨之故，我做了兩個，一個小帳篷包藏在內，大約帳篷在上，以油佈一大塊遮在最上面，這油布為我在船籃中所留下的，

And now I lay no more for a while in the bed which I had brought on shore, but in a [1]*hammock*, which was indeed a very good one, and [2]*belonged* to the mate of the ship.

Into this tent I brought all my provisions, and everything that would [3]*spoil* by the wet;and having thus [4]*inclosed* all my goods, I [5]*made up the entrance*, which till now I had left open, and so [6]*passed and repassed*, as I said, by a short [7]*ladder*.

When I had done this, I began [8]*to work my way into the rock*, and bringing all the earth and stones that I [9]*dug* down out through my tent, I laid them up within my [10]*fence*, [11]*in the nature of a terrace*, so that it raised the ground within about a foot and a half; and thus I made me a cave, just [12]*behind* my tent, which served me like a [13]*cellar* to my house.

It cost me much labor and many days before all these things [14]*were brougght to perfection*; and, therefore, I must go back to some other things which [15]*took up some of my thoughts*. At the same time it happened, after I [16]*had laid my scheme* for the [17]*setting up* my tent, and making the cave, that a storm of rain [18]*falling* from a thick, dark cloud, a [19]*sudden flash of lightning* happened, and after that, a [20]*great clap* of [21]*thunder*, as is [22]*naturally* the [23]*effect* of it. I was not so much surprised with the [24]*lightning* as I was with a thought which [25]*darted into my mind* as [26]*swift* as the [27]*lightning* itself,— "O my powder!" My very heart sank within me when I thought that, [28]*at one blast*, all my powder might be [29]*destroyed*; on which, not my [30]*defence* only, but the [31]*providing* my food, as I thought, [32]*entirely* [33]*depended*. I was nothing near so [34]*anxious* about my own danger, though, had the powder took fire, I should never have known what had [35]*hurt* me.

我現在再不睡在我帶到海岸的那隻牀上了，睡在一只很好的吊牀上了，這吊牀是船上同事的所有物，

我把我的糧食都帶進這個帳篷，凡要受潮溼損壞的每一件東西；我所有的貨物旣全巳如是貯藏完畢，我便關通門戶，門戶直到現在仍是開着，俾便出入，依我所說的，用短梯當門，

這個做完畢以後，我開始鑿石關路，我將我從我的帳篷所掘出的泥和石堆在我的籬笆中間，形如高蠹，如是一塊地皮壘高了一尺半；就在此我做一個洞，剛巧在我的帳篷後面，這好似爲我房屋內的地窖，

這費了我許多的苦工與很多的日子才得竣工；因此我須得轉思慮其他的事情了，同時，當我的帳篷，穴洞等布置巳安，忽然從黑烏重雲內降下暴雨，猝然閃電，繼之霹靂打雷，這是牠自然的功效，我並不爲着閃電而驚愕，因爲我的心中忽起了個念頭像閃電那麼快，———"啊我的火藥！"我一想到此點我的心嚇得魂不附體，因爲我想到一陣狂風，我全部的火藥就要裂爆，火藥這物，豈非將我用以保護自己的，但糧食的供給，我想，全然倚賴牠：我不是爲了自已的危險而着急，雖則，如果火藥着火，我永不知道我將怎樣的受害了，

1.吊牀.2.屬于.3.損壞.4.貯藏.5.關通門戶.6.出入.7.梯. 8.鑿石關路.9. 掘.10.籬笆.11.形如高蠹.12.後.13.地窖.14.竣工.15.令我念及，使予思慮.16.布置巳安17.豎直.18.落.19.猝然閃電.20.霹靂.21.打雷.22.此係其自然的功效所致（意卽雷電必隨暴風疾爾而至).23.電.24忽起于心.25.疾速.26.一陣狂風.27.裂壞.28.保護.29.供給.30.全然.31.倚賴.32損害,

Such [1]*impression* did this make upon me that, after the [2]*storm* was over, I [3]*laid aside* all my works, my [4]*building and fortifying,* and [5]*applied myself to make bags and boxes,* to [6]*separate* the powder, and to keep it [7]*a little and a little* in a parcel, in the hope that whatever might come it might not all take fire at once, and to keep it so [8]*apart* that it should not be [9]*possible* to make one part fire another. I [10]*finished* this work in about a [11]*fortnight*; and I think my powder, which in all was about two hundred and forty pounds [12]*weight,* was [13]*divided* in not less than a hundred parcels. As to the [14]*barrel* that had been wet, I [15]*did not apprehend any* [16]*danger* from that; so I placed it in my new cave, which, [17]*in my fancy,* I called my [18]*kitchen.* The rest I hid up and down in [19]*holes* among the rocks, so that no wet might come to it, [20]*marking* very carefully where I laid it.

[21]*In the interval of time* while this was doing, I went out once at least every day with my gun, as well [22]*to divert myself* as to see if I could kill anything fit for food; and, as near as I could, to [23]*acquaint* myself with what the island [24]*produced.* The first time I went out, I [25]*presently* discovered that there were [26]*goats* in the island which was [27]*a great satisfaction to me*; but then it was [28]*attended* with this misfortune to me, namely, that they were so [29]*shy,* so [30]*subtie,* and so [31]*swift of foot* that it was the most [32]*difficult* thing in the world [33]*to come at* them. But I was [34]*not discouraged at this,* not [35]*doubting* but I might [36]*now and then* shoot one, as it soon happened; for after I had found their [37]*haunts* a little,, [38]*I laid wait* in this manner for them: I observed if they saw me in the [39]*valleys,* though they were upon the rocks, they would run away, as in a [40]*terrible* [41]*fright*; but if they were [42]*feeding* in the valleys, and I was upon the rocks, they took

這個印像使我在狂風暴雨停之後，暫把別的工作都擱起；建築房舍及堡壘之事，而從事於製造甕箱等件，把火藥分開一些些貯放在包內，希望如果遇有不測，火藥不會立刻都燒去；隔開貯藏偉著火時不致漫延到別的，我用了兩星期做完這個工作；我想我的火藥，共重約二百四十磅，分開不下一百包，至於著了溼的琵琶桶，我並不懼有危險發生；所以我放牠在我的洞內，此洞，我心意中叶牠作我的廚房，其他的我藏在石的上下穴中，使不致受潮溼並詳細註明我放的地位，

在做這個的時間之中，每天我至少帶我的鎗出外一次，一方面藉以自娛，一方面招可殺作食物的獸類；以及努力認清這個島上的產物，第一次我出去，我立刻查見島上有山羊的這深愜予意；但是隨之有不利于我的，就是，牠們是易受驚；非常狹獪，非常疾快，要追護牠們倒是件極困難的事，但是我並不以此而灰心，並不躊躇，我也許有時可以射得一只的，這立刻應驗了；因為我尋到牠們的巢穴之後，我如此伏著待牠們；我窺見要是牠們見我在山下，雖然牠們在石上，牠們會突然嚇逃；但是如果牠們在山下吃草，而我在石上，牠們，

1.印像。2.狂風瀑雨。3.建築房舍及堡壘之事。4.從事。5.製造甕箱等件（以便置放火藥）。6.分。7.一些些。8.隔開。9.可能。10.兩星期。11.完畢。12.重量。13.分開。14.琵琶桶。15.並不懼有。16.危險。17.我心意中。18.廚房。19.穴。20.誌。21.中間之時。22.自娛。23.認清。24.產物。25.立刻。26.山羊。27.深愜予意。28.隨。29.畏避。30.狹獪。31.疾快。32.困難。33.追護。34.並不以此而灰心。35.躊躇。36.有時。37.巢穴。38.伏以待之。39.山下。40.可怕。41.突然的恐懼。42.吃草。

no notice of me; from whence I ¹*concluded* that by the position of their ²*optics*, their sight was so ³*directed* ⁴*downward* that they did not readily see ⁵*objects* that were above them. So afterwards I took this ⁶*method*,—I always ⁷*climbed* the rocks first, to get above them, and then ⁸*had* ⁹*frequently* ¹⁰*a fair mark.*

This first shot I made among these ¹¹*creatures*, I killed a ¹²*she-goat*, which had a little kid by her, which she ¹³*gave suck to.* This ¹⁴*grieved* me heartily, for when the old one fell, the ¹⁵*kid* ¹⁶*stood stock still* by her, till I came and took her up. And not only so, but when I carried the old one with me, upon my shoulders, the kid followed me quite to my ¹⁷*inclosure*; upon which I laid down the ¹⁸*dam*, and took the kid in my arms, and carried it over my ¹⁹*pale*, in hopes to have ²⁰*bred it up tame.* But it would not eat; so I was ²¹*forced* to kill it, and eat it myself. These two ²²*supplied* me with ²³*flesh* a great while, for I ate ²⁴*sparingly*, and saved my provisions, my bread especially, as much as ²⁵*possibly* I could.

Having now fixed my ²⁶*habitation*, I found it ²⁷*absolutely necessary* to provide a place to make a fire in, and ²⁸*fuel* to burn. What I did for that, and also how I ²⁹*enlarged* my cave, and what ³⁰*conveniences* I made, I shall ³¹*give a full account of* in its place; but I must now give some little account of myself, and of my thoughts about living, which, it may well be ³²*supposed*, were not a few.

CHAPTER XII

I HAD a ³³*dismal prospect* of my condition; for as I was not ³⁴*cast away* upon that island without being driven, as is said, by a ³⁵*violent* storm, quite out of the course of our

不會注意我；由此我決斷依牠們的視覺地位看着，牠們的視線直朝下面以致牠們看不見上面的物體。因此以後我探取這個方法，——我時常先爬上石，站在牠們的上面，於是幾次都易於射中了。

我第一次發鎗在這些動物的中間，我殺死了一每羊；在牠的旁邊有一只小羊，牠是哺乳這小羊的，這使我內心悲哀，因為，當老羊跌下去時，這小羊立定在旁，直待我去拿牠起來。非特如此，但是當我把老羊放在肩上，小的隨之而來很近我的圍籬，於是我把母羊放下，抱起小羊，帶過圍籬去，希望豢養而馴熟牠。但牠不肯吃食；所以我只得殺死牠，我自己吃牠，這兩隻供給我吃肉有好多時間，因為我吃得節省，俾得盡我所能的節省着食物，尤其是我的饅頭，

現在我既已定奪住所，我看出我必需預備一個地方可以燒火的，燒柴火的。這個我怎樣做了，我如何擴充我的洞，我如何做得便利安適，我將要詳述這個地方；但是我現在須得講一點關係自已的事，與我對於居住的意思，這些事情可以想像得出是不可少的

第 十 二 章

我的慘淡的情形；因為講到如果我不給已說過的一陣狂風吹我不會被拋在這個海島，上遠離着我們所計劃的

¹*intended* voyage, and a great way, namely, some ²*hundreds* of leagues, out of the ³*ordinary* ⁴*course* of the trade of mankind, I had great reason to consider it as a ⁵*determination of* ⁶*Heaven* that in this ⁷*desolate* place, and in this desolate manner, I should ⁸*end my life.* The tears would run ⁹*plentifully* down my face when I made these reflections; and sometimes I would ¹⁰*expostulate with myself* why ¹¹*Providence* should thus completely ruin his creatures, and ¹²*render* them so ¹³*absolutely* ¹⁴*miserable,* so without help, ¹⁵*abandoned,* so entirely ¹⁶*depressed,* that it could hardly be ¹⁷*rational* to be thankful for such a life.

But something always returned ¹⁸*swift* upon me to ¹⁹*check* these thoughts, and to ²⁰*reprove* me. Particularly one day, walking with my gun in my hand by the seaside, I was ²¹*very pensive upon the subject of my present condition,* when reason, as it were, ²²*expostulated* with me the other way, thus: "Well, you are in a desolate condition, it is true; but, ²³*pray remember,* where are the rest of you? Did not you come eleven of you in the boat? Where are the ten? Why were not they saved, and you lost? Why were you ²⁴*singled out?* Is it better to be here or there?" And than I ²⁵*pointed* to the sea. ²⁶*All evils are to be considered with the good that is in them, and with what worse attends them.*

Then it ²⁷*occurred* to me again how well I was ²⁸*furnished* for my ²⁹*subsistence,* and what would have been my case if it had not happened (which was ³⁰*a hundred thousand to one*) that the ship ³¹*floated* from the place where she first struck, and was driven so near to the shore that I had time to get all these things out of her. What would have been my case if I had been forced to live in the condition in which I at first came on shore, without ³²*necessaries of life,* or

海路線；很多路，就是：有幾百里路遠離普通人類貿易的路線，我有充分的理由考慮這是天命要我住在如此孤單的地方，以及在這樣孤單的情形之下終結我的生命．我想到這個地步之時，眼淚直如泉邊的流下我的面部；有時我自行勸導，說上天爲什麼要如此破壞他的生靈，使他們如是十分受苦，如是沒有助手，被棄如是憂鬱非凡，如此一個生命，眞招不出什麼可以感謝上帝的理由，

但是常常有反應；來得很快，阻止這些思想，同時警責着我。特在某日，手上拿着鎗在海邊走，我對此目前光景，能無廻腸九轉，正在此時，相反的有理的忠告出現了："好，你是在一孤單的情境之下，這是不錯的；但請同憶，你們中間其他的人往那兒去了呢？你們不是十一人進船的麼？十個到兒去了？他們爲什麼不遇救，而你失路？你爲什麼獨被選出？在這邊好呢還是在那邊好？"然以後我手指海．的想着有時禍中得福，不可因禍而忘福，然有時則禍上加禍，尤當因禍而戀禍。

此後又來了一個思想我的伙食如何完備，我的情形不知要怎樣，如果沒有遇到（這是十萬分中之一）這船從牠的第一次觸礁的地方漂流出去而被擱近海岸，使我有機會把船內貨物盡行取出。我的情形不知要怎樣如果我現在在初上岸的情境之下，沒有生命所必需的東西，或者

1．計備的。2．數百。3．普通。4．路程。5．命。6天。7．孤單。8．終我之生命。9．多。10．自行勸導。11．上天。12．使，致。13．十分。14．受苦。15．被棄。16．憂鬱。17．合理。18．快。19．阻過。20．警責。21．對此目前光景，能無廻腸九轉。22．忠告。23．請同憶。24．獨出。25．指手。26．有時禍中得福，不可因禍而忘福然有時則禍上加禍，尤當因禍而戀禍（卽禍不單行之說）。27．過。28．供備。29．伙食。30．十萬分中之一。31．漂海。32．生命所必需要者。

¹*necessaries* to supply and ²*procure* them ? " Particularly, " said I aloud (though to myself), " what should I have done without a gun, without ³*ammunition*, without any tools to make anything, or to work with, without clothes, "⁴*bedding*, a tent, or any manner of covering ?" Now I had all these ⁵*to sufficient quantity*, and was ⁶*in a fair way* to *provide* myself in such a manner as to live without my gun when my ammunition was spent. I had a ⁷*tolerable view of subsisting*, without any want, as long as I lived ; for I considered from the beginning how I would ⁸*provide for the accidents* that might happen and for ⁹*the time that was to come*, even not only after my ammunition should be spent, but even after my health and strength should ¹⁰*decay*.

And now being to enter into a ¹¹*melancholy relation of a scene of silent life* such, perhaps, as was never heard of in the world before, I shall take it from its beginning, and continue it in its order. It was, ¹²*by my account*, the 30th of ¹³*September*, when, in the manner as above said, I first ¹⁴*set foot upon* this ¹⁵*horrid* island ; when the sun, being to us in its ¹⁶*autumnal equinox*, was almost just over my head ; for I ¹⁷*reckoned* myself, by observation, to be ¹⁸*in the latitude of nine degrees twenty-two minutes north of the line*.

After I had been there about ten or twelve days, it ¹⁹*came into my thoughts* that I should lose my ²⁰*reckoning* of time for want of books and pen and ink, and should even forget the ²¹*Sabbath days*. To ²²*prevent* this I cut with my knife upon a large post, in ²³*capital letters*, and making it into a great ²⁴*cross*, I set it up on the shore where I first landed : " I came on shore here on the 30th of September, 1659."

供食的必須品和招得的必需品？"尤其是，"我喊道（雖然對自己）"我將怎樣辦，要是沒有一把鎗，沒有軍火，沒有做東西的傢伙，工作的器具，沒有衣服，牀帳被，一個帳篷，或者任何遮蓋的東西？現在我有這些足用的數量，如果我的軍火完了，我可希望如此住下去不用我的鎗。我於養生一道，得過且過，無容何求，旣是活着；因爲我自始考慮，要是遇到意外的事我當如何預防，以及在將來怎樣，不過我的軍火用完了怎樣，卽使我的康健和氣力衰殘之後怎樣。

現在旣已跨着進這寂寞而又抑鬱的身世，也許，世間從未聞過，我祇有依着開始的情形而繼續在這種秩序之下度日。這是，如我所算，九月三十日，如以上說的情形，當我起初到這可怕的島上，依我想；正是秋分時候因爲太陽，正將在頂上；因爲我自己計算，由觀察而得，是在北緯九度二十二分。

我住在那邊十或十二天之後，我念及我將要不復能計時日因爲缺乏書筆墨水之故，甚至禮拜日也要忘記。因爲欲免掉這個我用刀雕刻大楷在一根柱上做成大的十字架，我放在我起初登陸的海灘"我於一千六百五十九年九月四日在此測岸，"

1.必須品。2.招得。3，軍火。4.被褥。5.充足。6.有可望。7.於養生一道，得過且過。（意卽除衣食外，並不多求也）。8.預防不測。9，將來。10衰殘。11.寂寞而又抑鬱之身世。12.如予所算。13.九月。14."踏"到。15. 可怕。16.秋分。17.計算。18.北緯九度二十二分。19.念及。20.星期日。21.免掉。22.大楷。23.十字架。

Upon the sides of this [1]*square post* I cut every day a [2]*notch* with my knife, and every [3]*seventh* notch was [4]*as long again* as the rest, and every first day of the month, [5]*as long again as that long one*; and thus I kept my [6]*calendar*, or [7]*weekly*, [8]*monthly*, and yearly [9]*reckoning* of time.

[10]*In the next place* we are to [11]*observe* that among the many things which I [12]*brought out* of the ship in the several voyages which, as above [13]*mentioned*, I [14]*made to it*, I got serveral things of less value, but not at all less useful to me, which I [15]*omitted* setting down before; as, in particular, pens, ink, and paper; several parcels in the captain's, mate's, gunner's, and carpenter's keeping; three or four [16]*compasses*, some [17]*mathematical instruments, dials perspectives, charts*, and [18]*books of navigation*, all which I [19]*huddled together*, whether I might want them or no. Also, I found three very good [20]*Bibles*, which came to me in my cargo from England, and which I had [21]*packed up* among my things; some Portuguese books also; and, among them, two or three [22]*prayer books*, and several other books, all which I carefully [23]*secured*. And I must not forget that we had in the ship a dog and two cats, of whose [24]*eminent* history I [25]*may have occasion to say something in its place*; for I carried both the cats with me, and as for the dog, he [26]*jumped* out of the ship of himself, and swam on shore to me the day after I went on shore with my first cargo, and was a [27]*trusty* servant to me many years, I wanted nothing that he could fetch me, nor any company that he could [28]*make up to me*. I only wanted to have him talk to me, [29]*but that would not do*. As I observed before, I found pens, ink, and paper, and I [30]*husbanded* them to the utmost; and

在西方柱的旁邊我每天以刀刻一凹口，每第七個凹口的長度倍之，每月的第一天的長度又倍于較長之度，如是我保存我的日月歷，或者每星期，每月，每年這樣計算時日，

其次我們應該查看我幾次往船上去帶來的東西，已如上述，我拿獲幾件不重要的東西，但是並非對我絕對沒有効用的，這些不重要的東西我先前遺漏沒有寫出；至於，詳細而言，有筆墨水，紙；屬於船主，大副，掌礟者，與木匠的幾個包裹；三四只兩脚規，有幾個數學用具，日晷儀，望遠鏡，航海書，這些我都把牠們亂放，我也許用得着牠們，也許用不着，我亦招出幾本完好的聖經，這聖經是從英國船貨物中來的，這個我收拾在其他的東西一起；還有幾本葡萄牙書；其中有二三本祈禱書以及其他幾本書，這些書我都小心安放着，我必不可忘掉我們有一只狗兩只貓在船上，牠們的奇異歷史我或可乘機於適當的地方，說個大槪情形；我把兩只貓都帶走，至於這個狗，牠自己跳出船上，游到我的地方在我和我的貨物上岸的後一天，牠做了我的幾年忠心可靠的奴僕，我並不要牠能殼同我招什麼東西或替我作事，我不過要牠能殼和我談話，然而這個離難實行，如我以前查得的，有筆墨水和紙，我非常的節用；

1.四方柱。2.凹口。3.第七。4.其長度倍之。5.又倍於其較長之度。6.日月歷。7.每星期。8.每月。9.計算。10.其次。11.查得。12.帶。13.述及。4.往(指至船上言)。15.遺漏。16.兩脚規（亦可作衆數之羅盤解）。17.算學用具，日晷儀，望遠鏡，航海。18航海書。19.亂放。20.聖經。21.收拾。22.祈禱書。23.安放。24.奇異。25.或可乘機於適當的時候，說個大槪情形。26.跳。27.忠心可靠。28.備予之缺乏；與吾親近。29.但此離難實行。30.節用。

I shall show that while my ink *¹lasted*, I kept things very ²*exact*, but after that was gone I could not, for I could not make any ink ³*by any means that I could devise*.

And this ⁴*put me in mind* that I wanted many things, ⁵*notwithstanding* all that I had ⁶*amassed together*. Of these, ink was one ; as also a ⁷*spade*, ⁸*pickax*, and ⁹*shovel*, to dig or ¹⁰*remove* the earth ; ¹¹*needles, pins*, and ¹²*thread*. As for ¹³*linen*, I soon learned to want that without much ¹⁴*difficulty*.

This want of ¹⁵*tools* made every work I did go on heavily ; and it was near a whole year before I had ¹⁶*entirely* finished my little pale, or ¹⁷*surrounded* my ¹⁸*habitation*. The piles or stakes, which were as ¹⁹*heavy* as I could well lift, were a long time in cutting and preparing in the ²⁰*woods*, and more, ²¹*by far*, in ²²*bringing* home. I spent sometimes two days in cutting and ²³*bringing* home one of those posts, and a third day in ²⁴*driving* it into the ground ; for which purpose I got a heavy piece of wood at first, but at last ²⁵*bethought* myself of one of the iron ²⁶*crows* ; which, however, though I found it, made driving those ²⁷*posts* or piles very ²⁸*laborious and tedious work*. But what need I have been ²⁹*concerned at* the ³⁰*tediousness* of anything I had to do, seeing I had time enough to do it in ? Nor had I any other ³¹*employment*. if that had been over, at least that I could ³²*foresee*, except the ³³*ranging* the island to seek for food, which I did, ³⁴*more or less*, every day.

I now begon to consider ³⁵*seriously* my condition, and ³⁶*the. circumstances* I was ³⁷*reduced* to ; and I ³⁸*drew up* the state of my affairs in writing, not so much to leave them to any that were to come after me, as ³⁹*to deliver* ⁴⁰*my thoughts from daily poring over them*, and ⁴¹*afflicting* my mind. As my reason began now to ⁴²*master my despondency*, I began to

我將要敘出來當我的墨水存着，我記載事實非常眞確，但墨水用罄之後我便不能了，因爲我不能用什麼方法做墨水，

這件事使我想及我須要許多東西，不論我所已經收集的，這幾件事中，墨水是一件，還有鏟，鶴嘴斧，鐵鏟，用以掘泥土；針，別針，和線。至於夏布，我不久便招到易得的方法，

因爲缺乏工具，每件工作我都是難做；約近一年才把我的棚圍或我居所的圍牆完全完工．這椿．或頭尖木很不易拔起，費了好久時光在斬伐和聚集上面在森林之中，尤其是取至家中．我耗費二天去斬和拿其中的一根木頭到家，第三天則插入地中；爲着這個緣故，我起先用一塊重水，我後來想到一只鐵鏟我雖然尋到了，可是插起木樁來又辛苦而又厭煩。但是我既然有這充足的時間，對於無論何種的工作的漫煩又何必要關心呢？我亦沒有別的事務，如果這個做完了，至少我所能榖預見的；除非漫游此島尋食物，尋食物我每天多少總是必需去的，

我現在開始很勝重地考慮，我的情境，我的淪落情形；我將我所處之境況情形盡情描寫，一絲不漏在將來發見，俾每日得以流覽，同時發生意見而筆之以書，以免蓄於心中而傷我的胸懷，至於我的理由現在遏制我的失望心，我開始

comfort myself as well as I could, and [1]*to set the good against the evil*, that I might have something to [2]*distinguish* my case from [3]*worse*; and I stated very [4]*impartially*, like [5]*debtor* and [6]*creditor*, the comforts I enjoyed against the [7]*miseries* I [8]*suffered*, thus:

EVIL	GOOD
I am cast upon a [9]*horrible*, [10]*desolate* island, [11]*void of all* [12]*hope of recovery*.	But I am alive, and not [22]*drowned*, as all my ship's company were.
I am singled out and [13]*separated*, as it were, from all the world, to be [14]*miserable*.	But I am [23]*singled out*, too, from all the ship's [24]*crew*, [25]*to be spared from death*; and He that [26]*miraculously* saved me from death, can [27]*deliver* me from this condition.
I am [15]*divided from mankind* —a [11]*solitaire*; one banished from [17]*human society*.	But I am not [8]*starved* and [29]*perishing* on a [30]*barren* place, affording no sustenance.
I have not clothes to cover me.	But I am in a hot [31]*climate*, where, if I had clothes, I could hardly were them.
I am without any [18]*defence*, or means to [14]*resistany violence* of man or beast.	But I am [32]*cast on* an island where I see no wild beasts [33]*to hurt* me, as I saw on the coast of Africa; and what if I had been [34]*shipwrecked* there?
I have no [20]*soul* to speak to. or [21]*relieve* me.	But God [35]*wonderfully* sent the ship in near enough to the shore that I have got out as many [36]*necessary* things as will either [37]*supply* my wants or enable me to supply myself, even as long as I live.

極力安慰自己;並非禍福於兩端,使我從禍患中或可識別我的情形;我指定得非常公平,直類債戶與債主,我享樂的安慰對照我所受的痛苦,如此:

壞	好
我被拋在一個可怕的荒蕪的島上,全無復舊的希望	但是我是活着,沒有,像我船上的同伴都溺死;
我獨被選分離全世界而來受痛苦,	但我亦是從全船水手中獨被選出得免於死;他既經神奇低救我出死,當可救我出此情境,
我與人類分離 —— 隱居者;一自人類社會中逐出的人,	但我沒有在一荒蕪的地方餓斃與死,無衣無食,
我無衣遮蔽我身,	但我是在熱帶中,如果有衣服,我也不能穿牠,
我沒有保護物,我也沒有具工可抵禦人或獸的暴烈的攻擊,	但我被拋棄的島上我未見有野獸可以傷害我,像我在非洲海岸所看見的那樣;要是我的觸礁在非洲那末又將怎樣?
我沒有人來和我談話或者拯救我。	但是上帝奇奇地差船近岸,足使我把可供給我需要的,或可以供給我自己的所要的必需品都得取出,俾得與我的生命俱存,

1.並列禍福於兩端.2.識別.3.禍福.4.公平.5.債戶.6.債主.7.痛苦.8.受苦.9.可怕.10.荒蕪.11.全無希望.12.恢復元氣,復舊.13.分離.14.痛苦.15.哭人類分離.16.隱居者.17.人類社會.18.保護.19.抵禦暴烈之攻擊.20.人.21.拯救.22.溺死.23.獨被選出.24.水手.25.免死.26.神奇.27.餓死.28.斃.29.荒蕪.30.無衣無食.31.天氣.32.拋于.33.傷害.34.船觸礁.35.希奇.36.必需.27.供給.

¹*Upon the whole*, here was an ²*undoubted testimeony* that there was ³*scarce* any condition in the world so ⁴*miserable* but there was something to be thankful for in it ; and ⁵*let this stand as a direction*, from the ⁶*experience* of the most ⁷*miserable* of all conditions in this world, that we may always find in it something to comfort ⁸*ourselves* from, and to set, in the ⁹*description* of good and evil, ¹⁰*on the credit side* ¹¹*of the account.*

Having now ¹²*brought* my mind a little to ¹³*relish* my condition, and given over looking out to sea to see if I could ¹⁴*spy* a ship,—I say, giving over these things, I began to ¹⁵*apply* myself ¹⁶*to arrange my way of living*, and to make things as ¹⁷*easy* to me as I could.

CHAPTER XIII

I HAVE already ¹⁸*described* my ¹⁹*habitation*, which was a tent under the side of a rock, ²⁰*surrounded* with a strong pale of ²¹*posts* and ²²*cables*. But I might now rather call it a wall, for I raised a kind of wall up against it ²³*of turfs*, about two feet thick on the ²⁴*outside* ; and after some time (I think it was a year and a half) I raised ²⁵*rafters* from it, ²⁶*leaning to* the ²⁷*rock*, and ²⁸*thatched or covered it with boughs of trees*, and such things as I could get, ²⁹*to keep out the rain*, which I found at some times of the year ³⁰*very violent.*

I have already observed how I brought all my goods into this ³¹*pale*, and into the cave which I had made behind me. But I must ³²*observe*, too, that at first this was a ³³*confused* ³⁴*heap* of goods, which, as they ³⁵*lay in no order*, so they took up all my place. I had ³⁶*no room* to turn myself. So I ³⁷*set myself to enlarge* my cave, and work farther into the earth ; for it was a ³⁸*loose*, ³⁹*sandy rock*, which ⁴⁰*yielded* easily to the

總而言之，此地是確鑿的憑據，就是世上任何情境中少有絕對的痛苦，因爲痛苦之中必有可激謝的地方；以此爲標準，在世界上攏總情境中最痛苦的經驗裏，我們時常在債主帳之一項下招得可以安慰我們自己的事物，把好的和壞的一齊描寫出來，

現在旣巳轉移我的思想一，點使我喜悅我的情境，注意看着海上要是可以我望見一只船；── 我說，去掉這些事物，我開始潛心籌劃度日之計，努力安適事物，

第　十　三　章

我已經評論過我的居所這是在石邊的一個帳篷，有堅牢的柱子和錨鑱圍住，我現在寧可叫他爲牆，因爲我築的牆是以草皮作成的，外面約有二尺厚；過了幾時之後（我想是一年半載）我在牆上建築椽，靠於石上，覆蓋以樹枝，與這羣我能夠拿到的東西，防避雨水，我看出一年之中有一個時期是非常劇烈的，

我已經說過我如何把貨物搬進圍場與搬進在我後面所築的穴內，我必須加以評論，起初這是一堆雜亂的貨物，因爲牠們不整齊的亂放着，因此牠們佔了我所有的空地。我簡直沒有隙地可轉移我身，所以我從事擴充我穴，深掘到地低下去，因爲這是鬆泥石地，易於生出

labor I *¹bestowed on* it. And when I found I was *²pretty* safe as to *³beasts of prey*, I worked *⁴sideways*, to the right hand, into the *⁵rock*; and then, *⁶turning to the right* again, worked quite out, and made me a door to come out on the outside of my pale or *⁷fortification*. This gave me not only *⁸egress* and *⁹regress*, as it was a back way to my tent and to my *¹⁰storehouse*, but gave me room *¹¹to store* my goods.

And now I began to apply myself to make such *¹²neces- sary* things as I found I most wanted, *¹³particularly* a chair and *¹⁴a table*; for without these I was not able to enjoy the few *¹⁵comforts* I had in the world. I could not write, or eat, or do *¹⁶several* things with so much pleasure without a *¹⁷table*. So I went to work. And here I *¹⁸must needs* observe this as *¹⁹reason is the substance and origin of the mathematics*, so by *²⁰stating* and *²¹squaring* everything by reason, and by making the most *²²rational judgment* of things, every man may be, *²³in time*, master of every *²⁴mechanic art*. I had never *²⁵handled* a tool in my life; and yet, in time, by labor *²⁶application*, and *²⁷contrivance*, I found, at last, that I wanted nothing but I could have made it, *²⁸especially* if I had had tools. How- ever, I made *²⁹abundance* of things, even without tools: and some with no more tools than an *³⁰adze* and a *³¹hatchet*, which perhaps were never made that way before, and that with *³²infinite* labor. For example, if I wanted a *³³board*, I had no other way but to cut down a tree, *³⁴set it on an edge before me*, and *³⁵hew* it flat on either side with my ax, till I had brought it to be thin as a *³⁶plank*, and then *³⁷dub* it smooth with my *³⁸adze*. It is true, by this method I could make but one board out of a whole tree; but this I had *³⁹no remedy for* but *⁴⁰patience*, any more than I had for the *⁴¹prodigious*

加諸其上的工作効力，當我看出我沒有野獸來吃我而覺得很不隱，我向石內右邊工作；然後再轉向右門。這門非持給我一出路與返路，牠是到我的帳篷和貯藏所的後門，而且給我貯藏貨物的機會。

現在我起始潛心于辦這般必須品，依我看爲我非有不可的，尤其是一只椅子和一只桌子；因爲沒有這個我不能享受我在世界上應有的幾件慰藉。我不能狠高興地寫字，吃食和幾件事體，要是沒有一只桌子。於是我去工作，在此我必須批評理想爲數學之資料及本原，所以凡事祇須用理想來詳明和比較，極合理的明斷事物，每人終必能支配每種技藝。我生平從未處理一柄工具；但是將來只須加以工作，專心，計謀，我後來覺得我用不到什麼東西，是只須有了，尤其是工具，我便可把牠做成。然而，我做了許多東西，雖然沒有工具；有幾個我東西沒有用甚何工具，祇是一把斧和手斧，恐怕這是空前的工作，費了無限的工夫，譬如，如果我要一塊版，我沒有別的方法祇有斬樹，橫置於我前，拿我的斧頭兩頭斬平，直待平如木版，然後用我的斧使之平滑，不錯，這個方法一株大樹祇能做一塊木版；但這是無可奈何的事啊，祇須忍耐，與耗費許多時候

1.加諸.2.極.3.肉食獸.4.向一邊.5.石.6.轉.7.堡壘.8.出路.9.返路.10.貯藏所.11.貯藏.12.必須.13.尤其是.14.桌.15.安適.16.幾個.17.必須.19.理想爲數學之資料及本原.19.陳述，詳明.20.比較.21.明斷；合理之評斷.22.終必.23.技藝.24.技藝.25.處理.26.專心.27.機謀.28.尤其是.29.許多.30.斧.31.手斧.32.無限.33.桌版.34.橫置于前.35.斬.36.木版.37.使平滑.38.斧.39.無可奈何.40.忍耐.41.許多時候

[1]deal of time and labor which it took me to make a [2]plank or board. But my time or labor was little worth, and so it was as well [3]employed one way as another.

However, I made me a table and a [4]chair, as I [5]observed above, [6]in the first place; and this I did out of the short pieces of boards that I brought on my raft from the ship. But when I had [7]wrought out some boards as above, I made large [8]shelves, of the [9]breadth of a foot and a half, one over another all along one side of my [10]cave to lay all my [11]tools, nails, and [12]ironwork on; and, in a word, [13]to separate every-thing at large into their [14]places, that I might [15]come easily at them. I [16]knocked pieces [17]into the wall of the rock to hang my [18]guns and all things that would [19]hang up. Had my cave been to be seen, it looked like a general [20]magazine of all necessary things; and I had everything so [21]ready at my [22]hand that it was a great pleasure to me to see all my goods in such order, and [23]especially to find my [24]stock of all necessaries so great.

And now it was that I began to keep a [25]journal of every day's [26]employment; for, indeed, as first, I was [27]in too much hurry, and not only hurry as to [28]labor, but in too much [29]discomposure of mind; and my [30]journal would have been full of many [31]dull things. I shall here give you the [32]copy (though in it will be told all these [33]particulars over again) as long as it lasted; for having no more ink, I was forced [34]to leave it off.

THE JOURNAL

[35]September 30, 1659.—I, poor, [36]miserable Robinson Crusoe, being shipwrecked during a [37]dreadful storm in the [38]offing, came on shore on this [39]dismal, unfortunate island,

和工作做成一塊木版或桌版。但是我的時間和工作的價值細微,因此不是這樣服役就是那樣服役,

不論如何,我爲我自已做一隻桌子與一隻椅子,就是我在上面批評過的,第一;這個我由我的木扱從船上帶來的短木版做成的;但當我做成如上的幾塊版,我做個大的架子,一尺半闊,一塊隔在一塊的上面依着我的洞的一邊,這木架可以放工具,釘,鐵工具;總之,悉將各物分類而安置,俾我可以便於取拿此具,我把木塊敲入石牆掛我的鎗,以及其他可掛的東西,倘使有人來看我的洞,這洞看起來類如許多必須品的普通倉庫;我有每件東西近在手頭,這是件極快樂的事情看到我的貨物如是秩序并然,尤其是看到我的屯積貨物處的必須品之多,

現在我開始記載每天的工作;因爲,誠然,起初,我是過于急迫,非特工作上面急迫,但是過于心緒不寧;我的日記將要充滿許多憂悶抑鬱之事,我在此地給你這個原稿(雖然其中的詳細情形再要提講)至終;爲了沒有墨水,我祇得棄掉他不記,

日　記

一六五九年九月卅日,———— 我這可憐的受難的魯賓孫;爲了在一可怖的颶風的海面上觸礁,來到這昏暗,不幸的島岸上,

which I called ' [1]*The Island of Despair;*" all the rest of the ship's company being [2]*drowned,* and myself almost dead.

All the rest of the day I [3]*spent* in [4]*afflicting* myself at the dismal [5]*circumstances* I was brought to; namely, I had neither food, house, clothes, weapon, nor place to [6]*fly* to; and, [7]*in despair of any relief,* [8]*saw nothing but death before me,*—either that I should be [9]*devoured* by wild beasts, [10]*murdered* by [11]*savages,* or [12]*starved to death for want of food* [13]*At the approach of night* I slept in a tree, for fear of wild creatures; but [14]*slept soundly,* though it [15]*rained* all night.

[16]*October* I.—In the morning I saw, to my great [17]*surprise,* the ship had [18]*floated* with the [19]*high tide,* and was driven on shore again much nearer the island. This, as it was some comfort, [20]*on one hand.*—for, seeing her set [21]*upright,* and not broken to pieces, I hoped, if the wind [22]*abated,* I might get on board, and get some food and necessaries out of her for my [23]*relief,*—so, [24]*on the other hand*, it [25]*renewed* my grief at the loss of my [26]*comrades,* who, I [27]*imagined,* if we had all [28]*staid* on board, might have saved the ship, or, at least, that they would not have been all drowned, as they were; and that had the men been saved, we might perhaps have built us a boat [29]*out of* the [30]*ruins* of the ship, to have [31]*carried* us to some other part of the world. I spent great part of this day in [32]*perplexing* myself on these things; but, [33]*at length,* seeing the ship almost dry, I went upon the sand as near as I could, and then [34]*swam* on board. This day also it [35]*continued raining,* though with no wind at all.

From the 1st of [36]*October* to the 24th.—All these days [37]*entirely* spent in many several [38]*voyages* to get all I could [39]*out of* the ship, which I brought on shore every [40]*flood of tide*

我呼牠爲"絕望島，"船上的其他同伴均已溺死，而我自已幾乎要死，

處在此種暗淡的環境內我過着痛苦的日子；就是我沒有食物，房屋，衣服，軍器，也沒有可逃避的地方去，無拯救的希望，只有滿目淒涼，惟死而已，——或者我要被野獸吞食，被野人刺死，或因食絕而餓斃。臨夜我睡在一株樹中，爲怕野獸；不過倒可酣睡，雖則全夜下雨，

十月一日——在早晨我看見，不覺驚奇不已，這船隨大潮高漲而漂流，又被打至海灘，更近此島，這個一方面是些慰藉，——因爲看見牠豎起，沒有打成碎片，我希望，要是風減輕，我可上船，從船上招點食物或必需品籍以救濟我自己，——彼一方面，爲了我的同伴之死的悲哀又復哭起，我想如果他們歇在船內，或者可以使船安全，或者，最低限度，他們不致于溺死。如迄今他們已死；如此，要是這班人均告無恙，我們也許可以將破壞的船造成一隻船，而帶我們到世上別處去，我消磨我大半天在爲這些事情而困惱；但是終究，看看此船將乾，我奮勇走近海灘，然後游到船上。這一天，依舊繼續下雨，雖則全然無風，

自十月一號至念四號，——這許多日子完全消磨于航行之中，藉把船內的貨物竭力取出，每逢上潮時我把貨物

1.絕望島。2.溺死。3.過時，消磨。4.使痛苦。5.環境。6.逃避。7.無拯救之希翼。8.滿目淒涼，惟死而已。9.吞食。10.刺殺。11.野人。12.食絕而餓斃。13.臨夜。14.酣睡。15.下雨。16.十月。17.驚奇。18.漂流。19.大潮。20.一方面。21.豎直。22.減少。23.拯救。24.彼一方面。25.重起。26.同伴。27.幻想。28.歇近。29.出於。30.破壞。31.帶我們。32.困惱。33.終究。34.游。35.繼續。36.十月。37.完全。38.航海。39.出於。40.上潮。

upon rafts. Much rain also in the days, though with some
[1]*intervals of fair weather* : but it seems this was the [2]*rainy
season.*

Oct. 20.—I overset my raft, and all the goods I had got
upon it ; but, being in shoal water, and the things being
[4]*chiefly* heavy, I recovered many of them [5]*when the tide was
out.*

Oct. 25.—It rained all night and all day, [6]*with some gusts
of wind* ; during which time the ship broke in pieces, the
wind [7]*blowing* a little [8]*harder* than before, and was no more
to be seen, [9]*except* the wreck of her, and that only at low
water. I spent this day in covering and [10]*securing* the goods
which I had saved, that the rain might not [11]*spoil* them.

Oct. 26.—I walked about the shore almost all day, to find
out a place to [12]*fix* my [13]*habitaticn* greatly [14]*concerned* to secure
myself from any [15]*attack* in the night, either from wild [16]*beasts*
or men. Towards night I [17]*fixed upon* a proper place, under
a rock, and marked out a [18]*semicircle* for my [19]*encampment,*
which I resolved to [20]*strengthen* with a work, wall, or
fortification, made of double [21]*piles,* [22]*lined within with* cables,
and without, with [23]*turf.*

From the 26th to the 30th, I worked very hard in carrying all my goods to my new habitation, though some part
of the time [24]*it rained exceedingly hard.*

The 31st, in the morning, I went out into the island
with my gun, [25]*to seek* for some food, and discover the
country. I killed a she-goat, and her kid followed me home,
which I afterwards killed also, because it [26]*would not feed*

[27]*November* 1.—I set up my tent under a rock, and lay
there for the first night ; making it as large as I could, with
stakes driven in [28]*to swing my hammock upon.*

放在木排上運到岸上，白天下雨頗多，雖然間或天晴；不過看起來好像是黃霉天（多雨之時）。

十月二十日。——我的木排傾覆，同時我放在木排上的貨物都倒在海內；但是，因在淺水處，貨物大半頗重，當潮退之時我把牠們都取出。

十月二十五日。——終日夜降雨，間有猛烈的風；在此處這船被浪擊碎，風較前吹得更劇烈，這船不再有了，在下潮時祇見破船。這天我將撿得的貨物安放妥當，以免受風雨的打壞。

十月二十六日。——幾乎整日在河邊走着，尋招一處適宜我的居所，非常注意安寧使在夜間沒有危險，無論是野獸的害或人類的害。臨夜我擇定一個適當的地方，在石的底下，劃一個半圓形做我的營房，我決意將我的營房堅圍住一建築物或圍牆或堡壘，以雙重大椿做成，內層鑲以錨纜，外面蓋以草工。

自二十六日至卅日，我費了許多力把我的貨物都搬進新屋，雖則有時大雨傾盆。

卅一日早晨，我攜帶我的槍到島內去尋些食物，而發見這個地方。我殺死一隻雌羊，牠的小羊便隨我到家去，我後來也把小羊殺死，因爲牠不肯吃。

十一月。——在一石的底下我便豎建了我的帳篷，這是我第一天睡在那裏十；竭力擴大我的居所，並打入木椿懸掛我的吊牀。

159

Nov. 2.—I set up all my [1]*chests* and boards, and the pieces of [2]*timber* which made my rafts, and with them formed a fence round me, a little within the place I had [3]*marked* out for my fortification.

Nov. 3.—I went out with my gun, and killed two [4]*fowls* like [5]*ducks* which were very good food. In the afternoon went to work to make me a table

CHAPTER XIV

*Nov.*4.—This morning I [6]*began to order* my times of work, of going out with my gun, time of sleep, and time of [7]*diversion.* Every morning I walked out with my gun for two or three hours, if it did not rain ; then [8]*employed myself to work* till about eleven o'clock ; then ate what I had to [9]*live on*; and from twelve till two I lay down to sleep, the weather being [10]*excessively* hot ; and then, in the evening, to work again. The working part of this day and of the next was [11]*wholly* employed in making my table, for I was yet but a very [12]*sorry workman,* though time and necessity made me a [13]*complete natural mechanic* soon after, as I believe they [14]*would do any one else.*

Nov 5.—This day, [15]*went abroad* with my gun and my dog, and killed a wild cat ; her skin pretty [16]*soft*, but her flesh [17]*good for nothing.* Every creature that I killed I took off the skins and [18]*preserved* them. Coming back by the seashore, I saw many sorts of [19]*sea fowls,* which I did not understand; but was surprised, and almost [20]*frightened*, with two or three [21]*seals*, which, while I was [22]*gazing at*, not well knowing what they were, got into the sea, and [23]*escaped* me for that time.

十一月二日。——我安放我的箱子，桌子，以及做我木排的幾塊木板，將他們造成我的圍籬；籬內一小地我劃作我的堡壘。

十一月三日。——我攜帶我的槍出去，殺死兩隻類似鴨的禽類，鴨是很好的食品。下午我去工作一只桌子。

第 十 四 章

十一月四日。——這天早晨我始行酌定我工作的時間，游獵的時刻，睡的時刻，以及快樂的時刻，每天早晨我去游獵兩三個鐘點，如果不下雨；然後從事放工作直待將近十一時，此後我吃東西以養生：由十二時到二時為修息的時間，天氣很熱的緣故；然後，在黃昏，再工作。今天工作的時間加上明天的完全從事於做一桌子，因為我是個很拙劣的工人，雖然時間與須要不久造成我——完全天然的工匠，因為我相信這工作對於他人亦然。

十一月五日。——此日，帶我的槍，與我的狗出外，我殺死一隻野貓；牠的皮非常柔軟，不過牠的肉絕無用處。每個我所殺死的動物，我去了牠們的皮便把牠們保藏着，沿海岸區來時，我見有許多種類的海禽，可是我不悌是何禽；但是看見兩三隻的海狗。不覺驚奇而有些威懼，當我注視牠們時，不確實知道牠們為何物，牠們此時跳進海內而迴避我。

Nov. 6.—After my morning walk, I went to work with my table again, and finished it, though [1]*not to my liking*; nor was it long before I learned [2]*to ment* it.

[3]*Nov.* 7.—Now it began [4]*to be settled fair weather.* The 7th, 8th, 9th 10th, and part of the 12th (for the 11th was Sunday) I [5]*took wholly up* to make me a [6]*chair*, and [7]*with much ado brought it to a tolerable shape*, but never to please me; and even in the making I [8]*pulled it in pieces* several times.

Note.—I soon [9]*neglected* my keeping Sundays; for, [10]*omitting* my [11]*mark* for them on my [12]*post*, I forgot which was which.

Nov. 13.—This day it [13]*rained*, which [14]*refreshed* me *exceedingly*, and cooled the earth; but it was [15]*accompanied* with [16]*terrible thunder* and [17]*lightning*, which frightened me dreadfully, for fear of my powder. As soon as it was over, I resolved to [18]*separate* my [19]*stock of powder* into as many little parcels as possible, that it might not be in danger.

Nov. 14, 15, 16.—These three days I spent in making little square chests, or boxes, which might [20]*hold* about a pound, or two pounds at most, of powder; and so, putting the powder in, I [21]*stowed* it in places as [22]*secure* and [23]*remote* from one another as possible. On one of these three days I killed a large bird that was good to eat, but I knew not what to call it.

Nov. 17.—This day I began to dig behind my [24]*tent* into the rock, [25]*to make room for my further conveniency.*

Note.—Three things I wanted [26]*exceedingly* for this work; namely, a [27]*pickax*, a [28]*shovel*, and a [29]*wheelbarrow*, or basket; so I [30]*desisted from my work*, and began to consider how to supply that want and make me some [31]*tools*. As for

十一月六日。——我早晨散步之後,我再去做我的巢子,而竣工,雖則我不甚喜悅;不久我漸達改進。

十一月七日——現在天氣漸漸晴朗。七日,八日,九日,以及十二日的一部分(因爲十一日是星期),我盡日專門做椅,艱難盡至,才略成形式;但總不能使我滿意;就是當在做的時候我拆散了幾次。

注意。——我不久輕忽了維持星期日;因爲在柱上遺漏了星期日的記號,我忘記了那個是那個。

十一月十三日。——此日下雨,令予神清氣爽,微冷土地;但是接着就是可怕的打雷與電閃,令我恐怖不堪,猶恐我的軍藥着火。雷電雨完畢之後,我決定把我所藏有的軍火分做許多小包,俾不致發生危險。

十一月十四日,十五日,十六日,——這三日我消磨於做小方匣子,匣內可藏的約一磅或至多二磅的火藥;於是安放了火藥,我把牠藏在最妥當的地方,彼此隔離很遠。三日中的一天我殺死一隻可吃我鳥,可是我不知道怎樣叫牠。

十一月十七日。——此日我起始在我篷幄後面掘進石內,闢地以更求便利。

注意。——做這種工作有三物我非常須要;就是,一只丁字斧,一只鏟與一手車或籃;所以我停止工作,而開始考慮如何供給我的須要與做幾只工具。至於

1.不甚喜悅。2.改進。3.十一月。4.天氣晴朗。5盡日專以。6.椅。7.艱難盡至才略成形式。8.拆散。9.輕忽。10.遺漏。11.記號。12.柱。13.降雨。14.令予神清氣爽。15.接着。16.可怕的雷。17.電。18.分隔。19.貯藏的軍火。20.裝。21藏。22.平安。23.遠。24.帳蓬。25闢地以更求利便。26.非常。29.丁字斧。28.鏟。29.手車30.停止。31.工具。

the pickax, I made use of the iron crows, which were [1]*proper enough*, though heavy. But the next thing was a [2]*shovel*, or [3]*spade*. This was so [4]*absolutely necessary* that, indeed, I [5]*could do nothing effectually without it*; but what kind of one to make I knew not.

Nov. 18.—The next day, in [6]*searching* the woods, I found a tree of that wood, or like it, which, in Brazil, they call the iron tree, for its exceeding [7]*hardness*. Of this, [8]*with great labor*, and almost [9]*spoiling* my ax, I cut a [10]*piece*, and brought it home, too, with difficulty enough, for it was [11]*exceeding heavy*. The [12]*excessive* [13]*hardness* of the wood, and my having no other way, made me a long while upon this [14]*machine*, for I worked it [15]*effectually* by little and little into the form of a shovel or spade; the [16]*handle* exactly [17]*shaped* like ours in England, only that the [18]*broad part having no iron shod upon it at bottom*, it would not last me so long. However, it [19]*served well enough for the uses which I had occasion to put it to*; but never was a shovel, I believe, [20]*made after that fashion*, or so long in making.

I was still [21]*deficient*, for I wanted a basket or a [22]*wheel-barrow*. A basket I could not make [23]*by any means*, having no such things as [24]*twigs* that would [25]*bend to* make [26]*wicker ware*,—at least, none yet found out. As to a wheelbarrow, I [27]*fancied* I could make all but the [28]*wheel*, but that I [29]*had no notion of*, neither did I know [30]*how to go about it*; besides, I had no possible way to make the iron [31]*gudgeons* for the [32]*spindle or axis of the wheel to run in.* So I [33]*gave it over*, and for carrying away the earth which I [34]*dug out* of the cave I made me a thing like a [35]*hod* which the [36]*laborers* carry [37]*mortar* in when they serve the [38]*bricklayers*. This was not so difficult to me as the making the shovel; and yet this and the

丁字斧；我以鐵挺來替代，鐵挺頗適用，雖然重點，第二件東西就是鏟或鑿。這是萬不可少的，的確，無此不能成事；但做怎樣一個我可不知了。

十一月十八日。—— 第二天在尋招木料我招到一株這種木料的樹，或者類似的，在巴西國，他們叫牠為鐵樹，非常堅硬的緣故。這樹，大費工夫，幾乎斬壞我的斧頭，我斬去一塊，帶囘家，也非常困難，因為木料過重。這木過硬，同時我沒有別的方法，費了我許多辰光做這機器，因為我用十足力氣，一些些的把牠做成一鏟或鑿，柄的模樣正如我們在英國的，不過鋤之闊頭無鐵裝着，所以不能耐之，不論如何，牠頗能和合我所擬之用；但我相信從未有一個鏟子照此種形式製造，或者做了這好久時間。

我依舊缺乏，因為我要一只手車或籃。籃子我不論如何不能做的，因為沒有細小的樹枝可灣做柳枝編織之器具，—— 至少，我還沒有招到，講到小車，我想其他的我都可以做的就是車輪，我沒有想到，也不知道何從揷手；此外，我沒有方法可以做鐵軸之中樞為輪軸通過。所以我置諸度外，因為裝載我從洞內掘出的泥土我做了一隻類似灰沙桶，就是工人在服役泥水匠時帶灰泥用的，做這桶沒有像做鏟那麼困難；但是這個和這

shovel, and the [1]*attempt* which I made, [2]*in vain* to make a wheelbarrow, took me no less than four days,—I mean always [3]*excepting* my morning walk with my [4]*gun*, which I [5]*seldom* [6]*failed*, and very seldom failed also bringing home something fit to eat.

Nov. 23.—*My* other work having now [7]*stood still*, because of my making these tools. when they were finished I went on, and working every day, as my [8]*strength* and time allowed, I spent eighteen days [9]*entirely* in [10]*widening* and [11]*deepening* my cave, that it might hold my goods [12]*commodiously.*

Note.—During all this time I worked to make this room or cave [13]*spacious* enough to [14]*accommodate* me as a [15]*warehouse.* or [16]*magazine*, a [17]*kitchen*, a dining room, and a [18]*celler*. As for my [19]*lodging*, I [20]*kept to* the tent ; except that sometimes, in the wet seeson of the year, it [21]*rained* so hard that I could not keep myself dry, which caused me afterwards to cover all my place within my [22]*pale* with long [23]*poles*, in the form of [24]*rafters*, leaning against the rock, and load them with [25]*flags* and large leaves of trees, like a [26]*thatch.*

[27]*December* 10.—I began now to think my cave or [28]*vault* finished. when [29]*on a sudden* (it seems I had made it too large) a great [30]*quantity* of earth fell down from the top on one side ; [31]*so much that*, in short, it [32]*frighted* me, and not without reason, too, for if I had been under it, [33]*I had never wanted a gravedigger*. I had now a [34]*great deal* of work to do over again, for I had the loose earth to carry out ; and, which was of more [35]*importance*, I had the [36]*ceiling* to [37]*prop up*, so that I might be [38]*sure* no more would come down.

Dec. 11.—This day I went to work with it accordingly, and got two [39]*shores or posts pitched upright to the top*, with

鏟，試做小車而未成的小車，整個費了我四天，──我的意思，除去我時常在早晨攜帶鎗出去漫游，早晨散步這同事我少見不實行的，也少見不帶些食物回家的。

十一月二十三日。──我別的工作現在擱起，因為我在做這些工具，當工具竣工，我繼續每天工作，要是我的氣力與時間准我。我整個費了十八天在擴大和掘深我的洞的工作，俾便利貯藏我的貨物。

注意。──在這個時期內我從事工作，使此房間或穴寬闊足容我的棧房，雜物間，廚房，膳堂與地窖之用。至於我的住宿，我堅定於帳蓬內，除非有時，年內多雨的時期，雨下得過劇甚至不能保持乾燥，這使我後來在我的垣牆遮蓋長柱，似椽的形式，靠於石上，裝滿蔗和大樹葉，像一茅茨。

十二月十日。──我現在起始想我的穴或窖工程已告竣，猝然（好像我做得太大之故）多量的泥土由一邊的頂上落下；至如是之多，簡直嚇了我，也並非是沒理由的，因為如果我在低下，自必葬身其中而無需土工為我治壙矣。現在我有許多的工作要重做，因為我要把鬆下的泥土帶出去；這是最重大的工作，我得撐住天花板，如是使我確知再沒有泥土墜下。

十二月十一日。──此日我依舊如是工作，撐支兩柱插立直至其巔，有

two pieces of ¹*boards across* over ²*each post.* This I finished the next day; and setting more posts up with boards, in about a week more I had the roof ³*secured,* and the posts ⁴*standing* in rows, ⁵*served me for partitions to part off the house.*

Dec. 17.—From this day to the 20th I placed ⁶*shelves,* and ⁷*knocked up* ⁸*nails* on the posts to hang everything up that could be ⁹*hung up*; and now I began to be in some order within doors.

Dec. 20.—Now I carried everything into the cave, and began to furnish my house, and set up some pieces of boards like a ¹⁰*dresser,* ¹¹*to order my victuals upon*; but boards began to be very ¹²*scarce* with me. Also I made me another table.

Dec. 24.—Much rain all night and all day. ¹³*No stirring out.*

*Dec.*25.—Rain all day

Dec. 26.—No rain, and the earth much ¹⁴*cooler* than before and ¹⁵*pleasanter*

Dec. 27.—Killed a young goat, ¹⁶*and tamed another* so that I ¹⁷*caught* it and led it home on a ¹⁸*string*; when I had it at home, I bound and ¹⁹*splintered up* its leg, which was ²⁰*broken.*

N. B.—I ²¹*took such care of* it that it lived, and the leg grew well and as strong as ever; but, by my ²²*nursing* it so long, it grew tame, and fed upon the little ²³*green* at my door, and would not go away. This was the first time that I ²⁴*entertained a thought of breeding up* some tame creatures, that I might have food when my powder and shot was all ²⁵*spent.*

兩塊木板橫過每柱的上面，這個我第二天便完工；再豎起木柱與木板；約再過一星期我的屋頂做安；以及木柱排立着，籍以劃分我家區域之用。

十二月十七日。——從此日起至二十日我置架，並敲釘在柱上以便凡能掛的東西都得掛起；現在屋內的一切開始有秩序了。

十二月二十日。——現在我把每件東西搬進洞內，起始整齊我的房屋，放起幾塊板像碗碟架以次序排列我的食物於其上；但是我有的板漸次漸少，我又做了一只桌子。

十二月二十四日。——全夜與終日多雨，未出戶外。

十二月二十五日。——全天降雨。

十二月二十六日。——無雨，地上較先冷而爽快，

十二月二十七日。——殺死一隻山羊，而跛其一腿，於是被我促得，帶回家去，以繩縛住；我放在家內之後，我用布綁住軸和以夾骨板夾其斷肢；

注意。——我留心看顧，所以牠才得活着，肢張好了像先前那麼強壯；但是，我養了牠好久，漸漸馴服我了，在我的門前草地上吃草，不會逃走。

這是第一次我有志馴服幾個動物，俾我將來的軍火都用完了以後籍以有食物吃。

Dec. 28, 29, 30. 31.—[1]*Great heats*, and no [2]*breeze* so that there was no [3]*stirring* abroad, except in the evening, for food. This time I spent in putting all my things in order within doors.

CHAPTER XV

[4]*January* 1.—Very hot still; bu I went abroad early and late with my .gun, and [5]*lay still* in the middle of the day. This evening, going farther into the [6]*valleys* which lay towards the center of the island, I found there were plenty of [7]*goats*, [8]*exceedingly* [9]*shy*, and [10]*hard to come at*. However, I resolved to try if I could not bring my dog to [11]*hunt* them down.

Jan. 2.—Accordingly, the next day I went out with my dog, and [12]*set him upon* the goats; but I was [13]*mistaken*, for they all [14]*faced about* upon the dog, and he knew his danger too well, for he would not come near them.

Jan. 3.—I began my fence, or wall; which [15]*being still* [16]*jealous of* my being [17]*attacked* by somebody, I resolved to make very [18]*thick* and [19]*strong*.

N. B.—This wall being [20]*described* before, I [21]*purposely* [22]*omit* what was said in the [23]*journal*. It is [24]*sufficient* to observe that I was no less time than from the 3rd of January to the 14th of April working, finishing, and [25]*perfecting* this [26]*wall*, though it was no more than about twenty-four yards in length, being a [27]*half-circle* from one place in the rock to another place about eight [28]*yards* from it, the door of the cave being in the [29]*center* behind it.

All this time I [30]*worked very hard*, the [31]*rains* [32]*hindering* me many days, [33]*nay*, sometimes [34]*weeks* together; but I thought I should never be [35]*perfectly* [36]*secure* till this wall

十二月二十八日，二十九，三十，卅一日，——酷熱，毫無微風，所以沒有出去，除非在黃昏出去尋食。此時我把門內的一切貨物整頓完備。

第　十　五　章

一月一日。——依舊酷熱；但是在早晨與夜晚出去打獵白天靜臥。此日黃昏，深向著島中的山谷，我看見許多山羊，非常怕羞，而難以獲拿。然而，我決意帶我的狗來嘗試獵獲牠們。

一月二日。——於是，第二天我帶我的狗同去，使牠追擊山羊；但我錯誤了，因為牠們反身面向此狗，牠狠明白自己的危險，故牠不敢走近牠們。

一月三日。——我開始造我的圍籬或圍牆。猶慮受他物的攻擊，我決意建築厚而堅固的牆。

——注意。此牆前已敘述，我故意脫落日記上所說的這是足供批評，因為我自己一月三日至四月十四日從事這個工作，竣工與使此牆完善，雖則不達念四碼長，為是半圓形的，自石頭的一處到約離八碼的另一處，中央的洞門在石的後面。

完全這個辰光我工作甚為勞苦。雨阻滯我許多日子，不特如此，有時合共有數星期；但我想水不能全然安寧直至此牆。

was finished. It is *scarce credible* what *inexpressible labor everything was done with*, especially the bringing *piles* out of the woods, and *driving* them into the ground; for I made them much *bigger* than I needed.

When this wall was finished, and the outside *double-fenced*, with a turf wall raised up close to it, I *persuaded* myself that if any people were to come on *shore* there, they would not *perceive* anything like a *habitation*; and it was very well I did so, as may be observed *hereafter* upon a very *remarkable* *occasion*.

During this time I *made my rounds* in the woods *for game* every day when the rain *permitted* me, and made *frequent* *discoveries* in these walks of something or other *to my advantage*. Particularly I found a kind of wild *pigeons*, which build, not as wood *pigeons* in a tree, but rather as house *pigeons*, in the *holes* of the rocks. Taking some young ones, I *endeavored* to *breed* them up *tame*, and did so; but when they grew older they *flew away*, which perhaps was at first for want of *feeding* them, for I had nothing to give them. However, I *frequently* found their *nests*, and got their *young ones*, which were very good meat.

And now, in the *managing* my *household affairs*, I found myself wanting in many things, which I thought at first it was *impossible* for me to make; as, indeed, with some of them it was. *For instance*, I could never make a *cask* to be *hooped*. I had a *small* cask or two, as I *observed* before; but I *could never arrive at the capacity of making one by them*, though I *spent* many weeks about it. I *could neither put in the heads*, nor join the *staves* so true to one another as to make them hold water; so I gave that also over. In the next place, I was *at a great loss* for *candles*; so that *as*

完工以後。這是不易見信，凡所做的工作的辛苦，難以言語形容，尤其是椿拔出樹林與敲進土中的工作，因爲我把椿造得較我的須要更大。

此牆完工之後，外面重離，並黏着泥土的牆。我自信要是有人上岸來，他們決不能窺破這是像一座居所；我做得很不錯，因爲嗣後遇有意外之事，便可以顯明我的預斷是不錯的。

在此時期內，不下大雨的時候，我在樹林中邁巡，巡走時我屢屢發見這個或那個於我有益的生物。尤其是，我尋到一種野鴿，這類野鴿並不如樹林鴿住在樹內，而類似家鴿住在石穴內的。取幾只小鴿，我奮力養馴牠們，我得以成就；但是牠們長大了些牠們飛走了，起初也許牠們爲了缺乏食物，因爲我沒有給牠們吃的東西。然而我時常尋得牠們的巢，取幾個小鴿，牠們的肉是很好吃的。

現在，治理家務時，我覺得我缺少許多東西，起初我想誰能辦到；誠然有幾件是不能辦的，譬如，我永不能做一只箍圍住的籃子。我有一二只籃子，如我前面說過的；但我終不能達我欲仿製之目的，雖然我費了幾個星期專究，我既不能裝其低面，也不會裝製桶的薄狹木板使牠們貼緊而保留水量；所以我也置諸度外。第二件，我大爲缺乏燒燭，所以一到

1.不易見信．2．凡所做的工作的辛苦，難以言語形容．3．椿．4．敲．5．更大．6．重離．7．深信．8．海岸．9．窺知．10．居宅．11嗣後．12．堪注意的．13．事情．14．邁巡．15．爲田獵故．16誰．17屢次18．發見．19．有益於我．20．鴿．21穴．22．竭力．23．養．24．馴．25．飛走．26．給以食物．27．屢次．28．巢．29．小鴿．30．治．31．家務．32．不可能．33．譬如．34．桶．35．箍．36．小桶．37．說及．38．終不能達我欲仿製的目的．39．費．40．既不能裝其低面．41．製桶之薄狹木板．42．大爲缺乏．43．燒燭．44．一到．

soon as ever it was dark, which was generally by seven o'clock, I [1]*was obliged to go to bed.* I [2]*remembered* the [3]*lump* of [4]*beeswax* with which I made candles in my African [5]*adventure* ; that I had none of that now. The only [6]*remedly* I had was, that when I had killed a goat I saved the [7]*tallow* and with a little dish [8]*made of clay*, which I [9]*baked in the sun*, to which I added [10]*a wick of some oakum,* I made me a lamp. This gave me light, thought not a clear, [11]*steady* light like a [12]*candle.* In the middle of all my [13]*labors* it happened that, [14]*rummaging* my things, I found a little [15]*bag*, which, as I [16]*hinted before*, had been filled with corn [17]*for the feeding of* poultry,—not for this voyage, but before, as I [18]*suppose*, when the ship came from Lisbon. The little [19]*remainder* of corn that had been in the bag was [20]*all devoured* by the rats, and I saw nothing in the bag but [21]*husks* and [22]*dust*; and [23]*being* willing to have the bag for some other use, (I think it was to put powder in, when I divided it for fear of the lightning, or some such use,) I [24]*shook* the [25]*husks* of corn [26]*out of* it on one side of my [27]*fortification*, under the rock.

It was a little before the great [28]*rains* just now [29]*mentioned* that I threw this [30]*stuff* away, [31]*taking no notice*, and not so much as [32]*remembering* that I had thrown anything there. About a month after, or [33]*thereabouts*, I saw some few [34]*stalks* of something green [35]*shooting out of the ground*, which I [36]*fancied* might be some plant I had not seen : but I was surprised, and perfectly [37]*astonished*, when, after a little longer time, I saw about ten or twelve [38]*ears* come out, which were perfect green [39]*barley* of the same kind as our European—nay, as our English [40]*barley.*

It is impossible to [41]*express* the [42]*astonishment* and [43]*confusion* of my thoughts [44]*on this occasion.* I had [45]*hitherto* acted

天黑，普通是七句鐘，我不得不就寢。我記得我在非洲冒險之時做燒燭的那大塊鯨獵；我現在一些也沒有了。我唯一的辦法是，當我殺死一山羊，我把羊油留着，和一只泥土所製的盆，此盆爲我曝曬於日中，盆內的羊油中我加上一蔴根製的燈心，我便做了一隻燈。這給我一些光，雖然不像燭的光那麼淸明與屹然不動。在我工作的中間，恰好在搜查我的貨物之間，我尋到一只袋，前曾提及，充滿了穀爲飼家禽之用，——並不是備於此次船行而用，但是爲以前的，依我所想，當船從列史朋來。袋內剩餘的穀均爲老鼠咬食了，我不見袋內的什麼祇有穀糠與灰塵；爲了要把此袋做別的用處，（我想用以放軍火，分開時則怕電閃，或若別的類似的用處。）我將穀糠傾棄於圍籬的一邊，石的底下。

　就在我才將提及的大雨之前，我拋棄這廢物，不知不覺，我也沒有記憶。我拋在那邊的是何物，一月之後，大約相近，我瞧見幾根靑的莖突然發出於地中；這好像爲我從未見過的植物；但我覺得希奇，非常的驚奇，不久之後，我見約有十或十二株穗出來，這全然是靑麥，同我們歐洲的種類一樣——不：類似英國的麥

　這是不能把我遇見此事的驚奇的與紛亂的思想描寫出來。我迄今。

175

upon no religious foundation at all; indeed, I had very few [1]*notions of religion* in my head, nor had [2]*entertained* any sense of anything that had [3]*befallen* me otherwise than as chance, or, as we lightly say, what pleases God, without so much as [4]*inquiring into the end of Providence* in these things, or his [5]*order* in governing [6]*events* for the world. But after I saw [7]*barley* grow there, in a [8]*climate* which I knew was not [9]*proper* for corn, and [10]*especially* that I knew not how it came there, it [11]*startled me strangely*, and I began to [12]*suggest* that God had [13]*miraculously* caused his grain to grow [14]*without any help of seed sown*, and that it was so directed [15]*purely* for my [16]*sustenance* on that wild, [17]*miserable* place.

This [18]*touched my heart* a little, and brought tears out of my eyes, and I began to bless myself that such a [19]*prodigy of nature* should happen [20]*upon my account*. This was the more [21]*strange* to me, because I saw near it still, all along by the side of the rock, some other [22]*straggling* [23]*stalks*, which proved to be [24]*stalks* of rice, and which I knew because I had seen it grow in Africa when I was [25]*ashore* there.

I not only thought these the pure [26]*productions* of [27]*Providence* for my support, but, not doubting that there was more in the place, I went all over that part of the island where I had been before, [28]*peering in* every corner, and under every rock, to seek for more of it; but I could not find any. At last it [29]*occurred* to my thoughts that I [30]*shook* a bag of [31]*chicken's meat* out in that place. Then the wonder began to cease; and I must [32]*confess*, my [33]*religious* thankfulness to [34]*God's Providence* began to abate, too. upon the [35]*discovering* that all this was nothing but what was common. Yet I ought to have been as thankful for so [36]*strange* and

雖不遵照信仰宗教的根據而爲；誠然，我的頭腦中很少有宗教的思想，也沒有考慮我所遇到的事的意義，不過認牠爲一種偶然的而已，像我們輕易地說，什麼能喜悅上帝的，沒有根究在這事情中的天意，或者他的管理世務所下的命令。但是我看見那邊長起的麥，我知道這地的氣候是不合於穀類的，尤其是我不知道牠如何生長在那邊的之後，令我異常驚訝，我始覺這是上帝的奇蹟能力使他的穀增長而不必藉播種之助，這簡直是專供我在此荒野困苦的地方的食品。

這稍爲感動我心，使我流淚，我開始祝福我自己爲了我的起見有這天然的怪事出現。這於我是更奇怪的，因爲我瞧見靠近那穀生長的地方，沿石的旁邊，有別的散漫的穀，我證牠爲米穀，因爲我在非洲上岸時看見這類米穀生長着，故我知道的。

我不特想這是天帝專賜給我的出產品，但是，並不疑慮他處也有，我走遍了島上，我先前去過了的地方，至每個角處細查，以及每塊石頭低下，希望再招點出來；可是我一些也招不到。後來想出了一個念頭我曾在那邊拋棄一袋禽鳥之食品。然後我的驚訝漸次消滅；同時我必須承認感謝天助的宗教心也隨之減少，因爲看出這是沒有什麼稀罕的事情而是普通的。但是我也應該感謝如是稀奇的，

1.宗教思想。2.考慮。3.遇。4.根究天意。5.下令。9.事務。7.麥。8.氣候。9.和合。10.尤其是。11.令我異常驚訝。12.始覺。13.奇蹟能力。14.不必藉播動之助。15.全然。16.供食。17.困苦。18.感動我。19.天然悟事。20.爲我起見。21.驚訝。22.散漫。23.上岸。24.出產品。25.天帝。26.窺視。27.生出。28.拋棄。29.禽鳥之食品。30.承認。31.宗教。32.天助。33.看出。34.希奇。

¹*unforeseen* a ²*providence*, as if it had been ³*miraculous*; for it was ⁴*really* the work of Providence to me, that should order or ⁵*appoint* that ten or twelve ⁶*grains* of corn should remain ⁷*unspoiled*, when the rats had ⁸*destroyed* all the rest, as if it had been ⁹*dropped* from heaven; as also that I should throw it out in that ¹⁰*particular place*, where, it being in the ¹¹*shade* of a high rock, it ¹²*sprang up* immediately; ¹³*whereas*, if I had thrown it ¹⁴*anywhere else*, at that time, it had been burnt up and ¹⁵*destroyed*.

I carefully saved the ears of this ¹⁶*corn*, you may be sure, in their season, which was about the end of June; and, ¹⁷*laying up* every corn, I resolved to sow them all again, hoping, in time, to have some quantity, ¹⁸*sufficient* to supply me with bread. But it was not till the fourth year that I could allow myself the least grain of this corn to eat, and even then but ¹⁹*sparingly*, as I shall say afterwards, ²⁰*in its order*. I lost all that I sowed the first season, by not observing the proper time; for I sowed it just before the dry season, so that it never came up at all, at least not as it would have done; of which in its place.

Besides this ²¹*barley*, there were, as above, twenty or thirty ²²*stalks* of rice, which I ²³*preserved* with the same care and for the same use, or to the same purpose—to make me bread or rather food; for I found ²⁴*ways to cook* it without ²⁵*baking*, though I did that also after some time.

CHAPTER XVI

But to return to my Journal:

I worked ²⁶*excessively hard* these three or four months, to get my wall done; and the 14th of April, I ²⁷*closed* it ²⁸*up*,

不能覷見的庇佑，好似一種神跡；因為這真是上帝為我做的工作；他命令或指定這十粒或十二粒的穀存留未毀，當老鼠將其餘的都咬壞，好似由天上跌下來的；而且我恰會拋在這特定的地方，有高石的遮廠，他得立刻生出；反之，要是我拋棄在他處，當時，牠就要被焚滅或毀滅，

我小心保留此穀穗，你們可知道，到適當的時季，約在六月底；收藏每粒穀，我決意再播種，希望，遲早，收穫多量，使足以供我麵包，但是不滿四年一些穀我也不得吃，雖則可吃也是節食，其理由我在後依次說明，我第一季播種的穀全然耗費，因為我沒有遵守適當的時期，因為我播種在旱天之前，因此穀苗全然沒有出來，至少沒有見他生出照常應該生出的；就是在我播種的地方，

除此參外，有，如上所說，廿或卅整米我把米保留著同樣的小心，為着同樣的用處，或者同樣的目的——— 就是為我做麵包，還是說食物；因為我沒有烘的煑食方法，不遇以後我有時亦烘的，

第 十 六 章

但是回到我的日記上面：
我工作得非常辛勤在這三四個月裏，以期完成我的圍牆；四月十日，我將門封閉起來

¹*contriving* to go into it, not by a door, but over the ²*wall*, by ⁵ ³*ladder*, that there might be no sign on the ⁴*outside* of my ⁵*habitation*.

April 16.—I finished the ladder; so I went up the ladder to the top, and then ⁶*pulled* it up after me, and let it down on the ⁷*inside*. This was a complete ⁸*inclosure* to me; for within I had room enough, and nothing could come at me from without, unless it could first ⁹*mount* my wall.

The very next day after this wall was finished, I had almost had ¹⁰*all my labor overthrown* at once, and myself killed. The case was this:—As I was ¹¹*busy* in the inside, behind my ¹²*tent*, just at the ¹³*entrance* into my cave, I was ¹⁴*terribly* ¹⁵*frighted* with a most dreadful ¹⁶*surprising* thing ¹⁷*indeed*; for, all on a ¹⁸*sudden*, I found the earth come ¹⁹*crumbling down* from the ²⁰*roof* of my cave, and from the ²¹*edge* of the hill over my head, and two of the ²²*posts* I had set up in the cave ²³*cracked* in a frightful manner. I ²⁴*was heartily scared*; but thought nothing of what was really the cause, only thinking that the top of my cave was ²⁵*fallen in,* as some of it had done before. For fear I should be buried in it, I ran forward to my ladder, and not thinking myself safe there either, I ²⁶*got over* my wall for fear of the ²⁷*pieces* of the hill, which I ²⁸*expected* might roll down upon me. I had no sooner ²⁹*stepped down upon the firm ground*, than I plainly saw it was a ³⁰*terrible* ³¹*earthquake*. Then ground I stood on shook three times at about ³²*eight minutes' distance*, with three such ³³*shocks* as would have ³⁴*overturned* the strongest building that could be ³⁵*supposed* to have stood on the earth; and a great piece of the ³⁶*top* of a rock which stood about half a mile from me, next the sea, fell down with such a ³⁷*terrible* noise as I never heard in all my life. I ³⁸*perceived*

慮欲不從門戶走進，而由梯子過牆，俾在寓所的外面沒有人居住的記號，

　四月十六日我做好了梯子；於是我走上梯至顛，然後把他在我的後面拖起，放在裏邊，這我于是個很安全的圍籬，因爲裏邊有充足的房間，其外邊誰也不能打入，除非牠能登越我的牆，

　此圍牆完工後的第二天，我的前工幾乎立刻盡廢，以及我自已屠死，情形是如此：——我正在裏邊忙碌的時候，我的帳篷後面，適在我穴的出入處，我受到一種可怖奇特的遭遇，的確使我極端的驚駭；爲了，忽然之間，我覺察泥豪從我的穴顛，從上面山旁，及從我豎在穴內的兩柱邊，劈拍碎裂那種可怖的樣子，我大受驚慌；但想不出究境是什麼一會事，不過想到我的穴項在倒入，像以前也有過這種情形，惶恐被埋在其中，我向我的樓梯奔，無暇想及那邊能安逸與否，我越牆猶懼山塊，我想或者要滾在我的身上，我足踏實地不久，明白地看見這是空前的地震；我站立的地上在八分鐘內搖震三次，這三次的震動簡直可以傾覆聞到建築在此的最堅固的房屋；前我約半里路，石項上的一——大塊傾陷在海邊，所發出的可怕的聲很爲我平生從未老過，我又看見

1.意欲。2.牆。3.梯。4.外邊。5.住宅。6.拖起。7.起。8.圍籬。9.登越。10.前工盡廢。11.忙碌。12.帳篷。13.出入處。14.極端。15.驚駭。16.奇特。17.的確。18.忽。19.碎落。20.屋項。21.邊。22.柱。23.破裂。24.大受驚慌。25.倒入。26.越。27.塊。28.期待；想。29.起踏實地。30.可怖。31.地震。32.八分鐘之內。33.震動。34.傾陷。35.可料。36.項。37.可怕。38.見。

also the very sea ¹*was put into* ²*violent* motion by it; and I believe the ³*shocks* were stronger under the water than on the island.

I was so much ⁴*amazed* with the thing itself, having never felt ⁵*the like*, nor ⁶*discoursed* with any one that had, that I was like one dead or ⁷*stupefied*. The motion of the earth made my ⁸*stomach* sick, like one that was ⁹*tossed at sea;* but the noise of the falling of the rock awaked me, ¹⁰*as it were*, and ¹¹*rousing* me from the stupefied condition I was in, ¹²*filled me with horror*. I thought of nothing then but the hill falling upon my tent and all my ¹³*household* goods, and ¹⁴*burying* all at once; and this ¹⁵*sunk my very soul within me* a second time.

After the third ¹⁶*shock* way over, and I felt no more for some time, I ¹⁷*began to take courage*. Yet I had not heart enough to ¹⁸*go over* my wall again, for fear of being buried alive, but sat still upon the ground, greatly ¹⁹*cast down* and *disconsolate*, not knowing what to do. ²¹*All this while*, I had not the least ²²*serious* ²³*religious* thought; nothing but the common "Lord have ²⁴*mercy* upon me!" and when it was over that went away too.

While I sat thus, I found the air ²⁵*overcast* and grow ²⁶*cloudy*, as if it would rain. Soon after that the wind arose by little and little, so that in less than half an hour it blew a most dreadful ²⁷*hurricane*. The sea was all on a sudden covered over with ²⁸*foam and froth*; the shore was covered with the ²⁹*breach of the water*; the trees were torn up by the roots; and a terrible storm it was. This ³⁰*held* about three hours, and then began to ³¹*abate*; and in two hours more it was quite ³²*calm*, and began to ³³*rain* very hard.

就是這海被激成劇烈的震動；我相信水底的震動較島上的地震爲強烈，

　　我受着這種事情非尋驚駭，因爲我從沒有經歷類似之事，也沒有與有經歷的人談及，我簡直嚇得像死人般或昏迷了，地震使我的肚子不爽快，正似受海浪之顛簸而眩暈；但石落的響聲驚醒了我，正是令我驚惶無措，從我的昏迷的情境內提醒我，嗣後我所想到的不過此山倒落我的帳篷上以及我家內的一切貨物，立刻被埋沒了；想到此點我便受到第二次的心膽俱喪，

　　第三次的震動過了之後，我不覺得什麼，我始漸生出勇氣，然則我不敢再越牆查察，猶恐活埋，而靜坐地上，非常垂頭喪氣與憂鬱，不知如何做才好，當斯時，我毫無勝壯的宗教思想；沒有別的不過此類普通的呼喊，上帝救救我罷！"地震一停此種呼聲亦消滅了，

　　我如是坐着時，我看見雲霧蔽天，好似要下雨，不久風漸漸降臨，不滿半句鐘可怕的颶風來了。此海立刻充滿了浮泡；海灘蓋沒了海波；樹連根拔起，這是一劇烈的颶風啊，狂風約歷三句鐘之久，然後開始減輕；再過二句鐘，空氣平靜，而始下大雨，

1。秘激．2．劇烈．3．震動．4．驚駭．5．類似之事．6．談論．7．昏迷．8．肚．9．受海浪之顛簸而眩暈．10．正若．11．提醒．12．令我驚惶無措．13．屋內．14．埋沒．15．心膽俱喪．16．震動．17．始漸發生勇氣．18．越；查察．19．垂頭喪氣．20．憂鬱．21．當斯時．22．勝壯．23．宗教．24．救．25．雲霧蔽天．26．多雲．27．颶風．28．浮泡．29．海波．3。歷…．之久．31．減輕．32．平靜．33．降雨

All this while I sat upon the ground, very much *terrified and dejected*; when on a [2]*sudden* it came into my thoughts that these winds and rain being the [3]*consequences* of the [4]*earthquake*, the earthquake itself was [5]*.spent* and over, and I might [6]*venture into* my cave again. With this thought my [7]*spirits began to revive*; and the rain also helping to [8]*persuade* me, I went in and set down in my [9]*.ent*. But the rain was so [10]*violent* that my tent was ready to be [11]*beaten down* with it; and I was [12]*forced* to go into my cave, though very much [13]*afraid* and [14]*uneasy* for fear it should fall on my head. This violent rain forced me to a new work; [15]*namely*, to cut a hole through my new [16]*fortification*, like a [17]*sink*, to let the water go out, which would [18]*else* have [19]*flooded* my cave. After I had been in my cave for some time, and found still no more [20]*shocks* of the earthquake follow; I began to be more [21]*composed*: and now [22]*to support my spirits*, which [23]*indeed wanted it very much*, I went to my little store and [24]*took a small sup of rum*, which, however, I did then and always very [25]*sparingly*, knowing I could have no more when that was gone.

It [26]*continued* raining all that night, and great part of the next day, so that I could not stir abroad. But my mind being more [27]*composed*, I began to think of what I had best do; [28]*concluding* that if the island was subject to these earthquakes, there would be no living for me in a cave, but I must consider of building a little hut in an open place, which I might [29]*surround* with a wall, as I had done here and so make myself [30]*secure* from wild beasts or men; for I [31]*concluded* if I staid where I was, I should certainly, one time or other, be [32]*buried* alive.

　　我始終坐在地下，異常地驚駭而憂；突然來了一個念頭，這風雨無非是隨地震而發生的結果，地震自己是已經過了，我或者再冒險入穴，有了這個念頭，我的精神復振；同時雨助勢追逐我，我便被趕入而坐在我的帳篷內，但是雨下得非常狂暴甚至我的帳篷將要擊倒；我祇得走入洞內，雖則怕上面要傾覆，此暴雨擁迫我做一新的工作；郎，在我的新堡壘中掘一個洞，像一個溝，可讓水流出，否則水要淹沒我的洞，我住在洞內之後，仍舊不覺我地震的震動出現，我始覺泰然；現在提起精神，這是必要的，我走到貯藏室略飲糖酒少許；這個，不論如何，雖然我喝牠但是時常很節省的，因爲我明白喝完所有的以後，再也沒得了，

　　全夜與第二天的大半天不斷地下雨，所以我不得出外但我的心神旣是安寧，我開始考慮應該做什麼事，推斷要是此島時常有地震，那我不能住在洞內，而我得設法在空地上建築一草屋『四面圍住牆圈，如我在此做的一樣，如是可免野獸或人的攻擊；因爲我推斷如果我留在此地，必定有一個時期我要被活埋，

1.驚駭而憂悶。2.突然。3.隨…之後發生的結果。4.地震.5.完畢。6.冒險而入。7.精神復振。8.擁迫。9.帳篷。10.暴。11.擊倒。12.擁迫。13.怕。17.不安。15.郎。16.圍籬。17.溝。18.否則。19.淹沒。20'震動。21.泰然。22.提起精神。23.是爲必要。24.略飲糖酒可許。25.節省。26.不斷地。27.安寧。28.推斷。29.圍住。30.安安。31.推斷.32.埋。

185

With these thoughts, I resolved to ¹*remove* my tent from the place where it stood, which was just under the ²*hanging* ³*precipice* of the hill; and which, if it should be shaken again, would ⁴*certainly* fall upon my tent. I spent the next two days, being the 19th and 20th of April, in ⁵*contriving* where and how to ⁶*remove* my habitation. The fear of being ⁷*swallowed up* alive made me that I ⁸*never slept in quiet*; and yet the ⁹*apprehension* of lying abroad without any ¹⁰*fence* was almost equal to it. Still, when I looked about, and saw how everything was put in order, how ¹¹*pleasantly* ¹²*concealed* I was, and how safe from danger, it made me very ¹³*loath* to ¹⁴*remove*. ¹⁵*In the mean time*, it ¹⁶*occurred* to me that it would ¹⁷*require a vast deal of time* for me to do this, and that I must be ¹⁸*contented* to ¹⁹*venture* where I was till I had formed a ²⁰*camp* for myself, and had ²¹*secured* it so as to remove to it. So with this resolution I ²²*composed* myself for a time, and resolved that I would go to work with all ²³*speed* to build me a wall with ²⁴*piles* and ²⁵*cables*, etc., in a ²⁶*circle*, as before, and set my tent up in it when it was finished; but that I would ²⁷*venture to stay* where I was till it was finished, and fit to remove to. This was the 21st.

April 22.—The next morning I began to consider of means to ²⁸*put this resolve into execution*; but I was ²⁹*at a great loss* about my tools. I had three large ³⁰*axes*, and ³¹*abundance* of ³²*hatchets* (for we carried the hatchets ³³*for traffic* with the Indians); but with much ³⁴*chopping* and cutting ³⁵*knotty*, hard wood, they were all full of ³⁶*notches*, and ³⁷*dull*; and though I had a ³⁸*grindstone*, I could not turn it and grind my ³⁹*tools* too. This cost me as much thought ⁴⁰*as a statesman would have bestowed upon a grand point of politics, or a judge upon the*

有了這些念頭我決意遷移我的帳蓬從現在佔的地方，此處恰在山的懸崖底下；這個地方，如果再震動起來，當然會傾覆我的帳蓬。我用了次兩天的時間，是四月十九與二十日，計劃如何遷移我的住宅至何地，惶恐着我將被活埋，我終難安睡：但是睡在外面而沒有圍籬的恐懼心是一樣的程度。而且，當我四面觀察，看到各物處置井然，我居所的安逸深藏，以及沒有任何危險的時候，使我極不願遷移。同時，我覺得要遷移的話必須大費時日，而我還是心滿意足的冒一個險，直待我為自己做成一個住營，一切佈置妥當然後再搬。有了這個決意，我方才安寧一下子，我決定我要去即速造一座木樁與錨纜等造成的圍牆，造成圓圈，如前一般，散我的帳蓬於其中當牆完工之後；但一方面我得冒險住在原它直待新的住宅竣工與可以遷入的時候。這是二十一日。

四月二十二日——第二天早晨，我起始考慮將此意施諸實行的方法；但我的工具大為缺乏。我有三大斧，與許多小斧（我們攜帶手斧是為和印度人做生意用的）；但是為了時常斬與砍多節而硬的木頭，斧頭充滿了缺口，致不銳利：雖則我有塊礪石，可是我不能轉牠，也不能磨我的工具，這件事費了我許多的腦力，正如政治家之於國家大事，或如法官之

life and death of a man. At length, I *¹contrived* a wheel with a *²string*, to turn it with my foot, that I might have both my hands at *³liberty.*

Note.—I had never seen any such thing in England, or at least not to take notice how it was done, though since I have *⁴observed* it is very *⁵common* there; *⁶besides that*, my *⁷grindstone* was very large and heavy. This *⁸machine* cost me a full week's work *⁹to bring it to perfection.*

April 28, 29.—These two whole days I took up in *¹⁰grinding* my tools. my machine for turning my *¹¹grindstone* *¹²performing* very well.

April 30.—Having *¹³perceived* my bread had been *¹⁴low* a great while, now I *¹⁵took a survey of it*, and *¹⁶reduced* myself to one *¹⁷biscuit cake* a day, which made my heart very *¹⁸heavy.*

May 1.—In the morning looking towards the *¹⁹seaside*, the tide being low, I saw something lie on the shore bigger than *²⁰ordinary*, and it looked like a *²¹cask.* When I came to it, I found a small *²²barrel*, and two or three pieces of the *²³wreck* of the ship, which were driven on shore by the late *²⁴hurricane*; and looking towards the wreck itself, I thought it seemed to lie higher out of the water than it used to do. I examined the *²⁵barrel* which was driven on shore, and soon found it was a barrel of *²⁶gunpowder*; but it had *²⁷taken water*, and the powder was *²⁸caked* as hard as a stone. However, I rolled it farther on shore for the present, and went on upon the sands, as near as I could to the *²⁹wreck* of the ship, to look for more.

When I came down to the ship, I found it strangely removed. The *³⁰forecastle*, which lay before *³¹buried* in sand, was *³²heaved up* at least six feet, and the stern, which was broken in pieces and parted from *³³the rest* by the force of

決人之生死。後來,我巧製了一車輪又用了一根繩,我用了的我腳把牠旋轉,俾我兩手得以自由行動,

注意,—— 我在英國從未見有類此的東西,就是有的我也沒有注意怎樣做成,雖然以後我見過,但在那邊是很普遍的;而且,我的礪石是很大而重的。這機器整個費了我一星期方才成全其事。

四月二十八。二十九,——這兩天我完全費于磨我的工具,旋轉礪石的機器工作的很好。

四月三十日。—— 看到我的麵包減少很多,現在我視察一下,我自己減少到每日喫一塊餅乾,這使我非常憂心,

五月一日。——在早晨看看海灘上,好象是一只桶,在潮水底下,我見有一異常大的東西橫在海灘上,走近時,我見是一只小桶與船上剩下的二三塊舊物,為末次的大風雨所驅至岸灘的;看到舊物本身,好似較尋常的更覺遠出水外,我視察及到海灘上的桶,不久看出這是一桶的軍火;但已著水,火藥結成如石一般的硬塊。然而,我暫時把牠滾進岸去;我走往河濱,竭力走近船的剩餘舊物,希望再招得點東西。

當我走下船,我查見此船怪異地移動過了,這前艙,以前是埋在沙泥中,現在高出至少有六尺,以及船尾,本來受着風浪的打擊而碎成零片而已與他部分離。

the sea, soon after I had left [1]*rummaging* her, was [2]*tossed,* as it were, up, and [3]*cast on* one side. The sand was [4]*thrown* so high on that side next her [5]*stern,* that whereas there was a great place of water before, so that I could not come within a [6]*quarter* of a mile of the wreck without [7]*swimming,* I could now [8]*walk* quite up to her when the [9]*tide* was out. I was surprised with this at first, but soon [10]*concluded* it must be done by the earthquake. As by this [11]*violence* the ship was more broken open than [12]*formerly,* so many things came [13]*drily* on shore, which [14]*the sea had loosened,* and which the winds and water [15]*rolled* [16]*by degrees* to the land.

This wholly [17]*diverted* my thoughts from the [18]*design* of removing my habitation, and I [19]*busied* myself [20]*mightily,* that day especially, in [21]*searching* whether I could make any way into the ship; but I found nothing was to be [22]*expected* of that kind, for all the inside of the ship was [23]*choked up* with sand. However, as I had learned not to [24]*despair* of anything, I resolved to pull everything to [25]*pieces* that I could of the ship, [26]*concluding* that everything I could get from her would be of some use or other to me.

CHAPTER XVII

May 3.—I began with my [27]*saw,* and cut a piece of [28]*a beam* through, which I thought held some of the upper part, or [29]*quarterdeck,* together, and when I had cut it through, I [30]*cleared away* the sand as well as I could from the side which lay highest. But the tide coming in, I was [31]*obliged to* [32]*give over for that time.*

[33]*May 4.*—I went a-fishing, but caught not one fish that I [34]*durst* eat of, till I was [35]*weary* of my sport; when, just going to [36]*leave off* I caught a young [37]*dolphin.* I had made me a

在有搜查完畢離船之後，現在看牠樣子是被擧也後而拋在一邊，沙泥被傾覆在船尾的一邊疊得很高，至於以前此處是從之大洋，所以當時我非游囘不得到破餘船物的四分之一里之內，見在潮水一退我卽可徒步走近牠了，我起初覺得此點有些希奇，不過不久我便推斷這定是受到地震的結果．因爲遇着一番劇烈的震勯，此船較前更是破碎，許多的破物逐日邅到海灘，同時爲海溟所冲與惡風所逐，漸次滾近岸地，

　　此事把我懲移我的居所的計畫的思想全然打消，我自己忙極了，尤其是這天，在尋招往船內去的方法；但我着出此類希望完全沒有；因爲船的內部塞滿了沙泥，不論如何，因爲我學定對於不論何物不可絕望；我決意，凡是可能的，我把船上的每件東西都拖上岸去，推斷着我能從牠拿得的于我總有些用處，

第 十 七 章

　　五月三日，——我開始用我的鋸子割斷船梁，此梁我想是撐住船上面的幾部份，或船之後半甲板；當我割斷的時候，我將一邊高疊着的沙泥竭力清除；但是潮水一路進來，我祇好暫擱，

　　五月四日，——我去捕魚，可是我敢吃的魚--只沒有捉得，直待我厭倦我的娛樂；當時，我正在離去，我捉獲一只江豚，我爲自己做一根

long ¹*line* of some ²*rope yarn*, but I had no ³*hooks*; yet I ⁴*frequently* ⁵*caught* fish enough, as much as I cared to eat; all which I dried in the sun, and ⁶*ate* them dry.

May 5.— Worked on the ⁷*wreck*; cut another beam ⁸*asunder*, and brought three great ⁹*fir planks* off from the decks, which I tied together and made to ¹⁰*float* on shore when the flood ¹¹*of tide* came on.

May 6.—Worked on the wreck; got several iron ¹²*bolts* out of her, and other pieces of ¹³*ironwork*. Worked very hard, and came home very much tired, and had thoughts of giving it over.

May 7.—Went to the wreck again, ¹⁴*not with an intent* to work, but found the ¹⁵*weight* of the ¹⁶*wreck* had broken itself down, the beams being cut. Several pieces of the ship seemed to lie loose, and the inside of the hold lay so open that I could see into it; but it was almost full of water and sand.

May 8.—Went to the wreck, and carried an iron ¹⁷*crow* to ¹⁸*wrench up* the ¹⁹*deck*, which lay now quite clear of the water or sand. I wrenched open two ²⁰*planks*, and brought them on shore also with the tide. I left the iron crow in the wreck for next day.

May 9. Went to the wreck, and with the crow ²¹*made way into the body of the wreck*, and felt several ²²*casks*, and ²³*loosened* them with the crow, but could not break them up. I ²⁴*felt* also a roll of English ²⁵*lead*, and could ²⁶*stir* it, but it was too heavy to remove.

May 10-14—Went every day to the wreck, and got a great many pieces of timber, and boards, or plank, and two or three ²⁷*hundredweight* of iron.

絞繩的蔴絲的釣魚繩，但我沒有釣；可是我屢次挺獲的魚，足以供我想要吃的；魚我都麗在日光中，乾後再喫，

五月五日，————在破舟上工作；又割斷一根舟梁，從船頭上取去三塊松板，我縛三板在一起，潮水來時我便乘牠漂於岸上，

五月六日。————在破舟上工作；取出幾根鐵桿，以及其他鐵製之物。工得很辛苦，回家時非常乏力，意欲停止工作。

五月七日。————又在破舟上工作，無意工作，但是看見破舟受了壓力自己裂開了，舟梁割斷了，船上的幾塊板似乎鬆開，船艙廣闊；所以我可以窺入，但其中幾乎都充滿水和泥，

五月八日。————到破舟那邊去，帶了一個鐵挺用力扭去船頭，現在是沒有泥水了，我扭開兩塊木板，也隨潮帶上岸去。我留這鐵挺在破舟上以爲後天之用，

五月九日。————到破舟上去，以挺打入破之身，找到有幾個桶，以挺將牠們解鬆，可是不能打開牠。我也找得一捲英國鉛，我可以搖動牠，可是太重了故不能搬走牠，

五月十日至十四日。————每天去破船，獲得許多木材，與薄板或闊板，以及兩三個一百十二磅重的鐵，

1.釣魚繩，2. 絞繩之蔴絲，3.釣子。4.屢次。5.捉。6.喫。7. 破舟。8.折斷。9.松板。10.漂浮。11.潮水。12.鐵桿。13.鐵器。14.無意。15.重量。16.破舟。17.起貨鈎；鐵挺。18.扭去。19.船頭。20.木板。21.打入破舟之身。22.桶。23.放鬆。24.覺得。25.鉛。26.搖動。27.一百十二磅（重量名）。

May 15.—I carried two [1]*hatchets,* to try if I could not cut a piece off the [2]*roll* of lead, by [3]*placing* the edge of one [4]*hatchet,* and [5]*driving* it with the other; but as it lay about a foot and a half in the water, I could not make any blow to drive the hatchet.

May 16.—It had [6]*blown* hard in the night, and the wreck appeared more broken by the force of the water; but I staid so long in the woods, to get [7]*pigeons* for food, that the tide [8]*prevented* my going to the [9]*wreck* that day,

May 17,—I saw some pieces of the wreck blown on shore, at a great distance, near two miles off. I resolved to see what they were, and found it was a piece of the [10]*head,* but too [11]*heavy* for me to bring away.

May 24.—Every day, to this day, I worked on the wreck; and with hard labor I loosened some things so much with the crow that the first [12]*blowing tide* several casks floated out, and two of the seamen's chests. The wind blowing from the shore, nothing came to land that day but pieces of [13]*timber,* and a [14]*hogshead* which had some Brazil [15]*pork* in it; but the salt water and the sand had [16]*spoiled* it, I continued this work every day to the 15th of [17]*June,* except the time necessary to get food, which I always [18]*appointed,* during this part of my [19]*employment,* to be when the tide was up, that I might be ready when it was [20]*ebbed* out. By this time I had got timber and plank and iron-work enough to have built a good boat, if I had known how. I also got, at several times and in several pieces, near one [21]*hundredweight* of the [22]*sheet lead.*

June 16.—Going down to the seaside, I found a large [23]*tortoise* or [24]*turtle.* This was the first I had seen, which, it seems, was only my [25]*misfortune,* not any [26]*defect* of the

194

五月十五日。—— 我帶去兩把小斧，將一斧的邊放在鉛卷上，將另一斧敲牠進去，試割一條鉛；但是因爲鉛在水的下面一尺半，我不能將小斧敲入。

五月十六日。—— 在晚上大風已吹過，破船受水浪的衝擊顯出更大的裂裂；但是因爲我在樹林內獵食鴿子的時候太長久，潮水阻止我這天上破船去。

五月十七日。—— 我瞧見破船的幾塊碎片吹出很遠，近二里路之遙。我決意看看這是何物，我看出這是一塊船木頭；但是過重而不能帶走。

五月二十四日。—— 每天，迄於今日，我在破舟上工作；用了苦工我將數物以鐵挺解鬆了許多，一陣風潮把幾只桶，以及水手們的兩只巨箱。漂了出去從海灘吹的風，無物吹至岸地，這天只有幾根水料，以及一只大桶內藏有幾塊巴西國的猪肉的吹在岸上；但已爲鹹水和沙泥所損壞。我每天繼續工作下去迄至六月十五日，除非食物必須的時間，膳食的時間是我時常指定的，於這些事務，在上潮時，而下潮時我便可準備好了。此時我已有了木材，闊板，鐵器足以造成一只完好的船，如果我知道造法。我有時也得了幾片近乎一百十二磅的鉛板。

六月十六日。——走下海邊我尋見一只大龜或者說是鼈。這是我初次見到的，這似乎是我的不幸而已，並非是由於地方上稀少的缺點。

1.手斧 2.卷。3.置、4.小斧。5.敲。6.吹。7.鴿子。8.阻止。9.破船。10.船頭木。11.重。12.風潮。13.木料。14.木桶。15.猪肉。16.損壞。17.六月。18.指定。19.事務。20.下潮。21.一百十二磅。22.鉛板。23.龜。24.鼈。25.不幸。26.缺點。

place, or ¹*scarcity.* Had I happened to be on the other side of the ²*island*, I might have had hundreds of them every day, as I found afterwards; but ³*perhaps had paid dear enough for* them.

June 17.—I spent in ⁴*cooking* the ⁵*turtle.* I found in her ⁶*three-score* eggs; and her flesh was to me, at that time, the most ⁷*savory* and pleasant that ever I ⁸*tasted* in my life, having had no flesh, but of goats and ⁹*fowls*, since I landed in this ¹⁰*horrid* place.

June 18.—Rained all day, and I ¹¹*staid* within. I thought at this time, the rain felt cold, and I was something ¹²*chilly*, which I knew was not usual in that ¹³*latitude*.

June 19.—Very ill, and ¹⁴*shivering*, as if the weather had been cold.

Juue 20.—No rest all night; ¹⁵*violent pains* in my head, and ¹⁶*feverish*.

June 21.—Very ill; frighted almost to death with the ¹⁷*apprehensions* of my sad condition—to be sick, and no help. Prayed to God, for the first time since the storm off Hull, but ¹⁸*scarce* knew what I said, or why, my thoughts being all ¹⁹*confused*.

June 22.—A little better: but under dreadful apprehensions of sickness.

June 23ʻ—Very bad again; cold and ²⁰*shivering*, and then a violent ²¹*headache*.

June 24.—Much better.

June 25.—An ²²*ague* yery violent. The ²³*fit* held me seven hours: cold fit, and hot, with ²⁴*faint sweats* after it.

June 26.—Better: and having no ²⁵*victuals* to eat, took my gun, but found myself very weak. However, I killed a she-goat and with much ²⁶*difficulty* got it home, and ²⁷*broiled*

如果我住在島的另一邊，我每天可有數百只，照我以後莃見的算；但是作牠們非常費時費力，

　　六月十七日。—— 我消磨時間于責龜，我在牠裏邊招到六十個蛋；牠的肉于我，在那時，是在我一生所嚐的中間可謂最美味的與最使我愉快的了，因爲我自從登此可怕的陸地之後，除了羊肉與鳥肉之外一無其他的肉嚐，

　　六月十八日，—— 全天雨淋，我留住在內，我想，在此時，雨似乎很冷；我覺得有點寒冷，這種冷氣在這緯度以內是不常有的，

　　六月十九日。—— 天氣非常不好，與寒冷，好像天氣已經寒冷了，

　　六月二十日。—— 全夜未歇；頭內劇烈的疼痛，發着寒熱

　　八月二十一日。—— 病重；覺察到我的慘淡情境我幾乎嚇死 —— 生病而無醫生，祈求上帝，爲自從黑耳颶風後的第一次；但是我不十分知道我說的什麼或者爲何說此，因爲我的思想全然混亂了，

　　六月二十二日。—— 稍逢好；但知道有可危的病寬光臨

　　六月二十三日。— 病轉劇；冷與寒顫，繼之便是劇烈的頭痛，

　　六月二十四日。——多了許多，

　　六月二十五日。——極凶的瘧疾。寒熱發七旬鐘之久發冷與發熱，微汗隨之俱來，

　　六月二十六日。——稍逢；因無糧食，拿起我的鎗，但覺察自已太弱，無論如何，我殺了一只雌山羊，經過許多困難才拿到家中，責

some of it, and ate. I would faid have ¹*stewed* it and made some ²*broth*, but had no ³*pot*.

June 27.—The ague again so violent that I ⁴*lay abed* all day, and neither ate nor ⁵*drank*. I was ready to ⁶*perish for thirst*; but so weak I had not ⁷*strength* to stand up, or to get myself any water to drink. Prayed to God again, but was ⁸*light-headed*: and when I was not, I was ⁹*so ignorant* that I knew not what to say; only I lay and cried, "Lord, ¹⁰*look upon* me! Lord, pity me! Lord, have ¹¹*mercy* upon me!" I suppose I did nothing else for two or three hours: till, the fit ¹²*wearing off*, I fell asleep, and did not wake ¹³*till far in the night*. When I awoke I found myself much ¹⁴*refreshed*, but weak, and ¹⁵*exceeding* ¹⁶*thirsty*. However, as I had no water in my ¹⁷*habitation*, I was forced to lie till morning, and went to sleep again. In this second sleep I had this ¹⁸*terrible* dream.

I thought that I was sitting on the ground, on the outside of my wall, where I sat when the storm blew after the earthquake, and that I saw a man ¹⁹*descend* from a great black cloud, in a bright ²⁰*flame of fire*, and ²¹*light upon* the ground. He was ²²*all over* as ²³*bright* as a flame, so that I could but just ²⁴*bear* to look towards him. His ²⁵*countenance* was most ²⁶*inexpressibly* dreadful, ²⁷*impossible for words to describe*. When he ²⁸*stepped upon* the ground with his feet, I thought the earth ²⁹*trembled* just, as it had done before in the earthquake, and all the air looked, to my apprehension, as if it had been filled with ³⁰*flashes* of fire. He was no sooner landed upon the earth but he moved forward towards me, with a long spear or ³¹*weapon* in his hand, to kill me: and when he came to a ³²*rising ground*, at some distance, he spoke to me—or I heard a voice so terrible that it is im-

些與吃。我歡喜燉肉與煮些湯，可是無鍋子。

六月二十七日——瘧疾又變劇，使我終日僵臥牀上，不吃不渴；我將要渴死；可是身體太弱以致無力站起，或自己去水喝。再求上帝，但是昏暈；我不昏時，我是木然無知甚至我不知道說什麼話！不過我睡眠與喊"上帝，看顧我！上帝可憐我！上帝，救我罷！"我想我兩三個鐘頭未做他事，迄待，寒熱發作漸退，我才睡熟，遙至夜深方醒。醒來時我覺得爽快許多，但是軟弱無力而又極渴。不論如何，我因爲我的住宅內無水，我勉強俟待早晨，與再入睡鄉。在第二次的睡眠我做了些可怕的夢。

我想我是坐在地下，在我的圍牆外面，我坐着時颶風隨着地震而來，我見有一人從烏雲之間，在輝耀的火光中下降落於地下。他的全身亮似火光，所以我只能耐着性看他。他的容貌是不可言喻的可怕，非言語所能形容。他的腳踏在地下的時候，我覺得地在震動，誠似在地震時的模樣，全部的空氣，照我的感觸，好似充滿了火的閃光。他橙在地上不久，但他向我方走動，有一把長刀或軍器在他的手中，來殺我。當他走到一塊高地，稍遠，他對我講話——我聽得聲音非常可怕，這種可怕的情形

possible to [1]*express* the terror of it. All that I can say I understood was this: "Seeing all these things have not [2]*brought thee to repentance*, now thou shalt die;" at which words I thought he lifted up the spear that was in his hand to kill me.

No one that shall ever read this [3]*account* will expect that I should be able to [4]*describe* the [5]*horrors* of my [6]*soul* at this terrible [7]*vision*. I mean, that even while it was a dream, I even [8]*dreamed* of those horrors. Nor is it any more possible to describe the [9]*impression* that [10]*remained upon* my mind when I awaked, and found it was but a dream.

I had, alas! no knowledge of good. What I had [11]*received* by the good [12]*instruction* of my father was then worn out by [13]*an uninterruped series*, for eight years, of [14]*seafaring wickedness*, and a [15]*constant* [16]*conversation* with none but such as were, like myself, wicked and [17]*profane to the last degree*. I do not remember that I had, in all that time, one thought that so much as [18]*tended* either to looking upwards towards God, or [19]*inwards* towards a [20]*reflection* upon my own ways; but a certain [21]*stupidity of soul without desire of good, or conscience of evil*, had [22]*entirely* [23]*overwhelmed* me. I was all that the most [24]*hardened*, unthinking, [25]*wicked* creature among our common [26]*sailors* can be [27]*supposed* to be; not having the least [28]*sense*, either of the fear of, or [29]*thankfulness* to God. But now I was brought to a just sense of the difficulties I had to [30]*struggle* with, too great for even nature itself to support; and no [31]*assistance*, no help, no comfort, no [32]*advice*. Then I cried out, "Lord, be my help, for I am [33]*in great distress*." This was the first [34]*prayer*, if I may call it so, that I had made for many years.

非言語所能形容。我所能說我怖得的是此："看到這些事物倘不能使你懺悔，現在你將要死了"，他說了這幾個字我想他將舉起他手中的刀來殺我。

沒有一個看此記錄之事的人會希望我能夠把我在此可怖夢景內的精神的恐怖描寫出來。我意思，就是雖在夢中我還想像那種恐懼。也不能描寫我腦海中所留存的感觸之情在我醒的時候，尋出這不過是南柯一夢。

咳！我無一些善意，我從父親處所得到的良好的教導現已消滅於經歷綿綿不絕的八年航海之事，和不斷的交游象我自己一般的人，可惡和褻瀆達於極點的環境。在此時期，我不記得我有一種思想或者傾向到上帝方面，或者傾向到內心中回憶我自己的各種事情；但是一種生性的愚蠢，無好善而惡狠的良心，全然淹沒了。我可以算是在我們普通的水手之中最硬心的，最無思索的，最可惡的動物：毫無一些怕懼或感謝上帝的思想。我現在踏進一困難的情境我須得去打破牠，就是天地，萬物也不能解決如是大的問題，以及無援力，無輔助，無慰籍，無勸導。於是我喊道，"主宰，爲我的助者，爲了我是羅著大禍"，這是第一次的祈禱，倘使我以前早如是的叫牠，我已經可以祈禱多年了。

CHAPTER XVIII

June 28.—Having been somewhat [1]*refreshed* with the sleep I had had, and the fit being [2]*entirely* off, I got up; and though the [3]*fright* and terror of my dream was very great, yet I [4]*considered* that the the fit of the [5]*ague* would return again the next day, and now was my time to get something to refresh and [6]*support* myself when I should be ill. The first thing I did, I filled a large [7]*square* case bottle with water, and set it upon my table, [8]*in reach of* my bed; and [9]*to take off* the chill or [10]*aguish* [11]*disposition* of the water I put about a [12]*quarter* of a [13]*pint* of rum into it, and [14]*mixed* them together. Then I got me a piece of the goat's flesh, and [15]*broiled* it on the [16]*coals*, but could eat very little. I walked about, but was very weak, and [17]*withal* very sad and [18]*heavy-* [19]*hearted* under the sense of my [20]*miserable* condition, dreading [21]*the return of my distemper* the next day. At night I made my supper of three of the [22]*turtle's eggs*, which I [23]*roasted* in the [24]*ashes*, and ate, as we call it, in the [25]*shell*, and this was the first bit of meat I had ever asked God's blessing to, that I could remember, in my whole life.

After I had eaten I tried to walk, but found myself so weak that I could [26]*heardly* carry a gun, for I never went out without that. So I went but a little way, and sat down upon the ground, looking out upon the sea, which was just before me and very [27]*calm* and [28]*smooth*. As I sat here, some such thoughts as these [29]*occurred* to me: What is this earth and sea, of which I have seen so much? Whence is it [30]*produced*? And what am I, and all the other creatures, wild and tame, [31]*human and brutal*? Whence are we? Sure we are all made by some [32]*secret power*, who

第 十 八 章

六月二十八。——既已熟睡了以後精多少爽快了些，同時寒熱全然退減，我便起身，雖則夢的恐，恐懼怖極大，然而我推想瘧疾明天又要再發，所以現在是我的機會，準備些食物，俾在疾病時得以補養與供食我自己。第一件事我需做的，我將一只大而方的瓶盛滿了水，安置在我的桌上，近我的牀除去水中的冷性我參與四分之一升的酒於水內，把牠們調和蛋一起。此後我取了一塊山羊肉，在煤上薰燒，可是能吃很少。我走走，但是非常無力，並且想到處於這種困苦情境之下能不憂慮愁悶，猶恐明日舊病復發。在晚上我以三只龜蛋當了晚餐，蛋是我在灰燼中薰的，我吃，依我們叫牠，在蛋殼內，這是第一片肉我懇求上帝的祝福賜我喫，我需在一生中記着的。

　我吃完了以後我試着行走，但是覺得本身過羸，甚至我難能拿鎗，因為我從未外出而不帶鎗的。於是我走了一點路便坐在地下，望望海上，海在我前面很平靜的。我坐於此處時，有這種思想湧上我的頭腦：我時常見到的這種地與海是何物？牠產生於何處？我和其他的動物，野的和馴的，人類和獸類，是何物？我們自何處來的。誠然我們都是神力造成的，神力

1.爽神。2.全然。3.恐懼。4.推想。5.瘧疾。6.供食。7.方。8.近。9.除去10.冷。11.性質。12.四分之一。13.計。14.參雜。15.薰燒。16.煤。17.而且。18.愁悶。19.困苦。20.舊病復發。21.龜蛋22.薰。23.灰燼。24.蛋殼。25.難。26.靜。27.平。28.湧遇。26.產生。30.人類和獸類。31.神力，隱祕之力。

¹*formed* the earth and sea, the air and ²*sky*. And who is that? Then it followed most ³*naturally*, it is God that has made all.

But why has God done this to me? What have I done to be thus used? My conscience presently ⁴*checked* me in that ⁵*inquiry*, as if I had ⁶*blasphemed*, and ⁷*methought* it spoke to me like a voice : " ⁸*Wretch* ! dost ⁹*thou* " ask what thou hast done? Look back upon a dreadful. ¹⁰*misspent* life, and ask ¹¹*thyself* what thou hast not done. Ask, Why is it that thou wert not long ago ¹²*destroyed* ; why wert thou not ¹³*drowned* in Yarmouth Roads; killed in the fight when the ship was taken by the Sallee ¹⁴*man-of-war* ; devoured by the wild beasts on the coast of Africa ; or drowned here, when all the crew ¹⁵*perished* but thyself? Dost ¹⁶*thou* ask, What have I done? I was ¹⁷*struck dumb* with these ¹⁸*reflections*, as one ¹⁹*astonished*, and had not a word to say—no, not to answer to myself, but rose up ²⁰*pensive* and sad, walked back to my ²¹*retreat*, and went up over my wall as if I had been going to bed. But my thoughts were ²²*sadly* ²³*disturbed*, and I had ²⁴*no inclination* to sleep; so I sat down in my chair, and ²⁵*lighted* my lamp, for it began to be dark.

Now as the apprehension of the return of my ²⁶*distemper* terrified me very much, it ²⁷*occurred to my* thought that the ²⁸*Brazilians* take no ²⁹*physic* but their ³⁰*tobacco* for almost all distempers, and I had a piece of a roll of ³¹*tobacco* in one of the chests, which was quite ³²*cured*, and some also that was green, and not quite cured. I went, directed by Heaven no ³³*doubt* : for in this chest I found a ³⁴*cure* both for soul and body. I opened the chest, and found what I looked for, the tobacco ; and as the few books I had saved lay there too, I took out one of the Bibles which I ³⁵*mentioned* before,

製作地和海，空氣和靑天。神力爲何物？這是自然的結果；神力就是上帝。創造一切。

但是上帝爲何如是待我？我做了何事會如此被使用？我的良心立刻阻止我如是攷究，似乎我已褻瀆神明，我以爲似有一種聲音向我講："罪孽深重者你何不攷究汝的行爲,,回顧可怕妄費的生命，攷問你本人的行爲。攷問你爲何你這許多時候尚未忘滅；你何以未溺死於牙門河；死於戰塲當船給撒利兵艦擄去的時候；非洲岸的野獸吞食；或溺死於此，水手全死亡而只存汝一人？你曾否自問我所做的事？"我囘憶這些事情我目瞪口呆，一人驚奇時，一言發不出來——不，不囘覆我自己，但是默然愁眉不展地起立，走囘我的宿所，走上我的圍牆像去上牀睡覺一般：但是我的思想憂慮紛亂，我無意睡眠；於是我坐在我的椅內，點我的燈火，因爲天氣漸黑。

現在因爲杷憂我的病寬復發，使我畏縮不堪，然我來了一個念頭，就是巴西人不用藥品；以煙草治一切的病而巳，我在箱內有一卷煙草，草是還乾，還有些靑的，不十分乾。我去依上天的指示無疑的；因爲在此箱內我招到身心兩方的礎石。我打開此箱，看見我所尋求煙草；至於我留藏着的幾本書也在那邊，我取出聖經書中的一本遺是以前所提起的。

1.製作。2.靑天。3.自然。4.阻止。5.攷究。6.褻瀆神明。7.我以爲。8.罪孽深重者。9."汝,,10.妄費。11.汝自已。12.滅亡。13.溺死。14兵艦。15.死亡。16.汝。17.目瞪口呆。18.囘憶。19.驚奇。20.默然。21.宿所。22.憂慮。23.紛亂。24.無意。25.點火。26.生病。27.過。28.巴西人。29.藥品。30.煙草。31.乾 32疑慮。33.礎石。34.提及。

and which to this time I had not found [1]*leisure* of [2]*inclina-tion* [3]*to look into.* I say I took it out, and brought both that and the tobacco with me to the table.

What use to make of the tobacco I knew not, in my distemper, or whether it was good for it or no; but I tried several [4]*experiments* with it, as if I was resolved it should [5]*hit one way or other.* I first took a piece of a leaf and [6]*chewed* it in my mouth, which, indeed, at first almost [7]*stupefied* my brain, the tobacco being green and strong, and that I had not been much [8]*used to.* Then I took some, and [9]*steeped* it for an hour or two in some rum, and resolved to take [10]*a dose* of it when I lay down. Lastly, I [11]*burnt* some upon a [12]*pan* of [13]*coals*, and held my nose close over the [14]*smoke* of it as long as I could bear it, as well for the heat as almost for [15]*suffocation.* [16]*In the interval of this operation* I took up the Bible and began to read; but my head was too much [17]*disturbed* with the tobacco to bear reading, at least at that time. Only, having opened the book [18]*casually*, the first words that [19]*occurred* to me were these: "Call on me in the day of trouble, and I will [20]*deliver* thee, and thou shalt [21]*glorify* me."

These words were very [22]*apt to* my case, and made some [23]*impression* upon my thoughts at the time of reading them, though not so much as they did afterwards; for, as for being " [24]*delivered,* " the word had no sound, as I may say, to me; the thing was so [25]*remote*, so [26]*impossible* in my apprehension of things, that I began to say, as the [27]*Children of Israel* did when they were [28]*promised* flesh to eat, " Can God [29]*spread* a table in the [30]*wilderness*?" so I began to say, "Can God himself deliver me from this place?" And as it was not for many years that any hopes [31]*appeared*, this

此時我沒有閒暇想去翻閱。我說我把牠取出，聖經和煙草我都放在桌上。

我不知如何使用煙草以治我的病，也不知能否對症下藥：但是我嘗試着幾種方法，似乎我決斷無論如何是必有效的。我起先取一葉，放在口內嚼，這一嚼，誠然，起初幾乎失去我的知覺，因為煙草是青的性質猛烈，而且我是不慣於這樣的。於是我取點煙草放在酒內一二時，決意睡時一服。末後，我放在一盆煤上燒些煙，我盡我所能耐的將鼻薰在煙上，因為薰熱氣亦是足以塞住氣息的。此行工作之時我拿起這本聖經開始看讀；但是我的頭腦受煙霧的擾亂太烈之故，至少在此時致不能看書；不過，偶然打開了書，我碰見的首先數字是"在危難的日子，你在叫我，我要拯救你，你將要歸榮於我。"

這數字很合我的情境，在念的時候我的思想中有了些印像，雖則這種印像並不深刻；因為，講到"拯救，"此字於我，我可以說，沒有意思，因為拯救之事遙遙無期，在我的觀察事物實是不可能的，於是我開始說，宛似以色列人當允許他們有肉吃時所說，"上帝能否在荒野地上鋪張一桌？"所以我開始說，"上帝你自己能否救我出這個地方？"因為非等待多年沒有任何希望發現，這個

1.暇閒。2.有意，想。3.翻閱。4.試檢。5.無論如何，必有效也。6.嚼。7.昏迷。8.慣。9.浸。10.一服。11.燒。12.一盆。13.煤。14.煙。15.望息。16.行此工作之時。17.擾亂。18.偶然。19.碰着。20.救。21.歸榮於。22.合宜。23.印像。24.救。25.甚遠。26.不可能。27.以色列人。28.允許。29.鋪張。30.荒地。31.發現

1prevailed　very　often　upon　my　*thoughts*.　But　the　words made a ` great *2impression* upon　me,　and　I　*3mused upon* them very　often.

It now grew late, and the tobacco had, as I said, *4dozed* my head so much that I *5inclined* to sleep; so I left my *6lamp* burning in the *7cave*, lest I should want anything in the night, and went to bed. But before I lay down, I did what I never had done in all my life,—I *8kneeled* down, and prayed to God to *9fulfil the promise* to me, that if I called upon him in *10the day of trouble*, he would *11deliver* me. After my broken and *12imperfect* prayer was over, I drank the rum in which I had *13steeped* the tobacco, which was so strong and *14rank* of the tobacco that I could *15scarcely* get it down; *16immediately* upon this I went to bed. I found *17presently* it flew up into my head violently; but I fell into a sound sleep, and waked no more *18till*, by the sun, it must necessarily be near three o'clock in the afternoon the next day—nay, to this hour *19I am partly of opinion* that I slept all the next day and night, and till almost three the day after. Otherwise, I know not how I should *20lose* a day out of my *21reckoning* in the days of the week, as it *22appeared* some years after I had done. It I had lost it by *23crossing* and *24recrossing* the line, I should have lost more than one day. But *25certainly* I lost a day *26in my* account, and never knew which way.

But that, however, one way or the other, when I waked I found myself *27exceedingly* *28refreshed*, and my spirits *29lively* and *30cheerful*, When I got up I was stronger than I was the day before, and my *31stomach* better, for I was *32hungry*. In short, I had no fit the next day, but *33continued much altered for the better*. This was the 29th.

當發現於我心。但是此字於我有了深刻的印象，我時常沉思着十字。

天氣漸黑，煙草巳經；如我說的，沉醉我的頭腦使我想睡；我讓我的燈在我的穴所燃着，也許在夜晚我須要任何物件，於是我去睡了。但是我在睡的以前，我做了一件我一生從未做過的事，——我跪下，懇求上帝對我實踐其約，就是要我在受難之時呼救時，他必須救我。我斷斷續續的向祈求之後，我渴我浸煙草的酒，煙酒非常的凶與觸鼻，使我很難飲下；渴後我立刻睡去。我卽刻覺察酒性很劇烈地湧進我的頭腦；我睡得很熟，依時光觀察，迄至第二天的下午近三時未醒——不特如此我也半信半疑的以爲睡了第二天的全日夜，或者竟巳睡第三天了不然，我不知我的計算日期如何少去一天，因爲幾年以後顯出我巳少算一天。是否我遺漏劃十字或再又於此線上遺漏去一天以上的記號。但是的確在我的記載中我遺漏一天，永不知如何遺漏的。

但是，不論如何，我醒來的時候我覺得自身異常的爽快我的精神活潑和暢快。我起身的時候，我較前天強健，我的胃部較佳，因爲我感覺飢餓。總之，次日我沒有發瘧，而且逐漸復元。這天是二十九日。

The 80th was my well day, [1]*of course,* and I went abroad with my gun, but did not care to [2]*travel* too far. I killed a [3]*sea fowl* or two, something like a [4]*brand goose,* and brought them home, but was not very [5]*forward* to eat them; so I ate some more of the [6]*turtle's eggs,* which were very good. This evening I renewed the [7]*medicine* which I had supposed did me good the day before,—the tobacco [8]*steeped in* [9]*rum*; only I did not take so much as before nor did I [10]*chew* any of the [11]*leaf,* or hold my head over the [12]*smoke.* However, I was not so well the next day, which was the first of [13]*July,* as I hoped I should have been; for I had a little [14]*spice* of the [15]*cold fit,* but it was not much.

July 2.—I [16]*renewed* the [17]*medicine* all the three ways; and *dosed* myself with it as at first, and doubled the [18]*quantity* which I drank.

July 3.—I missed the fit [19]*for good and all,* though I did not recover my full [20]*strength* for some weeks after. While I was thus gathering strength my thoughts ran [21]*exceedingly* upon this [22]*scripture,* " I will [23]*deliver* thee ; " and the impossibility of my [24]*deliverance* lay much upon my mind, [25]*in bar of* my ever expecting it. But as I was [26]*discouraging* myself with such thoughts, it [27]*occurred* to my mind that I pored so much upon my [28]*deliverance* from the main [29]*affliction* that I [30]*disregarded* the deliverance I had [31]*received,* and I was as it were made to ask myself such questions as these, namely : " Have I not been delivered, and wonderfully too, from sickness—from the most [32]*distressed* condition that could be, and that was so [33]*frightful* to me ? and what notice have I taken of it ? Have I [34]*done my part* ? God has delivered me, but I have not [35]*glorified* him ; that is to say, I have not owned and been thankful for that as a

六月三十日當然是我的幸福的日子，我攜着槍出外，走得太遠，也不介意。我殺了一二隻海鳥，瞧起來像雁鵝一般，把牠們帶到家內；然而沒有膽量去吃牠們；於是乎我多吃了幾個龞蛋，到也很有味的。當晚我把昨天使我料想於我有益的療治術重行試驗一下，——煙草浸在甜酒內；不過我沒有上次用得多，我也不嚼煙葉，我也不把我的頭放在煙霧上面。然而第二天我是狠不舒適，這天就是七月一號，照我希望，我應當覺着舒適的；因爲我稍發寒戰，却也無關緊要。

七月二日。——我用三種方法把療治術重行試驗起來；像從前一樣，我照方服藥，把我的飲料的分量加了一倍。

七月三日。——我然究不受寒戰的襲擊了，雖然在數星期以後，我方能完全恢復了健康。當我體力逐漸加增之時，我的思想非常地奔向聖經上面，"我將援助爾"；我的心裏滿貯着援助的不可能意念，雖然我對於援助是朝夕希冀。我雖被這些思想弄灰了心，我心中忽然覺着我從根本的苦痛上面太注重我的脫離危難了，反而把我已經得着的拯救，不以爲意，我宛如預備着問問自己以下的問題，就是："我未曾從疾病之中，從極困苦境遇之中，對我是這樣地可怕，狠奇異地被援救出來嗎？我對這事注意了嗎？我盡了天職嗎？上帝援助了我，我却未曾使他光榮；這就是說，我對於他的援助雖未加以承認和感謝像是拯救一般；我如何能希望着較大的拯救呢？"這些問題很觸動我的心；我立即下

¹*deliverance*; and how can I expect greater ²*deliverance*?" This ³*touched* my heart very much; and immediately I knelt down, and gave God thanks aloud for my recovery from my sickness.

July 4.—In the morning, I took the Bible; and, beginning at the ⁴*New Testament*, I began ⁵*seriously to read it*, and ⁶*imposed upon myself* to read ⁷*awhile* every morning and every night; ⁸*not tying myself to the number of chapters*, but ⁹*as long as my thoughts should engage me*. It was not long after I set ¹⁰*seriously* to this work, till I found my heart more deeply and ¹¹*sincerely* ¹²*affected* with ¹³*the wickedness of my past life*. The ¹⁴*impression* of my dream ¹⁵*revived*; and the words, "All these things have not brought thee to ¹⁶*repentance*," ran seriously in my thoughts.

Now I began to ¹⁷*construe* the words ¹⁸*mentioned* above, "Call on me, and I will deliver thee," in a different sense from what I had ever done before. Then I had no notion of anything being called "deliverance" but my being delivered from the ¹⁹*captivity* I was in; for though I was indeed ²⁰*at large* in the place, yet the island was certainly a ²¹*prison* to me, and that ²²*in the worst sense in the world*. But now I learned to take it ²³*in another sense*; now I looked back upon my past life with such horror, and my ²⁴*sins* appeared so dreadful, that my soul ²⁵*sought nothing of God but deliverance* from ²⁶*the load of guilt* that ²⁷*bore down all my comfort*. As for my ²⁸*solitary life*, it was nothing. I did not so much as pray to be delivered from it, or think of it; ²⁹*it was all of no consideration in comparison to this*. And I add this part here, ³⁰*to hint* to ³¹*whoever* shall read it, that ³²*whenever* they come to a true sense of things, they will find deliverance from sin a much greater blessing than deliverance from ³³*affliction*.

跪，對於我的疾病復原，大聲感謝上帝。

七月四日。——早上，我拿了一本聖經；從新約篇起頭，我恭敬地讀着，我自定一種規例以後每早和每晚，誦讀聖經片刻，章數不限幾何，誦讀時候的長短：隨意所之，不加限制。很嚴肅地進行這種工作不久以後，我於是覺着心中受了很深切的感觸，覺着往日的行爲是惡劣了。我的夢中的感應重行振作起來；這些話，"這一切的事物未曾使得你懊悔，"嚴重地在我的思潮中奔流着。

現在我把上面所說的話解釋出來，"祈禱我，我將拯爾，"這是和我從前所做的，意義完全兩樣。當時我除却在束縛之中被拯救出來之外，我對於"拯救"這種名稱，絲毫沒有觀念；因爲我雖然在這個地方是自由自在，然而這座島對我實在是一座囚牢，是世界上最難堪的地位。但是現在我又作別念了；現在用這樣的恐怖去囘看我過去的生活，罪惡很可怕的表現出來：以致於我的心靈所祈求於上帝的，沒有別的東西，不過請他把我從那個消磨我的樂趣的大罪裏面拯救出來罷了。至於我的寂寞身世，那是絲毫無礙的。我並不祈求從這種身世裏面被拯救出來，却也未曾想到；其他各事皆不足重輕，決不能與靈魂的拯救，相提並論。我在這裏加了這一部份，指示着讀這書的人們，無論何時，他們一經得了事物的真實的意念；他們從罪惡之中所得到的拯救却比從苦痛之中所得到的拯救，其幸福還要來得大呢。

1.援助。2.救助。3.感觸。4.新約。5.恭讀。6.自定。7.片刻。8.不限章數。9.隨意。10.嚴重貌。11.影響；12.劣行13.往日。14感應。15.重振。16.悔悟。17.解釋。18.述。19.束縛。20.自由。21.囚牢。22.最惡。23.別意。24.罪惡。25.惟欲上帝拯救。26.重罪。27.消磨樂趣。28.孤寂的生活。29.以彼比此，其地各事，無足重輕，30.暗示。31.任誰人。32無論何時。33.苦痛。

CHAPTER XIX

But leaving this part, I return to my [1]*Journal* :

My condition now began to be, though not less [2]*miser able* as to my way of living, yet much easier to my mind. my thoughts being directed, by a [3]*constant* reading the [4]*scripture* and praying to God, to [5]*things of a higher nature*, I had a [6]*great deal* of [7]*comfort* within, which, till now, I knew nothing of. Also, my health and strength returned. I [8]*bestirred myself* to [9]*furnish* myself with everything that I wanted, and make my way of living as [10]*regular* as I could.

From the 4th of July to the 14th, I was chiefly [11]*employed* in walking about with my gun in my hand, a [12]*little and a little at a time*, as a man that was [13]*gathering up* his strength after a fit of [14]*sickness* ; for it is hardly to be [15]*imagined* how [16]*low* I was and to what weakness I was [17]*reduced*. The [18]*application* which I made use of was [19]*perfectly* new, and perhaps had never [20]*cured* an [21]*ague* before ; neither can I [22]*recommend* it to any to practice, by this [23]*experiment*. Though it did [24]*carry off* the fit, yet it rather [25]*contributed to weakening me* ; for I had [26]*frequent* [27]*convulsions* in my [28]*nerves* and [29]*limbs* for some time. I learned from it also this, [30]*in particular*, that being abroad in the [31]*rainy season* was the most [32]*pernicious* thing to my health that could be, especially in those rains which came [33]*attended with* storms and [34]*hurricanes* of wind. As the rain which came in the dry season was always [35]*accompanied with* such storms, so I found that rain was much more dangerous than the rain which fell in September and October.

第十九章

丟開了這部份，我要囘到日記上面去。

現在我的景況，雖然生活方法不見得稍減困苦，在心中是較覺恬適的了。我的思想，因爲常常地讀聖經和祈禱上帝，途被引導到神聖事物方面上去，心中我覺着甚爲安適，這種安適，直到現在，我尚未知悉。我的健康和力量也恢復了，我深自勉勵着凡我所需要的東西必設法供給自己，並且竭力使我生活的方式有條不紊。

從七月四日到七月十四日，大半的光陰是消磨在攜槍出外步行上面，路程逐漸加增，如同一個人在病症發作之後，恢復體力一樣；因爲我這樣的疲荼和弄到這樣衰弱的地步，決不能猜料於萬一的。我所施用的方法是狠新的，大槪以前尚還未曾治愈一個寒瘧；我也不能因爲經過了試驗就介紹給人去實行。雖然牠除脫了寒戰，然而牠却大傷我的元氣，因爲有時我的筋脈和四肢覺得常常地抽搐着。我從牠也尤其明白了這個，在多雨的季候出外，對於我身體的健康是非常有害的，在暴風暴雨交作的時候尤甚。在乾燥的季候下的雨常常是隨着大風而來，所以我覺着這種雨較之九月和十月下降的雨是更爲有害的。

1. 日記。2. 不幸的。3. 不住的。4. 聖經。5. 神。聖事物。6. 狠多。7. 安慰。8. 自勉。9. 供給。10. 有次序。11. 用。12. 逐漸增加。13. 恢復體力。14. 病。15. 猜料。16. 疲荼。17. 降至。18. 用法。19. 完全。20. 治愈。21. 寒瘧。22. 介紹。23. 試驗。24. 除去。25. 傷我體氣。26. 常常。27. 抽搐。28. 筋脈。29. 四肢。30. 特地。31. 多雨的季候。32. 最有損害的。33. 相隨而來。34. 大風雨。35. 鹽以

I had now been in *th*is ¹*unhealthy* island above ten months. All possibility of deliverance from this ²*condition* seemed to be ³*entirely* taken from me ; and ⁴*I firmly believe* that no human ⁵*shape* had ever ⁶*set foot upon* that place. Having now ⁷*secured* my ⁸*habitation,* as I thought, fully to my mind, I had a great desire to make a more perfect discovery of the island, and to see what other ⁹*productions* I might find, which I yet knew nothing of.

It was on the 15th of July that I began to take a more particular ¹⁰*survey* of the island itself. I went up the ¹¹*creek* first, where, as I ¹²*hinted*, I brought my rafts on shore. I found, after I came about two miles up, that the ¹³*tide* did not flow any higher, and that it was no more than a little brook of running water, very ¹⁴*fresh* and good ; but this being the dry season, there was hardly any water in some parts of it,,—at least, not enough to run in any ¹⁵*stream* so as it could be ¹⁶*perceived.*

On the banks of this ¹⁷*brook* I found many pleasant ¹⁸*savannahs,* or ¹⁹*meadows*, plain, ²⁰*smooth,* and covered with grass ; and on the ²¹*rising parts* of them, next to the higher grounds, where the water, as might be ²²*supposed,* never ²³*overflowed*, I found a great deal of ²⁴*tobacco,* ²⁵*green*, and growing to a great and very strong ²⁶*stalk.* There were ²⁷*divers* other plants, which I had ²⁸*no notion of or **under**standing about*, that might, perhaps, ²⁹*have virtues of their own*, which I could not find out.

I ³⁰*searched* for the ³¹*cassava root,* which the Indians, in all that ³²*climate,* make their bread of, but I could find none. I saw large plants of ³³*aloes*, but did not understand them. I saw several ³⁴*sugar canes*, but wild, and, ³⁵*for want of cultivation,* ³⁶*imperfect.* I ³⁷*contended* mysel fwith these dis-

　　現在我居留在這座不衞生的島上有十個月以上了。對於這種景況一切可能的拯救大概是完全無望的了；我却堅信這個地方永遠未曾被人踐踏過。照我想起來，我已經得了一座住所，甚是滿足心意的，我還狠希望在這島上再有更完美的發現，瞧瞧我能否島獲那些我不知道的產物。

　　在七月十五那一天，我開始在島的上面特別地查勘。起頭我走向小河方面去；在那裏，像我曾經暗示着，我曾把我的木筏拿上岸去。走了兩（英）里後，我覺着潮水漲得不狠高，那個小河不過是一座流着新鮮和佳妙的水的小溪而已；但是現在是乾燥的季候，河的各部份，水却極少：——至少，水却不足以流到傍的溪內，而被人所瞧見。

　　在小溪的兩岸，我找着了許多悅目的草原，牧場，平坦的，光滑的；而且被草蓋住；在她們聳起的部份上，在較高的平地附近，在那裏，水兒可以懸想得出，永遠不會溢溢；我找着許多青的和長得又大又堅壯的桿兒的烟草。還有別的草木，其名我不能知；牠們當然各有特別功用，我却不能尋出找來。

　　我搜尋薯根，（印度）人一年四季用牠作糧食用的，然而我却毫無所獲。我看見大的沉香木，但是不能明白牠。我瞧見幾根甘蔗，但是野的，因爲缺少培養之功，長得不完全。

coveries for this time, and came back, ¹*musing with myself* what ²*course* I might take to know the virtue and ³*goodness* of any of the ⁴*fruits* or plants which I should discover, ⁵*but could bring it to no conclusion*; for, ⁶*in short*, I had made so little ⁷*observation* while I was in Brazil that I knew little of the plants in the field; at least, very little that might ⁸*serve to any purpose* now in my ⁹*distress*.

The next day, the 16th, I went up the same way again; and, after going something further than I had gone the day before, I found the brook and ¹⁰*savannahs* ¹¹*cease*, and the country became more woody than before. In this part I found different fruits, and particularly I found ¹²*melons* upon the ground, in great ¹³*abundance,* and ¹⁴*grapes* upon the trees. The ¹⁵*vines* had ¹⁶*spread*, indeed, over the trees, and the ¹⁷*clusters of grapes* were just now in ¹⁸*their prime*, very ¹⁹*ripe* and rich. _This was a ²⁰*surprising* discovery, and I was ²¹*exceeding* glad of them; but I was warned by my ²²*experience* to eat ²³*sparingly* of them; ²⁴*remembering* that when I was ²⁵*ashore* in ²⁶*Barbary,* the eating of ²⁷*grapes* killed several of our Englishmen, who were slaves there, by throwing them into ²⁸*fluxes* and ²⁹*fevers*. But I found an excellent use for these ³⁰*grapes*; and that was to ³¹*cure or dry them in the sun*, and keep them as dried ³²*grapes* or ³³*raisins* are kept, which I thought would be, as indeed they were, ³⁴*wholesome* and ³⁵*agreeable to eat* when no grapes could be had.

I ³⁶*spent* all that evening there, and went not back to my ³⁷*habitation*; which, ³⁸*by the way*, was the first night, as I might say, I had ³⁹*lain from home*. In the night I took my first ⁴⁰*contrivance*, and got up in a tree, where I slept well. The next morning I ⁴¹*proceeded upon* my discovery, traveling nearly four ⁴²*miles*, as I might ⁴³*judge* by

日前我以所曾經發現之物自相辨論;同來以後,自己忖度着:對於我將要尋出的果木用什麼步驟能夠明白牠們的功效和美質來;但是終究想不出歸結;因為,總而言之,當我在（布勒喜爾）的時候,對於田中的草木,並未詳細考察過;現在處於厄難之境;此點也無補於用。

第二天,十六日,我重行往原路去;比上次略走遠了幾步以後,我見那個小溪和草原終結了;曠野比較以前格外多木了。在這部份中,我找着許多種類的果子,尤其是我尋着多量的西瓜在地上,葡萄在樹上。葡萄樹在別的樹上伸展開來,許多族葡萄球正在極豐盛的時候,熟透而且眾多。這是一樁可驚的發見,我對於牠們是非常快樂的;但是我的經驗警告我要慢慢地去吃她們;想起我在（巴巴利）登岸的時候在那裏的（英）國奴隸因為吃多了葡萄,罹着痢疾和熱症而死。然而我對於這些葡萄找出了一個狠好的用場,就是把牠們在太陽裏曝乾,把牠們收藏起來,好像收藏乾葡萄一樣,我想牠們應當是,實在牠們是這樣,滋補和適口的,當沒有葡萄的時候。

那一天晚上我未曾離開那個地方,不回到我的住所;順便說起來,這就是我留宿在外的第一夜。中夜,我用了初次的計劃爬上樹去,安安穩穩地睡在樹上。第二天早晨,我繼續進行我的發明,差不多走了四（英）里,因為我用山谷的長度判斷出來,

1.自忖 2.步驟 3.美質 4.果 5.終難定斷 6.總括 7.觀察 8.略可合川 9.厄難 10.草原 11.終止 12.西瓜 13.多量 14.葡萄 15.葡萄樹 16.展開 17.葡萄球 18.極盛之時 19.熟 20.可驚的 21.甚 22.經驗 23.略 24.記憶 25.上岸 26.(巴巴利) 27.葡萄 28.痢疾 29.寒熱 30.葡萄 31.曝乾於日中 32.葡萄 33.葡萄乾 34.滋補 35.可口 36.敷去 37.住所 38.順便言及 39.在外住宿 40.計劃 41.繼進 42.(英)里 43.判斷

the length of the ¹*valley*, ²*keeping still due north*, with a ³*ridge* of ⁴*hills* on the south and north sides of me At the end of this ⁵*march* I came to an opening, where the country seemed to ⁶*descend* to the west, and a little spring of *fresh water*, which ⁷*issued out of* the side of the hill by me, ran the other way,--that is ⁹*due east*. The country appeared so fresh, so green, so ¹⁰*flourishing*, everything being in ¹¹*a constant verdure* ¹²*or flourish of spring*, that it looked like a ¹³*planted* garden.

I ¹⁴*descended* a little on the side of that ¹⁵*delicious vale*, ¹⁶*surveying* it with a secret kind of pleasure, though mixed with my other ¹⁷*afflicting* thoughts, to think that this was all my own; that I was king and lord of all this country ¹⁸*indefeasibly*, and had ¹⁹*a right of possession.* If I could ²⁰*convey* it, I might ²¹*have it in inheritance* as completely as an ²²*lord of a manor in England.* I saw here ²³*abundance* of ²⁴*cocoa* trees ²⁵*orange*, and ²⁶*lemon*, and ²⁷*citron* trees, but all wild, and very few bearing any fruit, at least not ²⁸*then.* However, the green ²⁹*limes* that I gathered were not only pleasant to eat, but very wholesome. I mixed their ³⁰*juice* afterwards with water, which made it very wholesome, and very cool and ³¹*refreshing.* I found now I had business enough, to gather and carry home; and I resolved to ³²*lay up a store*, as well of grapes as limes and lemons, ³³*to furnish* myself for the ³⁴*wet* season, which I knew ³⁵*was approaching.*

In order to do this, I gathered a great heap of grapes in one place, a lesser heap in another place, and a great ³⁶*parcel* of limes and lemons in another place. Taking a few of each with me, I traveled ³⁷*homewards.* resolving to come again, and bring a ³⁸*bag* or ³⁹*sack*, or what I could make, to carry the rest home. Accordingly, having spent three days in this journey, I came home (so I must now call my

我仍繼續向正北而行，羣山的脊背在我身傍南北兩面。路程完了的時候，我來到一座曠地，在那裏曠野好像是向西方降下：一座小泉中的清新的水，是從我身傍山側中流出來出的，馳向對方而去，一就是：向正東而去。曠野是這樣的清新，活潑，茂盛，各樣東西皆有欣欣向榮的氣象，瞧起來宛如一座種有草木的花園。

我在那風景秀麗的山谷的傍邊降下幾步，用一種靜俏的快樂態度來查勘牠，雖然心中還參雜着別的苦痛的思想，以爲這些東西皆歸于我，我儼然自以爲是曠野中的王與主子，並有占領的權。倘使我能把牠過渡，我將把牠傳與後裔，如同（英國）領有封地的諸侯一般。在那裏，我瞧見許多椰子樹，橘子，檸檬，佛手等樹，牠們都是野的，其中狠少產有果子的，在這時尤其沒有。然而我收集的青佛手非特可口而且狠滋養的。後來我把牠的汁用水調和，吃起來涼爽而滋補現在我有事情做了，把牠們收集帶回家去，我決定把她們貯藏起來，葡萄，佛手，檸檬等等，預備等潮濕季候作食料：這種季候我知道快要到了。

爲做這事，在一個地方，我聚集一大堆葡萄，別的地方，堆兒較小，另外一個地方，一大堆佛手和檸檬。隨身帶了些，我走向家中而去，決定再來，並帶一袋或一囊，或其他我能製的物件，把其餘的運回家去。這個行程費去我三天光陰，我回家去（現在我必須叫牠作帳幕和山穴）；但是在我未曾到那裏以前，

1.山谷。2.繼向北行。3.山脊。4.山。5.行程。6.降下。7.清水。8.從……出。9.正東。10.茂盛。11.欣欣向榮之狀。12.陽春時草木皆青。13.種草木的。14.下降。15.秀美山谷。16.查勘。17.困苦的。18.儼然。19.占領權。20.讓渡。21.傳與子孫。22.（英）國諸侯。23.衆多。24.椰子樹。25.橘子。26.檸檬。27.佛手。28.當時。29.佛手。30.汁。31.爽快。32.貯藏。33.供給。34.濕。35.將臨。36.堆。37.向家而行。38.袋。39.囊

tent and my cave); but before I got thither the grapes were [1]*spoiled*. The richness of the fruit and the weight of the [2]*juice* having broken them and [3]*bruised* them, they were good [4]*for little or nothing*, As to the [5]*limes*, they were good, but I could bring but a few.

The next day, being the nineteenth, I went back, having made me two small bags to bring home my [6]*harvest*. But I was [7]*surprised*, when coming to my heap of grapes, which were so rich and fine when I gathered them, to find them all [8]*spread about, trod to pieces*, and [9]*dragged* about, ome here, some there, and [10]*abundance* eaten and [11]*devoured*. By this I [12]*concluded* there were some wild creatures [13]*thereabouts*, which had done this; but what they were I knew not.

However, as I found there was no laying them up on [14]*heaps*, and no carrying them away in a [15]*sack* but that one way they would be [16]*destroyed*, and the other way they would be [17]*crushed* with their own weight, I took another [18]*course*. I gathered a large quantity of the grapes and hung them upon the out [19]*branches* of the trees, that they might [20]*cure* and dry in the sun. Of the limes and lemons, I carried as many back as I [21]*could well stand under*.

When I came home from this journey, I [22]*contemplated with great pleasure* the [23]*fruitfulness* of that [24]*valley*, and the pleasantness of the [25]*situation* the [26]*security* from storms on that side the water, and the wood; and I [27]*concluded* that I had [28]*pitched upon* a place to fix my [29]*abode* which was [30]*by far the worst part* of the country. [31]*Upon the whole*, I began to consider of [32]*removing* my habitation, and looking out for a place [33]*equally safe* as where now I was [34]*situate*, if possible, in that pleasant, fruitful part of the island.

葡萄已經腐爛了。果實的多量和汁液的重量把牠們弄碎榨破了，牠們是毫無用處了。至於佛手，牠們是好的，可是我只拿一些。

第二天，十九日，我囘轉去，做好兩隻小袋爲把我的收穫物取囘家去之用。然而當我走到堆集葡萄的地方，我不禁駭怪起來，當我收集葡萄的辰光，牠們是豐而美，現在牠們亂散在四處，踏碎無遺，被人曳至各處，此處若干，彼處若干，大多數皆被人吞吃。由此我決定在近必有野人及野獸，彼等曾做此事；彼等究爲何物，我不知之。

我於是不將牠們聚集成堆，不將牠們置於袋中而攜去，但是一期牠們將被人損壞，一期牠們將被自己的重量壓碎，我於是用其他方法。我收集多量的葡萄，把牠們掛在樹的外枝上面，使得牠們能夠在日中曝乾。盡我的力量，我把佛手和檸檬取了若干囘家。

從這個行程返了家，我狠快活地想着山谷的谷的豐盛的出產，地點的悅意，在水和樹林那邊，可以免去暴風雨的襲擊；我決定我已擇定一個地方來安定我的寓所，那是曠野中的最劣的一部份。總而言之，我開始着想遷移住所，要找出一個同我現在所住的地方一樣安全的場所，倘使事勢可能，在這個島上使人欣悅和出產豐富的部份。

This thought ran long in my head, and I was [1]*exceeding* fond of it for some time, the [2]*pleasantness* of the place [3]*tempting* me. But when [4]*I came to a nearer view of it*, I considered that I was now by the [5]*seaside*, where it was at least possible that something might happen to my [6]*advantage*; and, by the same ill [7]*fate* that brought me hither, might bring some other unhappy [8]*wretches* to the same place. Though it was [9]*scarce* probable that any such thing should ever happen, yet to [10]*inclose* myself among the [11]*hills* and [12]*woods* in the center of the island [13]*was to anticipate my bondage*, and to [14]*render* such [15]*an affair not only improbable*, [16]*but impossible*. Therefore I ought not by any means to [17]*remove*.

However, I was so [18]*enamored* of this place that I spent much of my time there for the whole of the [19]*remaining* part of the month of July ; and though, upon second thoughts, I resolved not to [20]*remove*, yet I built me a little kind of a [21]*bower*, and [22]*surrounded* it at a distance with a strong [23]*fence*, being a double [24]*hedge*, as high as I could reach, *well staked*, and filled between with [25]*brushwood*. Here I lay very [26]*secure*, sometimes two or three nights together, always going over it with a [27]*ladder* ; so that I [28]*fancied* now I had my country house and my seacoast. house. This work took me up to the beginning of [29]*August*.

I had but newly finished my fence, and begun to enjoy my labor, when the rains came on, and made me [30]*stick* close to my first habtiation ; for though I had made me a tent like the other. with a piece of a [31]*sail*, and [32]*spread* it very well, yet I had not the [33]*shelter* of a hill to keep me from storms nor a cave behind me to [34]*retreat* into when the rains were [35]*extraordinary*.

這種思想在我腦中轉了許久，我有時極喜歡牠，那個地方的欣悅的樣子把我引誘了。但是當我仔細思量的時候，我想現在我是居於海濱：這個地方各事或將於我有益，同樣的不幸的命運把我帶到這裏來；或者也會帶些別的不幸的災禍到同樣的地方來。雖然這是很不可能的這些事件將要發生，然而把我自己關在島中的山和樹林裏面，這就好比是禁錮一般，使得這事非但不能有，而且亦不能行。所以無論如何我不應遷移。

然而，我對於把七月餘剩下來的日子一齊消耗的地方很是迷戀的；雖然過了第二次思想，我決意不遷移：我製了一座小的亭子，繞亭四周，在一定距離範圍以內，用堅固的垣護著；這是一座雙層的籬笆，其高我所能及，以椿護衛，其中用矮樹充塞之。我睡在這裏很安全，有時完全兩三夜，常常用一座梯子跑上去；這樣我幻想著我現在有了曠野的房屋和海濱的房屋了。這個工作使我到了八月初頭方纔罷手。

我不過纔完畢我的短垣，開始享受我的勞作，兩兒驟然來了，使我躲在家中，不能出來，雖然我另外製成了一座帳幕，和其他一座相似，這是用打破了船帆製成的，然而我尚缺一山中的隱身所，使我避免暴風雨，又缺一洞穴，當雨勢極大的時候，使我能入內藏身。

1. 極。2. 欣悅之狀。3. 引誘。4. 進而思之。5. 海濱。6. 益處。7. 命運。8. 災害。9. 稀少。10. 封。11. 山。12. 林。13. 是卽所以禁錮之。14. 使得。15. 非但不能有，16. 而且亦不能行。17. 遷移。18. 迷戀。19. 餘剩。20. 移家。21. 小亭。22. 圍以。23. 垣。24. 籬笆。25. 矮樹。26. 安全。27. 梯。28. 幻想。29. 八月。30. 貼住。31. 船帆。32. 廣佈。33. 藏身之地。34. 退入。35. 非常的。

CHAPTER XX

ABOUT the beginning of August, as I said, I finished my bower, and began to ¹*enjoy* myself. On the 3rd of August, I found the grapes I had hung up were ²*perfectly* ³*dried*, and indeed were excellent good ⁴*raisins* of the sun. I began to take them down from the trees, and it was very happy that I did so, for the rains which followed would have ⁵*spoiled* them, and I had lost the best part of my winter food; for I had above two hundred large ⁶*bunches* of them. No sooner had I taken them all down, and carried most of them home to my cave, than it began to rain; and ⁷*from hence*, which was the 14th of August, it rained, ⁸*more or less*, every day till the middle of October; and sometimes so ⁹*violently* that I could not ¹⁰*stir out* of my cave for several days.

From the 14th of August to the 26th, ¹¹*incessant rain*, so that I could not ¹²*stir*, and was now very careful not to be much wet, In this ¹³*confinement* I began to be ¹⁴*straitened for food*; but, ¹⁵*venturing* out twice, I one day killed a goat, and the last day, which was the 26th, I found a very large ¹⁶*tortoise*, which was ¹⁷*a treat to me*. My food was ¹⁸*regulated* thus: I ate a bunch of raisins for my ¹⁹*breakfast*; a piece of the ²⁰*goat's* flesh, or of the ²¹*turtle*, for my dinner, broiled, (for, to my great misfortune, I had no ²²*vessel* to boil or stew anything,) and two or three of the turtle's eggs for my ²³*supper*.

During this ²⁴*confinement* in my cover by the rain, I worked daily two or three hours at ²⁵*enlarging* my cave, and by degrees worked it on towards one side till I came to the outside of the hill, and made a door or way out, which came beyond my fence or ²⁶*wall*. So I came in and out this

大約在八月初頭，像我前此所說，我完成了小亭，開始自相娛樂。八月三日，我瞧見我所懸掛的葡萄已完全晾乾了，實在是被陽光曝成的上好的葡萄乾。我把牠們從樹上拿下來，我做這事實在是很快樂的，因爲雨兒或將損壞牠們，我失去了我的冬日糧食最好的一部份；因爲我有二百大縏以上的葡萄，一經把牠們拿下來，把一大牛帶到家中洞穴裏面去以後，天就降雨了；從此以後，那是八月十四日，雨兒下得或多或少，每日如此，直到十月中旬始住；有時下得這樣厲害，以致於我幾天不能夠出洞去。

從八月十四日到二十六日，陰雨連綿，我是不能行動的了，現在我是很小心不要把身上弄的太溼了。困守家中，食物缺乏；但是，冒險出外兩次，一天我殺了一隻山羊，最後的一天，就是二十六日，我找着了一隻很大的龜，這就是犒饗我的東西了。我的食物這樣的整理：早餐吃一縏葡萄乾；午餐吃一塊山羊肉，或者龜肉，烤熟了吃，（我是困苦之極，沒有器皿來煑或燉東西吃，）晚餐吃兩個或三個龜蛋。

在因爲天雨困居穴中的時候，每天我工作二三小時把我的洞穴放寬，漸漸的向一邊工作下去，後來直到了山的外面；我做成一個門或是一個出路，那個是在我的垣或牆的外面。

way. But I was not [1]*perfectly* easy at lying so open; for, as I had managed myself before, I was in a perfect [2]*inclosure*; whereas now I thought I lay [3]*exposed*, and open for anything to come in upon me. Yet I could not [4]*perceive* that there was any living thing to fear, the biggest creature that I had yet seen upon the island being a [5]*goat*. Sept. 30.—I was now come to the unhappy [6]*anniversary* of my landing. I cast up the [7]*notches* on my post, and found I had been on [8]*shore* three hundred and [9]*sixty-five* days. I [10]*kept this day as a solemn fast*, setting it apart for [11]*religious exercise*, [12]*prostrating myself on the ground* [13]*with the most serious humiliation, confessing my sins to God* [14]*acknowledging his righteous judgments upon me* and praying to him to [15]*have mercy on* me through [16]*Jesus Christ*. Not having tasted the least [17]*refreshment* for twelve hours, even till the going down of the sun, I then ate a [18]*biscuit* cake and a [19]*bunch* of grapes, and went to bed, finishing the day as I began it.

I had all this time [20]*observed* no Sabbath day; for as at first I had [21]*no sense of religion* upon my mind, I had, after some time, [22]*omitted* to [23]*distinguish* the weeks by making a longer [24]*notch* than ordinary for the Sabbath day, and so did not really know what any of the days were. But now, having cast up the days as before, I found I had been there a year. So I divided it into weeks, and set [25]*apart* every seventh day for a Sabbath; though I found at the end of my [26]*account* I had lost a day or two in my [27]*reckoning*.

A little after this my ink [28]*began to fail me*, and so I [29]*contended* myself to use it more [30]*sparingly*, and to write down only the most [31]*remarkable* events of my life, without [32]*continuing* a [33]*daily memorandum* of other things.

我就從那裏進來出去。然而我露天而臥，覺得很不安適；因為，像我從前處置自己一樣，我是在一個完全的圍地之內；現在我想倘使我露天而臥，必定有東西來到我的面前。我還不能知道有使人可怕的生物，在這島上，我瞧見的最大的生物就是一隻山羊。

九月三十日——我現在到了不幸的登陸的紀念日了。我在我的柱子上面計算我所刻的痕跡，我曉得我上岸已經有三百六十五天了。我謹守這一天作為齋戒的日子，把這日別置着，行禮拜之禮，用極虔誠和卑謙的態度，跪伏於地，向上帝懺悔過失，祈求他賜我正當的裁判，求他看耶穌的面子衷憐饒恕我。十二個鐘頭，一點點心都未下肚，直到日落西山，我於是方喫了一塊餅乾和一束葡萄，上床安息，完成了這一天的光陰像我開始牠一樣。

這多時以來，我曾遵守着安息日了；因為起初我心中毫無宗教的觀念，過了些時，我對於安息日忘記用東西刻一較長的刻痕來區別週期，以致於不知道其餘的日子是件麼了。現在仍究計算着日子，我知道來到這裏已一年了。這樣我把一年分作週日，把每第七日別置着，作為安息日；在我核算的終點，我覺着我算的時候遺去了一二日了。

不久以後，我的墨水將盡，這樣我遂要省儉用牠，只把我生活上最重要的事記下來，對於其他事件，不再每日作記了。

1.完全。2.圍地。2.露宿。4.想。5.山羊。6.紀念日。7.刻痕。8.岸。9.六十五。10.守此日為齋戒日。11.行禮拜之禮。12.跪伏於地。13.虔誠謙卑之概。14.認罪於天，求賜正當裁判。15.憐宥。16.耶穌。17.點心。18.餅乾。19.束。20.遵守。21.無宗教觀念。22.遺漏。23.區別。24.刻痕。25.分開。26.計算。27.計算。28.將完。29.自辦。30.省儉。31.可注意的。32.繼續。33.日記。

The [1]*rainy* season and the dry season began now to appear [2]*regular* to me, and I learned to [3]*divide* them so as [4]*to provide for them accordingly.* But I bought all my [5]*experience* before I had it, and this I am going to [6]*relate* was one of the most [7]*discouraging* [8]*experiments* that I made.

I have mentioned that I had saved the few ears of [9]*barley* and rice which I had so [10]*surprisingly* found [11]*spring up,* as I thought, of themselves. I believe there were about thirty [12]*stalks* of rice, and about twenty of barley; and now I thought it a proper time to [13]*sow* it, after the rains, the sun being in its southern position,—going from me. Accordingly, I dug up a piece of ground as well as I could with my wooden [14]*spade*, and, dividing it into two parts, I sowed my [15]*grain*. But as I was sowing, it casually [16]*occurred* to my thoughts that I would not sow it all at first, because I did not know when was the proper time for it; so I [17]*sowed* about two thirds of the seed, [18]*leaving about a handful of each*, It was a great comfort to me afterwards that I did so, for not one grain of what I [19]*sowed* this time [20]*came to anything*. The dry months following, the earth having had no rain after the seed was [21]*sown*, it had [22]*no moisture to assist its growth*, and never came up at all till the wet season had come again, and then it [23]*grew* as if it had been but newly [24]*sown*.

Finding my first seed did not grow, which I easily [25]*imagined* was [26]*by the drought*, I sought for a [27]*moister* piece of ground to [28]*make another trial in.* I dug up a piece of ground near my new [29]*bower*, and [30]*sowed* the rest of my seed in [31]*February*, a little before the [32]*vernal equinox.* This having the [33]*rainy* months of [34]*March* and April to water it, sprung up very [35]*pleasantly*, and [36]*yielded* a very good [37]*crop;*

　　現在乾燥和多雨的時候對我是狠有秩序的了，我把牠們分將開來；以作未雨綢繆之計。在我未有經驗之前，我是把牠賣到手的；以下所述的就是我的最失意的試驗的一節。

　　我曾說過我保存着幾株大麥和米的穗，照我想起來，牠們自己發芽萌生被我驚異地找着的。我想信大概有三十隻米梗，二十隻大麥梗；現在我想是播種的合宜的時候了，雨降之後，太陽在南面，——從我的方面而去。我用木鍁竭力地掘起了一塊土地，把牠分作兩個部份，我播種穀子。但是當我播種的時候，心中偶然想到我不應起頭把穀子完全種盡，因為我不知道何時對於穀子是合宜的時期；這樣我種了三分之二的種子，各留了一點兒。我做了這事，後來我是狠安慰的，因為我現在播種的穀一粒也未曾結實。乾燥的月份連續來了，穀子種過後，地土未曾得着雨水沾潤，又無潮氣來助牠生長，永遠不生長直到潮溼時期重來，於是牠生長起來好像是剛剛纔播種的一般。

　　瞧見我第一次種的種子不生長，我料想着是因爲久旱的緣故；我找尋一塊較潮溼的地土再行試驗。在靠近我的新造成功的小亭傍邊，我掘起一塊地土，在二月裏，稍在春分之前，我把我的種子完全播種下去。這些種子受着三月和四月多雨的月來灌漑牠，狠欣悅地萌生出來，致成一極好的大收成；

1.多雨。2.有秩序。3.分。4.未雨綢繆。5.經驗。6.述。7.失意的。8.試驗。9.大麥。10.可驚狀。11.萌生。12.梗。13.種。14.鍁。15.穀。16.遇到。17.播。18.各留少許。19.播。20.生實。21.播。22.無潮氣助之生長。23.生長。24.種。25.猜想。26.因久旱故。27.較經。28.再試。29.小亭。30.播。31.二月。32.春分。33.多雨。34.三月。35.欣悅狀。36.致生。37.收成

but having part of the seed left only, and not [1]*daring* to [2]*sow* all that I had I had but a small [3]*quantity* at last, my whole crop not [4]*amounting to* above half a [5]*peck* of each kind. But by this [6]*experiment* I was made master of my business, and knew exactly when the proper season was to sow, and that I might expect two [7]*seedtimes* and two [8]*harvests* every year.

While this corn was growing, I made a little [9]*discovery* which was of use to me afterwards. As soon as [10]*the rains were over*, and the weather began to settle, which was about the month of November, I made a visit up the country to my [11]*bower,* where, though I had not been for some months, yet I found all things just as I left them. The [12]*circle* or double [13]*hedge* that I had made was not only firm and [14]*entire*, but the [15]*stakes* which I had cut out of some trees that grew [16]*thereabouts* were all [17]*shot out* and grown with long [18]*branches*, as much as a [19]*willow* tree usually [20]*shoots* the first year after [21]*lopping* its head.

I could not tell what tree to call it that these stakes were cut from. I was surprised, and yet very well pleased, to see the young trees grow. I [22]*pruned* them, and led them up to grow as much alike as I could ; and it is [23]*scarce credible* how beautiful a [24]*figure* they grew into in three years ; so that though the hedge made a circle of about twenty-five yards in [25]*diameter*, yet the trees—for such I might now call them—soon covered it, and it was a complete shade, [26]*sufficient* to lodge under all the dry season. This made me resolve to cut some more stakes, and make me a hedge like this in a [27]*semicircle* round my wall (I mean that of my first [28]*dwelling*) which I did. Placing the trees or stakes in a double row, at about eight

但是僅僅留下了一部份，不敢把我所有的一齊播種下去，我最後只有些小的分量，收成的總數；統計起來，每種不上半斗。然而因為這個試驗，我對於這事可以措置裕如了，而且的確地明白什麼是合宜播種的時候，每年我能夠希望着有兩個播種的時期和兩個收穫時期。

當穀子生長的時候，我得了一個小小的發見，後來於我很有益的。一經雨止和天氣定規以後，大約是十一月光景，我就到曠地上面去拜訪我的小亭，在那裏，雖然我有幾個月不去了，各種東西，景況如舊；像我告別牠們的時候一樣。我做成的一圈或是雙層籬笆非但堅牢和完美不缺，而且我從那些生長在左近地方的樹林裏面所割取的椿木，都一齊發出，生出長的枝兒，好像一株楊柳樹一般，常常在被修截了頭的第一年後發芽。

我不能說出這些椿兒是從什麼樹兒裏割取出來的。瞧見幼樹生長，我是又驚又喜。我修削牠們，盡我的能力來讓牠們生長；這簡直令人難以相信，三年以內，她們竟長成得這樣美麗的形狀；雖然籬笆做成大約有二十五碼直徑的一個圓圈，然而這些樹，——現在我能這樣地叫牠們了，——立即把她掩蓋，可說是一個完全的蔭地，足以居留，在乾燥的時期。我遂決定再多割些椿木，做成一座籬笆，半圓的式樣，來圍繞我所造的牆。（我的意思就是說我第一次的住所。）

1.敢．2.播種．3.分量．4.統計．5.斗．6.試驗．7.種子期．8.收成．9.發見．雨止．11.小亭．12.圓圈．13.籬笆．14.完美．15.椿木．16.左近．17.發出．18.枝．19.柳．20.萌芽．21.修剪．22.修削．23.難以相信．24.形狀．25.直徑．56.足以．27.半圓形．28.住所

yards' distance from my first fence, they grew [1]*presently*, and were at first a fine cover to my habitation, and after-wards served for a [2]*defense* also, as I shall observe in its order.

I found now that the seasons of the year might [3]*generally* be divided, not into summer and [4]*winter*, as in Europe, but into the [5]*rainy* seasons and the dry seasons, which were generally thus :—

The half of [6]*February*, the whole of [7]*March*, and the half of April,—[8]*rainy*, the sun being then on or near the [9]*equator*.

The half of [10]*April*, the whole of [11]*May*, [12]*June*, and [13]*July*, and the half of [14]*August*,—dry, the sun being then to the north of the [15]line.

The half of August, the whole of September, and the half of [16]*October*,—rainy, the sun being then come back.

The half of October, the whole of [17]*November*, [18]*December*, and [19]*January*, and the half of February,—dry, the sun being then to the south of the line.

The rainy seasons sometimes held longer or [20]*shorter* as the winds [21]*happened* to blow, but this was the general [22]*observation* I made. After I had found, by [23]*experience*, the [24]*ill consequences* of being abroad in the rain, I took care to furnish myself with [25]*provisions* [26]*beforehand*, that I might not be [27]*obliged* to go out, and I sat within doors as much as [28]*possible* during the wet months. This time I found much [29]*employment*. and very [30]*suitable* also to the time, for I found great [31]*occasion* for many things which I had no way to furnish myself with [32]*but by hard labor and constant application.* Particularly I tried many ways to make myself a [33]*basket*, but all the [34]*twigs* I could [35]*get for the purpose* [36]*proved so brittle that they would do nothing.*

把樹或椿木排成兩行；大約離開我的牆垣有八碼遠近，牠們立即生長；起初對於我的住所是一個良好的遮蔽物，後來也可以當作防禦物之用；照我觀察她們生長的次序而論。

現在我覺着一年四季大概可以分作，並不是像在(歐洲)分作夏天和冬天一樣；但是分作多雨的季候和乾燥的季候那個大概是這樣。——

二月的一半，三月的全月，四月的一半。——多雨，太陽那時候是在或是貼近赤道上面。

四月的一半，五月六月，和七月的全月，以及八月的一能——乾燥；太陽那時候是在經線的北面。

八月的一半，九月的全月，十月的一半，——多雨，太陽那時候回來了。十月的一半；十一月，十二月，正月全月，和二月的一半，——乾燥，太陽那時候是在經線的南面。

有時多雨的時季長或短是以風的吹括爲轉移，不過這是我的大概的觀察。憑了經驗，明白了雨天出外的惡果以後，我就小心地預防着備辦齊了食物，那末我不一定要出外，在多雨的月，我儘能坐在家中了。這時我尋着許多的事務，對於辰光也狠合宜的；因爲我找到了狠大的機會，對於供養生活的東西，非用勞力和恆心是無法到手的。特別地我試了許多的方法去製造一個籃子，但是攏總我能得到作爲此用的小樹枝，簡直是過於脆薄，無能爲用的了。

It *¹proved* of excellent advantage to me now, that when I was a boy I used to take great *²delight* in standing at a *³dasket maker's* in the town where my father lived, to see them make their wicker ware. Being, as boys usually are, very *⁴officious to help*, and a great observer of the manner in which they worked those things, and sometimes *⁵lending a hand*, I *⁶had by these means full knowledge of the methods of it*, and I wanted nothing but the *⁷materials*. It came into my mind that the twigs of that tree from whence I cut my stakes that grew might possibly be as *⁸tough* as the *⁹sallows*, *¹⁰willows*, and *¹¹osiers* in England, and I resolved to try.

Accordingly, the next day I went to my *¹²country house*, as I called it, and *¹³cutting* some of the smaller twigs, I found them *¹⁴to my purpose* as much as I could desire; *¹⁵whereupon* I came the next time prepared with a *¹⁶hatchet* to cut down a quantity, which I soon found, for there was great *¹⁷plenty* of them. These I set up to dry within my *¹⁸circle*, or hedge, and when they were fit for use I carried them to my cave. Here, during the next season, I employed myself in making, as well as I could, a great many baskets, both to carry *¹⁹earth* and to carry or lay up anything, *²⁰as I had occasion*. Though I did not finish them very *²¹handsomely*, yet I made them *²²sufficiently serviceable for my purpose*; and thus, afterwards, I took care never to be without them. As my *²³wicker* ware *²⁴decayed*, I made more, *²⁵especially* strong, deep baskets to place my corn in, instead of *²⁶sacks*, when I should come to have any quantity of it.

Having *²⁷mastered this difficulty*, and *²⁸employed a world of time about it*, I *²⁹bestirred* myself to see, if possible, how to supply two wants. I had no *³⁰vessel* to hold anything that

現在這事是對我狠有益處的了，當我是一個小孩子的時候，我常常喜歡立在製籃子的人的店門口，店是在我父親住的城中，瞧他們製造柳枝編的器具。如同小孩子習慣一樣：我喜歡贊助不干己的事，一個瞧他們如何製造那些東西的觀察者，有時候給他們一臂之力；因此我深知其製造的法子，除去材料以外，我是毫無所缺的了。心中忽然想着我從那些樹裏割下來的椿木，牠們的樹枝或者能夠長得和（英國）的楊柳一般地堅硬，我逐決定試上一試。

第二天，我往我的村舍中去，我就這樣地叫牠，割了些較小的樹枝，我覺着牠們合我之用如我所希望一樣；於是第二次去的時候，我預備了一把小斧去砍下若干分量來，我立即成功，因為樹枝是非常之多的。我把牠們放在籬笆的中間晾乾；一經合用，我把牠們帶到洞穴中去。在那裏，在第二個季候的辰光，我儘力地製造了許多的籃子，為盛泥土和盛放傍的東西的用場，當我需要的時候。雖然我完成了牠們，不狠巧妙，然而使得牠們足以供我之用了；後來我狠小心，每逢出外：必定攜着牠們。柳枝作的器具朽爛了，我再製些堅固和深的籃子來放我的穀子，當我有了若干分量的穀子的時候，不再把牠們放在袋子裏面去了。

克服了困難，耗去了光陰，我起來觀察，如事勢可能，怎樣來供給兩個需要。

was [1]*liquid*, except two [2]*casks*. which were almost full of rum, and some glass bottles,—some of the common [3]*size*, and others which were case bottles, square, for the holding of water, [4]*spirits*, etc. I had not so much as a [5]*pot* to [6]*boil* anything, except a great [7]*kettle* which I saved out of the ship, and which was too big for such as I desired it, namely to make [8]*broth*, and stew a bit of meat by itself. The second thing I fain would have had was a tobacco [9]*pipe*, but it was [10]*impossible* to me to make one; however, I found a [11]*contrivance* for that, too, at last.

I employed myself in planting my second [12]*rows* of stakes or [13]*piles*, and in this wicker working, all the summer or dry season, when another business took me up more time than it could be [14]*imagined* I could [15]*spare*.

CHAPTER XXI

I MENTIONED before that I had a great mind to see the whole island, and that I had [16]*traveled* up the [17]*brook*, and so on to where I built my bower, and where I had an opening quite to the sea, on the other side of the island. I now resolved to travel quite [18]*across* to the seashore on that side. Taking my gun, a [19]*hatchet*, and my dog, and a larger quantity of powder and [20]*shot* than usual, with two biscuit cakes and a great bunch of [21]*raisins* in my [22]*pouch* for my store, I began my journey. When I had passed the vale where my bower [23]*stood*, as above, I [24]*came within view of* the sea to the [25]*west*. It being a very clear day I [26]*fairly descried* land—whether an island or a [27]*continent* I could not tell; but it lay very high, [28]*extending* from the west to the [29]*west-southwest* at a very great [30]*distance*. [31]*By my guess* it could not be less than fifteen or twenty [32]*leagues* off.

我沒有器皿來裝那些流汁的東西，除去兩個夠滿了甜酒的酒桶和幾隻玻璃瓶之外，——有幾隻是普通的樣子，其他皆是架上瓶，四方形的，為盛水，酒精之用的。我甚至連貯東西吃的罐兒都沒有，除去我從船中保留着的一隻大的鍋以外，牠是太大了對於我所希望用牠的去處，就是煨湯，和炎一塊肉。我極願要得的第二樁東西就是一隻烟管，然而我是不能製造出來；末了，我畢竟找出了一個計劃。

我忙着去種我的第二行椿木或是杙，一個乾燥的夏天就用在編這些東西上面，又有一種別的事務把我能夠節省下來的光陰耗去了不少，這是不能猜料得出的。

第 二 十 一 章

我先前曾說過我極有心來觀察全島，我走到了小溪上面；在那裏我造了一座小亭：在島的別一方面，完全對着海面（我有一座開豁的地方。現在我決定橫過去走到那方面海濱上去。拿了槍，小斧，和小狗；以及比平常多些的火藥和彈丸；兩塊餅乾和一大束葡萄乾；放在小袋裏面，貯藏起來，我開始我的路程。當我經過我的小亭豎立的地方的谷口；像從前一樣，我望見海的西面。天氣是非常晴朗，我遠遠望見陸地，或是一座島，或是大陸，我不能夠知道，但是牠立得非常之高；在很大的距離以內；從西方直向西偏西南方向舒展過去。照我思想起來，簡直不下於四十五或六十（英）里之遙。

（League—三英里）

I could not tell what part of the world this might be, otherwise than that I knew it must be part of America, and, as I [1]*concluded* by all my [2]*observations*, must be near the [3]*Spanish dominions*, and perhaps was all [4]*inhabited* by [5]*savages*, where, if I had landed, I had been in a [6]*worse* condition than I was now. Therefore I [7]*acquiesced in the dispositions of Providence*, which I began now to own and to believe ordered everything [8]*for the best*. I say I quieted my mind with this, and left off [9]*afflicting* myself with [10]*fruitless wishes* of being there.

Besides, after some thought upon this [11]*affair*, I considered that if this land was the Spanish [12]*coast*, I should certainly, [13]*one time or other*, see some [14]*vessel* pass or [15]*repass* one way or other; but if not, then it was the savage [16]*coast* between the Spanish country and Brazil, where are found the worst of [17]*savages*; for they are [18]*cannibals*, or [91]*men-eaters*, and [20]*fail not to murder* and [21]*devour* all the [22]*human bodies* that [23]*fall into their hands*.

With these [24]*considerations*, I [25]*walked very leisurely forward*. I found that side of the island where I now was much [26]*pleasanter* than mine,—the open or [27]*savannah* fields sweet, [28]*adorned with* flowers and grass, and full of very fine woods, I saw [19]*abundance* of [30]*parrots*, and fain would have [31]*caught* one, if possible, to have kept it to be [32]*tame*, and taught it to speak to me. I did, [33]*after some painstaking*, catch a young [34]*parrot*, for I [35]*knocked* it down with a [36]*stick*, and having [37]*recovered* it, I brough' it home. It was some years before I could make him speak; however, at last, I taught him to call me by name very [28]*familiarly*. But the [39]*accident* that followed, though it be a [40]*trifle*, will be very [41]*diverting* in its place.

　　我不知道這裏是世界上的那一部份，否則我想起來，這裏必是(美洲)的一部份，照我所有的觀察方面推斷，這裏必定靠近西班牙領土，或者是完全被野人占居着，倘使我在那裏登岸，我的景況一定比現在更劣。於是我把一切，委諸天命，現在我承認和相信上天，牠是吩咐着萬物都要向盡善盡美的方面行去。我說我用這思念來安慰我的心；把那些在那裏困苦我心身的妄想，一齊拋開。

　　其外，對於這事想了幾想以後，我注意着倘使這個陸地是(西班牙)的海岸，終究我一定能瞧見取徑不同來來往往的船舶；但是若非如此，那末這是在(西班牙)國和(巴勒喜爾)的中間的荒野的海岸了；在那裏有最壞的野人；因爲他們是吃人肉的東西，人體一經落在他們手中，必定殺而吞噬之。

　　有了這些考慮，我途緩步前進。我覺着現在我來到的這座島的側面是比我的那座島格外來得使人適意；——甘美的曠地和草地，花草繽紛，林木繁茂。我瞧見了許多鸚哥，倘使能夠這樣做，我極想捉住一隻來馴養和教牠對我說話。略費勞力之後，我捉住了一隻幼的鸚哥，我用手杖把牠打下來，使得牠恢復了元氣，我就把牠帶到家中。費了幾年工夫我纔能使得牠會說話；後來，我教牠用極慣熟的態度來叫喚我的名字。但是以下所遇的不測之事：雖然是瑣屑不足道，在牠的地位觀或者是很足賞心的呢。

1.決定.2. 觀察.2.西班牙領土。4.住居.5.野人.6.更壞。7.聽天由命.8. 俾可盡善.9.苦痛.10.妄想.11.事情.12. 海岸.13.終必.14. 船隻.15.重過.16.海濱.17.野人.18.吃人者.19.吃人者.20.必得而殺之.21.吞吃.22.人身.23.落於彼手.24.注意.25.緩步前行.26.較欣悅.27.平原.28.飾以.29.多量.30.鸚鵡.31.捉.32.馴之.33.略費辛苦.34.鸚哥.35. 敎.36. 棍. 37.使復元氣。38.慣熟.39.不測.40.小事.41.賞心。

I was [1]*exceedingly* diverted with this [2]*journey*, I found in the low grounds [3]*hares* (as I thought them to be) and foxes; but they differed greatly from all the other kinds I had met with, nor could I [4]*satisfy* myself to eat them, though I killed several. But I [5]*had no need to be venturous*, for I had no want of food, and of that which was very good, too, especially these three sorts, [6]*namely*: [7]*goats*, [8]*pigeons*, and turtle, or [9]*tortoise*, which, added to my grapes, Leadenhall market in London could not have [10]*furnished* a table better than I, [11]*in proportion to the company*. [12]*Though my case was deplorable enough*, [13]*yet I had great cause for thankfulness* [14]*that I was not driven to any extremities for food*, but had rather plenty, even to [15]*dainties*.

I never [16]*traveled* in this journey above two miles [17]*outright* in a day, or [18]*thereabouts*; but I [19]*took so many turns and returns* to see what [20]*discoveries* I could make, that I came weary enough to the place where I [21]*resolved* to sit down for all night. Then I either [22]*reposed* myself in a tree, or [23]*surrounded* myself with a [24]*row* of stakes set [25]*upright* in the ground, either from one tree to another, or so that no [26]*wild creature* could come at me without [27]*waking* me.

As soon as I came to the seashore, I was surprised to see that I had [28]*taken up my lot* on the [29]*worst* side of the island, for here, indeed, the shore was covered with [30]*innumerable* [31]*turtles*, whereas [32]*on the other side* I had found but three in a year and a half. Here also was an [33]*infinite number* of fowls of many kinds,—some which I had seen, and some which I had not seen before,—and many of them very good meat but such as I knew not the names of, [34]*except* those called [35]*penguins*.

我對於此次行程，非常賞心愜意。在低的地面上，我瞧見了野兔（我想起來或者是的）和狐狸；但是牠們同我曾經遇見的各種，樣子很是不同，雖然我殺了幾個，我也不能滿足自己來吃牠們。然而我也不必冒這險，因為我並不缺乏食物，所有的食物都是很好的，尤其是下面三種，就是：山羊，鴿子，鼈或龜，再加上葡萄，照人數比例起來說。就是（倫敦）城中的（利登）菜館也辦不出比我所辦的較好的一桌筵席，雖然我的景況是很為可憫的，然而我有感謝上天的原因，我不至於受絕糧的困阨，不過食物不能豐盛，珍饈不能到口而已。

我永不在這次行程中，一時間於一天內就走上兩（英）里左近；但是俳徊往來，瞧瞧能發見什麼東西，等我來到我所決定坐而度夜的地方，已經甚是疲乏了。於是我或者在樹中憩息，或者把樹立地上的椿木圍住我的身子，或者從此樹往彼樹，這樣那些野的生物，在我睡眠之中，不會來侵襲我了。

一經到了海岸，我很驚異地瞧我已經在這島上最劣的一面擇定了命運了，這裏，實在，海岸上充滿了無數的鼈；然而在岸的那一面，在一年有半的辰光，我僅僅找着了三隻。這裏也有各種無限數的禽鳥，——有些我曾見過，有些我未曾見過，—— 牠們之中有許多是很好的饌饈，除去那些叫做企鵝的以外，其餘的叫什麼名字，我是一概不知。

I could have shot as many as I ¹*pleased*, but was very
²*sparing* of my ³*powder* and shot, and therefore had more
mind to kill a she-goat, if I could, which I could better
feed on. Though there were many ⁴*goats* here, more than
on my side the island, yet it was with much more ⁵*difficulty*
that I could come near them, the country being ⁶*flat and
even*, and they saw me much sooner than when I was on
the ⁷*hills*.

I ⁸*confess* this side of the country was much ⁹*pleasanter*
than mine; but yet I had not the least ¹⁰*inclination* to
¹¹*remove*, for as I was fixed in my habitation it became
natural to me. I seemed all the while I was here to be as
it were upon a journey, and from home. However, I
traveled along the shore of the sea towards the east, I
¹²*suppose* about twelve miles. Then, ¹³*setting up* a great
pole upon the shore for a ¹⁴*mark*, I concluded I would go
home again, and that the next ¹⁵*journey* I took should be
on the other side of the island, east from my ¹⁶*dwelling*,
and so round till I came to my post again.

I took another way to come back than that I went,
thinking I could ¹⁷*easily* ¹⁸*keep* all the island so much in my
view that I could not ¹⁹*miss* finding my first ²⁰*dwelling* by
²¹*viewing* the country. But I found myself ²²*mistaken*, for,
being come about two or three miles, I found myself
²³*descended* into a very large ²⁴*valley*, but so ²⁵*surrounded* with
hills, and those hills so covered with wood, that I could
not see which was my way by any ²⁶*direction* but that of
the sun, ²⁷*nor even then*, unless I knew very well the
²⁸*position* of the sun at that time of the day. It happened,
to my further ²⁹*misfortune*, that the weather ³⁰*proved* ³¹*hazy*
for three or four days while I was in the ³²*valley*, and not

我願意射擊多少，就能射擊多少；但是藥粉和彈丸必須要省儉着使用，所以我極願射殺一隻母山羊，若果可能，那末我就能享用得較好了。這裏雖然有許多山羊，比較島上我的那一方面更加的多，然而要想靠近牠們，必定要費去許多勞力方可，地方是平坦得狠，一經我到小山上面，牠們已經很仔細地瞧見我了。

我承認這地方的這一面比起我的那一面來是更使人欣悅，但是我毫無遷移的念頭，因爲我已經擇定了我的住所，牠對我已是很自然的了。一時瞧起來好像我在這個地方是從家中出去旅行一樣。我沿着海岸向東方行去，我想大約是十二(英)里，於是在海岸上插立一根大柱作爲標記，我決定再回家去，下次行程，須到島的別面，從我住所的東面，這樣兜轉，直到木柱爲止。

我走另外的一條路回家，想想我能夠很容易地把全島的景色，一覽無餘，察看這個地方，我就不至於尋不着我的第一次的住所了。但是我又自覺錯誤，因爲，走了大約二三(英)里遠近，我覺得降到一座很大的山谷裏面，四圍皆小山，小山被林木□蓋，除去被太陽的指示以外，其他的指示皆不能使我尋出我的歸路來，在這天那個辰光，若是我不很明白太陽所在的地位，恐怕此事也是無濟。更加使我不幸，天氣忽然靄障起來，有三四天之久，當我在山谷裏面的時候，

being able to see the sun, I wandered about very ¹*uncomfortably*. At last I was ²*obliged* to find the ³*seaside*, look for my ⁴*post*, and come back the same way I went. Then, by easy journeys, I ⁵*turned homeward*, the weather being exceeding hot, and my gun, ⁶*ammunition*, hatched, and other things, very heavy.

In this journey my dog surprised a young ⁷*kid*, and ⁸*seized upon* it; and I, running in to ⁹*take hold of it*, caught it, and saved it alive from the dog. I had a great mind to bring it home if I could, for I had often been ¹⁰*musing* whether it might not be possible to get a kid or two, and so ¹¹*raise* a ¹²*breed* of tame goats, which might supply me when my powder and shot should all be ¹³*spent*. I made a ¹⁴*collar* for this little creature, and with a ¹⁵*string*, which I made of some ¹⁶*rope* ¹⁷*yarn*, which I always carried about me, I led him along, though with some ¹⁸*difficulty*, till I came to my bower. There I ¹⁹*inclosed* him and left him, for I was ²⁰*very impatient to be at home*, from whence I had been ²¹*absent above a month*.

I cannot ²²*express* what a ²³*satisfaction* it was to me to come into my old hut, and lie down in my ²⁴*hammock* bed. This little wandering journey, without ²⁵*settled* place of abode, had been so ²⁶*unpleasant* to me that my own house, as I called it to myself, was a perfect ²⁷*settlement* to me compared to that; and it ²⁸*rendered* everything about me so ²⁹*comfortable* that I resolved I would never go a great way from it again, while it should be my lot to ³⁰*stay on* the island.

I ³¹*reposed* myself here a week, to rest and ³²*regale* myself after my long journey: during which, most of the time was ³³*taken up in* the ³⁴*weighty affair* of making a ³⁵*cage* for

我不能瞧見太陽，很不安地漫步行。最後，我是必須要尋出海岸，搜尋我所插立的柱子，囘到我來的路上去。於是，經過一次很容易的行程，我轉身向家而行，天氣熱極，我的槍，彈實，斧，以及傍的東西都是很重的。

在這次行程之中，我的狗驚起了一隻幼的小山羊，捉住了牠；我跑去執着牠，捉着牠，把牠從狗的口內活活地救了出來。倘使我能夠這樣地做，我極願把牠帶囘家中，因爲我常常地沉思着不知道能不能得着一二隻小山羊，豢養成功一羣馴的山羊，當我藥粉和彈丸耗盡之時，牠們可以供給我作食料。我爲這個小生物做了一個頸圈，我用隨身帶着的繩線做了一根小索，我稍爲感着些困難來牽著牠走，直到我的小享爲止。在那裏我圈住牠，離開牠，因爲我是急欲囘家，我離家已有一月餘了。

來到了舊茅舍和睡在吊床上面以後。我不知用什麼言詞來表示我的滿意纔好。這次流蕩無歸宿地的旅行對於我恨不快意的，我自稱屬我的房屋和那個比較起來，簡直可稱爲完全的寓所了；牠使我身旁的東西這樣的安適，以致於我決定了以後我再不離牠還去，我居留在這島上，大概是我命運使然的。

我在這裏休憩了一星期，長途旅行之後，必須休養和享樂的；一牛的辰光是用在爲鸚哥製造一隻籠兒的緊要的事情上面去，牠

my [1]*Poll,* who began now to be a [2]*mere domestic,* and to be well [3]*acquainted* with me.　Then I began to think of

the poor kid which I had [4]*penned in* within my little circle, and resolved to go and [5]*fetch* it home, or give it some food.

Accordingly I went, and found it where I left it, for indeed it could not, get out but, was [6]*almost starved for* [7]*want of food.*　I went and cut [8]*boughs* of trees, and [9]*branches*

現在是一隻純全的家畜了，對於我是很熟識的了。于是我開始想着那個被我關閉在小圈裏面的可憐的小山羊，決定去把牠帶回來，或者去給牠些食物。

我立卽前往，在我離開牠的地方找着了牠，牠實在是不能夠出外，差不多因缺少食物而餓斃了。我去割些樹的嫩枝和灌木的枝子，我找得着便割將下來，投而飼之，喂了牠之後，我像以前一樣的繫着牠，領牠走，牠因爲肚裏餓所以這樣馴，隨着我走像一匹狗一般，我竟不必要去繫着牠了。

1. 鸚哥. 2. 純然家畜.
3. 熟悉. 4. 關閉於. 5.
帶來. 6. 幾乎餓死. 7.
因缺乏食物. 8. 嫩枝.
9. 枝葉.

of such ¹*shrubs* as I could find, and ²*threw over to it,* and having fed it, I tied it as I did before, to lead it away, but it was so tame with being ³*hungry* that I had no need to have ⁴*tied* it, for it followed me like a dog. As I ⁵*continually fed it,* the creature became so loving, so gentle, and so ⁶*fond,* that it became from that time one of my ⁷*domestics* also, and would never leave me afterwards.

The ⁸*rainy season* of the ⁹*autumnal equinox* was now come, and I kept the 30th of September in the same ¹⁰*solemn* manner as before, it being the ¹¹*anniversary* of my landing on the ¹²*island,* having now been there two years, with no more ¹³*prospect* of being ¹⁴*delivered* than the first day I came there. I ¹⁵*spent* the whole day in ¹⁶*humble* and thankful ¹⁷*acknowledgments* of the many wonderful ¹⁸*mercies* which my ¹⁹*solitary* condition was ²⁰*attended* with, and without which it might have been ²¹*infinitely* more ²²*miserable.* I gave ²³*humble* and hearty thanks that God had been pleased to discover to me that it was possible I might be more happy in this ²⁴*solitary* condition than I should have been in the liberty of ²⁵*society* and in all the pleasures of the world.

It was now that I began ²⁶*sensibly* to feel how much more happy this life I now led was, with all its miserable ²⁷*circumstances,* than the ²⁸*wicked,* ²⁹*cursed,* ³⁰*abominable* life *I* led all the past part of my days. Now I ³¹*changed* both my ³²*sorrows* and my joys; my very desires ³³*altered,* ³⁴*my affections changed their gusts,* and my delights were perfectly new from what they were at my first coming or, indeed, for the two years past.

Before, as I walked about, either on my ³⁵*hunting,* or for ³⁶*viewing* the country, the ³⁷*anguish* of my ³⁸*soul* at my

我常常飼養牠，這個生物變得這樣的可愛，這樣的柔和，和這樣地討歡喜，從此以後，牠便變成我的一個馴僕，永遠不離開我。

秋分多雨時季現在來了，我像從前一樣很恭重的保守著九月三十日，這天是我登陸的紀念日，現在在島上有二年了，無有更多的獲救希望如我第一日到這裏一樣。這一天的一個整日子我都用在用謙卑不和感謝的態度來答謝那些希奇的恩惠上面，牠們是伴着我的孤獨的景況的，沒有牠們，我格外的不幸了。我謙卑和誠心感謝着，上帝願使我明白我在這個孤獨的景況裏面是比在那些自由的社會和快樂的世界裏面還要樂意得多呢。

現在我覺得我過着這種不幸的景況的生活是比我從前一部份時候過的卑下，可惡，可憎的生活是要快樂的多呢。現在我把憂愁和快樂都改變過來；我的願望也轉移了，我的性情也頓改了，我的樂趣比我第一次來的時候，或者，實在講起來，兩年以前的樂趣是完全趣於新的途徑了。

以前，當我俳徊散步之時，或者去打獵，或者去察看地方光景，對於我的處境心中的悲慘念頭，突然地便會發現，

1,灌木。2.投而飼之。3.飢。4.繫。5.常飼之。6.可愛。7.奴。8.多雨之季。9.秋分。10.莊重。11.紀念日。12.島。13.希望。14.獲救。15.用。16.卑下。17.答謝。18.恩惠。19.孤寂。20.伴以。21.無限地。22.不幸。23.卑下。24.孤寂。25.社會。26.覺得。27.情形。28.卑賤。29.可惡。30.可憎。31.改變。32.憂愁。33.改換。34.性情頓然改變。35.打獵。36.察看。37.悲慘。38.心靈。

condition would ¹*break out upon me on a sudden* and my very heart would die within me, to think of the ²*wood*, the mountains, the deserts I was in, and how I was a ³*prisoner*, ⁴*looked up* with the ⁵*eternal bars* and ⁶*bolts* of the ocean, in an ⁷*uninhabited* ⁸*wilderness*, ⁹*without redemption*. In the ¹⁰*midst* of the greatest ¹¹*composure of my mind*, this would ¹²*break out* upon me like a ¹³*storm*, and make me ¹⁴*wring my hands* and ¹⁵*weep* like a child. Sometimes it would take me in the middle of my work, and I would ¹⁶*immediately* sit down and ¹⁷*sigh*, and look upon the ground for an hour or two together; and this was still worse to me, for if I could ¹⁸*burst out into tears*, ¹⁹*or vent myself by words*, it would go off, and the ²⁰*grief*, having ²¹*exhausted* itself, would ²²*abate*.

But now I began to exercise myself with new thoughts. I ²³*daily* read the word of God, and ²⁴*applied* all the ²⁵*comforts* of it to my present state. One morning, being very sad, I opened the Bible upon these words: " I will never, never leave thee, nor ²⁶*forsake* thee." Immediately it ²⁷*occurred* that these words were to me. Why else should they be ²⁸*directed* in such a manner, just at the moment when I was ²⁹*mourning* over my condition as one ³⁰*forsaken* of God and man? " Well, then," said I, " if God does not forsake me, ³¹*of what ill consequence can it be*, or what matters it, thought the world should all forsake me, seeing on the other hand, ³²*if I had all the world*, and should lose the favor and ³³*blessing* of God, ³⁴*there would be no comparison in the loss*?"

From this ³⁵*moment* I began to ³⁶*conclude* in my mind that it was possible for me to be more happy in this forsaken, ³⁷*solitary condition*, than it was ³⁸*probable* I should ever have been in any other particular state in the world. Though I could not say I thanked God for being there, yet I sincerely

我的心在胸中也要死去了，只要想着樹林，山，我現住在的荒地，以及我如何變成拘囚，受海洋中關塞和障壁永遠的禁錮；在一個無人隱住的荒島上面，毫無拯救的希望。在我心最甯靜的中間，這個思想像暴風雨一般突然向我發現，使得我堅握着手，號泣起來和小孩子一樣。有時在我工作之中，這種思念便佔據着我了，我便立刻坐下來嘆息，注視着地面一二個整鐘頭不少瞬，這對於我尤其不好，因為倘使我能放聲大哭，或用言語發洩，那末牠便離去了，憂愁旣經殫竭，亦可稍抑了。

現在我開始着用新思想來訓練自已。每天我念誦上帝的話，把他話中的一切安慰用到我現在的景況上來。一天早晨，身體很倦，我展開了聖經，瞧見了這些話："我將永遠地，永遠地不離開你，亦不捨棄你。"馬上我覺得這些話是對我說的，當我恰正在被上帝和人類抛棄，觸景傷情的時候，為什麼這些話用這樣的態度來指點呢？"那末很好"，我說，若是上帝不抛棄我，結果那能夠比這個更甚，又有什麼關係，雖然全世界抛棄我，在別一方面瞧起來，倘使我得世界上的人心，和失去了上帝的福佑和恩眷，那末所受的損失，還尋得出比較嗎？"

從此以後，我心中決定着在這種秘棄和孤獨的景況中，或者能夠更為快樂，比較在世界上其他特別的景況中尤甚。雖然我不能說因為我在那裏便感謝着上帝，然而我卻誠誠懇懇

1.忽然發現．2.林．3.囚．4.關閉．5.永濱禁錮．6.海洋的關塞．7.無人住的．8.荒野．9.無拯救之機．10.中間．11.心中泰然．12.發現．13.暴風雨．14.緊握手．15.哭．16.立卽．17.歎．18.放聲大哭．19.用言語發洩．20.憂愁．21.殫竭．22.減．23.每月．24.施用．25.安慰．26.捨卻．27.偶遇．28.指點．29.觸景傷情．30.被天人所棄．31.結果不能較劣於此．32.倘得人望．33.福佑．34.所受損失，矛能比較．35.時間．36.決斷．37.孤寂生活．38.或者

gave thanks to God for opening my eyes to see the ¹*former* condition of my life, and to ²*mourn for my wickedness*, and ³*repent*. I never opened the Bible, or shut it, but my very soul within me *blessed* God for directing my friend in England, without any order of mine, to pack it up among my goods, and for ⁵*assisting* me afterwards to save it out of the ⁶*wreck* of the ship.

CHAPTER XXII

THUS, and in this ⁷*disposition of mind*, I began my third year. Though I have not given the ⁸*reader* the trouble of so particular ⁹*an account of* my works this year as the first, yet in general it may be observed that I was ¹⁰*very seldom idle*, having ¹¹*regularly* divided my time according to the several ¹²*daily* ¹³*employments* that were before me; such as first, my duty to God, and the reading the ¹⁴*Scriptures*, which I ¹⁵*constantly* ¹⁶*set apart some time for*, thrice every day; secondly, the going abroad with my gun for food, which ¹⁷*generally* took me about three hours in every morning, when it did not rain; thirdly, the ordering, ¹⁸*cutting*, ¹⁹*preserving*, and ²⁰*cooking* what I had killed or ²¹*caught* for my supply. These took up great part of the day. Also it is to be considered that in the middle of the day, when the sun was in the ²²*zenith*, the ²³*violence* of the ²⁴*heat* was too great ²⁵*to stir out*. About four hours in the evening was all the time I could be ²⁶*supposed* to work in, with this exception, that sometimes I changed my hours of ²⁷*hunting* and working, and went to work in the morning, and abroad with my gun in the afternoon.

地獄給他我的謝意，因爲他使我瞧着我以前生活的狀況，悲痛我從前的過失和悔恨着。一經展開或是合攏着聖經，我的心靈就感謝着上帝，因爲他在(英)國指點着我的朋友；沒有我的囑咐，就把聖經包裹在我的行李裏面，他又幫助我後來從船的破壞中把他保存著出來。

第 二 十 二 章

在這種心境之中，我的第三年開始了。雖然這一年我不像從前給讀者我的工作的特別的報告，然而大概可以說我是不常常偷嬾的，照每日當前的事務而斷，我按秩序把時光分派起來；例如，第一，我對上帝的本分，誦讀聖經，爲作這事，我特定了幾個時刻，每日三次；第二，攜搶出外尋食，每早大概須費三小時在這事上面，當不落雨的時候；第三，整理，削割，醃製，烹調那些我所殺或捉住的東西，以供佐餐之用。這些事務把一天的光陰耗去了一大半。雖然也應當注意着在日中的時候，太陽高及天頂，熱度強烈已極，不能出外。大約在晚上四個鐘頭，這就是我料想着我所能工作的時間了，除去這個例外，有些時候，我把我的打獵和工作的時候改變過來，早上去作工，下午攜着槍出外。

To this short time allowed for labor I desire may be added the [1]*exceeding* [2]*laboriousness* of my work; the many hours which, for want of tools, want of help, and want of skill, everything I did took up out of my time. For example I was full two and forty days in making a board for a long shelf which I wanted in my cave; whereas two [3]*sawyers*, with their tools and a [4]*saw pit*, would have cut six of them out of the same tree in half a day.

My [5]*case* was this. It was to be a large tree which was to be [6]*cut down*, because my board was to be a broad one. This tree I was three days in cutting down, and two more cutting off the boughs and [7]*reducing* it to a [8]*log*, or piece of [9]*timber*. With [10]*inexpressible* [11]*hacking* and [12]*hewing* I reduced both the sides of it into [13]*chips*, till it began to be [14]*light* enough to move. Then I turned it, and made one side of it [15]*smooth* and flat as a board [16]*from end to end*. Then, turning that side [17]*downward*, I cut the other side till I brought the [18]*plank* to be about three inches thick, and smooth on both sides. Any one may [19]*judge* the labor of my hands in such a piece of work; but labor and [20]*patience* carried me through that, and many other things.

I only observe this [21]*in particular*, to show the reason why so much of my time went away with so little work; namely, that what might be a little to be done with help and tools, was a vast labor and [22]*required* a [23]*prodigious* time to do alone, and by hand. But [24]*notwithstanding* this, with patience and labor I [25]*got through* everything that my [26]*circumstances* made necessary to me to do, [27]*as will appear by what follows*.

I was now, in the months of November and December, expecting my [28]*crop* of barley and [29]*rice*. The ground I had

對於我希望工作的短的辰光可以再加上我極勞苦的工作；許多辰光，因爲缺少器具，缺少幫助，缺少技能，我所做的事都費去我的時候。例如，我整整費去四十二天光陰去製造一個木板來放在一隻長的架子上面，這樣東西我的穴中是不能夠缺少的；然而兩個鋸木匠，用他們的器具和鋸木坑，在半天辰光，從同樣的樹中可以作成六個。

我的事務是這樣。須把一株大樹砍來，因爲我的木板是很寬的。費去三天辰光，我把這樹砍下，又費去兩天工夫，把牠的枝葉削去，使牠變成一根大木頭，或者是一大塊木料。用了非言語所能形容的斫砍工夫，我把樹的兩邊弄成了木片，直到牠輕而易動爲止。於是我把牠翻轉來，把一邊弄得光滑和平坦，從頭至尾，像木板一樣。於是，把那一邊向下翻過去，我削這一邊，直到板兒約有三寸厚和雙面光滑方止。在這樣工作的裏面，我兩手的勞苦，任是誰都能評判得出的；然而勞力和忍耐力却使我弄成功了這個工作和別的事務。

我僅僅特別地考察這個，說出爲什麼做這種小工作却費去這許多的辰光的緣故來；就是，得了幫助和器具不很費力的工作，用起手來，就要費去很大的勞力並且需要一個極長的時候，方能做畢。但是雖然如此，用了忍耐力和勞力，我把環境裏面我所需要的事都做成了，對於這點，下文當詳述之。

我現在是，在十一月和十二月裏面，希望着大麥和米的收穫。

[1]*manured* and dug up for them was not great; for, as I observed, my seed of each was not above the [2]*quantity* of half a [3]*peck*, for I had lost one whole [4]*crop* by [5]*sowing* in the dry season. But now my crop [6]*promised* very well, when on a [7]*sudden* I found I was [8]*in danger of losing it* all again by [9]*enemies* of several [10]*sorts*, which it was [11]*scarcely* possible to keep from it. First the goats, and wild [12]*creatures* which I called hares, who, [13]*tasting* the [14]*sweetness* of the [15]*blade*, lay in it night and day, as soon as it came up, and ate it so [16]*close* that it [17]*could get no time to shoot up into stalk*.

This I saw no [18]*remedy* for but by making an [19]*inclosure* about it with a [20]*hedge*, which I did [21]*with a great deal of toil*; and the more, because it [22]*required* [23]*speed*. However, as my [24]*arable land* was but small, [25]*suited* to my [26]*crop*, I got it totally well fenced in about three weeks' time; and [27]*shooting* some of the creatures in the daytime, I set my dog to guard it in the night, tying him up to a stake at the gate, where he would stand and [28]*bark* [29]*all night long*; So in a little time the [30]*enemies* [31]*forsook* the place, and the corn grew very strong and well, and began to [32]*ripen* [33]*apace*.

But as the beasts [34]*ruined* me before, while my corn was in the [35]*blade*, so the birds were as likely to [36]*ruin* me now, when it was in the ear; for, going along by the place to see how it [37]*throve*, I saw my little crop surrounded with fowls, of I know not how many sorts, who stood, as it were, [38]*watching* till I should be gone. I immediately [39]*let fly* among them, for I always had my gun with me. I had no sooner shot, but there rose up a little [40]*cloud* of fowls, which I had not seen at all, from among the corn

我爲牠們壅糞和搰起的土地是不寬大的；照我觀察而論，我的各種種子的分量不在半斗之上，因爲我在乾燥時季播種，已把整個的收成失去了。但是現在我的收穫到很有希望，忽然之間，我覺察因有幾樣的敵人，我的收穫又有全失的危險，這種敵人到很不容易防備的呢。第一，山羊們和野的生物，我叫做野兔的，嚐着了葉子的甘味，一經葉子長出，牠們就日夜躺在葉兒裏面：把葉子喫得這樣的短，以致於牠來不及發生，變成梗子了。

除去造一籬笆來圍着以外，我覺得沒有別的補救的方法了，我費了許多工夫方把圍牆造成，因爲這個工作需要的是急速，所以力氣更費了不少。可耕種和合乎收穫的田地是很小的，費了大約三個星期的辰光，我把田地完全掩護好了；白天的時候，射擊了幾個生物，晚上我叫狗看守田地，把牠繫在門旁椿上，在那裏，牠可以通宵達旦地站住和狂吠。這樣過了些時，那些敵人便捨棄了這個地方，穀子長得很高很好，開始着趕快的結熟了。

在前，野獸損壞我，當我的殼子在葉子裏面的時候；現在鳥兒又來損壞我，當殼子在穗的裏面；到那個地方去看殼子怎樣的生殖起來，我見許多禽鳥圍繞着我的小的殼子，這些禽鳥，我不知道是何種類，牠們站在那裏宛如候我動身一般。我立卽在牠們中間放槍，因爲我槍是不離身的。一經開槍，從殼子裏面立刻飛起了一小羣禽鳥；起頭我到未曾瞧見牠們呢。

1.壅糞. 2.分量, 3.斗. 4.收成. 5.種. 6.有望. 7.突然. 8.有全失望之虞. 9.敵. 10.種. 11.很少. 12.生物. 13.嚐. 14.甘味. 15.葉. 16.短. 17.不及發生成莖. 18.救藥. 19.圍地. 20.籬笆. 21.大費氣力. 2?.需要. 23.急速. 24.可耕之地. 25.合乎. 26.收穫. 27.射. 28.吠. 29.通夜. 30.敵. 31.捨去. 32.熟. 33.快. 34.損壞. 35.葉. 36.損壞. 37.生殖. 8.守候. 39.放射. 403羣.

This touched me [1]*sensibly*, for I [2]*foresaw* that in a few days they would [3]*devour* all my hopes, that I should be [4]*starved*, and never be able to raise a crop at all ; and what to do I could not tell. However, I resolved not to lose my corn, if possible, though I should watch it night and day. In the first place, I went among it, to see what [5]*damage* was already done, and found they had [6]*spoiled* a good deal of it. But as it was yet too green for them, the loss was not so great but that the [7]*remainder* was likely to be a good [8]*crop*, if it could be saved.

I [9]*staid* by it to load my gun, and then coming away, I could easily see the thieves sitting upon all the trees about me, as if they only [10]*waited* till I was gone away. The event [11]*proved* it to be so ; for as I walked off, as if I was gone, I was no sooner [12]*out of their sight* than they [13]*dropped down* one by one into the corn again. I was so [14]*provoked* that I could not have [15]*patience* to stay till more came on, knowing that every [16]*grain* that they ate now was, as it might be said, [17]*a peck loaf* to me in the [18]*consequence* : but coming up to the hedge, I fired again, and killed three of them. This was what I wished for. I took them up, and [19]*served* them as we serve [20]*notorious thieves* in England,— [21]*hanged them in chains, for a terror to others*. It is [22]*impossible* to imagine that this should have such an [23]*effect* as it had, for the [24]*fowls* would not only not come at the corn, but, in short, they [25]*forsook* all that part of the island, and I could never see a bird near the place as long as my [26]*scarecrows* hung there. This I was very glad of, you may be sure, and about the latter end of December, which was our second [27]*harvest* of the year, I [28]*reaped my corn*.

這事使我很受着感觸，我預料幾天以內，牠們將要把我所有的收穫完全喫掉，我必要捱餓，永遠不能再培養成功一個收穫；我應當做些什麼，我却不能知道哩。然而，我决意不使失去我的穀子，假使能行的話，那末我到要日夜地來守着牠了。第一步，我走到穀子裏面去看看，已經釀成了什麼損害，覺察了鳥兒已經損害了不少的穀子。但是穀子對於牠們是很生的，損失到不過於大，倘然餘留的可以保存起來，或者還可以得一好的收成。

我站在牠的旁邊裝好了槍彈，漫步前進，我很容易地看見那些偷穀的賊坐在我身旁的樹上，好像牠們是候着我動身一般。事實證明是這樣；我漫步前行，宛如我離去一樣，我一經在牠們視線以外，牠們便一個一個的重行下降到穀的裏面去了。我是這樣地被激怒了，不能再忍耐下去，等到再有許多鳥兒來，我明白現在牠們喫的每粒穀子，可以這般地講，結果對於我却是一斗大的麵包呢；但是來到籬邊，我重行放槍，殺了三隻鳥兒。這就是我所希望做的事了。我把牠們拿起來，待遇牠們好像我們在(英)國待遇劇盜一樣，一懸以鐵鍊，以警傚尤。這種舉動所得的效果是不能預料着的，禽鳥非特不來到穀子裏面，而且離開了這座島的各部份，一經那個鏈鎖的鳥兒繫在那裏，我沒有看見一隻鳥兒飛近這個地方。你可以確知，這事使我很快樂，大約十二月下旬，那是我們一年中的第二次收穫期，我於是收穫了禾穀。

1.感觸狀。2.預知。3.吞吃。4.捱餓。52損害。6.損壞。7.餘留。8.收成。9.站。10.等。11.證明。12.在視線以外。13.下降。14.激怒。15.忍耐心。16.穀子。17.一斗大之麵包。18.結果。19.優遇。20.劇盜。21.懸以鐵鍊以警傚尤。22.不能。23.效果。24.禽鳥。25.捨去。26.草人。27.收穫期。23.收穫禾穀。

I [1]*was sadly put to it for a scythe or sickle* to cut it down, and all I could do was to make one, as well as I could, out of one of the [2]*broadswords*, or [3]*cutlasses*, which I saved among the [4]*arms* out of the ship. However, as my first [5]*crop* was but small, I had no great [6]*difficulty* to cut it down. In short, I [7]*reaped* it in my way, for I cut nothing off but the ears, and carried it away in a great basket which I had made, and so [8]*rubbed* it out with my hands. At the end of all my [9]*harvesting*, I found that out of my half peck of seed I had near two [10]*bushels* of rice, and about two [11]*dushels* and a half of barley; that is to say, [12]*by my guess*, for I had no [13]*measure* at that time.

However. this was a great [14]*encouragement* to me, and I [15]*foresaw* that, in time, it would please God to [16]*supply* me with bread. And yet here I was [17]*perplexed* again, for I neither knew how to [18]*grind*, or [19]*make meal of my corn*, or, indeed, how to clean it and part it; nor, if made into meal, how to make bread of it; and if how to make it, yet I knew not how [20]*to bake* it.

These things being added to my desire of having a good quantiy for [21]*store*, and to [22]*sesure* a [23]*constant* supply, I [24]*resolved* not to taste any of this crop, but to [25]*preserve* it all for seed agaiust the next season; and, in the mean time, to employ all my study and hours of working to [26]*accomplish* this great work of [27]*providing* myself with corn and bread.

It might be truly said that now I worked for my bread. I believe few people have thought much upon the [28]*strange* [29]*multitude* of little things necessary in the providing, [30]*producing*, [31]*curing*, [32]*dressing*, making, and finishing [33]*this one article of bread*.

　　因爲割穀子要有一把鐮刀的緣故，我是很爲困難的；我所能做的事就是要儘力從我的腰刀上面去製造一把出來，腰刀是我從船中軍器裏面保留出來的。第一次收穫分量是很少的，割牠下來到不大費事。總而言之，我用我的方法來收穫穀子，我僅把穗兒割去，用我製的一個大籃子把牠帶走，用我的手把牠摩擦掉。在收穫期終止以後，我覺着我從半斗種子當中得着了差不多兩斗米；大約兩斗大麥；這是照我猜測而斷定的，因爲在那個時候，我沒有量器。

　　這事對於我是很鼓勵的，我預知不久上帝將要用麵包來供給我了。然而我卻又困憊起來，因爲我旣不知道怎樣去研，磨穀成粉，實在說起來，怎樣去把牠弄乾淨和把牠分開；就是做成粉了，我又不知道怎樣把牠做成麵包；卽使成麵包，我又不知道怎樣去焙炙牠呢。

　　這些東西使我希望着貯藏一個很多分量的穀來，因爲想得着常久的供給物，我決定不去賣這些收穫物，把牠們保存起來做下季種子的用場；在平均的時候，利用我的研究和工作的時候來完成用穀子和麵包供給自己的一種大的工作。

　　這是可以照實說的，現在我做着麵包的工作。我相信很少的人們曾經想到許多很小的工作是需要于做麵包的工作，如同，生產，炒，賣，以及製造等事，

I, that was [1]*reduced* to a [2]*mere state of nature*, found this to my daily [3]*discouragement*; and was made more [4]*sensible* of it every hour, even after I got the first [5]*handful* of seed corn, which, as I have said, came up [6]*unexpectedly*, and indeed as a [7]*surprise*.

First, I had no [8]*plow* to [9]*turn up* the earth, no [10]*spade* or [11]*shovel* to dig it. Well, this I [12]*conquered* by making me a wooden spade, as I observed before. But this did my work but in a [13]*wooden* manner; and though it cost me a great many days to make it, yet for want of iron, it not only wore out soon, but made my work the [14]*harder,* and made it be [15]*performed* much [16]*worse*. However, this I [17]*bore with*, and was [18]*content* to [19]*work it out* wiih [20]*patience*, and bear with the [21]*badness of the performence*. When the [22]*corn* was [23]*sown*, I had no [24]*harrow*, but was forced to [25]*go over* it myself, and [26]*drag* a great [27]*heavy* bough of a tree over it, to [28]*scratch* it, as it may be called, rather than [29]*rake or harrow* it.

When it was [30]*growing*, and grown, I have observed already how many things I wanted to fence it, [31]*secure* it, [32]*mow* or [33]*reap* it, cure and carry it home, [34]*thrash* it, [35]*part it from the chaff* and save it. Then I wanted a [36]*mill* to [37]*grind* it, [38]*sieves* to dress it, [39]*yeast* and salt to make it into bread, and an [40]*oven* to bake it. [41]*All these things I did without,* as shall be observed, and yet the corn was an [42]*inestimable* comfort and advantage to me, too. All this, as I said, made every thing [43]*laborious* and [44]*tedious* to me; but that [45]*there was no help for.* Neither was my time so much loss to me, because, as I had divided it, a [46]*certain part* of it was every day [47]*appointed* to these works. And as I had resolved to use none of the corn for bread till I had a greater [48]*quantity* by me, I had the next six months to

弄到一身之外，別無長物的時候，我覺着每日對於這個皆是失望，就是我得着我曾經說過那些出乎意外和使我吃驚生長的第一把穀子以後，每個時辰我還是覺得更加有感觸。

第一，我沒有犁來鋤掘地土，沒有鏟子或是鍬來剗牠。像我從前觀察着一樣，我造成一隻木鏟，這個困難便克服了。但是這個鏟兒工作起來，非常愚蠢；雖然費去許多日子方能把牠造好，然而因爲缺少鐵貨，牠不但馬上就被用壞了，而且把我的工作弄得更難，使得我的工作進行更劣。對於這事，我權且忍耐住，滿意地想用堅忍心把工作成就，和 忍受着工作惡劣。當穀子播種下去的時候，我沒有耙子，強迫着走穀子上面行過去，在牠上面，我拖曳着一根重的樹枝，抓搔牠，可以這樣地講，並不是去把耙鋤牠。

當穀子漸長和長成的時候，我已經覺察了要想圍住牠，保存牠，芟刈牠或是收穫牠，晾乾牠帶回家去，打牠，簸去牠的粃糠，貯藏牠，我是缺少很多的物品呢。我缺少一個窖子去研牠，一隻火爐去焙炙牠。篩子去調和牠，酵和鹽去把牠製成麵包，這些物品我都沒有，可以觀察出來的，然而穀子對我却也是一種無價值的安慰和利益呢。攏總這些東西，如我所說的一樣，使得各種事務對於我皆覺費力和煩厭；然亦無可如何。我也不失去許多的辰光，因爲我把牠分開來，每日時間的一部份是用在這些工作上面。我決定非俟我有較多分量穀子的時候，我不將我製成麵包，

1. 使成。2. 一身以外無他物。3. 失意。4. 感覺。5. 一把。6. 非意料所及。7. 驚異。8. 犁。9. 掘起。10. 鏟。11. 鍬。12. 克服。13. 笨拙。44. 較難。15. 進行。16. 較劣。17. 忍受。18. 自滿。19. 成就。20. 忍耐心。21. 工作之拙劣。22. 穀。23. 種。24. 耙。25. 步行而過。26. 曳。27. 重。28. 搔。29. 耙。30. 漸長。31. 保存。32. 刈。33. 收穫。34. 打。35. 簸去粃糠。36. 磨。37. 研。38. 篩子。39. 酵。40. 火爐。41. 予皆無所有。42. 無價的。43. 勞力。44. 煩厭。45. 無可奈何。46. 一部份。47. 指定。48. 分量

apply myself [1]*wholly*, by labor and [2]*invention*, to [3]*furnish* myself with [4]*utensils* proper for the [5]*performing* all the [6]*operations* necessary for making the corn, when I had it, fit for my use.

But first I was to [7]*prepare* more land, for I had now seed enough to sow above an [8]*acre of ground*. Before I did this, I had a week's work, at least, to make me a [9]*spade*, which, when it was done, was but a [10]*sorry* one indeed, and very heavy, and [11]*required* [12]*double* labor to work with it. However, I got through that, and [13]*sowed* my seed in two large, flat [14]*pieces* of ground, as, near my house as I could find them to my mind, and [15]*fenced* them in with a good hedge, the stakes of which were all cut off that wood which I had set before, and knew it would grow; so that in a year's time, I knew I should have a [16]*quick or living* hedge, that would want but little [17]*repair*. This work did not take me less than three months, because a great part of that time was the wet season, when I could not go [18]*abroad*.

Within doors, that is when it [19]*rained*, and I could not go out, I found employment in the following [20]*occupations*, always observing that all the while I was at work, I [21]*diverted* myself with talking to my [22]*parrot*, and [23]*teaching* him to speak. I [24]*quickly* taught him to know his own name, and at last to speak it out [25]*pretty* loud,—"Poll," which was the first word I ever heard spoken in the island by any mouth but my own. This, therefore, was not my work, but an [26]*assistance* to my work; for now, as I said, I had a great [27]*employment* upon my hands, as follows: I had long [28]*studied* to make, by some means or other, some [29]*earthen vessels*, which, indeed, I [30]*wanted sorely*, but knew not where to [31]*come at* them. However, [32]*considering* the

以下六個月，我便不得不完全地用勞力和發明來利用着自己，使自己得着那些種穀所必需和合宜進行攏總工作的器具；當我得着了牠們，就合我的用場。

　　第一步，我必須預備較多的士地，因為現在我有可種一畝以上的種子了。在我做這事以前，至少，我必須工作一星期去達成一個鏈子，做好了牠，瞧瞧實在拙劣的狠，而且又笨重，拿牠工作須費兩倍勞力。然而我却完成了牠，把我的種子種在兩塊寬而平的地上，貼近我的住所，我能記憶着牠們，用一座好的籬笆把牠們圍繞起來，以前我植立的木頭的椿兒一齊割去了我知道牠要生長的；經過了一年工夫，我將有一座活的籬笆，稍加修茸，便成美觀。這個工作費去我不下三個月的工夫，因為那個時候有一大半是潮溼的時期，我不能夠出外。

　　在家中，當下雨我不能出去的時候，我找出以下所做的事務來。常常觀察着正當我工作的辰光，我向鸚哥說話和教牠發言；這是我自娛的方法。我迅速地教牠知道牠自己的名字，最後，用狠大的聲音說出來，一"波兒，"除去我自己一張口說話以外，這句話是我在島上第一次聽見說的。這不是我的工作，不過工作中一個幫助而已；因為現在，我曾說過，我手中有一個狠大的事務，就是：用某種方法。我曾研究着可以製成泥器，我實在亟需着牠們，但是不知道從什麼地方可以獲得牠們。然而，照氣候的熱度而論，我毫不懷疑地想我一定能夠

heat of the [1]*climate*, I did not [2]*doubt* but if I could find out any clay, I might make some [3]*pots* that might, being [4]*dried* in the sun, be hard [5]*enough* and strong enough to [6]*bear handling*, and to hold anything that was dry and [7]*required* to be kept so. As this was [8]*necessary* in the [9]*preparing* corn, [10]*meal*, etc., which was the thing I was doing, I [11]*resolved* to make some as large as I could, and fit only to stand like [12]*jars*, to hold what should be put into them.

CHAPTER XXIII

It would make the reader pity me, or rather laugh at me, to tell how many [13]*awkward* ways I took to [14]*raise* this [15]*paste*; what [16]*odd*, [17]*misshapen*, [18]*ugly* things I made; how many of them [19]*fell in*, and how many [20]*fell out*, the [21]*clay* [22]*not being stiff enough to bear its own weight*; how many [23]*cracked* by the [24]*over-violent* heat of the sun, being [25]*set out* too [26]*hastily*; and how many fell in pieces with only [27]*removing*, as well before as after they were [28]*dried*; and, in a word, how often, having [29]*labored* hard to find the [30]*clay*, to dig it, to [31]*temper* it, to bring it home, and work it, I could not make above two large, [32]*earthen*, [33]*ugly* things (I cannot call them jars) in about two months' [34]*labor*.

However, as the sun [35]*baked* these two very dry and hard, lifted them very gently up, and [36]*set them down again in two* great wicker [37]*baskets*, which I had made on purpose for them, that they might not [38]*break*. As between the pot and the [39]*basket* [40]*there was a little room to spare*, I [41]*stuffed it full* of the rice and [42]*barley* [43] *straw*. These two pots, being to stand always dry, I thought would hold my dry corn, and perhaps the meal, when the corn was [44]*bruised*.

得着些泥灰，我必須製些罐兒，在月光中晾乾以後；牠可以變硬了，變堅固了，足以使用，能夠放些乾的和必須保存的東西在內。這對於預備穀和粉是必要的物件。現在我正製造着，我決定儘力製造些大的，豎立起來宛如大口瓶一般：那末任何東要都可以放進去了。

第 二 十 三 章

讀者必定要哀憐我，倘使我敍述出我用怎樣笨拙的法子來弄到泥漿；我製成怎樣奇形怪狀的物件；有若干不合用；泥土不能固結以自載牠的重量；有多少因爲受着太陽驟然發出的猛烈的熱光而爆裂了；有些在晾乾以後和末晾乾以前，因爲被搬開而碎成齏粉了；總而言之，狠常常地，在費勞力來尋找泥灰，掘起牠，調和牠，帶牠回家，製造牠以後，我僅能製成兩隻大的，泥製的，醜陋的東西（我不能叫牠們作瓶），却大約費了二個月的勞功呢。

太陽把這兩隻東西焙炙得狠乾狠堅固，我把牠們慢慢地舉起來，放牠們在兩隻柳枝製的大籃子裏面，籃子我是特地爲牠們製的，這樣一來，牠們便不會碎了。在罐兒和籃子的中間，略有空隙，我用米和大麥稈把牠塞滿了。這兩隻兒常常是乾的立在那裏，我想當穀子打碎的時候，可以盛放着乾的穀子，或者還能貯放着粉呢。

1.氣候。2.懷疑。3.罐。4.晾乾。5.足以 6.可以使用。7.需要。8.必須。9.預備。10.粉。11.決定。12.大口瓶。13.粗劣。14.收穫。15.泥漿。16.怪異。17.怪狀。18.惡劣。19.合用。20.不合用。21.泥灰。22.不能固結載重。23.裂。24.太猛。25.發出。26.速。27.移動。28.乾。29.勞力。30.泥灰。31.調和。32.泥製。33惡劣34.勞力。35.焙炙。36.放入。37.籃子。38.碎。39.籃子。40.略有空隙。41.塞滿。42.大麥。43.稈。44.打碎

Though I [1]*miscarried* so much in my [2]*design* for large pots, yet I made several smaller things with better [3]*success*; such as little round pots, flat dishes, [4]*pitchers*, and [5]*pipkins*, and any things my hand [6]*turned to*; and the heat of the summer [7]*baked* them quite hard.

[8]*But all this would not answer my end*, which was to get an earthen [9]*pot* to hold what was [10]*liquid*, and [11]*bear* the fire,—which [12]*none* of these could do. It happened after some time, making a [13]*pretty* large fire for [14]*cooking* my meat, when I went to [15]*put it out* after I had done with it, I found a broken [16]*piece* of one of my [17]*earthenware* [18]*vessels* in the fire, [19]*burnt* as hard as a stone, and red as [20]*a tile*. I was [21]*agreeably* surprised to see it, and said to myself that certainly they might be made to [22]*burn* whole, if they would burn broken.

This [23]*set me to study* how to order my fire so as to make it burn some pots. I had no notion of a [24]*kiln*, such as the [25]*potters* burn in, or of [26]*glazing* them with lead, though I had some lead to do it with; but I placed three large [27]*pipkins*, and two or three pots, in a [28]*pile*, one upon another, and placed my [29]*firewood* all round it with [30]*a great heap* of [31]*embers* under them. I [32]*plied* the fire with fresh fuel round the outside, and upon the [33]*top*, till I saw the pots in the [34]*inside* *red hot quite through*, and observed that they did not [35]*crack* at all. When I saw them [36]*clear red*, I let them stand in that heat about five or six hours, till I found one of them, though it did not [37]*crack*, did [38]*melt or run*; for the sand which was [39]*mixed* with the clay [40]*melted* by the [41]*violence* of the heat, and would have run into glass if I had gone on. So I [42]*slacked* my fire [43]*gradually* till the [44]*pots* began to [45]*abate* of the [46]*red* color; and, [47]*watching* them all night, that I might not let the fire abate too [48]*fast*, in the morning I had

雖然我要製造大罐的計劃是完全失敗了，然而製造些較小的物件却成了功；例如小的圓的罐，平坦的碟子，水盂，瓦鍋，以及我製造的其他的東西；夏天的熱度把牠們焙炙得狠硬。

但是這些東西終究不能使我達到目的，就是要得着一隻泥罐來盛放流質的東西和熬得住火：—— 這兩個問題，這些東西皆不能夠解決。過了些時，我偶然地去弄些較大的火來煮我的食物，當我煮好了把火熄滅以後，我瞧見了在火中有一隻泥製的器具的碎塊一片，燒得和石頭一樣硬，紅得像瓦片一般。我瞧見了這個，歡喜得了不得，自己向自己說倘使牠們能夠燒碎，牠們一定能夠燒成整個的。

這事使得我研究怎樣去整理火，使得牠能夠燒成功幾隻罐兒。我心中沒有瓦窰的念頭，像那些陶器工在其中燒和用鉛去磨光陶器，雖然我到有些鉛來作這層工作；但是我放三隻大的瓦鍋，兩三隻罐，在一根木椿上面，一個累一個，四面放了柴薪；下面放了一大堆燃屑。繞着外層，和頂面我燃燒了火，用的是新的燃料，直到我瞧見其中的罐十分透紅為止，並且注意着不使牠們炸裂；當我見牠們甚紅之時，我使牠們直立在熱度裏面大約五六個鐘頭，後來我找着一隻，雖然未曾炸裂，已經鎔化了；因為和泥灰調和的沙土，受了強烈的熱，便融化了，倘使我使牠繼續下去，必定要鎔成玻璃了。這樣我便漸漸地減去了火勢，直至罐減去了紅的顏色為止；整夜地看守着牠們，我必須不讓火減却得太快，早間，我得了三隻狠

three very good (I will not say handsome) [1]*pipkins*, and two other earthen pots, as hard [2]*burnt* as could be derised, and one of them perfectly [3]*glazed* with the running of the sand.

After this [4]*experiment*, I need not say that I wanted no sort of [5]*earthenware* for my use, but I must [6]*needs* say as to the [7]*shapes* of them, they were very [8]*indifferent*, as any one may [9]*suppose* when I had no way of making them but as the children make [10]*dirt pies,* or as a woman would make pies that never learned [11]*to raise paste.*

No joy at a thing [12]*of so mean a nature* was ever equal to mine when I found I had made an [13]*earthen* pot that would bear the fire. I had hardly [14]*patience* to stay till they were cold before I set one on the fire again, with some water in it, to [15]*boil* me some meat, which it did [16]*admirably well*. With a piece of a kid I made some very good broth, though I wanted [17]*oatmeal,* and several other [18]*ingredients* [19]*requisite* to make it as good as I would have had it.

My next concern was to get me a stone [20]*mortar* to [21]*stamp* or beat some corn in; for as to the mill, there was no thought of [22]*arriving at that perfection of art* with one pair of hands. To supply this want I [23]*was at a great loss*; for of all the [24]*trades* in the world, I was as perfectly [25]*unqualified* for a [26]*stone cutter* as for any [27]*whatever*. Neither had I any tools [28]*to go about it* with. I spent [29]*many a day* to find out a great stone big enough to [30]*cut hollhw*, and make fit for a mortar, and could find none at all, [31]*except* what was in the [32]*solid* [33]*rock,* and which I had no way to [34]*dig* or cut out. Nor indeed were the [35]*rocks* in the island of hardness [36]*sufficient*, but were all of a sandy, [37]*crumbling* stone, which neither would bear the [38]*weight* of a heavy [39]*pestle*, nor would break the corn without [40]*filling* it with sand. So,

好的(我却不說是美麗)瓦釜和兩隻陶罐，燒得堅固的狠，如我所希冀的一樣；其中一隻，因爲沙土流動，被磨得狠光滑。

在這次試驗以後，我不須說我不缺少應用的陶器；但是我須說；關於牠們的形式，這是無關緊要的事，任是何人都能猜想得出，我沒有法子來製造出樣子，像小孩子做泥包子，和像未曾學過怎樣去調粉漿，便來做包子的婦女一樣。

當我瞧見我製成了一隻能夠耐火的罐子，我對於這個性質低微的東西的快樂，是無物可與比較的。我簡直沒有忍耐心去等着牠們冷透，便把一隻重行擺在火上，裏面放了些水，燒些食物來吃，到是燒得極妙。拿了一塊小山羊肉，我做了些好吃的湯，雖然我缺少燕麥粉和傍的必需的參雜品來把牠做成如我所希望的那麼好。

我的第二次的事務就是要得着一個石臼來搗碎或是打碎穀子；至於磨子，用了一雙手，決計不能使技藝達於盡善盡美的境地。爲供給這個缺乏之故，我是茫然不知所措；因爲在世界上所有的業務裏面，我是毫無資格地去做一個石匠以及其牠任何工匠的。我也沒有器具來着手工作。費了許多天工夫，我找着一大塊石頭，其大足以鑿空和合宜作石臼之用；除去在堅固的石岩內以外，其他各處皆無有，對於這個我却沒有方法來掘起或割開。這島上的石頭的堅固的力量也不充分，都是多沙，破碎的石頭，旣不能受重杵的量重，若不用沙土充滿牠，又不能礳碎穀子。

1.瓦釜．2．燒．3.磨光．4.試驗．5.陶製．6.須．7.樣式．8.無關緊要．9.猜想．10. 泥包子．11.調粉漿．12.性質低下．13.陶器．14.忍耐力．15.燒．16.極妙．17.燕麥粉．18.物質．19.必需．20. 白．31.搗．22. 達彼技藝完全之境地．23.不知所措．24.行業．25.不合格．26.石匠．27.不拘其他．28.着手．29.多日．30.鑿空．31.除去．32.堅固．33.岩石．34.掘．35.岩石．36.克分．37.碎．38.重量．39.杵．40.充滿．

after a great deal of time lost in ¹*searching* for a stone, I gave it over, and ²*resolved* to look out for a great ³*block* of hard wood, which I found indeed much ⁴*easier*. Getting one as big as I had ⁵*strength* to stir, I ⁶*rounded* it, and formed it on the outside with my ax and ⁷*hatchet*, and then, with the help of fire, and infinite labor, made a ⁸*hollow* place in it, as the Indians in Brazil make their ⁹*canoes*. After this. I made a great heavy, ¹⁰*pestle*, or ¹¹*beater*, of the wood called the iron wood. This I ¹²*prepared* and laid by against I had my next ¹³*crop* of corn, which I ¹⁴*proposed* to myself to ¹⁵*grind*, or rather ¹⁶*pound*, into meal, to make bread.

My next difficulty was to make a sieve, to dress my meal and to part it from the ¹⁷*bran* and the ¹⁸*husk*; without which I did not see it possible I could have any ¹⁹*bread*. This was a most ²⁰*difficult* thing even to think on, for to be sure I had nothing like the ²¹*necessary* thing to make it,— I mean fine, thin ²²*canvas* or ²³*stuff* to ²⁴*sift* the meal through.

And here I was ²⁵*at a full stop* for many months; nor did I really know what to do. Linen I had none left but what was mere ²⁶*rags*. I had ²⁷*goat's hair*, but neither knew how to ²⁸*weave* it or ²⁹*spin* it; and had I known how, here were no ³⁰*tools* to work it with. All the ³¹*remedy* that I found for this was that at last I did ³²*remember* I had, among the seamen's clothes which were saved out for the ship, some ³³*neckcloths* of ³⁴*calico* or ³⁵*muslin*. With some pieces of these I made three small sieves proper enough of the work; and thus I ³⁶*made shift* for some years. How I did afterwards, I shall show in its place,

The baking part was the next thing to be ³⁷*considered*, and how I should make bread when I came to have corn;

這樣費了許多辰光還找不出一塊石頭，我遂放棄此舉，決定要尋出一大塊硬木來，我狠容易地把牠找出來了。得了一塊其大如我的力量能搬得動的木料，我弄圓牠，在外面我用斧和小斧把牠製成形式，後來，靠了火的助力；以及無限的力量的後盾，在牠的裏面做了一個空凹的地方，好像（印第安人）在(布勒喜爾)造木艇一般。這事做畢以後，我造了一隻大而重的杵，或是椎，是用所謂鐵木製成的。我預備牠和把牠收藏起來，等到穀子第二次收穫的時候再用，我自己提議我必須把穀子磨碎或搗碎，使牠成粉，俾作製麵包之用。

第二次我的困難就是造一篩子，為調和粉和播去糠和殼之用；沒有篩子，我想要得麵包大概是不可能的。想起來這就是一椿最困難的事，因為我實在沒在製造這個篩的必需的物件，——我的意思就是說：好的，薄的網眼布或是布料來把粉子篩過。

我這裏就停了工許多月；我也不知道怎樣是好。除去破爛麻布以外，我沒有整塊的餘留了。我有山羊毛，但是不知道怎樣地去編製和紡織牠；就使我知道，也沒有器具來工作。對於這點我尋出的補救方法，就是後來我想起，在從船中保留出來的水手衣服裏面，我有些棉布或是毛紗製的頸巾。拿了幾塊，我就作成三隻小篩子，足以工作；於是我就這樣敷衍了若干年。後來怎樣呢，我就要表示出來。

第二種事件要考察的就是焙炙的部份了，以及有了穀子怎樣

1.找．2.決心．3.塊．4.較易．5.力量．6.作圓．7.小斧．8.凹的．9.木艇．10.杵．11.椎．12.預備．13.收成．14.提議．15.磨．16.搗碎．17.糠．18.殼．19.麵包．20.困難．21.必須的．22.網眼布．23.布料．24.篩．25.停止．26.破布．27.山羊毛．28.編．29.紡．30.器具．31.補救方法．32.記憶．33.頸巾．34.棉布．35.洋紗．36.將就．37.考察．

for, first, I had no yeast. As to that part, [1]*there was no supplying the want*, so I [2]*did not concern myself much about it*. But for an oven, I was indeed in great [3]*pain*. At length I found out an [4]*experiment* for that also, which was this: I made some earthen [5]*vessels*, very broad, but not deep,—that is to say, about two feet [6]*diameter*, and not above nine inches [7]*deep*. These I [8]*burned* in the fire, as I had done the others, and [9]*laid them by*; and when I [10]*wanted* to bake, I made a great fire upon my [11]*hearth*, which I had [12]*paved* with some square [13]*tiles*, of my own baking and [14]*burning* also; but I should not call them [15]*square*.

When the [16]*firewood* was burnt [17]*pretty* much into [18]*embers*, or [19]*live coals*, I drew them forward upon this hearth, so as to cover it all over, and there I let them lie till the hearth was very hot. Then, [20]*sweeping away* all the embers, I set down my loaf or loaves, and turning down the earthen pot to cover them, drew the embers all round the outside of the pot, [21]*to keep in* and add to the [22]*heat*. Thus, as well as in the best oven in the world, I baked my barley loaves, and became, in a little time, a good [23]*pastry cook into the bargain*; for I made myself several [24]*cakes* and [25]*puddings* of the rice. But I made no [26]*pies*, neither had I anything to put into them, supposing I had, except the flesh either of fowls or goats.

It need not be wondered at if all these things took me up most part of the third year of my [27]*abode* here; for it is to be observed that in the [28]*intervals* of these things I had my new harvest and [29]*husbandry* to manage. I [30]*reaped* my corn [31]*in its season*, and carried it home as well as I could, [32]*and laid it up*, [33]*in the ear*, in my large [34]*baskets*, till I had time to [35]*rub* it out, for I had no floor to [36]*thrash* it on, or [37]*instrument* to thrash it with.

去製成麵包；因爲，第一步，我沒有酵。至於那個部份，無法供其缺乏；所以我就不甚關懷了。但是對於一隻火爐，實在我是煞覺周章的。最後，我也尋出一種試驗來了，那就是這樣：我製成了若干很寬而不甚深的陶器；——就是說，大約二尺直徑，不上九寸深。我把牠們放在火內燒，好像我處置其他的一樣；收藏起來；當我要燴煑東西的時候，在火爐底我生了一個大的火；這隻火爐底是我用幾塊方瓦砌起來的，也是我自已焙燒起來的；但是我不應當叫牠們方形。

當柴薪將要燒成燃屑或熾炭的時候，我把牠們帶到火爐上去；以致把爐兒掩蓋住了，我讓牠們在那裏置着直到爐兒透熱爲止。於是把燃屑都掃去了，我放下我的幾塊麵包，把陶罐翻轉來將牠們蓋好；把燃屑放在罐的四周外面，爲着保存和加熱的緣故。這簡直可稱世界上的最好的火爐，我焙煑大麥麵包，不久以後，我又變成一個製餅大司務了；因爲我用米製了些餅和布丁。但是我沒有作包子，也沒有餡子放在裏面，就是有，也不過禽鳥或山羊的肉而巳。

倘使這些事務把我住在這裏第三年的光陰耗去了一大半，那也不須驚異的；但是應當注意着，在這些事務的間隙裏面，我得着了新的收穫和處置農務。我應時收穫穀子，儘力攜牠囘家，連穗把牠藏起；放在籃中，直到我有功夫來摩擦牠，方把牠拿出來，因爲既沒有打穀的地板，又沒有打穀的器具。

1. 無法供其缺乏. 2. 不甚關心. 3. 痛苦. 4. 試驗. 5. 器皿. 6. 直徑. 7. 深. 8. 燒. 9. 收藏. 10. 需要. 11. 火爐底. 12. 砌. 13. 瓦. 14. 燒. 15. 方形. 16. 柴. 17. 稍. 18. 燃屑. 19. 熾炭. 20. 掃去. 21. 保存. 22. 熱. 23. 魯濱孫製餅師. 24. 餅. 25. 布丁. 26. 包子. 27. 住所. 28. 間隙. 29. 農務. 30. 收穫. 31. 當其時. 32. 收存. 33. 連穗. 34. 籃子. 35. 摩擦. 36. 打穀. 37. 器具.

And now, indeed, my ¹*stock* of corn ²*increasing*, I really wanted to build my ³*barns* bigger. I wanted a place to lay it up in, for the increase of the corn now ⁴*yielded* me so much that I had of the barley about twenty ⁵*bushels*, and of the rice as much, or more. I now resolved to begin ⁶*to use it freely*; for my bread ⁷*had been quite gone a great while*. Also I resolved to see what quantity would be ⁸*sufficient* for me a whole year, and to sow but once a year.

Upon the whole, I found that the forty bushels of barley and rice were much more than I could ⁹*consume* in a year; so I resolved to sow just the same quantity every year that I sowed the last, in hopes that such a ¹⁰*quantity* would fully provide me with bread.

CHAPTER XXIV

ALL the while these things were doing, you may be sure my thoughts ran many times upon the ¹¹*prospect* of land which I had seen from the other side of the island. I was not without ¹²*secret wishes* that I were on shore there, fancying that, seeing the ¹³*mainland* and an ¹⁴*inhabited* country, I might find some way or other to ¹⁵*convey* myself farther, and perhaps at last find some means of ¹⁶*escape*.

But all this while I ¹⁷*made no allowance for* the ¹⁸*dangers* of such an undertaking, and how I might ¹⁹*fall into the hands of* ²⁰*savages*, and perhaps such as I might have reason to think far ²¹*worse* than the lions and ²²*tigers* of Africa; that if I once came in their power, I should ²³*run a hazard of* more than ²⁴*a thousand to one of being killed*, and perhaps of being eaten, for I had heard that the people of the Caribbean coast were ²⁵*connibals*, or ²⁶*man-eaters*, and I knew by the ²⁷*latitude* that I could not be far from that ²⁸*shore*. Then,

現在，實在，我的穀子的存儲是加增起來了，我一定須要把我的倉廩造得大些了。我需要一個地方來貯藏牠，因為穀子的加增使我想到現在我大約有二十斛大麥和同量或較多的米。現在我決定我可以用之不吝了；因為我的麵包早已告罄。我也決定去考察，一個整年我需要若干分量方能足夠自給，並決定一年中只要播種一次。

總而言之，我覺着在一年內我吃不完四十斛大麥和米；所以我決定每年播種同樣的量數，我最後播種，並希望着這樣的分量儘可供給我麵包了。

第二十四章

正逢作這些事的時侯，讀者可以確定我的思想是在土地的期望上面流動着，這個土地就是我從島的那一面瞧見的。我在那裏登岸，心中有些私願，幻想着，瞧見了大地和居住的地方以後，我或能尋出些方法來把我帶得較遠的地方上去，或者最後能尋出逃走的法子來。

但是當其時我對於這種舉動的危險並未顧及，我或者將落於野人之手，我有理由來想起，他們是比(亞非利加)洲的獅虎還要來得惡劣；倘使我墜入彼等牢籠，我將要冒千死而無一生之險了；或是被他們吃掉，我聽見說過(卡利賓)海濱的人是吃人的，從緯線上面，我知道我是離開海岸不甚遠的。

¹*supposing* they were not ²*cannibals*, yet they might kill me, as many Europeans who had fallen into their hands had been ³*served*, even when they had been ten or twenty together; much more I, that was but one, and could make little or no ⁴*defense*. All these things, I say, which I ought to have considered well, and which did come into my thoughts afterwards, yet gave me no ⁵*apprehensions* at first, and ⁶*my head ran mightily upon the thought of getting over to the shore.*

Now I ⁷*wished for* my boy Xury, and the longboat with ⁸*shoulder-of mutton* ⁹*sail*, with which I sailed above a thousand miles on the ¹⁰*coast* of Africa; but this was ¹¹*in vain.* Then I thought I would go and look at our ship's boat, which, as I have said, was blown up upon the shore a great way in the storm, when we were first ¹²*cast away*. She lay almost where she did at first, but not quite, and was turned, by the force of the waves and the winds, almost ¹³*bottom upward* against a high ¹⁴*ridge of beachy*, ¹⁵*rough sand*, but no water about her. If I had had hands to ¹⁶*refit* her, and to ¹⁷*launch her into the water*, the boat would have done well enough, and I might have gone back to Brazil with her easily enough; but I might have ¹⁸*foreseen* that I ¹⁹*could no more turn her and set her upright upon her bottom, than* I could ²⁰*remove* the island. However, I went to the woods, and cut ²¹*levers* and ²²*rollers,* and brought them to the boat, resolving to try what I could do; ²³*suggesting* to myself that if I could but turn her down, I might ²⁴*repair the damage* she had ²⁵*received,* and she would be a very good boat, and I might go to sea in her very ²⁶*easily.*

I ²⁷*spared no pains*, indeed, in this piece of ²⁸*fruitless toils* and ²⁹*spent,* I think, three or four weeks about it. At last

猜想着他們不是吃人的東西，然而他們或者殺了我，好像許多(歐)洲人落在他們手中所受的待遇一般，就是十個或是二十個一隊走，也是於事無濟；而況我是孤另另地一人，一點自衛力都沒有。我想，這些事情我是應當仔細考察的，後來牠們也跑到我的思想裏面來，起初使得我毫無恐怕之念，我是極欲登岸去的。

現在我想望我的孩子(許利)和我在(亞非利加)海濱乘了走了一千(英)里以上的那隻用羊肩帆行的大舢板船了；然而這是徒然無益。後來我想去瞧我們大船的小艇，這隻艇我曾經說過，是被暴風雨吹到很遠的海岸上去了，當我們先前被浪花打走的時候。牠差不多仍舊在牠從前躺的地方，但是不十分正確了，經過風浪猛力攻擊，翻過來了，差不多顛倒過來靠在粗亂沙石的高脊上，四面却沒有水。倘使我能修理牠和放牠入水，艇兒必甚合用，我狠容易地乘着牠同到(布勒喜爾)去；但是我必須預料着我不能翻轉牠的底面，使牠豎立起來，正如我不能移動這座島一樣。然而我却走到林木中去，割下檳杆和轉木來，把牠們拿到艇旁邊去，決定儘我能力試試看；自己提議着倘使能夠把牠翻下來，我可以修理牠所受的破壞，牠或將成為一隻好的船，我狠容易地乘着牠到海內去了。

實在，我對於這件無結果的工作，是不辭勞瘁的，我想，大約費去三四個星期的光陰在這個上面。後來，

1.猜想。2.吃人者。3.待遇。4.防衛。5.恐怕。6.急欲上岸。7.想望。8.羊肩形。9.帆。10.海濱。11.徒然。12.打走。13.翻轉。14.脊。15.粗亂沙石。16.修理。17.放之入水。18.預知。19.不能翻轉底面使之豎立。20.移動。21.檳木。22.轉木。23.提議。24.修理損傷。25.得着。26.容易地。27.不辭勞瘁。28.無結果的工作。39.費去。

finding it ¹*impossible* to ²*heave it up* with my little ³*strength*
I ⁴*fell to* ⁵*digging away* the sand, to ⁶*undermine* it, and so to
make it fall down, setting pieces of wood to ⁷*thrust* and
guide it right in the fall.

But when I had done this, I was unable to stir it up
again, or to get under it, much less to move it forward
towards the water ; so I was ⁸*forced* to given it over. Yet,
though I gave over the hopes of the boat, my desire to
⁹*venture* over for the main ¹⁰*increased*, rather than ¹¹*decreased*,
as the means for it seemed ¹²*impossible*.

This ¹³*at length* put me upon thinking whether it was
not possible to make myself a ¹⁴*canoe*, or ¹⁵*periagua*, such as
the natives of those ¹⁶*climates* make, even without tools,—
or, as I might say, without hands,—of the ¹⁷*trunk* of a
great tree. This I not only thought possible but easy, and
pleased myself ¹⁸*extremely* with the thoughts of making it,
and with my having much more ¹⁹*convenience* for it than
any of the ²⁰*negroes* or Indians ; but ²¹*not at all* considering
the ²²*particular inconveniences* which I ²³*lay under* more than
the Indians did ; namely, the ²⁴*want of hands* to move it,
when it was made, into the water,—a ²⁵*difficulty* much
²⁶*harder* for me to ²⁷*surmount* than all the ²⁸*consequences* of
want of tools could be to them ; for what was it to me if,
when I had ²⁹*chosen* a vast tree in the woods, and with
much trouble cut it down, if I had been able with my
tools to hew and ³⁰*dub* the outside into the proper shape of
a boat, and burn or cut out the inside to make it ³¹*hollow*,
so as to make a boat of it,—if, after all this, I must leave
it just there where I found it, and not be able to ³²*launch* it
into the water.

覺着我的微細的力量是不能把牠舉起來，我於是從事於掘起沙土，使牠落下來，這樣便使牠墜落，放些本塊在旁邊以便讓牠落下來的時候，把牠弄正。

但是做完這事以後，我不能再把牠弄起來，又不能把牠弄下去，狠難的把牠推向水邊去；這樣我是不得不拋棄這層工作。雖然我放棄了乘船的企圖，我欲往大洋去的希望是有增無減，然而欲往那裏去的方法看來是不能尋到的。

最後，這事使我想着我能不能造一木艇，或是獨木舟，像這些地方土人造的一樣，卽使沒有器具，—— 或者我能夠說，沒有手工，——這舟的材料是從一顆大樹的幹上着想的。我不但想這個是可能而且容易，要造成小舟的思想使我欣喜萬狀，尤其欣慰的是我比較那些黑人或是(印第安)人所有的便利是來得大；但是我將要比(印第安)人受特別的不方便，這事我却絕未注意及之；就是，缺少人手來移動牠，當牠造好了的時候，到水裏去，——這個困難對於我是更難克服的，比較缺乏器具所得的結果尤甚；我將得着什麼益處，當我在樹林中找着了一顆大樹，狠費力的把牠砍下來，倘使我能用器具來斫牠，弄平牠，外面弄成小舟的形式，燒或割牠的裏面，把牠弄凹，那末船是成功了，——倘使，各事完畢以後，我却要把牠放在我找着牠的原地方，而不能放牠下水。

1. 不能。2. 舉起。3. 力量。4. 始從事於。5. 掘出。6. 使落下。7. 推。8. 不得不。9. 敢。10. 加增。11. 減。12. 不能。13. 後來。14. 木艇。15. 獨木舟。16. 地方。17. 幹。18. 極。19. 便利。20. 黑人。21. 絕不。22. 特別不便。23. 受。24. 缺少人手。25. 困難。26. 較難。27. 克服。28. 結果。29. 選。30. 弄滑。31. 凹的。32. 放……入水。

One would think I [1]*could not have had the least reflection upon my mind of my circumstances*, while I was making this boat, but I should have immediately thought how I should get it into the sea ; but my thoughts were so [2]*intent upon* my [3]*voyage* over the sea in it that I never once [4]*considered* how I should get it off the land ; and it was [5]*really*, [6]*in its own nature*, more easy for me to [7]*guide* it over forty-five miles in sea, than about forty-five [8]*fathoms* of land, where it lay, [9]*to set it afloat in the water.*

I went to work upon this boat the most like a [10]*fool* that ever man did who had any of his [11]*senses* awake. I pleased myself with the [12]*design*, without [13]*determining* whether I was ever able to [14]*undertake* it. Not but that the [15]*difficulty* of [16]*launching* my boat came often into my head ; but I [17]*put a stop to* my [18]*inquiries into it* by this foolish answer, which I gave myself : "Let me first make it ; I [19]*warrant* I will find some way or other to [20]*get it along* when it is done."

This was a most [21]*preposterous* method ; but [22]*the eagerness of my fancy prevailed,* and to work I went. I [23]*felled* a [24]*cedar tree,* and I question much whether [25]*Solomon* ever had such a one for the building of the [26]*Temple of Jerusalem.* It was five feet ten inches [27]*diameter* at the lower part next the [28]*stump,* and four feet eleven inches [29]*diameter* at the end of twenty-two feet, after which it [30]*lessened for a while,* and then parted into [31]*branches.* It was not without [32]*infinite* labor that I felled this tree. I was twenty days hacking and [33]*hewing* at it at the bottom, I was fourteen more getting the [34]*branches* and [35]*limbs* and the vast, [36]*spreading* head cut off, which I [37]*hacked* and hewed through with ax and hatchet and [38]*inexpressible* labor. After this, it cost me a month to shape it and dub it [39]*to a proportion,* and to

　　有人或者要想我對於所處的境地是毫不自察的，當我正在造船的時候，但是我却立刻想着怎樣方能把牠弄下水去；然而我的思想是這樣地注在乘舟入海的上面；這種行程我早巳在念了，我御未曾思及怎樣方能使船離岸；依其本性而論，把牠在海中領到四十五（英）里以上的程途是比較從牠所在的四十五尋以上的陸地上面弄到水裏實在更爲容易些。

　　我進行造船工作，好像理智清明的人去做愚笨的事一樣；未曾斷定究竟能否承辦這事，我却欣然以此計劃爲慰。弄船下水的困難常常在我腦內出現；但是我用這個愚蠢的囘答來使得腦中的詢問停止，我說：“起頭讓我試試看；我担保當船造好了以後，我將要找出些方法來使牠進行。”

　　這是一個極不合理的方法；但是我的思想縈切，我遂進行工作。我所斫下的一顆柏樹，我詢問着：(沙羅孟)當造(耶路撒冷)廟的時候，有否這樣的一顆大樹。在靠樹株較下的部份，直徑是五尺十寸，在二十二尺的末端；直徑是四尺十一寸；以下漸次減少，分成樹枝。將樹斫下，費力甚多。砍斫樹的下部，費去二十日光陰。又費去十四日工夫，用斧和小斧以及非言語所能形容的勞力，方把樹枝，大枝，大的和放開的樹頭削去。這事做完，費了一月光陰，把牠弄成形式；弄得光滑，按度配合，使牠像船

something like the [1]*bottom* of a boat, that it might swim
[2]*upright* as it ought to do. It cost me near three months
more to clear the inside, and work it out so as to make an
[3]*exact* boat of it. This I did, [4]*indeed*, without fire, by
mere [5]*mallet* and [6]*chisel*, and [7]*by the dint of* [8] *hard labor*, till
I had [9]*brought it to be* a very handsome [10]*periagua*, and
big enough to have carried [11]*six-and-twenty* men, and
[12]*consequently* big enough to have carried me and all my
[13]*cargo.*

When I had [14]*gone through this work*, I was [15]*extremely*
delighted with it. The boat was really much bigger than
ever I saw a canoe or [16]*periagua*, that was made of one tree,
in my life. [17]*Many a weary stroke it had cost*, you may be
sure ; and had I gotton it into the water, I make no
question but I should have begun the [18]*maddest voyage*,
and the most [19]*unlikely to be performed*, that ever was
[20]*undertaken.*

But all my [21]*devices* to get it into the water [22]*failed* me ;
thorgh they cost me [23]*infinite* labor too. It lay about one
hundred yards from the water, and not more ; but the first
[24]*inconvenience* was, it was [25]*up hill towards the creek*. Well,
to take away this [26]*discouragement*, I resolved to dig into
the [27]*surface* of the earth, and so make a [28]*declivity*. This I
began, and it cost me a prodigious deal of pains ; but
when this was worked through, and this [29]*difficulty* [30]*managed*,
it was [31]*still much the same*, for I could no more [32]*stir* the
[33]*canoe* than I could the other boat.

Then I measured the distance of ground, and resolved
to cut a [34]*dock* or [35]*canal to* bring the water up to the [36]*canoe*,
[37]*seeing* I could not bring the canoe down to the water.
Well, I began this work ; and when I [38]*began to enter upon*

底一般的東西，那末牠就可直立地在水中浮泛起來，如牠應做的一樣。把牠內部弄得清淨和把牠造成恰如一隻小船，差不多費去我三月餘功夫。實在，我做了這個，沒有火的幫助，僅僅有賴於槌，鑿，以及苦力，後來我便造成一隻狠好看的獨木舟，其大足容二十六人，於是載我和攏總我的貨物是綽然有餘裕了。

當我完畢了這個工程之後，我是狠爲欣慰的，這隻船實在是比我一生所見從樹木造成的木艇或獨木舟來得大。你可以確定這事當然是費經營的；倘使我把牠放下水去，那末我就要一心一意地來開始我那久巳在心而甚不可行的瘋狂的行程了。

但是使牠下水的各種的計劃皆使我失望；雖然費去勞力極多，也是於事無濟。牠躺在離水大約一百碼的地面上；第一個不便的事就是牠斜上而逹於河。好，要把這個失望丟開，我遂決定去掘地的面層，使成一個斜坡。我開始這件工作，却使我受了狠大的痛苦；但是工作完成以後，困難制服以後，牠却依然如故，因爲我不能移動這隻木艇像我不能移動別的船隻一般。

我於是丈量地的距離，决定開一船塢或水道，把水帶到木艇方面來，因爲我是不能夠把木艇帶到水邊去。好，我開始着這件工程；當我從事之初，我計算着要把牠掘得怎樣深，怎樣寬，以及怎樣把無用的料實拋去，

ti, and ¹*calculate* how deep it was to be ²*dug*, how oroad, and how the ³*stuff* was to be ⁴*thrown out*, I found that, by the number of hands I had, being none but my own; it must have been ten or twelve years before I could have gone through with it; for the shore ⁵*lay* so high that at the upper end it must have been at least twenty feet deep. So at ⁶*length*, ⁷*though with great reluctancy*, I gave this ⁸*attempt* over also.

This ⁹*grieved me heartily*. Now I saw, though too late, the ¹⁰*folly* of beginning a work before we ¹¹*count* the ¹²*cost*, and before we judge rightly of our own strength to go through with it.

In the middle of this work I finished my fourth year in this place, and ¹³*kept* my ¹⁴*anniversary* with the same ¹⁵*devotion*, and with as much comfort, as ever before. By a ¹⁶*constant* study and ¹⁷*serious* application to the word of God, and ¹⁸*by the assistance of his grace*, I ¹⁹*gained* a different knowledge from what I had before. I ²⁰*entertained different notions of things*. I looked now upon the world as a thing ²¹*remote*, which I ²²*had nothing to do with*, ²³*no expectation from*, and, indeed, ²⁴*no desires about*. In a word, I had nothing indeed to do with it, ²⁵*nor was ever likely to have*. So I thought it looked as we may ²⁶*perhaps* look upon it hereafter; namely, as a place I had lived in, but was come out of it; and well might I say, as ²⁷*Father Abraham* to ²⁸*Dives*, "Between me and thee is a great gulf fixed."

In the first place, I was ²⁹*removed* ³⁰*from all the wickedness of the world* here. I had neither ³¹*the lusts of the flesh, the lusts of the eye*, nor ³²*the pride of life*. I ³³*had nothing to covet*, for I had all that I was now capable of ³⁴*enjoying*. I was lord of the whole ³⁵*manor*; or, if I pleased, I might call

我覺着，倘使用我獨自一人的手工，我必須費去十年或十二年的辰光方能把這件工作弄得完成；因為海岸所在的地位是這樣的高，在牠的上面的尾端，水至少有二十尺深。這樣，後來，雖非所願，我也把這個企圖放棄了。

這事令我憂恨不已，現在我明白，雖然是太晚了，在未計算費用以前，在未曾正當地評判自己的力量能否完成以前便着手工作的愚笨了。

在這件工作之中，我在這個地方度過了我的第四年，用了同等的虔心和像以前同等的安慰，我保守着這個紀念日。經過時常研究和勝重注意上帝的言語以後，有賴於上帝的恩眷，我得了一個和從前不同的知識。對於各種事物的見解與前大異。現在我看世界像一個不足注意的東西了，牠和我絕不相關，於彼無所希望；實在，也是一無所求於牠。總而言之，實在我和牠無關係了，而且將來也不見得再有關係。這樣，我想我們現在瞧世界或者能夠和以後所瞧的是一樣；就是，好像是我住的一塊地方，然而不久便要離開牠了；我也可以說，像（亞伯拉罕）長老向（戴扶斯）說的一樣，"在我和窗之中，有一大坑存焉。"

第一步，我在這裏是不蹈世俗惡習。我既無肉慾，目慾之念，又無人生尊榮之心。我無貪求之物，因為現在所有者已儘夠享受的了。我是這個領地上面的貴爵；如其我願意，我可以自稱為我所佔領的土地上面的王或皇帝。我沒有和我爭競的人。

1. 計算。2. 掛。3. 嚴料。4. 拋去。5. 躺。6. 長。7. 雖非所願。8. 企圖。9. 大傷予懷。10. 愚笨。11. 數。12. 費用。13. 保守。14. 紀念日。15. 虔心。16. 常常。17. 勝重。18. 賴天之恩。19. 得。20. 對於事物有不同之見解。21. 不足重輕。22. 絕不相關。23. 於彼無望。24. 於世無求。25. 將來永無關係。26. 或者。27. （亞伯拉罕）28. （戴扶斯）29. 離開。30. 世上的惡習。37. 肉慾，目慾。32. 人生之榮華。33. 無所貪求。34. 享受。35. 領地。

myself king or [1]*emperor* over the whole country which I had [2]*possession* of. There were no [3]*rivals.* I had no [4]*competitor*, none to [5]*dispute* [6]*sovereignty* or [7]*command* with me. I might have [8]*raised shiploadings* of corn, but I had no use for it; so I let as little grow as I thought enough [9]*for my occasion.* I had tortoise or turtle enough, but now and then one was as much as I could put to any use. I had timber enough to have built [10]*a fleet of ships;* and I had grapes enough to have made [11]*wine,* or to have cured into [12]*raisins,* to have loaded that [13]*fleet* when it had been built.

But all I could make use of was all that was [14]*valuable.* I had enough to eat and [15]*supply* my wants, and what was all [16]*the rest* to me? If I killed more flesh than I could eat, the dog must eat it, or [17]*vermin.* If I [18]*sowed* more corn than I could eat, it must be [19]*spoiled.* This trees that I cut down were lying to [20]*rot* on the ground; I could make no more use of them but for [21]*fuel,* and that I [22]*had no occasion for* but to [23]*dress* my food.

In a word, the nature and [24]*experience* of things [25]*dictated* to me, upon just [26]*reflection,* that all the good things of this world are no farther good to us than they are for our use. Whatever we may heap up to give others, we enjoy just as much as we can use, and no more. The most [27]*covetous, griping miser* in the world would have been cured of [28]*the* [29]*vice of covetousness* if he had been in my case; for I possessed [30]*infinitely* more than I knew what to do with. I had [31]*no room for desire,* [32]*except* it was of things which I had not, and they were but [33]*trifles,* though, indeed, of great use to me.

I had, as I hinted before, a parcel of money, [34]*as well gold as silver,* about thirty-six [35]*pounds* [36]*sterling,* Alas! there

我無與我爭勝之人；又無人與我爭櫃爭勢。我可以收穫一船的載量的穀子，但是我却用不着牠；所以我不過讓穀子少少的生長，心想只要能應不時之需就足夠了。我有足量的龜和鼈，但是時常地一隻已經夠應我各項需求了。我有足量的木料，足以造船一隊；我有足量的葡萄，足以造酒，或者把牠晾乾，製爲葡萄乾，等船造好就可以把這些東西放上船去。

但是我所能利用的都是些有價值的東西。我有足量吃的東西和供給我的需要的物件，其餘復何所求？倘使我殺了多的肉食，我一個人吃不了，狗或蟲子將要吃完牠。倘使穀子種的多吃不盡，牠必定至損壞爲止。我割下來的那些樹現在躺在地上腐爛了，除去把牠們當薪柴，其餘便無用牠們的地方了，然而除去用牠們烹煑食物外，並無他用。

總而言之，由正直的追想上面說起來，事物的本性和經驗指示我說：世間之物，無有貴於適用者。我們可以把東西聚積起來贈與旁人，我們僅能享受我們所能用的而已。世界上的最貪婪的，一錢如命的慳吝人，倘使他處在我的境地，或者能夠把他貪婪之念消除了；因爲我有無限量的東西；以致我不知道怎樣來處置他們。除去我所無的東西以外，我並無欲望，這些東西雖是瑣屑之物，却對於我實在是很有用的呢。

我從前說過，我有一袋錢幣，金銀兼備；大約純粹三十六鎊。

1.皇帝．2.有．3.爭勝者．4.競爭者．5.爭競．6.櫃柄．7.命令．8.一船之載量．9.爲我不時之需．10.一隊船．11.酒．12.葡萄乾．13.船隊．14.有價值．15.供給．16.其餘．17.蟲．18.播．19.損壞．20.腐爛．21.柴．22.並無他用．23.烹煑．24.經驗．25.指示．26.同憶．27.貪婪之徒．28.惡念．29.貪婪．30.無量．31.無所欲望．32.除去……以外．33.瑣屑之物．34.金銀兼有．35.鎊．36.純粹的。

the sorry, useless [1]*stuff* lay. I had no manner of business for it, and often thought with myself that I would have given a handful of it for a [2]*gross* of tobacco [3]*pipes*, or for a [4]*hand mill* to [5]*grind* my corn. Nay, I would have given it all for a [6]*sixpenny* worth of [7]*turnip* and [8]*corrot seed* out of England, or for a handful of [9]*peas and beans*, and a bottle of ink. [10]*As it was*, I had not the least [11]*advantage* by it or [12]*benefit* from it. There it lay in a [13]*drawer*, and [14]*grew moldy with the damp* of the cave in the wet seasons; and if I had had the [15]*drawer* full of [16]*diamonds*, it had been [17]*the same case*; they had been of no manner of value to me, because of no use.

I had now brought my state of life to be much [18]*easier in* itself than it was at first, and much easier to my mind as well as to my body. I [19]*frequently* [20]*sat down to my meat* with [21]*thankfulness*, and [22]*admired* the mind of God's providence, which had thus [23]*spread* my table in the [24]*wilderness*. I learned to look more upon [25]*the bright side of my condition*, and less upon [26]*the dark side*, and to consider what I enjoyed rather than what I wanted. This gave me sometimes such secret comforts that I cannot [27]*express* them; and this I take notice of here, to [28]*put those discontented people in mind of it* who cannot enjoy [29]*comfortably* what God has given them, because they see and covet something that he has not given them. All our [30]*discontents* about what we want appeared to me to spring from the want of thankfulness for what we have.

CHAPTER XXV

I HAD now been here so long that many things which I had brought on [31]*shore* for my help were either quite gone,

可惜！憂慮所在的地方，無用之物便存在焉。我和牠沒有事務往來，常常想着我願意拿一把錢幣去換十二打烟袋或一隻磨麥的手磨。豈止如此，我願意把所有的錢幣去換由英國出產的價值六辨士的蘿蔔和萊菔種子或一把豆類和一瓶墨水。但是現在呢，我由牠得不到些微益處和從中得些利益。錢幣放在抽斗內；因為洞中天氣潮濕的緣故便發霉了；倘使我有一抽斗的金剛鑽，也不過同此景况；牠們因為沒有用場，就對於我毫無價值了。

現在我使我的生活狀况較前更為安適，身心泰然，煩慮盡除。我常常用感謝的態度來坐而飲食，崇仰上帝的先見的心，在荒野之中我的食桌上充滿了上帝的恩賜。我於是看重我處境好的方面，而看輕壞的方面，並狠注重我所享受的東西，而忽略我所缺少的東西。有時這些思想給我說不出的私心的安慰；我在這裏注意着這個，使得那些不知足的人們得以想及，他們不能安逸地享受着上帝所賜予的東西，因為他們心想和貪求那些上帝所未曾賜予的東西。照我看起來，我們對於需要的東西的不自足的心是由于我們對於所有的東西享用缺少感謝心發生的。

第 二 十 五 章

現在我在這裏狠久了，許多東西被我帶到岸上來備用的

1. 無用之物。2. 十二打。3. 烟管。4. 手磨。5. 磨。6. 六辨士。7. 萊菔。8. 紅萊菔子。9. 豆。10. 而今則。11. 利益。12. 利益。13. 抽屜。14. 因濕發霉。15. 抽斗。16. 鑽石。17. 亦如是耳。18. 較安逸。19. 常常。20. 坐食。21. 感謝。22. 崇仰。23. 鋪開。24. 荒野。25. 好的方面。26. 壞的方面。27. 表示。28. 令不知足之人得以想及。29. 安逸之狀。30. 不知足之心。31. 海岸。

or very much [1]*wasted* and near [2]*spnet*. My ink, as I
[3]*observed*, had been gone some time, all but a very little
which I [4]*eked out* with water, a little and a little, till it was
so pale it [5]*scarce* left any [6]*appearance* of [7]*black* upon the
paper. As long as it lasted I made use of it to [8]*minute*
down the days of the month on which any [9]*remarkable*
thing happened to me. [10]*By casting up times past*, I remembered that there was a strange [11]*concurrence of days* in the
[12]*various* [13]*providences* which befell me, and which, if I had
been [14]*superstitiously* inclined to observe days as [15]*fatal* or
[16]*fortunate*, I might have had reason to have looked upon
with a great deal of [17]*curiosity*.

First, I had [18]*observed* that the same day that I broke
away from my father and friends, and ran away to Hull,
in order to go to sea, the same day afterwards I was taken
by the Sallee [19]*man-of-war*, and made a [20]*slave*. The same
day of the year that I [21]*escaped* out of the [22]*wreck* of that
ship in Yarmouth Roads, that same day of the year afterwards I made my escape from Sallee in a boat. The same
day of the year I was born on, namely, the 30th of September, that same day I had my life so [23]*miraculously* saved
twenty-six years after, when I was cast on shore on this
island; so that my [24]*wicked life* and my [25]*solitary* life began
both on a day.

The next thing to my ink being [26]*wasted*, was that of my
bread, I mean the biscuit which I brought out of the ship.
This I had [27]*husbanded* to the [28]*last degree*, [29]*allowing* myself
but one cake of bread a day for above a year; and yet I
was quite without bread for near a year before I got any
corn of my own. Great reason I had to be [30]*thankful* that
I had any at all, the getting it being as has been already
observed, [31]*next to miraculous*.

或是完全失去了，或是大牛用盡和差不多用耗了。照我觀察而論，我的墨水用罄已久，只有些須留存，我用水調和補湊，一點一點的，後來墨水這樣的淡；牠簡直在紙上留下很少的黑跡來。牠一日不斷絕，我就用牠把一月中我所做的可記載的事的日子錄將下來。同憶往日的事跡，我想起在上天種種護佑我的境遇中，到有一個狠奇異的符合的日期呢，假使我迷信地注重日子的吉或凶，我一定很有理由地來用驚異的眼光去瞧牠了。

第一步，我注意着我和父親以及友人離開，跑到（赫爾）去，爲的是要到海中去，那個同樣的日子，以及以後我被（沙利）戰艦拘囚作奴的那個同樣的日子。在（夏爾毛斯）路，我從船的損壞中逃走出來的那年那個日子，後來我乘一只小船從（沙利）中逃走出來的那年那個日子。我誕生的那年那個日子，就是九月三十日，二十六年以後，當我被風浪打到這座小島上面的岸上來，我狠奇妙地被救的那個日子；於是我的惡劣的生活和我的孤寂的生活在一日中都開始了。

在我缺乏墨水以後，我的麵包也隨卽用耗了，我的意思就是從船中帶下來的餅乾。我對牠用得極爲節省，大約一年光景，我一天只吃一塊麵包，然而在我未曾收穫穀子以前，差不多一年沒有麵包吃了。我有極大緣故來感謝，因爲我居然能得着了，而且得着牠的法子，像我從前所說的一樣，簡直是奇異非常。

1.耗去。2.用去。3.注意。4.補足。5.少6.樣子。7.黑色。8.記下。9.可異的。10.同憶往事。11.日期符合。12.種種的。13.護佑。14.迷信地。15.凶的。16.吉的。17.奇異心。18.注意。19.戰船。20.奴。21.逃。22.破損。23.奇怪。24.惡劣。25.孤寂。26.用去。27.節省。28.極點。29.允許。80.感謝。31.絕無僅有。

My clothes, too, began to [1]*decay.* As to [2]*linen,* I had had none a good while, except some [3]*checkered shirts* which I found in the [4]*chests* of the other seamen, and which I carefully [5]*preserved.* Many times I could bear no other clothes on but a [6]*shirt*; and it was a very great help to me that I had, among all the men's [7]*clothes* of the ship, almost three dozen of [8]*shirts.* There were also, indeed, several thick [9]*watch coats* of the seamen's which were left, but they were too hot to wear; and though it is [10]*true* that the weather was so [11]*violently* hot that there was no need of clothes, [12]*yet I could not go quite without them.*

I have [13]*mentioned* that I saved the skins of all the creatures that I killed,—I mean [14]*four-footed ones,*—and I had them hung up, [15]*stretched out* with stichs in the sun, [16]*by which means* some of them were so dry and hard that they were [17]*fit for little*; but others were very useful. The first thing I made of these was a great [18]*cap* for my head, with the hair on the outside [19]*to shoot off the rain.* This I [20]*performed* so well that afterwards I made me [21]*a suit of clothes* wholly of these skins,—that is to say, a [22]*waistcoat,* and [23]*breeches open at the knees,* and both [24]*loose,* for they were rather wanting to keep me [25]*cool* than to keep me warm. I [26]*must not omit to acknowledge* that they were [27]*wretchedly made*; for if I was a bad carpenter, I was a worse [28]*tailor.* However, they were such as I [29]*made very good shift with,* and when I was out, if it [30]*happened* to rain, the hair of my [31]*waistcoat* and cap being [32]*outermost.* I was kept very dry.

After this, I spent a great deal of time and pains to make an [33]*umbrella.* I was indeed in great want of one, and had a great mind to make one. I had seen them made in Brazil, where they are very useful in the great heats

　　我的衣服也開始破損了。至於蔴布；除去在我好好地保存着別的水手所有的箱子裏面找出些印有棋盤花格的襯衫以外，我所有的並不甚多。許多次，我除襯衫外不能穿別的衣服；我有牠實在是一個大幫助；在船中許多水手的衣服當中，差不多有三打襯衫。實在，還有些遺留下來的幾件水手的厚的守夜着的衣服；但是着起牠們；却嫌太暖；雖然不錯，天氣是非常的熱，無須衣服，然而我不能不用牠來遮蔽身體。

　　我曾說過我保存着許多被我殺死的生物的皮，—— 我的意思是說四足動物，——我把牠們懸掛起來，用棍子在太陽中撑開來；因此，有幾張皮是變得這樣地乾和硬，遂至不甚合用了；但是其餘的到狠有用的。我用牠們第一次所製的東西是頭上的一項小帽；毛放在外面，使雨不得進去。這事進行得甚佳，後來我完全用這些皮來製一套衣服，——就是說，一件背心，幾件長及膝的褲子，全是寬闊的，因為牠們不大使我暖却狠使我覺冷呢。我不得不承認牠們是製得狠劣的；因為倘使我是一個惡劣的木匠；我更是一個較劣的裁縫。然而着起牠們來可以將就過日子，當我出外之時，倘使天雨，背心和帽子上面的毛穿向外面，我覺着狠乾燥的。

　　這事完後，我費了許多時候和痛苦去製一根洋傘。我實在需要着牠，並且狠願意造製一根。在（布勒喜爾）我瞧見人們

which are there, and I felt ¹*the heats every jot as graet here*, and greater too, being nearer the ²*equator*. Besides, as ³*I was obliged to be much abroad*, it was a most useful thing to me, as well for the rains as the ⁴*heats*. I ⁵*took a world of pains* with it, and was a great while before I could make anything likely to hold. Nay, after I thought I ⁶*had hit the way*, I ⁷*spoiled* two or three before I made one ⁸*to my mind*; but at last I made one that ⁹*answered indifferently well*. The ¹⁰*main* difficulty I found was to make it ¹¹*let down*. I could make it ¹²*spread*, but if it did not let down too, and ¹³*draw in*, it was not ¹⁴*portable* for me any way but just over my head, which would not do. However, at last, as I said, I made one to ¹⁵*answer*, and covered it with shins, the hair ¹⁶*upwards*, so that it ¹⁷*cast off the rain like a shed*, and ¹⁸*kept off* the sun so ¹⁹*effectually* that I could walk out in the hottest of the weather with greater advantage than I could before in the coolest, and, when I had no need of it, could close it and ²⁰*carry* it under my arm.

Thus I lived ²¹*mighty comfortably*, my mind being entirely ²²*composed* by ²³*resigning myself to the will of God* and ²⁴*throwing myself wholly upon the disposal of his providence*. This made my life better than ²⁵*sociable*, for when I began to ²⁶*regret* the want of ²⁷*conversation*, I would sak myself whether thus ²⁸*conversing* ²⁹*mutually* with my own thoughts, and (as I hope I may say) with even God himself, by ³⁰*ejaculations*, was not better than the utmost enjoyment of ³¹*human society* in the world.

I cannot say that after this, for five years, any ³²*extraordinary* thing happened to me, but I ³³*lived on in the same course*, in the same ³⁴*posture* and place as before. The chief things I was ³⁵*employed* in, besides my yearly labor

製作傘兒，在那個地方，天氣狠是燒熱，所以牠們是狠有用的，我覺着此種熱氣之劇烈正和彼處相似，而且更属害些，因爲貼近於赤道的緣故。而且是從不得不常常出外的，所以無論天雨或天熱，傘兒對於我是一件狠有用的東西。我製造牠辛苦萬狀，在我製成可握的東西以前費了不少的時候呢。豈止如此，在我想已得其法以後，弄壞了兩三柄，然後方能製成如我心意的一柄；後來我製成一柄，用起來甚爲合式。我覺着最主要的困難就是把牠垂落下來。我能把牠張開來，倘使牠不垂落下來和收縮，除去在頭上撐起來外，沒有別的法子來攜帶牠，就是撐在頭上也覺不狠合宜。最後，我說過，我製成合用的一柄，用獸皮把牠蓋住，毛向上，這樣牠像廬舍一般能夠禦雨，狠有效力地把太陽遮住，在氣候極熱的天時，我也能出外，所得的利益比較最冷的天氣尤大，當我無需此物，便把牠摺起，夾在臂中。

　　我度日甚安適，我的心是十分泰然，各事悉由天命，一切聽天安排。這樣使我生活比較際尤好，當我悔恨缺少交談之時，我自問能否我思想互相敍談，以及（我希望我可以說）用禱告和上帝接談，是不是世界上人類社會之中最大的快樂。

　　我不能說，在這事以後，過了五年，有什麼特別的大事到我身上來，但是我居處一仍舊貫，情形地位，與前無異。在我每年所費的種植大麥和米以及晾曬葡萄乾勞力以外，這

1. 此處熱氣劇烈與彼處相似。2. 赤道。3. 逼予外出。4. 熱度。5. 辛苦異常。6. 已得其法。7. 損壞。8. 如心。甚合式。10. 主要。11. 垂落。12. 張開。13. 收縮。15. 可攜。15. 合用。16. 向上。17. 如廬舍能禦雨。18. 拒。19. 有力地。20. 攜。31. 甚安適。22. 安心。23. 悉由天命。24. 由天安排。25. 交際。26悔恨。27. 交談。23. 敍談。29. 互相。30. 禱祝。31. 人類社會。32. 特別的。33. 居處如昔。34. 情形。35. 從事。

of planting my [1]*barley* and [2]*rice*, and curing my [3]*raisins*, of both which I always kept up just enough to have [4]*sufficient* stock of one year's [5]*provision* [6]*beforehand*,—I say, besides this yearly labor, and my [7]*daily pursuit of going out with my gun*, I had one labor, to make a canoe, which at last I finished. By [8]*digging* a canal to it six feet [9]*wide* and four feet deep, I brought it into the [10]*creek*, almost half a mile. And though I [11]*was near two years about it*, yet I [12]*never grudged* my labor, in hopes of having a boat to go off to sea at last.

Though my little [13]*periagua* was finished, yet the size of it [14]*was not at all answerable to the design* which I [15]*had in view* when I made the first; I mean of [16]*venturing* over to the [17]*terra firma*, where the sea was above forty miles broad. Accordingly, the smallness of my boat [18]*assisted* [19]*to put an end to that design*, and now I thought no more of it.

As I had a boat, my next [20]*design* was [21]*to make a cruise round the island*. I had been on the other side in one place, [22]*crossing*, as I have already [23]*described* it, over the land, and the [24]*discoveries* I made in that little journey made me [25]*very eager to see other parts of the coast*. Now I had a boat, I thought of nothing but [26]*sailing* round the island.

[27]*For this purpose*, and that I might do everything with [28]*discretion* and consideration, I [29]*fitted up* a little mast in my boat, and made a sail to it out of some of the pieces of the ship's sails which [30]*lay in store*, and of which I had a great [31]*stock* by me. Having fitted my mast and sail, and tried the boat, I found she would sail very well. Then I made little [32]*lockers*, or boxes, at each end of my boat, to put provisions, [33]*necessaries*, [34]*ammunition*, etc., into, to be kept dry either from rain or [35]*the spray of the sea*. A little, long,

幾類東西我常常預先存儲足夠一年供給的十足分量，一就是說，在我費去這種每年的勞力以外，和每日攜槍出獵之事以外，我有一種工作，去製一木艇，後來到底弄成功了。這就是我所從事的業務了。向木艇方面掘了一條六尺寬四尺深的水道，我把木艇帶到小河內去，差不多有半(英)里路。雖然我為此事工作兩年，然而我對於工作殊無怨恨的心思，僅希望最後能得一船駛向大海而去。

雖然小獨木舟已經完工，然而牠的式樣和我以前有意製造牠的時候所擬的全然不合；我的意思就是冒險駛到陸地上面去，在那裏，海大約有四十(英)里以外的寬。然而船體甚小把我的意念全消除了，現在我已不再瞧牠。

我既然有了一隻船，第二次的計劃就是要巡邏全島。我是曾經往島的那一方面的地方上去過，我巳經把牠的形勢詳述過了，我橫過了陸地，在那次小的行程中所得着新發見的事物使我亟欲一視岸上各區。現在我有一隻船，除去駛繞全島以外，我無其他意念了。

因此之故，我必須用謹慎和思慮的態度來處理各事，我在船上裝備一根小帆柱，用我藏貯甚多的幾塊船帆來和小船作了一張帆。裝備好了帆柱和帆，試試小船，我覺着牠駛行得很好。於是我製造櫃和箱，在船的兩邊末端上，去放入食物，必需品，軍實等等，保守牠們乾燥使不受雨淚的襲擊。在船的內部，我挖了一個

hollow place I cut in the ¹inside of the boat, where I could lay my gun, making a ²flap to hang down over it to keep it dry.

I ³fixed my ⁴umbrella, also, in a ⁵step at the ⁶stern, like a mast, to ⁷stand over my head and keep the ⁸heat of the sun off me, like an ⁹awning. Thus I ¹⁰every now and then took a little voyage upon the sea; but never ¹¹went far out, nor far from the little ¹²creek. At last, being ¹³eager to view the ¹⁴circumference of my little kingdom, I ¹⁵resolved upon my cruise; and accordingly ¹⁶I victualed my ship for the voyage, putting in two dozen of ¹⁷loaves (cakes I should rather call them) of barley bread, an earthen ¹⁸pot full of ¹⁹parched rice (a food I ate a great deal of) a little ²⁰bottle of ²¹rum, half a goat, and powder and shot for killing more, and two large watch coats, of those which, as I mentioned before, I had saved out of the seamen's chests. These I took, one ²²to lie upon and the other to cover me in the night.

It was the 6th of November, in the sixth year of my ²³reign,—or my ²⁴captivity, which you please,—that I set out on this voyage. I found it much longer than I ²⁵expected, for though the island itself was not very large, yet when I came to the east side of it, I found a great ²⁶ledge of rocks lie out about two ²⁷leagues into the sea, some above water, some under it, and beyond that a ²⁸shoal of sand, lying dry half a league more; so that I was obliged to go a great way out to sea to ²⁹double the point.

When first I discovered these ³⁰difficulties, I was going to give over my ³¹enterprise, and come back again, not knowing how far it might ³²oblige me to go out to sea; and, ³³above all, doubting how I should get back again. I ³⁴came ³⁵to an anchor; for I had made a kind of an ³⁶anchor with a

小的，長的和凹的地方，在那裏，我可以放槍，製造了一塊垂板，在牠上面垂下來因，爲要使牠乾燥。

　　我也把傘插在船尾的架上。像一根帆柱一般，遮蓋我的頭，使得太陽熱氣離開我，像一張天幔一樣。這樣我不時地在海上作一小小的旅行；但是不走得太遠，也不離開小河太遠。最後，因爲極想察看我的小王國的周圍地方，我決意駛船巡游海岸；於是把糧食儲於船上，準備旅行，放入兩打麵包（我應當叫作牠們餅餌），大麥粉作的，一大陶罐烘乾的米（這是我吃得狠多的一種食品），一小瓶甜酒半隻山羊，因爲殺更多些山羊又帶着藥粉和子彈，二件大的守夜衣，這就是我以前說過從水手們的箱中保存出來的。我拿了牠們，一件以爲睡臥之用。一件以爲夜間蓋身之用。

　　這是九月六日，我的御宇，——或是拘囚，隨你的便，——第六年間，我開始着這次旅行。我覺旅行比我所料的日子來得長，因爲島雖不十分大，然而當我到牠東面的時候，我瞧見一大塊石礁躺在海中約有兩海里之遠，有些石頭露出水面，有些石頭深藏水底，此外尚有一堆淺沙，乾燥地伸長到半海里餘之遠；這樣我便不得不駛到老遠的海外去，繞角而行。當我初次發見這些困難之時，我將要放棄此擧，重行回家，不知道我應當去海多遠，最要者，我疑惑着不知怎樣的地方能同到舊路。我拋了錨；這是我用我從船中所得到的一塊

piece of a broken ¹*grappling iron* which I got out of the ship.

Having ²*secured* my boat, I took my gun and went on shore, ³*climbing* up a hill which seemed to ⁴*overlook* that point, where I ⁵*saw the full extent of it*, and ⁶*resolved to* ⁷*venture*.

In my ⁸*viewing* the sea from that hill where I stood, I ⁹*perceived* a strong and, indeed, a most ¹⁰*furious current*, which ran to the east, and even came close to the point. I took the more notice of it because I saw there might be some ¹¹*danger* that, when I came into it, I might be carried out to sea by the strength of it, and not be able to ¹²*make* the island again. Indeed, had I not ¹³*got first upon this hill*, I ¹⁴*believe* it would have been so; for there was the same ¹⁵*current* on the other side the island, only that it ¹⁶*set off* at a farther ¹⁷*distance*, and I saw there was a strong ¹⁸*eddy* under the shore; so I had nothing to do but to get out of the first current, and I should presently be in an ¹⁹*eddy*.

I lay here, however, two days, becuase the wind ²⁰*blowing* pretty fresh at ²¹*east-southeast*, and that being just ²²*contrary* to the ²³*current*, ²⁴*made a great breach of the sea* upon the point; so that it was not safe for me to keep too close to the shore for the ²⁵*breach*, nor to go too far off because of the ²⁶*stream*.

The third day, in the morning, ²⁷*the wind having abated over night*, the sea was calm, and I ventured, But I am a ²⁸*warning* again to all ²⁹*rash* and ³⁰*ignorant* ³¹*pilots*; for no sooner was I come to the point, when I was not even my ³²*boat's length from the shore*, but I found myself in a great depth of water, and a current like the ³³*sluice of a mill*. It carried my boat along with it with such ³⁴*violence* that all

碎的小鐵錨製成了錨。

把船停穩了，我拿槍上岸，爬上一座可俯臨該地的小山，在山上，我望見牠的全部面積，決心去冒險嘗試。

在我站立的小山上面觀察海面，我見強烈和實在而且是急而猛的湍流，牠向東方流去，並流到靠近這個地方，我對於這個更加注意，因爲我想那邊或者有些危險，當我駛進去，我或者被急流冲出海去，不能再到島上去了。實在，倘使我不卽行登山，我相信必有這層危險；因爲在島的那一方面也有同樣的急流，不過牠出發的地方距離稍遠而已，我看見在海岸之下有陣強烈的急水；我於是除去駛出這第一層急流以外，別無事情可做，我現在却身處急水之中呢。

我在那裏兩天，因爲風在東偏東南方面括得很清新的，却正是和急流趨向不同，在海角上，大興波濤；倘使我貼近海岸以避波濤，實在是甚不安全，也不要因爲水流之故去得太遠。

第三日，早間，風勢昨夜已減，海水平靜，我乃冒險前進，但是我仍可以作鹵莽和愚昧的領港人的鑒誡；因爲一經到了海角，我離岸未嘗有一船之遠，我覺着我是在水的極深處，和在像水磨開門放出的水的急流當中。急流用極猛烈的力量把我的船帶去，儘我之力，我不能使牠離開溜頭，

1.碎鐵。2.停穩。3.爬。4.俯臨。5.望見全部面積。6.決心。7.冒險。8.觀看。9.見。10.急流。11危險。12.到。13.卽行上山。14.相信。15.急流。16.出發。17.距離。18.急水。19.同水。20.括。21.束偏東南。22.相反。23.急流。24.大興波濤。25.破處。36.流。27.風勢昨夜已減。28.鑒誡。29.鹵莽。30.愚昧。31.領港人。32.離岸一舟之遙。33.水閘放出之水。34.強烈

I could do could not keep her so much as on the ¹*edge* of it ; but I found it hurried me farther and farther out from the eddy, which was on my left hand. There was no wind ²*stirring* to help me, and all I could do with my ³*paddles signified nothing.* Now I began ⁴*to give myself over for lost* ; for as the current was on both sides of the island, I knew in a few ⁵*leagues'* distance they must join again, and then I was ⁶*irrecoverably* gone. Nor did I see any ⁷*possibility* of ⁸*avoiding* it ; so that I had no ⁹*prospect* before me but of ¹⁰*perishing* not by the sea, for that was calm enough, but of ¹¹*starving* from ¹²*hunger.* I had, indeed, found a ¹³*tortoise* on the shore, as big almost as I could lift, and had ¹⁴*tossed* it into the boat ; and I had a great jar of fresh water, that is to say, one of my earthen pots ; but what was all this to being ¹⁵*driven into* the vast ocean, where, to be ¹⁶*sure*, there was no shore, no ¹⁷*mainland* or island, for a thousand leagues at least?

And now I saw how easy it was for the ¹⁸*providence* of God to make even the most ¹⁹*miserable* condition of ²⁰*mankind* worse. Now I looked back upon my ²¹*desolate*, ²²*solitary* island as the most pleasant place in the world, and all the happiness my heart could wish for was to be but there again. I ²³*stretched out* my hands to it, with eager wishes. " O happy ²⁴*desert* !" said I, "²⁵*I shall never see thee more.* O ²⁶*miserable* creature ! whither am I going?" Then I re-²⁷*proached* myself with my unthankful ²⁸*temper*, and that I had ²⁹*repind at* my ³⁰*solitary* condition ; and now what would I give to be on shore there again ! Thus we never see the ³¹*true state* of our condition till it is ²²*illustrated* to us by its ³³*contraries*, nor know how to ³⁴*value* what we enjoy but by the want of it.

但是我覺着急流把我還遠的迸出靠我左手旁的旋水外面。沒有風來幫助我，我盡力地用着槳，然而毫無進步。現在我以爲生命一定要失去了；因爲急流是在島的兩方面，我知道在不多的海里的距離中，牠們將要合併起來，那末我是無可救濟了。我想要避免急流也是不可能的事，這樣我除死以外，在我目前，沒有別的希望了，並不是死於海，因爲牠是很平靜的，却要死於飢餓了。我在岸上找着一隻龜，其大如我所能舉起，把牠擲入船中；我有一大瓶鮮潔的水，就是說，我的陶器罐中的一隻；但是我被追入於大洋中，在那裏，當然地，沒有海岸，沒有大地或島，至少有一千海里遠，那末這些東西對我有何益呢？

　　我現在狠容易地明白了，上帝的護佑也能把人類中的最困苦的境况弄得更壞。現在我囘看我的孤立寂寞的島，覺着牠是世界上最快樂的地方，我心中希望的幸福就是能够再回到那邊去。我用懇切的願望向着島伸出手來。我說："哦，快樂的荒野呀！我將永遠地瞧不見了。峩，苦惱的生物呀！我往那兒去呢？"於是我用不感謝的態度來自己責備，我曾在孤寂境况中怨恨過的；現在我重到了海岸上，又將如何呢！我們非俟我們的景况的實在情形被相反之事表彰出來後，決計不會明白的，我們也不知道怎樣地去寶貴我們所享用的東西，但是需求牠時，便明白了。

1，邊。2．動。3．毫無用處。4．自度不免。5．海里。6．無可挽救。7．可能。8．避免。9．希冀。10．死。11．飆。12．餓。13．龜。14．擲。15．被驅入。16．一定。17．大地。18．保佑。19．困苦。20．人類。21．孤立。22．寂寞23．伸出。24荒地。25．永不見爾。26．困苦。27．責備。28．性情。29．悔恨。30．孤獨。31．眞相。32．表彰。33．相反之事。34．寶貴。

CHAPTER XXVI

IT is ¹*scarcely* possible to imagine the ²*consternation* I was now in, being driven from my ³*beloved* island (for so it ⁴*appeared* to me now to be) into the ⁵*wide ocean*, almost two leagues, and ⁶*in the utmost despair of ever recovering it again.* However, I worked hard, till indeed my ⁷*strength* was almost ⁸*exhausted*, and kept my boat as much to the northward—that is towards the side of the current which the eddy ⁹*lay on*—as possibly I could; when about noon, as the sun passed the ¹⁰*meridian*, I thought I felt a little ¹¹*breeze* of wind in my face, ¹²*springing up* from ¹³*south-southeast.* This ¹⁴*cheered* my heart a little, and ¹⁵*especially* when, in about half an hour more, it blew a pretty gentle ¹⁶*gale.* By this time I had ¹⁷*got at a frightful distance* from the island, and had the least cloudy or ¹⁷*hazy* weather ¹⁹*intervened,* I had been ⁰*undone* another way, too; for I had no compass on board, and should never have known how to ²¹*steer* towards the island if I had but once lost sight of it. But the weather continuing clear, I ²²*applied* myself to get up my mast again, and spread my sail, standing away to the north as much as possible, to get out of the current.

Just as I had set my mast and sail, and the boat began to ²³*stretch away*, I saw even by the clearness of the water some ²⁴*alteration* of the current was near; for where the current was so strong the water was ²⁵*foul.* But per-²⁶*ceiving* the water clear, I found the current ²⁷*abate*; and presently I found to the east, at about half a mile, a breach of the sea upon some ²⁸*rocks.* These rocks I found caused the current to part again, and as the ²⁹*main stress* of it ran

第二十六章

這是狠不可能的去猜想我現在的驚慌失措的態度，從我的可愛的島中被驅到(現在我覺着牠是可愛的)汪洋裏面，差不多兩海里寬；我恐怕不能再回到舊島上面去了。然而，我竭力地工作，直到力量用盡爲止，儘力使我的小舟向北方，——就是朝旋水打擊的急流的一面——，當大約中午之時，太陽過了子午線，我覺着有微風拂面，從南偏東南吹來，這個稍微把我的心鼓礪一下，大約半個多鐘頭裏面。天上起了一陣狠平和的狂風，這更使我欣慰了。這個時候，我纔到離開島的甚遠的地方，天上間或多雲多霧，我又是不得了；因爲在船上沒有羅盤，一經不瞧見了島，我就永遠不會知道怎樣地方能駛向島方而去。但是天氣仍舊清新，我把帆柱樹起來，船帆張起來，儘力地朝北面豎立，使船出于急流之外。

剛剛把船帆柱和帆安好，船開始着駛行，從水的清澈當中，我瞧見急流馬上要改變方向了；因爲在那裏，急流是強烈的，而水却是淺濁的。但是瞧見水清澈，我覺着急流的勢漸減：現在，在大約半(英)里之遙的東方，我瞧見在石上有海水的斷流處。我瞧見這些石頭使急流重行分開，急流的大勢傾向南面流去，在東北方面，離開了石頭，於是別的濫流被石頭打擊囘來，

away more southerly, leaving the ¹*rocks* to the northeast, so the other returned by ²*the repulse of the rocks*, and made a strong eddy, which ran back again to the northwest, with a very ³*sharp stream.*

They who know what it is to have a ⁴*reprieve* brought to them upon the ⁵*ladder*, or to be ⁶*rescued* from ⁷*thieves* just going to ⁸*murder* them, or who have been in such ⁹*extremities*, may ¹⁰*guess* what my present surprise of joy was, and how gladly I put my boat into the ¹¹*stream* of this eddy; the wind also ¹²*freshening*, how gladly I ¹³*spread* my sail to it, running ¹⁴*cheerfully* before the wind, and with a strong ¹⁵*tide* or eddy under foot.

This eddy carried me about a league in my way ¹⁶*back* again, directly towards the island, but about two leagues more to the northward than the current which carried me away at first; so that when I came near the island, I found myself open to the northern shore of it,—that is to say, the other end of the island, ¹⁷*opposite* to that which I went out from,

When I had made something more than a league of way by the help of this ¹⁸*current* or eddy, I found it was spent, and ¹⁹*served me no farther.* However, I found that being between two great currents,—namely, that on the south side, which had hurried me away, and that on the north, which lay about a league on the other side,—I say, between these two, ²⁰*in the wake of the island*, I found the water at least still, and ²¹*running no way*; and having still a breeze of wind fair for me, I kept on ²²*steering* directly for the island, though not making such ²³*fresh* way as I did before.

遂成一陣強烈的漩水，又向西北流轉，帶着很大的急湍。

　　凡是那些人們明白他們在刑梯上忽然得着赦放的命令，或是剛剛要被盜賊謀殺便得救出來，或是遇着極大的困難的光景，那末他們可以料想得到我現在的驚喜交集的情形了；我是多麼快樂把船放到漩水的急流裏面；風勢加增，我是怎樣地快活向風張帆，快樂地在風前駛船；足下有強烈的潮水和漩水流着。

　　茌我取道而歸的程途中，漩水把我帶了大約一海里遠，直向島的方面，向北駛行。比起頭把我帶走的急流大約多了兩海里有餘；以致當我來近島面之時，我覺着到了島的北面海岸了，——那就是說，島的別一面的末端，是我所離開的方面的對向。

　　因爲溜流之助，駛行了一海里多路，我覺着溜流已用盡，不能再助我前進了。我覺着身處兩大溜流之中，——就是說，南方面的溜流把我帶走，北方的溜流，躺在大約一海里遠的別一方面；——我說，在這兩層急流之中，和島相接，後來水便靜寂，不稍流動；我仍舊遇着些微風，我直向島方**不停地駛去**，雖然路程却不如以前順利。

About four o'clock in the ¹*evening*, being then within a league of the island, I ²*stretched* across another eddy, ³*slanting northwest*; and in about an hour came within about a ⁴*mile* of the shore, where, it being ⁵*smooth water*, I soon got to land.

When I was on shore, I fell on my ⁶*knees* and gave God thanks for my ⁷*deliverance*, resolving to lay aside all thoughts of my deliverance by my boat; and ⁸*refreshing* myself with such things as I had, I brought my boat close to the ⁹*shore*, in a little ¹⁰*cove* that I had ¹¹*spied* under some trees, and laid me down to sleep, being quite ¹²*spent* with the labor and ¹³*fatigue* of the voyage.

I was now at a great loss which way to get home with my boat. I had run so much ¹⁴*hazard*, and knew too much of the case to think of ¹⁵*attempting* it by the way I went out. What might be at the other side (I mean the west side) I knew not, nor had I any mind to run any more ¹⁶*ventures*. So I only resolved on the next morning to make my way ¹⁷*westward* along the shore, and to see if there was no creek where I might ¹⁸*lay up my frigate in safety*, so as to have her again if I wanted her. In about three miles, or thereabouts, ¹⁹*coasting the shore*, I came to a very good ²⁰*inlet or bay*, about a mile over, which ²¹*narrowed* till it came to a very little ²²*rivulet or brook*, where I found a very ²³*convenient* harbor for my boat, and where she lay as if she had been in a little dock ²⁴*made on purpose for her*. Here I put in, and having ²⁵*stowed* my boat very safe, I went on shore to look about me, and see where I was.

I soon found I had but a little passed by the place where I had been before, when I ²⁶*traveled on foot to that shore*. So, ²⁷*taking* nothing out of my boat but my gun and

大約在晚上四點鐘，離島只在一海里之中的路程了。我橫過了另外的一層瀲水，偏斜向西北進駛；大約在一個鐘頭以內，駛到海岸邊的一英里之中，在那裏，水是光滑的，我卽刻便上了岸。

當我上了岸的時候，我跪下地去，謝上帝救我出險，決定把所有拯救的希望託付於船；用了我所有的東西來休憩自己，我把船靠攏了岸，在樹下我曾經發見的一個小灣裏面泊住，躺下來睡覺，因爲勞力和旅程把我弄得疲乏極了。

現在我茫然不知所措，不曉得乘船從那道囘去。我冒了許多險，我想最好從我出去的那條路囘家。那一邊究竟什麼光景（我的意思就是指兩邊而言），我不知道，我也再無心去冒險了。所以第二天清晨，我僅僅決心沿岸向西而進，瞧瞧有沒有可以停泊小船的小河，那末倘使我要用船的時候便可以再乘牠了。大約三英里之內，沿岸而駛，我來到了一座很好的海門或是海灣，大約從頭到尾有一英里濶，漸漸變狹，直抵一條小溪爲止，在那裏，我找着一座很好的泊船港，牠停在那裏好似停在爲牠而造的一所小船塢內一般。我進了港口，很安全地泊了我的船，上岸去四面一望，瞧瞧我在何處。

卽刻的覺察我不過離開從前所處的地方一點點遠，當我步行而登彼岸的時候。這樣，僅從船中把我的槍

umbrella, for it was [1]*exceedingly* hot, I began my [2]*march.* The way was [3]*comfortable* enough after such a voyage as I had been upon, and I reached my old [4]*bower* in the [5]*evening*, where I found everything [6]*standing as I left it*; for I always kept it in good order, it being, as I said before, my country house.

I got over the fence, and laid me down in the [7]*shade* to rest my [8]*limbs*, for I was very [9]*weary*, and fell [10]*asleep.* Judge you, if you can, that read my story, what a surprise I must be in when I was awaked out of my sleep by a [11]*voice* calling me by my name several times : " Robin, Robin, Robin Crusoe; poor Robin Crusoe ! Where are you, Robin Crusoe ? Where are you ? Where have you been ?"

I was so [12]*dead asleep* at first, being [13]*fatigued* with [14]*rowing,* or [15]*paddling* as it is called, the first part of the day, and with walking the latter part, that I [16]*did not wake thoroughly.* But [17]*dozing between sleeping and waking*, I [18]*dreamed* that somebody spoke to me, and as the voice continued to [19]*repeat*, " Robin Crusoe, Robin Crusoe, " at last I began to wake more [20]*perfectly*, and was at first dreadfully [21]*frightened*, and [22]*started* up in the utmost [23]*consternation.* But no sooner were my eyes open but I saw my Poll [24]*sitting on* the top of the hedge, and [25]*immediately* knew that it was he that spoke to me; for just in such [26]*bemoaning* language I had used to talk to him and teach him. He had learned it so [27]*perfectly* that he would sit upn my finger, and lay his [28]*bill* close to my face, and cry " Poor Robin Crusoe ! Where are you ? Where have you been ? How come you here ?" and such things as I had [29]*taught* him.

和傘拿了出來，因爲天氣熱得非凡，我開始進行前往。在我經過了那次旅程之後，我覺得島上的路程是很安適的，在晚上我到了我的從前造的小亭內，在那裏，我見各物毫無變更的情狀；因爲我是常常地把物件擺得合乎次序的，像我從前所說一樣，這裏就是我的村居了。

我走過了籬笆，在樹蔭中躺下來，休息我的肢體，我是疲乏極了，於是呼呼入睡。你讀了我的故事，倘使你能夠這樣做，那末你可以評判着我是怎樣地驚異，當我從睡眠中被一種屢次呼喚我的名字的聲音所驚醒：“魯賓，魯賓，魯賓克路索；可憐的魯賓克路索！你在那裏，魯賓克路索？你在那裏，你曾往那裏去？”

起頭我睡得恨熟，因爲搖船和打漿之故，那一天上半天，又因爲那一天下半天走了許多路而困乏了，我並未完全地醒來。但是將睡將醒，我夢見了有人向我說話，聲音仍舊重復着說：“魯賓克路索，魯賓克路索，”最後，我完全地醒了，不覺大驚，很慌迫地跳將起來。但是我的眼睛剛剛睜開，我就看見我的波爾座在籬笆頂上，馬上我明白就是牠向我說話；因爲我常常用這種悲哀的言詞來教牠和同牠談話。牠讀得很熟，牠時常歇在我的手指上面把牠的嘴貼近我的臉叫道：”可憐的魯賓克路索呀！你在那裏？你曾在那裏？你怎樣來到這裏？”這就是我教牠說的話。

However, even though I knew it was the [1]*parrot*, and that [2]*indeed* it could be nobody else, it was a good while before I could [3]*compose* myself. First, I was [4]*amazed* how the creature got thither ; and then, how he should just keep about the place, and nowhere else. But as I was well [5]*satisfied* it could be nobody but honest Poll. I [6]*got over it* ; and holding out my hand, and calling him by his name,' ' Poll, " the [7]*sociable* creature came to me, and sat upon my [8]*thumb*, as he used to do, and continued talking to me—Poor Pobin Crusoe ! and how did I come here ? and where had I been ?—just as if he had been [9]*overjoyed* to see me again. So I carried him home along with me.

I had now had enough of [10]*rambling* to sea for some time, and had enough to do for many days to sit still and [11]*reflect* upon the danger I had been in. I should have been very glad to have my boat again on my side of the island ; but I knew not how it was [12]*practicable* to [13]*get it about*. As to the east side of the island, which I had gone round, I knew well enough there was no [14]*venturing* that way. My [15]*very heart would shrink*, and my [16]*very blood run chill*, but to think of it. As to the other side of the island, I did not know how it might be there ; but [17]*supposing* the [18]*current* ran with the same force against the shore at the east as it passed by it on the other side, I might run the same [19]*risk* of being driven down the [20]*stream*, and carried by the island, as I had been before of being carried away from it. With these thoughts, I [21]*contented* myself to be without any boat, though it had been the [22]*product* of so many months' labor to make it, and of so many more to get it into the sea.

雖然我知道是鸚鵡說話，實在沒有旁人，然而過了半天工夫，我的心纔安靜。第一步，我是很詫怪的這個生物怎樣會到那裏去；後來，我又奇怪牠爲什麼株守一地，並不他往。我是滿意了。除去誠實的波爾以外，並無他人，我還不以爲意；伸出手來，叫牠名字。"波爾"，這個慓交際的生物來到我面前，坐在我的大拇指上，—一如舊例不停地向我說；——可憐的魯賓克路索呀！以及我怎樣到這裏來？我曾到那裏去？——好像牠是不勝欣喜似的又看見了我。我於是把牠帶到家裏去。

有時我常常到海內去乘船行，有時許多天靜靜地坐下來回想我從前所遇的危險。重行在島旁得着了船，我應當是很快樂的，但是我不知道用怎樣可取的方法方能把牠取來。至於我曾經巡游的島的東面，我很明白那邊的行程是不冒險的。只要想着了，我的心膽俱喪，血液冰冷。至於島的別一方面，我不知道那裏的情形；但是懸想着：在東方，急溜衝擊海岸當有同樣的力量像在別一方面流過海岸一般，我或者要冒同樣的危險被驅到急流裏面，被島帶去，好像我以前被波浪帶得離開牠一樣。用了這些思想，我自已很滿足，就是無船，也不要緊，雖然費了許多月的勞力方能得着結果，把牠造成，又費了許多月的工夫方能放牠下水。

¹*In this government of my temper* I ²*remained* near a year, and lived a very ³*sedate*, ⁴*retired* life, as you may well ⁵*suppose*. My thoughts being very much composed as to my condition, and fully ⁶*comforted* in ⁷*resigning* myself to the ⁸*dispositions* of Providence, I thought I lived really very happily in all things except that of ⁹*society*.

I ¹⁰*improved* myself in this time in all the ¹¹*mechanic* ¹²*exercises* which my necessities put me upon applying myself to. I believe I should, upon ¹³*occasion*, have made a very good carpenter, especially ¹⁴*considering* how few ¹⁵*tools* I had.

Besides this, ¹⁶*I arrived at an unexpected perfection in my earthenware*, and ¹⁷*contrived* well enough to make them with a wheel, which I found ¹⁸*infinitely* easier and better, because I made things round and ¹⁹*shaped*, which before were ²⁰*filthy*

差不多一年工夫我保留着我的自制的性質,度着一種沈靜的,僻處的生活,這是你可以懸想得到的。至於我的境地,我的思想是很安慰的,將我自己的命運去順從上天的處置,我是完全地自適的,我想除去社會交際以外,在各種事物裏面,我是過得很快樂的。

這個時候,我的工藝的練習實在是有進益了,這種工藝是我的需要品迫我去做的。遇着機會,我相信我自己能夠成爲一個技藝精良的木匠,特別地應當注意着,我所有的工具是如何的少啊。

除此以外,我製造陶器的優美的結果實在出乎我意料之外,我設了計劃去用一輪子來製造牠們,我覺着這個方法又很便易,又較好些,因爲我製造圓的物件和把牠們弄成形式,起頭所造成的東西瞧起來是很粗俗的。

things indeed to look on. But I think I was never more vain of my own [1]*performance*,or more joyful for anything I found out, than for my being able to make a [2]*tobacco pipe*. Though it was a very [3]*ugly*, [4]*clumsy* thing when it was done, and only burned red, like other earthenware, yet as it was [5]*hard* and [6]*firm*, and would [7]*draw* the smoke, I was exceedingly [8]*comforted* with it. I had always been [9]*used to* smoke, and there were [10]*pipes* in the ship, but forgot them at first, not thinking there was [11]*tobacco* in the island ; and afterwards, when I [12]*searched* the ship again, I could not [13]*come at* any [14]*pipes*.

In my wicker ware, also, I [15]*improved* much, and made [16]*abundance* of necessary baskets, as well as my [17]*invention* showed me. Though not very handsome, yet they were such as were very handy and [18]*convenient* for laying things up in, or [19]*fetching* things home. [20]*For example*, if I killed a goat abroad, I could [21]*hang* it up in a tree, [22]*flay it*, dress it, and cut it in pieces, and bring it home in a [23]*basket*. And the like by a [24]*turtle* ; I could cut it up, take out the eggs and a piece or two of the flesh, which was enough for me, and bring them home in a basket, and [25]*leave* the rest behind me, Also, large, deep [26]*baskets* were the [27]*receivers* of my corn, which I always [28]*rubbed out* as soon as it was dry, and [29]*cured*, and kept it in great baskets.

I began now to [30]*perceive* my powder abated considerably. This was a want which it was impossible for me to supply, and I began [31]*seriously* to consider what I must do when I should have no more powder ; that is to say, how I should kill any goats. I had, as I observed, in the third year of my being here, kept a young kid, and bred her up tame, and I was in hopes of getting a [32]*he-goat*. But I could not

但是我想倘使我能製造一隻烟管，那末我對於我所從事的業務的自誇和對於我所尋出的東西的快樂就無逾於此了。當烟管製成以後，雖然牠是一個狠惡劣，笨拙，和像旁的陶器一樣，一燒就紅的東西，然而牠是堅而實，可以引煙。我有了牠，覺得狠爲安適。我慣常是吸烟的，船上有許多烟管，起初把牠們忘懷了未曾想到島上會有烟草；後來，當再去搜檢船上，一隻烟管都找不到了。

我也在我的柳枝編製的器具的工藝上面弄得狠有進益，製成了許多有用的籃子，依着我的發明來指示我。雖然不狠好看，然而牠們是輕而易舉，便於置物，以及帶物回家，例如，倘使我在外面殺了一隻山羊，我能把牠懸在樹上，剝去牠的皮，調理牠，把牠割成碎塊，放在籃中，攜之回家。得了鼈也照樣施行；我把牠剖開來，拿出蛋和一兩塊肉，這些已足夠我用，放在籃內，取回家去，把其餘的都留下。寬的，大的，深的籃子也是我的貯穀器，穀子一經乾了，我便把牠磨出，晾曬，和把牠放在大的籃子裏面。

現在我見我的子彈的藥粉的量數大減了。這是我不能供給的一個缺乏，我開始勝重地注意着，當我沒有藥的時候，我將怎麼辦；就是說，我怎樣去殺山羊呢。照我觀察，在這裏第三年之中，我保養了一隻小山羊，把牠弄馴了，我希望再得一隻雄山羊。但是我不能

by any means [1]*bring it to pass* till my kid grew an old goat; and as I could never find in my heart to kill her, she [2]*died at last of mere age.*

CHAPTER XXVII

BEING now in the eleventh year of my [3]*residence,* and, as I have said, my *ammunition* [5]*growing low,* I set myself [6]*to study some art to trap and snare the goats,* to see whether I could not [7]*catch* some of them [8]*alive.* For this purpose I made [9]*snares* to [10]*hamper* them, and I do believe they were more than once taken in them; but my [11]*tackle* was not good, for I had no [12]*wire,* and I always found them broken, and my [13]*bait* [14]*devoured.* At length I resolved to try a [15]*pitfall.* I [16]*dug* several large [17]*pits* in the earth, in places where I had [18]*observed* the goats used to feed, and over those pits I placed *hurdles,* [19]*of my own making,* too, with a great [20]*weight* upon them. Several times I put [21]*ears* of barley and dry rice, without [22]*setting the trap*; and I could easily perceive that the goats had gone in and eaten up the [23]*corn,* for I could see the marks of their feet.

At length I set three [24]*traps* in one night, and, going the next morning, I found them all standing, and yet the [25]*bait* eaten and gone. This was very [26]*discouraging.* However, I [27]*altered* my [28]*traps*; and, [29]*not to trouble you with particulars,* going one morning to see my traps, I found in one of them a large, old he-goat, and in one of the others three kids, a [30]*male* and two [31]*females.*

As to the old one I knew not what to do with him. He was so fierce I [32]*durst* not go into the [33]*pit* to him; that is to say, to bring him away alive, which was what I wanted. I could have killed him, but that was not my [34]*business,* [35]*not*

無論用什麼方法，把這事弄成功，直至我的小山羊變成了一隻老山羊的時候；我毫無心思去殺牠，牠遂死於天年。

第 二 十 七 章

現在是我寓居島上的第十年了，我曾經說過，我的彈藥日漸短少，我遂開始研究捕羊之法，瞧瞧我能不能捉住幾隻活的。因為這個緣故，我造了些陷穽來誘致牠們，我相信牠們墜入穽中不止一次；但是捕機不佳，因為我沒有金屬線，常常瞧見牠們斷了，誘牠們的餌却被牠們吃去了。最後，我決計去造一陷阱試試，在地土裏面，我掘了幾座大穴擺在我所注意着山羊常常吃食的地方，在那些穴上面，我放了些木欄，是我自己造的，在牠們上面，放了重壓之物。有幾次，我放大麥穗和乾的米在地上，那末陷阱就不設了；我狠容易地瞧見山羊們進來把穀子吃掉，因此我能夠瞧見牠們的足跡了。

最後，一夜之間，我闓放了三座捕機，第二天早上去看，我見機器仍舊樹立在那裏，餌却被吃去了。這是狠灰心的事。我遂改良我的陷阱，不必把那些瑣屑情形來煩擾讀者，一天早晨，跑去看陷阱，我看見在一座陷阱裏面有一隻大而老的雄山羊，在別的一座裏面有三隻小山羊，一隻公的，二隻毋的。

老的山羊我不知道怎樣來對待牠。牠是這樣的猛烈，我竟不敢到穴中去拿牠；就是說，活活地把牠帶走，這就是我願意做的事。我能把牠殺却，但是那到不是我的事務，

would it answer my end. So I even let him out, and he ran away as if he had been [1]*frightened out of his wits.* But I did not then know what I afterwards learned, that [2]*hunger* will [3]*tame* a lion. If I had let him [4]*stay* there three or four days without food, and then have carried him some water to drink, and then a little corn, he would have been as tame as one of the [5]*kids*; for they are mighty [6]*sagacious,* [7]*tractable* creatures where they are well used.

However, [8]*for the present* I let him go, knowing no better at that time. Then I went to the three kids, and, taking them one by one, I tied them with [9]*strings* together, and with some [10]*difficulty* brought them all home.

It was a good while before they would feed; but, throwing them some sweet corn, it [11]*tempted* them, and they began to be [12]*tame.* And now I found that if I [13]*expected* to [14]*supply* myself with goats' [15]*flesh*, when I had no powder or shot [16]*left*, [17]*breeding* some up tame was my only way, when, perhaps, I might have them about my house like [18]*a flock of sheep.* But then it [19]*occurred* to me that I must keep the tame from the [20]*wild*, or else they would always run wild when they [21]*grew up.* The only way for this was to have some [22]*inclosed* piece of ground, well [23]*fenced* either with hedge or pale, to keep them in so [24]*effectually* that those within might not [25]*break out*, or those without [26]*break in.*

This was a great undertaking for one pair of hands. Yet, as I saw there was [27]*an absolute necessity* for doing it, my first work was to find out a proper piece of ground, where there was likely to be [28]*herbage* for them to eat, water for them to drink, and [29]*cover* to keep them from the sun.

Those who understand such [30]*inclosures* will think I had very little [31]*contrivance*, when I [32]*pitched* upon a place very

又不能達我目的。這樣我逐讓牠出來，像驚呆般地逃走了。我後來知道的事，那時却不明白，原來飢餓却能使獅馴服呢。倘使我讓牠在那裏三四天沒有食物，後來帶些水給牠喝，後來再給牠一點穀子，牠或者將同那些小山羊一般地馴服，因爲在牠們習慣的地方，牠們是聰慧和易教的。

目下我且讓牠走，當時我却想不出較好的法子來。我於是走到三隻小山羊面前，一隻一隻的把牠們拿出來，用繩子把牠們繫在一處，費了些力把牠們帶回家去。

過了許多辰光，牠們方緩吃食；但是擲給牠們若干甘美的穀子，牠們却被穀子引誘而馴服了。現在我覺着假使我希望拿山羊肉來供給自己，當火藥和子彈告罄的時候，養馴牠們幾隻，這是唯一的法子，不久，牠們或者能繞行我的屋子像一羣羊一般。但是後來我想我應把馴的羊和野的羊分開，如其不然，當牠們長大了，牠們必定要全變野了。做這事的唯一方法就是把幾隻圈在地中，用籬笆或杙來圍住，保守得牠們這樣地精密，那些在內的不會衝出來，那些在外的不會衝進去。

對於一雙手這事實在是一件大工作。然而我覺得這事是萬難缺少的，第一次的工作是要找出一塊合宜的地來，在那裏，牠們必須有菜蔬吃，有水喝，有遮蓋陽光的東西。

懂得這種園地的人們將要想着我所用的計劃是很

proper for all these, (being a plain, open piece of ¹*meadow* land, or "²*savannah*" as our people call it in the ³*western* ⁴*colonies*,) which had two or three little ⁵*drills* of fresh water in it, and at one end was very ⁶*woody*; I say they will smile at my ⁷*forecast*, when I shall tell them I began by inclosing this piece of ground in such a manner that my ⁸*hedge* or ⁹*pale* must have been at least two miles about. Nor was the ¹⁰*madness* of it so great as to the ¹¹*compass*, for if it was ten miles about, I was like to have time enough to do it in; but I did not consider that my goats would be as wild in so much ¹²*compass* as if they had had the whole island, and I should have so much room to ¹³*chase* them in that I should never ¹⁴*catch* them.

My hedge was begun and ¹⁵*carried on*, I believe, about fifty yards when this thought ¹⁶*occurred* to me. So I presently ¹⁷*stopped short*, and, for the beginning, I ¹⁸*resolved* to inclose a piece of about one hundred and fifty yards in length, and one hundred yards in ¹⁹*breadth*, which, as it would ²⁰*maintain* as many as I should have in any ²¹*reasonable* time, so, as my stock ²²*increased*, I could add more ground to my ²³*inclosure*.

This was acting with some ²⁴*prudence*, and I went to work with ²⁵*courage*. I was about three months ²⁶*hedging in* the first piece; and, till I had done it, I ²⁷*tethered* the three kids in the best part of it, ond ²⁸*accustomed* them to feed as near me as possible, to make them ²⁹*familiar*. Very often I would go and carry them some ears of barley or a handful of rich, and ³⁰*feed them out of my hand*, so that after my ³¹*inclosure* was ³²*finished*, and I ³³*let them loose*, they would follow me up and down, ³⁴*bleating after me* for a handful of corn.

淺近的，我為這些山羊們擇定了一座合宜的地點，（是一座平坦開曠的草原地，或者是"草原"，像在西方的殖民地裏面我們國人叫着的一樣），在牠的中間有兩三座流水鮮潔的小川，一邊的末端是多木的；我知道當我告訴那些人們我把那塊地圈成這種樣子，以致籬笆或者至少有兩英里周圍的時候，他們一定要譏笑我的計劃了。地的範圍也其大無外，却有十英里周圍，我願意有工夫來造成牠；但是我未曾注意山羊們在這樣大的區域中將要長成得和牠們生活在全島地面上一樣地野。那末我將要到處去追逐牠們，永不能捉住牠們。

　　我的籬笆開始了和繼續着製造，我相信，大約造了五十碼的時候，這個思想才想到，我決定去圈長約一百五十碼，寬約一百碼的地。這塊地，牠必定容留我在合理的時間內所得着的山羊，這樣，羊羣加增之時，我能再擴張地面到圈地上去。

　　用了謹慎態度來辦這事，狠勇敢地去進工行作。在第一塊地上，費事大約三個月工夫去製造籬笆；直到完畢為止，我把三隻小山羊繫在地的最好的部份上面，使得牠們習慣着靠近我的身旁來吃食，使牠們和和我相熟。狠常常地我帶去些大麥穗，一把米我給牠們吃，用手來喂牠們，這樣在圈地完工以後，我釋放牠們，牠們必定上下都跟着我走，在我後面叫着要想吃…把穀子。

This answered my end, and in about a year and a half I had a ¹*flock* of about twelve goats, kids and all. In two years more I had three and forty, ²*besides several* that I took and killed for my food. After that, I inclosed five several pieces of ground to feed them in, with little ³*pens* to ⁴*drive* them into, to take them as I wanted, and ⁵*gates* out of one piece of ground into another.

⁶*But this was not all.* Now I not only had ⁷*goats flesh to feed* on when I pleased, but ⁸*milk* too,—a thing which, indeed, in the beginning, I did not so much as think of, and which, when it came into my thoughts, was really an ⁹*agreeable* ¹⁰*surprise*, for now I ¹¹*set up my dairy*, and had sometimes a ¹²*gallon* or two of milk in a day. And as ¹³*Nature*, who gives ¹⁴*supplies* of food to every creature dictates even naturally how to make use of it, so I, that had never milked a cow, much less a goat; or seen ¹⁵*butter* or ¹⁶*cheese* made ¹⁷*very readily and handily*, though after a great many ¹⁸*essays* and ¹⁹*miscarriages,* made both ²⁰*butter* and ²¹*cheese* at last, also salt (though I found it partly made to my hand by the heat of the sun upon some of the ²²*rock* of the sea), and never wanted it afterwards.

.²³*How mercifully can our Creator treat His creatures,* even in those conditions in which they seem to be ²⁴*overwhelmed* in ²⁵*destruction*! How can He sweeten the ²⁶*bitterest* ²⁷*providences*, and give us cause to ²⁸*praise* Him for ²⁹*dungeons and prisons*! What a table was here ³⁰*spread* for me in the ³¹*wilderness*, where I saw nothing at first but to ³²*perish* for hunger!

It would have made a ³³*stoic* smile to see me and my little family sit down to dinner. There was my ³⁴*majesty*, the prince and lord of the whole island. ³⁵*I had the lives of*

Robinson Crusoe

這事應了我的目的，大約在一年有半當中，我有了十二隻山羊，小山羊和其他等等。再過兩年，除去殺了做膳的幾隻以外，我得着了四十三隻山羊。從此以後，我圈了五塊別的地來飼養牠們，驅牠們入小的欄去內，願意的時候便把牠們取出，又有門定一塊地方開到另一塊地方之內。

非但如此。現在我不但當我願意吃的時候有山羊肉喫，而且還有乳呢，——一樣東西，起初我却實在未曾想到，當我想着牠時，實在是一樣令人可喜驚異的東西，現在我建設了造乳所，有時一天有一二加侖的乳。那賜給各種生物食物的造化主宰，狠自然地指示着人們怎樣地去利用乳，我永遠未曾榨過牛的乳，山羊的乳更沒有擠過，永遠未曾見人做過牛油或牛乳餅，雖然經過了許多試驗和失敗，我最後却狠敏捷和伶巧地做成了牛油和牛乳餅，而且還做了鹽（牠到我手一半是由太陽的熱度在海面石上造成功的），以後永遠不曾少鹽。

造物待人何其慈善，就是生物們在那些將臨滅亡的境況當中，也受着上天的好的待遇！他如何能把最苦的天意變得最甘，給我們因由去禱告他，就是身處牢獄之中，也是如此！在荒野中，在我起頭除餓死以外找不出東西的地方，我竟能有這樣一桌的食品鋪在我的面前！

要是瞧見我和我的小家庭坐下來午餐，人們恐怕要發出一陣不動情的微笑了。在全島上，我有王子和貴爵的威儀。我操我的人民的生死之權。

¹*all my subject at my absolute command.* I could hang, draw, give ²*liberty*, and take it away, and no ³*rebels* among all my subjects. Then, to see how like a king I ⁴*dined*, too, ⁵*all alone*, ⁶*attended* by my servants! Poll, as if he had been my ⁷*favorite*, was the only person ⁸*permitted* to talk to me. My dog, who was now grown old and ⁹*crazy*, sat always at my right hand; and two cats, one on one side of the table, and one on the other, ¹⁰*expecting* now and then ¹¹*a bit* from my hand, ¹²*as a mark of special favor.*

But these were not the two ¹³*cats* which I brought on shore at first, for they were both of them dead, and had been ¹⁴*interred* near my ¹⁵*habitation* by my own hand. These were two of ¹⁶*a litter of kittens* which I had ¹⁷*preserved* tame, whereas the rest ran wild in the woods, and became indeed ¹⁸*troublesome* to me at last, for they would often come into my house, ¹⁹*and plunder me too*, till at last I was ²⁰*obliged to* shoot them, and did kill a great many. ²¹*At length they left me.* With this ²²*attendance* and in this ²³*plentiful* manner I lived; neither could I be said to want anything but society. Of that, some time after this, I was likely to have much.

I was something ²⁴*impatient*, as I have observed, to have the use of my boat, though ²⁵*very loate to run any more hazards*, Therefore sometimes I sat ²⁶*contriving* ways to get her about the island, and at other times I sat myself down ²⁷*contented* enougth without her. But I had a ²⁸*strange* ²⁹*uneasiness in my mind* to go down to the point of the island where, as I have said, in my ³⁰*last ramble* I went up the hill to see how the ³¹*shore* lay, and how the current set, that I might see what I had to do. This ³²*inclination* increased upon me every day, and at length I resolved *to*

我能縱殺人，引曳人，給人自由，取消人自由。我的臣民之中，沒有叛反之徒。瞧瞧我用膳的時候，像國王一般，獨自一人享用，我的庸人們伺候着我！(波爾)，牠是我的幸臣，僅有向我說話的權柄。我的狗現在長大和發癲了，常常靠在我的右手坐着；兩匹貓，一匹在桌子的這一面，一匹在那一面，時時地希望着從我手中得一點點食物，好像特恩曠典的標幟一樣。

但是這兩匹貓並不是我起初上岸帶來的，牠們都已死去；已經由我親手葬在貼近我的寓所的地內。這兩匹是從一窠小貓中得來的，我把牠們養馴，其餘的變野了，跑到樹林中去，後來牠們實在給我煩擾，因為牠們常常跑到我的屋內偷竊我的東西，我於是不得不射擊牠們，結果殺死許多匹，後來牠們離我遠行。用了這些隨從者，在富裕的境地中我生活着；除去社交之外，我不缺少任何物件了。遇了些時以後，關於社交，我也同樣的有了。

我曾注意過，我雖然不欲再行冒險，然而對於駕駛小艇已覺着不能忍耐了。有時我坐下來設計怎樣把船弄到岸上來，另外有些時，我狠自足地坐下來，雖然沒有牠。但是我心中甚為不暢，當我走至島角的時候，在那裏，在我前次游行中，我跑上小山去看海岸的形勢，急流的出處，那末我可以明白我應當怎樣行事。這個傾向每日在我心中增加。

¹*travel thither by land,* ²*following the edge of the shore.* I did so ; but had any one in England met such a man as I was, it must either have ³*frightened* him, or ⁴*raised a great deal of laughter* ; and as I ⁵*frequently* stood still to look at myself, I could not but smile at the notion of my ⁶*traveling* through Yorkshire with such an ⁷*equipage*, and in such a ⁸*dress.* Be pleased ⁹*to take a sketch of my* gure, as follows :—

I had a great, high, ¹⁰*shapeless* cap made of a goat's ¹¹*skin* with a flap ¹²*hanging* down behind as well to keep the sun from me as to ¹³*shoot* the ¹⁴*rain off* from running into my neck, nothing being so ¹⁵*hurtful* in these ¹⁶*chimates* as the rain upon the flesh under the clothes.

I had a short ¹⁷*jacket* of goat's ¹⁸*skin* the ¹⁹*skirts* coming down to about ²⁰*the middle of the thighs,* and a pair of ²¹*open-kneed* ²²*breeches* of the same. The breeches were made of the skin of an old he-goat, whose ²³*hair* ²⁴*hung down* such a length on either side that, like ²⁵*pantaloons,* it reached to the ²⁶*middle* of my legs. Stockings and ²⁷*shoes* I had none, but had made me a ²⁸*pair* of somethings, I ²⁹*scarce* know what to call them, like ³⁰*buskins,* ³¹*to flap over* my legs, and ³²*lace* on either side like ³³*leggings,* but of a most ³⁴*barbarous* ³⁵*shape,* as indeed were all the rest of my clothes.

I had on a broad ³⁶*belt* of goat's skin ³⁷*dried,* which I drew together with two ³⁸*thongs* of the same ³⁹*instead of buckles* ; and in a kind of a ⁴⁰*frog* on either side of this, instead of a ⁴¹*sword* and ⁴²*dagger,* hung a little saw and a ⁴³*hatchet,* one on one side and one on the other. I had another ⁴⁴*belt,* not so broad, and ⁴⁵*fastened* in the same manner, which hung over my ⁴⁶*shoulder* ; and at the end of it, under my left arm, hung two ⁴⁷*pouches,* both made of goat's skin too, in one of

起來,後來我決定沿岸邊而行,陸行到那邊。我這樣做了;但是假使無論何人在(英)國遇到像我這樣的人,他若不吃驚,必定要大笑,我常常靜立着瞧我自己,對於我帶這些行裝,着這些衣服,想去經過(約克)州旅行的觀念;必要匿笑不止了。略述我的形狀如下,以娛讀者:────

我有着山羊皮的大的,高的,無形式的小帽一頂,後面掛有懸垂的東西,避却陽光和那流到我的頸中去的雨,在這些地方,沒有再比雨在衣服下沾人皮肉的重傷害人東西了。

我有一件山羊皮的小衫,衣裾大約達到我的大腿中部,兩件同樣質料皮的開膝短褲。短褲是用一隻老公山羊皮製的,牠的毛在兩邊懸下來這樣長,像長袴一般,直伸到我的腿中為止。我沒有襪和鞋,但是做了一套相似的東西,我不道怎樣去稱呼牠們,好像半截靴,垂蓋我的兩腿,兩邊的紐帶像脛衣一般,但是形式最拙劣,我其餘的衣服的式樣,實在也是如此。

我繫一條乾山羊皮的寬帶,我把牠和兩條皮帶曳在一處,以代扣子;在兩邊做成紐扣一般,懸了一把小鋸和一柄小斧,以代刀和七首,一個在這邊,一個在那邊。我另外有一條帶,不甚寬,同樣的繫在身上,牠懸下來經過我的肩膀;在牠的末端,在我左臂之上,掛了兩只袋,都是山

1.陸行至彼處.2.沿岸而行.3.使吃驚.4.令其大笑.5.常常.6.旅行.7.行裝.8.衣衫.9.略述予之形狀.10.無形式.11.皮.12垂下.13.射.14.雨.15.損傷.16.地方.17.小衫.18.皮.19.衣裾.20.大腿中部.21.開膝.22.褲.23.毛.24.垂下.25.長袴.26.中間.27.鞋.28.雙.29.少.30.半截靴;31.垂蓋.32.紐帶.33.脛衣34.拙劣.35.形式.36.帶.37.乾.38.皮帶.39.以代扣子.40.紐扣.41.刀.42.七首.43.小斧.44.帶.45.繫.46.肩.47.袋.

which hung my powder, in the other my [1]*shot*. At my
back I carried my basket, and on my shoulder, my gun,
and over my head a great, [2]*clumsy*, ugly, goat-skin [3]*umbrella,* but which, after all, was the most necessary thing
I had about me, next to my gun. As for my face, the
color of it was really not so [4]*mulattolike* as one might
expect from a man [5]*not at all careful of it*, and living
within nine of ten degrees of the [6]*equator*. My beard I
had once [7]*suffered* to grow till it was [8]*about a quarter of a
yard long*; but as I had both [9]*scissors* and razors [10]*sufficient*,
I had cut it [11]*pretty* short, except what grew on my upper
lip. which I had [12]*trimmed* into a large pair of [13]*Mahometan
whiskers,* such as I had seen worn by some [14]*Turks* at Sallee.
The Moors did not were such, though the Turks did. Of
these [15]*mustachios*, or [16]*whiskers*, I will not say they were
long enough to hang my hat upon them, but they were of
a length and shape [17]*monstrous* enough, and such as in
England [18]*would have passed for* frightful.

But all this is by the boy; for, as to my [19]*figure*, I had so
few to observe me that it was [20]*of no manner of consequence*;
so I say no more of that. In this kind of dress I went my
new journey, and was out five or six days. I [21]*traveled*
first along the seashore, directly to the place where I first
brought my boat to an anchor to get upon the [22]*rocks*.
Having no boat now to take care of, I went over the land
a nearer way to the same [23]*height* that I was upon before,
when, looking forward to the points of the rocks which
lay out, and which I was obliged to [24]*double* with my boat,
as is said above, I was surprised to see the sea all smooth
and [25]*quiet*—[26]*no rippling*, no motion, no current any more
there than in any other places.

羊皮做的，在一只袋裏面放了藥粉，在另外一只裏面放了子彈。我把籃子載在背上，在肩上扛了槍，在頭上撐了一項大身的，粗笨的，惡劣的，山羊皮做的傘，但是此後傘却是我隨身牠帶的物件裏面最要要的東西，除去槍以外而言。至於我的臉。的顏色不像白人又不像黑人，那種不小心的模樣，應當是這樣的，這個人是住在赤道九或十度之中的。我讓我的鬍子去生長，後來直長到大約一碼四分之一的長度；但是我却有充分的剪子和刀，我把牠割得很短，除長在上唇上面的以外，我把牠修剪得像回教人的煩鬚一樣，在(沙利)地方，我瞧見(土耳其)人有這樣的鬍子，(摩爾)人却不是這樣。雖然(土耳其)人是這樣。這些髭鬚，我不說他們是這樣的長，足以把我的帽子掛在上面，但是牠們的長度和形式到確是非常可怕的。在(英)國，必將爲可怖之物。

這些都是閒話；至於我的面容，我不曾注意過，無關緊要，不復題及。着了這種衣彩，我進行新的旅程，出去了五六天了。我起初沿岸而行，直赴我從前把船靠在石上停錨的那匾地方。現在沒有船掛着心，我經過陸地，走較近的路到我從前站立的高山上去，向前瞧瞧伸出的石角，就是以前說過船不得不繞行的石角，我驚喜地看着海水光滑而平靜——沒有漪紋，沒有動作，沒有急溜，好像別的地方一樣。

1.子彈。2.粗笨。3.傘。4.如黑白人.合生之雜種人.5.不留心。6.赤道。7.受。8.長約一碼四分之一。9.剪.10.足量。11.狠。2.修剪。13.回教人之鬍。14.(土耳基人)15.髭。16.鬚。7.可驚。18.以爲。19.面容。20.無關緊要。21.行.22.石。23.高山.24.繞行.25.平靜。26.無漪紋

I ¹*was at a strange loss to understand this*, and resolved to spend some time in the observing it, to see if nothing from the ²*sets of the tide had occasioned it*. But I was ³*presently* ⁴*convinced* how it was; namely, that ⁵*the ebb of tide setting from the west*, and ⁷*joining* with the current of waters from some great river on the shore, must be the ⁸*occasion* of this current, and that, according as the wind ⁹*blew* more ¹⁰*forcibly* from the west or from the north, this current came nearer, or went farther from the shore. ¹¹*Waiting* thereabouts till enening, I went up to the rock again, and then the ¹²*ebb* of ¹³*tide* being made, I plainly saw the current again as before, only that it ran farther off, being near half a ¹⁴*league* from the shore; whereas in my case it set close upon the shore, and ¹⁵*hurried* me and my ¹⁶*canoe* along with it, which at another time it would not have done.

This ¹⁷*observation* convinced me that I had nothing to do but ¹⁸*to observe* the ebbing and the ¹⁹*flowing* of the tide and I might very easily bring my boat about the island again. But when I began to ²⁰*think of putting it in practice*, I had such terror upon my ²¹*spirits* at the ²²*remembrance* of the danger I had been in that I could not think of it again with any ²³*patience*, but, on the ²⁴*contrary*, I took up another ²⁵*resolution*, which was more safe, though more ²⁶*laborious*; and this was that I would build, or rather make, me another ²⁷*periagua* or canoe, and so have one for one side of the island, and one for the other.

CHAPTER XXVIII

You are to understand that now I had, as I may call it, two ²⁸*plantations* in the island,—one, my little ²⁹*fartification* or tent, with the wall about it, under the rock, with

我不明其故，決心費些工夫來觀察，瞧瞧是不是潮流的方向使牠這種樣的。但是我馬上明白牠怎麼會這樣，就是那個下退的潮水，自西流行，和大河岸邊的急湍相會，這就是急流的起由了，依照從西方北方括得狠有力的風的鼓動，急流或是靠近了岸，或是離岸遠去。等到了晚間，我重行到石上去，那時潮水正退，我狠明顯的又瞧見了從前瞧見過的急湍，不過牠流得較遠，差不多離岸半海里遠；然而在我當時所處的情形之中，急湍是緊衝海岸，把我和木艇一齊驅走，在別的時候，急湍不會這樣做的。

這個觀察解去我的疑惑，使我明白除去注意潮退和潮漲以外，沒有旁的事可做，我可以狠容易地再駛船游行全島。但是當我想把這個計劃付諸實行之時，我的心靈中回憶著從前身受的危險不覺驚駭起來，以致於不能再有忍耐力去想牠了，相反地，我有了另外的一個決心，那是較為安全的，雖然較為費力；就是我將再行造一隻獨木舟或木艇，這樣在島的這一方面有一隻，在那一方面有另外的一隻。

第 二 十 八 章

你可以明白現在我有，我可以叫牠，是兩處新闢地，在島的裏面，——一處，我的小的堅固的防禦地或是帳有牆將牠圍住，在石之下，

the cave behind me, which by this time I [1]*had enlarged into several apartments*, or caves, one within another.　One of these, which was the [2]*driest* and largest, and had a door out [3]*beyond* my wall or [4]*fortification*, — that is to say, beyond where my wall joined to the rock,—was all [5]*filled up* with the large earthen pots of which I [6]*have given an account*, and with fourteen or fifteen great baskets, which would hold five or six [7]*bushels* each, where I laid up stores of [8]*provisions*, especially my corn, some in the ear, cut off short from the [9]*straw*, and the other [10]*rubbed out* with my hand.

As for my wall, made, as before, with long [11]*stakes* or [12]*piles*, those piles grew all like trees, and were by this time grown so big, and [13]*spread* so very much, that there was not the least [14]*appearance*, to any one's view, of any [15]*habitation* behind them.

Near this [16]*dwelling* of mine, but a little [17]*farther* within the land, and upon lower ground, lay my two pieces of [18]*corn land*, which I kept [19]*duly* [20]*cultivated* and [21]*sowed*, and which [22]*yielded* me their [23]*harvest* in its season ; and whenever I [24]*had occasion for* more corn, I had more land [25]*adjoining* as fit as that.

Besides this, I had my [26]*country seat,* and I had now a [27]*tolerable* [28]*plantation* there also,　First I had my little bower, as I called it, which I [29]*kept in repair*,—that is to say, I kept the [30]*hedge*, which [31]*circled* it in [32]*constantly fitted up to its usual height*, the [33]*ladder* standing always in the inside.　I kept the trees, which at first were no more than stakes, but were now grown very firm and tall, always cut, so that they might [34]*spread* and grow [35]*thick* and wild, and make the more agreeable [36]*shade*, which they did [37]*effectually*

有著石洞在我後面，那個洞我已經將他造大，分成幾間：或者說是分成幾個洞，還有一間在另一個洞中，其中的一座洞穴，牠是最乾燥的和最寬大，有一扇門在牆或者說是防禦物的外面，——就是說，在牆和石岩相接的地方，——被那些大的陶器充塞滿了，這些陶器我已經詳細地敍述過了，還有十四隻或十五隻大的籃子，每隻可以容納五六斛，在那裏，我貯藏食物，特別地是穀子，有些是在籃子裏面，直接從梗上割將下來，其餘的係用手搓出。

至於牆壁，像從前一樣，用長的木椿和栈造成，那些栈生起來像樹一般，這個時候，牠們是長得這樣地大，鋪開得這樣地遠，無論誰來觀察，簡直看不出來在牠們的後面還有我的住居呢。

貼近我的住所，但是在陸地之中稍微遠一些，在較低的地土上，有兩塊種穀地，用適當的方法，我培養和播種牠們，季候到了，牠們給我收穫；無論何時，我多要穀子時，我有許多靠近這些地土的同樣的地土

其次，我有一所村舍，現在我也有一座頗佳的新闢地了，第一，我有一座小亭，我這樣地叫牠，不時地把牠修理——就是說，我把圍住牠的籬芭常常就其尋常高度，加以修茸，梯子是常常放在裏面。我那些樹，在先牠們僅僅是木椿，但是現在長得又厚實又高大了，常常地修割，這樣牠們可以鋪張開來，長得厚而大，做成最可意的樹蔭，牠們把牠緊得實隨我心。

1.擴增數屋。2.最乾。3.在外。4.防護物。5.充滿。6.已詳述之。7.斛。8.食物。9.草梗。10.搓。11.椿。12.栈。13.鋪。14.顯示。15.住所。16.住所。17.較遠。18.種穀地。19.合宜。20培養。21.播222.使給。23.收成。24.多用。25.附近。26.村舍。27.尚可。28.新闢地。29.隨時修理。30.籬芭。31.圍住。32.常就其尋常高度而修改之。33.梯。34.張開。35.厚。36.蔭。37.有實效。

to my mind.   In the middle of this I had [1]*my tent always standing*, being a piece of a sail [2]*spread over poles set up for that purpose*, and which [3]*never wanted any repair or renewing*.   Under this I had made a [4]*squab*, or [5]*couch* with the skins of the creatures I had killed, and with other soft things, and a [6]*blanket* laid on them, such as belonged to our sea [7]*bedding*, which I had saved ; and a great watch coat to cover me.   And here, whenever I had [8]*occasion* to be [9]*absent* from my chief seat, I took up my country [10]*habitation*.

Adjoining to this I had my [11]*inclosures* for my [12]*cattle*,— that is to say, my goats,—and I [13]*had taken an inconceivable deal of pains* to fence and inclose this ground.   I was so [14]*anxious* to see it [15]*kept entire*, lest the goats should [16]*break* through, that I never left off till, with [17]*infinite* labor, I had [18]*stuck the outside* of the hedge so full of small stakes, and so near to one another, that it was rather a pale than a hedge, and [19]*there was scarce room* to put a hand through between them,   When those stakes [20]*grew*, as they all did in the next rainy season, this made the [21]*inclosure* strong like a wall,— indeed stronger than any wall.

This will [22]*testify* for me that I was not [23]*idle*, and that I [24]*spared no pains to bring to pass* whatever appeared [25]*necessary* for my [26]*comfortable* support.   I considered the [27]*keeping up* a [28]*breed* of tame creatures thus [29]*at my hand* would be a [30]*living* [31]*magazine*, or [32]*storehouse*, of [33]*flesh*, [34]*milk*, [35]*butter*, and [36]*cheese* for me as long as I lived in the place, if it were to be forty years ; and that keeping them in my reach [37]*depended* entirely upon my [38]*perfecting* my inclosure to such a degree that I might be sure of keeping them together.   By this method, indeed, I so [39]*effectually* [40]*secured* this that when

340

在牠的中間，我把幕常常地張開，就是一塊船帆，張掛於幾根竿子上，這些竿子是專爲此用而樹立的，幕旣無須修理又不須重建。在幕的下，我造了一張睡椅或者說是臥榻，用我殺却的生物的皮造的，還用了別的柔軟的東西，把我們海船床具上用的一張毛毯蓋在上面，這張毛毯我好好地保留着的，一件大的守夜衣掩蓋着我。在這裏，無論何時，只要有從我的主要的坐位上離開的機會，我就往我的村居而去。

附近這個地方，我有着放畜生的圈地，——就是說，我的山羊，——我費了說不出的困苦來把這塊地圍好了籬笆來圈住這塊地方。我是狠担心的，希望牠完善，恐怕山羊衝過去，我永遠沒有離開牠，直到，費了無限的力量，我用小木尉插滿了籬笆的外面，木椿一根靠一根爲止，這樣瞧起來狠像是柵欄，却不像是籬笆，在牠們之中，沒有把手放進去的餘地。這些木椿生長了，在下次多雨的時季內生長，使得圈子堅固得像城牆一般，——實在比平常的牆堅固。

這個是爲我證明我是不偷嬾的，凡對於我的適意的供給的需要發見了，我是不辭勞苦的去把牠做成功，我注意着豢養在我手頭的一羣馴的生物，將要變成一所肉，牛油，乳酪餅的活庫或是貯廠室，就是在這裏住上四十年，這些東西都是取之不盡，用之不竭的，要使牠們在我範圍之內，這完全倚靠着我要把籬笆圍得這樣的完善，那末一定能夠把牠們插到一處。用了這個方法，實在，我這樣有效力的確信着當這些小木椿開始生長的時候，我曾經把牠們種植得狠厚，我不得不再將牠們之中拔起幾根。

these little stakes began to grow, I had ¹*planted* them so very ²*thick* that I was forced ³*to pull* some of them up again. In this place, also, I had my ⁴*grapes* growing, upon which I ⁵*principally depended* for my winter store of ⁸*raisins*, and which I never failed to ⁷*preserve* very carefully, as the best and most agreeable ⁸*dainty* of my whole ⁹*diet*. And indeed they were not only agreeable, but ¹⁰*medicinal*, ¹¹*wholesome*, ¹²*nourishing*, and ¹³*refreshing in the greatest degree.*

As this was also about ¹⁴*holy way* between my other habitation and the place where I had laid up my boat, I generally stayed and lay here in my way thither, for I used ¹⁵*frequently* to ¹⁶*visit* my boat ; and I kept all things about, or belonging to her, in very good order. Sometimes I went out in her to ¹⁷*divert* myself, but no more ¹⁸*hazardous* voyages would I go, nor ¹⁹*scarcely* ever above ²⁰*a stone's cast* or two from the shore, I was so ²¹*apprehensive of being hurried out of my knowledge again by the currents*, or winds, or any other ²²*accident*. But now I come to a ²³*new scene* of my life.

It happened one day, about noon, going towards my boat I was exceedingly surprised with the ²⁴*print* of a man's ²⁵*naked foot* on the shore, which was very ²⁶*plain* to be seen on the sand. I stood like one ²⁷*thunderstruck*, or ²⁸*as if I had seen an apparition.* I ²⁹*listened*, I looked round me, but I could hear nothing, nor see anything. I went up to a ³⁰*rising ground* to look farther. I went up the shore, and down the shore, ³¹*but it was all one.* I could see no other ³²*impression* but that one. I went to it again to see if there were any more, and to ³³*observe* if it might not be my fancy ; but ³⁴*there was no room for that,* for there was ³⁵*exactly* the print of a foot,—³⁶*toes, heel,* and every part of a foot. How it came thither I knew not, ³⁷*nor could I in the least*

在這塊地方，我也有生長的葡萄，對於我冬天葡萄乾的貯積，我是完全倚靠着牠的，我常常地狠留心地保留牠，牠是我食品中的最好的和最可口的珍品。實在牠們不僅僅是可口，而且宜於治病，滋養的，補身的，和能使精神爽快達於極點。

這塊地方大約有一牛的路在我別的住所和放船的地方當中，我到那邊去的時候，大概停留這裏一會。因為我常常地去看我的船；我把船的四周的東西和附屬牠的物件做得井井有條。有時我出去到船中去自娛着，但是不去作冒險的旅行了，也不走得離岸較投一二石可達之遠的路程，我是這樣地恐懼着重行再被急湍，狂風，或其他不幸之事所迫，使我昏暈不知所措。但是現在我來到生活的新景象裏面了。

一天大約在中午，我偶然向船而行，在岸上見了一個人赤足的脚印，我是非常地恐懼起來，脚印在沙上狠明顯地發見出來。我站立着如被雷轟，或者像見了鬼怪一般。我聽，我臼周望了一望；但是聽不見什麼，看不見什麼。我跑到高地上面去遠望。我跑到岸上去，岸下去，不過僅此而已。除去這一塊足印，不能瞧見別的。我又跑去瞧；看看再有沒有，注意着是不是我的幻想；但是毫無疑義，因為實在有一塊足印，趾印，踵印，以及一隻足的各部份的印。牠怎樣會來，我

[1]*imagine.*   After [2]*innumerable* [3]*fluttering thoughts,* like a man [4]*perfectly confused* and [5]*out of himself,* I came home to my fortification, not feeling, as we say, the ground I went on, but [6]*terrified* [7]*to the last degree,* [8]*looking behind me at every* [9]*two or three steps,* [10]*mistaking* every bush and tree, and [11]*fancying every stump at a distance to be a man.* Nor is it possible to [12]*describe* how many [13]*various shapes* my [14]*affrighted imagination represented* things to me in, how many wild ideas were found every moment in my [15]*fancy,* and what [16]*strange,* [17]*unaccountable whimseys* came into my thoughts [18]*by the way.*

When I came to my [19]*castle* (for so I think I called it [20]*ever after this*), I fled into it like one [21]*pursued.*   Whether I went over by the [22]*ladder,* as first [23]*contrived,* or went in at the hole in the rock, which I had called a door, I cannot [24]*remember.*   No, nor could I [25]*remember* the next morning; for never [26]*frightened hare fled to cover,* [29]*or fox to earth,* with more [28]*terror* of mind than I to this [27]*retreat.*

I [30]*slept* none that night. The farther I was from the [31]*occasion* of my fright, the greater my [32]*apprehensions* were, which is something [33]*contrary* to the nature of such things, and [34]*especially* to the usual [35]*practice* of all creatures in fear, But I was so [36]*embarrassed* with my own frightful ideas of the thing that I formed nothing but [37]*dismal* [38]*imaginations* to myself. How was it possible a man should come there? Where was the vessel that brought him? What marks were there of any other footsteps?

I presently [39]*concluded,* then, that it must be some dangerous creature: namely, that it must be some of the [40]*savages* of the [41]*mainland* [42]*opposite,* who had wandered out to sea in their [43]*canoes,* and, either driven by the currents

不知道，我亦無從測度。在無數的騷動的思想之後，像一個
心意紛紜不知所措的人一般，我回到我的家中去，不覺着
，我們可以說，我所往的路，但是驚嚇達於極點，行了兩三步
必囘首望望，誤會了每一根樹枝和一棵樹，遠遠的一根樹幹
，皆把牠們當作了人。這是不可能的事去把我驚慌的意像向
我表現出事的各種形式，多少的騷亂的意念時時在幻想中
尋着，因此許多奇怪的幻想來到我的思想裏面，一一敍述出
來。

　　當我抵我的堡壘的時候，（自此以後，我就這樣地叫牠）
，我飛奔入內好像被追逐一樣。或者我是由梯子上（如起初
設計一般，或者從石的洞中進去，就是我叫作們的，我不能
夠記憶了。第二天早晨我也不能記憶；那吃驚逃入林中的兔
子和竄入窩中的狐狸都沒有我逃入這個退避所的恐嚇。

　　那天夜裏沒有睡着。我離開恐懼的機會愈遠，我的思慮
愈大，這是相反這種事物的天性的東西，尤其相反各種恐嚇
中的生物的普通的實行。但是我對於自已可怕的意念是這
樣的困苦，除去造成憂悶的幻想以外，別無其他事物。一個
人怎樣會到這裏來？載他的船在那裏？還有什麼旁的足跡嗎
？

　　我馬上結論，這必定是可危的生物的足印；就是，那對
遍大地上的野人的足印，他們在木艇中遊出大海，

or by ¹*contrary* winds, ²*had made the island,* and had been
on shore, but were gone away again to sea ; being as ³*loath,*
perhape, to have stayed in this ⁴*desolate* island as I would
have been to have had them.

While these ⁵*reflections* were ⁶*rolling in my mind,* I was
very thankful in my thoughts that I was so happy as not to
be thereabouts at that time, or that they did not see my
boat, by which they would have ⁷*concluded* that some
inhabitants had been in the place, and perhaps have
⁸*searched* farther for me,

Then ⁹*terrible* thoughts ¹⁰*racked my imaginatinn* about
their having found out my boat, and that there were people
here ; and that, if so, I should ¹¹*certainly* have them come
again in greater unmbers, and ¹²*devour* me ; that if it should
happen that they should not find me, yet they would find
my inclosure, ¹³*destroy* all my. corn, and carry away all my
flock of tame goats, and ¹⁴*I should perish at last for mere want.*

Thus my fear ¹⁵*banished* all my ¹⁶*religious* hope,—all that
former ¹⁷*confidence* in God, which was ¹⁸*founded* upon such
wonderful ¹⁹*experience* as I had had of his goodness ; as if
he that had fed me by ²⁰*miracle* hitherto could not preserve,
by his power, the ²¹*provision* which he had made for me by
his goodness. I ²²*reproached myself with my laziness,* that
would not sow any more corn one year, than would just
²³*serve* me till the next season, as if no ²⁴*accident* could
²⁵*intervene* to ²⁶*prevent* my enjoying the ²⁷*crop* that was upon
the gound. This I thought so just a ²⁸*reproof* that I re-
²⁹*solved* for the future to have two or three years' corn
³⁰*beforehand,* so that, whatever might come, I might not
³¹*perish* for want of bread.

或被急湍，或被逆風驅逐，到了島上，上了岸；但是又往悔裏去；或者他們不願居留在這個孤寂的島上，好像我曾經有了他們一樣。

當這些囘想輾轉在我心中之時，在我思想中，我是深自慶幸，當時未曾在他們左近，他們未曾瞧見我的船，若使他們瞧見了船，他們必要決斷着在這個地方定有居民，或者要老遠的來搜尋我了。

可怖的思想把我的幻覺磨難得不停，關於他們已經找着了我的船和有人在這個地方等等；倘然是這樣，他們不久一定要結隊而來，把我吃去；倘使他們找不着我，他們將要尋出我的圍地，損壞我的穀子，把我的成羣的馴的山羊一齊帶走，那末最後我將因缺乏食物而死了。

我的恐懼把宗教上帝希望一齊驅走了，——從前信仰上帝，信仰心我從他的仁慈中所得的奇異經驗上面樹立的，好像他用不可思議的奇蹟，用他的能力，用他的仁慈，把他爲我所設備的食物來喂養我。我自責我的偸惰，我一年之中未曾多播種些穀子直到下一個季候能夠供我之用爲止，好像是沒有不幸之事來阻礙我享受地上穀子的收成一般。我想這個對我實在是一種責罰，我決定將來必要預先存留供兩三年之用的穀子，那末，無論何事發生，我不致因缺乏食物而餓死了。

How strange a [1]*checkerwork* of [2]*Providence* is the life of man! and [3]*by with different*, [4]*secret springs are the affections hurried about*, as different [5]*circumstances* present!　To-day we love what to-morrow we hate; to-day we [6]*seek* what to-morrow we [7]*shun*; to-day we desire what to-morrow we fear,—nay, [8]*even tremble at the apprehensions of*.　This was [9]*exemplified in me*, at this time, in the most lively manner [10]*imaginable*; for I, whose only [11]*affliction* was that I seemed [12]*banished* from human society, that I was [13]*alone*, cut off from mankind, and [14]*condemned* to what I call [15]*silent life*, so that to have seen one of my own [16]*species* would have seemed to me a raising me from death to life, and the greatest [17]*blessing* that Heaven itself could [18]*bestow*; I say, that I should now [19]*tremble* at the very [20]*apprehensions* of seeing a man, and was ready to sink into the ground at but the shadow or silent [21]*appearance* of a man having set his foot in the island!

These thoughts took me up many hours, days—nay, I my say weeks and months; and one [22]*particular effect* of my [23]*cogitations* on this [24]*occasion* [52]*I cannot omit*,　One morning early, lying in my bed, and [26]*filled* with thoughts about my danger from the [27]*appearance* of [28]*savages*, I found it [29]*discomposed me very much*; upon which these words of the Scripture came into my thoughts: "Call upon me in the day of trouble, and I will [30]*deliver* thee, and thou [31]*shalt glorify* me."

In the middle of these [32]*cogitations*, apprehensions, and [33]*reflections*, it came into my thoughts one day that all this might be a mere [34]*fancy* of my own, and that this foot might be the [35]*print* of my own foot when I came on shore from my boat.　This [36]*cheered* me up a little, too, and I began

上天賜給生命與人，宛如雜色細工一般，奇異非言可喻！在各種環境之中，人的感情因受各種原動力而變化！明日我儕所恨者今日則愛之；明日我儕所趨避者今日則尋求之。明日我儕所恐懼者今日則希望之，——豈止恐懼甫一念及則戰慄不已。這就是我的現身說法，在這個時候，在可幻想的最活潑的態度中；我的惟一的苦痛就是為人類社會所屏棄，我孤身一人，為人類所削除，謫我幽居，以為我的刑罰，那末倘使瞧見了一個和我種類相同的人，在我想起來，可說是把我出死入生，這就是上天所能賜予的最大的福澤了；我想，現在當我看見一個人出現，必定要恐怖失措，只要瞧見人的影兒或是祕密出現的人在這島上置足，我便要立刻到地內去！

這些思想消磨了許多鐘頭，日子，——豈止如此，可以說許多星期和月份；在這個時會裏面，我不能忘却我的思想的一個特別的效果。一天早晨，躺在床上，心中充滿了野人出現對於我將有危險的思想，我覺着這個令我甚為不安；聖經上的這些話又來到我的思潮之中："在困難之中呼喚我，我將援助爾，爾將使我光榮"。

在這些思想恐怖，和回憶之中，一天，心中偶然想着這些東西大概都自由於我自己幻覺所致，那個足印或者是我自己從船上往岸上所留下來的足跡。這個思想。

1. 雜色細工. 2. 上天. 3. 受各種的. 4. 原動力. 5. 環境. 6. 尋求. 7. 避. 8. 一念及則戰慄. 9. 現身說法. 10. 可幻想的. 11. 困苦. 12. 驅去. 13. 孤單. 14. 戀. 15. 孤寂生活. 16. 種類. 17. 福. 18. 給予. 9. 顛戰. 20. 恐怖. 21. 現形. 22. 特別效力. 3. 思想. 24. 機會. 25. 不能忘. 26. 充滿. 27. 現形. 28. 野人. 29. 令我不安. 30. 援助. 31. 將. 32. 光榮. 34. 思想. 35. 足跡. 36. 使我欣慰.

to ¹*persuade* myself it was all a ²*delusion* ; that it was nothing else but my own foot.　Why might I not come that way from the boat, as well as I was going that way to the boat? Again I considered, also, that I could by no means tell, ³*for certain*, where I had *trod*, and where I had not.　If, at last, this was only the print of my own foot, I had played the part of those fools who try to make stories of ⁵*specters* and ⁶*apparition*⁺, and then are ⁷*frightened* at them more than anybody.

Now I began to take ⁸*courage*, and ⁹*to peep abroad* again, for I had not ¹⁰*stirred out* of my ¹¹*castle* for three days and nights, so that I began to ¹²*starve for provisions* ; for I had little or nothing within doors but some barley cakes and water.　Then I knew that my goats wanted to be ¹³*milked* too, which usually was my evening ¹⁴*diversion* ; and the poor creatures were in great pain and ¹⁵*inconvenience* for want of it.　Indeed, it almost ¹⁶*spoiled* some of them. and almost dried up their ¹⁷*milk*.　¹⁸*Encouraging* myself, therefore, with the ¹⁹*belief* that this was nothing but the print of one of my own feet, and that I might be truly said to start at my own ²⁰*shadow*, I began to go abroad again, and went to my country house to milk my flock.　But to see with what feer I went forward, how often I looked behind me, how I was ready, every now and then, to lay down my basket and ²¹*run for my life*, it would have made any one think I was ²²*hounted with an evil conscience*, or that I had been lately most ²³*terribly* frightened ; and so, indeed, I had.

However, I went down thus two or three days, and having seen nothing, I began to be a little ²⁴*bolder*, and to think there was really nothing in it but my own imagina-

稍為鼓勵我一些，我開始着勸誘自己說這完全是一種幻覺；除我自己的足印而外，別無他物。為什麼我不可以從船上到那條路上去；既然我從那條路往船上去？我重行又注意着一定不能確切地說那條路我曾踐踏過，那條路我未曾踐踏過。倘使，最後，這僅是我自己的足印，我簡直做了呆事了，像那些作鬼怪出現故事的人，自己到比旁人來得害怕。

現在我始覺着膽大了，重行出外；不出堡壘已經三日三夜了，那末我將因乏食而餓斃了；因為在家中我僅有些大麥餅和水。我知道山羊也要擠乳了，擠乳就是我晚間慣常的消遣之事；可憐的生物需要擠乳的時候，是狠痛苦和狠不便利的。實在，擠乳差不多要損壞牠們幾隻，差不多把牠們的乳都弄乾了。自己鼓勵着，想信那個足印不過是我自己的，我可以真實地講我是恐怕我自己的影兒了，我重行外出，到我村舍內去擠羊乳。但是想想看我向前走是如何的恐怖，常常回轉頭來向身後望，時時我預備着把籃子放下來逃命，人們或要猜想我是被惡心所崇了，或者我是近來被物恐嚇太甚了；實在，我是如此。

然而兩三日來我就這樣地走下去，沒有瞧見什麼東西，我開始着較為勇敢一些了，想除去我自己的幻想以外，實在沒有什麼東西存在着。

tion. But I [1]*could not persuade myself fully of this* till I should go down to the shore again, and see this print of a foot, and measure it by my own, and see if there was any [2]*similitude* or [3]*fitness*, that I might be [4]*assured* it was my own foot. But when I came to the place, first, it appeared [5]*evidently* to me that when I laid up my boat, I could not possibly be on shore anywhere [6]*thereabouts*; [7]*secondly*, when I came to measure the [8]*mark* with my own foot, I found my foot [9]*not so large by a great deal*. Both these things filled my head with new [10]*imaginations*, and [11]*gave me the vapors* again to the highest degree, so that I shook with cold like one in ague. I went home again, filled with the belief that some man or men had been on shore there; or, in short, that the island was [12]*inhabited*, and I might be [13]*surprised* before I [14]*was aware*. What course to take for my [15]*security* I knew not.

Oh, what [16]*ridiculous* resolutions men take when [17]*possessed* with fear! It [18]*deprives them of* the use of those means which reason offers for their relief. The first thing I proposed to myself was to throw down my inclosures, and turn all my tame cattle wild into the woods, lest the [19]*enemy* should find them and then [20]*frequent* the island [21]*in prospect of* the same or [22]*the like booty*; then the simple thing of [23]*digging up* my two [24]*cornfields*, lest they should find such a grain there, and [25]*still be prompted* to [26]*frequent* the island; then to [27]*demolish* my bower and tent, that they might not see any vestiges of habitation and be [28]*prompted* to look farther in order to find out the persons [29]*inhabiting*.

CHAPTER XXIX

THIS [30]*confusion* of my thoughts kept me awake all night. But in the morning I fell asleep; and, having by

但是我不能完全地自信，直至我再往島岸上，看那個足印，用我自已的足來測量牠，瞧瞧形樣是否相同，大小是否適合為止，那末我便可以確信那是我自已的足印了。但是當我來到那個地方，第一步，我顯然地覺着當我停船的時候，我是不可能的到岸上左近的地方上去；第二步，當我去用自已的足來測量那個足印，我覺着我自已的足遠不如牠大。這兩種事把我的腦中充滿了新的幻想，使我憂鬱重行達於極點；我遂渾身抖戰起來，像人發瘧疾一般。我重行囘家，心中充滿思潮，相信有人或有些人曾到那邊岸上去過的；總而言之，這座島是有人居住的，在我未曾得知以前，我將要被人襲擊。將取何種方法，方能使我安全，我不知道。

哦，當人們爲恐怖之念所佔有之時，他們將取怎樣可笑的決心！理性給予人們的援助却被恐怖把那些方法奪去了。我自已主張的第一步是把我的圍地打倒，把那些馴的羊使他們到林中去變野，恐怕敵人們尋着牠們，於是乎時常來到這座島上，希望再得些同樣的掠獲物；後來又想把我的兩座穀的堀起，恐怕他們在這裏尋出穀子，那末他們更爲激動，格外要常臨此島了；後來又想把我的小亭和帳幕弄壞，那末他們便瞧不出有人住居的痕跡，便不致於急速地向遠方觀察，想把住居的人尋找出來了。

the [1]*amusement* of my mind been, as it were, [2]*tired*, and my [3]*spirits exhausted*, I slept very soundly, and [4]*waked* much better [5]*composed* than I had ever been before. And now I began [6]*to think sedately*; and, [7]*upon debate with myself*, I [8]*concluded* that this island, which was so [9]*exceedingly* pleasant, [10]*fruitful*, and no farther from the [11]*mainland* than as I had seen, was not so [12]*entirely abandoned* as I might imagine; that although there were no [13]*stated inhabitants* who lived on the [14]*spot*, yet that there might sometimes come boats off from the shore, who, either with [15]*design*, or perhaps never but when they were [16]*driven* by [17]*cross winds*, might come to this place; that I had lived here fifteen years now, and had not met with the least shadow or [18]*figure* of any people yet; and that, if [19]*at any time* they should be driven here, it was [20]*probable* they would go away again as soon as ever they could, seeing they had never thought fit to fix here [21]*upon any occasion*; that the most I could [22]*suggest* any danger from, was from any [23]*casual*, [24]*accidental landing* of [25]*straggling people* from the main, who, [26]*as it was likely*, if they were driven hither, [27]*were here against their wills*, so they made no [28]*stay* here, but went off again [29]*with all possible speed*, [30]*seldom* staying one night on shore, lest they should not have the help of the [31]*tides* and [32]*daylight* back again; and that, therefore, I had nothing to do but to consider of some safe [33]*retreat*, in case I should see any savages land upon the [34]*spot*.

Now I began [35]*sorely to repent* that I had [36]*dug* my cave so large as to bring a door through again, which door, as I said, came out beyond where my fortification [37]*joined* to the rock. [38]*Upon maturely considering this*, therefore, I resolved to [29]*draw* me a second fortificatinn' [40]*in the manner of a*

第 二 十 九 章

　　紛亂的思潮使我終夕不寐。但是早上我却睡着了；心中娛樂煩倦了，精神困乏了，我睡得狠熟，醒來的時候覺得比前來得安寧。現在我開始沉思默想；自巳心內忖度，我決斷這座島，牠是這樣地令人極爲欣悅的，出產豐富，離開我所見的大地不甚遠，不是全然被人所棄，如我料想所及；雖然沒有住在那裏的固定的居民，然而有時或者有船舶從岸邊出發，船舶或者是在計劃中，或是被逆風所驅逐，就來到這個地方；現在我住在這裏有十五年了，然而尙未曾碰着人的影兒或臉兒；倘使無論何時他們被追到這裏來，大槪當他們瞧見這裏是不慣停留的，一經能走，便重行再離開這裏；我所猜想得着的危險就是從那些由大海中偶然登岸的游蕩之民身上來，他們大槪是這樣，倘使被追到這裏來：是非心中所願的，所以不停留在這裏，盡其速力離去此處，狠少在岸上停留一夜，恐怕是失去幫助他們囘去的潮水和日光；所以我除想找一個安全的避身處之外，別無他的可爲，一經在這個地方瞧見了野人，我便藏藏起來。

　　現在我深自懊悔着我把洞穴掘得這樣寬大，再要關一座大門，那座大門，我未曾經說過，從相連岩石的我的堡壘外面伸將出來。精密地熱思了以後，我決定畫一個第二個堡壘的圖樣，半圓形，離開我的牆壁，就在大

¹*semicircle*, at a distance from my wall, just where I had planted a double row of trees about twelve years before ²*of which I made mention*. These trees having been planted so thick before, they wanted but a few ³*piles* to be driven between them, that they might be ⁴*thicker* and stronger, and my wall would be soon ⁵*finished*.

Thus I had now a ⁶*double* wall; and my outer wall was thickened with pieces of timber, old ⁷*cables*, and everything I could think of, to make it strong; having in it seven little holes, about as big as I ⁸*might put my arm out at*. In the inside of this I thickened my wall to about ten feet thick with ⁹*continually* bringing earth out of my cave, and laying it at the foot of the wall, and walking upon it. Through the seven holes I ¹⁰*contrived* to ¹¹*plant the muskets*, of which I took ¹²*notice* that I had got seven on shore out of the ship. These, I say, I planted like my ¹³*cannon* and ¹⁴*fitted them into* ¹⁵*frames* that held them like a ¹⁶*carriage*, so that I could fire all the seven guns in two minutes' time. This wall I was ¹⁷*many a weary month in finishing*, and yet never thought myself ¹⁸*safe* till it was done.

When this was done, I ¹⁹*stuck* all the ground without my wall, ²⁰*for a great length every way*, as full with stakes or ²¹*sticks* of the ²²*osierlike wood*, which I found so ²³*apt to grow*, as they ²⁴*could well stand*; ²⁵*insomuch that* I believe I might ²⁶*set in* near twenty thousand of them, leaving a ²⁷*pretty* large space between them and my well, that I might have room to see an ²⁸*enemy*, and they might have no ²⁹*shelter* from the young trees, if they ³⁰*attempted* to ³¹*approach* my outer wall.

Thus, in two years' time, I had a ³²*thick grove*; and in five or six years' time, I had a wood before my ³³*dwelling*, growing so ³⁴*monstrously* thick and strong that it was indeed

約十二年以前我種植雙行樹的那個地方，這事我已經說過了。這些樹是種得這樣地厚，在牠們之中，若是不缺幾根木椿，那末牠們還可以厚些堅固些，我的牆壁便馬上完成了。1

現在我有雙層牆；外面的牆是用木塊，舊的船索，以及我能想及的東西把牠弄厚使得牠堅固；其中有七個小穴其大足容予臂之出入。牆的裏面，我把牠弄得大約十尺厚，不停地從洞穴中帶出泥土來，把牠放在牆腳，在牠上面行走。穿過七個小穴，我預備安置短槍，短槍共有七隻，是我從船中帶上岸來的。這些，我說，我樹立起來像大礮一樣，用架子裝配起來，好像裝在車中一般，這樣在兩分鐘的辰光，我可以把七隻短槍一齊開放。我幸苦數月方把這座牆壁造成，直到工竣以後，方覺已身安全。

這事做畢，在牆的外面，我用木椿和棒我想是易於生長的，又能耐久；甚至於我相信我可以設置牠們二萬根，在牠們和牆的中間留下稍寬的地位，我可以有地位去看敵人們倘使他們企圖走近我的外牆，他們在幼檻當中得不着遮蔽所的。

在兩年中，我有了一座叢林，在五六年中，在住所外，我有了一

perfectly ¹impassable. No men, ²of what kind soever, could ever imagine that there was anything beyond it, much less a ³habitation. As for the way which ⁴I proposed to myself to go in and out (for I left no ⁵avenue), it was by setting two ⁶ladders, one to a part of the rock which was low, and then ⁷broke in, and ⁸left room to place another ⁹ladder upon that. So when the two ladders were taken down, no man living could come down to me without ¹⁰doing himself mischief; and if they had come down, they were still on the outside of my outer wall.

Thus I ¹¹took all the measures human ¹²prudence could ¹³suggest for my own ¹⁴preservation. It will. be seen, at length, that they were not ¹⁵altogether without just reason; though I ¹⁶foresaw nothing at that time more than my mere fear suggested to me.

While this was doing, I was not altogether ¹⁷careless of my other ¹⁸affairs; for I ¹⁹had a great concern upon me for my little ²⁰herd of goats. They were not only a ²¹ready supply to me on every ²²occasion, and began to be ²³sufficient to me, ²⁴without the expense of powder and shot, but also without the ²⁵fatigue of ²⁶hunting after the wild ones; and I was ²⁷loath to lose the advantage of them, and to have them all to ²⁸nurse up over again.

For this purpose, after long ²⁹consideration, I could think of but two ways to ³⁰preserve them. One was, to find another ³¹convenient place ³²to dig a cave underground, and to drive them into it every night. The other was to inclose two or three ³³little bits of land, remote from one another, and as much ³⁴concealed as I could, where I might keep about half a dozen young goats in each place; so that if any ³⁵disaster happened to the ³⁶flock ³⁷in general, I might be able to raise

座大樹林，長得堅厚異常，實在是無路可以通過。無論那一種類的人不能夠猜料得着有像住所一般的東西在牠的外面存着。至於我想進出的那一條路（因爲我未曾留下小路），就是放了兩座梯子，一座靠在低的石頭的一面，後來凹進去，留下餘地來放第二座梯子上面。這樣當兩座梯子取下之時，凡是人想走下來到我面前，一定要傷害他自己的；就使他們下來了，他們仍舊是在我外牆的外面。

我用了人類的智慧能夠計算的種種方法來保存我的生命。後來，可以瞧得出這些方法不見得全不合理；雖然在那個時候，除去我的恐懼之念提醒我以外，我沒有瞧見任何東西。

遭事進行的時候，對於別的事務，我也未曾忽視；我是極其關心我的一小羣山羊。無論何時，牠們不但對我是不時的供應，對我是滿足的供給，不必耗費藥粉和彈丸，而且還無須費去獵逐野獸之勞；我是不願失去牠們給我的利益，於是重行豢養牠們。

爲了這個緣故，在深思遠慮之後，我僅能想出兩個法子來保留牠們。一個就是尋出別的合宜的地方，掘穴於地下，每晚把牠們驅進去。其他一個方法就是圍兩三塊小地，彼此相隔略遠，須極其隱密，在那裏每一塊地方我可以保留大約牛打小山羊；倘使有災難降到全體山羊身上來，我可以費些力氣和時間再把牠們飼養起來。

1.不能行過。2. 無論何種。3. 住所。4. 我意欲。5. 徑。6. 梯。7. 凹入。8. 留出餘地。9. 梯。10. 傷害自身。11. 盡情設法。12. 智慧。13. 提議。14. 保存。15. 完全。16. 見。17. 不留心。18. 事務。19. 我極關心於。20. 羊羣。21. 不時之供應。22. 機會。23. 滿足。24. 不必耗費。25. 困乏。26. 獵。27. 不欲。28. 再行飼養。29. 思慮。30. 保留。31. 合且。32. 掘穴地下。33. 小塊地，彼此相隔略遠。34. 隱密。35. 災難。36. 羊羣。37. 全體

them again with little [1]*trouble* and time. This, though it would [2]*require* a good deal of time and labor, I thought was the [3]*most rational design.*

Accordingly, I spent some time to find out the most [4]*retired parts* of the island; and I [5]*pitched upon one* which was as [6]*private*, indeed, as my heart could wish for. It was a little, [7]*damp* piece of ground, in the middle of the [8]*hollow* and thick woods, where, as is [9]*observed*, I [10]*almost lost myself* once before, [11]*endeavoring* to come back that way from the eastern part of the island. Here I found a clear piece of land, near three acres, so [12]*surrounded* with woods that it was almost an inclosure [13]*by nature.* At least, it did not want near so much labor to make it so as the other piece of ground I had worked so hard at.

I immediately went to work with this piece of ground; and, in less than a month's time, I had so fenced it round that my flock, or [14]*herd*, call it which you please, which were not so wild now as at first they might be [15]*supposed* to be, [16]*were well enough secured* in it

So, without any further delay, I [17]*removed* ten young she-goats and two he-goats to this piece. When they were there, I continued to [18]*perfect* the fence, till I had made it as [19]*secure* as the other; which, however, I [20]*did at more* [21]*leisure*, and it took me up more time by a great deal. [22]*All this labor I was at the expense of*, [23]*purely* from my apprehensions on account of the print of a man's foot; for, as yet, I had never seen any human creature come near the island.

I had now lived two years under this [24]*uneasiness*, which indeed, made my life much less [25]*comfortable* than it was before, as may be well [26]*imagined* by any who know what it

這個事情，雖然必需費着許多的時候和工作，但是我想是最好的合理的方法。

依着貫例我費着許多的時候尋訪島上的幽僻之處．我於是擇選了一塊 做着私宅；的確的這是我心上所極喜歡的地方。這是一塊小的潮潤我地方，在深沉和濃厚的樹林中間那個地方，我觀察起來，我以前曾經迷落在那裏過的；那時我竭力地尋覓着路同去在島的東部份。在此處我找到一塊清爽的地，相近有一畝地大小，如此的圍繞着樹林，因此好像是有着天然的包圍物。所以至少，牠可以不必費極大的工作像其他的地方我費着極大的工作。

我就立卽去開始工作在這塊地上；差不多不到一月的時光，我已經如此的圍着籬笆在我的羊羣或者說是牧蓄的周圍，讀者可以隨便的稱呼他罷，這個籬笆並不遣樣的大，像我以前所設想的那樣大，但是在其中極可以保持平安了。

如此，我並不延擱時光，我就移殖十只小雌山羊和兩只雄山羊到遣個地方來。當牠們已經移殖過去以後，我依舊繼續着完成那個籬笆，佈置至我做得和其他的一樣堅固；那個籬笆我從從容容建造的，遣個費去我許多的時光。我之所以做着遣種工作，完全是爲着發見了人的足跡之故，因爲。雖然我並不再看見其他的生人來至此島。

我已經住了兩年在遣種不安逸的狀態之下，遣種不安適的狀態，的確使我的生命不十分的安適像以前一般，不論何人都可以想像到一個入在恐嚇的情形之中的態度。

is to live ¹*in the constant snare of* the fear of man. And this I must observe, with grief, too, that the ²*discomposure* of my mind ³*had great impression also upon* the ⁴*religious* part of my thoughts ; for the dread and ⁵*terror* of falling into the hands of savages and ⁶*cannibals* ⁷*lay so upon my spirits* that I ⁸*seldom* found myself with the ⁹*sedate* ¹⁰*calmness* and ¹¹*resignation* of ¹²*soul* which I ¹³*was wont to have.* I rather prayed to God as ¹⁴*under great affliction and pressure of mind,* surrounded with danger, and in ¹⁵*expectation* every night of being ¹⁶*murdered* and devoured before morning ; and I must ¹⁷*testify,* from my experience, that a temper of peace, thankfulness, love, and ¹⁸*affection* is much the more proper ¹⁹*frame* for prayer than that of terror and discomposure.

But to go on. After I had thus ²⁰*secured* one part of my little ²¹*living stock,* I went about the whole island, searching for another ²²*private* place to make such another ²³*deposit* ; when, wandering more to the went point of the island than I had ever done yet, and looking out to sea, I thought I saw a boat upon the sea, at a great distance. I had found a ²⁴*perspective glass* or two in one of the seamen's ²⁵*chests* which I saved out of our ship, but I had it not about me ; and this was so ²⁶*remote* that I could not tell what to make of it, though I looked at it till my eyes were ²⁷*not able to hold* to look any longer. Whether it was a boat or not, I do not know ; but as I ²⁸*descended* from the hill I could see no more of it, so I gave it over : only I resolved to go no more out without a ²⁹*perspective* glass in my ³⁰*pocket.*

³ When I was come down the ³¹*hill* to the end of the island, where, indeed, I had never been before, I was presently ³²*convinced* that the seeing the print of a man's foot was not such a ³³*strange* thing in the island as I imagined ; and but that it was a special ³⁴*providence* that I was cast upon the side of the island where the ³⁵*savages* never came, I should

我也要用憂愁態度來注意道個，就是我心中的不安大有形響於我思想中的宗教部份；因為將落於野人和吃人者的手中的恐懼，深印在我的腦中；我不常常覺着神志沈靜和心靈滿足，這個却是我平常常覺着的。被危險所環繞之故，心中大受困苦；每晚預想等不到早晨便要被殺和被吃的時候，我就向上帝禱告；從我的經驗上，我必須證明，一個安逸的，感謝的，相愛的。有情感的人禱告比較一個人在恐懼和不安逸的人的禱告要來得鎮靜。

但是繼續着說去。我把牲畜一部份安置好了以後，我去周游全島，搜尋別的隱僻場所來再弄一個存儲的地方；當我漫游島的西部比平常走的遠，瞧着海水，我想我瞧見遠地裏有一隻船。在海員箱子中，我曾找着一兩隻望遠鏡。那隻箱子是我從船中保留下來的；但是望遠鏡却不在路傍；船是這樣地遠，我不知道他是怎麼樣子，雖然我看着牠至目力不能再望遠為止。牠是不是一隻船，我不知道；但是當我從小山下降之時，我不能再瞧見牠了，這樣我便放棄牠；不過我決定以後出外袋中應當放一隻望遠鏡。

當我下山到島的末端之時，在那裏，實在，我未曾去過，我立刻明白瞧見一個人的足跡印在這島上不是如我所猜想的那樣奇怪；不過是我在那些野人永不蒞臨的島側這是一個特別的天賜之助。

1. 常受…束博。2. 不安。3. 大為感動。4. 宗教。5. 恐怕。6. 吃人者。7. 深印於腦。8. 不常。9. 沉默。10. 安靜。11. 服從天意。12. 靈。13. 常有。14. 心中受困。15. 希冀。16. 殺。17. 證明。18. 感情。19. 性情。20. 安全。21. 牲畜。22. 隱僻。23. 存貯。24. 望遠鏡。25. 箱。26. 遠。27. 不能支持。28. 降。29. 望遠。30. 袋。31. 小山。32. 悟433. 奇怪。34. 天賜之助。35. 野人。

easily have known that nothing was more ¹*frequent* than for the canoes from the main, when they happened to be a little too far out at sea, ²*to shoot over to that side of the island for harbor.* Likewise, as they often met and ³*fought* in their canoes, the ⁴*victors*, having taken any ⁵*prisoners*, would bring them over to this shore, where, according to their dreadful ⁶*customs*, being all ⁷*cannibals*, they would kill and eat them ; of which more hereafter.

我應當老早狠容易地知道僅僅只有那些從大海中來的木艇時常光顧此島，沒有別的東西；當這些木艇偶然離岸入海較爲過遠了，爲尋覓港口的緣故，所以向島的對岸急駛而去。野人們常常在木艇裏面遇着和打架，勝利的人，獲有幾個囚俘，把他們帶到岸上來，在那裏，依照他們可怖的習慣，他們都是吃人的東西，他們便把俘處殺而食之；後來那些習慣却更加多了。

1.常常來往。2.爲覓港口之故，所以向彼岸急駛而去。3.打架。4.勝利之人。5.囚俘。6.習慣。7.吃人者

365

When I was come down the hill to the shore, as I said above, being the southwest point of the island I was perfectly [1]*confounded and amazed*, nor is it [2]*possible* for me to [3]*express* the horror of my mind, at seeing the shore [4]*spread* with [5]*skulls*, hands, feet, and other bones of [6]*human bodies*. Particularly, I observed a place where there had been a fire made, and a circle [7]*dug* in the earth, like a [8]*cockpit*, where I supposed the [8]*savage wretches* had sat down to their [10]*inhuman feastings* upon [4]he bodies of their [11]*fellow-creatures*.

I was so [12]*astonished* with the sight of these things that I [13]*entertained* no notions of any danger to myself from it for a long while. All my apprehensions were [14]*buried* in the thoughts [15]*of such a pitch of inhuman brutality*, and the horror of the [16]*degeneracy of human nature*, which, though I had heard of it often, yet I never had so near a view of before. In short, I turned away my face from the [17]*horrid spectacle*. My [18]*stomach* grew sick, and I was [19]*just at the point of fainting*, when nature [20]*discharged the disorder from my stomach*. [21]*I was then a little relieved*, but could not bear to stay in the place a moment; so I got up the hill again with all the [22]*speed* I could, and walked on towards my own [23]*habitation*

When I came a little out of that part of the island, I stood still awhile, as [24]*amazed*. Then, [25]*recovering* myself, I looked up with the utmost [26]*affection* of my soul, and [27]*with a flood of tears in my eyes*, gave God thanks that he had cast my first lot in a part of the world where I was [28]*distinguished* from such dreadful creatures as these; and that, though I had [39]*esteemed* my present condition very [30]*miserable*, yet he had given me so many [31]*comforts* in it that I had still more to give thanks for than [32]*to complain of*; and this [33]*above all,*

當我下山赴海岸之時，我已經說過，那裏是島的西南角，我非常驚惶失措起來，我是不能將心中的恐懼表明出來，我瞧見海岸上面鋪滿了骷髏，人手，人足，以及人身上的骨骼等等。特別地，我注意着一座地方，在那裏却有火生着，地中掘了一個圈，像鬥雞場一般，我猜是野人們在那裏坐下來享受他們的野蠻的飲宴，吃他們同類的身體。

看見這些東西，我是異常地恐懼，過了半天，我並未懷有自身危險的觀念。我所看的恐怖都藏在野蠻之極的思想裏面，人格墮落的恐嚇當中，雖然我曾經聽見過這種事情，然而以前我却永遠未曾逼視過呢。總之，我從這種可怖的景象上面掉過來。我的腹中有病了，當我剛剛要昏暈的時候，體氣却把我腹中的疾病排泄出來。我覺稍為舒適一點，但是不能再一刻停留於此處了；這樣我又下了山。竭力地速行，向我的住所而往。

當我稍微離開了島的那一部份，我站了一會，好像驚呆了一樣。後來，復原了，我用滿腔熱誠，涕淚如雨的態度向上望。謝謝上帝，他把我支配到的這一部份，在那裏，我同那些可怕的生物分開來；雖然我以為現在身處的境況是不幸的然而他賜予我許多安慰，我應多加感謝，而不應稍存怨恨之心，最要者。即使在這種不幸境況之中，我被他的

1.驚惶失措。2.可能。3.表示。4.鋪開。5.骷髏。6.人身。7.掘。8.鬥雞場。9.野人。10.野蠻之宴。11.同類生物。12.吃驚。13.有。14.埋。15.野蠻已極。16.人格墮落。17.可怖之狀。18.胃口。19.將暈。20.掘泄腹中之疾病。21.我覺稍適。22.快。23.住居。24.吃驚。25.囘復。26.情感。27.淚如雨下。28.分出。29.以為。30.不幸的。31.安慰。32.怨訴。33.尤甚者。

that I had, even in this miserable condition, been [1]*comforted* with the knowledge of himself, and the hope of his [2]*blessing*, which was a [3]*felicity* more then [4]*sufficiently* [5]*equivalent* to all the [6]*misery* which I had [7]*suffered*, or could suffer.

In this [8]*frame* of thankfulness I went home to my [9]*castle* and began to be much [10]*easier* now, as to the [11]*safety* of my [12]*circumstances*, than ever I was before. For I [13]*observed* that these [14]*wretches* never came to this island in search of what they could get; perhaps not seeking, not [15]*wanting*, or not expecting anything here; and having often, no [16]*doubt*, been up in the covered, woody part of it without finding anything [17]*to their purpose*. I knew I had been here now almost eighteen years, and never saw the least [18]*footsteps* of [19]*human* creature there before; and I might be eighteen years more as entirely [20]*concealed* as I was now if I did not discover myself to them, which I [21]*had no manner of occasion to do*, it being my only [22]*business* to keep myself entirely concealed where I was, unless I found a better sort of creatures than [23]*cannibals* to make myself known to.

Yet I [24]*entertained* such an [25]*abhorrence* of the savage wretches that I have been speaking of, and of the wretched, [26]*inhuman* [27]*custom* of their [28]*devouring* and eating one another up, that I continued [29]*pensive and sad*, and [30]*kept close within* my own circle, for almost two years after this. When I say my own [31]*circle*, I mean by it my three [32]*plantations*,—namely my castle, my country seat (which I called my bower), and my inclosure in the woods; nor did I look after this for any other use than as an inclosure for my goats. I did not so much as go to look after my boat all his time, but began rather to think of making me another;

知識所安慰，爲他的福澤的希望所安慰，那是一種幸福，决不能和我所受的以及我所能受的一切不幸之事，等量齊觀的。

在這種感謝的情感中，我同到我的堡壘中去，現在覺得比較安逸些，對於我的環境的安全，比到從前較好。因爲我注意着這些野蠻的東西永遠不是爲搜尋他們所能得的東西而來島上；或者未曾尋找，未曾需要，和未曾在這裏希望着任何物件；一定無疑，他們常常地來到島的掩蓋的部份，多木的部份上面來，從未得着合意的東西。我知道現在我在島上差不多十八年了，以前永遠不曾見過人的足印，我或者還要再隱居十八年，像我現在一樣，倘使我不向他們現形，這事我却無機可乘，我惟一的事務就是把我自己完全藏匿於我居住的地方；若是我找不着比較吃人的野人稍好種類的生物，使他們知道我的行蹤的話。

我却痛恨那些野人，就是我述及的那般野蠻東西：和他們互相吞噬那些無人道的習慣，我愁悶不已，緊匿於我的圓圈裏面，在此事以後差不多藏了兩年。當我說我的圓圈，我的意思就是說我的三處新闢地，——就是，堡壘，村舍（我叫作牠涼亭），和在樹林中圍地，除去作圍住山羊以外，不作他用，我不時常地去看守小船，但是開始着想再製造一隻；

1.安慰. 2.福澤. 3.幸福. 4.滿足. 5.同等. 6.不幸之事. 7.受. 8.性情. 9.堡壘. 10.較易. 11.安全. 12.環境. 13.注意. 14.壞的東西. 15.需要. 16.疑惑. 16.合意. 18.足印. 19.人的. 20.隱匿. 21.無機可乘. 22.事務. 23.吃人者. 24.懼. 25.恨. 26.無人道的. 27.習慣. 28.吞. 29.憂悶不已. 30.緊匿於家中. 31.圓圈. 32.新闢地

for I could not think of ever making any more [1]*attempts* to bring the other boat round the island to me, lest I should meet with some of these creatures at sea; in which case if I happened to have fallen into their hands, I knew what would have been my [2]*lot*.

CHAPTER XXX

TIME, however, and the [3]*satisfaction* I had that I [4]*was in no danger of* being discovered by these people, began to [5]*wear off* my [6]*uneasiness* about them. I began to live just in the same [7]*composed manner* as before, only with this [8]*difference*, that I used more [9]*caution*, and kept my eyes more about me than I did before, lest I should happen to be seen by any of them; and particularly, I was more cautious of firing my gun, lest any of them, being on the island, should happen to hear it. It was, therefore , a very good [10]*providence* to me that I had [11]*furnished* myself with a tame breed of goats, and that I had no need to [12]*hunt* any more about the woods, or shoot at them. If I did catch any of them after this, it was by [13]*traps* and [14]*snares*, as I had done before, so that for two years after this I believe I never [15]*fired* my [16]*gun off* once, though I never went out without it; and, what was more, as I had saved three [17]*pistols* out of the ship, I always carried them out with me,—or at least two of them,—[18]*sticking* them in my goat-skin belt. I also [19]*furbished up* one of the great [20]*cutlasses* that I had out of the ship, and made me a belt to hang it on also; so that I was now a most [21]*formidable fellow* to look at when I went abroad, if you add to the former [22]*description* of myself the particular of two pistols, and a great [23]*broadsword* hanging at my side in a belt, but without a [24]*scabbard*.

在此時我也不十分去留意着我的船了，但是我却開始着想我另外再去造一只船；因為我不能再想還有其他的船會衝到這個島的四圍來了，除非我還會在海中遭遇到其他相同的建築物，在這種情形之中，倘使我能夠遭到這樣的落在他們手中，那麼我可以知道我的命運應該怎樣了。

第 三 十 章

無論如何，依時間，說並且我也有充足的理由想着，被這些野人發見已決無這種危險了，因此我解除了對他們的不安逸的心思。如此我又泰然自若的住着像以前的情形一般，不過這是有差別的；我是特別的留心注意着他們，我時常自行四處看清；否則我想，或者會被他們不論何人所看見，其中最重要的是這樣，我極謹慎着放我的槍，否則，無論他們之中的那一個，在這個島上的，或者會聽到槍聲。這個，所以就是對於我的一個天賜的良機了，因為我有着馴順的山羊可以供給我的食品，我不必再在樹林中去打獵了，或者再去打山羊，即使此後我捉到幾只山羊，這是用機關或陷阱捉到的，像我以前所做的一般，如此我居住兩年永不開放一槍，雖然我出外必需帶鎗，並且此外，我曾在船中得到手鎗三枝，我時常帶着出外。至少我要帶兩枝，縛在我的羊皮帶上。我也磨快了一柄短刀，那個刀是我殺羊的，也做着一條帶繫在身上，所以我現在一跑出去就是一個非常可怕的人物，倘使你加上了以前描寫我的特別的情形，兩只手鎗，一柄大的腰刀掛在皮帶上在我的身邊；不過刀是沒有劍鞘的。

Things going on thus, as I have said, for some time, I seemed, [1]*excepting* these cautions, to be [2]*reduced* to my former calm, [3]*sedate* way of living. All these things [4]*tended to* show me, more and more, how far my condition was from being [5]*miserable*, [6]*compared* to some others,—nay, to many [7]*other particulars of life*, which it might have pleased God to have made my lot. [8]*It put me upon reflecting* how little [9]*repining* there would be among [10]*mankind* at any [11]*condition of life*, if people would rather [12]*compare* their condition with those that were worse, in order to be thankful, than be always [13]*comparing* them with those which are better, [14]*to assist their murmurings and complainings*.

As in my present condition there were not [15]*really* many things which I [16]*wanted*, so, indeed, I thought that the [17]*frights* I had been in about these savage wretches, and the concern I had been in for my own [18]*preservation*, [19]*had taken off the edge of my invention for my own conveniences*. I had [20]*dropped* a good design, which I had once [21]*bent* my thoughts too much upon, and that was to try if I could not make some of my [22]*barley* into [23]*malt*, and then try to [24]*brew* myself some beer. This was really a [25]*whimsical thought*, and I [26]*reproved myself often for the simplicity of it*; for I presently say there would be the want of several things [27]*necessary* for the making my beer, that it would be [28]*impossible* for me to supply. First, I needed [29]*casks* to [30]*preserve* it in, which was a thing that; as I have [31]*observed* already, I [32]*could never compass*,—no, though I spent not only many days, but weeks, nay months, in [33]*attempting* it, [34]*but to no purpose.* In the next place, I had no [35]*hops* to make it keeps, no yeast to make it work, no [36]*copper or kettle* to make it boil. Yet [37]*with all these things wanting*, I [38]*verily believe*, had not the frights

一切事情是如此的過去：我以前已經說過了，我似乎在有些時光丟開了那些謹慎之心，恢復了我以前的平安態度，過着恬靜的生活。一切向着我的事情一些一些的煩惱，如何我的情形是如此的卑劣，倘使和其他的人比較起來；——噎，不過其他許多的特別事情，那些事情或者是上帝所喜歡的，上帝將我的命運做成這樣。這個事情使我回想到人類怨恨着各種的環境生活的痛苦是何等的少，倘使人們將他們自己的環境和比他們更劣的比較，這個或者會使他們感激上帝了。倘使他們時常和比較他們地位較好的人比較，那麼就會造成他一切的默愁和怨恨。

至於我目前的境況，其實我所其缺乏的東西已經狠少，因此，的確，我想着恐怕那些野人的思想完全消挫了我創製我自用便利品的銳氣和保存我生命的一切有關係的事情。我丟棄了一個好的計畫，這是我以前專心想着的，這個計畫就是我想試着是否能夠將麥做麥酒，再試着去做成皮酒，這個眞是一種幻想，於是我就時常賣着自己的思想 怪誕；現在我可以說，那裏有着許多的必要的工作做皮酒，這些工作是我萬不能辨到的。第一我需要木箱來保存他在裏面，這個事情我早已觀察到了，這個是我萬難成功的，———不，雖然我費不少的日子，星期，月份，去試驗他，但是終無佳果。第二就是我沒有酵花去保存他，沒有酒母去調製他，沒有銅鍋燒沸他。

1.去除。2.降低，減少。3.安靜。4.注向。5.卑鄙。6.比較。7.其他人生的特別事務。8.使我回想。9.怨恨。10.人類。11.人生的環境。12.比較。13.比。14.助成默愁和怨恨。15.眞。16.需要。17.怕。18.保存。19.創製我自用物品的銳氣全爲消滅。20.丟棄。21.衷心。22.大麥。23.麥酒。24.釀酒。25.妄想。26.自責怪想。27.必需。28.不能。29.箱。30.保存。31.觀察。32.不能成爲事實。33.試。34.無佳果。35.酵母花。36 銅器或銅鍋。37.缺此數事。38.確信。

and [1]*terrors* I was in about the savages [2]*intervened*, I had [3]*undertaken* it, and [4]*perhaps brought it to pass*, too; for I [5]*seldom gave anything over without accomplishing it*, when once I had it in my head enough to begin it.

But my [6]*invention* now ran quite another way; for, night and day, I could think of nothing but how I might [7]*destroy* some of these [8]*monsters* in their [9]*cruel*, [10]*bloody* [11]*entertainment*; and, if possible, save the [12]*victim* they should bring hither to [13]*destroy*. It would take up a larger [14]*volume* than this whole work is [15]*intended* to be, [16]*to set down* all the [17]*contrivances* I [18]*hatched*, or rather [19]*brooded upon*, in my thoughts, for the destroying these creatures, or at least [20]*frightening* them so as to [21]*prevent* their coming hither any more; but [22]*all this came to nought*. Nothing could be possible [23]*to take effect* unless I was to be there to do it myself: and what could one man do among them, when perhaps there might be twenty or thirty of them together, with their [24]*darts*, or their [25]*bows and arrows*, with which they could [26]*shoot* as true to a [27]*mark* as I could with my gun?

Sometimes I thought of [28]*digging* a [29]*hole* under the place where they made their fire, and putting in five or six pounds of [30]*gunpowder*, which, when they [31]*kindled their fire*, would [32]*consequently* [33]*take fire*, and [34]*blow up* all that was near it. But as, in the first place, I should be [35]*unwilling* to waste so much powder upon them, my store being now within the quantity of one [36]*barrel*, so neither could I be sure of its [37]*going off* at any certain time, when it might surprise them; and, [38]*at best*, that it would do little more than just blow the fire about their ears and fright them, but not [39]*sufficient* to make them [40]*forsake the place*. So I [41]*laid it aside*: and then [42]*proposed* that I would place myself [43]*in*

就使缺少這些東西，我確信，假使我心中沒有恐懼野人的觀念來煩擾着，我已經試辦着了，或者可以成功，也未可知；因為當我腦中想進行一事的時候，不把牠做成功我是不肯把牠丟棄下來的。

但是現在我的發明又另尋一條路徑了；因為，整日整夜，我除想法子把那些野蠻動物的殘暴和流血的宴飲來損壞以外，別無他念；若果能行，把他們帶到這裏預備殺害的遇難人救將出來。倘使要把我心中所籌畫的把這些野人消滅：或者至少恐嚇他們使他們下次不敢再到這裏來的計劃——記錄下來，這一本小書決不夠登載，恐怕再要撰述一本較大的卷帙呢；但是所有這些計畫均成泡影。倘使我自己不到那裏去做，沒有一樁事能望生效：在他們當中，我一人能做些什麼，他們差不多有二十或三十人在一起，有標鎗，有弓箭，用這些東西他們射擊目標和我用鎗射擊東西一樣地準？

有時我想掘一個穴。在他們生火的地方下面，放入五六磅火藥，當他們燃火的時候，火藥立刻著火，把靠近牠的東西一齊轟去。但是第一層，我不願在他們身上費却許多火藥，現在所藏的僅有一桶之量了，我也不能夠確定牠在何時可以炸裂，當牠可以驚嚇他們的時候；究竟，這事不過比在他們耳旁吹火驚嚇他們較為厲害一些，但是不會使他們離此他適。這樣我遂放棄此法；提

ambush in some convenient place, with my three guns all
[1]*double loaded*, and [2]*in the middle of their bloody ceremony let
fly at them*, when I should be sure to kill or wound perhaps two or three at every [3]*shot*; and then [4]*falling in upon*
them with my three pistols and my sword, I made no
[5]*doubt* but that, if there were twenty, I should kill them
all. This fancy pleased my thoughts for some weeks, and
I was so full of it that I often [6]*dreamed* of it, and sometimes that I was just going to let fly at them in my sleep.
I went so far with it in my imagination that I [7]*employed*
myself several days to find out proper places to put myself
[8]*in ambuscade*, as I said, to watch for them, and I went
frequently to the place itself, which was now grown more
[9]*familiar* to me. But while my mind was thus filled with
[10]*thoughts of revenge* and of a [11]*bloody* putting twenty or thirty
of them to the [12]*sword*, as I may call it, the horror I had at
the place, and at the [13]*signals* of the [14]*barbarous* wretches
devouring one another, [15]*abetted my malice*.

Well, at length I found a place in the side of the hill,
where I was [16]*satisfied* I might securely wait till I saw any
of their boats coming; and might then, even before they
would be ready to come on shore, [17]*convey* myself unseen
into some [18]*thickets of trees*, in one of which there was a
hollow large enough to [19]*conceal* me entirely. There I
might sit and [20]*observe* all their [21]*bloody doings*, and [22]*take my
full aim at their heads*, when they were so close together as
that it would be [23]*next to impossible* that I should miss my
shot, or that I could fail of [24]*wounding* three or four of them
at the first shot. In this place, then, I resolved [25]*to fulfill
my design*; and accordingly I prepared two [26]*muskets* and
my [27]*ordinary* [28]*fowling piece*. The two [29]*muskets* I [30]*loaded with*

讓在合宜的地方，我去埋伏着，把三隻鎗都加倍地裝滿彈藥，在他們舉行兇殘儀式之，發放而射擊之，當我能夠確定每鎗的發射或者能殺傷他們二三人之時，方始射擊。後來便用三只手鎗和刀來毆擊他們，我是毫無疑惑的，倘使他們有二十人，我能把他們一齊殺完。這種幻想使我的思念愉快了幾個星期，我腦中充滿了牠，竟至常常地夢見實行牠，有時我在睡夢之中便要發鎗射擊他們。在幻想中，我想得這樣地遠，我費了幾天工夫找着了合宜的地方來埋伏着，像我說過的一樣，等候他們，我常常地到那個地方去，現在我是狠熟悉該地了。但是當我心中充滿了報復之念和要把他們二三十人來染血我刃的思想之時，我可以這樣地叫牠，在那個地方所覺着的恐怖，那些殘暴野人互相吞噬時的暗號，把我的怨恨心激起來了。

喝，最後我在山側找到一座地方，在那裏我是滿意的，我可以安靜地等着直至我瞧見他們的船來；我可以，在他們預備上岸之前，藏匿到森林內，使得不被他們所見，森林之中有一穴，其大足藏我全身。我可以坐在那裏，注視着他們的兇殘的行動，舉鎗對準其首而射擊之，當他們聚集一處的時候，這樣我的鎗可以能夠無虛發，第一次射擊，便不會不傷他們三四人，在這個地方，我決定實行我的計劃；我隨卽預備二只小銃和我平常用的打鳥鎗。兩只小銃，每只裏面我裝了雙彈丸，

1.加倍裝彈 .2.當其血肉相交之時，發放而射擊之.3.射.4.襲攻.5.疑.6.夢.7.用.8.埋伏.9.相稔.10.報復之念.11.流血.12.刀.13.暗號.14.野蠻.15.激我怨心.16.滿足.17.途.18.森林.19.藏匿.20.注意.21.兇殘之行為.22.舉鎗對準其首而射.23.幾不能.24.傷.25.將我意念施諸實行.26.鎗.27.普通的.28.打鳥鎗.29.小銃.30.裝以雙彈

a brace of slugs each, and four or five *[1]smaller [2]bullets*, about the size of pistol bullets; and the fowling piece I loaded with near a *[3]handful* of *[4]swan shot* of the largest size. I also loaded my pistols with about four bullets each; and, in this *[5]posture*, well provided with *[6]ammunition* for a second and third *[7]charge*, I *[8]prepared myself for my expedition.*

After I had thus *[9]laid the scheme* of my *[10]design*, and in my imagination *[11]put it in practice*, I continually made my *[12]tour* every morning to the top of the hill, which was from my castle, as I called it, about three miles, or more, to see if I could observe any boats upon the sea, coming near the island, or *[13]standing* over towards it; but I began *[14]to tire* of this hard duty, after I had for two or three months *[15]constantly kept my watch*, but always came back without any discovery. There had not, in all that time, been the least *[16]appearance*, not only on or near the shore, but on the whole ocean, *[17]so far as my eyes or glass could reach every way.*

As long as I kept up my daily *[18]tour* to the hill to look out, so long also I *[19]kept up the vigor of my design*, and my spirts seemed to be all the while in a *[20]suitable [21]frame* for so *[22]outrageous* an *[23]execution* as the killing twenty or thirty *[24]naked* savages, for an *[25]offense* which I had not at all entered into any *[26]discussion* of in my thoughts, any farther than my passions were at first fired by the horror I *[27]conceived* at the *[28]unnatual custom* of the people of that country. But now, when, as I have said, I began to be weary of the *[29]fruitless excursion* which I had made so long and so far every morning in vain, so *[30]my opinion of the action itself began to alter.* I began, with *[31]cooler* and *[32]salmer* thoughts, to consider what I was going to engage in; *[33]what authority or call I had to pretend to be judge* and *[34]executioner* upon these men

和四五粒較小的彈丸，大約有手鎗彈丸大小，把鳥鎗裝了差不多一把最大的形式的長形彈丸。我也把手鎗每只大約裝有彈丸四粒；在這種狀態中，彈藥充足，可作第二次射擊之用，戰途預備出征野人。

在我把計劃把我的幻想施諸實行以後；我每早不停地到山頂上去巡行，那個山離我的堡壘，我這樣地叫牠，大約有三英里遠，或更多些，瞧瞧我能不能在海上看見船，向峭駛近，或是對島面停住。但是我對於這種艱難的職務開始覺著厭倦，在時常注意着兩三月之後，常常地得不着發見物而悵然回家。撇總那些時候，在那邊毫無東西發見，不僅僅在岸上或靠着岸是如此，而且在全個大洋中也是如此，以我目力或望遠鏡之力達於四周各處而論。

我一經保守着每日到山上巡視的課程，和維持我計畫的精神於不疲的地位，我的心靈好像是始終在一種合宜的性情裏面，想作豪勇的事業，像欲殺死二三十赤身的野人，為了一種竟未經過我詳細斟酌的冒犯，我的怒火也被那個國度裏面的野人們的不合天理的風俗所給我的恐怕心燃燒起來了。但是現在，我曾經說過，當我開始厭倦着這個無效果的行程，我保守得了狠長久，每早出去，總是失望；這樣我對於這事的方針始行改變了。我開始用較冷靜和較沉寂的思想去考察着我應如何進行§我有何種權勢與何種

as [1]*criminals*, whom Heaven had thought fit, for so many ages, [2]*to suffer*, [3]*unpunished*, *to go on*; *how far these people were offenders against me*, and what [5]*right* I had to [6]*engage* in the [7]*quarrel* of that [8]*blood* which they [9]*shed* [10]*promiscuously* [11]*upon one another*. I [12]*debated* this very often with myself thus: "How do I know what God himself judges in [13]*this particular case*? It is certain these people [14]*do not commit this as a crime*; [15]*it is not against their own consciences* reproving, or their light [16]*reproaching* them; they do not know it to be an offense, and then [17]*commit* it [18]*in defiance of divine justice*, as we do in almost all the sins we [19]*commit*. They think it no more a [20]*crime* to kill a [21]*captive taken in war*, than we do to kill an ox; or to eat human [22]*flesh*, than we do to eat [23]*mutton*."

When I considered this a little, it followed necessarily that I was certainly in the [24]*wrong*; that these people were not [25]*murderers* in the sense that I had before [26]*condemned* them in my thoughts. In the next place, it occurred to me that although [27]*the usage they gave one another* was thus [28]*brutish and inhuman*, yet it was really nothing to me. These people [29]*had done me no injury*. If they [30]*attempted* me, or I saw it necessary [31]*for my immediate preservation to fall upon them*, something might be said for it; but I was yet out of their power, and they really had no knowlebge of me, [32]*and consequently no design upon me*.

CHAPTER XXXI

In this [33]*disposition* I continued for near a year after this; and so far was I from desiring an [34]*occasion* for falling upon these [35]*wretches*, that in all that time I never once

職司去冒充司法官和劊子手來處決他們,視同罪犯,經過了許多世紀,上天想着是合宜的任他們自然而不加以刑罰;他們又未曾冒犯於我,我有何權利去從事爭論他們互相殘殺,流血的舉動。我常常用這些話來自相辨駁:"上天對於這種特別的事如何評判我怎樣能夠知道?這是一定的這些人民不必因此而犯罪;並不違背他們的天良而斥責之,或者違背他們的見解去斥責他們;他們不知道做這種事是一種過失,於是乎便不顧上天的公道來從事於此了,如同我們所犯的各種的過失一樣。他們想想殺一個戰爭得來的俘囚,不是一種罪惡;就同我們殺一只牛一般;他們吃人肉,就同我們吃羊肉一般。"

當我稍稍注意這個,一定無疑地我是錯了;這些人民按諸字義說起來,決不是殺人的兇徒;如同先前我思想中懲責他們一般。第二層,我偶然地想着雖然他們彼此待遇之法是這樣地兇惡而殘忍,然而實在與我何傷。這些人民並未加損害於我。倘使他們企圖着我,或者我想這是必需地爲保存我自已的生命去襲擊他們,有些事可以這般地講;但我尚未曾在他們能力以內,他們實在也不知道有我這樣一個人,所以無謀害我的心思。

第 三 十 一 章

在這種情勢裏面,我繼續着過了差不多一年;我不想找一機會。

1.罪人.2.受.3.不加罪.4.他們又未冒犯我.5.權利.6.從事.7.爭端.8.血.9.流.10.混雜.11.彼此.12.辨駁.13.特別之事.14.不以此爲犯罪.15.並不違背天良.16.斥責.17.犯.18.不顧天理.19.犯.20.罪.21.戰時俘囚.22.肉.23.羊肉.24.錯.25.殺人者.26.懲責.27.彼此待遇之法.28.兇殘.29.於我無傷.30.企圖.31.爲自已保存而加以攻擊.32.故亦無害我之心.33.情勢.34.機會.35.壞東西.

went up the hill to see ¹*whether* there were any of the·n ²*in
sight*, or to know whether any of them had been, on shore
there or not. I went and ³*removed* my boat, which I had
on the other side of the island, and carried it down to the east
end of the ⁴*whole* island, where I ran it into a little ⁵*cove*,
which I found under some high rocks, and where I knew,
by reason of the currents, the savages ⁶*durst not*—at least
would not—come with their boats ⁷*upon any account whatever*. With my boat I carried away everything that I had
left there belonging to her, though not necessary for the ⁸*bare
going thither*,—namely, a mast and ⁹*sail* which I had made
for her, and a thing like an ¹⁰*anchor*, but which indeed
could not be called either anchor or ¹¹*grapnel*; however, it
was the best I could make of its kind. All these I
¹²*removed*, that there might not be the least shadow for
discovery, or appearance of any boat, or of any human
¹³*habitation* upon the island.

Besides this, I kept myself, as I said, more ¹⁴*retired* than
ever, and ¹⁵*seldom* went from my cell ¹⁶*except* upon my
¹⁷*constant* employment,—to milk my she-goats, and manage
my little ¹⁸*flock* in the wood, which, as it was quite on
the other part of the island, ¹⁹*was quite out of danger*. For
²⁰*certain* it is that these savage, people, who sometimes
²¹*haunted this island*, never came with any thoughts of
finding anything here, and ²²*consequently* never wandered
off from the coast, and I doubt not but they might have
been several times on shore after my ²³*apprehensions* of
them had made me cautious, as well as before. Indeed, I
looked back with some horror upon the thoughts of what
my condition would have been if I had ²⁴*chanced upon* them
and been discovered before; when, ²⁵*naked*, and ²⁶*unarmed*,

來攻打這些野人，一總我未曾到山上去過一次；瞧瞧或者看見他們幾個人；或者瞧瞧他們曾否在那邊上岸。我去移開我的小船，我曾經把牠停泊在島的那一方，把牠帶到全島上的東方的末端上，在那裏，我把牠放入小灣內，這座小灣是我在高的石岩下面尋着的；在那裏我知道，因爲急湍的緣故，野人不敢——至少我是不願。——無論何種情形，駛他們的船進來。我把在那裏曾經留下來的屬於船的各樣東西和牠一齊帶走，雖然不需要空船駛往彼處，——就是，我爲牠製造的一根檝和一張帆，一個像錨般的東西，牠實在不能夠被喚作錨或是小錨；然而牠却是我能竭力造成的一種東西。這些東西我都把牠們遷走了，那末以後或者沒有絲毫的跡象，由牠發見曾有船的發現而島上有人居住的現象。

　　此外，我曾說過：我把自已隱藏得較前更密，不常常地從穴洞中出外，除去進行日常的事務以外，——擠山羊乳，在樹林中處置一羣山羊，樹林是在島的完全的別一部份，所以絕無危險。一定這些野人們有時常常來往此島，却永遠未曾想到在這裏能找出些東西來，所以就永遠未曾從海濱上往各處遨遊，我是毫不疑惑，在我恐懼他們的心使我小心之後，他們如同從前一樣有幾次曾往岸上來。實在，我很恐怖地回想着那些意念：倘使以前我偶然地碰着他們或是被他們所發見，那末我的境地不知道要變成什麼樣子了；當寸銶不掛，未帶兵器，

[1]*except* with one gun, and that [2]*loaded* often only with small shot, I walked everywhere, [3]*peeping and peering* about the island to see what I could get. What a surprise should I have been in if. when I discovered the print of a man's foot, I had, instead of that, seen fifteen or twenty savages, and found them [4]*pursuing* me, and, by the [5]*swiftness* of their running, [6]*no possibility of my escaping them*! The thoughts of this sometimes [7]*sank my very soul within me*, and [8]*distressed* my mind so much that I could not soon [9]*recover* it, to think what I should have done, and how I should not only have been [10]*unable to resist* them, but even should not have had [11]*presence of mind* enough to do what I might have done; much less what now, after so much [12]*consideration* and [13]*preparation*, I might be able to do. Indeed, after [14]*serious* thinking of these things I would be [15]*melancholy*, and, sometimes, it would last a great while.

I believe the reader of this will not think it strange if I [16]*confess* that these [17]*anxieties*, these constant dangers I lived in, and [18]*the concern that was now upon me, put an end to* all invention, and to all the contrivances that I had laid [19]*for my future accommodations and conveniences*. I had the care of my [20]*safety* more now upon my hands than that of my food. I cared not to drive a [21]*nail*, or [22]*chop a stick* of wood now, for fear the noise I might make should be heard. Much less would I fire a gun, for the same reason; and, above all, I was [23]*intolerably uneasy* at making any fire, lest the [24]*smoke*, which is [25]*visible at a great distance* in the day [26]*should betray me*. For this reason I removed that part of my business which [27]*required* fire, such as [28]*burning* of pots and [29]*pipes*, etc., into my new [30]*apartment* in the woods; where, after I had been some time, I found to my [31]*unspeak-*

除去一艙以外，僅常裝有小彈，我散步各處，窺探一切，窺視鳥上以搜求我所能得之物。我將怎樣地恐怖，倘使，當我尋出人的足印之後，我瞧見了十五或二十個野人；覺著他們追逐我，藉着他們跑逐輕捷之力，使我不能逃避他們！思想及此，有時使我心灰意沮，使我的心這樣地痛苦不能立刻回復原狀；想想我應當作了些什麼，我如何的非但不能夠抵抗他們；而且還不會有膽識來作我應作的事；現在所應作的尤其不知道，在這些考慮和預備以後，我可以能夠去做了。實在，對於這些事物加以嚴重思想以後，我或者要憂鬱起來，有時，竟想了很久。我想讀者不會覺得這事可怪，假使我承認這些焦慮；這些我身處的危險，令我關懷的事，使得我攏總的發明消滅始盡，使得我對於將來爲膳宿方便計的所懷的各種計劃一齊打破。

　　我現在手頭上所有的爲安全的焦慮比食物尤甚。我不大注意去釘一只釘或削伐樹枝，恐怕我弄出來的聲音會使人聽見。我更不去放槍，爲了同樣的緣故；尤要者，我極不愉快地去生火，恐怕煙在白天老遠地可以望見，洩漏我的祕密。爲了這個緣故。我把需火的那種事務移往別處，如燒罐及煙管等等，遷移到樹林中我的新房內去；在那裏，我居住了些時以後，我覺着欣慰無似，在地土中，我找着一處純乎天成的洞穴，

able [1]consolation a [2]mere natural cave in the earth, which when in a vast way, and where, I dare say, [3]no savage, had he been at the mouth of it, [4]would be so hardy as to venture in; nor, indeed, would any man else, but one who, like me, wanted nothing so much as a safe [5]retreat.

The mouth of this [6]hollow was at the [7]bottom of a great rock, where, by mere [8]accident, I would say, if I [9]did not see abundant reason to ascribe all such things now to Providence, I was cutting down some thick [10]branches of trees to make [11]charcoal. Before I go on I must observe the reason of my making this [12]charcoal, which was this : I was afraid of making a smoke about my [13]habitation, as I said before; and yet I could not live there without [14]baking my bread, cooking my meat, etc. So I contrived to burn some wood here, as I had seen done in England, under turf, till it became [15]chark or dry coal. Then [16]putting the fire out, I preserved the coal to carry home, and [17]perform the other [18]services for which fire was [19]wanting, without danger of smoke. But this is by the bye.

While I was cutting down some wood here, I [20]perceived that behind a very thick [21]branch of low [22]brushwood or underwood, there was a kind of [23]hollow place. I was [24]curious to look into it; and getting with difficulty into the mouth of it, I found it was pretty large,—that is to say, [25]sufficient for me to [26]stand upright in it, and perhaps another with me. But I must [27]confess to you that I made more haste out than I did in, when, looking farther into the place, which was perfectly dark, I saw two [28]broad, [29]shining eyes of some creature, whether [30]devil or man I knew not, which [31]twinkled like two stars, the dim light from the cave's mouth shining directly in and making the [32]reflection.

那個洞伸長得很寬，在那裏，我敢說，沒有野人，倘使他在穴口能夠有冒險而入的瞻量；實在，不常的人也不敢進內，但是除非一個人，像我一樣，除去急欲得着一個安全的退避所，別無他求，絕敢入內。

穴的口在大石的底面，在那裏，經過僅有的不幸之事，我可以說，假使我決不能以此等事歸諸天命，我割下樹的厚的枝來作炭。在我進行之前，我必須考察着我作炭的理由，那就是這樣：在我住所的四圍，我怕有煙冒起來，我已經敘述過了；然而我却不能生活在那裏假使不去焙麵包，燒食物，等等。這樣我設計在這裏燒些林木，像我從前在英國做的一般，在草泥的下面，直到牠們變成焦炭或乾炭方止。於是把火熄去，我保留着炭把牠帶回家去，進行別種事務，為這種事務火是缺少不得的，却沒有生煙的危險。但是這個不過是一種閒話而已。

當我在這裏砍下林木的時候，我看見，在一株低的矮叢林的很厚的樹枝後面，有一處凹的地方。我是奇怪極了，望裏面考察了一會；很困難的走到牠的口內去，我覺着牠是狠寬的，——就是說，足夠容我立在裏面，或者還能另外來一個人，和我立在一處。但是我必須承認，告訴讀者，我出來的時候比進去來得忽促，當向這個地方的極裏面望了一望，那是十分的黑暗，我瞧見了兩只寬的，發光的動物的眼睛，或者是鬼還是人我不能得知道，那兩只眼睛鑠着好像兩顆星一般。從洞穴的口裏來的黯淡的光直按地點進去，於是發現這種回光。

However, after some pause, I ¹*recovered* myself, and began to call myself a thousand fools, and to think that he that was ²*afraid* to see the ³*devil*, was not fit to live twenty years in an island all alone, and that I might well think there was nothing in this cave that was more ⁴*frightful* than myself.　Upon this, ⁵*plucking up my courage*, I took up a ⁶*firebrand*, and ⁷*in I rushed again*, with the ⁸*stick* ⁹*flaming* in my hand.　I had not gone three ¹⁰*steps* in, before I was almost as much ¹¹*frightened* as before ; for I heard a very loud sigh, like that of a man in some pain, and it was followed by a ¹²*broken noise*, as of words half ¹³*expressed*, and then a deep sigh again.　I ¹⁴*stepped* back, and was indeed ¹⁵*struck* with such a ¹⁶*surprise* that it ¹⁷*put me into a cold sweat*, and if I had had a hat on my head, I ¹⁸*will not answer for it* that my hair might not have ¹⁹*lifted it off*.　But ²⁰*still plucking up my spirits* as well as I could, and ²¹*encouraging* myself a little with considering that the power and ²²*presence of God was everywhere*, and was able to ²³*protect* me, I ²⁴*stepped* forward again.

By the light of the ²⁵*firebrand*, holding it up a little over my head, I saw lying on the ground a ²⁶*monstrous*, ²⁷*frightful*, old he-goat, ²⁸*gasping for life*, and dying, indeed, of mere old age.　I ²⁹*stirred* him a little to see if I could get him out, and he ³⁰*essayed* to get up, but was not able to ³¹*raise* himself.　I thought with myself he might even lie there ; for if he had ³²*frightened* me, so he would ³³*certainly* frighten any of the savages, if any of them should be so hardy as to come in there while he ³⁴*had any life in him*.

I was now ³⁵*recovered* from my surprise, and began to look round me, when I found the cave was but very ³⁶*small*,

雖然，稍息之後，我便復原了，開始着呼喚我自己做萬愚之人，想想凡是怕見鬼的人，是不相稱的獨自一人在荒島上面居住了二十年；我可以好好地想在這洞穴裏面，除去我自己以外，沒有再可怖的東西了。因此，壯壯膽量，我拿了一根火把，重行衝入，手中抓着發亮的火棍。我進去還未曾有三步，我忽然和前次一樣，吃驚起來；因爲我聽見一種很高的歎聲，像一個人在痛苦之中所發出的一般，歎聲又被一種破碎的聲音相續着，好像半吞半吐的說話一般，後來又是一聲長的歎息。我退後，實在被這種驚訝打擊了，渾身冷汗，假使我頭上有頂帽子，我將不任其咎，我的頭髮是否將要把帽兒揭去。但是仍舊竭力振起精神，鼓勵自己一下，注意着上帝的權力和神的現顯之處是無所不在的，他能夠保佑我，我於是邁步前進。

得了火把的光熖之助，把牠稍舉起來，經過了我的頭，我看見躺在地上有一隻巨大的，可怖的，老的公山羊在極力喘息，實在因爲年紀太大將要死了。我動了牠一下去瞧瞧我能不能把牠帶出去，牠企圖着立起來，但是不能站起。我自己想想牠最好仍舊躺在那裏，假使牠驚嚇了我，牠一定能夠驚嚇那些野人，若是他們之中有大胆的竟來到那裏，當牠尚有餘生的時候。

現在我從驚訝之中回復過來了，開始着四面望了一望，

that is to say, it might be about ¹*twelve* feet over, but in no manner of ²*shape*, neither round nor ³*square*, no hands having ever been ⁴*employed* in making it, but those of mere nature. I ⁵*observed* also that there was a place at the farther side of it that went in farther, but was so low that it ⁶*required* me to ⁷*creep* upon my hands and ⁸*knees* to go into it, and whither it went I knew not. So, having no ⁹*candle*, I gave it over for that time, but ¹⁰*resolved* to go again the next day, ¹¹*provided* with ¹²*candles* and a ¹³*t inder box*, which I had made of the lock of one of the ¹⁴*muskets*, with some ¹⁵*wildfire* in the pan.

Accordingly, the next day I came ¹⁶*provided* with six large candles of my own making, (for I made very good ¹⁷*candles* now of ¹⁸*goat's tallow*, but was ¹⁹*hard set for* candle ²⁰*wicks*, using sometimes ²¹*rags* or ²²*rope-yarn*, and sometimes the dried ²³*rind* of a weed like ²⁴*nettles* ;) and going into this low place I was obliged ²⁵*to creep upon all fours*, as I have said, almost ten yards; which, ²⁶*by the way*, I thought was a ²⁷*venture* bold enough, considering that I knew not how far it might go, nor what was beyond it. When I ²⁸*had got through the strait*, I found the ²⁹*roof* rose higher up, I believe near twenty feet. But never was such a ³⁰*glorious* sight seen in the island, I dare say as it was to look round the sides and roof of this ³¹*vault* or cave. The wall ³²*reflected* a hundred thousand lights to me from my two candles, What it was in the rock,—whether ³³*diamonds* or any other ³⁴*precious stones*, or gold, which I rather ³⁵*supposed* it to be,— I knew not. The place I was in was a most ³⁶*delightful* ³⁷*cavity*, ³⁸*or gratto*, though perfectly dark. The ³⁹*floor* was dry and ⁴⁰*level*, and had a sort of ⁴¹*small*, ⁴²*loose*

陡然之間，我覺着這座洞穴是狠小的，就是說，牠周圍大約有十二尺，毫未具有形式，旣不圓又不方，沒有手工曾經來製作牠，但不過是天然之而已。我也注意着在牠的稍遠的部份上有一所伸長得很遠的地方，但是這樣的底下，我必須手膝爬行，方能入內，牠伸長到什麼地方去，我不知道。這樣，沒有燭，當時我遂放棄此舉，但是決心第二天走進去，備辦着燭和火絨盒，這隻盒子是從我的一隻小銃槍機上面製造出來的，在槍機藥池裏面放了些烈火種。

立刻，第二天我來了，備有六只大燭，是我自己製的，（因為我現在拿山羊的油來製了些很好的燭，但是燭芯不易得着，有時用破布或是繩紗，有時用乾皮，是像苧蔴的種子的皮一般；）去到我不得不爬行的那個低下的地方裏面，我曾經說過了，差不多有十碼地；順便說起來，那是一種冒險的舉動，注意着我不知道那個地方究竟有多遠，也不知道在牠外面有些什麼。當我過了這個山峽，我覺着屋頂高起，我相信差不多有二十尺高。但是在島上永遠沒有瞧見過這種光榮的景象，我敢說，如同圍繞着這地穴或洞穴的兩傍和屋頂所見的一樣。從我的兩只燭光中，牆壁向我反射着千萬道光鋩。在石岩內有什麼，——或是鑽石，或是別的寶石，或是金子，這個我却未曾想及，——或不知道。我所在的地方是一座令人可愛的洞穴，雖然是十分的黑暗。

¹*gravel* upon it, so that there was no ²*nauseous* or ³*venomous* creature to be seen, neither was there any ⁴*damp* or wet on the sides or ⁵*roof*.

The only difficulty in it was the ⁶*entrance*, which, however, as it was a ⁷*place of security*, and such a ⁸*retreat* as I wanted, I thought was a ⁹*convenience*; so that I was really ¹⁰*rejoiced* at the ¹¹*discovery*, and ¹²*resolved*, ¹³*without any delay*, to bring some of those things which I was most anxious about to this place. ¹⁴*Particularly*, I ¹⁵*resolved* to bring hither my ¹⁶*magazine* of powder, and all my ¹⁷*spare arms*; namely, two fowling pieces—for I ¹⁸*had three in all*—and three ¹⁹*muskets*— for of them I had ²⁰*eight* in all. So I kept in my ²¹*castle* only five, which stood ready ²²*mounted* like pieces of ²³*cannon* on my ²⁴*outpost fence*, and were ready also to take out upon any ²⁵*expedition*. Upon this ²⁶*occasion* of removing my ammunition I happened to open the ²⁷*barrel* of ²⁸*powder* which I took up out of the sea, and which had been ²⁹*wet*, and I found that the water had ³⁰*penetrated* about three or four ³¹*inches* into the powder on every side, which ³²*caking* and growing hard, had ³³*preserved* the inside ³⁴*like a kernel in the shell*, so that I had near sixty ³⁵*pounds* of very good powder in the ³⁶*center* of the ³⁷*cask*. This was a very agreeable ³⁸*discovery* to me at that time; so I carried all away thither, never keeping above two or three pounds of powder with me in my ³⁹*castle*, for fear of a surprise of any kind. I also carried thither all the lead I had left for bullets,

I fancied myself now like one of the ⁴⁰*ancient giants* who were said to live in caves and ⁴¹*holes* in the rocks, where ⁴²*none could come at them*. I ⁴³*persuaded* myself, while I was here, that if five hundred ⁴⁴*savages* were to ⁴⁵*hunt* me, they

地面乾而平，有一種小的，鬆的小石在上面，所以沒有令人厭惡的和有毒的動物能夠發現，在牠的兩側和屋頂上也沒有潮溼的地方。

　　裏面所最困難的地方就是入口，牠誠然如同平安之所一般，和我所希望的退避所無二，我想這處是一所便利場地；我於是實在地欣悅着這個發見，決定，不稍遲延，把我所急欲需求的東西帶到這個地方來。特別地，我決定去把我的貯藏火藥庫和攏總餘下來的兵器攜來；就是，兩只鳥槍，──因爲我却共有三只── 和三只小銃── 我攏總有八只。這樣我在堡壘中僅保留着五只槍，牠們被安置於架上而提高，口徑，好像我的外籬上面安放的幾架礮一般，也是預備好了逢到任何出征之時，把牠們帶出。在我還移軍火的機會上面，我偶然地把我從前從海中取上岸來的一桶火藥打開，牠是溼了，我瞧見水曾經透進去，在每一邊火藥裏面約浸入三四寸深，火藥凝結成塊，變硬了，把內裏保存起來好像果仁在殼內一般，以至於我差不多有六十磅很好的火藥在桶的中央。當時這對於我實在是一種合意的發見；這樣我一概攜往那邊，在堡壘中，永遠未曾保留着兩三磅以上的火藥，恐怕發生任何恐嚇。我把做彈丸用的鉛也一概帶到那邊。

　　現在我自已幻想着我像古時代的巨人一般，人家說他是住在山洞或山穴裏面，在岩石的當中，在聖裏，無有能及他的。我自已勸誘着，當我在這裏的時候，假使有五百野人來追逐我，他們永遠不會找出我來；卽使找着我，他們也不敢在這裏攻打我。

could never find me out; or if they did, they would not
¹venture to ²attack me here.   The old goat whom I found
³expiring, died in the mouth of the cave the next day after
I made this discovery; and I found it much ⁴easier to dig a
great hole there, and throw him in and cover him with
earth, than to ⁵drag him out.

I was now in the twenty-third year of my ⁶residence in
this island, and was so ⁷naturalized to the place and the
⁸manner of living that, could I but have ⁹enjoyed the certainty
that no savages would come to the place to ¹⁰disturb me,
I could have been ¹¹content to ¹²capitulate for ¹³spending the
rest of my time there, even to the last moment, till I had
laid me down and ¹⁴died, like the old ¹⁵goat in the cave.   I
had also arrived to some little ¹⁶diversions and ¹⁷amusements,
wich made the time pass a great deal more pleasantly
with me than it did before.   First, I had ¹⁸taught my Poll,
as I named before, to speak; and he did it so ¹⁹familiarly,
and talked so ²⁰articulately and plain, that it was very
²¹pleasant to me; and he lived with me no less than six-
and-twenty years.   How long he might have lived ²²after-
wards I know not, though I know they have a ²³notion in
Brazil that they live a hundred years.   My dog was a
pleasant and loving ²⁴companion to me for no less than
sixteen years of my time, and then died of mere old age.
As for my cats, they ²⁵multiplied, as I have observed, to that
degree that I was obliged to ²⁶shoot several of them at first,
to keep them from devouring me and all I had; but, at
length, when the two old ones I borught with me were
gone, and after some time ²⁷continually driving them from
me, and letting them have no ²⁸provision with me, they all
ran wild into the woods, except two or three ²⁹favorites

我尊着的那個將死的老山羊，在我這個發見以後的第二天在山穴的口內死去了；我覺着這是格外容易在那裏去掘一個大穴，把牠攜進去，用泥土把牠蓋好，後來再把牠拖出。在這座島上，我現在寓居了第二十三年，對於這個地方很是習慣，謀生的現象，我也覺着很慣常的，假使我能以爲一定沒有野人會到這裏來煩惱我，我必能自足地列一規定辦事時刻的表，藉以消耗餘生，至最後的一刻，直至我躺下身來死去爲止；好像老山羊在穴中一樣。我也從事於小的消遣之事和娛樂之法，這些事使得光陰過去比以前更爲欣快些。第一，我教我的波爾，我以前曾述及過牠，說話；牠說得這樣的純熟，而且講得聲音清楚，字眼明白，對於我是很欣快的；牠和我相處了不下二十六年。以後牠能再活若干年，我不知道，雖然我知道在布納喜爾牠們有一種觀念，說牠們能活一百年。我的狗是我的欣快的可愛的伴侶，隨我不下十六年，後來因爲年紀老而死去了。至於我的那些貓，牠們增加起來，我曾注意過，直到了那個等數以致於我不得不起頭打死牠們幾隻，爲着不使牠們把我所有的食物吃完；但是，後來，當我帶到這裏來的兩只老貓死去之時，過了些時，不停地把牠們從我身旁驅逐，讓牠們不和我同食，牠們一齊在樹林中變野了，除去兩三隻我所喜愛的以外，

which I kept [1]*tame,* and whose young, when they had any, I always [2]*drowned* ; and these were part of my family.

Besides these I always kept two or three [3]*household* kids about me, which I [4]*taught* [5]*to feed out of my hand.* And I had two more [6]*parrots,* which talked [7]*pretty well,* and would all call "Robin Crusoe," but none like my first; nor, indeed, did I [8]*take the pains* with any of them that I had done with him. I had also several tame [9]*sea fowls,* whose name I knew not, that I [10]*caught* upon the shore, and cut their wings; and the little [11]*stakes* which I had [12]*planted* before my castle wall being now grown up to a good thick grove, these fowls all lived among these low trees, and bred there, which was very [13]*agreeable* to me; so that, as I said above, I began to be [14]*very well contented with the life I led,* if I could have been [15]*secured* from the dread of the savages.

But it was otherwise directed; and it may not be [16]*amiss* for all people who shall meet with my story to make this [17]*just observation* from it, namely, how [18]*frequently,* [19]*in the course of our lives,* the evil which in itself we [20]*seek most to shun,* and which, when we [21]*are fallen into,* is the most dreadful to us, is [22]*oftentimes the very means or door of our deliverance,* by which alone we can be raised again from the affliction we are fallen into. I could give many [23]*examples* of this in the [24]*course* of my [25]*unaccountable* life; but in nothing was it more particularly [26]*remarkable* than in the [27]*sircumstances* of my last years of [28]*solitary* residence in this island.

CHAPTER XXXII

IT was now the mouth of December. as I said above, in my twenty-third year; and this, being the [29]*southern*

我把牠們養馴；他們的幼貓，當牠們生育了若干的時候，我常常地把牠們沈入水中；這些東西是我家庭中的一部份。在這些東西之外，我常常在我身邊養了兩三隻家居的小山羊，我教牠們到我手內來吃東西。我還有另外兩只鸚鵡：說話說得很不錯；兩只都會叫"魯賓克路沙，"但是皆不像第一只鸚哥；實在，我對牠們也不甚勞心費力像我對那第一只一樣。我還有些馴的海禽，他們的名兒我不知道，我在海岸上捉住了牠們，把牠們的翅膀割掉；在我堡壘牆壁之前。我所種植的那些小木樁現在長成了一座很厚密的森林，海禽們就住在低樹之中，在那裏生育，這對我很欣悅的；以致於，如我先前述及的一般，我開始着度此生活：心滿意足，假使我從恐懼野人之中而得到安全。

但是這事從別的方面判斷起來；或者不是錯誤，對於擾總人們，他們或將個攫我這樣的遭際，從這個上面，作一公平判斷的話；就是，怎樣常常地，在我們在世之日，我們亟欲滋遍壞處，當我們陷入牠的裏面之時，牠對於我們是一極可怖的東西，牠常常也是我們被救的根由，單單由牠，我們可以從我們陷入的苦痛裏面振拔起來。在我怪異的生活當中，我可以示出許多的例子來；但是這個在旁的事物裏面沒有在我孤寂居於島上過去的若干年中的環境裏面更加來得特別地可注意。

第 三 十 二 章

現在是十二月了，我先前曾說過，在我的第二十三年中；

¹*solstice* (for winter I cannot call it), was the particular
time of my ²*harvest*, and ³*required* me to be pretty much
⁴*abroad* in the ⁵*fields*.　Going out early in the morning, even
⁶*before it was thorough daylight*, I was ⁷*surprised* with seeing
a light of some fire upon the shore, at a ⁸*distance* from me
of about two ⁹*miles*, toward that part of the island where
I had observed some savages had been before ; not on the
other side,—but, to my great ¹⁰*affliction*, it was on my side
of the island.

I was indeed ¹¹*terribly* ¹²*surprised* at the sight, and
¹³*stopped short* within my ¹⁴*grove* not daring to go out, lest
I might be ¹⁵*surprised*.　And ¹⁶*yet I had no more peace within*,
from the ¹⁷*apprehensions* I had that if these savages, in
¹⁸*rambling* over the island, should find my corn standing or
cut, or any of my works or ¹⁹*improvements*, they would
immediately ²⁰*conclude* that there were people in the place,
and would then never rest till they had found me out. ²¹*In
this extremity* I went back directly to my ²²*castle*, pulled up
the ladder after me, and made all things without look as
wild and natural as I could,

Then I prepared myself within, putting myself in a
²³*posture of defense*. I ²⁴*loaded* all my ²⁵*cannon*, as I called
them,—that is to say my muskets,—which were mounted
upon my new fortification, and all my pistols, and ²⁶*resolved*
²⁷*to defend myself to the last gasp*, not ²⁸*forgetting* ²⁹*seriously* ³⁰*to
commend myself to the divine protection*, and ³¹*earnestly* to
pray to God to ³²*deliver* me out of the hands of the
barbarians.　I continued in this ³³*posture* about two hours,
and began to be ³⁴*impatient for intelligence abroad*, for I had
no ³⁵*spies* to send out.　After sitting a while longer, and
³⁶*musing* what I should do in this case, I ³⁷*was not able to*

冬至日到了(我不能叫牠作冬天)，這是我收成的特別的時期，需要着我常常出外到田中去。早上很早的出外，天尚未大亮，我却吃驚起來了；瞧見有些火光在岸上，距離着我約有兩英里之遠，向島上那個部份，在那裏我以前曾經瞧見來了幾個野人；不是在另外的一面，————但是，對我是苦痛得很，就在島上的這一面。

瞧了這種景況，我實在是非常的吃驚，在森林那面突然地止了步，不致出去，恐怕我將要彼襲擊。然我的心中也甚安定，因為有了幾個恐怖之念，假使這些野人，在島的四周漫步，或將找着了我的樹立或是割下的穀子，或者我的工作，或者改善的事物，他們立刻便要決定在這個地方是有人居住的，那末他們非把我找到，不肯休息。在這種逆境之中，我立即同到堡中去，在我身後把梯子拖下，竭力使得外面各種東西瞧起來荒野而自然。

後來我在裏面預備，置身於防禦之狀態中。把礮全裝置好了，我這樣地稱呼牠們，————就是說，我的小銃，都裝在我的新造的礮台上面，以及我所有的手槍；決心盡死力以自衛，毫不忘記委身以求上帝的保佑，誠懇地祈求上帝把我從野蠻人手中援救出來。我繼續着在這種狀態中約兩個時辰，開始着急欲探聽外邊的消息，因為我却沒有探子，遣他出外。坐了稍久之後，默想着在這種情況中我應

bear sitting in ignorance longer, So, setting up my ladder to the side of the hill, where there was a flat place, as I [1]*observed* before, and then [2]*pulling* the ladder after me, I set it up again and [3]*mounted the top of the hill,* and pulling out my [4]*perspective* glass, which I had taken [5]*on purpose,* I [6]*laid me down flat on the ground,* and began to look for the place. I [7]*presently* found there were no less than nine naked [8]*savages* sitting round a small fire they had made, not to warm them, for [9]*they had no need of that,* the weather being [10]*extremely* hot, but, as I supposed, to dress some of their barbarous diet of [11]*human flesh* which they had brought with them, whether alive or dead I could not tell,

They had two canoes with them, which they had [12]*hauled up* upon the shore; and [13]*as it was then ebb of tide,* they seemed to me to wait for the return of the [14]*flood* to go away again. It is not easy to imagine what [15]*confusion* this sight put me into, especially seeing them come on my side of the island, and so near to me. But when I considered their coming must be always with the current of the [16]*ebb,* I began afterwards to be more [17]*sedate* in my mind, being satisfied that I might go abroad with safety all the time of the flood of [18]*tide,* if they were not on shore before. Having made this observation, I went abroad about my [19]*harvest* work with the more [20]*composure.*

[21]*As I expected so it proved*; for, as soon as [22]*the tide made to the westward,* I saw them all take boat, and row (or [23]*paddle* as we call it) all away. I should have observed that for an hour or more before they went off they were [24]*dancing,* and I could easily [25]*discern* their postures and [26]*gestures* by my [27]*glasses.*

當如何從事；我不能惘然久坐以待。這樣，把梯子放置在小山之側，在那裏有一所平坦的地方，我以前曾注意過，我把梯子從身後拖曳著，我把牠重行放好，登山之巔，拿出我的望遠鏡，我是有意地把牠帶在身邊，我俯伏於地上，開始朝那個地方注視著。我立卽瞧見了不下九個赤身的野人圍著他們所坐的微火而坐，並不是取暖，因爲他們無需於此，天氣極熱，但是，照我所料，他們是在調理人肉的野蠻的食品，他們把人肉帶了來，或是活的，或是死的，我不知道。

他們帶來了兩隻木艇，他們把牠們拖曳到岸上來；因爲那時恰正潮退，我想他們大概坐等候潮水重來，始行動身。這是不容易去猜想，這種景象使得我到怎樣的紛亂的情況裏面，尤其是瞧見他們來到島上我的這一方面，這樣地貼近我。但是我想他們所以來此必是常常隨潮流以俱至，我後來心中又更幽默起來，很滿意地我可以趁潮水漲的時候，無論何時，皆可安然在外面，假使他們以前不在岸上。有了這種觀念，我狠安心地出外做我收穫的工作。

果如予之期望；因爲，一經潮向西流，我見他們一淘上船，搖（或者是划如我們所說的一般）去了。我應當注意著，在他們將去的一個或幾個時辰之前，他們跳著舞，我狠容易地能辨別得出他們的狀態和手勢來，依著我的望遠鏡的助力。

1.注意。2.拖。3.登山巔。4.望遠。5.有意。6.俯伏於地。7.立卽。8.野人。9.彼等不需之。10.極。11人。肉。12.拖曳。13.彼時適潮退。14潮流。15.混亂16.退潮。17幽默。18潮。19.收成。20.心安。21.果逐我望。22.潮向西流。23.划。24.跳舞。25.看見。26.手勢。2

As soon as I saw them [1]*shipped* and gone, I took two guns upon my shoulders, and two [2]*pistols* in my [3]*girdle,* and my great sword by my side, without a [4]*scabbard*, and, [5]*with all the speed I was able to make,* went away to the [6]*hill* where I had discovered the first appearance of all. As soon as I got thither, which was in not less than two hours, (for I could not go [7]*quickly,* being so [8]*loaded* with arms as I was,) I [9]*perceived* there had been three canoes more of the savages at that place; and, looking out farther, I saw [10]*they were all at sea together, making over for the main.* This was a [11]*dreadful sight* to me, especially as, going down to the shore, I could see the marks of horror which the [12]*dismal work* they had been about had left behind it; namely, the blood, the [13]*bones,* and part of the flesh of human bodies, eaten and [14]*devoured* by thoes [15]*wretches* with [16]*merriment* and [17]*sport.*

I was so filled with [18]*indignation* at the sight, that I now begen to [19]*premeditate* the [20]*destruction* of the next that I saw there, let them be whom or how many soever. It seemed [21]*evident* to me that the visits which they made thus to this island were not very [22]*frequent,* for it was above fifteen months before any more of them came on shore there again,—that is to say, I neither saw them nor any [23]*footsteps* or [24]*signals* of them in all that time; for as to the [25]*rainy* [26]*seasons,* then they are sure not to come abroad, at least not so far. Yet all this while I lived [27]*uncomfortably,* [28]*by reason* of the [29]*constant* [30]*apprehensions* I was in of their coming upon me by [31]*surprise;* whence I observe that the [32]*expectation* of evil is more bitter than the [33]*suffering,* especially if [34]*there is no room to shake off* that [35]*expectation,* or those apprehensions.

我一經瞧見他們登船開駛而去：便把兩隻槍扛在肩上，兩隻手槍繫在腰帶上，大刀掛腰旁，沒有鞘，盡我速力進行，跑到小山上去，在那裏，我曾經發見攏總東西的第一次出現。方到那裏，走了不下兩個鐘頭，（因為我不能走得快，身上裝置了這許多武器；）我看見在那個地方還有裝滿了野人的三隻木艇；向較遠的場所望了一望，我看見他們都在海中，正向大洋進駛。這個對於我是一可怖的景象，尤其是當我下山到岸上來的時候，我還能看見恐怖的遺跡，就是他們留下來的他們所做的慘懷殘忍之事的跡象；血，骨，人體上一部份的肉，被那些壞坯用快樂和遊戲的法子吞吃了。

我見此光景怒不可遏，現在我預備殺戮將來我看見到這裏來的野人們，無論他們是誰，或者無論他們有多少人。這事向我顯然表示着，他們來拜訪這座島，決不是常常的事，因為在他們重行來到這裏以前，已經過了十五個多月了，——就是說，在攏總那些時候，我也沒有看見他們，也沒有發見足跡，或者暗號；因為至於多雨的季候，他們一定是不出外的，至少出去得不很遠。然而這些時候我生活得不安逸；因為我有了他們將出我不意來襲擊我的常生的恐怖；由此我注意着：希望災禍來比較忍受災禍更為苦痛，尤其是假使無隙可以棄脫那個希望，或是那些恐怖之念。

I [1]*spent* my days now in great [2]*perplexity* and [3]*anxiety* of mind, expecting that I should one day or other fall into the hand of these [4]*merciless* creatures. If I did at any time [5]*venture* abroad, it was not without looking around me with the greatest care and [6]*caution* [7]*imaginable.* And now I found, to my great [8]*comfort*, how happy it was that I had [9]*provided* a [10]*tame* [11]*flock*, or herd, of goats, for I [12]*durst not upon any* [13]*account* fire my gun, [14]*especially* near that side of the island where they usually came, lest I should [15]*alarm* the savages; and if they had [16]*fled* from me now, I was [17]*sure* to have them come again, with perhaps two or three hundred [18]*canoes* with them, in a few days, and then I knew what to expect.

I slept unquietly, [19]*dreamed* always frightful dreams, and often [20]*started* [21]*out of my sleep* in the night. In the day, great [22]*troubles* [23]*overwhelmed* my mind; and in the night, I [24]*dreamed* often of killing the savages, and of the reasons why I [25]*might justify the doing of it.*

It was in the middle of May, on the sixteenth day, I think, as well as my poor wooden [26]*calendar* would [27]*reckon*,—for I marked all upon the post still;—I say, it was on the sixteenth of May that it [28]*blew* a very great storm of wind all day, with a [29]*great deal* of [30]*lightning* and [31]*thunder*, and a [32]*very foul night* it was after it. I knew not what was the particular [33]*occasion* of it; but as I was reading in the Bible, and taken up with very [34]*serious* thoughts about my present [35]*condition*, I was surprised with the [36]*noise* of a gun, as I thought, fired at sea. This was, to be sure, a surprise quite of a different nature from any I had met with before; for the [27]*notions* this put into my thoughts were quite of another kind. I [38]*started up* in the greatest haste [39]*imaginable*; and, in a trice, [40]*clapped* my [41]*ladder* to the middle place of

現在我心迷意亂而度時光，預料着終有一日我陷入於那些無人情的生物手中。在無論何時，假使我冒險出外，我總是十分謹愼地向四面望一望。現在我覺着，對我是很安逸的，這是怎樣的快樂我曾養了一羣馴的山羊，因爲我決不敢開放槍，尤其是在貼近島的那側，在那裏他們是常常溜止的；恐怕我將驚動那些野人們；假使他們現在從我這裏逃去，我是一定他們將要重來，或者駕了兩三百隻木艇來；在不多幾天的工夫，那末未來的結果我就不能預期了。

我不安靜地睡眠，常常夢見可怖的夢，在夜裏，常常驚醒。白天裏，大的困惱來煩擾我的心；夜間，我常常夢見殺死野人，以及爲什麼我可實行其事，而證明爲正當的理由。

這是五月中旬，在第十六日，我想，照我的可憐的水歷能夠敷算而言，——因爲我仍把一切事物記在柱上；——我說，這是在五月十六日，整天的起了很大的暴風，雷電交作，過後，夜間仍舊是狂風暴雨。我不知道什麼是這個的特別的機會；但是我在聖經內讀着，對於我現在的情況，起了勝重的思想，我陡被礮擊所驚訝，我想，礮是在海中發的。一定地，這是一種和我以前所遇着的性質不同的驚訝；因爲在我思想中的觀念是完全的另外的一類。我急速立起；頃刻之間，移置我的梯子到岩石的中間的地方去，在我身

1.去賣．2.迷亂．3.靈慮．4.無情的．5.冒險．9.留心．7.想得到．8.安逸．6.養．10.馴．11.羊羣．12.決不敢．13.無論如何．14.尤其是．15.紛擾．16.逃去．17.一定．18.木艇．19.預期．20.夢見．21.驚醒．22.困惱．23.煩擾．24.夢見．25.或可實行其事而表明之．26.歷．27.敷．28.括．29.很大．30.電．31.雷．32.狂風暴雨之夜．33.機會．34.勝重．35.情況．36.一定．37.觀念．38.起立．39.可猜想．40.急移置．41.梯．

the rock, and [1]*pulled* it after me; and [2]*mounting* it the second time, got to the top of the hill the very moment that a [3]*flash* of fire bid me [4]*listen* for a second gun, which, [5]*accordingly*, in about half a minute, I heard. By the sound I knew that it was from that part of the sea where I was driven down the current in my boat,

I [6]*immediately* [7]*considered* that this [8]*must be some ship in distress*, and that they had some [9]*comrade*, or [10]*some other ship in company*, and fired these for [11]*signals* of [12]*distress*, and to [13]*obtain* help. I had the [14]*presence* of mind, at that minute, to think that though I could not help them, it might be they might help me So I brought together all the dry wood I could get at hand, and, [15]*making a good*, [16]*handsome pile*, I [17]*set it on fire* upon the hill. The wood was dry, and [18]*blazed* freely; and, though [19]*the wind blew very hard*, yet [20]*it burned fairly out*. I was [21]*certain*, if there was any such thing as a ship, they must see it. And no [22]*doubt* they did: for as soon as ever my fire [23]*blazed up*, I heard another gun, and after that several others, all from [24]*the same quarter*. I [25]*plied my fire all night long till daybreak*.

When it was [26]*broad day*, and [27]*the air cleared up*, I saw something at a great distance at sea, [28]*full east of the island*, whether a sail or a [29]*hull* I could not [30]*distinguish*—no, not with my glass; the distance was so great, and the weather still something [31]*hazy* also.

I looked [32]*frequently* at it all that day, and soon [33]*perceived* that it was [34]*a ship at anchor*; and being [35]*eager* you may be sure, to be [36]*satisfied*, I took my gun in my hand, and ran towards the south side of the island, to the [37]*rocks* where I had [38]*formerly* been carried away by the current. Getting up there, the weather by this time being [39]*perfectly* clear, I

後拖曳牠；第二次我使梯上升，一經到了山頂，一陣火的閃光使我聽着或有第二礮來；於是大約在半分鐘工夫，我就聽見了。從聲音上面，我知道這是從海的那邊來的；在那裏，我在船中曾被急湍驅下去。

我立即想着必定是有船遇難，他們有些同伴，或者有他船同行，放了這些在困難中的號礮，希望得救助。我心靜神安，在那時，想想雖然我不能救助他們，他們或者能夠救助我。這樣我便把所有的在手頭能得到的乾木聚集一處，造成既高且大的一堆，在山上我焚燒起來；木是乾的，很自然地焚燒起來；雖然風勢很烈，然而木却焚燒將盡。我是一定，假使有船這樣的東西，他們必能看見火光。撫疑地他們是瞧見了；因為一經火燒起來，我聽見了又一礮聲，以後又有幾響，都是從同一方向而來。我把火徹夜燃燒達旦始止。

當白天來了，天氣晴朗，我看見有種東西在距離很遠的海中，在島的極東面，或者是一張帆，或是一隻船身，我不能分別出來——否，用望遠鏡也不能；距離是這樣的遠，天氣也仍舊是烟霧曚曨。

我整天注視這個不停，立刻看見那是一只碇泊的船；很切望的，你可以一定，要滿遖，我在手中拿了槍，跑向島的南側而去，到岩石上，在那裏，我從前曾被急湍帶去。上了岩石，這時天氣

could plainly see, to my great ¹*sorrow*, the wreck of a ship, cast away in the night upon those ²*concealed* rocks which I found when I was out in my boat; and which rocks, as they ³*checked the violence of the stream*, were the occasion of my recovering from the most ⁴*desperate*, ⁵*hopeless condition* that ever I had been in ⁶*all my life*. Thus, what is one man's safety is another man's ⁷*destruction*; for it seems these men, whoever they were, ⁸*being out of their knowledge*, and the rocks being wholly under water had been ⁹*driven* upon them in the night, the wind blowing hard at ¹⁰*east-northeast*. Had they seen the island, as I must ¹¹*necessarily* ¹²*suppose* they did not, they must, as I thought, have endeavored to have saved themselves on shore by the help of their boat.

It was now calm, and I had a great mind to ¹³*venture* out in my boat to this wreck, not ¹⁴*doubting* but I might find something on board that might be useful to me. But that did not ¹⁵*altogether* ¹⁶*press* me so much as the ¹⁷*possibility* that there might be yet some living ¹⁸*creature* on board, whose life I might not only save, but might, by saving that life, comfort my own ¹⁹*to the last degree*. ²⁰*This thought so clung to my heart* that I could not be quiet night or day, but I must ²¹*venture* out in my boat on board this wreck; and ²²*committing* the rest to ²³*God's providence*, I thought ²⁴*the impression* was so strong upon my mind that it could not be ²⁵*resisted*,—that it must come from some ²⁶*invisible* direction, and that I should be ²⁷*wanting to myself* if I did not go.

Under the power of this impression, I ²⁸*hastened back* to my castle, ²⁹*prepared* everything for my voyage, took a quantity of bread, a great pot of fresh water, a ³⁰ *compass* to steer by, a bottle of rum (for I had still a great deal of that

十分晴朗，我能明白地看見，對我是很憂悶的，一隻船的破損，在夜間，在那些隱藏不能見的岩石上面撞碎了，這些岩石就是當我乘船出外之時找着的；這些岩石，牠們阻止川的急流，是我從終身所處的最絕望的境况當中回復過來的一個機遇。一個人的安完全就是另外一個人的損害；因爲瞧起來這些人，無論他們是誰，是茫然不知，岩石是深藏水低，在夜間衝擊他們，風兒東偏東北吹得很厲害。假使他們瞧見了島，我一定必須要猜想着他們未曾看見了牠，他們一定，我想起來是這樣，竭力救助自己到岸上去，用他們的船的助力。

　　現在天氣安靜，我極欲冒險出外，乘船到那破損的船的場所去，無疑地，在船上我或者可以找着些對我有用的東西。但是那個意念並不十分地迫着我去這樣做，我想這是能夠的，船上或者有些活的生物；我不但可以救了他們的命，而且還可以，救了他們的命，把我自己的生命安慰到了極點。此意縈縴在我的心中，整日整夜，我不能安處，但是我一定要冒險乘出船外，到那隻破損船的裏面去；其餘各事悉委諸於天命，我想此意深印於我心中，不能抵抗，——牠必是從不可見的指示中來的，我自己必有所缺乏，若是我不去的話。

　　在這個印象的權力之下，我急速回到堡中，預備着各樣旅行所需要的物件，拿了若干分量的麵包，一大罐新鮮的水，一隻用以駕駛的羅盤，一瓶醋酒（因爲我還有許多的存着），以及一籃葡萄乾；

left), and a basket of ¹*raisins* ; and thus ²*loading* myself with everything ³*necessary*, I went down to my boat, got the water out of her, ⁴*got her afloat* loaded all my ⁵*cargo* in her, and then went home again for more. My second cargo was a great ⁶*bag* of rice, the ⁷*umbrella* to set up over my head for a ⁸*shade*, another large pot of ⁹*fresh water*, and about two dozen of small loaves, or barley cakes, more then before, with a bottle of goat's milk, and a ¹⁰*cheese*.

All this with great labor and ¹¹*sweat* I carried to my boat; and praying to God to direct my voyage, I ¹²*put out*, and ¹³*rowing* or ¹⁴*paddling* the canoe along the shore, came at last to the ¹⁵*utmost point* of the island on the northeast side. And now I was to ¹⁶*launch out into the ocean*, and either to ¹⁷*venture* or not to venture. I looked on the ¹⁸*rapid* currents which ran ¹⁹*constantly* on both sides of the island at a distance, and which were very terrible to me, from the ²⁰*remembrance* of the ²¹*hazard* I had been in before, and my heart began to fail me. ²²*I foresaw* that if I was driven into either of those currents, I should be carried a great way out to sea, and ²³*perhaps out of my reach*, ²⁴*or sight of the island again*; and that then, as my boat was but small, if any little gale of wind should rise, I ²⁵*should be inevitably lost*.

I first made a little out to sea, full north, till I began to feel the ²⁶*benefit* of the current, which ²⁷*set eastward*, and which carried me ²⁸*at a great rate*, and yet did not so hurry me as the current on the south side had done before, so as to take from me all ²⁹*government* of the boat. Having a strong ³⁰*steerage* with my ³¹*paddle*, I went at a great rate directly for the ³²*wreck*, and in less than two hours I came up to it. It was a ³³*dismal*, sight to look at. The ship, which, by its building, was Spanish, ³⁴*stuck fast*, ³⁵*jammed* in between two

用了必需的東西來供給着自己，我走下船去，把水弄出去，將船浮起，在船內裝了我所有的船貨，後來重行又轉回家中。我的第二次的船貨是一大袋米，傘撑在頭上當作遮陰，另外一大罐新鮮的水，大約兩打小麵包塊，或是大麥餅，比從前較多，一瓶山羊乳，以及乳酪。

費盡了氣力我把這些東西帶上船去；懇求上帝指引我的航程，我於是出發，搖或划着木艇，沿岸而駛，最後到了島的盡頭處，在東北方面。現在我預備駛入洋中，或者要冒險，或者可以不冒險。我注視着急流，牠在島的兩側，經若干距離，不停地流着；牠對我是狠可怖的，憶及了上次所經的危險，我的勇氣漸消滅了。我預測假使我被驅到任何急流的一面，我將彼老遠地帶出去到海中，恐怕不能再抵，或是再見那座島了；既然我的船是小的倘使括了一陣大風，我難免沒頂之災。

起初我略向海中駛行，向正北，直至我覺着急湍的盆處，牠向東流，牠把我帶走得狠快，然而並不驅迫我像南側的急流以前所做的一般，以致於令我不能駕駛。極力鼓槳前駛，我狠快地直向那破船之處而去，不到兩個鐘頭，我到了船的那裏。景況瞧起來實在是悲慘得很。船，照構造的樣子而論，是西班牙的，擱淺了，緊擠於兩塊岩石之中。

1.葡萄乾. 2.備給. 3.必需. 4.將船浮起. 5.船貨. 6.袋. 7.傘. 8.遮陰. 9.新鮮水. 10.乳酪. 11.汗. 12.出發. 13.搖. 14.划. 15.盡頭處. 16.駛入洋中. [1] 7.冒險. 18.快. 19.常常. 20.憶及. 21.危險. 22.預料. 23.恐不能再逢. 24.或再見此島. 25.難免溺死. 26.盆處. 27.向東流. 28.甚快. 29.駕駛之力. 30.駕駛. 31.槳. 32.破船. 33.悲慘. 34.擱淺. 35.緊擠於兩石之中

¹*rocks*. **When** I came close to her, a dog appeared upon her, who, seeing me coming, ²*yelped* and cried, and, as soon as I called him, ³*jumped into* the sea to come to me. I took him into the boat, but found him almost dead with hunger and ⁴*thirst*. I gave him a cake of my bread, and he ⁵*devoured* it like a ⁶*ravenous wolf* that had been ⁷*starving* a ⁸*fortnight* in the snow. I then gave the poor creature some fresh water, with which, if I would have let him, he would have ⁹*burst* himself. After this I went on board; but ¹⁰*the first sight I met with* was two men ¹¹*drowned* in the ¹²*cookroom*, or ¹³*forecastle* of the ship, with their arms fast about one another. I ¹⁴*concluded*, as is indeed ¹⁵*probable*, that when the ship ¹⁶*struck*, it being in a storm, the sea broke so high and so ¹⁷*continually* over her that the men were not able to bear it, and were ¹⁸*strangled* with the ¹⁹*constant* ²⁰*rushing* in of the water, as much as if they had been under water.

Besides the dog, there was nothing left in the ship that had life; nor any goods, that I could see, but what were ²¹*spoiled* by the water. I saw several ²²*chests*, which I believe, belonged to some of the seamen; and I got two of them into the boat, without ²³*examining* what was in them.

I found, besides these ²⁴*chests*, a little cask full of liquor, of about twenty ²⁵*gallons*, which I got into my boat with much ²⁶*difficulty*. I took a ²⁷*fire shoved* and ²⁸*tongs*, which I wanted ²⁹*extremely*; as also two little ³⁰*brass* ³¹*kettles*, a copper pot to make ³²*chocolate*, and a ³³*gridiron*; and with this cargo, and the dog, I came away, the tide beginning to ³⁴*make home* again. The same evening, about an hour within night, I reached the island again, ³⁵*weary* and ³⁶*fatigued to*

當我走進船身之時，在船上出現一匹狗；牠，瞧見我走來，吠將起來；一經我叫喚牠，牠就跳入水中，浮至我處。我把牠放入船中，但是見牠差不多因饑渴而將死了。我給牠我的麵包的一塊餅。牠吞噬了，好像在雪中餓了兩星期的餓狼一般。後來我給這個可憐的生物若干新鮮水，用了這水，假使我任牠喝，牠必定要把自己來裂開了。這事完畢，我去到那只船中；我所見的第一個景況就是兩個人溺死在船中廚室裏面，或是船的前部，彼此用手臂緊抱着。我決定，實在這是可能的，當這隻船撞擊的時候，牠是在暴風雨的裏面，海浪奔騰甚高，不停地冒上船身，裏面的人不能再支持了，被時常衝入船中的水窒塞死了，好像他們是置身水底一般。

在狗以外，沒有旁的有生命的東西留在船上了；也沒有貨物，我所能見的都被海水損壞了。我看見幾只箱子，我相信，牠們是屬於幾個水手的；我拿了兩只到我的小船上去，沒有考察裏面裝的是什麼東西。

我尋着，在這些箱子之外，一隻裝滿了流質的小桶，大約有二十加侖，很費力的我把牠拿到小船上去。我拿了一把火爐鏈和火鉗，這些是我急需的東西；也拿了兩隻小黃銅鍋，做諸古律的銅罐一只和一柄鐵鈀；帶了這些貨物和狗，我走了，潮水方退。當天晚上，大約一點鐘在夜間，我重抵原島

1.岩石。2.吠。3.跳入。4.渴。5.吞噬。6.餓狼。7.餓。8.兩星期。9.裂開。10.我所首先見者。11.溺。12.船中廚室。13.前部。14.決定。15.或能。16.撞擊。17.不停。18.局死。19.不停。20.衝突。21.損壞。22.箱。23.考察。24.箱。25.加侖。26.困難。27.火爐鏈。28.火鉗。29.盂。30.黃銅。31.鍋。32.諸古律。33.鐵鈀。34.退同去。35.濱。36.爐

the last ¹*degree*. I reposed that night in the boat; and in the morning I ²*resolved* to harbor what I had got in my new cave, and not to carry it home to my ³*castle*. When I came to open the chests, I found several things of great use to me. For example, I found in one a fine case of bottles, of and ⁴*extraordinary* kind, and filled with ⁵*cordial* waters, fine and very good. The ⁶*bottles* held about three ⁷*pints* each, and were ⁸*tipped* with silver, I found two pots of very good ⁹*succades*, or ¹⁰*sweetmeats,* so fastened also on the top that the ¹¹*salt* water had not hurt them; and two more of the same, which the water had ¹²*spoiled*. I found some very good ¹³*shirts*, which were very ¹⁴*welcome* to me; and about a ¹⁵*dozen* and a half of white ¹⁶*linen* ¹⁷*hankerchiefs* and colored ¹⁸*neckcloths*. The former were also very welcome, being exceedingly ¹⁹*refreshing* to ²⁰*wipe* my face in a hot day. Besides this, when I came to the ²¹*till* in the chest, I found there three great bags of pieces of ²²*eight*, which held about elevn hundred pieces in all; and in one of them, ²³*wrapped* up in a paper, six ²⁴*doubloons* of gold, and some small ²⁵*bars* ²⁶*or widges of gold*; I ²⁷*suppose* they might all ²⁸*weigh* near a pound.

²⁹*Upon the whole,* I got very little by this ³⁰*voyage* that was of any use to me; for, as to the money, I ³¹*had no manner* of ³²*occasion* for it; it was to me as the ³³*dirt under* my feet, and I would have given it all for three or four pair of English shose and ³⁴*stockings* ⁴ which were things I greatly ³⁵*wanted,* but had had none on my feet for many years.

Having now brought all my things on shore, and se- ³⁶*cured* them, I went back to my ³⁷*boat*, and rowed ³⁸*or paddled* her along the shore to her old ³⁹*harbor*, where I ⁴⁰*laid her up,* and ⁴¹*made the best of my way to* my old ⁴²*habitation*, where I

疲憊達於極點。那天晚上我在船中休息；在早晨，我決定把我所得着的東西藏在我的新山穴內，不把牠們帶同堡中去。當我開箱子的時候；我找着幾椿對於我很有用的東西。例如，在一只箱子裏面，我找着一只精美的裝滿了瓶子的盒子，樣子特別，瓶中貯有補血藥水，美妙異常。每瓶容量約三品脫，以銀鑲頂。我找着兩罐狠好的蜜餞；糖果，在頂上繫得這樣地緊，海水未嘗損壞他們；同樣的還有兩只，海水卻把他們弄壞了。我找着幾件很好的襯衫；這對於我是極受歡迎的；大約一打有半的。洋布手巾和着色的頭巾。洋布手巾也是很受歡迎的，因爲在一個炎的日子，用牠揩面，是非常爽快的。其外，當我找到箱子內的銀匣，我尋着那裏有三只大袋裝滿了值八數的銀塊，攏總差不多裝有一千一百銀塊；其中一袋裏面，包在一張紙的當中，有六個金都不龍以及若干小的金條或金塊；我想牠們一齊橫衡起來約有一磅的重量。

　　總之；這次旅行我所得有限對我有益的東西；因爲；至於銀錢，我無有用牠的機會；牠對於我宛如足下的泥士一般我願把所有的銀錢來換取三四雙英國製造的鞋襪；這些是我亟需的東西，但是許多年來，脚空無所有！現在把所有物件拿上岸去，保留牠們，我囘到小船上去，搖牠或划牠，沿着岸而行，往牠的舊泊所而去，在那那裏，我卸去船載而置船入塢，由捷徑囘至舊寓所，

found everything safe and ¹*quiet*. I began now to ²*repse* myself, ³*live after my old fashion*, and ⁴*take care* of my ⁵*family affairs*. For a while I lived easy enough, only that I was more ⁶*vigilant* than I ⁷*used to be*, looked out ⁸*oftener*, and did not go ⁹*abroad* so much. If at any time I did stir with any ¹⁰*freedom*, it was always to the east part of the island, where I was pretty well ¹¹*satisfied* the ¹²*savages* never came, and where I could go without so many ¹³*precautions* and such a load of arms and ¹⁴*ammunition* as I always carried with me if I went the other way. I lived in this ¹⁵*condition* near two years more; but my ¹⁶*unlucky* head, that was always to let me know it was born to make my body ¹⁷*miserable*, was all these two years filled with ¹⁸*projects* and ¹⁹*designs*, how, if it were possible, I might get away from this island.

CHAPTER XXXIII

I⊤ was one of the nights in the rainy season in March, the four-and-twentieth year of my first setting foot in this ²⁰*island of solitude*, I was lying in my bed or ²¹*hammock*, awake, and very well in health; I had no pain, no dis-²²*temper*, no ²³*uneasiness* of body nor any uneasiness of mind more than ²⁴*ordinary*, but ²⁵*could by no means* close my eyes,—that is, so as to sleep,—no, ²⁶*not a wink*. I ran over the whole ²⁷*history* of my life ²⁸*in miniature*, or ²⁹*by abridgment*, as I may call it, to my coming to this island, and also of that part of my life since I came to this island.

In my ³⁰*reflections* upon the state of my case since I came on shore on this island, I was ³¹*comparing* the happy ³²*posture* of my affairs in the first years of my habitation here, with the life of ³³*anxiety*, fear, and care, which I had

在那裏，我見各種事物皆安靜如常。我現在開始休息我自己，照常度日，料理家務，我生活着安逸了些時，不過我較平日為謹慎，常常地注意着，不很出外。假使在無論何時，我可自由行動，這就是常常到島的東旁一部份上去，在那裏，我是很滿足的野人們永遠不來，在那裏我能夠去，無需想出許多的預防之策和像我平常所帶的甚多的兵器和軍實，假使我向別道而去的話。我在這種景況之中生活了差不多兩載有餘；但是我不幸的頭腦，她常常使我明白着她是為使我身體受痛苦而生的，她在這兩年之中充滿了計策和謀劃，怎樣，若果可能，我可以離島而去。

第 三 十 三 章

這就是在多爾的季候三月中的某晚上，我第一次置足於此絕島的第二十四週年。我躺在我的床或吊床上，醒着身體甚好；我毫無痛苦，為病，體無不適之處，較之平常，心中也無不安之處，但是無論如何閉不起眼睛來，——就是說，去睡覺，—— 否，連一刻都不能睡。我潦草地翻開我生活的全個的記事來看看，僅就再縮小和大略之處而觀之，我可以這樣地記述我來到這島的事而且還有自從我來到這島生活的一部份。

在我回想的境況的情形，自從我在島上登岸以來，我拿我住在這裏頭幾年事物的快樂的情狀和我自從發見沙中足跡以後所過的憂慮的，恐怖的，留心的生活兩相比較。

lived in ever since I had seen the ¹*print* of a foot in the sand. Not that I did not belive the ²*savages* had frequented the island even all the while, and might have been several hundreds of them at times on shore there; but I had never known it, and was ³*incapable* of any ⁴*apprehensions* about it. I had walked about in the greatest ⁵*security* and with all ⁶*possible* ⁷*tranquillity*, even when perhaps nothing but the ⁸*brow of a hill*, a great tree, or the ⁹*casual* ¹⁰*apprach* of night, had been between me and the ¹¹*worst* kind of ¹²*destructions*; namely, that of falling into the hands of cannibals and ¹³*savages*, who would have ¹⁴*seized on* me with the ¹⁵*same view* as I would on a goat or ¹⁶*turtle*; and would have thought it no more crime to kill and devour me, than I did of a ¹⁷*pigeon* or a ¹⁸*curlew*. I would unjustly ¹⁹*slander* myself if I should say I was not ²⁰*sincerely* thankful to my great ²¹*Preserver*, to whose singular ²²*protection* I ²³*acknowledged*, with great ²⁴*hnmility*, that all these unknown ²⁵*deliverances* were ²⁶*due*, and without which I must ²⁷*inevitably* have fallen into their ²⁸*merciless* hands.

When these thoughts were over, my head was for some time taken up in considering what part of the world these ²⁹*wretches* lived in; how far off the ³⁰*coast* was from whence they came; what they ³¹*ventured* over so far from home for; what kind of boats they had; and why I might not ³²*order* myself and my ³³*business* so that I might be as able to go over thither as they were to come to me. Perhaps I might ³⁴*fail in with* some Christian ship that might take me in; and if the ³⁵*worst* came to the ³⁶*worst*, I could but die, which would put an end to all these ³⁷*miseries* at once.

When this had ³⁸*agitated* my thoughts for two hours or more, with such ³⁹*violence* that it ⁴⁰*set my very blood into a*

雖不是我不相信野人們時時來往此島，有時在那邊海岸上或者來有數百人；但是我永不知此事，所以毫無恐怖之心。我用了極安全和平靜的態度來散步，就是當(我)或者不過(我走在)山崖，一棵大樹，或者夜之將近，在我和最劣的一種破壞的中間；就是，或將陷入於吃人者和野人們的手中了，他們將要在同一光景裏面來捕捉我好像我去捕捉山羊和鼈一般；他們想想這是不犯罪的來殺和吞噬我，宛如我殺和吞噬鴿和鳶鳥一樣。我或者要不正直的來毀謗我自己；假使我要說我是不誠謹地來感謝我的保佑人，我感謝他的特別的保佑，用了極謙下的態度，我所得着的莫名其故的救助都是有賴於他，沒有那些救助，我是必不可免地早已陷入於野人們無情的手中了。

　　當這些思潮想過了以後，經過若干時，我的腦中極力注意着究竟這些壞坯住在世界上的那一個部份之中；海濱離開他們所來的地方究竟有若干遠近；他們冒險外出，去家甚遠，究竟為着何來；他們所有的船是何種形式；為什麼我不可以整理我自身和料理我的事務，這樣我便能到他們那邊去如同他們到我這邊來一般。或者我將遇着些基督教的船，牠可以載我往內，假使遭時不幸，我惟一死而已，那末我的一切苦難立刻便被死神消滅淨盡了。當這個激起了我的思潮兩個多鐘頭之時，牠來得這樣

¹*ferment*, and my ²*pulse beat* as if I had been in a ³*fever*, merely with the ⁴*extraordinary* ⁵*fervor of my mind* about it, nature—as if I had been ⁶*fatigued* and ⁷*exhausted* with the very thoughts of it—⁸*threw* me into a ⁹*sound sleep*. One would have thought I should have ¹⁰*dreamed* of it, but I did not, nor of ¹¹*anything relating to it*. But I dreamed that as I was going out in the morning as ¹²*usual*, from my ¹³*castle*, I saw upon the ¹⁴*shore* two ¹⁵*canoes* and eleven ¹⁶*savagess* coming to land, and that they brought with them another savage, whom they were going to kill in order to eat him ; when, on a sudden, the savage that they were going to kill ¹⁷*jumped* away, and ¹⁸*ran for his life*. And I thought, in my sleep, that he came running into my little thick grove before my fortification, to hide himself ; and that I, seeing him alone, and not ¹⁹*perceiving* that the others ²⁰*sought* him that way, showed myself to him and smiling upon him, ²¹*encouraged* him.　He ²²*kneeled* down to me. seeming to pray me to ²³*assist* him ; upon which I showed him my ²⁴*ladder*, made him go up, and carried him into my cave, and he became my servant. As soon as I had got this man, I said to myself. "Now I may certainly ²⁵*venture* to the ²⁶*mainland*, for this fellow will ²⁷*serve* me as pilot and will tell me what to do, and whither to go for ²⁸*provisions*, and whither not to go for fear of being ²⁹*devoured* ; what places to venture into, and what ³⁰*to shun*." I awoke with this thought ; and was under such inexpressible ³¹*impressions* of joy at the ³²*prospect* of my escape in my dream, that the ³³*disappointments* which I felt ³⁴*upon coming to myself*, and finding that it was no more than a dream, were equally ³⁵*extravagant* the other way, and threw me into a very great ³⁶*dejection of spirits*.

的強烈，以致把我的熱血激動起來了，我的脈跳起來好似我發寒熱一般，不過這種光景是由於我心中非常的熱誠所致，天然，——我一想到牠便困乏和疲倦，——把我驅到睡鄉中去了。人們或將妄想，我將夢想着牠，但是我卻未曾如此，與之有關繫者我亦未曾夢及。但是我夢見，我和平常一樣，早上從堡中出門；在岸上我看見兩隻木艇和十一個野人，到陸地上來；他們帶來了另外的一個野人，他們就要把他殺而食之；徒然之間，這個將要被他們所殺的野人跳將起來，脫身而逃。我想，在我睡夢之中，他是向我堡壘前面小而厚的森林中跑來，藏着他的身子；我看見他獨自一人，未曾看見那些野人從這條路來追逐他，跑到他面前去，對他笑着，撫慰他。他向我下跪，好像是求我幫助他一般；因此有指示着他我的梯子，叫他爬上去，把他帶入穴中，他於是做了我的生人。我一經得了這個人，我自己對自己說道，"現在我一定可以冒險到大地上去，因爲這個人可以充我的領導者，他將要告訴我應當做什麼事，到什麼地方去尋食物，什麼地方不應當去，恐怕是被吞噬了；那處地方可以冒險而入，那處地方應當趨避。"因這個思想我醒了；我是不勝愉快想起我夢中逃走的希冀，醒後我覺着失望，心想這不過是一場大夢，於從一方面觀之，亦同一的荒謬，失望之餘，心神遂極其的愁悶了。

1.沸．2.脈跳．3.寒熱．4.非常的．5.熱誠．6.困乏．7.疲倦．8.攫入．9.熱睡．1.夢．11.與之有關係者．12.如常．13.堡．14.海岸．15.木艇．16.野人．17.跳．18.脫身逃命．19.見．20.尋．21.安慰．22.跪．23.幫助．24.梯．25.冒險．26.大地．27.充任．28.食物．29.吞噬．30.趨避．31.印象．32.期望．33.失望．34.醒後．35.荒謬．36.心神愁悶

Upon this, however, I made this [1]*conclusion* : that my only way to go about to [2]*attempt* an escape was to [3]*endeavor* to get a savage into my [4]*possession*. If possible, it should be one of their [5]*prisoners*, whom they had [6]*condemned* to be eaten, and should bring hither to kill.

With these resolutions in my thoughts, I set myself upon the [7]*scout* as often as [8]*possible*, and indeed so often that I was [9]*heartily* [10]*tired* of it. I went out to the west end, and to the [11]*southwest* [12]*corner* of the island almost every day, to look for canoes, but none appeared. The longer they seemed to be [13]*delayed*, the more eager I was for them. In a word, I was not at first so [14]*careful* to shun the [15]*sight* of these savages, and [16]*avoid* being seen by them, as I was now [17]*eager to be upon them*. Besides, I [18]*fancied* myself able to [19]*manage* one, nay, two or three savages, if I had them, so as to make them [20]*entirely* slaves to me, to do whatever I should [21]*direct* them, and to [22]*prevent* their being able at any time to do me any [23]*hurt*. It was a great while that I pleased myself with this [24]*affair* ; but [25]*nothing still presented itself*. All my fancies and schemes [26]*came to nothing*, for no savages came near me for a great while.

About a year and a half after I had [27]*entertained* these [28]*notions*, I was [29]*surprised* one morning early by seeing no less than five canoes all on shore together on my side the island, and the people who [30]*belonged* to them all landed and [31]*out of my sight*. The [32]*number* of them [33]*broke all my measures* ; for seeing so many, and knowing that they always came four or six, or sometimes more, in a boat, I could not tell what to think of it, or how [34]*to take my measures* to [35]*attack* twenty or thirty men [36]*single-handed*. So I lay still in my [37]*castle*, [38]*perplexed* and [39]*discomforted*.

因此，我有了這個斷定：我企圖着逃走的惟一方法就是要竭力地去得着一個野人在我掌握之中。假使可能，他必須是那些野人們的俘虜，他們定他被吞噬之罪，把他帶到這裏來殺死他。

我的思想中有了這些決定，我就隨時偵探着，實在地狠常常這樣，以致於不勝其厭倦。我去到西方末端，每日差不多總要往島的西南角上去，去看木艇，但是一隻都不發現。牠們愈是延捱着不來，我愈是渴望着牠們。總而言之，起初我是這樣的留心去逃避這些野人的目光，和趨避着不爲他們所見，現在我却亟欲和他們相遇。其外，我自已幻想着我能處置一人，豈止如此，兩個或三個野人，假使我有了他們的話，那末便使他們完全地做我的奴隸，做我指示着他們所做的事，禁止他們在無論何時能加我以傷害。很長久我因此事而自娛着；但是仍一無所見。所有我的幻想和方法歸於無效，因爲許久沒有野人們來靠近我。

在我懷了這些觀念一年有半之後，一天很早的早晨我是驚訝起來瞧見了不下五只木艇，一齊在島的我這邊的海岸上，艇的人們都上了岸，不得而見之。他們的數目把我的計劃破壞了；因爲我看見許多人，平常知道他們是四人或六人相偕而來，有時則較多，在一只小船中，我不能知道怎樣地去想，以及怎樣去設法獨自一人攻打二十或三十人。這樣我仍究縮在堡中，困惱而不安。

However, I put myself into the same ¹*position* for an attack that I had formerly ²*provided*, and was just ³*ready for action*, if anything had ⁴*presented*.

Having ⁵*waited* ⁶*a good while*, ⁷*listening* to hear if they made any noise, at length, being very ⁸*impatient*, I set my guns at the foot of my ladder, and ⁹*clambered up* to the top of the hill, by my two ¹⁰*stages*, as usual; standing so, however, that my head did not ¹¹*appear* above the hill, so that they could not ¹²*perceive* me ¹³*by any means*. Here I observed by the help of my ¹⁴*perspective* glass, that they were no less than thirty in number; that they had a fire ¹⁵*kindled*, and that they had meat ¹⁶*drssed*. How they had ¹⁷*cooked* it, I knew not, or what it was; but they were all ¹⁸*dancing* in I know not how many ¹⁹*barbarous* ²⁰*gestures* and figures, their own way, round the fire.

While I was thus looking on them, I ²¹*perceived*, by my ²²*perspective* glass, two ²³*miserable* wretches ²⁴*dragged* from the boats, where, it seems, they were laid by, and were now ²⁵*brought out* for the ²⁶*slaughter*. I perceived one of them ²⁷*immediately* fall, being ²⁸*knocked down*, I ²⁹*suppose*, with a ³⁰*club*, or wooden ³¹*swords*, for that was their way; and two or three others were at work immediately, cutting him open for their ³²*cookery*, while the other ³³*victim* was left standing by himself, till they should be ready for him. In that ³⁴*very moment*, this poor wretch, seeing himself ³⁵*at liberty*, and ³⁶*unbound*, Nature ³⁷*inspired* him with hopes of life, and he ³⁸*started away* from them, and ran with ³⁹*incredible swiftness* along the ⁴⁰*sands*, directly toward me; I mean, toward that part of the ⁴¹*coast* where my ⁴²*habitation* was. I was ⁴³*dreadfully* ⁴⁴*frightened*, I must ⁴⁵*acknowledge*, when I perceived him run my way; and ⁴⁶*especially* when, as I thought,

然而，我置身在同一的情形中，預備我以前所想的攻擊；假使任何事物發現，我就馬上預備交戰。

等候了許久，留心去聽他們是否發出些聲音來，後來，我是極其不耐，我放槍在梯足下，用我的兩只架子，和平常一樣，爬登山頂；這樣地立着，我的頭不曾在山上發見，以致於無論如何他們決計看不見我。在這裏，我注意着，藉了我的望遠鏡之助，他們不下於三十人；他們生了火，他們煑肉。他們怎樣地烹調牠，我不知道，或者牠是什麼東西；但是他們一齊跳着舞，我不知道是用了多少的野蠻的手勢和樣子，他們惟一的方法，圍着了火。

當我注意他們之時，我看見，藉了望遠鏡之助，兩個不幸的人被他們從船中拖曳出來，在船裏，好像是，他們是被收藏着，現在被牽出待人屠殺。我看見他們之中一人立卽倒地，我猜想着，是被木棍或是木刀打倒了，這就是野人們的方法；別的兩三個野人卽行從事，把他剖將開來，供他們烹調而爲食品之用，那另外一個被害者獨自地立在那裏，直至他們預備好了再動他的手。就在這個時候，這個可憐的人，看見自己自由而無束縛，自然之神啓發他有生命的希望，他從他們之中衝走了，用了極神速的快步而逃，沿着沙土而行直向我處而來；我意，就是向在我的住所海濱那邊而行。我驚愕失措，我必須承認，當我看見他向我處跑來之時；尤其是，我想起是這樣，當我見他被野人全體所追逐着之時。

I saw him ¹*pursued* by the whole body. I ²*expected* that part of my dream was ³*coming to pass*, and that he would certainly ⁴*take shelter* in my ⁵*grove* ; but I could not ⁶*depend*, by any means, upon my dream, that the other savages would not pursue him thither, and find him there. However, I ⁷*kept my station*, and my ⁸*spirits* began to ⁹*recover* when I found that there were not above three men that followed him. Still more was I ¹⁰*encouraged*, when I found that he ¹¹*outstripped* them ¹²*exceedingly* in running , and ¹³*gained* ground of them ; so that if he could but bold out for half an hour, I saw ¹⁴*easily* he would ¹⁵*fairly* get away from them all.

There was between them and my castle, the ¹⁶*creek*, which I ¹⁷*mentioned* often in the first part of my story, where I landed my ¹⁸*cargoes* out of the ship. This I saw ¹⁹*plainly* he must ²⁰*necessarily* ²¹*swim over*, or the poor wretch would be taken there. But when the savage escaping came thither, he made nothing of it, though the tide was then up , but ²²*plunging in* swam through in about thirty ²³*strokes*, or ²⁴*thereabouts*, landed, and ran with exceeding ²⁵*strength* and ²⁶*swiftness*. When the three persons came to the creek, I found that two of them could swim , but the third could not . and that , standing on the other side . he looked at the others , but went no ²⁷*farther*, and soon ofter went softly back again ; which , as it happened, was very well for him in the end. I ²⁸*observed* that the two who ²⁹*swam* were yet more than ³⁰*twice as long* swimming over the creek as the fellow was that ³¹*fled from* them. It came very warmly upon my thoughts; and indeed ³²*irresistibly* , that now was the time to get me a servant , and perhaps a ³³*companion* or ³⁴*assistant* ; and that I was ³⁵*plainly* called by ³⁶*Providence to* save this poor creature's life.

我希望我的夢的第二個部份應驗、他一定要逃到我的森林中來躲避；但是無論如何，我不能倚賴着我的夢，別的野人們不把他追到那裏去，在那裏找着他。然而，我保守我的地位，我的精神復振了，當我看見祇有不上三人跟着他之時。我自已仍究竟鼓勵着；當我看見他走得比他們更快，佔他們的上風；假令他再能支持半小時之久，我很明白地知道他可以安然逃出他們之手。

在他們和我的我堅壘的中間，有一小溪；在我故事的第一部份我常常述及牠；在那裏，我從船中把船貨運上了岸。我明白地知道他必須游泳過這座小溪，如其不然，這個可憐的東西將要在那裏被捉住了。但是當逃走的野人來到那裏之時，他不知所以，雖然那時潮水是高漲；但是，他投入水中游泳經過了大約三十划速力的左右，上了岸，用了有力量和輕捷的步伐而跑。當那三個人來到小溪之時，我看見他們之中有二人能泅水，第三人不能，立在對岸，瞧着別人；但是不再走遠，旋卽慢步而歸，這事實在是於他有益無損。我意着泅水的二人；他們在小溪中泅水，游泳得比從他們手中逃走的那個人相差有一倍之久。我的思潮陡然熱烈起來，實在是不能能抵抗的；現在是我要得着用人的時候了，或者是一個伴侶或助手；我是很明白地被上天叫着去救這個可憐生物的命。

I immediately ran down the [1]*ladders* with all possible [2]*expedition*, [3]*fetched* my two guns, for they were both at the foot of the ladders, as I observed before, and getting up again with the same [4]*haste* to the top of the hill, I [5]*crossed toward* the sea. Having a very [6]*short cut*, and all [7]*downhill*, I placed myself in the way between the [8]*pursuers* and the pursued, [9]*hollowing* [10]*aloud* to him that [11]*fled*, who, looking back, was at first perhaps as much [12]*frightened* at me as at them. But I [13]*beckoned* with my hand to him to come back; and, in the mean time, I slowly advanced towards the two that followed. Then [14]*rushing* at once upon the [15]*oremost*, I [16]*knocked* him down with the stock of my piece. I was [17]*loath* to fire, because I would not have the rest hear; though, at that [18]*distance*, it would not have been easily heard, and being out of sight of the [19]*smoke*, too, they would not have known what to make of it, Having knocked this fellow down, the other who pursued with him stopped, as if he had been frightened, and I [20]*advanced* quickly towards him; but as I came nearer, I perceived presently he had a [21]*bow* and [22]*arrow*, and was fitting it to [23]*shoot* at me. So I was then [24]*obliged* to shoot at him first, which I did, and killed him at the first shot. The poor savage who fled, but had [25]*stopped*, though he saw both his [26]*enemies* fallen and killed, as he thought, yet was so frightened with the fire and noise of my piece that he stood [27]*stock-still*, and neither come forward, nor went backward, though he seemed [28]*rather inclined* still to fly than to come on. I hollowed again to him, and made signs to come forward, which he easily [29]*understood*, and came a little way; then stopped again, and then a little farther, and stopped again. I could then perceive that he stood [30]*trembling*, as if he had been taken

我立卽盡我的速力把梯子放下來,拿了兩只槍,因爲牠們全在梯的足下,我曾經逃過了,爬起來用了同樣的急速跑到山頂上去;我橫過了山向海而去。有了一個捷徑,是斜下的,我置身於追者和被迫者之間,向逃走的人大聲疾呼,他,朝後望了一望,起初像是怕我好像怕他們一樣。但是我用手向他作手勢,叫他囘來;卽於此時,我慢慢地向前去:向跟隨的那兩個人面前行去。後來立卽衝到最前的一人面前,用槍柄把他打倒。我不欲開槍,因爲我不願其他野人們聽見;雖然,距離尙遠。槍聲或不能聽見得狠容易,又不得見烟,他們不知道這是作什麼事。把這人打倒之後,同他一淘追趕的那一個停了步,宛如吃驚地一般,我狠快地跑到他的面前;但是當我走得較近之時,我立卽看見他有一弓和一箭,預備向我發射。這樣我是不得不先射擊他,我做了這事,第一彈就把他打死了。逃走的那個可憐的野人,現在却停了步,雖給他瞧見他的兩個敵人,一仆地,一被殺,如他所想一般,然而他是這樣地恐怕着我的槍的火光和聲音,他於是立定了絲毫不動,也不向前來,也不向後退,雖然他瞧起來還是寧願逃走而不願來前。我重行向他高呼,作手勢叫他來前,他狠容易地明白了,走了幾步路;後來重行停止,於是再走上幾步,重行又停下來。我能夠看見他站着發抖,好像他是被獲而將爲

¹*prisoner*, and were just about to be killed as his two enemies had been.　I ²*beckoned* to him again to come to me, and gave him all the signs of ³*encouragement* that I could think of. He came nearer and nearer, ⁴*kneeling down* every ten or twelve ⁵*steps*, in token of ⁶*acknowledgment* for saving his life. I ⁷*smiled* at him, and looked ⁸*pleasantly*, and beckoned to him to come still nearer.　At length he came close to me; and

囚虜，將要和他的兩個敵人同樣地被殺一般。我以手招他來，把我所能恨像得到的一切鼓勵的手勢，給示於他。他一步一步地走近，每隔十步或二十步便跪將下來，以示感謝我救他性命之意。我向他微笑着；做出和悅的樣子，作手勢叫他再走近些。最後，他來到我的面前；

1. 囚虜。2. 以手招他來前。3. 鼓勵。4. 跪下。5. 步。6. 以手示感謝救命之意。7. 微笑。8. 和悅。

then he ¹*kneeled* down again, kissed the ground, and laid his head upon the ground, and, taking me by the foot, set my foot upon his head. This, it seems, was in token of ²*swearing* to be my slave ³*forever*.

I took him up and ⁴*made much of him*, and ⁵*encouraged* him all I could. But there was more work to do yet; for I perceived the savage whom I had ⁶*knocked down* was not killed, but ⁷*stunned* with the blow, and began to ⁸*come to himself*. So I ⁹*pointed* to him, and showed him the ¹⁰*savage*, that he was not dead. Upon this he spoke words to me and though I could not understand them, yet I thought they were ¹¹*pleasant to hear*; for they were the first sound of a man's voice that I had heard, my own excepted, for above twenty-five years.

But ¹²*there was no time* for such ¹³*reflections* now. The savage who was knocked down ¹⁴*recovered* himself so far as to sit up upon the ground, and I perceived that my savage began to be afraid. But when I saw tnat, I presented my other piece at the man, as if I would ¹⁵*shoot* him. Upon this, my savage,—for so I call him now;—made a motion to me to lend him my sword, which hung ¹⁶*naked* in a ¹⁷*belt* by my side; which I did. He no sooner had it, but he ran to his enemy, and at one blow cut off his head so ¹⁸*cleverly*, no ¹⁹*executioner* in Germany could have done it sooner or better; which I thought veay strange for one who , I had reason, to believe,. never saw a sword in his life before , except their own wooden ²⁰*swords*. However, it seems, as I learned afterwards, they make their wooden swords so sharp, so heavy, and the wood is so hard, that they will even cut off heads with them,—²¹*ay*, and arms, and that at one blow too. When he had done this, he came laughing to me ²²*in sign*

於是他重行下跪，吻了地土，放他的頭在地上，拿我一只足，把我的足放在他的頭上。這個，瞧起來，是表示永遠作我的奴隸的誓約記號。

我扶他起來，善加待遇，竭力地安慰着他。但是尚有許多的事要做；因爲我看見被我打倒的那個野人尚未曾死去，但是因被擊而暈倒了，開始着蘇醒了。這樣，我向他指示着，向他表示着那個野人未曾死去。因此他途向我說話，雖然我不能懂他的言語；然而我想那些話是很好聽的；因爲這是我所聽見的一個人第一次說話的聲音，我自己的聲音

但是現在無暇去憶及這些回想。那個被打倒的野人復原了，竟爬起來坐在地上，我看見我的野人立刻吃驚起來。但是當我看見那事之時，我拿別的一只槍對着他，好像要射擊他一般。因此，我的野人，——現在我這樣地叫着他了，——向我作手勢，叫我把刀借給他，刀是出着鞘，掛在我腰旁皮帶上面；我做了這事。他一經有了刀，立卽跑到他的敵人面前，一擊之下，便敏捷地把他的頭割下，在德國的劊子手無人能做的更加快和更加好；我想這事是很奇怪的對於一個人；我有理由去相信，他畢生永遠未曾見過刀，除去他自己的木刀之外。然而，睡起來，後來我知道了，他們把木刀弄得這樣尖利，這樣重，木頭是這樣堅固，他們能用牠們去割下膠袋的，——唯，以及兵器，也能一擊之下，便可成功

當他做畢此事，他達到我的面前，向我微笑着，表出得勝之象，

of triumph, and brought me the sword again, and, [1]*with abundance of gestures* which I did not understand, laid it down, with the head of the savage that he had killed, just before me.

But that which [2]*estonished* him most was to know how I killed the other [3]*Indian* so far off. Pointing to him, he [4]*made signs to me* to let him go to him ; and I bade him go, as well as I could. When he came to him, he stood like one [5]*amazed,* looking at him, turning him first on one side, then on the other ; looked at the [6]*wound* the [7]*bullet* had made, which it seems was just in his breast, where it had made a hole, and no great [8]*quantity* of blood had followed, but he had [9]*bled inwardly,* for he was quite dead. He took up his bow and arrows, and came back. I[10]*turned to go away,* and [11]*beckoned* him to follow me, making [12]*signs* to him that more might come after them. Upon this he made signs to me that he should bury them with sand, that they might not be seen by the rest, if they followed. I made signs to him again to do so. He fell to work ; and in an instant he had [13]*scraped a hole* in the sand with his hands, big enough to bury the first in, and then [14]*dragged* him into it, and covered him. He did so by the other also ; I believe he had buried them both in a quarter of an hour. Then, calling him away, I carried him, not to my [15]*castle,* but quite away to my cave on the farther part of the island ; so I did not let my [16]*dream* come to pass in that part, that he came into my [17]*grove* for [18]*shelter.* Here I gave him bread and a [19]*bunch* of [20]*raisins* to eat, and a [21]*draught* of water, which I found he was indeed [22]*in great distress for,* from his running. Having [23]*refreshed* him, I made signs for him to go and lie down to sleep, showing him a place where I had laid some

434

重行把刀帶給我，演出了種種的手勢，我一些都不懂，放下刀，把他所殺的那個野人的頭剛剛放在我的面前。

　　但是最使他吃嚇的就是他要明白我怎樣地能老遠的把那個土人打死。他用手指着他，以手向我示意，求我讓他到死的土人那裏去；我吩咐他去，盡我之力去做。當他走到土人面前，他立在那裏好像吃驚的人一般，瞧着他，起頭把他翻到一面去，後來又把他翻到另一面去，注視着鎗彈所擊的傷口，好像是正在胸口，在那裏，鎗彈穿了一個洞，血流的不多，但是血向內流，他是完全地死去了。他拿起了弓和箭，走囘來。我轉身行去，做手勢叫他跟我來，向他做記號說或者還有許多野人隨他們之後而來。因此，他向我作手勢說他將用沙土把他們埋起來，假使其餘的人追來，他們將不被其他野人所見。我向他作手勢叫他這樣地做。他立卽從事；瞬息之間他用手在沙土中挖了一個洞，其大足夠埋進那第一個野人，後來把他曳進洞去，蓋好了他。另外的一個他也照樣對待；我相信他在一刻鐘之中就把二人一齊埋好。我於是叫他走，我不把他帶到堡中去，但是往島不較遠的部份我的洞穴中去；這樣我不使我的夢在那個部份見諸實驗，就是他逃到森林中來躱避。在那裏我給他麵包一束葡萄乾吃，一些的水這些東西我想他是實在亟欲得着的，因爲跑的路太多了。補養了他以後，我向他作手勢叫他躺下去睡覺，指示他一個傷所，在那裏，

rice *straw,* and a *blanket* upon it, which I used to sleep upon myself sometimes. So the poor creature lay down, and went to sleep.

CHAPTER XXXIV

HE was *comely,* handsome fellow *perfectly well made,* with *straight* strong *limbs*; not too large, tall and well shaped, and, *as I reckon,* about twenty-six years of age. He had a very good *countenance,* not a *fierce* and surly *aspect,* but seemed to have something very *manly* in his face : and yet he had all the *sweetness* and *softness* of a European in his *countenance* too, especially when he smiled. His hair was long and black, *not curled like wool,* his *forehead* very high and large, and a great *vivacity* and *sparkling* *sharpness* in his eyes. The color of his skin was not quite black, but very *tawny*; and yet not an *ugly,* yellow, *nauseous* tawny, as the Brazilians and *Virginians,* and other natives of America are, but of a bright kind of a *dun olive-color,* that had in it something very agreeable, though not very easy to *describe.* His face was *round and plump*; his nose small, not *flat* like the negroes ; a very good mouth, thin lips, ane *his fine teeth well set,* and *as white as ivory.*

After he had slept about half an hour, he awoke again and came out of the cave to me. I had been *milking* my goats, which I had in the *inclosure* *just by.* When he *espied* me, he came running to me, laying himself down again upon the ground, with all the possible *signs* of a *humble,* thankful *disposition,* making a great many *antic* *gestures* to show it. At last he laid his head flat upon the ground, close to my foot, and set my other foot upon his

我曾經放了些米梗，在上面放一塊氈子，有時我自已常常睡在上面。這樣，這個可憐的人躺下去，睡覺去了

第三十四章

他是清秀美好的人，身材修短合宜，肢體挺直堅強；不太寬大，高，形式甚好；照我計算而言，大約有二十六歲。他面貌端正，面目並不獰惡可憎，但是臨起來在他的臉上有些丈夫氣概；然而在他的面容之中，尤其是當他微笑之時，他還有像歐洲人溫柔和靄的形狀。他的髮長而黑，不似羊毛之鬈，他的額高而寬，目光銳利而又活潑如流星。腐色並不甚黑但是很是棕黃的；然而不是醜陋的，黃的可憎的棕黃色像布勒喜爾人，浮及利亞省人，以及美洲其他種族的人一般，但是像棕黑橄欖色光亮的一種，其中有些使人可悅的東西，巋然是不狼容易去揣寫。他的臉圓而肥；鼻子是小的，不像黑人的平；一張狼好的嘴，薄的唇，牙齒白潔而齊整，白如象牙一般。

大約睡了半個鐘頭以後，他重行醒來，走出洞來，到我面前。我正擠山羊乳，山羊是在近處的圍地之內。當他見了我之時，他跑到我的面前，重行躺在地上，演示手勢，極表其謙下降服感謝之心，做出許多古怪的手勢將心意表示出來。最後，他把他的頭平放在他上，靠近我的足，把我的另外的一只足放在他的頭上，像他以前所做的一般。

head, as he had done before. After this, he made all the
signs to me of ¹*subjection*, ²*servitude*, and ³*submission* ⁴*imaginable*, to let me know how he would serve me so long as
he lived. I understood him in many things, and let him
know I was very well pleased with him. In a little time I
began to speak to him, and teach him to speak to me; and,
first, I let him know his name should be FRIDAY, which
was the day I saved his life. I called him so ⁵*for the memory
of the time.* I likewise ⁶*taught* him to say "Master," and
then let him know that was to be my name. I likewise
⁷*taught* him to say "yes" and "no," and to know the
meaning of them. I gave him some milk in an earthen
pot, and let him see me drink it before him, and ⁸*sop* my
bread in it; and gave him a cake of bread to do the like,
which he quickly ⁹*complied with,* and made signs that it was
very good for him.

I kept there with him all that night; but, as soon as
it was day, I beckoned to him to come with me, and let
him know I would give him some clothes. As we went by
the place where he had buried the two men, he pointed
exactly to the place, and showed me the marks that he had
made to find them again, making ¹⁰*signs* to me that we
should ¹¹*dig* them up again and eat them. At this, I appeared very angry, ¹²*expressed* my ¹³*abhorrence* of it, made as if
I would ¹⁴*vomit* at the thoughts of it, and beckoned with my
hand to him to come away, which he did ¹⁵*immediately*, with
great submission. I then led him up to the top of the
hill, to see if his enemies were gone. Pulling out my
glass, I looked, and saw plainly the place where they
had been, but no appearance of them or their ¹⁶*canoes*; so

後來，他向我做了各種歸服而甘爲奴隸可猜想的順從的手勢，使我知道他在世一日他怎樣地甘心來服侍我。許多事我明白了他，使他知道我是很喜愛他的。不久，我開始向他說話，敎他向我說話；第一，我使他知道他的名字將要叫作他星期五，就是在那一天我救了他的性命。我這樣地叫他因爲紀念著那個時日。我又敎他說"主人，"使他知道那是我的名字。我又敎他說"是"和"不是，"使他知道牠們的義意。我在一只泥製的罐內給他些乳吃，使他瞧我在他以前怎樣地去飲牠，在乳中浸我的麵包；給他一塊麵包使他照樣而行，他立卽依從，做出手勢來表示著這些食物對他是很好的。

那一夜的工夫，我和他都在那裏；但是，一經天亮，我做手勢叫他隨我走，使他知道我要給他些衣服穿。當我們走過他埋那兩個人的地方時，他準確的指出那個地方來，向我表示著我們應當把那兩個人重行掘出來，把他們吃掉。我對於這事甚爲憤怒，表示我厭惡這種擧動，好像是一經思及便要嘔吐一般，用我的手向他作手勢叫他走開，他立刻用極順從的態度遵命而行。後來我把他領到小山的頂上去，瞧瞧他的敵人們走了沒有。拿出我的望遠鏡，我瞧，明顯地看見他們先前所在的那個地方，但是他們和他們的木艇都不見了；這樣

1.歸服。2.奴役。3.降服。4.可想著的。5.薑爲時日之紀念起見。6.敎。7.敎。8.浸。9.依從。10.手勢。11.掘。12.表示。13.厭惡。14.嘔吐。15.立卽。16.木艇。

439

that it was plain they were gone, and had left their two
¹*comrades* behind them, without any ²*search* after them.

But I was not ³*content* with this ⁴*discovery*; but having
now more ⁵*courage*, and ⁶*consequently* more ⁷*curiosity*, I took
my man Friday with me, giving him the sword in his hand,
with the bow and arrows at his back, which I found he
could use very ⁸*dexterously*, making him carry one gun for
me, and I two for myself; and away we ⁹*marched* to the
place where these ¹⁰*creatures* had been; for ¹¹*I had a mind* now
to get some ¹²*fuller* ¹³*intelligence* of them. When I came to the
place, my very blood ran ¹⁴*chill* in my ¹⁵*veins*, and my heart
sank within me, at the horror of the ¹⁶*spectacle*. Indeed, it
was a dreadful sight,—at least it was so to me, though
Friday made nothing of it. The place was covered with
human bones, and the ground ¹⁷*dyed* with their ¹⁸*blood*.
Friday, by his signs, made me understand that they
brought over four ¹⁹*prisoners* to feast upon; that three of
them were eaten up, and that he, pointing to himself, was
the fourth; that there had been a great battle between
them and their next king, of whose ²⁰*subjects*, it seems, he
had been one, and that they hrd taken a great number of
²¹*prisoners*; all which were carried to several places, by those
who had taken them in the fight, in order to ²²*feast upon*
them, as was done here by there ²³*wretches* upon those they
brought hither.

I ²⁴*caused* Friday to gather all the ²⁵*skulls*, bones, flesh, and
²⁶*whatever remained*, and lay them together in a ²⁷*heap*, and
make a great fire upon it, and ²⁸*burn them all to ashes*. I
found Friday had still a ²⁹*hankering* ³⁰*stomach* after some of the
flesh, and was still a ³¹*cannibal* in his nature; but I showed
so much ³²*abhorrence* at the very thoughts of it, and at the

很明顯地他們是走了，把他們的兩個伴侶留下來，並不去搜尋他們。

　　但是我對於這個發見並不自足；但是現在我有更多的勇氣和更大的好奇心；我把我的人星期五帶着走，把刀遞給他手中，弓和箭在他的背上，我知道他用這些東西是很伶巧的，使他爲我負一枝槍，我自己負兩隻；我們往那個地方去；在那裏，這些生物曾經置足的；因爲我有心去刺探他們的完全的消息。當我到了那個地方，我血管的血，忽然冰冷起來，我的勇氣消洗了，見了這種驚駭的景象。實在，這是一種可怖的光景，——至少對我是如此，雖然星期五不以爲意。這個地方蓋滿了人的骨，地上染有人血。星期五，用他的手勢，使我知道他們帶來了四個囚虜來飲宴；三個是被吃掉了，他，指着他自己，是第四人；在他們和他們的第二的王之中曾有一場大戰，瞧起來，他曾經是那個王的臣民，他們得了許多的囚虜；都被他們帶到各處，被那些在戰爭中捉住他們的人帶走的；以致於把他們作爲飲宴之食品，好像那些野人們把那些囚虜帶到這裏所做的一般。

　　我使星期五把所有的骷髏，骨，肉，以及所餘之物都案集起來，把牠們弄成一堆在上面生了大的火，把牠們付之一炬。我見星期五仍有愛食人肉的口胃，食人肉的天性猶存；但是我一經思及便覺非常厭惡，

1.同伴．2.搜．3.自足．4.發見．5.勇氣．6.於是．7.好奇心．8.伶俐．9.行．10.生物．11.有心．12.完全．13.消息．14.冰冷．15.血管．16.景象．17.染．18.血．19.囚虜．20.臣民．21.囚虜．22.飲宴．23.壞坏．24.使．25.骷髏．26.所餘．27.堆．28.付諸一炬．29.愛食人肉．30.胃口．31.食人肉的．32.厭惡．

least appearance of it, that he durst not discover it; for I had, by some means, let him know that I would kill him if he ¹*offered* it.

When he had done this, we came back to our ²*castle*, and there I fell to work for my man Friday. First of all, I gave him ³*a pair* of ⁴*linen* ⁵*breeches*, which I had out of the poor gunner's ⁶*chest* I mentioned, which I found in the wreck, and which, with a little ⁷*alteration*, fitted him very well; and then I made him a ⁸*jerkin* of goat's skin, as well as my skill would allow (for I was now grown a ⁹*tolerably* good tailor): and I gave him a cap which I made of hare's skin, very ¹⁰*convenient*, and fashionable enough. Thus he was clothed, for the present, ¹¹*tolerably* well, and was ¹²*mighty well pleased* to see himself almost as well clothed as his master. It is true, he went ¹³*awkwardly* in these clothes at first. Wearing the ¹⁴*breeches* was very awkward to him, and the ¹⁵*sleeves* of the ¹⁶*waistcoat* ¹⁷*galled* his shoulders and the inside of his arms; but with a little ¹⁸*easing* them where he ¹⁹*complained* they hurt him, and using himself to them, he took to them at length very well.

The next day after I came home to my hut with him, I began to consider where I should lodge him; and, that I might do well for him and yet be perfectly easy myself, I made a little ²⁰*tent* for him in the ²¹*vacant* place between my two ²²*fortifications*, in the inside of the last, and in the outside of the first. As there was a door or ²³*entrance* there into my cave, I made a ²⁴*framed doorcase*, and a door to it of boards, and set it up in the ²⁵*passage*, a little within the entrance; and, causing the door to open in the inside, I ²⁶*barred* it up in the night, taking in my ²⁷*ladders*, too. So Friday could no way come at me in the inside of my ²⁸*inner-*

只要發見這個，他不敢表示出來；因爲我，無論如何，決心使他明白假使他再提及吃人肉事之，一定要殺死他。

當他做完這事，我們囘到堡中，在那裏，我爲我的人星期五開始工作。首先，我給一條洋布褲，這是我從我曾經敍述過那個可憐的砲手的箱中得着的，我在破船中找着這燒箱子，略加修改，褲子對他甚爲合式，後來我用山羊皮替他做了一件短外衣，極我手藝之所能而爲之，（因爲現在我成爲一個手藝尙好的裁縫了）；我用兔皮做了一頂帽子給他，很合式的而且甚時髦的。他這樣地穿戴起來，在目下是頗好的，他是樂不可支地瞧瞧他自己差不多穿戴得和他的主人一般。這是實在的，他起首行動不便，致顯醜陋之形。他穿了褲子瞧起來狠醜陋的，背心的袖子把他的兩只肩膀和他的膀臂裏面都擦傷了；但是把他訴說傷害他的地方稍爲放鬆一點，常常着之，最後他狠喜穿着牠了。

第二日在我和他囘家到了茅舍以後，我開始想着我將使他住在何處；我最好使他安適，爲我自己也要十分安逸，我爲他造了一座小的帳幕在我的兩座堡壘之中的空地的裏面，在第二個堡壘之內，在第一個堡壘之外。因爲在我的洞穴之中有一座門或入口，我做了一座有架的門框，安了一座木板的門，放牠在通路上，稍爲在入口的裏面；使門朝裏開，在夜裏我將門閂好，把梯子也拿進來。這樣星期五無法可以來到我的身傍，在最靠近的牆的裏面，

most wall, without making so much noise in getting over that it must needs awaken me; for my first wall had now a [1]*complete* roof over it of long [2]*poles*, covering all my tent, and [3]*leaning up* to the side of the hill; which was again [4]*laid across* with smaller [5]*sticks* instead of [6]*laths*, and then [7]*thatched* over a great thickness with the rice [8]*straw*, which was strong, like [9]*reeds*. At the hole or place which was left to go in or out by the ladder, I had placed a kind of [10]*trapdoor*, which, if it had been [11]*attempted* on the outside, would not have opened at all, but would have fallen down and made a great noise. As to [12]*weapons*, I took them all into my side every night.

But I needed none of all this [13]*precaution* : for never man had a more faithful, loving, [14]*sincere* servant than Friday was to me. He was without [15]*passions* [16]*sullenness*, or [17]*designs*, perfectly obliged and [18]*engaged*. His very [19]*affections* were tied to me like those of a child to a father; and I dare say he would have [20]*sacrificed* his life to save mine, upon any occasion [21]*whatsoever*. The many [22]*testimonies* he gave me of this put it out of [23]*doubt*, and soon [24]*convinced* me that I needed to use no [25]*precautions* for my safety [26]*on his account*.

I was greatly [27]*delighted* with him, and made it my business to teach him everything that was proper to make him useful, handy, and helpful; but especially to make him speak, and understand me when I spoke. And he was the [28]*aptest scholar* that ever was; and particularly was so merry, so [29]*constantly* diligent, and so pleased when he could but understand me, or make me understand him, that it was very pleasant to me to talk to him. Now my life began to be [30]*so easy* that I began to say to myself

444

假使他經過上面不弄出狠大的聲音來把我驚醒；因爲現在我的第一座牆的上面有一座長柱子的完美的屋頂，把帳幕全遮蓋起來。斜上直達山邊；那個仍是被橫置於其上，用小的棍子而不用條板，用木梗狠厚地把牠掩蓋好，木梗是狠堅固的，像蘆葦一般。在洞穴或用梯子進出的地方，我放了一種活板門，假使外面有人試圖推開，決計不會開的，但是必定傾倒下來，發出大的聲音。至於武器，每晚我把牠們一齊帶在身傍。

但是我無須這些預防：因爲無論何人沒有像星期五對我是這樣的一個忠心的，可愛的，誠實的用人。他沒有情欲，慓悍之性，圖謀他是甚爲邇就而又熱心。他愛我深切之情宛如小孩對於父親一般；我敢說他願意犧牲生命來救我，在無論何時用得着他的時候。他對於這個所給我的證據使我不用疑念，立刻使我覺悟我無須因他之故從事預防以求生命之安全。

我狠喜愛他，我視爲我的事務去教他各種對他有用，伶巧，有助的事物；特別地是令他說話，使他怖我所說的是什麼。他是敏而好學之人；尤其是這樣快樂，勤而不倦，這樣地快活當他怖我的話之時，或使我怖得他的話之時，我是狠欣悅地去和他談話。現在我的生活是開始着這樣地舒適，我向自己說

1. 完全。2. 柱。3. 斜上。4. 橫置其上。5. 棍。6. 條板。7. 蓋草。8. 梗。9. 蘆葦。10. 活板門。11. 試。12. 武器。13. 預防。14. 誠實。16. 情欲。16. 慓悍之性。17. 圖謀。18. 熱心。19. 感情。20. 犧牲。21. 無論如何。22. 證據。23. 懷疑。24. 使悟。25. 預防。26. 因彼之故。27. 欣悅。28. 敏而好學之人。29. 時常。30. 這樣的安逸。

445

that could I but have been safe from more savages, I cared
not.if I was never to ¹*remove* from the place while I lived.

CHAPTER XXXV

AFTER I had been two or three days returned to my
castle, I thought that, in order to bring Friday off from his
²*horrid* way of ³*feeding*, and from the ⁴*relish* of a ⁵*cannibal's*
⁶*stomach*, I ought to let him ⁷*taste* other ⁸*flesh*, so I took him
out with me one morning to the woods. I went, indeed,
⁹*intending* to kill a kid out of my own ¹⁰*flock*, and bring it
home and dress it ; but as I was going, I saw a she-goat
lying down in the ¹¹*shade*, and two young ¹²*kids* sitting by
her. I ¹³*caught hold of* Friday. "*Hold*" said I, "¹⁴*stand
still*;" and made signs to him not to stir. Immediately,
I presented my piece, ¹⁵*shot*, and killed one of the kids. The
poor creature, who had, at a distance, indeed, seen me kill
the savage, his enemy, but did not know, nor could
imagine, how it was done, was ¹⁶*sensibly* surprised ; he
¹⁷*trembled*, and shock, and ¹⁸*looked so amazed* that I thought
he would have sunk down. He did not see the kid I shot
at, or perceive I had killed it, but ¹⁹*ripped* up his ²⁰waistcoat,
to feel whether he was not ²¹*wounded*; and, as I found
presently, thought I was resolved to kill him. He came
and kneeled down to me, and ²²*embracing* my ²³*knees*, said a
great many things I did not understand ; but I could easily
see the meaning was to pray me not to kill him.

I soon found a way to ²⁴*convince* him that I would do
him no harm. Taking him up by the hand, I laughed at
him, and pointing to the kid which I had killed. I ²⁵*beckoned*
to him to run and fetch it, which he did. While he was

假使我能不爲野人們所危，我將不措意我是否永遠不能從我現在所住的地方遷移而去。

第 三 十 五 章

在我同到堡中二三天以後，我想，要把星期五的用可怖的方法來吃東西，和喜愛吃人肉的胃口戒掉；我應當讓他吃別種肉類；這樣一天早晨我把他帶到我的樹林中去。我想，實在說起來，從我的羊羣裏面殺却一只小山羊，把他帶同家去烹調；但是當我走的時候，我看見一只母山羊躺在林蔭之中，兩只小山羊坐在牠的身旁。我握住星期五。"止步，"我說，"立定；"做手勢教他不要動。立卽，我描準了鎗，放射，殺了一只小山羊。這個可憐的生物，他曾在遠處，實在瞧見了我殺了一個野人，他的敵人，但是不知道，也不能夠猜想，是怎樣做的，現在心中大爲驚懼；他抖戰起來，面色驚惶，我想他或者要傾跌下去。他未曾看見我所射擊的小山羊，或者看見我殺了牠，但是解開他的背心，看看他是否受了傷；我立卽明白他的意思，他想我是决心去殺他。他走來向我跪下，抱住我的雙膝，說了許多我不能懂得的話；但是我能容易地明白話中的意思，就是求我不要殺他。

我馬上找着一個法子來使他明白我不加害於他。用手把他扶起，我嘲笑他，指示着我所殺的小山羊，我向他作手勢，叫他跑去把牠拿來，牠應命而行。

wondering, and looking to see how the creature was killed,
I ¹*loaded* my gun again. By and by I saw a great ²*fowl*,
like a ³*hawk,* sitting upon a tree ⁴*within shot.* To let Friday
understand a little what I would do, I called him to me
again, pointed at the ⁵*fowl,*—which was indeed a ⁶*Parrot*,
though I thought it had been a ⁷*hawk,*—I say, pointing to
the parrot, and to my gun, and to the ground under the
parrot, to let him see I would make it fall, I made him
understand that I would shoot and kill that bird. Accordingly I fired, and bade him look, and immediately he saw
the parrot fall. He stood like one ⁸*frightened* again, notwithstanding all I had said to him. I found he was the
more ⁹*amazed* because he did not see me put anything into
the gun, but thought that there must be some wonderful
¹⁰*fund of death* and ¹¹*destruction* in that thing able to kill
man, ¹²*beast,* bird, or anything near or far off; and the
astonishment this created in him was such as could not
¹³*wear off* for a long time. I believe, if I would have let him
he would have ¹⁴*worshiped* me and my gun. As for the gun
itself, he would not so much as ¹⁵*touch* it for several days
after; but he would speak to it, and talk to it, as if it had
answered him, when he was by himself; which, as I
afterwards learned of him. was to desire it not to kill him.

Well, after his ¹⁶*astonishment* was a little over at this, I
pointed to him to run and fetch the bird I had shot, which
he did, but stayed some time; for the parrot, not being
quite dead, had ¹⁷*fluttered away* a good distance from the
place where she fell, However he found her, took her up,
and brought her to me; and as I had ¹⁸*perceived* his
¹⁹*ignorance* about the gun before, I took this ²⁰*advantage* to
charge the gun again, and not to let him see me do it, that

正當他奇怪之時，和看這個生物怎樣地被殺之時，我重行又把子彈裝進槍去。不久，我看見一只大的禽鳥，像鷹一般，坐在彈丸所能及的一株樹上。讓星期五稍爲明白我將做些什麼事我重行把他叫到面前來，指着那只禽鳥，———那實在是一只鸚鵡，雖然我想牠是一只鷹，———我說指着那隻鸚鵡，我的槍，在鸚鵡下面的地土，使他明白我將要把牠打下來，我使他知道我將射擊和殺死那只鳥兒。我立卽發槍，叫他看，馬上他看見鸚鵡掉下地來。他站住仍舊好像是吃驚的人一般，雖然我把一切使得他明白。我覺着他是更加驚惶，因爲他未曾瞧見我把東西放入槍內，但是他想必定有些奇怪的可致命的可損傷的東西在槍的裏面，能夠把人，獸，鳥，以及遠近各物來殺死；他受着的驚惶長久竟然不能消滅。我相信，假使我讓他去，他一定要崇拜我和我的槍。至於槍的本身，過了幾天以後，他方纔敢稍微觸牠一下；但是他向牠說話，向牠談心，好像牠能同答他一般，當他獨居之時；我後來詢問他，他說他是希望槍不來殺死他。

　　不錯，在他對於這事的驚懼過了以後，我指示他叫他驅去把我射死的鳥兒拿來，他應命而行，但是停了些時；因爲那只鸚鵡，未曾完全死去，撲翼而飛，從牠被射擊下來的地方飛了好遠。然而他尋着了牠，把牠拿起，把牠帶給我；我曾見他以前對於槍的愚昧的觀念，我乘此机會把槍彈重行裝好，不讓他看見有做這事，

1.裝好。2.禽鳥。3.鷹
。4.彈丸所能久。5.禽
鳥。6.鸚鵡。7.鷹。8.
吃驚。9.吃驚。10致命
之由。11.損害。12.獸
。13消滅。14.崇拜。15
。觸。16.驚惶。17.撲
翼飛去。18.見。19.愚
昧。20.機會。

I might be ready for any other mark that might present,
But nothing more offered at that time ; so I brought home
the kid, and the same evening I took the skin off, and cut
it out as well as I could ; and having a pot fit for that
¹purpose, I boiled or *²stewed* some of the flesh, and made some
very good broth. After I had begun to eat some, I gave
some to my man, who seemed very glad of it, and liked it
very well ; but that which was strangest to him was to see
me eat *³salt* with it. He made a sign to me that the salt
was not good to eat ; and putting a little into his own
mouth, he seemed to *⁴nauseate* it , and would *⁵spit* and *⁶sputter*
at it, washing his mouth with fresh water after it. On the
other hand, I took some meat into my mouth without salt ,
and I pretended to spit and *⁷sputter* for want of *⁸salt*, as
much as he had done at the salt . But it would not do ; he
would never care for salt with meat or in his *⁹broth* ; at
least, not for a great while, and then but a very little.

Having thus *¹⁰fed* him with boiled meat and broth, I was
resolved to feast him the next day by *¹¹roasting* a piece of
the kid. This I did by hanging it before the fire on a
¹²string , as I had seen many people do in England, setting
two *¹³poles* up, one on each side of the fire, and one across
the top, and *¹⁴tying* the string to the *¹⁵cross* stick; letting the
meat turn continually. This Friday admired very much ;
but when he came to taste the *¹⁶flesh*, he took so many ways
to tell me how well he liked it, that I could not but
understand him. At last he told me, as well as he could ,
he would never eat man's flesh any more, which I was very
glad to hear .

The next day, I set him to work beating some corn out,
and *¹⁷sifting* it in the manner I used to do, as I *¹⁸observed*

我可以預備着射擊其他在目前之物。但是那個時候沒有東西發見；這樣我遂把小山羊帶回家去；當晚我把牠的皮剝掉，盡力地把牠割成塊；有一只適於這事之用的罐子，我煑或炙幾塊羊肉，做了些很好的湯。在我吃了些以後，我給些我的人吃，他瞧起來狠喜歡這個，對我的給予非常樂意；但是他最奇怪的就是看見我和鹹一淘吃羊肉。他向我作手勢說鹹是不好吃的；放了少許到牠自己的內口，他好像要把牠嘔出一般，要想嘖而吐之，後來他用新鮮的水，洗他的嘴。在別的一只手中，我放了些肉到我的口中，沒有放鹹，我假裝要把肉嘖而吐之，因爲少鹹之故，好像他因爲有鹹而嘖吐一樣。但是這事是徒然的；他永遠未曾注意着肉內湯中是否需鹹；至少，鹹用得時候不多，但是用得狠少。

用煑好的肉和湯給他吃以後，我決心第二天烤一塊羊肉來餉他。我做了這個，把肉懸在火前的一根繩子上，好像在英國我看見許多人做的一樣，立起兩根柱子，一根在火的這面，一根火的那面，一根是橫在頂上，繫着繩子倒橫置在上面的棍子上，讓肉常常地翻身。星期五狠驚異這事；但是當他來嚐肉之時，他用種種方法來告訴我他是怎樣地喜愛牠，我當然懂得他的意思。後來他告訴我，竭他的能力而說，他永遠不再吃人肉了，這話我聽了狠樂意。

1.用處。2.炙。3.鹹。4.起惡心。5.嘖。6.吐。7.嘖。8.鹹 9.湯。10.喂。11.烤。12.繩。13.柱。14.繫。15.橫置其上。16.肉。17.篩。18.已詳述於前矣。

before. He soon understood how to do it as well as I, especially after he had seen what the meaning of it was, and that it was to make bread of. After that, I let him see me make my bread, and bake, it, too; and in a little time, Friday was able to do all the work for me, as well as I could do it myself.

I began now to consider that, having two mouths to feed instead of one, I must [1]*provide* more ground for my [2]*harvest,* and plant a larger [3]*quantity* of corn than I used to do. So I [4]*marked out* a larger piece of land, and began the fence in the same manner as before, in which Friday not only worked very willingly and very[6]hard, but did it very [5]*cheerfully.* I told him what it was for,—that it was for corn to make more bread, because he was now with me, and that I might have enough for him and myself too. He [6]*appeared very sensible* of that part, and let me know that he thought I had much more labor upon me on his account than I had for myself; and that he would work the [7]*harder* for me, if I would tell him what to do.

This was the [8]*pleasantest* year of all the life I led in this place. Friday began to talk [9]*pretty well,* and understand the names of almost everything I had [10]*occasion* to [11]*call for*, and of every place I had to send him to, and talked a great deal to me, so that, in short, I began now to have some use for my [12]*tongue* again, which, indeed, I had very little occasion for before. Besides the pleasure of talking to him, I had a singular [13]*satisfaction* in the fellow himself. His simple, [14]*unfeigned* honesty appeared to me more and more every day, and, I began really to love the creature; [15]*and on his side,* I believe he loved me more than it was possible for him ever to love anything before.

第二天,我叫他,工作,打些穀子出來,照我平常所做的樣子來篩牠;這種方法我先前已經詳述過了。他立刻知道怎樣去做,做的同我一樣,尤其是在他知道了這事是什麼意思和用穀子可以做麵包之後。這事完畢,我讓他看我做麵包,焙牠;不久,星期五可以替我做這些工作, 好像我自己所做的一樣。

現在我注意着,不是一張嘴,但是兩張嘴要吃,我必須多供備些地來收穫:比從前要植較多量的穀子了.這樣我標示一大塊地,像從前一樣去造籬笆;星期五非但很願意和很困苦的做這事,而且欣然爲之,我告訴他爲什麼做這事,——就是爲得着穀子來做更多的麵包,因爲現在他和我在一處,我必須有足夠的分量,方能供給我和他二人。他瞧起來甚爲明白對於那個部份,讓我知道他想我爲他費了比較爲我自己更多的勞力;他願爲我做較難的工作,假使我告訴他怎樣去做。

這是我在這個地方生活的第一個最欣快的年頭。星期五話講得頗好,懂得所有我有時需要物件的名字,和我教他去的各地方的名稱,同我講許多的話;總而言之,現在我再對於舌頭又有用場了,實在,前此我却不甚用得着牠。在和他談話的快樂以外,我異常滿意他的爲人。他的簡單的;不詭詐的誠實態度每天向我表現出來,我開始實在地喜愛這個生物;至於他的一方面,我相信他愛我比較他以前所愛的東西更甚。

1.供備.2.收成.3.分量.4.標示.5.欣然.6.似甚明白.7.較難.8.最欣悅的.9.顏好.10.有時.11.需用.12.舌.語言.13.滿意.14.不詭詐.15.至彼一方面.

I had a mind once to try if he had any [1]*inclination* for his own country again; and having taught him English so well that he could answer me almost any question, I asked him whether the nation that he [2]*belonged* to never [3]*conquered* in [4]*battle*, at which he smiled, and said, "Yes, yes, we always [5]*fight the better*;" that is, he meant, always get the better in [6]*fight*; and so we began the following [7]*discourse*;

Master.—You always fight the better! How came you to be taken [8]*prisoner* then, Friday?

Friday.—My [9]*nation beat much for all that*.

Master.—How beat? If your nation beat them, how came you to be taken?

Friday.—They more many than my nation, in the place where me was; they take one, two, three, and me. My nation [10]*over-beat* them in the yonder place. where me no was; there my nation take one, two, great thousand.

Master.—But why did not your side [11]*recover* you from the hands of your enemies then?

Friday.—They run, one, two, three, and me, and make go in the canoe; my nation have no canoe that time.

Mastr.—Well, Friday. and what does your nation do with the men they take? Do they carry them away and eat them, as these did?

Friday.—Yes, my nation eat mans too; eat all up.

Master.—Where do they carry them?

Friday.—Go to other place, where they think.

Master.—Do they come hither?

Friday.—Yes, yes, they come hither; come other else place.

Master.—Have you been here with them?

　　有一次我有心試試他是否仍舊愛戀着他的祖國；把他英語教得這樣地好，他差不多能囘答我各項問題，我問他他所屬的國度是否永遠未曾戰擊過，他對這問題，笑了一笑，說，"是的，是的，我們常常戰擊；"他的意思就是常常在戰爭中得着上風；這樣我們開始下面的談話；

　　主人。——你常常打勝！那末你爲什麼被俘而爲囚呢，星期五？

　　星期五。——無論如何，吾國常常得以打敗他人。

　　主人。——怎樣打法？假使你的國家打敗他們，你因甚被俘？

　　星期五。——他們的人比我們多，在我所在的那個地方；他們捉了一人，二人，三人，和我。我的國家在另方面打敗他們，我不在那裏，彼處我的國家捉了一，二，許多千人。

　　主人。——爲什麼你的一方不把你從敵人手中取囘呢？

　　星期五。——他們趨，一，二，三，我，使水艇走；那時我國沒有木艇。

　　主人。——好，星期五，你的國家捉住了那些人怎樣處置？他們將俘虜帶走，吞噬他們，像這些人所做的一樣嗎？

　　星期五。——是，我國也吃人；吃盡了一切人。

　　主人。——他們把囚虜帶到那兒去？

　　星期五。——到別的地方去，在那裏他們想着。

　　主人。——他們到這裏來嗎？

　　星期五。——是的，是的，他們到這裏來；又到別的地方去。

　　主人。——你和他們一處到這裏來過嗎？

1.意向所在。2. 所屬。3.勝利。4. 戰爭。5.戰勝。6.戰鬥。7.談話。8.囚虜。9.無論如何，我國得以戰勝他人。10.戰擊。11.克復，取囘。

Friday.—Yes, I been here. (Points to the northwest side of the island, which, it seems, was their side.)

By this I understood that my man Friday had formerly been among the savages who used to come on shore on the farther part of the island, on the same [1]*man-eating* [2]*occasions* he was now brought for. Some time after, when I took the courage to carry him to that side, being the same I [3]*formerly mentioned*, he presently knew the place, and told me he was there once when they ate up twenty men, two women, and one child. He could not tell twenty in English, but he [4]*numbered* them by laying so many stones in a row, and pointing to me [5]*to tell them over.*

I asked him how far it was from our [6]*island* to the shore, and whether the canoes were not often lost. He told me there was no [7]*danger*, no canoes ever lost; but that, after a little way out to sea, there was a [8]*current* and wind, always one way in the morning, the other in the afternoon. This I understood to be no more than the [9]*sets of the tide*, as going out or coming in. But I afterwards understood it was occasioned by the great [10]*draft* and [11]*reflux* of the [12]*mighty river Orinoco*, in the mouth of which river, as I found afterwards, our island lay; and that this land which I [13]*perceived* to be west and northwest, was the great island [14]*Trinidad*, on the north point of the mouth of the river. I asked Friday a thousand questions about the country, the inhabitants, the sea, the coast, and what nations were near. He told me all he knew, with the greatest openness [15]*imaginable*. I asked him the names of the several nations of his sort of people, but could get no other name than Caribs. I easily understood that these were the Caribbees. which our [16]*maps* place on the part of

456

星期五．——是，我曾經到過這裏。(指示着島的西北面，那個瞧起來是他們的一面°)

因爲這次談話，我明白了我的人星期五從前也是在那些野人當中，他們常常來到岸上，在島的較遠的部份上，他現在在吃人之時而被帶來了。過了些時，當我鼓起勇氣把他帶到那邊之時，就是我以前所述的同樣的地力，樣立刻知道了這地方，告訴我他曾經來過一次，當他們吃了二十人之時，還吃了二個女人，一個小孩子。他不能說出英文的二十來但是他數他們把許多石頭放在一列，指示着我去計算。

我問他從我們的島上到岸邊有多少遠，木艇是否不常常失事。他告訴我毫無危險，木艇未曾失過事；但是，離了海較遠，有急流和風常常早上在這個方向，下午在那個方向。我明白了這個，這不過是潮流之向，出去或回來。但是後來我明白了這事發生是因俄里羅哥大河的漲潮和退潮，在那河的口中，我後來知道了，我們的島躺在那裏；我看見的那個陸地是在西方和西北方的，就是特立里答特大島，在河口的角上。我問星期五許多問題，

關於城市，人民，海，海濱，什麼國度靠近這裏。他把他知道的告訴了我，極其爽直。我問他如他種類的人的國度的名字，但是我只得着了加里卜一個名字。我容易地明白這些是加里卜人，我們的地圖把這個地方放在美州部份上，從俄里羅哥河口到格伊耶那，向上直至聖瑪爾達。

1.吃人．2.時候．3.前已述及．4.數．5.計數．6.島．7.危險．8.急流．9.潮流之向．10潮之漲退．11.退潮．13.大河．13.見．14.特立里答特島．15.可猜想的．16.地圖．

America which reaches from the mouth of the river Orinoco to ¹*Guiana*, and onwards to ²*St Martha*. He told me that up a great way beyond the moon,—that is, beyond ³*the setting of the moon*, which must be west from their country,—there ⁴*dwelt* white, bearded men like me,—and pointed to my great ⁵*whiskers*, which I mentioned before,—and that they had killed "much mans,"—that was his word. By all which I understood he meant the Spaniards, whose ⁶*cruelties* in America had been ⁷*spread over* the whole cuuntry, and were ⁸*remembered* by all the nations from father to son.

I inquired if he could tell me how I might go from this island, and get among those white men. He told me, "Yes, yes, you may go in two canoe." I could not understand what he meant, or make him ⁹*describe* to me what he meant by "two canoe," till at last, with great difficulty, I found he meant it must be in a large boat, as big as two canoes. This part of Friday's discourse I began to ¹⁰*relish* very well; and from this time I ¹¹*entertained* some hopes that, ¹²*one time or other*, I might find an ¹³*opportunity* to make my ¹⁴*escape* from this place, and that this poor savage might be a means to help me.

CHAPTER XXXVI

DURING the long time that Friday had now been with me, and that he began to speak to me, and understand me I was not wanting in laying a ¹⁵*foundation* of ¹⁶*religious* knowledge in his mind ; particularly I asked him, one time, who made him. The poor creature did not understand me at all, but thought I had asked who was his father ; but I took it up by another ¹⁷*handle*, and asked him who made the sea,

他告訴我那裏在月亮之外離了甚遠，——就是說，在月落之處以外，那裏是他們國度的西方，——在那裏住有白色的，有鬚的人像我一樣，——他指着我的鬍子；我曾經敍述過他——他說他們曾經殺了"許多的人，"這就是他的語法。我所能悸得他的話，他就是指斯巴利亞達人，在美洲他們的殘忍是傳播全國的；從父親到兒子，各國的人都記憶着的。

　　我問他能否告訴我我怎樣能從此島遠去，到那些白色人裏面去。他告訴我，"是，是，你可以在兩只木艇之中而去。"我不能明白他的意思，或者使他爲我描寫他所說的"兩只木艇"是何意思，直到最後，用了狠困難的法子，我覺着他的意思就是說一只大船，像兩只木艇一般大。星期五談話的這一部份，我是很喜歡的；從此以後，我懷着希望，終有一日，我可以找着机會從這個地方逃走，這個可憐的野人可以充作教我的一個方法。

第 三 十 六 章

　　在星期五現在和我共處的長時間之內，他和我談心，明白了我，我在他的心中便開始立着宗教知識的基礎；特別地我一時詢問他誰把他造成功。這個可憐的生物一點都不明白我的話，但是想我是問他誰是他的生父；但是我易一法再問他，向他詢問誰是造成了海，我們走的地土，以及小山和樹林。

the ground we walked on, and the ¹*hills* and ²*woods*. He told me it was one old Benamuckee, that lived beyond all. He could ³*describe* nothing of this great person but that he was very old,—much older, he said, than the sea or land, than the moon or the ⁴*stars*. I asked him, then, if this old person had made all things, why all things did not ⁵*worship* him. He looked very ⁶*grave*, and, with a perfect look of ⁷*innocence*, said, "All things say O to him." I asked him if the people who died in his country went away anywhere. He said yes, they all went to Bena-muckee. Then I asked him whether those they ate went up thither too. He said, "Yes"

From these things I began to ⁸*instruct* him in the knowl-edge of the true God. I told him that the great Maker of all things lived up there (pointing up towards ⁹*heaven*); that he ¹⁰*governed* the world by the same power and ¹¹*provi-dence* by which he made it; that he was ¹²*omnipotent,* and could do everything for us, give everything to us, take everything from us. Thus, ¹³*by degrees,* I opened his eyes. He heard with great ¹⁴*attention* of Jesus Christ, and of the manrer of making our ¹⁵*prayers* to God, and his being able to hear us, even in heaven. He told me one day that if our God could hear us, up beyond the sun, he must needs be a greater God than their Benamuckee, who lived but a little way off, and yet could not hear till they went up to the great mountains where he dwelt to speak to him. I asked him if ever he went thither to speak to him. He said no, they never went that were young men; none went thither but the old men, whom he called their "¹⁶*Oowokakee*"; that is, as I made him explain to me, their ¹⁷*religious,* or ¹⁸*clergy*; and that they went to say

他說這是一個老倍那母克伊所造成的，他生活在各種生物以外。他不能描寫出這個偉大人物的別種特質，只知道他是老的，——更老，他說，比到海或陸地；比到月或星。那末我就問他，假使這個老人造成了這些東西，爲什麼各種東西不崇拜他。他正其容色，用了無識無知的狀態來說道，"所有這些東西向他說"哦。"我問他在他們國裏死了是否到別處去。他說不錯，他們到倍那母克伊那裏去。我於是問他他們所吃的那些人是否也到他那裏去。他說，"是的"。

從這些事物上面，我開始教訓他真實上帝的智識。我告訴他萬物的大造化主住在那邊（向天上指着）；他用同樣的權力和意旨來管理世界，世界是他造成的；他是全能的，能爲我們做各種事情，給予我們各種事物；把各種事物從我們身邊拿去；漸漸地，我把他眼界開開來。他用狠留心的態度來聽講耶穌，以及我們禱告上帝的態度方法，他能聽見我們，就是住在天上。一天，他告訴我假使上帝能聽見我們，在太陽以外的上面，他必定是比較他們倍那母克伊還要大的一位上帝；他住得不狠遠，然而不能聽見，直至他們跑上山去，方能聽見，在山上他住着，他向他們說話。我問他他是否到山上去過同他說過話。他說否，少年人永不到那裏去，除去老年人，無人到山上去，他叫老年人作

" O " (so he called saying prayers), and then came back and told them what Benamuckee' said. By this I observed that there is [1]*priestcraft* even among the most blinded, [2]*ignorant* [3]*pagans* in the world

I [4]*diverted* the present [5]*discourse* between me and my man by sending him for something a good way off. I then [6]*seriously* prayed to God that he would enable me to [7]*instruct* this poor savage, [8]*assisting*, *by his* [9]*Spirit*, the heart of the poor, ignorant creature to receive the light of the knowledge of God in Christ, [10]*reconciling* him to himself, and would [11]*guide* me so to speak to him from the Word of God that his [12]*conscience* might be [13]*convinced*, his eyes opened, and his [14]*soul* saved. When he came again to me, I entered into a long discourse with him upon the subject of the [15]*redemption* of man by the Savior of the world, and of the [16]*doctrine* of the [17]*gospel* [18]*preached* from heaven ; namely, of [19]*repentance towads* God, and faith in our blessed Lord Jesus

I had, God knows, more [20]*sincerity* than knowledge in all the methods I took for this poor creature's instruction, and must [21]*acknowledge*—what I believe all that [22]*act upon the* same principle will find—that in laying things open to him, I really informed and [23]*instructed* myself in many things that either I did not know, or had not fully considered before, but which [24]*occurred naturally to my mind* upon [25]*searching into* them for the [26]*information* of this poor savage. I had more [27]*affectinn* in my [28]*inquiry after* things upon this occacion than ever I felt before. Whether this poor, wild wretch was the better for me or no, I had great reason to be thankful that ever he came to me, my [29]*grief sat lighter* upon me, my habitation grew [30]*comfortable* to me [31]*beyond measure*, and I [32]*frequently* rejoiced that ever I was brought

"哦哦烏家格伊;"就是說，我叫他向我解釋，他們的牧師；他們去說"哦"（他說這就是做禱告），後來回來告訴他們倍那母克伊說了些什麼。因此，我注意著在世界之中，就是在最盲昧，最愚蒙的耶教徒之內也有一種宗教的權術。

在我和我的人之中，我把現在所談論的題目改變了，我把他遣出去到較遠的地方去做些事。我於是慇重地禱告上常，他將要使我能教訓這個可憐的野人，幫助我，用他的聖靈感動可憐的愚昧的人的心在基督之中接受上帝的智識之光，使他和合自己；指引我這樣地和他說，從上帝意旨之中他的良心可以感悟，他的眼界可以開展，他的靈魂可以得救。當他重行回到我處之時，我和他長談；談及世間救主的拯救世人，以及從天上所宣傳的福音書中的道理；就是，悔罪於上帝之前，信仰我們可愛的主子耶穌。

上帝知道，我用誠意去開化他比較用知識的方法去訓導這個可憐的生物格外注重，必須承認—— 我所相信的，所有遵守此同一的道理的東西將要找出來—— 把事物向他昭示，我實在改進和訓導自己許多我不知道的事物，以及以前我未詳加注意的，但是自然地牠在我心中發現出來了，在研究牠們因為想啟示野人之時。在我研求事物之中，在這個時候我有許多的情感，當此之時，較我以前所覺著的尤甚。或者這個可憐的野的東西對我是好的或是不好的，我有狠大的緣故去感謝著，自從他到我這裏來以後，我的憂愁頓然減去。我的住所對我是非常的安逸，我常常地欣悅那個，自從我到此處以來，我常常想著那些臨在我身上的所有的一切苦痛的恐怖。

to this place, which I had so often thought the most dread-full of all [1]*afflictions* that could possibly have [2]*befallen* me.

I continued in this thankful frame all the [3]*remainder* of my time; and the [4]*conversation* which employed the hours between Friday and me was such as made the three years which we lived there together perfectly and [5]*completely* happy, if any such thing as complete happiness can be found in a [6]*sublunary state*. This savage was now a good Christian, a much better than I; though I have reason to hope, and bless God for it, that we were equally [7]*penitent*, and [8]*comforted*, [9]*restored penitents*. We had here the Word of God to read, and were no [10]*farther off* from his Spirit to instruct than if we had been in England. I always [11]*applied* myself, in reading the [12]*Scripture*, to let him know, as well as I could, the meaning of what I read.

After Friday and I became more [13]*intimately acquainted*, and he could understand almost all I said to him, and speak pretty [14]*fluently*, though, in broken English, to me, I [15]*acquainted* him with my own history, or at least so much of it as [16]*related to* my coming to this place; how I had lived there, and how long. I let him into the [17]*mystery*—for such it was to him—of [18]*gunpowder* and [19]*bullet*, and taught him how to [20]*shoot*. I gave him a knife, which he was [21]*wonderfully* [22]*delighted with*; and I made him a belt with a [23]*frog* hanging to it, such as in England we wear [24]*hangers* in; and in the frog, instead of a hanger, I gave him a [25]*hatchet*, which was not only as good a [26]*weapon* [27]*in some cases*, but much more useful upon other occasions.

I [28]*described* to him the countries of Europe, particularly England, which I came from; how we lived, how we [29]*worshiped* God, how we [30]*behaved* to one another, and how we

464

其餘的時日我繼續着在這種感謝情形之中；在我和星期五之中，消磨時日的談話，是像我們一淘在這個地方完全地快活地生活着三年以來所說的一樣，假使像完美的幸福能在世間的境況裏面所找着的話，這個野人現在是一好的基督教徒，比我還要好些；雖然我有緣故去希望和祝福上帝，爲了這個，我們是同等的懺悔的，安心的和因悔罪而得復原的人。在這裏我們有上帝的意旨來念，並不遠離他的訓導的聖靈，如同我們在英國一般。我常常用心，念着聖經，讓他明白，竭我的能力去做我所讀的意義。

在星期五和我更加熟識之後，他差不多能懂所有我對他說的話，他對我說的頗流利，雖然英語是不完全的，我告訴他我的生平的歷史，或者至少是關於我來到這個地方的原由：我在那裏怎樣生活，住了多少時候。我引他到奧妙之事的裏面去——因爲對於他是如此的——就是炮藥和子彈，教他如何去放射牠們。我給他一把刀，他非常喜歡牠；我替他做一根皮帶，繫在帶上有一大鈕扣，如同在英國我們懸掛腰刀用的一樣；在大衣鈕之中，沒有腰刀，我給他一柄小斧，不僅是在某種工作之間是一種好的武器，而且在別種的工作中之也很有用。

向他描寫歐洲各國，尤其是英國，我是從那處來的，我們怎樣生活，我們怎樣崇拜上帝，我們怎樣彼此交際，以及我們怎樣在船中和世界上各部份通商貿易。

¹*traded* in ships to all parts of the world. I gave him an account of the wreck which I had been on board of, and showed him, as near as I could, the place where she lay. She was all beaten in pieces before, and gone. I showed him the ²*ruins* of our boat, which we lost when we escaped, and which I could not stir with my whole ³*strength* then, but was now fallen almost all to pieces. Upon seeing this boat, Friday stood ⁴*musing* a great while, and said nothing. I asked him what it was he ⁵*studied upon*. At last he said, "Me see such boat like come to place at my nation." I did not understand him a good while; but at last, when I had ⁶*examined* further into it, I understood by him that a boat such as that had been, came on shore upon the country where he lived; that is, as he ⁷*explained* it, was driven thither by ⁸*stress of weather*. I presently imagined that some European ship must have been ⁹*cast away* upon their coast, and the boat might get loose and drive ashore; but was so ¹⁰*dull* that I never once thought of men making their escape from a wreck thither, much less whence they might come.

Friday described the boat to me well enough; but brought me better to understand him when he added with some ¹¹*warmth*, "We save the white mans from drown." Then I presently asked if there were any "white mans," as he called them, in the boat. "Yes," he said; "the boat full of white mans." I asked him how many. He told me upon his ¹²*fingers*, seventeen. I asked him then what became of them. He told me, "They live, they ¹³*dwell* at my nation."

This put new thoughts into my head. I presently imagined that these might be the men belonging to the

我告知他我乘的船的損壞的情形，指示着他，竭力地指示着較近的地方，船所在的塲所。牠爲風雨波浪所擊碎而失去了。我指着他我們船的殘留，當我們逃走之時我們失去了船，當時用了我所有的力量我不能把牠推動，但是現在差不多成爲紛碎了。看見了這隻船，星期五立定默想了良久，一語不發。我問他他考察着什麼。最後他說，"我看這只船像到我的國度中去的一般"我好些時不明白他的話；但是最後，當我詳加考察牠以後，我由他而明白了有像這只船一樣的一艘，曾經去到他生活的地方海岸上；就是，如他所表明的一般，被狂風大浪驅到那裏去。我立卽猜想有些歐洲的船一定曾在他們的海濱上沈沒　船或者被放鬆着，衝到海岸上去；但是我是這樣的愚蠢，我永遠連一次都未曾想及那些人從那邊破船中逃走出來，對於他們或者從什麼地方來的尤未曾想及。

　　星期五向我竭力地描寫着那只船；但是使我更加明瞭他，當他更懇切地說，"我們救了白色人使他們不致於溺斃。我馬上問是否有些白色人，如他所說的一般，在船的裏面。是的，"他說；"船中滿載白色人。"我問他有多少人。他在手指上告訴我，十七人我問他，他們後來怎樣。他告訴我，"他們活着，他們住在我的國中。"

　　這個添進我腦中的新的思想。我立卽猜想這些或者是那些人，屬於那只沈沒在我的島中船上的人，現在我把島叫作我的島了；

ship that was [1]*cast away* in the sight of my island, as I
now called it; and who, after the ship was [2]*struck on* the
rock and they saw her [3]*inevitably lost*, had saved themselves
in their boat, and were landed upon that wild shore among
the savages. Upon this I [4]*inquired* of him more [5]*critically*
what was become of them. He [6]*assured* me they lived still
there; that they had been there about four years; that the
savages left them alone, and gave them [7]*victuals* to live on.
I asked him how it [8]*came to pass* they did not kill them and
eat them. He said, "No, they make brother with them";
that is, as I understood him a [9]*truce*. Then he added,
"They no eat mans but when make the war fight," that
is to say, they never eat any men but such as come to fight
with them and are taken in [10]*battle.*

It was after this some conisderable time that, being
upon the top of the [11]*hill,* at the east side of the island, from
whence, as I have said, I had, in a clear day, discovered
the main or [12]*continent* of America, Friday, the [13]*weather*
being very serene, looks very earnestly towards the mainland, and, in a kind of surprise, falls [14]*a-jumping* and
[15]*dancing,* and calls out to me, for I was at some distance
from him. I asked him what was the matter. "O
joy!" says he; "O glad! there see my country! there
my nation!"

I observed an [16]*extraordinary* sense of pleasure appeared
in his face, and his [17]*eyes sparkled,* and his [18]*countenance* discovered a strange [19]*eagerness,* as if he had a mind to be in
his own country again. This [20]*observation* of mine put a
great many thoughts into me, which made me, at first,
not so easy about my new man Friday as I was before;
and I made no doubt but that, if Friday could get back to

他們在船觸礁和被見難免沈沒以後，從船中逃了生命，在野人之中的荒野的海岸上登了岸。因此，我更加詳細地問他，他們後來怎麼樣。他向我確切地說他們仍舊住在那裏；他們在那裏大約四年了；野人們讓他們獨自活着，給他們供養生的糧食。我問他何故他們不把他們殺而食之。他說，"否，他們和他們作爲兄弟；"這就是，我明白了他，一種休戰之約。後來他又說，"他們不吃人除非在戰爭之時，"那就是說，他們永遠不吃人，除非和他交戰的以及在戰爭中被俘的人。

　在這事以後，幽了若干時，我在小山的頂上，在島的東邊，從那裏，我曾經說過，我曾，在一個天氣清新的日子中，發見了大洋或美洲的大陸，星期五，天氣是爽朗的，狠懇切地朝大地而望，在一種驚奇之中，忽然跳舞起來，叫喚着我，我那時在離開他較遠的地方。我問他爲着什麼事。"哦快樂！"他說；"哦，樂意！看見我的國度了！看見我的國家了！"

　我注意着在他的臉上現出了一種欣喜非常的樣子，他的目光閃爍，面露一種奮發殷勤之色，好像他是有心重行同國去一般。我的這個觀察使我有了許多的思想，那些思想使得我，起頭，對於我的新人星期五不如從前那樣安適了；我是無疑的，假使星期五能夠重行囘轉到他的國中去，他不但要忘却了所有他的宗教，而且還要忘却他對於我感謝之心，

his own nation again, he would not only forget all his ¹*religion* but all his ²*obligation* to me, and would be forward enough to give his countrymen an account of me, and come back, perhaps, with a hundred or two of them, and make a feast upon me, at which he might be as merry as he used to be with those of his enemies, when they were taken in war.

But I ³*wronged* the poor, honest creature very much, for which I was sorry afterwards. However, as my ⁴*jealousy* increased, and held some weeks, I was a little more ⁵*circumspect*, and not so familiar and kind to him as before. In this I was certainly wrong, too; the honest, ⁶*grateful* creature having no thought about it but what ⁷*consisted* with the best ⁸*principles*, both as a religious Christian, and as a grateful friend, as appeared afterwards to my full ⁹*satisfaction*.

While my jealousy of him lasted, you may be sure I was every day ¹⁰*pumping* him, to see if he would discover any of the new thoughts which I ¹¹*suspected* were in him; but I found everything he said was so honest and so innocent that I could find nothing ¹²*to nourish* my suspicion. In spite of all my ¹³*uneasiness*, he made me at last ¹⁴*entirely* his own again; nor did he in the least ¹⁵*perceive* that I was uneasy, and therefore I could not ¹⁶*suspect* him of ¹⁷*deceit*.

One day, walking up the same hill, but the weather being ¹⁸*hazy* at sea, so that we could not see the ¹⁹*continent*, I called to him, and said, "Friday, do not you wish yourself in your own country, your own nation?" "Yes," he said. "I be much O glad to be at my own nation," "What would you do there?" said I; "would you ²⁰*turn wild again*, eat men's flesh again, and be a savage, as you

或者將要很爽直地去把我的故事告訴他國人，重行和他們一二百人同來；把我作飲食品，他們吃我或者是同樣地快樂像他們習慣吃他們在戰爭之中所俘虜的敵人一樣。

但是我冤枉了這個可憐的，誠實的生物：後來我是很懊悔的。然而，我的猜忌之心加增起來，保留了幾個星期，我是稍加小心；不像以前一樣和他親密和待他寬厚了。對於這事我也是一定錯誤了；這個誠實的感恩的生物對於這事毫未想及，然而心懷好意，同時是一宗教的基督教徒，又是一個感恩的朋友，以後我發見他是這樣，我就非常滿意的。

當我的猜忌他的心未息之時，你可以一定知道我每天探問他，看看我能不能在他心中探詢出來我所猜疑的他的新思想；但是我覺他所說的話都是誠實和無知，以致於我找不出東西來供我猜疑。雖然我是一切地不安，他終究是使我再行信服他；他一點也未曾覺察我的不安之狀，所以我不能疑他有詐。

一天，走到同樣的那個小山上面，在海上天氣是矇矓的，我們於是看不見大陸，我叫他，說道，"星期五，你不希望你自己到你家鄉去，到你國中去?""是的，"他說。"我很樂意地去到我自己的國中。""你在那裏將要做些什麼?"我說；"你，將要再變野了，再吃人的肉，成為野人，像你從前一樣嗎?

1.宗敏。2.感謝之心。3.冤枉。4.妒忌。5.細心。6.感恩。7.相待。3.理。9.滿意。10.探問。11.猜疑。12.供，助。13.不安。14.完全。15.見。16.猜疑。17.詭詐。18.矇矓。19.大陸。20.再變野蠻。

were brfore?" He *looked full of concern,* and *shaking* his head, said, "No, no, Friday tell them to live good; tell them to *pray* God; tell them to eat corn bread, cattle flesh, milk; no eat man again." "Why, then," said I to him, "they will kill you," He looked *grave* at that, and then said, "No, no, they no kill me, they willing love learn." He meant by this, they would be willing to learn. He added, "They learn much of the *bearded mans* that come in the boat." Then I asked him if he would go back to them. He *smiled* at that, and told me that he could not *swim* so far. I told him I would make a canoe for him. He told me he would go if I would go with him. "I go!" says I; "why, they will eat me if I come there." "No, no," says he, "me make they no eat you; me make they much love you," He meant, he would tell them how I had killed his enemies, and saved his life, and so he would make them love me.

CHAPTER XXXVII

FROM this time, I *confess*, I had a mind to *venture over*, and see if I could possibly join with those *bearded* men, who, I made no *doubt*, were Spaniards and Portuguese; not doubting but, if I could, we might find some method to escape from thence, being upon a *continent*, and a good company together, better than I could from an island forty miles off the shore, alone, and without help. So, after some days, I took Friday to work again, by way of *discourse*, and told him I would give him a boat to go back to his own nation. Accordingly, I carried him to my *frigate*, which lay on the other side of the island, and

他正其顏色；搖着頭；說道，"不是；不是；星期五告訴他們要好好地生活；告訴他們要祈求上帝；告訴他們去吃穀麵包，牛羊肉，乳；再不要吃人肉。""那末，"我說，"他們將要把你殺掉。"他聽了這話面色極其莊重，後來說道，"不對，不對，他們不殺我，他們情願學習。"他說這話的意思，就是他們甘心學習。他又說道，"他們從乘船而來的那些多鬍子的人學了許多。"我於是問他，他是否要囘到他們那裏去。他聽了微笑，告訴我說他不能游泳得這樣遠。我告訴他我將爲他造一只木艇。他告訴我他情願去，假使我和他一淘去。"我去！"我說；"唉，他們將要吃我假使我去到那裏。""否，否，"他說，"我叫他們不要吃你；我使他們喜愛你。"他的意思就是，他將要告訴他們我怎樣殺了他的敵人們，救了他的性命，這樣他使他們喜愛我。

第 三 十 七 章

從這時以來，我自認，我有意冒險前往，看看我能不能去和那些多鬍的人聯合，他們，我是無疑的，是斯巴里耶達人葡萄牙人；也是無疑的，假使我能去，我們大家可以找出從那裏逃走的計劃來，是在一座大陸上，許多人在一處，比到我獨自一人，沒有救助之人，在離海岸四十英里遠的一座島上逃走起來當然更爲便利。這樣，過了幾天，我叫星期五重行工作，閒談之時，我告訴他我將給予他一只船囘到他的本國去。於是我把他領到我的三支桅的船那裏去，船躺在島的別一面，

having ¹*cleared* it of water (for I always kept it sunk in water), I brought it out, showed it him, and we both went into it. I found he was a most ²*dexterous* fellow at ³*managing* it and would make it go almost as ⁴*swift* again as I could. So when he was in, I said to him, "Well, now, Friday, shall we go to your nation?" He looked very ⁵*dull* at my saying so; which, it seems, was because he thought the boat was too small to go so far. I then told him I had a bigger; so the next day I went to the place where the first boat lay which I had made, but which I could not get into the water. He said that was big enough; but then, as I had taken no care of it, and it had ⁶*lain* two or three and twenty years there, the sun had ⁷*split* and dried it, and it was ⁸*rotten*. Friday told me such a boat would do very well, and would carry "much enough ⁹*vittle*, drink, bread;"— this was his way of talking.

Upon the whole, I was by this time so ¹⁰*fixed upon my* ¹¹*design* of going over with him to the ¹²*continent*, that I told him we would go and make one as big as that, and he should go home in it. He answered not one word, but looked very grave and sad. I asked him what was the matter with him. He asked me again, "Why you ¹³*angry* mad with Friday? what me done?" I asked him what he meant, and told him I was not angry with him at all. "No angry!" says he, ¹⁴*repeating* the words several times; "Why send Friday home away to my nation?" "Why," says I, "Friday, did not you say you wished you were there?" "Yes, yes," says he, "wish be both there; no wish Friday there, no master there." In a word, he would not think of going there without me. "I go there! Friday," says I, "what shall I do there?" He ¹⁵*turned*

474

把船的水清去了以後，（因爲我常常使牠沈在水內），我把牠拿出來，向他指示，我們兩人走到船內去。我覺着他對於行駛一道到是一個伶俐的人，他使船走差不多和我駕駛得一樣地敏捷。這樣當他走進船來，我和他說，"好，現在，星期五，我們將要到你的國中去嗎？"他聽了我的話面上現出不知所以的樣子；好像是因爲他想這只船是太小了，不能行駛過還，我於是告訴他我有一只較大的船，這樣第二天，我去到我第一次製造的那只船所在的地方，但是我却未曾能夠使牠下水呢。他說牠是狠大的了；但是，自從我未曾照顧牠以來，牠被棄置在那邊已經有二十二三年了，太陽把牠弄得破碎和乾枯了，牠是朽爛了。星期五告訴我這樣的船於事是狠有濟的，可以裝載許多食糧，飲料，麵包；"—— 這就是他說話的方法。

總之，這時我對於和他一同去到大陸的計劃是這樣的解決，我告訴他我們可以去製造和那只一樣大的一只船，他乘坐其中而回去。他一語不答，瞧起來是狠莊重而憂愁。我問他爲什麼這樣。他重行問我，"爲什麼你向星期五發大怒？我做了什麼事？"我問他他是什麼意思，告訴他我不向他發絲毫之怒。"不發怒！"他說，再三覆述這句話；"爲何這星期五囘家去？""唯，"我說，"星期五，你不曾說過你希望着到那裏去嗎？""是的，是的，"他說，"我希望兩人一淘到那裏去，不希望星期五一人到那裏去，主人却不在那裏。"總而言之，他不和我偕往是不願到那裏去的。"我去到那裏！星期五，"我說，"我在那裏做什麼？"

very quick upon me at this. "You do great deal much good," says he; "you teach wild mans be good, [1]*sober*, [2]*tame* mans; you tell them know God, pray God, and live new life." "Alas, Friday!" says I, "thou knowest not what thou sayest; I am but an [3]*ignorant* man myself." "Yes, yes," says he, "you [4]*teachee* me good, you [5]*teachee* them good." "No, no Friday," says I, "you shall go without me; leave me here to live by myself, as I did before." He looken [6]*confused* again at that word; and running to one of the [7]*hatchets* which he used to wear, he takes it up [8]*hastily*, and gives it to me. "What must I do with this?" says I to him. "You take kill Friday," says he. "What must I kill you for?" said I again. He returns very quick, "What you send Friday away for? Take kill Friday; no send Friday away." This he spoke so [9]*earnestly* that I saw tears stand in his eyes. In a word, I so [10]*plainly* discovered the utmost [11]*affection* in him to me, and a [12]*firm resolution* in him, that I told him then, and often after, that I would never send him away from me, if he was willing to stay with me.

[13]*Upon the whole*, as I found by all his discourse a [14]*settled affection* to me, and that nothing could part him from me, so I found all [15]*the foundation of his desire* to go to his own country was laid in his [16]*ardent* affection to the people, and his hopes of my doing them good; a thing which, as I had no [17]*notion* of myself, so I had not the lest thought, or [18]*intention*, or desire, of undertaking it. But still I found a strong [19]*inclination* to [20]*attempting* my escape, founded on the [21]*supposition*, gathered from the [22]*discourse*, that there were seventeen bearded men there. Therefore, without any more delay, I went to work with Friday to find out

他因這話急急地回答我。"你將要做許多的好事，"他說；"你教野人做好的，清醒的，馴服的人；你使他們知道上常，祈求上帝，度着新的生活。"，唉，星期五！"我說，"你不知道你說的是什麼話；我自已也不過是一個愚昧的人。""是的，是的，他說，"你教我好，你教他們好。""否，否，星期五，"我說，"你將不和我一淘去；讓我一人在這裏生活，如我以前一樣。'他瞧起來又茫然不知所措，聽了這話以後，跑到他常佩的一只小斧那裏去，狠忽促地把牠拿起來，把牠遞給了我。"我拿這斧做些什麼？"我向他說。"你殺了星期五罷，"他說。"我爲什麼要殺你？"我重行說。他很快地回答，"你爲什麼遣星期五去？殺了星期五罷；不要遣星期五去。"他這樣地誠懇說了這些話，我看見眼淚在他眼中流着。總之，我狠明顯地發見他心中對我的最深的感情，他心中的堅決的志向，我於是告訴，他後來常常這樣，我將永遠不遣他離我而去，假使他願意和我在一處。

總而言之，我從他的談話中發見他對我堅定的愛情，無物足以使他和我分別，這樣我覺着他所有想同國的欲望的根是由他的愛慕同種的熱心，和希望我爲他們做好事所致；這是一種我自已沒有觀念的事，所以我一點也沒有思想，傾向，或是願望去從事於牠。但是我仍舊覺着一種強力的傾向去試圖我的逃走，以推測之意爲基礎，從談話聚集而來，在那邊常十七個多髯的人。所以，不再延摭，我和星期五去工作，去尋出一株大樹，爲砍伐是合宜的，製造一只大獨木舟，或是木艇，以便從事旅行。

.1.清醒.2.養馴.3.愚昧.4.教.5.教.6.茫然.7.小斧.8.忽促.9.誠懇.10.顯明. 11.感情.12.堅決之心.13.總而言之心.14.堅定之愛情.15.其欲望之根原.19.熱心.17.觀念.18.意志.19.傾向.20.企圖.21.推測.22.談話.

a great tree proper to fell, and make a large ¹*periagua,* or canoe, to undertake the voyage. There were trees enough in the island to have ²*built a little fleet,* not of periaguas or canoes but even of good large ³*vessels.* But the main thing I looked at was to get one so near the water that we might ⁴*launch* it when it was made, ⁵*to avoid* the ⁶*mistake* I ⁷*committed* at first. At last Friday ⁸*pitched upon* a tree; for I found he knew much better than I what kind of wood was ⁹*fittest* for it. Nor can I tell, to this day, what wood to call the tree we cut down, except that it was very like the tree we call ¹⁰*fustic,* or between that and the ¹¹*Nicaragua wood,* for it was much of the same color and smell.

Friday wished to burn the hollow, or ¹²*cavity,* of this tree out, to make it for a boat, but I showed him how to cut it out with tools; which after I had showed him how to use, he did it very ¹³*handily.* In about a month's hard labor we finished it, and made it very ¹⁴*handsome;* ¹⁵*especially* when, with our ¹⁶*axes,* which I showed him how to ¹⁷*handle,* we cut and ¹⁸*hewed* the outside into the true ¹⁹*shape* of a boat. After this, however, it cost us near a ²⁰*fortnight's* time to get her along, as it were ²¹*inch by inch,* upon great ²²*rollers* into the water; but when she was in, she would have carried twenty men with great ease.

It amazed me to see with what ²³*dexterity* and how ²⁴*swift* my man Friday could manage her, turn her, and ²⁵*paddle* her along. So I asked him if he would, and if we might ²⁶*venture* over in her. "Yes," he said, "we ²⁷*venture* over in her very well, though great blow wind." However, I had a ²⁸*farther* ²⁹*design* that he knew nothing of, and that was to make a mast and a sail, and ³⁰*to fit* her with an

在島上有樹足夠造成小隊戰艦，不是獨木舟或是木艇，但是是很大的船只。我注意的主要的事是得着一只靠水的船；當我們把牠製好便可放牠下水，不致再犯前次的過失。最後星期五擇定了一株大樹；因爲我覺着他比我知道得多，那種木對造船最爲合宜。直至今日，我也不能明白我們砍下來的樹木究竟叫做什麼名字，除非很像是那種我們叫做產黃顏料之樹一般，或是在那種和蘇木之中，因爲顏色和氣味都相似。

星期五希望把洞或穴從樹上燒去，把牠造成一只船，但是我指示着他怎樣用器具來把牠砍下來；我後來向他表示怎樣去利用器具，他很輕巧地用牠。大約在一月的困苦的工作中我們把船造好，造得很美麗的；尤其是當着，用我們的斧子，我指示着他，怎樣去處置牠，我們割和砍樹的外面使牠成爲船的實在形式之時。此事做畢，牠費去我差不多兩星期的光陰去從事工作，像逐步地在大的轉木上面把牠擋下水去；但是當牠下了水之時，牠很容易地可載二十人。

我是吃驚地去看着用了何等的伶巧，何等的輕捷，我的人星期五能夠駕駛着牠，掉轉牠，把牠搖走。這樣我問他他是否情願和我們，是否可以在船中冒險前進。"是的，"他說，"我們很好的在船中冒險前進，雖然天上括大風。"然而，我另存他念，他却不能知道，就是去製造一根桅柱，一張帆，以及用錨和纜繩來配置牠。

1. 獨木舟。2. 造小艦隊。3. 船。4. 放入水。5. 避。6. 過失。7. 踏。8. 擇定。9. 最合宜。10. 產黃顏料之樹。11. 一種蘇木。12. 穴。13. 輕巧。14. 美好。15. 尤其是。16. 斧。17. 握。18. 研。19. 形式。20. 二星期。21. 逐步。22. 轉木。23. 伶巧。24. 敏捷。25. 搖走。26. 冒險。27. 冒險。28. 深邃。29. 計劃。30. 配置。

¹*anchor* and ²*cable*. As to a mast, that was easy enough to get ; so I pitched upon a ³*straight* young ⁴*cedar* tree, which I found near the place, and which there were great ⁵*plenty* of in the island, and I set Friday to work to cut it down and gave him ⁶*directions* how ⁷*to shape* and order it. But as to the sail, that was my ⁸*particular care*. I knew I had old sails, or rather pieces of old sails, enough ; but as I had had them now six and twenty years by me, and had not been very careful to preserve them, not imagining that I should ever have this kind of use for them, I did not doubt but they were all ⁹*rotten*. Indeed, most of them were so However, I found two pieces which appeared pretty good, and with these I went to work. With a great deal of pains, and ¹⁰*awkward* ¹¹*stitching*, you may be sure, for want of ¹²*needles*, I at length made a ¹³*three-cornered* ugly thing, like what we call in England a ¹⁴*shoulder-of-mutton sail*, to go with a ¹⁵*boom at bottom*, and a little short ¹⁶*sprit* at the top, such as usually our ships' ¹⁷*longboats* sail with, and such as I best knew how to manage, for it was such a one as I had to the boat in which I made my escape from Barbary, as related in the firit part of my story.

I was near two months ¹⁸*performing* this last work, namely, ¹⁹*rigging* and fitting my mast and sails ; for I finished them very complete, making a small ²⁰*stay*, and a sail or ²¹*foresail* to it, to assist if we should ²²*turn to windward*. Then, what was more than all, I fixed a ²³*rudder* to the stern of her to ²⁴*steer* with. I was but a ²⁵*bungling shipwright*, yet as I knew the ²⁶*usefulness*, and even the necessity, of such a thing, I ²⁷*applied* myseif with so much pains to do it that at last I ²⁸*brought it to pass* ; though, considering

至於檣柱，那是很容易得着的；這樣我擇定一株直而小的柏樹，我在近處找着牠的，在這島上有許多這樣種類的樹，我叫星期五去工作，把牠砍下來，示他方法怎樣去削成形式而處理牠。但是關於船帆一事，我却特別留心。我知道我舊的船帆，或是舊的船帆破壞，但是我有了牠們現在已經二十六年了，未曾好好地保留着牠們，未曾猜想着我將要把牠們作這種用場。我是一定無疑地牠們完全是朽爛了。實在，牠們之中有許多是這樣。然而，我找着兩塊，瞧起來頗好，用了這個我去工作。用了許多的勞力和拙劣的縫補，你可以確知，因爲缺乏針的原故，我最後却製造功一個三角醜陋的東西，像在英國我們叫做三角帆的一般，在牠的低下用一根帆檣上的橫木去行駛，在頂上有一較短的橫杠，好像常常地我們的船的長艄板用牠行駛的一樣，我很明白怎樣去駕駛牠，因爲牠像那只船，在其中我從巴巴利人手中逃走出來的，在故事的第一部份我已經敘述過了。

　　差不多有二月的工夫，我進行最後的工程，就是，裝備帆索和配置檣柱和帆；我很完美地把牠們造好，造了一根小檣纜，一張帆，一張船頭的三角帆，以作我們迎風而駛之助。尤要的，我置了一把舵在船的後面，以使行駛。我僅是一個拙劣的船匠，然而我知道這種東西的有用和需要，費了許多氣力我利用着自已去製造這個，後來我成了功；雖然，注意着我爲這個把許多的愚鈍的計謀都弄得失敗了，我想這事費了我差不多同樣的氣力和造船時所費的一般

1.錨.2.纜.3.直. 4.柏.5.許多.6.指揮.7.使成形式.8.特別留心.9.朽爛.10.拙劣.11.縫補.12.針. 13.三角.4.三角帆.15.在船低帆檣上橫木.16.篷上之橫杠.17.長艄板.17.進行.19.備帆索.20.檣纜.21.三角帆.22.迎風而駛.23.舵.24.行駛.25.拙劣之船匠.27.利用.28.成功.

the many dull ¹*contrivances* I had for it that ²*failed*, I think it cost me almost as much labor as making the boat.

After all this was done, I had my man Friday to teach as to what belonged to the ³*navigation* of my boat. Though he knew very well how to ⁴*paddle* a canoe, he knew nothing of what belonged to a sail and a rudder, and was the most amazed when he saw me work the boat to and again in the sea by the ⁵*rudder*, and how the sail ⁶*jibbed*, and filled this way or that way, as the course we sailed changed; I say, when he saw this, he stood like one astonished and amazed. However, whith a little use I made all these things familiar to him, and he became an ⁷*expert sailor*, except that of the ⁸*compass* I could make him understand very little. On the other hand, as there was very little cloudy weather, and ⁹*seldom* or never any fogs in those parts, there was the less occasion for a compass, seeing the ¹⁰*stars* were always to be seen by night, and the shore by day, except in the ¹¹*rainy* seasons, and then nobody cared to stir abroad either by land or sea.

I was now entered on the seven and twentieth year of my ¹²*captivity* in this place; though the last three years, that I had this creature with me, ought rather to be left out of the account, my ¹³*habitation* being quite of another kind than in all the rest of the time. I kept the ¹⁴*anniversary* of my landing here with the same thankfulness to God for his mercies as at first. And if I had such ¹⁵*cause of acknowledgment* at first, I had much more so now, having such additional ¹⁶*testimonies* of the care of ¹⁷*Providence* over me, and the great hopes I had of being ¹⁸*effectually* and ¹⁹*speedity* ²⁰*delivered*; for I had an ²¹*invincible* impression upon my thoughts that my ²³*deliverance* was ²³*at hand*, and that I should

這些事情一齊完畢以後，我去教我的人星期五駕駛船舶所必要的方法。雖然他很明白怎樣去搖行一只木艇，他不知道怎樣去處置帆和舵，他大大地吃驚，當他看見我去駕駛這船，用了舵把船駛入海中；帆是怎樣地轉移，或左或右，或前或後，照行駛之路程而改變；我說，當他看見這個，他立着好像一個驚怪詫愕的人一樣。用了幾次的教授，我把這些東西使他熟悉，他遂成爲一個老練的水手，除去羅盤以外，我不能使他十分明白牠。其外，多雲的天氣是不常常有的，罕有或永遠沒有霧在那些部份中，羅盤是無需的；夜間星辰常常可見，日間海岸可見，除去多雨的時期以外那時沒有人留心到外面去，或是在海岸上，或是在海中。

現在我在這個地方被拘留了二十七週年了；雖然最後三年，我有這個生物和我作伴，似應不必去記載了，我的住居的方法和其餘的時候完不同。我保守着登岸到這裏的紀念日，用了同樣的感謝上帝的恩惠的心，如從前一般。假使我有感謝的原因在起頭的時候，現在我却更加的有了，有了上天對我留意的增加的證據，以及我願有效力地和迅速地被救的大希望；因爲我的心意中有確切的感動，我的被救就在目前，我不會再在這個地方又住上一年了。我不停地去從事農務，掘地，植樹，圍籬等等，與前所做的無二。我聚集和晾曬葡萄，和從前一樣，進行各種需要之事。

not be another year in this place. I went on, however, with my [1]*husbandry*, [2]*digging*, planting, and [3]*fencing*, as usual. I gathered and cured my grapes, and did every necessary thing as before.

The [4]*rainy season* was in the mean time upon me, when I kept more within doors than at other times. We had [5]*stowed* our new vessel as [6]*secure* as we could, bringing her up into the [7]*creek*, where, as I said in the beginning, I landed my [8]*rafts* from the ship; and [9]*hauling* her up to the shore at high-water mark, I made my man Friday dig a little [10]*dock*, just big enough to [11]*hold* her, and just deep enough to gave her water enough [12]*to float in*. Then, when the [13]*tide* was out, we made a strong dam across the end of it, to keep the water out; and so she lay dry as to the tide from the sea. To [14]*keep the rain off* we laid a great many [15]*boughs* of trees, so thick that she was as well [16]*thatched* as a house; and thus we waited for the months of November and December, in which I [17]*designed* to make my adventure.

When the [18]*setiled season* began to come in, as the thought of my design returned with the [19]*fair weather*, I was preparing [20]*daily* for the voyage. And the first thing I did was [21]*to lay by* a certain quantity of [22]*provisions*, being the stores for our voyage; and I intended, in a week or a fortnight's time, to open the dock and [23]*launch* out our boat. I was busy one morning upon something of this kind, when I called to Friday, and bid him to go to the seashore, and see if he could find a [24]*turtle* or [25]*tortoise*, a thing which we generally got once a week, [26]*for the sake of* the eggs as well as the flesh. Friday had not been long gone when he came running back, and [27]*flew over* my outer wall, or fence, like one that felt not the ground, or the steps he sat his feet on:

當其時多雨的時期却來了，於是我守在家中比較任何時候都長久。我們把新造的船竭力地保藏安全，把牠帶到小溪中，在那裏，我起初曾經說過，我把筏從船中拿上岸去；把牠牽到岸上，在滿潮標上，我使我的人星期五去掘一座小船塢，其大正足以容放牠，其深正足以給牠夠量的水，以便浮於其上。當潮退時，我們築了一座壩，橫著船的末端，使水出外，這樣牠從海潮中乾燥地躺著。爲遮蔽風雨，我們放了許多樹枝，這樣繁密，牠好像房子被茅草蓋著一般；我們等候著十一月和十二月，在那時，我設計要從事冒險旅程。

當天氣晴朗之時來了，我的圖謀之念也隨著晴天而來，我每日頹備著旅行。我所做的第一種事，就是貯藏若干分量的糧食，作我們旅行的儲藏；我意欲，在一個星期或兩個星期之中，把船塢開啓，把船拿出。一天早晨，我是看他能不能找著一只鼈或龜，這是我們每星期能夠得著的東西，爲了蛋和肉的原故。星期五走了不多遠，忽然跑回來，跳過了我的外牆，或是籬笆，像一個人不覺著有地，或是不覺著他放脚步在地上行走一般：在我未曾有暇向他說話之前，他向我大叫起來，"哦，主人！哦，主人！哦，不好！哦，壞了！"

1.農務.2.掘.3.圍籬.4.多雨之季.5.貯藏.6.安全.7.小溪.8.筏.9.牽.10.塢.11.容收.12.浮於其上.13.潮.14.遮蔽風雨.15.枝.16.蓋茅.17.設計.18.天晴之時.19.晴天.20.每日.21.儲藏.22.食物.23.領出.24.鼈.25.龜.26.爲…之故.27.跳過.

and before I had time to speak to him, he cries out to me, "O master! O master! O sorrow! O bad!" "What's the matter, Friday?" says I. "O yonder, there," says he, "one, two, three canoe; one, two, three!" By this way of speaking, I [1]*concluded* there were six; but on [2]*inquiry* I found there were but three. "Well, Friday," says I, "do not be [3]*frightened.*" So I [4]*heartened* him up as well as I could.

However, I saw the poor fellow was most [5]*terribly* [6]*scared,* for nothing ran in his head but that they were come to look for him, and would cut him in pieces and eat him; and the poor fellow [7]*trembled* so that I [8]*scarcely* knew what to do with him. I comforted him as well as I could, and told him I was in as much danger as, he and that they would eat me as well as him. "But," says I, "Friday, we must [9]*resolve* to fight them. Can you fight, Friday?" "Me shoot," says he, "but there come many great number." "[10]*No matter* for that," said I, again; "our guns will frighten them that we do not kill." So I asked him whether, if I resolved to defend him, he would [11]*defend* me, and [12]*stand by* me, and do just as I bid him. He said, "Me die when yon bid die, master." So I made him take the two [13]*fowling* pieces, which we always carried, and loaded them with large [14]*swan shot,* as big as small [15]*pistol bullets.* Then I took four [16]*muskets,* and [17]*loaded* them with two [18]*slugs* and five small bullets each; and my two pistols I loaded with a brace of bullets each. I hung my great sword, as usual, naked by my side, and gave Friday his [19]*hatchet.*

When I had thus prepared myself, I took my [20]*perspective* glass, and went up to the side of the [21]*hill,* to see what

"什麼事，星期五？"我說哦，在那邊，那面，"他說，"一，二，三只木艇；一，二，三，"照這樣方法的說話，我決斷那裏是有六只木艇；但是詢問之下，我方知僅有三只○"好，星期五，"我說，"別害怕。"這樣我遂竭力地去壯他的胆量。

　　然而，我看見這個可憐的人是驚惶失措，因為在他的膶筋中沒有別的思想，只是以為他們是來找他的，要，把他切成塊而吃他；這個可憐的人抖戰起來，我竟不知道如何處置他。我竭力去安慰他，告訴他我是和他在同一危險之中，他們或者要吃我和吃他一樣。"但是，"我說，"星期五，我們必須決定和他們一戰。你能打嗎，星期五？""我射擊，"他說，"但是那邊來了許多人。""此何足道，"我說，重行說；'我們的槍將使他們驚嚇，我們可以不殺死他們。"我於是問他是否，假使我決心保護他，他能夠保護我，幫助我，做我吩咐他做的事。他說"我死當你吩咐我死，主人。"這樣，我叫他拿了二只打鳥槍，我們常常帶着那個，用寬的大彈去裝軸，其如大同小手槍內的子彈一般。我於是拿了四只槍，每只用兩粒斜形彈，五粒小彈子去裝上；我的兩只小手槍，每只裝有一對彈子。我掛我的大刀，照常一樣，出鞘掛在腰間，把小釜給了星期五。

　　當我這樣地預備好了以後，我拿了望遠鏡，跑到山側上

1．決斷．2．詢問．3．吃嚇．4．壯胆．5．異常．6．驚惶．7．抖．8．鮮．9．決心．10．無足重輕．11．保護．12．助．13．打鳥的．14．子彈．15．手槍．16．槍．17．裝載．18．斜形彈．19．小斧．20．望遠．21．小山．

I could discover. I found quickly by my glass that there were one and twenty savages, three [1]*prisoners*, and three canoes; and that their whole business seemed to be the [2]*triumphant* [3]*banquet* upon these three human bodies,—a [4]*barbarous feast*, inded! but nothing more than, as I had observed, was usual with them. I observed, also, that they had landed, not where they had done when Friday made his escape, but nearer to my [5]*creek*, where the shore was low, and where a thick wood came almost close down to the sea. This, with the [6]*abhorrence* of the [7]*inhuman* [8]*errand* these [9]*wretches* [10]*came about*, filled me with such [11]*indignation* that I came down again to Friday, and told him I was [12]*resolved* to go down to them, and kill them all; and asked him if he would stand by me. He had now got over his fright, and told me, as before, he would die when I bid die.

CHAPTER XXXVIII

In this fit of [13]*fury* I divided the arms, which I had charged as before, between us. I gave Friday one pistol to [14]*stick* in his [15]*girdle*, and three guns upon his shoulder. I took one pistol and the other three guns myself; and in this [16]*posture* we [17]*marched out*. I gave Friday a large bag with more powder and bullets; and as to orders, I [18]*charged* him to keep close behind me, and not to stir, or [19]*shoot*, or do anything till I bid him, and in the mean time not to speak a word. In this posture I made a [20]*circuit* to my right hand, of near a mile, as well to get over the creek as [21]*to get into* the wood, so that I could come within shoot of them before I should be [22]*discovered*, which I had seen by my glass it was easy to do.

去，看看我能發見什麼東西。用了望遠鏡，我馬上看見，十二一個野人，三個四麼，三隻木艇；他們所有的事看起來是拿那三個人的肉體來開一個慶賀勝利之宴，——一個殘暴的宴飲，實在是的！但是，照我曾述過的而言，他們對於這事是很覺尋常的。我也曾注意他們上了岸，不是在星期五逃走的那個地方，但是在較近我的小溪，在那裏，海岸是低的，在那邊，有一座深密樹林差不多舒展下去，和海相近。這個，加之那些壞坯做的令人可怖的殘忍不仁之事，使我滿腔憤怒，我重行跑下山去，到星期五那裏，告訴他我決心到他們那邊去，把他們斬盡殺絕；問他肯不肯幫助我。他現在不害怕了，告訴我像以前一樣，他情願死，當吩咐他死。

第 三 十 八 章

當此憤怒之際，我在我們之中，把前此頁載的兵器分派一下。我給星期五一隻手槍，插在帶上，三隻槍放他肩上。我自己拿了一隻手槍和其他三隻槍；在這種情勢之中，我們出發。我給星期五一大袋火藥和子彈；至於命令，我吩咐他緊隨我後而行，不要動，或射擊，或做別的事，須待我吩咐他方可，在這時不得發言。在這種情勢之中，我向右繞行一周，差不多有一英里，為着便於過小溪，入樹林，那末在我未被他們發見以前我能用彈丸來射擊他們，我用望遠鏡看了一看，知道這事是很容易做的。

I entered the wood, and, with all possible *¹wariness* and silence, Friday following close at my heels, I marched till I came to the *²skirt* of the wood on the side which was next to them, only that one corner of the wood lay between me and them. Here I called softly to Friday, and showing him a great tree which was just at the corner of the wood, I bade him go to the tree, and bring me word if he could see there *³plainly* what they were doing. He did so, and came *⁴immediately* back to me, and told me they might be plainly *⁵viewed* there; that they were all about their fire, eating the flesh of one of their prisoners, and that another *⁶lay bound upon the sand*, a little from them, whom he said they would kill next. This fired *⁷the very soul* within me. He told me it was not one of their nation, but one of the bearded men he had told me of, that came to their country in the boat. I was filled with horror at the very naming of the white, bearded man; and going to the tree, I saw plainly by my glass a white man, who lay upon the beach of the saa, with his hands and his feet tied with *⁸flags*, or things like *⁹rushes*, and that he was a European, and had clothes on.

There was another tree, and a little *¹⁰thicket* beyond it, about fifty yards nearer to them than the place where I was, which, by going a little way about, I saw I might come at *¹¹undiscovered*, and that then I should be within half a shot of them. So I *¹²withheld my passion*, though I was indeed *¹³enraged* to the highest degree; and going back about twenty *¹⁴paces*, I got behind some *¹⁵bushes*, which held all the way till I came to the other tree; and then I came to a little rising ground, which gave me a full view of them at the *¹⁶distance* of about eighty yards.

我進了樹林，用了極其小心和審靜的態度，星期五緊隨我的身後而行，我行走直至我來到林邊，在靠近他們的一邊不過樹林的一角躺在我和他們之中。在這裏，我輕輕地叫星期五，指示他一座大樹，我正在樹林的角上，我吩咐他上樹去，向我傳話他能不能明顯地看見他們在那邊做什麼。他照樣做，立即囘到我面前來，告訴我在那邊他們將很清楚被我們看見；他們圍繞着火，吃着一個囚虜的肉，還有一個被縛着，睡在沙上，離他們稍遠，他說他們第二次便要殺他。這個報告大激我怒。他告訴我說這不是他們一國的人，是他上次告訴過我乘船來到他國的多鬚人的一種人。一聞說及白色人，多鬚的人，我便恐怖起來；跑上樹去，我用望遠鏡明顯地看見一個白色人，他躺在海濱上，手足被旗幟，或被像蘆葦一般的東西綑着，他是歐洲人，身上穿着衣服。

又有一株樹，和一座小森林在這個以外，大約比現在我所在的地方較靠近他們五十碼，走了幾步，我明白我可以去不被他們發見，那末我將要能夠在射擊他們的一個彈丸之牛當中，這樣我抑制我的情感，雖然我是怒不可遏；囘來了大約二十步，我走到叢林後面，那叢樹沿路生着，直到我來到別的一株樹為止；於是我來到了一座聳高的地上，牠使我得以暢觀他們在大約在八十碼距離的地方。

1.小心. 2.邊. 3.顯明.4.立即.5.見. 6.被縛而臥於沙上. 7.心靈.8.旗. 9.蘆葦. 10.森林. 11.不為所見.12抑制我的情感. 13.怒. 14.步.15.叢樹.16.距離.

I had now not a ¹*moment* to lose, for nineteen of the dreadful ²*wretches* sat upon the ground, all close ³*huddled* together, and had just sent the other two to ⁴*butcher* the poor Christian, and bring him, perhaps ⁵*limb, by limb*, to their fire, and they were ⁶*stooping* down to ⁷*untie the bands* at his feet. I turned to Friday. "Now, Friday," said I, "do as I bid thee." Friday said he would. "Then, Friday," says I, " do exac.ly as you see me do; ⁸*fail in nothing*" So I set down one of the ⁹*muskets* and the fowling piece upon the ground, and Friday did the like by his, and with the other musket I took my aim at the savages, bidding him to do the like. Then, asking him if he was ready, he said, "Yes." "Then fire at them, said I; and at the same moment I fired also.

Friday took his aim so much better than I that on the side that he shot he killed two of them, and ¹⁰*wounded* three more; and on my side I killed one, and wounded two. They were, you may by sure, in a dreadful ¹¹*consternation*; and all of them that were not hurt jumped upon their feet, but did not immediately know which way to run, or which way to look, for they knew not from whence their destruction came. Friday kept his eyes close upon me, that, as I had bid him, he might ¹²*observe* what I did. As soon as the first shot was made, I threw down the piece, and took up the ¹³*fowling* piece, and Friday did the like. He saw me ¹⁴*cock* and ¹⁵*present*; he did the same again. "Are you ready Friday? " said I. " Yes, " says he. " ¹⁶*Let fly*, then," says I,"in the name of Cod!" and with that I fired again among the amazed ¹⁷*wretches*, and so did Friday. As our pieces were now ¹⁸*loaded* with what I call swan shot, or small pistol bullets, we found only two drop; but so many

當此時際,不容稍懈,因爲十九個可怖的壞坯于坐在地上,擠作一團,剛剛遣另外二人去殺那個可憐的基督敎徒,把他帶到,大槪是一肢一肢的,火旁,他們正屈身來解他足上的縛。我轉向星期五。"現在,星期五,"我說,"做我吩咐你做的事。"星期五說他遵命而行。"那末,星期五,"我說,"確實地做,看我所做的事;不可失事。"這樣我把一枝槍和打鳥槍放在地上,星期五把他的槍依樣爲之,拿着別的一枝槍,我向野人們描準,吩咐他依樣而行。於是,我問他預備好了沒有,他說,"好了。""那末射擊他們罷,"我說,同時我也放射。

星期五描準標的比我還要好些,在他放槍的那一邊,他殺死了二人,傷了三人;在我的一邊,我殺死一人,傷二人。他們是,你可以確知,嚇得魂不附體;沒有受傷的人一齊跳將起來,但是他們不能馬上知道向那條路逃跑,向那條路張望,因爲他們不明白殺傷他們同伴的東西究從那裏來的。星期五向我注目而視,像我吩咐他一樣,他可以注視我的行動。一經第一排槍放過以後,我把槍擲下來,拿起打鳥槍,星期五也這樣做。他看見我睨目斜視和對準;他又照樣從事。"你預備好了嗎,星期五?"我說。"好了"他說。"放罷,"我說,"惟上帝是賴!"說完後,我在那些驚惶的壞坯于當中又放了槍,星期五也照樣而行。我們的槍現在是裝載了我叫做的大彈,或是小手槍內彈丸,我們僅看見二人跌仆下來;但是許多受了傷,他們跑着,喊叫起來像癲的生物一般,都出血了,他們之中有許多是重傷了;又有三人後來立卽跌仆下來,雖然未曾完全死去。

were wounded that they ran about [1]*yelling* and [2]*scraming* like mad creatures, all [3]*bloody,* and most of them [4]*miserably wounded* ; whereof three more fell quickly after, though not [5]*quite dead.*

"Now, Friday," says I, laying down the [6]*discharged pieces,* and taking up the [7]*musket* which was yet loaded, "follow me, " which he did with a great deal of courage ; upon which I [8]*rushed out* of the wood and showed myself, and Friday [9]*close at my foot.* As soon as I perceived they saw me, I [10]*shouted* as loud as I could, and bade Friday do so too, and running as fast as I could,—which, by the way, was not very fast' being [11]*loaded with* arms as I was,— I made directly towards the poor [12]*victim,* who was, as I said, lying upon the beach or shore, between the place where they sat and the sea. The two [13]*butchers* who were just going to work with him had left him at the surprise of our first fire, and fled in a [14]*terrible* fright to the seaside, and had [15]*jumped into* a canoe, and three more of the rest made the same way. I turned to Friday, and [16]*bade* him [17]*step forward* and fire at them. He understood me immediately, and running abort forty yards, to be nearer them, he shot at them. I thought he had killed them all, for I saw them all fall of [18]*a leap* into the boat, though I saw two of them up again quickly. However, he killed two of them, and wounded the third, so that he lay down in the bottom of the boat as if he had been dead.

While my man Friday fired at them, I [19]*pulled out* my knife and cut the [20]*flags* that bound the poor victim ; and [21]*loosing* his hands and feet, I lifted him up, and asked him in the [22]*Portuguese tongue* what he was. He answered in Latin, " [23]*Christianus,* " but was so [24]*weak and faint* that he

　　"現在，星期五，"我說，把放過了的槍放下來，把已經裝置好了的槍拿起來，"隨我來，"他用了狠多勇氣來做這事；因此我衝出林中，現出身來，星期五緊隨予後。一經我看見他們瞧見了我，我竭力地大叫起來，吩咐星期五也這樣做，我竭力地跑，——那是，聞說起來，不狠快的，因爲我身上載有兵器，——我直向那個被害人的方面前進，他是，我曾說過，躺在海灣上或海岸上，在他們所坐的地方和海的中央。那正要來動他手的兩個屠夫因爲聽見我們第一次所發射的槍，驚駭而離開他了，狠發慌地跑到海側去。跳入一只木艇，其餘的三人也這樣行事。我轉向星期五，吩咐他向前行去，射擊他們。他立即明白了我，跑了大約四十碼，靠近些他們，他途射擊他們。我想把他們殺完了，因爲我看見他們在船中跌作一團，雖然我看見他們之中有二人馬上又立起來。他畢竟殺了二人，傷了第三人，以致使他躺到船的底下去，好像死去一般。

　　當我的人星期五射擊他們之時，我曳出刀來；割掉縛著那個可憐的被難的人的旗子；鬆開手足之縛，我舉他起來，用了葡萄牙言語來問他是什麼人。他用臟丁話來囘答說，"我是基督教徒，"但是他這樣的偹乏，

1．喊．2、叫．3．出血．4．不幸的．5．完全死去．6．已放過之槍．7．槍．8．衝出．9．緊跟我後．10．叫．11．裝載．12．被害人．13．屠夫．14．可怖．15．跳入．16．吩咐．17．走向前去．18．一堆．19．曳出．20．旗．21．鬆開．22．葡萄牙語．23．基督教徒．24．疲乏．

could ¹*scarce* stand or speak. Then I asked him what countryman he was, and he said "²*Espagniole*"; and being a little recovered, he let me know, by all the signs he could possibly make, how much he was in my ³*debt* for his ⁴*deliverance*. "⁵*Seignior*," said I, with as much Spanish as I could make up, "we will talk ⁶*afterwards*, but we must fight now. If you have any strength left, take this ptisol and sword, and lay about you." He took them very thankfully; and no sooner had he the arms in his hands, but, as if they had put new vigor into him, he flew upon his ⁷*murderers* like a fury, and had cut two of them in pieces in an instant. The truth is, as the whole was a surprise to them, so the poor ⁸*creatures* were so much ⁹*frightened* with the noise of our pieces that they fell down for mere ¹⁰*amazement* and fear, and had no more power to ¹¹*attempt* their own escape than their flesh had to ¹²*resist* our shot. That was the case of those five that Friday shot at in the boat; for as three of them fell with the ¹³*hurt* they ¹⁴*received*, so the other two fell with the fright.

I kept my piece in my hand still without firing, being willing to keep my charge ready, because I had given the ¹⁵*Spaniard* my pistol and sword. So I called to Friday, and bade him run up to the tree from whence we first fired. and ¹⁶*fetch* the arms which lay there that had been ¹⁷*discharged*, which he did with great ¹⁸*swiftness*. Then giving him my ¹⁹*musket*, I sat down myself to load all the rest again, and bade them come to me when they wanted. While I was loading these pieces, there happened a ²⁰*fierce engagement* between the Spaniard and one of the savages, who ²¹*made at* him with one of their great wooden swords, the weapon that was to have killed him before, if I had

以致他竟不能立起來或說話。我於是問他是那一國的人，他說，"我是西班牙；"因為稍稍復原，他使我知道，用他所能做的種種手式，他得有我的救助，實在感激得了不得。"先生；"我說，竭力地用我能說的西班牙話來說，"以後我們再談罷，現在我們必須戰鬥。假使你有餘力，把這個手槍和刀拿了，你就亂打罷。"他很感謝地拿了牠們；一經武器在手，好像牠們給了他新的膂力一般，他就憤激起來，攻擊他的屠夫，頃刻之間，便把他們殺死了二人，砍成數塊。眞理是這樣，這些事對於他們是出其不意的，所以那些可憐的生物聽了我們的槍聲是這樣地害怕，以致他們僅因驚恐而倒下地去，再沒有能力去試圖逃走，好像他們的肉沒有能力來抵抗彈丸一般。那就是星期五射擊在船中的那五個人的情形；因為三人因受傷倒下，其餘二人因恐懼而傾跌。

　我仍把槍拿在手上未曾放射，我願把子彈預備好，因為我把手槍和刀都給了西班牙人了。我於是叫星期五，吩咐他跑上樹去，從我們初次放槍的那個地方去，把在那裏的放過了的槍拿來，他很敏捷地做了這事。我於是把槍遞給他，假使他們要用。當我把槍裝上子彈之時，在西班牙和野人中的一人之中，却有一場劇戰，野人用他的大木刀來攻打他，就是以前預備用來殺他的武器，假使我未曾阻止這事。

1.鮮能. 2.西班牙人.
3.債. 4.拯救. 5.先
生. 6.以後. 7.兇手.
8. 人物. 9.使吃驚.
10.吃驚. 1.企圖. 12.
抵抗. 13.傷害. 14.
遭. 15.西班牙人. 16.
拿來. 17.放射. 18.輕
捷. 19.槍. 20.劇戰. 2
1.攻打.

not [1]*prevented* it.　The Spaniard, who was as bold and brave as could be imagined, though weak, had [2]*fought* the Indian a good while, and had cut two great wounds on his head.　But the savage, being a [3]*stout* [4]*lusty* fellow, closing in with him, had thrown him down, being faint, and was [5]*wringing* my sword out of his hand; when the Spaniard, though undermost, wisely [6]*quitting* the sword, drew the pistol from his [7]*girdle*, shot the savage through the body, and killed him [8]*upon the spot,* before I, who was running to help him, could come near him

Friday, being now left to his [9]*liberty*, pursued the [10]*flying* [11]*wretches,* with no weapon in his hand but his hatchet. With that he [12]*dispatched* those three who, as I said before, were wounded at first, and fallen, and all the rest he could [13]*come up with.* The Spaniard coming to me for a gun, I gave him one of the fowling pieces, with which he [14]*pursued* two of the savages, and wounded them both.　But, as he was not able to run, they both got from him into the wood, where Friday [15]*pursued* them, and killed one of them; but the other was too [16]*nimble* for him, and though he was wounded, yet had [17]*plunged* himself into the sea, and [18]*swam* with all his might off to those two who were left in the canoe; which three in the canoe, with one wounded, were all that escaped our hands out of one and twenty.

Those that were in the [19]*canoe* worked hard to get out of [20]*gunshot,* and though Friday made two or three shots at them, I did not find that he [21]*hit* any of them.　Friday would [22]*fain* have had me take one of their canoes, and [23]*pursue* them; and, indeed, I was very [24]*anxious* about their [25]*escape,* lest carrying the news home to their people, they should came back perhaps with two or three hundred of

西班牙人，他的勇毅之態是可想而知的，雖然疲弱，和印第安人打了許久，在他頭上割了兩道大傷痕。但是那個野人，他是肥壯而力強，靠近了他，把他打翻，暈了過去。從他的手中把我的刀強奪過去；西班牙人雖然在下面，狠聰明地把刀捨棄了，從帶上拿出手鎗來把野人身上打穿了，當場把他殺死，在我，我是跑去幫助他的，未曾來到貼近他身之處以前。

星期五，現在是由他自由了，追逐那些逃走的壞坯子，除小斧外手中別無武器。用了那個，他殺了三人，他們，我曾經說過，起先是受了傷，跌下去，其餘的他能追及之。西班牙人到我面前來討一只鎗，我給他打鳥鎗一只，用了那個，他去追逐兩野人，把他們全打傷了。但是，既然他是不能夠跑，他們兩人從他身邊跑到樹林中去，在那裏，星期五去追逐他們。殺了一人；但是另一人是比他敏捷，雖然受了傷，然而還能跳入海中，用了平生之力去游泳，汨到留在木艇中的兩個野人那裏去；於是三人在木艇之中，一人受了傷，這就是在二十一人之中能從我們手中逃走的所有的人。

在木艇中的人奮力逃出鎗彈所及**之處**，雖然星期五射擊他們二三彈，我不能覺着他放中了任何人。星期五極欲我把他們的一只木艇取來，追隨他們；實在，我深以他們逃走為慮，恐怕他們帶信息回家去，告訴他們的人，他們或將重來，或者將帶來二三百木艇；僅賴人多一端，便可將我們吞噬。

1.阻止。2.攻打。3.肥壯。4.強有力。5.強取。6.捨却。7.帶。8.當場。9.自由。10.逃過。11.壞坏。12.殺。13.追及。14.追隨。15.追隨。16.敏捷。17.浸入。18.游泳。19.木艇。20.彈丸。21.擊中。22.願。23.追隨。24.掛慮。25.逃走。

the canoes, and *devour* us *by mere multitude*.　So I consented to pursue them by sea, and running to one of their canoes, I *jumped* in, and bade Friday follow me.　But when I was in the canoe, I was surprised to find another poor creature lie there, bound hand and foot, as the Spaniard was, for the *slaughter*, and almost dead with fear, not knowing what was the matter; for he had not been able to look up over the side of the boat, he was *tied* so hard neck and *heels*, and had been tied so long that he had really but little life in him

I immediately cut the *twisted* flags or *rushes*, which they had bound him with, and would have helped him up; but he could not stand or speak, but *groaned* most *piteously*, believing, it seems, still, that he was only *unbound* in order to be killed.　When Friday came to him, I bade him sperk to him, and tell him of his *deliverance*; and the news of his being delivered *revived him*, and he sat up in the boat.　But when Friday came to hear him speak, and look in his face, it would have *moved any one to tears* to see how Friday *kissed* him, *embraced* him, *hugged* him, cried, laughed, *halloed*, jumped about, danced, sang; then cried again, *wrung* his hands, beat his own face and head, and then sang and jumped about again like a *distracted* creature.　It was a good while before I could make him speak to me, or tell me what was the matter; but when he *came* a little to himself, he told me that it was his father.

It is not easy for me to *express* how it moved me to see what *ecstasy* and *filial affection* had worked in this poor savage at the sight of his father, and of his being delivered from death.　Nor, indeed, can I *describe* half the *extravagances* of his *affection* after this; for he went into the boat,

這樣我允許在海上去追逐他們，跑到他們的一只木艇旁邊，我跳進去，吩咐星期五跟着我。但是當我在木艇中之時，我是很驚異地找着了另外一個可憐的生物躺在那裏，手足被縛，好像那西班牙人一般，因為殺人者，幾因恐怖而死，不知如何措手；因為他不能向船的那邊望過去，他是自頂至踵悉被綑綁，縛得這樣地長久，僅有一息存在。

我立刻割斷扭曲的旗或蘆葦；他們用這個來縛住他，要扶他起來；但是他不能立起或說話，僅僅呻吟歎息，使人可憫，他仍相信，瞧起來是這樣，他是被解開來以便被殺的。當星期五來到他前，我吩咐他向他說話，告訴他他被救了；他的被救的消息使他復蘇，他在船上坐起來。但是由星期五走進聽他說話，和望他的臉之時，這實在要令人淚下，看着星期五怎樣地去吻他，摟他，抱他：叫，笑，吼，跳起來，打他自己的臉和頭，後來唱起來像一個顛癡的生物一般。歇了許久，我方能使他和我說話，告訴我這是做什麼；但是當他略為甦醒之時，他告訴我那個人是他的父親。

這對於我是狠不容易去表示我是怎樣地驚訝看這個可憐的野人在他見父親從死中被救活之時是如何歡欣和孝心發見。實在，我也不能夠描寫出他見了父親以後所表示過度的愛情一半來；因為他走進船去，又走出船來，好多次數。

1.吃.2.賴其人多.3.跳入.4.殺人者.5.縛.6.踵.7.扭曲的.8.蘆葦.9.歎息.10.憫然.11.解縛.12.援助.13.使復蘇.14.令人下淚.15.吻.16.抱.17.抱住.18.叫.19.扭.20.顛狂.21.甦.22.表明.23.欣喜.24.孝心.25.描述.26.過度.27.愛情.

and out of the boat, a great many times. When he went in to him, he would sit down by him, open his [1]*breast*, and hold his father's head close to his [2]*bosom* for many minutes together, to [3]*nourish* it. Then he took his arms and [4]*ankles*, which were [e]*numbed* and [5]*stiff* with the [7]*binding*, and [8]*chafed* and [9]*rubbed* them with his hands.

This affair put an end to our [10]*pursuit* of the canoe with the other savages, who were now almost out of sight. It was happy for us that we did not, for it blew so hard within two hours after, and before they could be got a [11]*quarter* of their way, and [12]*continued* [13]*blowing* so hard all night, and that from the northwest, which was against them that I could not suppose their boat could live, or that they ever reached their own [14]*coast*.

CHAPTER XXXIX

BUT to return to Friday. He was so [15]*busy* about his father that I could not find in my heart to take him off for some time. But after I thought he could leave him a little, I called him to me, and he came [16]*jumping* and [17]*laughing*, and pleased to the highest [18]*extreme*. Then I asked him if he had given his father any bread. He shook his head, and said, "None; [19]*ugly* dog eat all up self." I then gave him a cake of bread out of a little [20]*pouch* I carried [21]*on purpose*. I had in my pocket two or three [22]*bunches* of raisins, so I gave him a handful of them for his father.

We had no sooner given his father these raisins, but I saw him come out of the boat, and run away as if he had been [23]*bewitched*, for he was the [24]*swiftest* fellow on his feet that ever I saw. I say, he ran at such a [25]*rate* that he was

當他進船到他面前之時，他就坐下來在他的旁邊：把他的胸打開，把他父親的頭貼緊在他的胸前，過了許多分鐘，去撫慰牠。後來他拿了他的膀臂和脚踝，都因受束縛之故而廠木僵硬了，他用他的手去摩擦着牠們。

這個事情把我們要乘木艇去追逐那些野人的舉動攪得終止了，他們差不多走得不可見了。這對於我們是有幸的我們未曾做這事，因爲後來在兩小時之內，風括得非常厲害，在他們能走了四分之一的路以前，整夜繼續着括大風，從西北方吹來，向他們吹着，我不能猜想他們的船能夠脫免於難，或者他們能到他們自已的海岸。

第 三 十 九 章

但是再說到星期五。他爲他的父親是這樣地忙碌，在我的心中，我不能找出些方法來把他帶走若干時候。但是在我想他能離開他一些時候之時，我把他叫到我的面前來，他跳笑而來，快樂達於極點。我問他曾否給些麵包與他父親。他搖頭，說道，"沒有；醜陋的狗全把牠吃完了。"我於是在我有意帶出來的小袋之中取出一塊麵餅遞給他。在我口袋內，我有兩三束葡萄乾，這樣我給他一把叫他給父親。

我們一經把這些葡萄乾給了他的父親，我就看見他從船中出來，跑去了好像他是被迷地一般，因爲他是我曾見過步伐最輕捷的人。我的意思是說，他跑得這樣地速，

[1]*out of sight*, as it were, in an [2]*instant* ; and though I called, and [3]*hollowed out*, too, after him, it was all one,—away he went. In a quarter of an hour I saw him come back again, though not so fast as he went, and, as he came nearer, I found his [4]*pace* was [5]*slacker* because he had something in his hand. When he came up to me, I found he had been quite home for an [6]*earthen jug or pot,* to bring his father some [7]*fresh water*, and that he had got two more [8]*cakes*, or loaves of bread. The bread he gave me, but the water he carried to his father. However, as I was very [9]*thirsty* too, I took a little of it.

When his father had [10]*drunk*, I called to him to know if there was any water left. He said "Yes; and I bade him give it to the poor Spaniard, who was in as much want of it as his father ; and I sent one of the cakes that Friday [11]*brought*, to the Spaniard, too, who was indeed very weak, and was [12]*reposing* himself upon a green place under the [13]*shade* of a tree ; and whose limbs were also very [14]*stiff*, and very much [15]*swelled* with the [16]*rude bandage* he had been tied with. When I saw that upon Friday's coming to him with the water he sat up and drank, and took the [17]*bread* and began to eat, I went to him and gave him a handful of raisins He looked up in my face with all the tokens of [18]*gratitude* and [19]*thankfulness* that could appear in any [20]*countenance* ; but was so weak, notwithstanding he had so [21]*exerted* himself in the fight, that he [22]*could not stand up upon his feet.* He tried to do it two or three times, but was really not able, his [23]*ankles* were so [24]*swelled* and so painful to him ; so I bade him sit still, and [25]*caused* Friday to [26]*rub* his ankles, as he had done his father's.

片刻之間，就看不見他了；雖然我叫，大叫，在他後面，他也置諸不答，——他去了。在一刻鐘以內，我見他重行回來了，雖然不及去時走得快，然而當他走近之時，我覺着他行得稍緩，因為他的手上拿着些東西。當他來到我前，我知道他已經回了家又重行回來了，因為去拿一個泥罐，帶些清水來給他父親喝，他又拿了兩塊餅，或是麵包塊。他把麵包給我，但是把水給他的父親。然而，我也是很渴的，我也就吃了一些。

當他的父親喝了水，我叫他看看還沒有餘下的水。他說，"有的；"我吩咐他給些水與那西班牙人，他急需着水好像他的父親一般；我把星期五帶給我的麵餅的塊也給了西班牙人，他實在是很疲弱的，休息他自己在樹蔭之下，在青綠草地上面；他的肢體是很彊硬的，因為受粗帶束縛之故而腫脹了。當我看見星期五把水帶到他面前，他坐起來喝着，拿了麵餅就吃，我走到他面前，給他一把葡萄乾。他用了種種感謝的表示朝我臉上望，感激之情現於容色；但是他是這樣的疲弱，雖然他曾因戰鬥而用力過度以致困乏，他竟不能起立。他試着兩三次，但是實在不能，他的腳踝脹起，對於他很痛苦；這樣我囑咐他靜坐勿動，命星期五去摩擦他的腳踝，

I observed the poor, [1]*affectionate creature*, every two minutes, or perhaps less, all the while he was here, turn his head about, to see if his father was in the same place and [2]*posture* as he left him sitting. At last he found he was not to be seen; at which he [3]*started up*, and, without speaking a word, flew with that swiftness to him that one could [4]*scarce* perceive his feet to [5]*touch* the ground as he went. But when he came, he only found he had laid himself down [6]*to ease his limbs*, so Friday came back to me presently. Then I spoke to the Spaniard to let Friday help him up, if he could, and lead him to the boat, and then he should carry him to our [7]*dwelling*, where I would take care of him. But Friday, [8]*a lusty*, strong fellow, took the Spaniard upon his back, and carried him away to the boat, and set him down softly upon the side or [9]*gunnel* of the canoe, with his feet in the [10]*inside* of it; and then lifting him quite in, he set him close to his father. Presently stepping out again, he [11]*launched* the boat off, and [12]*paddled* it along the shore faster than I could walk, though the wind [13]*blew* pretty hard, too. So he brought them both safe into our [14]*creek*, and leaving them in the boat, ran away to fetch the other canoe. As he passed me I spoke to him, and asked him whither he went, He told me, "Go fetch more boat." So away he went like the wind, for sure never man or horse ran like him; and he had the other canoe in the creek almost as soon as I got to it by land. He [15]*wafted* me over, and then went to help our new [16]*guests* out of the boat, which he did. But they were neither of them able to walk; so that poor Friday knew not what to do.

[17]*To remedy* this, I went to work in my thought, and calling to Friday to bid them sit down on the bank while he

我注意這個可憐的生物，每隔兩分鐘，或較此爲少，他在這裏的時候，掉過他我頭去，看看他的父是否和他離開坐着之時是在同樣的地位和狀況之中。最後，他覺着他不爲他所見了；他忽然跳起來，一言不發，用了這樣輕捷步伐跑到他面前去，人們鮮能看見他走時脚是否觸着地。但是當他到了那裏，他僅僅看見他父親躺下身來舒伸手足的筋骨，於是星期五馬上回到我處。我就向西班牙人說讓星期五幫助他起來，假使他能，領他到船上，他把他帶到我們住所中去，在那裏，我可以照應他。但是星期五，是個康健強壯的人，把西班牙人放在背上，把他帶到船上，輕輕地把他放下來，放他在木艇的沿側，他的脚是放在艇的內部；把他舉起來放入艇中，他把他放在貼近他的父親身邊。馬上重行走出，他將艇駛行着沿着岸搖牠，比我走得還要快，雖然風括得很大。這樣他把二人狠安全地帶到小溪中，在船中離開了他們，跑去拿別一只木艇。他走過我身傍，我向他說話，問他到何處去。他告訴我，"去再拿一只木艇來。"他於是像風一般跑去了，這是一定的人或馬永遠不能夠跑得和他一樣；他把別一只木艇拿到了小溪中，差不多貼正我陸行而至彼處。他泛舟渡過我，後來去幫我們新客人們從船中出來，他做了這事。但是二人都不能走；這樣星期五不知如何措手。

爲補救之計，我腦中想着，叫星期五來，吩咐他們坐在岸邊，

came to me, I soon made a kind of ¹*handbarrow* to lay them on, and Friday and I carried them both up together upon it between us. But when we got them to the outside of our wall, or fortification, we ²*were at a worse loss* than before, for it was impossible to get them over, and I was resolved not to break it down. So I set to work again, end Friday and I, in about two hours' time, made a very ³*handsome* tent, covered with old ⁴*sails*, and above that with ⁵*boughs* of trees, being in the space without our outward fence, and between that and the ⁶*grove* of young wood which I had planted. Here we made them two beds of such things as I had; namely, of good rice ⁷*straw*, with ⁸*blankets* laid upon it to lie on, and another to cover them, on each bed.

My island was now ⁹*peopled*, and I thought myself ¹⁰*very rich in subjects*. It was a merry ¹¹*reflection*, which I frequently made, how like a king I looked. First of all, the whole country was my own property, so that I had an ¹²*undoubted* right of ¹³*dominion*. Secondly, my people were perfectly ¹⁴*subjected*. I was ¹⁵*absolutely lord* and ¹⁶*lawgiver*. They all owed their lives to me, and were ready to lay down thir lives, if there had been occasion for it, for me. It was ¹⁷*remarkable*, too, I had but three subjects, and they were of three different ¹⁸*religions*. My man Friday was a ¹⁹*Protestant*, his father was a Pagan and a ²⁰*cannibal*, and the Spaniard was a ²¹*Roman Catholic*. However, I ²²*allowed liberty of conscience* throughout my dominions. But this is by the way.

As soon as I had secured my two weak, ²³*rescued prisoners*, and given them shelter and a place to rest them upon, I began to think of making some ²⁴*provision* for them. The first thing I did, I ordered Friday to take a ²⁵*yearling*

當他來到我面前之時，我立卽造了一種手車，把他們放進去，星期五和我把們兩人一淘帶上車去，在我們之中。但是當我們把他們帶到我們的牆外之時，我們較前更茫然不知所措了，因爲這是不可能的把他們帶過牆去，我也不決心去把牆打碎。這樣我又進行工作，星期五和我，在大約兩小時之中，做成了一座很美好的帳幕，用舊船帆蓋着，在帆上面有樹枝，是造在我們外籬外面的地方，在離和我種植的幼木的森林之中。在這裏，我們爲他們做了兩座牀，拿我所有的東西來做着；就是用，好的米粳，氈覆在上面，以備睡臥之用，另外用一條氈，在每座牀上，掩蓋着他們。

現在我的島是有人居住了；我想我自己已有很繁盛的人民了。這是一個快樂的同憶，我常常想着，我想起來簡直像王一般。第一，全個國家都是我的私產，我有統轄領土的確實的主權。第二，我的人民甚爲歸順。我是全權主宰，立法人。他們的性命皆賴我拯救，他們是預備捐棄生命，假使我有需用他們之時。這也是可注意的，我僅有三個人民，他們却是信三種不同的宗教的。我的人星期五是耶穌教徒，他的父親是拜偶像者，吃人者，西班牙人是羅馬教徒。然而，我允許信教自由，在我領土之中。但是這不過是閒話而巳。

一經我使我的兩個疲弱者，得救的俘虜安定了以後，給他們住和一座休憩的地方，我開始想着爲他們做些食物。

goat, ¹*betwixt* a kid and a goat, out of my particular flock, to be killed. Then I cut off the ²*hinder quarter*, and chopping it into small pieces, I set Friday to work to ³*boiling* and ⁴*stewing*, and made them a very good dish, I ⁵*assure* you, of flesh and broth. As I ⁶*cooked* it ⁷*without doors*, for I made no fire within my inner wall, so I carried it all into the new ⁸*tent*, and having set a table there for them, I sat down, and ate my own dinner also with them, and, as well as I could cheered them and ⁹*encouraged* them. Friday was my ¹⁰*interpreter*, especially to his father, and, indeed, to the Spaniard, too; for the Spaniard spoke the ¹¹*language* of the savages pretty well.

After we had dined, or rather ¹²*supped*, I ordered Friday to take one of the canoes, and go and fetch our ¹³*muskets* and other ¹⁴*firearms*, which, ¹⁵*for want of time*, we had left upon the place of battle. The next day, I ordered him to go and ¹⁶*bury* the dead bodies of the savages, which ¹⁷*lay open to the sun*. I also ordered him to bury the ¹⁸*horrid* ¹⁹*remains* of their ²⁰*barbarous* feast, which I could not think of doing myself;—nay, I could not bear to see thim, if I went that way. All this he ²¹*punctually* performed, and ²²*effaced* the very appearance of the savages being there; so that when I went again, I could ²³*scarce* know where it was, otherwise than by the corner of the wood pointing to the place.

I then began to enter into a little ²⁴*conversation* with my two new subjects. First, I set Friday ²⁵*to inquire* of his father what he thought of the escape of the savages in that canoe, and whether we might expect a return of them, with a power too great for us ²⁶*to resist*. His first opinion was that the savages in the boat never could live out the storm which blew that night they went off, but must, of

第一個我做的事，我命星期五拿一只一年大的山羊來，介乎小山羊和山羊之中，從我的特別的羊羣中拿出來，殺了牠。我於是割下後部來，切成小塊，我叫星期五去燒炙牠們，做成了一味好菜，我向你切實地說，是一盆好的肉和湯。我在戶外燒她，因爲在裏牆之內，我未嘗生火，我把牠一齊帶到新帳幕裏面，在那裏爲他們設置一桌，我坐下來，和他們一淘吃我的午筵，竭力地來使他們歡欣和鼓勵他們。星期五是我的翻話人，尤其是爲他的父親，實在，也爲西班牙人；因爲西班牙人說野人的話說得很好。

我們午膳完畢以後，或者是晚膳，我命星期五拿一只木艇來，去把槍和火器取來，因時候偱促，我們把牠們留在戰場上了。第二天，我命他去把那些野人們的屍首埋起來，牠們都是在日光中曝露着。我也命他把那些殘忍的飲宴留下來的可怖的屍骨埋奜，我自己不想去做這事；——豈止如此，我不忍見之，假使我往那裏去。他把這些事立卽做好，把在那裏野人的跡象都抹去了，這樣當我重至其地，我鮮能知道牠是在什麼地方，若非他在樹林之角，指出那個地方。

我於是開始和我的兩個新人民談話。第一，我使星期五去問他的父親他對於在木艇逃走的野人們有什麼思想，我們是否要掛慮着他們的重來，其力之強大，非我們所能抵抗。他的第一次的意見是說，在木艇內的野人永遠不能經過風浪而達目的地，他們去的那晚，風是這樣的大，但是必須，勢必這樣，是被溺斃了，或被驅到南方別的海岸上，在那裏，他們將被吃掉，好像他們是被淹死了一樣，假使他們的船沈了。

[1]*necessity*, be [2]*drowned*, or [3]*driven* south to those other shores, where they were as sure to be [4]*devoured* as they were to be drowned if they were [5]*cast away*. But, as to what they would do if they came safe on shore, he said he knew not. It was his opinion that they were so dreadfully frightened with the manner of their being [6]*attacked*, the noise, and the fire, that he believed they would tell the people they were all killed by [7]*thunder* and [8]*lightening*, not by the hand of man; and that the two which appeared, namely Friday and I, were two [9]*heavenly spirits*, or [10]*furies*, come down to [11]*destroy* them, and not men with [12]*weapons*. This, he said, he knew; because he heard them all cry out so, in their language, one to another. It was [13]*impossible* for them to [14]*conceive* that a man could [15]*dart fire*, and [16]*speak thunder*, and kill at a distance, without lifting up the hand, as was done now. This old savage was [17]*in the right*; for, as I learned [18]*since*, the savages never [19]*attempted* to go over to the island afterwards. They were so [20]*terrified* with the accounts given by those four men (for it seems they did escape the sea), that they believed whoever went to that [21]*enchanted* island would be destroyed with fire from the gods.

This, however, I knew not; and therefore was under [22]*continual* [23]*apprehensions* for a good while, and kept always upon my [24]*guard*, with all my army. As there were now four of us, I would have [25]*ventured* upon a hundred of them, fairly, in the [26] *open field*, at any time. In a little time, however, no more canoes appearing, the fear of their coming [27]*wore off*, and I began to take my former thoughts of a voyage to the main into [28]*consideration*; being likewise [29]*assured* by Friday's father that I might [30]*depend upon* good [31]*usage* from their nation, on his account, if I would go.

但是假使他們上了岸，做些什麼，他說他不能知道。這是他的意見，他們是被攻擊他們的方法，聲音，火，所大加恐怖了。他相信他們將要告訴國人，我們同伴都被雷電所殺死了，不是經人的手；那兩個發見的人，就是我和星期五，是兩個天上仙人，或是報仇之神，降下地來殺傷他們，不是用武器的人，這個我說，是他能知道的；因爲他聽見他們一淘這樣地喊着，用了他們的言語，互相說着。這對於他們是不能想着的一個人居然能發火，發聲如雷，老遠地殺人，不舉起手來，像現在所做的一般。這個老野人說得合理；因爲，我以後明白了野人們從不再企圖到這島上來。他們是這樣地吃嚇，聽了那四人的報告（瞧起來那就是逃走的人），他們相信無論何人去到那邪怪的島上，便要被天神所發的火殺傷。

然而，我不知道這個，是以常存恐怖之心，時時小心防守。我們現在是四個人，我可以冒險地去攻打一百個野人很順利的，在空地上，在無論何時。不久，再沒有木艇發見，恐怖他們再來之心漸漸消滅了，我開始復將我從前想旅行到大洋中的思念詳加攷慮；其外又被星期五的父親向我確定我在他們國中可得善遇，爲了他的原故，假使我情願去。

1.必至.2.溺.3.騙.4.吞吃.5.破舟.6.攻擊.7.雷.8.電.9.天上仙人.10.報仇神.11.死壞.12.武器.13.不能.14.想.15.發火.16.發聲如雷.17.合理.18.以來.19.企想.20.吃嚇.21.邪妖的.22.時常.23.恐怖.24.防守.25.冒險.26.空地.27.漸漸消滅.28.思慮.29.確定.30.可得.31.善遇.

But my thoughts were a little [1]*suspended* when I had a
[2]*serious* [3]*discourse* with the Spaniard, and when I understood that there were sixteen more of his countrymen and
Portuguese, who, having been cast away and made their
escape to that side, lived there at peace, indeed, with the
savages, but were very sore put to it for [4]*necessaries*, and,
indeed, for life. I asked him all the [5]*particulars* of their
voyage, and found they were a Spanish ship, [6]*bound from*
the [7]*Rio de la Plata to Havana*, being directed to leave their
[8]*loading* there, which was [9]*chiefly* [10]*hides* and silver, add to
bring back what European goods they could meet with
there. They had five Portuguese seamen on board, whom
they took out of another [11]*wreck*. Five of their own men
were drowned when first the ship was lost, and these
escaped through [12]*infinite* dangers and [13]*hazards*, and [14]*arrived*,
almost [15]*starved*, on the cannibal coast, where they expected
to have been devoured every moment. He told me they
had some arms with them, but they were perfectly [16]*useless*,
for that they had neither powder nor ball, the [17]*washing* of
the sea having [18]*spoiled* all their powder but a little, which
they used at their first landing to [19]*provide* themselves with
some food.

I asked him what he thought would become of them
there, and if they had formed any [20]*design* of makeng their
escape. He said they had many [21]*consultations* about it; but
having neither [22]*vessel*, nor tools to build one, nor [23]*provisions*
of any kind, their [24]*councils* always ended in tears and [25]*despair*.
I asked him how he thought they would receive a [26]*proposal*
from me, which might tend towards an escape; and whether,
if they were all here, it might not be done. I told him,
with [27]*freedom*, I feared mostly their [28]*treachery* and [29]*ill-usage* of

但是我的思想中止了些時候，當我和西班牙人接了一次嚴重的談話之後，以及當我明白了還有十六個他的同國之人和葡萄牙人們，他們，船破了，逃到那邊去，和野人們相處至善；但是因爲需物之故甚爲困難，爲生命故，實係如此。我問我他們旅行的詳情，知道了他們是乘西班牙船，由里阿得拉白拿大河到哈發那島去，把船貨在那裏卸載，船貨大部是皮和銀子，把他們在那裏能遇着的歐洲貨物帶回去。在船上他們有五個葡萄牙水手，他們從別的破船中救出來的。他們自己的五個水手是溺斃了，當船初次失事之時，那些人歷盡無限危險逃走了，差不多快餓死之時，到了吃人者的海濱，在那裏，他們預期時時有被吞吃之虞。我告訴我他們帶了些兵器，但是完無用，因爲他們旣無火藥，又無子彈，海水把他們的火藥弄壞了，所餘無幾，他們初次上岸用那個去拿些食物來供養着自己。

我問他想起來他們在那邊將要變成什麼樣，假使他們設法逃走。他說，他們對於這事，會議多次；但是旣無船，又無造船之具，又無任何糧食，所以他們的會議常以涕淚和失望爲終結。我問他想怎樣，假使他們納我提議，或可助成他們的逃走；倘使他們全在那邊，這事是否未曾做畢。我告訴他，直言不諱，我最怕他們的奸詐和苛待我，假使我將生命置於他們的手中。

me, if I put my life in their hands. I told him it would be very hard that I should be the [1]*instrument* of their [2]*deliverance*, and that they should [3]*afterwards* make me their [4]*prisoner* in New Spain, where an Englishman was certain to be made [5]*a sacrifice*, what necessity or what [6]*accident* [7]*soever* brought him thither.

He answered, with a great deal of [8]*candor*, that their condition was so [9]*miserable*, and that they were so [10]*sensible* of it, that he believed they would [11]*abhor* the thought of using any man [12]*unkindly* that should [13]*contribute* to their deliverance; that if I pleased he would go to them, with the old man, and [14]*discourse* with them about it, and return again, and bring me their answer. He would make [15]*conditions* with them, upon their [16]*solemn oath*, that they should be [17]*absolutely* under my [18]*direction*, as their commander and captain. He told me they were all of them very [19]*civil*, honest men, under the greatest [20]*distress* [21]*imaginable*, having neither weapons nor clothes, nor any food, but at the [22]*mercy* and [23]*discretion* of the savages, and out of all hopes of ever returning to their own country; and that he was sure, if I would [24]*undertake* their relief, they would live and die by me.

CHAPTER XL

[25]*Upon these assurances*, I resolved to [26]*venture* to relieve them, if possible, and to send the old savage and this Spaniard over to them [27]*to treat*. But when we had got all things in [28]*readiness* to go, the Spaniard himself started an [29]*objection*, which had so much [30]*prudence* in it on one hand, and so much [31]*sincerity* [32]*on the other hand*, that I could not but be very well [33]*satisfied* in it; and, by his advice, I put off the deliverance of his comrades for at least half a year.

我告訴他這是很困苦的，我將要爲他們的被救之器具，以後他們在新西班牙將要使我做他們的囚俘，在那個地方。一個英國人一定要被作爲犧牲品。無論何種需要或何種不幸之事把他帶到那個地方去。

我囘答，甚爲誠實，說他們的境況是這樣的不幸，他們非常感覺着這個，他相信他們將要厭惡虐待他人的思想，而這個人卻是拯救他們的助力；他說假使我情願，他將到他們那裏去，和老野人一淌去和他們說及此事，重行囘來，給我他們的囘答。他將要和他們定立約章，以正式立誓爲實，他們必須完全受我的指揮，好像是他們的領袖和統領一般。他告訴我他們全是文明，誠實的人，在極困難的境遇之中，旣無武器，又無衣着，又無食物：僅在野人們掌握之中，囘國一擧，已經絕望；他是一定，假使我允爲他們之助，他們將生死與我相共。

第 四 十 章

有此堅信之心，我決心冒險去救助他們，假使可能，這老野人和西班牙人到他們那邊去商議。但是當我們諸物備齊，預備就道之時，西班牙忽起而反對，一則他是顧盧周詳再則又是眞誠無比，我遂不能不對他的反對表示着十分滿意；依照他的勸告，我至少要把拯救他的同伴之念延擱上半年。

The case was thus. He had been with us now about a month, during which time I had let him see in what manner I had [1]*provided*, with the [2]*assistance* of [3]*Providence*, for my support; and he saw [4]*evidently* what stock of corn and rice I had [5]*laid up*. Though it was more than [6]*sufficient* for myself, yet it was not sufficient, without good [7]*husbandry*, for my family, now it was [8]*increased* to four. But much less would it be sufficient if his countrymen, who were, as he said, fourteen still alive, should come over; and, least of all would it be sufficient [9]*to victual* our vessel, if we should build one, for a voyage to any of the Christian [10]*colonies* of America. So he told me he thought it would be more [11]*advisable* to let him and the other two dig and [12]*cultivate* some more land, as much as I could [13]*spare* seed [14]*to sew*, and that we should wait another [15]*harvest*, that we might have a supply of corn for his countrymen, when they should some; for want might be a [16]*temptation* to them to disagree, or not to think themselves delivered, otherwise than [17]*out of one difficulty into another*.

His caution was so [18]*seasonable,* and his advice so good, that I could not but be very well pleased with his [19]*proposal*, as well as I was satisfied with his [20]*fidetliy*. So we fell to [21]*digging*, all four of us, as well as the [22]*wooden tools* we were [23]*furnished* with [24]*permitted*; and, in about a month's time, by the end of which it was [25]*seed-time*, we had got as much land [26]*cured* and [27]*trimmed up* as we sowed two and twenty bushels of [28]*darley* on, and sixteen jars of rice; which was, in short, all the seed we had [29]*to spare*.

Having now society enough, and our number being usfficient to put us out of fear of the savages, if they had come, unless their number had been very great, we went

情形是這樣。他現在和我們住了將及一月，在那些時候之中我使他看我用何方法來備辦食物；得了上天之助，支持我的生存；他顯然地看見我存貯了多少米和穀。雖然這對於我是很足夠的，然而還是不足夠，若不好爲耕種，對於我的家人現在人口增至四人了。但是尤其是不足夠了，假使他的同國之人，他們是，他說過，十四人生存着，到這裏來；至少當要足夠的量來供備食物在船上，假使我們要製造一只船，預備旅行到無論那個耶教殖民地去。這樣他告訴我他想這是很合宜的讓他和別的二人去掘和培植若干土地，足數我所貯藏的穀種散播之用，我們當俟下次收成，我們將有供給他的國人的穀子了，當他們來了的時候；迫於飢寒或至大家意見不合，或者他們不想着自己是被救了，否則不過出入是危險而巳。

他的小心是很合時，他的勸告是很好，所以我對於他的提議是非常欣悅的；他的忠心我也十分滿足。這樣，我們開始掘地，四人一齊工作，盡我等所有之木器作事；在大約一月的工夫，一月以後就是播種之時了，我們有了許多的地，修理佈置整齊，足夠播種二十二桶多麥在上面，以及十六袋米；總而言之，那個是我們攏總餘留的種子。

現在有了足夠的社交了，我們的人數足以使我們對於野人不懷恐怖之心，假使他們來此，除非他們的人數是狠多的，我們當有機會之時，狠自在地周游全島。

freely all over the island, whenever we found [1]*occasion*. As
we had our escape or deliverance upon our thoughts, it
was [2]*impossible*, at least for me, to have the means of it out
of mine. For this purpose I marked out several trees,
which I thought fit for our work; and I set Friday and his
father to cut them down; and then I caused the [3]*Spaniard*,
to whom I [4]*imparted* my thoughts on that [5]*affair*, to [6]*oversee*
and direct their work. I showed them with what [7]*indefati-
gable* [8]*pains* I had hewed a large tree into [9]*single planks*, and
I caused them to do the like, till they had made about a
dozen large [10]*planks* of good oak, near two feet broad,
thirty-five feet long, and from two inches to four inches
thick. What [11]*prodigious* labor it took up, any one may
imagine

At the same time, I [12]*contrived* to increase my little
flock of [13]*tame goats* as much as I could. For this purpose,
I made Friday and the Spaniard go out one day, and myself with Friday the next day (for we took our turns). By
this means we got about twenty young kids [14]*to breed up*
with the rest; for whenever we shot the [15]*dam*, we saved the
kids, and added them to our flocks But, above all, the
season for curing the [16]*grapes* coming on, I caused such a
[17]*prodigious* quantity to be [18]*hung up* in the sun that I
believe, had we been at [19]*Alicant*, where the [20]*raisins* of the
sun are [21]*cured*, we could have filled sixty or eighty [22]*barrels*.
These, with our bread, [23]*formed* a great part of our food.—
very good living too, I [24]*assure* you, for they are [25]*exceedingly*
[26]*nourishing*.

It was now harvest, and our crop [27]*in good order*. It
was not the most plentiful [28]*increase* I had seen in the island,
but it was enough [29]*to answer our end*. From twenty-two

我們腦筋中既然有了逃走和被救的思想，這是不可能的，至少對於我，把設法拯救之事，置諸度外。爲了這個緣故，我至標記了幾株樹，我想牠們是合於我們工作之用；我使星期五和他的父親把牠們砍下來；我於是使西班牙人，我把欲得拯救之意告訴他，監視養指揮工作。我表示他們我曾歷盡艱苦把一株大樹砍成細薄木片，我教他們照樣工作，直至他們做成差不多有一打的好樣樹的寬大的木片，大約二尺寬，三十五尺長，從二寸到四寸厚。其工程之大，可以想見。

　同時，竭力地想法把馴的羊羣的數目加增起來。爲了這事，我使星期五和西班牙人在某一天走出去，我自己和星期五第二天出外（因爲我們輪流着）。用了這個方法，我們得着了大約二十只小山羊，和其餘的羊一淘豢養；因爲無論何時我們射擊母羊，我們留下小山羊，把牠們加到羊羣內去。但是尤要者，晾曬葡萄的時期來了，我把這樣大的分量來在日光中懸着；我相信，卽使我們是在阿里剛，在那裏，葡萄是在日光中晾曬的，我們能夠滿盛六十或八十大桶。這些，以及麵包造成了我們的食物的大部份，——生活也是很好的，我對你確說，因爲牠們是非常滋着的。

　現在是收成之時了，我們的收穫甚爲佳妙。這不是在島上我看見的最豐盛的加增的出產，但是却足夠適合我等之用了。

1. 機會. 2. 不能. 3. 西班牙人. 4. 授以. 5. 事. 6. 監視. 7. 極點. 8. 痛苦. 9. 細薄木片. 10. 木板. 11. 很大. 12. 意欲. 13. 馴山羊. 14. 養. 15. 母羊. 16. 葡萄. 17. 狠大. 18. 吊起. 19. 阿里剛. 20. 葡萄乾. 21. 晾. 22. 桶. 23. 做成. 24. 確定. 25. 非常. 26. 滋養. 27. 整齊. 28. 加增. 29. 達我目的

bushels of barley we brought in and [1]thrashed out above two hundred and twenty bushels, and the like; in [2]proportion, of the rice ; which was store enough for our food to the next harvest, though all the fourteen Spaniards had been on shore with me. Or, if we had been ready for a voyage, it would very [3]plentifully have [4]victualed our ship to have carried us to any part of the world,—that is to say, any part of America. When we had thus [5]housed and [6]secured our [7]magazine of [8]corn, we fell to work to make more wicker ware ; namely, great baskets, in which we kept it. The Spaniard was very handy and [9]dexterous at this part, and often [10]blamed me that I did not make some things for [11]defense of this kind of work ; but I saw no need of it.

And now, having a full supply of food for all the [12]guests I expected, I gave the Spaniard leave to go over to the main, to see what he could do with those he had left behind him there. I gave him a [13]strict charge not to bring any man who would not first swear, [14]in the presence of himself and the old savage, that he would [15]in no way [16]injure, fight with, or [17]attack the person he should find in the island, who was so kind as to send for them in order for their [18]deliverance ; but that they would [19]stand by him and [20]defend him against all such [21]attempts, and, wherever they went, would be [22]entirely under and subjected to his command; and that this should be put in writing, and signed in their hand/. How they were to have done this, when I knew they had neither pen nor ink, was a question which we never asked.

Under these [23]instructions, the Spaniard and the old savage, the father of Friday, went away in one of the canoes which they might be said to have come in,—

從二十二斗大麥我們帶進來的裏面，我們打出了兩百二十斗以上，在比例上，米的量也是如此，在下次收成以前，那是我們食物足量的存貯了，雖然十四個西班牙人一齊在岸上和我們生活。假使我們預備旅行，這在船中是很豐豐的備辦的食品，無論駛向那裏都行，——就是說，隨便往美洲那一部都成。當我們這般地將穀取藏穩固，我們起始工作，再做些柳枝編製品；就是，大籃子，在裏面我們放好穀子。西班牙人對於這事是很伶俐和技巧的，常常怪我不曾製些像這些東西的防備品；但是我却以爲無需於此。

現在，對於我所希望來的攏總的客人有了足夠的量食品的供給，我准西班牙人往大洋中去，看看他和在那裏他留下來的人們能做些什麼事。我切切訓諭他，凡是起先不發誓的人不可帶他來，在他自己和老野人面前立誓，他決不傷害，戰鬥，或攻打他能在島上尋出來的人，他是這樣的仁慈遣人去招他們來，藉以拯救他們，但是他們當幫助他，保護他，抵抗一切的企圖，無論他們到那方去，當唯他的命是聽，這個綱約要寫下來，親筆簽押。他們怎樣來做了這事，當我知道了他們既無筆又無墨，這是我們永遠未曾問及的一個問題。

在這些訓令之下，西班牙人和老野人，星期五的父親去了，在一只木艇中那只木艇，可以說是他們曾經進去過的，——寧可說是被帶進去的，——當他們被囚虜而來，將要被野人們吃去之時。

1.打出。2.比例。3.多量。4.供備食物。5.收藏。6.穩固。7.倉。8.穀。9.技巧。10.責怪。11.抵抗。12.客人。13.切諭。14.在....之前。15.決不。16.詢。17.攻打。18.拯救。19.助。20.保護。21.企試。22.完全。23.訓令。

or rather were brought in—when they came as [1]*prisoners* to be [2]*devoured* by the savages. I gave each of them a musket, what a [3]*firelock* on it, and about [4]*eight charges of powder* and ball, [5]*charging them to husband bath*, and not to use either of them but upon [6]*urgent occasions.*

This was a cheerful work, bring the first [7]*measures used* by me [8]*in view of* my deliverance for now twenty-seven years and some days. I gave them [9]*provisions* of bread and of dried grapes sufficient for themselves for many days and sufficient for all the Spaniards for about eight days' time; and wishing them a good voyage, I saw them go, [10]*agreeing with them about* a signal they should [11]*hang out* at their return, by which I should know them again when they came back, at a distance, before they came on shore. They went away with [12]*a fair gale* on the day that the moon was at full, by my account in the month of October. As for an [13]*exact* [14]*reckoning* of days, after I had once lost it, I could never recover it again.

It was no less than eight days I had [15]*waited* for them, when a strange and unforeseen accident [16]*intervened*, of which the like has not, perhaps, been heard of in history. I was fast asleep in my hut one morning, when my man Friday came running in to me, and called along, "Master, master, they are come, they are come!" I [17]*jumped up*, and, [18]*regardless of danger*, I went, as soon as I could get my clothes on, through my little grove, which, by the way, was by this time grown to be a very thick wood. I say' regardless of danger, I went without my arms, which was not my custom to do. But I was surprised when, turning my eye to the sea, I presently saw a boat at about a [19]*league* and a half distance, standing in for the [20]*shore'* with a

我給他們每人一只槍，在上面有一只燧發槍，大約有八管火藥和子彈之量，二者均囑他們須要節用；若非緊急之時，二者皆不必用。

這是一件欣悅的工作，是我第一次實行的法子；爲我的拯救之故，現在已是二十七年和若干日了。我給他們食物，麵包，乾葡萄，足以供給他們多日之用，足以供給所有西班牙人大約八日之用；希望他們一路順風來，由此我將要知道他們，當他們轉來之時；老遠地，在他們未抵岸之前。他們乘着順風去了，在那一天，月正圓滿，照我計算起來是十月裏。至於核準的日期，一經我忘記了，我却永遠不能再想起來。

我等候他們不下於八日，有一意外之事，忽然發現，和這事相似的事，在歷史上，或者人們還未聽見說過。一天早晨，我在茅舍中睡熟了，我的了星期五忽然跑到我面前來，大叫着，"主人，主人，他們來了，他們來了！"我跳起身來，不顧危險，我是不帶兵器出外，這却不是我的習慣。但是我被驚駭了，當我轉眼向海觀望，我立卽看見一只船，大約在一哩里有牛的距離之中，向岸駛行，

1. 囚牢．2. 吞吃．3. 燧發槍．4. 八管彈藥之量．5. 兩皆令其節用．6. 緊急之時．7. 法子．8. 爲....之故．9. 食物．10. 彼此商定．11. 掛出．12. 順風．13. 核準．14. 日期．15. 等．16. 發見．17. 跳起．18. 不顧危險．19. 海里．20. 海岸．

shoulder-of-[1]*mutton* sail, as they call it, and the wind blowing [2]*pretty* fair to bring them in. Also I [3]*observed*, presently, that they did not come from that side which the shore lay on, but from the southernmost end of the island.

Upon this I called Friday in, and bade him [4]*lie close*, for these were not the people we looked for, and that we might not know yet whether they were freinds or [5]*enemies*. In the next place, I went in to fetch my [6]*perspective* glass, to see what I could make of them ; and, having taken the [7]*ladder* out, I [8]*climbed up* to the top of the hill, as I used to do when I was [9]*apprehensive* of anything, and to take my view the [10]*plainer*, without being [11]*discovered*. I had scarce set my foot upon the hill when my eye plainly discovered a ship lying at [12]*anchor*, at about two leagues and a half distance from me, [13]*south-southeast,* but not above a league and a half from the shore. By my [14]*observation* it appeared plainly to be an English ship, and the boat appeared to be an [15]*English* [16]*longboat.*

I cannot express the [17]*confusion* I was in, though the joy of seeing a ship, and one that I had reason to believe was manned by my own countrymen, and [18]*consequently* friends, was such as I cannot [19]*describe*. Yet I had some secret [20]*doubts hung* [21]*about me*—I cannot tell from whence they came—[22]*bidding* me keep upon my guard. In the first place, it [23]*occurred* to me to consider what business an English ship could have in that part of the world, since it was not the way to or from any part of the world where the English had any [24]*traffic*, I knew there had been no storms to drive them in there, in [25]*distress* ; and that if they were really English, it was most [26]*probable* that they were here [27]*upon no good design* ; and that I had better continue

撐了羊屑帆，他們這樣叫牠，風括得頗順利，把他們帶進來，我也注意着，立即，他們不是從海岸躺着的那邊而來，似是從島的最南的末端而至。

因此，我把星期五叫進來，盼咐他緊隨着我，因為這些不是我們所盼望的人們，我們不能知道他們來此還是友人還是敵人。第二步°我進去把望遠鏡拿出來，看看能否辨別他們是誰；把梯子拿出來，我爬到小山頂上面去，如我向來所做一般，當我恐怖某事之時，使我看得更加清楚，不為他人所見。我剛剛踏上山巔，我的眼睛就看見一只船，在離我大約兩海里有半的距離之中下了錨，在南偏東南，但是離岸不及一海里有半之遠。照我覺察，牠顯明地是一只英國船，看起來像一只英國的長舢板。

我不能把我的混亂的狀態表明出來，雖然快樂地看了一只船，我有理由去相信這只船上所載的是我的同國之人，那末就是友人了，我竟不能把牠描寫出來。然而我有些私慮繞在我的心中——我不能明白他們由何方而來——使得我自己小心防守着。第一步，我偶然想着去注意英國船在世界上那個部份能夠有何事務須進行，旣然這不是那條路或從任何世界上的部份，在那裏英國人有生意可做。我知道沒有風浪把他們驅到那裏去，在苦痛之中；假使他們眞是英國人，那末大概來到這裏，他們是不存好心了；我最好繼續着我從前那樣，不要陷入盜賊和殺人者的手中。

as I was, than fall into the hands of [1]*thieves* and [2]*murderers.*

I had not kept myself long in this [3]*posture*, till I saw the boat [4]*draw* near the shore, as if they looked for a [5]*creek* to [6]*thrust* in at, for the [7]*convenience* of landing. As they did not come quite far enough, they did not see the little inlet where I formerly landed my rafts, but ran their boat on shore upon the beach, at about half a mile from me; which was very happy for me, for otherwise they would have landed just at my door, as I may say, and would soon have [8]*beaten me out of my castle*, and perhaps have [9]*plundered* me of all I had. When they were on shore, I was fully satisfied they were Englishmen,—at least most of them. One or two I thought were Dutch, but it did not prove so. There were [10]*in all* eleven men, whereof three of them I found were [11]*unarmed*, and, as I thought, bound.

When the first four or five of them were jumped on shore, they took those three out of the boat as prisoners. One of the three I could [12]*perceive* using the most [13]*passionate* [14]*gestures* of [15]*entreaty*, [16]*affliction*, and [17]*despair*, even to a kind of [18]*extravagance*. The other two, I could [19]*perceive*, lifted up their hands sometimes, and appeared concerned indeed, but not to such a degree as the first. I was [20]*perfectly* [21]*confounded* at the sight, and knew not what the meaning of it could be. Friday called out to me in English, as well as he could, "O master! you see English mans eat prisoner as well as savage mans." "Why, Friday." says I, "do you think they are going to eat them, then?" "Yes," says Friday, "they will eat them," "No, no," says I, "Friday; I am afraid they will [22]*murder* them, indeed; but you may be sure they will not eat them."

　　我在這種狀況之中不甚久長，直至我看見船拉攏了岸，為上岸便利起見。好像是他們要找尋一座小溪把船弄進去，他們既然走得不十分遠，他們遂未曾看見那個小灣，在那裏，我先前曾把木筏攏上了岸，但是海灣上，他們把船攏上了岸大約離開我半英里，這對於我是很快樂的，因為否則他們將要正在我的門前上岸，我可以這般說，那末馬上便驅我出堡，或者把我所有的東西一齊搶去。當他們上了岸，我 很滿意地他知道們是英國人，——至少有一大半是的。一兩個我想起來是荷蘭人，但是不確。一共有十一人，他們之中有三人我看見是沒有兵器的，我想起來，是被縛著。

　　當第一次四五個人跳上了岸，他們把那三個人像囚虜般從船中拖將出來。三人內的一人，我能看見他用了最感動人的祈求，困苦，和失望的樣子來表示著乞憐，甚至於過了常度。另外二人，我能看見，時時舉起手來，實在也表示憂慮的樣子，但是不像第一人的厲害。我一見之下，心神紛亂，不知這是何意。星期五用英語叫我，竭力地說，"哦，主人！你看英國人吃囚虜好似野人一般。""星期五，"我說，"你為什麼想着他們將要去吃那些人？""是的，"星期五說"他們將要吃那些人。""否，否，"我說，星期五；我恐怕他們將要殺害那些人，實在是這樣；但是你可以確定他們不會去吃掉他們。"

1.賊。2.殺人者。3.狀況。4.曳。5.小溪。6.驅進。7.傾利。8.逐我出堡。10.一共。11.無兵器。12.見。12.可憐。14.樣子。15.哀求。16.苦痛。17.失望。18.過度。19.見。20.完全。21.紜亂。22.殺害。

All this while I had no thought of what the matter really was, but stood [1]*trembling* with the horror of the sight [2]*expecting* every moment when the three prisoners should be killed. Nay, once I saw one of the [3]*villains* lift up his arm with a great [4]*cutlass*, as the seamen call it, or sword, [5]*to strike* one of the poor men. I [6]*expected* to see him fall every moment; at which all the [7]*blood* in my body seemed to run [8]*chill* in my veins. I wished [9]*heartily* now for the Spaniard, and the savage that was gone with him, or that I had any way to have come [10]*undiscovered* within shot of them, that I might have [11]*secured* the three men, for I saw no [12]*firearms* they had among them, But it fell out to my mind another way. After I had [13]*observed* the [14]*outrageous* usage of the three men by the [15]*insolent* seamen. I observed the fellows run [16]*scattering* about the island, as if they wanted to see the country. I observed that the three other men had liberty to go also where they pleased; but they sat down all three upon the ground, [17]*very pensive*, and looked like men [18]*despair*. This put me in mind of the first time in when I came on shore, and began to look about me; how I gave myself over for lost, how wildly I looked round me, what dreadful [19]*apprehensions* I had, and how I lodged in the tree all night, for fear of being [20]*devoured* by wild beasts.

CHAPTER XLI

IT was just [21]*at high water* when these people came on shore; and while they [22]*rambled about* to see what kind of a place they were in, they had carelessly staid till the [23]*tide* was spent, and the water was [24]*ebbed* [25]*considerably* away, leaving their boat aground. They had left two men in the

攬總這些時候我未嘗想及這事實在是什麼，但是因為看見這種可怖的景象，立在那裏發抖；時時期望着這三人不知在何時將要被殺却。豈止如此，一次我看見一個棍徒舉起了他的膀臂，用了一把腰刀，如同水手叫牠一般；或是刀，去擊那一個可憐的人。我希望着時時看他跌仆下來；想到這個：我渾身的血在血管中好像是冰冷起來。我現在很希望着那個西班牙人，以及和他同去的野人，假使我可以到他們彈丸可及而不被他們所見的地方，那末我便能保全那三人，因為我看見在那些人之中，沒有兵器。但使我別生一種意念。在我觀察那三人被鹵莽的水手加以虐待之後；我看見人們在島上四散去了，如同他們要觀察這個地方一樣。我看見三個別的人來往自由；但是三人一淘坐下來，非常愁悶，瞧起來好似失望的人一般。這個使我想起我第一次上岸的光景，在我四面望着；我怎樣地自以為無救，我在我四圍看起來怎樣的荒野，我有怎樣的恐怖之心，整夜我怎樣地睡在樹中，因為恐怕被野獸所吞噬。

第 四 十 一 章

貼正水漲起來，當這些人上了岸之時；當他們游行觀覽，他們究竟在什麼地方，他們不留心地堅定了，直至潮退，水蓋乾去後，把他們的船留在地上。他們留下二人

boat, who, as I found afterwards, having ¹*drunk* a little too much ²*brandy*, fell asleep. One of them, waking a little sooner than the other, and finding the boat too fast aground for him to stir it, ³*hallooed* out for the rest, who were ⁴*straggling* about; upon which they all soon came to the boat. But it was ⁵*past all their strength* to launch her, the boat being very ⁶*heavy*, and the shore on that side being a soft, ⁷*oozy* sand, almost like a ⁸*quicksand*. In this condition, like true seamen, who are, perhaps, the least of all ⁹*mankind* given to ¹⁰*forethought*, they gave it over, and away they ¹¹*strolled* about the country again; and I heard one of them say aloud to another, ¹²*calling* them ¹³*off* from the boat, " Why, let her alone, Jack, can't you? ¹⁴*she'll* ¹⁵*float* next tide;" by which I was fully ¹⁶*confirmed* in the ¹⁷*main inquiry* of what countrymen they were.

All this while I kept myself very close, not once daring to stir out of my castle any farther than to my place of ¹⁸*observation* near the top of the hill ; and very glad I was to think how well it was ¹⁹*fortified*. I knew it was no less than ten hours before the boat could float again, and by that time it would be dark, and I might be at more liberty to see their motions, and to hear their discourse, if they had any. In the mean time I fitted myself up for a battle, as before, though with more ²⁰*caution*, knowing I had to do with another kind of enemy than I had at first. I ordered Friday also, whom I had made an ²¹*excellent* ²²*marksman* with his gun, to load himself with arms. I took myself two fowling pieces, and I gave him three muskets. ²³*My figure*, indeed, was very ²⁴*fierce*; I had my ²⁵*formidable* ²⁶*goat-skin* ²⁶*coat* on, with the great cap I have mentioned, a naked sword by my side, two pistols in my belt, and a gun upon each shoulder.

在船中，他們，後來我知道了，喝了較多的百蘭地酒，睡得狠醉熟了。他們之中一人，比其餘的早醒了些時，看見船擱淺過牢，難以行動，把其餘的人叫起來，他們四散游行；他們一齊因此不久便都上了船。但是要行駛牠？非他們能力所及，船是太重了，那邊的海岸是一座泥灣的沙地，差不多似流沙一樣。在此情况之中，如同眞實水手一般，他們是，大概如此，毫不先事預防；他們放棄此事，他們重行在這地方遨游着；我聽見其中一人大聲向別的人說，叫他們離開了船，"爲什麼，讓牠去，甲克，你不能？下次潮流來，牠將要浮起來；" 聽了這話，我是很確定的了，在主要問題中，他們是那一國的人。

這些時候我使我自己貼近了，一次也不敢從我的堡中翻外到比我的靠近小山之頂的觀察所的更遠的地方去；我是很快活地去想這裏防禦得是多麼好。我知道這是不下於十個鐘頭，在這只船能浮起以前，在那時，天色要暗了，我將要很安全地來注視他們的行動，聽他們的談話，假使他們這樣做。其中之時，我預備開戰，像前一樣，雖然更加小心，知道我將和我以前所遇的不同的敵人們去從事。我也命令星期五，我把他敎成一個伶巧的善放射槍的人，去把槍彈上好。我自己拿了兩只打鳥槍，我給他三只槍。我的形狀實在是狠可怖的，穿了我可怕的山羊皮製的衣彩，戴了我曾經敍述過的帽子，腰間掛了出鞘的刀，帶內插有手鎗兩只，每只肩上杠有一只鎗。

It was my ¹*design,* as I said above, not to have made any ²*attempt* till it was dark ; but about two o'clock, being ³*the heat* of the day, I found that they were all gone straggling into the woods, and as I thought, were laid down to sleep. The three poor ⁴*distressed* men, too ⁵*anxious* for their condition to get any sleep, had, however, sat down under the ⁶*shelter* of a great tree, at about a quarter of a mile from me, and, as I thought, out of sight of any of the rest. Upon this I ⁷*resolved* to discover myself to them,

　　這是我的計劃；我先前已經說過了，非俟天晚，不作若何企圖；但是大約在兩點鐘的辰光，日中最熱之時，我看見他們一共都到樹林中散步去了，我想。他們是躺下去睡覺了。那三個可憐的受困苦的人，對於他們所處的境況，非常的焦慮，竟致不能入睡；然而，他們却坐在一株大樹的遮陰之下，大約離開我有一英里四分之一的遠，我想起來；其餘之人均不得而見之。因此之故，我決心把我自已向他們顯示出來；探悉關於他們的境況的事。立刻我向前進，我的人星期五在我身後好遠的地方，他帶的兵器使人可怖好似我帶的一般，但是他不像有如怪物，有令人注視之形狀。我竭力地去靠近他們，而不使他們看見，在他們之中任何人看見我以前；我用西班牙語向他們大叫道，"你們是誰，先生們?"

1.計謀.2.企圖.3.熱.4.困苦的.5.焦慮.6.蔭.7.決心。

and learn something of their [1]*condition.* [2]*Immediately* I [3]*marched,* with my man Friday at a good distance behind me, as formidable for his arms as I, but not making quite so [4]*staring* a [5]*specter-like* figure as I did. I came as near them [6]*undiscovered* as I could and then, before any of them saw me, I called aloud to them in Spanish, "What are ye, gentlemen ?"

They [7]*started up* at the noise, but were ten times more [8]*confounded* when they saw me, and the [9]*uncouth figure* that I made. They made no answer at all, but I thought I [10]*perceived* them just going to fly from me, when I spoke to them in English : "Gentleman," said I, "do not be [11]*surprised* at me ; perhaps you may have a friend near, [12]when you did not expect." "He must be sent directly from Heaven then ;" said one of them very [13]*gravely* to me and [13]*pulling off* his hat at the same time to me; "for our condition is past the help of men." "All help is from Heaven, sir, " and I : "but can you put a [14]*stranger* in the way to help you ? for you seem to be in some great [15]*distress.* I saw you when you landed ; and when you seemed to make [16]*application* to the brutes that came with you, I saw one of them lift up his [17]*sword* to kill you. "

The poor man, with tears running down his face, and [18]*trembling,* looking, like one [19]*astonished,* returned, "Am I talking to God, or man ? Is it a real man, or an [20]*angel* ?" "Be in no fear about that, sir " said I ; "if God had sent an angel to relieve you, he would have come better clothed, and [21]*armed after another manner* than you see me. Pray lay [22]*aside* your fears. I am a man, an Englishman, and [23]*disposed* to [24]*assist* you, you see. I have one servant only we have arms and [25]*ammunition* ; tell us freely, can we serve

他們跳起身來，聽見了聲音之後，但是當他們看見了我之時，他們是十倍地混亂起來，就是因爲我做出的奇形怪狀的原故了。他們並不囘答，但是我想我看見他們正要逃走離開我當我用英語向他們說話之時："先生們，"我說，"不要恐怖着我，或者你們馬上就可以有一個友人，當你們未曾料及之時。""那末他一定是直接從天上派遣下來的；"他們之中的一人向我很莊重地說，隨卽脫帽向我致敬；"因爲我們的境況已非人力所能助。""各種助力皆係從天上而來，先生，"我說："但是你們能使一個不相識之人想法子幫助你們嗎？因爲你們看起來是在些大困難之中。我看見你們當你們上岸之時；當你們好像向那些和你們同來的野蠻之人用語哀求之時？我看見他們之中的一人舉起刀來要想殺你們。

那個可憐的人，淚流於面，抖着好似吃驚的人一樣，囘答道，"我是向上帝說話，還是向人說話？這是一個實在的人，或是一位天使？""對於這個不必驚懼，先生，"我說；"假使上帝遣天使來救助你們，他一定着好的衣彩而來，着別樣裝束不像你們看見的這樣。請把恐怖之心放下。我是人，一個英國人，專意來救助你們，你們知道的。我只有一個僕人；我們有兵器和軍實；誠實地告訴我們，我們能夠爲你們効力嗎？你們的情形是怎樣？""我們的情形，先生，"他說，"是太長了，不好告訴你，當我們的屠夫是在我們附近之時。總而言之，先生，我是船上的首領。我的水手反叛了我。

1.狀況.2.立卽.3.前進.4.注視.5.如鬼怪.6.不見.7.跳起.8.混亂.9.奇異之狀.10.見.11.驚駭.12.莊.13.脫去.14.不相識之人.15.困苦.16.哀求.17.刀.18.抖.19.驚駭.20.天使.21.別樣裝束.22.去.23.專意.24.助.25.軍實.

you? What is your case?" "Our case, sir," said he, "is too long to tell you, while our ¹*murderers* are so near us. In short, sir, I was ²*commander* of that ship. My men have ³*mutinied against* me. They have been hardly ⁴*prevailed* on not to ⁵*murder me*, and, at last, have set me on shore in this ⁶*desolate* place, with these two men with me,—one my mate, the other a ⁷*passenger*,—where we expected to ⁸*perish*, believing the place to be ⁹*uninhabited*, and know not yet what to think of it."

"Where are these brutes, your ¹⁰*enemies*?" said I; "do you know where they are gone?" "There they lie, sir," said he, pointing to a ¹¹*thicket* of trees; "my heart ¹²*trembles* for fear they have seen us, and heard you speak. If they have, they will certainly murder us all." "Have they any ¹³*firearms*?" said I. He answered, "They had only two pieces, and one which they left in the boat." "Well, then," said I, "¹⁴*leave the rest to me*. I see they are all ¹⁵*asleep*; it is an easy thing to kill them all; but shall we rather take them ¹⁶*prisoners*?" He told me there were two ¹⁷*desperate* ¹⁸*villains* among them that it was ¹⁹*scarce* safe to show any ²⁰*mercy* to; but if they were ²¹*secured*, he believed all the rest would return to their ²²*duty*. I asked him which they were. He told me he could not at that distance ²³*distinguish* them, but he would obey my orders in anything I would dirdct. "Well," says I, "let us ²⁴*retreat* out of their view or hearing, lest they awake, and we will ²⁵*resolve* further." So they willingly went back with me, till the woods covered us from them.

"Look you, sir," said I; "if I venture upon your deliverance, are you willing to make two conditions with me?" He ²⁶*anticipated* my ²⁷*proposals*, by telling me that both he and the

他們對於不殺害我一事是很難說服的，最後，他們使我上岸，把我放到這所孤寂的地方，使這兩人和我在一處，——一個是我的同伴，另外一個是搭客，——在那裏我們希望死去，相信這個地方是無人居住的，不知道想怎樣是好。」

「那些野蠻之人，你們的敵人，在什麼地方？」我說，「你知道他們到何處去了？」「他們睡在那邊，先生，他說，指着樹中的厚密之處；「我的心抖戰起來，恐怕他們看見我們，聽見你說話。假使他們如此，他們一定要把我們一齊殺却。」「他們有些火器嗎？」我說。答：「他們只有兩枝槍；一枝他們留在船上。」「好，那末，我說，「把其餘各事委託於我便了。我知道他們是全睡着了；把他們殺盡，這是一樁很容易的事；但是我們不能，寧可使他們作俘囚嗎？」他告訴我在他們之中有兩個怙惡不悛的棍徒，這是很不安全的去給予他們以恩惠；但是假使他們是拘禁，他相信餘之人將要恢復原職。我問他那兩個人是什麼樣子，他告訴我他在那個距離之中不能把他們分別出來，但是他將服從我的命令，無論何事，他都受我指揮。「好，」我說，「讓我們略為後退，不使他們看見，或聽見，恐怕他們醒來，我們再另想別法。」這樣，他們很心願地和我一淘退回來，直至樹林把我們從他們目光中遮蓋起來。

「你看，先生，」我說，「假使我為救助你們而冒着危險，你們情願和我訂立兩種條約嗎？」他預知我的提議，告訴我他和他的船，一經能夠復原，將要各事都聽我的指揮和命令。

ship, if recovered, should be wholly [1]*directed* and commanded
by me in everything.   If the ship was not recovered,
he would lived and die with me in what part of the world
soever I would send him.   The two other men said the
same.   "Well," says I, "my conditions are but two; first:
that while you [2]*stay* in this island with me, you will not
[3]*pretend* to any [4]*authority* here; and if I put arms in your
hands, you will, [5]*upon all occasions*, give them up to me
and do no [6]*prejudice* to me or mine upon this island, and in,
the mean time be [7]*governed* by my orders, Secondly: that
if the ship is, or may be, recovered, you will carry me and
my man to England, [8]*passage free*."

He gave me all the [9]*assurances* that the invention or
faith of man could devise, that he would comply with these
most [10]*reasonable demands,* and besides would owe his life to
me, and [11]*acknowledge it* upon all occasions as long as he
lived.   "Well, then," said I, "here are three muskets
for you, with powder and ball.   Tell me next what you
think is proper to be done."   He showed all the [12]*testimonies*
of his [13]*gratitude* that he was able, but offered to be wholly
guided by me.   I told him I thought it was hard [14]*venturing*
anything; but the best [15]*method* I could think of was to fire
on them at once as they lay, and if any were not killed at
the first [16]*volley,* and offered to [17]*submit,* we might save them,
and so put it wholly upon God's [18]*providence* to direct the shot.
He said, [19]*very modestly,* that he was loath to kill them, if he
could help it; but that those two were [20]*incorrigible* [21]*villains,*
and had been the authors of all the [22]*mutiny* in the ship, and
if they [23]*escaped*, we should be undone still, for they would
go on board and bring the whole ship's company, and destroy us all.   "Well, then," says I, " necessity [24]*legitimates*

假使船不能復原，他將生死與我相共；在世界上任何部份他
都願去，若使我遣他去。那兩個人也這樣地說。"好，"我說，"
我所提的條件，僅有兩件；第一：當你們在島上和我同居之
時，你們將要不在這裏冒僭權力；假使我置武器在你們的手
中，無論何時，你們須把牠們交給我，在這島上不要和我發
生意見，在島之時，須聽我的命令來管理你們。第二：假使那
只船是，或者可以是，復原了，你們將要載我和我的人同英
國去，不索我們的船費。"

他給我所有的保證而能為人們的思想和信心所能想着
的，他將要依從這些最合理的要求，其外，他的性命將惟我是
賴，在任何時，一經活着，他將感激這事。"好，那末就是如此
，"我說，"這裏有三枝鎗給你們，藥粉子彈皆備。再告訴我你
想最合宜的是做些什麼事。"他竭力把所有的感激的憑證一
齊示出來，他情願在我完全指揮之下行事。我告訴他我想
要去冒險是困苦的；但是我能想出最好的方法就是乘他們
睡覺之時馬上去射擊他們，假使第一排鎗未嘗殺傷任何人，
遂向我們歸順，我們便可饒恕他們，這樣，彈丸之能否打中，
悉聽上天之命。他很和平地說他是不願去殺害他們，若能為
力；但是那兩個怙惡不悛的棍徒，船中叛變的主謀人，假使
他們逃走，我們恐怕仍要受害，因為他們將要跑上船去，把
全船的人帶來，把我們一齊殺害。"好，那末，"我說，"至萬不
得巳之時，我的計劃也可算作正當的辦法，因為這是救助我
們生命的惟一方法。"然而，看見他們仍舊顧慮到流血之舉，
我告訴他，他們將去自行處理，去進行對於他們便利之事。

my [1]*advice,* for it is the only way to save our lives."
However, seeing him still [2]*cautious* of [3]*shedding* [4]*blood,* I told
him they should go themselves, and manage as they found
[5]*convenient.*

In the middle of this [6]*discourse* we heard some of them
awake, and soon after we saw two of them on their feet. I
asked him if either of them was at the head of the mutiny.
He said, "No." "Well, then," said I, "you may let
them escape; and Providence seems to have [7]*awakened* them
on [8]*purpose* to save themselves. "Now," said I, "if the rest
[9]*escape* you, it is your fault." [10]*Animated with this,* he took
the musket I had given him in his hand, and a pistol in
his belt, and his two [11]*comrades* with him, with each a piece
in his hand. The two men who were with him going first
made some noise, at which one of the seamen, who was
awake, [12]*turned about,* and seeing them coming, cried out to
the rest; but it was too late then, for the moment he cried
out they fired,—I mean the two men, the captain wisely
[13]*reserving* his own piecs.

They had so well [14]*aimed their shot* at the men they
knew that one of them was killed [15]*on the spot,* and the other
very much [16]*wounded;* but not being dead he [17]*started up* on
hie feet, and called [18]*eagerly* for help to the other. But the
captain stepping to him, told him it was too late to cry for
help, he should call upon God to [19]*forgive* his [20]*villainy;* and
with that word [21]*knoeked* him [22]*down* with the [23]*stock* of his
musket, so that he never spoke more. There were three
more in the company, and one of them was slightly
wounded. By this time I was come; and when they saw
their danger, and that it was [24]*in vain* [25]*to resist,* they begged
for [26]*mercy.* The captain told them he would [27]*spare* their

在談話之中，我們聽見他們之中有幾人醒了，立刻我們看見二人立起來。我問他這兩人是不是叛變的主要人物。他說，"不是。"，"好，那末，"我說，"你可以讓們逃走；看起來好似上天把他們弄醒，特意地來救助他們。""現在，"我說，"假使其餘的人從你們方面逃走，這就是你們的過失了。"被這話所激厲，他把我給他的鎗拿在手中，帶中藏有一把手鎗，他的同伴二人和他一同去，每人手執一只鎗。和他們同走的兩個人在前面走發出了些聲音，聽見了聲音，水手中的一人，他是醒了，掉轉身去，看見他們來了，向其餘的人大聲叫着；但是太遲了：因爲當他喊叫之時，他們發了鎗—— 我的意思是那兩人，船長很聰明地把他的鎗留而不發。

他們把鎗彈向水手們描得這樣地準，他們知道他們之中的一人是立卽被殺了，另外一個受了重傷；但是未死，他忽立起而奔逃，懇切地向其餘的人呼救。但是船主向他的面前，告訴他這是太遲了，來不及呼救了，他將呼上帝之名而赦他的罪惡；說了這話，他用鎗幹把他打倒，他遂不再說話了。在一羣中尙有三人，其中一人受有輕傷。這時我走來了；當他們看見危險臨頭之時，抵抗是徒然的，他們遂乞憐的求恕。船主告訴他們他將饒恕他們的性命，假使他們給

lives if they would give him any ¹*assurance* of their ab-
²*horrence* of the ³*treachery* they had been ⁴*gnilty* of, and
would swear to be faithful to him in recoveing the ship,
and afterwards in carrying her back to Jamaica, from
whence they came. They gave him all the ⁵*protestations* of
their ⁶*sincerity* that could de desired ; and he was willing
to believe them, and spare their livs, which I was not
against. Only I ⁷*obliged* him to keep them bound hand and
foot while they were on the island.

.　While this was doing, I sent Friday with the captain's
mate to the boat, with orders ⁸*to secure* her, and bring away
the ⁹*oars* and ¹⁰*sails*, which they did. By and by three
¹¹*straggling* men, that were (happily for them) parted from
the rest, came back upon hearing the guns fired ; and
seeing the captain, who was before their prisoner, now
their ¹²*conqueror*, they ¹³*submitted* to be bound also. So our
¹⁴*victory* was complete.

CHAPTER XLII

Iᴛ now ¹⁵*remained* that the capain and I should ¹⁶*inquire*
into one another's ¹⁷*circumstances*. I began first, and told him
my wholl history, which he heard with an ¹⁸*attention* even
to ¹⁹*amazement*, and particularly at the wonderful manner
of my being ²⁰*furnished* with provisions and ²¹*ammunition*;
and indeed, as my story is a whole ²²*collection* of wonders,
it ²³*affected* him ²⁴*deeply*. But whem he ²⁵*reflected* from thence
upon himself, and how I seemed to have been preserved
there on purpose to save his life, the tears ran down his
face, and he could not speak a word more. ✺ After this
²⁶*communication* was at an end, I carried him and his two
men into my ²⁷*apartment*, leading them in just where I came

544

他他們曾經犯了奸詐之事以後發生憎惡的確證，以及立誓忠心對他，重行使船復原，以後把船駛往賈妹加去，從那裏他們是出來的。我們給他他們所能表示得出誠實心的所有的申明的話；他很情願地相信他們，饒了他們的生命，我對遣事不加以反對。不過我命他把他們手足都綑綁起來；當他們在島上之時。

當做遣事之時，我遣星期五和船主的同伴到船上去，命他們將船扣留，把槳，船帆帶走，他們做了這事。不久，那三個散步的人；他們是（對他們是有幸）和其餘的人分別了的，聽了發槍的聲音走回來了；看見了船主，他以前是他們的囚虜，現在却是他們的征服者了，他們也都甘心受縛這樣我們的勝利是完全了

第四十二章

現在船主和我有暇來彼此互詢境況了。我起頭開言，告訴他我的完全的故事，他用留心的態度甚至於吃驚來聽我講，尤其是聽了我用奇怪的方法來供備我的食物和軍實；實在我的故事是奇事的總集，牠使他甚為感動。但是當他從那裏想到他自己身上，瞧起來我怎樣地像是有意留在這裏來救他的生命一般，淚珠流在他的臉上他不能再發一言了。談論終止了以後，我帶他和他的兩個人到我室中去，領他們進去，貼正

out, namely, at the top of the house, where I [1]*refreshed* him
with such provisions as I had, and showed them all the
[2]*contrivances* I had make during my long, long [3]*inhabiting*
that place.

All I showed them, all I said to them, was perfectly
[4]*amazing.* But above all the captain admired my [5]*fortification*, and how perfectly I had [6]*concealed* my [7]*retreat* with a
grove of trees, which, having been now planted nearly
twenty years, and the trees growing much faster than in
England, was become a little wood, [8]*so thick* that it was
[9]*impassable* in any part of it but at that one side where I
had [10]*reserved* my little [11]*winding passage* into it. I told him
this was my castle and my [12]*residence*, but that I had a seat
in the country, as most princes have, whither I could
retreat upon occasion, and I would show him that, too,
another time; but at present our business was to consider
how to recover the ship. He agreed with me as to that,
but told me he was perfectly at a loss what [13]*measures* to take,
for that there were still six and twenty hands on board,
who, having entered into a [14]*cursed* [15]*conspiracy*, by which they
had all [16]*forfeited* their lives to the law, would be [17]*hardened* in
it now by [18]*desperation,* and would carry it on, knowing that
if they were [19]*subdued* they would be brought to the [20]*gallows* as
soon as they came to England or to any of the English
[21]*colonies.* Therefore, there would be no [22]*attacking* them
with so small a number as we were.

I mused for some time on what he had said, and found
it was a very [23]*rational conclusion*, and that therefore something
thing was to be resolved on [24]*speedily*, as well to draw the
men on board into some [25]*snare* for their [26]*surprise*, as to
[27]*prevent* their landing upon us, and destroying us. Upon

在我從那裏出來的地方，就是，在房子的頂上，在那裏我用我所有的東西來調養他們：指示着他們我所做成的各種計劃在我在那個地方居住得很久的時候之中。

我指示他們一切，我告訴他們一切，都是使他們吃驚的事物。但是最要者船主歡賞我的堡壘，我怎樣地完美地把我的隱居之所在樹林之中遮蓋起來，樹林現在差不多種植了二十年了，樹比在英國長得還要快，變成了小樹林了.這樣地厚，在無論那一方面都不能通過，除卻在那一方面，在那裏，我在其中留下了一條小曲徑。我告訴他這是我的堡和住所，但是我在村舍中還有一座別墅，好像王子們所有的一般，無論何時，我可以在那裏退隱，我將要把那個也向他表示，在別的時期之中；但是現在我們的事務是注意着怎樣去找尋那只船。他對於這事和我同意，但是告訴我他是毫不知道將要用何計劃，因為在船上仍舊我二十六人，他們，已經結黨謀叛，做了那事，按法當以性命抵償，將要因絕望而其心愈忍，將要繼續進行，知道假使他們被克服了，他們將受絞死之刑，一經到了英國，或是到了英國的殖民地裏面。所以，我們的人數是這樣的少，最好不要去攻打他們。

我默然想了若干時他所說的話，覺着這是很合理的結彄，所以馬上要另行設法，去把在船上的人弄到陷穽中去，使他們吃驚，以及去阻止他們上岸來攻打我們，殺害我們。

1.調養。2.計謀。3.居住。4.可驚。5.堡。6.遮蔽。7.隱居所。8.如此厚。0.不能通過。10.留下。11.曲徑。12.住所。13.法子。14.可惡的。15.反叛。16.抵償。17.使殘忍。18.絕望。19.克服。20.縊架。21.殖民地。22.攻打。23.合理之結論。24.速。25.陷阱。26.吃驚。27.阻止。

this, it presently [1]*occurred* to me that in a little while the ship's crew, wondering what was become of their comrades and of the boat, would certainly come on shore in their other boat to look for them, and that then, perhaps, they might come armed, and be too strong for us. [2]*This he allowed to be rational.* Upon this, I told him the first thing we had to do was [3]*to stave the boat*, which lay upon the beach, so that they might not carry her off, and, taking everything out of her, leave her so far useless as not to be fit to [4]*swim*. Accordingly we went on board, took the arms which were left on board out of her, and whatever else we found there,—which was a bottle of [5]*brandy*, and another of rum, a few [6]*biscuit* cakes, a horn of powder, and a great lump of [7]*sugar* in a piece of [8]*canvas*. The sugar was five or six pounds. All this was very welcome to me, especially the brandy and sugar, of which I had had none left for many years.

When we had carried all these things on shore, (the [9]*oars*, [10]*mast*, [11]*sail*, and [12]*rudder* of the boat were carried away before,) we knocked a great hole in her bottom, that if they had come strong enough to master us, yet they could not carry off the boat. Indeed, it was not much in my thoughts that we could be able to recover the ship. But my view was that if they went away without the boat, I did not much question to make her again fit to carry us to the [13]*Leeward Islands*, and call upon our friends the Spaniards in my way ; for I had them still in my thoughts.

While we were thus preparing our designs, and had first, by [14]*main strength*, heaved the boat upon the beach so high that the tide would not float her off at high-water mark, and, besides, had broken a hole in her bottom too

因此之故，馬上我想着在不久之時，船上的水手們，奇怪着不知他們的同伴和小船怎樣了，一定要上岸來，在他們別一只小船中，找尋他們，那末，或者，他們挾有武器而來，太強橫了，非我們所能抵抗。他也以此意爲然。因此之故，我告訴他我們要做的第一件事就是要去把船鑿成一洞，使水流入而沈沒之，船是橫在海濱之上，這樣他們可以不把牠帶去，把船中所有物件都取出來，讓牠成爲無用的東西，不合宜在水上游着。立刻我們到船上去，把在船中的兵器一齊拿出來，以及別的能夠尋得着的東西，——一瓶白蘭地酒，另一瓶醋酒，幾塊餅干，一只裝火藥的角形物，在一塊帆布中有一大塊糖。糖重至五或六磅。這些東西對我是歡迎的，尤其是白蘭地和糖，那些東西多少年我已未曾有餘下的了。

當我們把這東西帶上岸去，(槳，船椼柱，船帆和舵以前巳被帶走了，)在船底我們打了一個大洞，假使他們有強大的力量足以戰勝我們，然而他們却不能把船帶走。實在，我的思想之中却未曾多想着我們竟能找着那只船。但是我的意見是那樣，假使他們不乘船而走了，我不難把船重行攏得合用，把我們載到李宛而特羣島去，在路上招呼我們的友人西班牙人們；因爲在腦筋中，我仍舊想念着他們。

當我們這樣地預備着我們的計謀之時，起初，用了主要的力量，把船扛到海濱上面這樣高，在水漲高之時，潮水可以不把牠漂流而去，其外，在船的底下，我們也碎了一個洞，

big to be quickly stopped, and were sat down *¹musing* what
we should do, we heard the ship fire a gun, and saw her
made ²a *waft* with her ³*ensign* as a signal for the boat to
come on board. But no boat ⁴*stirred,* and they fired several
times making other ⁵*signals* for the boat. At last, when all
their signals and firing ⁶*proved fruitless,* and they found
the boat did not stir, we saw them, by the help of my
glasses, ⁷*hoist* another boat out, and row towards the
shore. We found, as they ⁸*approached,* that there were no
less than ten men in her, and that they had ⁹*firearms*
with them.

As the ship lay almost two ¹⁰*leaguse* from the shore, we
had a full view of them as they came, and plain sight even
of their faces; because the tide having set them a little
to the east of the other boat, they rowed up under shors,
to come to the same place where the other had landed, and
where the boat lay. By this means, I say, we had a full
view of them, and the captain knew the persons and
¹¹*characters* of all the men in the boat, of whom, he said,
there were three very honest fellows, who, he was sure,
were led into this ¹²*conspiracy* by the rest, being ¹³*overpowered*
and ¹⁴*frightened;* but that as for the ¹⁵*boatswain,* who, it
seems, was the ¹⁶*chief officer* among them, and all the rest,
they were as ¹⁷*outrageous* as any of the ship's crew, and
were no doubt made ¹⁸*desperate* in their now ¹⁹*enterprise.*

We had, upon the first appearance of the boats coming
from the ship, considered of ²⁰*separating* our prisoners; and
we had, indeed, secured them ²¹*effectually.* Two of them,
of whom the captain was less ²²*assured* than ²³*ordinary,* I sent
with Friday and one of the three delivered man, to my
cave, where they were ²⁴*remote* enough, and out of danger

太大了而不能陡然地停下來，我們坐下來默想着應當做什麼，我們聽見船上發了一鎗；看見牠搖旗以為記號，為着小船中的人要上船去了。但是沒有船行駛，他們又放了幾次鎗，向船敬別的記號。最後，當他們所有的記號和放鎗皆歸無效之時，他們見船不動，我們看見他們，賴了我的望遠鏡之助，把別的一只小船升了起來，向海岸搖曳而去。我們看見，當他們臨近之時，在畧中不下於十人，他們帶有火器。

船泊在離岸約有兩海里遠的地方，他們來了，我們完全地看見他們，他們的面目都明顯地可見；因為潮水使他們稍為到別的一只船的東面去，他們在岸下搖上去，到同一的地點上去；在那裏，別的人曾上岸，在那裏，船泊着。用這個方法，我說，我們完全地看見他們；船主知道船中所有人的人格和品行，在他們之中，他說，有三個很誠實的人，他們，他可以確定，是被其餘的人牽引到謀叛裏面去，是被人強迫而驚嚇的；至於那個水手長，他，瞧起來是如此，是他們中的大副，其餘的人，他們是和任何船上的水手一樣的橫暴，一定無疑，他們的新事業使得他們尤為兇悍了。

在小船從船中第一次出見之時，我們曾想着要把我們的囚虜們分開；實在，我們很有效地把他們拘禁了。他們之中二人，船主對於他們是比平常的人不甚確信的，我遺星期五和被救的三人中的一人，到我山穴中去，在那裏，他們是很遠的了，不致有被聽見或被發見的，或者是覓路而出了樹林的危險，假使他們能夠解放了自己。

1.默想。2.搖。3.旗。4.行駛。5.記號。6.無效。7.升起。8.臨近。9火器。10.海里。11.品格。12.謀叛。13.強迫14.驚嚇。15.水手長。16.船中大副。17.橫暴。18.兇悍。19.事業。20.分開。21.有效。22.確定。23.平常。24.遠。

of being **heard** or discovered, or of finding their way out of the woods if they could have delivered themselves. Here they left them bound, but gave them [1]*provisions*, and [2]*promised* them, if they [3]*continued* there [4]*quietly*, to give them their [5]*liberty* in a day or two; but that if they [6]*attempted* their [7]*escape*, they should be put to death without mercy. They promised [8]*faithfully* to bear their [9]*confinement* with [10]*patience*, and were very thankful that they had such good [11]*usage* as to have provisions and light left them. Friday gave them [12]*candles* for their [13]*comfort*; and they did not know but tnat he stood [14]*sentinel* over them at [15]*the entrance*.

The other prisoners had better usage. Two of them were kept [16]*pinioned*, indeed, because the captain was not able [17]*to trust* them; but the other two were token into my service, upon the captain's [18]*recommendation*, and upon their [19]*solemnly* [20]*engaging* to live and die with us. So with them and the three honest men we were seven man, well armed; and I made no [21]*doubt* we should be able to deal well enough with the ten that were coming, considering that the captain had said there were three or four honest man among them also.

. As soon as they got to the place where their other boat lay, they ran their boat into the beach and came all on shore, [22]*hauling* the boat up after them, which I was glad to see, for I was afraid they would rather have left the boat at an [23]*anchor* some distance from the shore, with some hands in her, to [24]*guard* her, and so we should not be able to [25]*seize* the boat. Being on shore, the first thing they did, they all ran to their other boat. If was easy to see they were under a great surprise to find her [26]*stripped* of all that was in her and a great hole in her bottom. After they had [27]*mused*

在這裏，他們是綑着而被留下了，但是他們給他們食物，並且允許他們，假使他們繼續着平靜地在那裏，在一二日之內，就可以給他們自由了；但是假使他們要想企圖着逃走，他們是死無赦的。他們允許着誠實地監禁，耐着心腸，他們感謝着這樣好的待遇，例如給他們食物和光亮。星期五為他們的安慰之故，給了他們幾枝燭；他們不知道他巡邏於門外而防守着他們呢。

別的囚虜也受着較好的待遇。兩個人是被綁着，實係如此，因為船主不能相信他們；但是另外兩人是歸我差遣，接受了船主的介紹，以及接受了他們允許和我們共禍福的隆重的誓詞。這樣，和了他們以及那三個誠實的人，我們是七個人了，武裝齊備；我毫不懷疑我們能夠抵抗那將要來的十個人，想着船主曾說過在他們之中我也三四個誠實的人呢。

一經他們來到了他們另外一只小船停泊的地方，他們把小船駛到海濱內去，一齊上了岸；在他們身後把船曳上來，我是很快樂地看見這事，因為我怕他們將要把小船下了錨，在離岸若干距離的地方，在小船中有若干人守着，這樣我們便不能去取那只小船了。上了岸，他們第一次所做的事，就是跑到他們的另外一只小船那裏去。很容易地看見他們是驚異了，看見船上的東西都被取去了，船底下還有一個大洞。他們默想了一會以後，

1.食物. 2.允許. 3.繼續. 4.平靜. 5.自由. 6.企圖. 7.逃走. 8.忠心地. 9.監禁. 10.忍耐. 11.待遇. 12.燭. 13.安慰. 14.巡邏. 15.門外. 16.綑. 17.相信. 18.介紹. 19.莊重. 20.允. 21.疑. 22.曳. 23.錨. 24.防守. 25.捉. 26.取. 27.默念.

awhile upon this, they set up two or three great ¹*shouts,* ²*hallooing* with all their might, to try if they could make their ³*companions* hear. But all was to no ⁴*purpose.* Then they ⁵*came all close in a ring,* and fired a ⁶*volley* of their small arms, which, indeed, we heard, and the ⁷*echoes* made the woods ⁸*ring.* But it was all ¦one; those in the cave, we were sure, could not hear; and those in our ⁹*keeping,* though they heard it well enough, yet ¹⁰*durst* give no answer to them. They were so ¹¹*astonished* at this that, as they told us afterwards, they resolved to go all on board again to their ship, and let them know that the men were all murdered, and the longboat ¹²*staved.* Accordingly, they ¹³*immediately* ¹⁴*launched* their boat again, and got all of them on board.

The captain was ¹⁵*terribly* ¹⁶*amazed,* and even ¹⁷*confounded,* at this, believing they would go on board the ship again and set sail, giving their comrades over for lost, and so he should stil lose the ship, which he was in hopes we should have recovered. But he was ¹⁸*quickly* as much frightened the other way.

They had not been long put off with the boat, when we ¹⁹*perceived* them all coming on shore again, but with this new measure, which it seems they ²⁰*consulted* together upon; namely, to leave three men in the boat, and the rest to go on shore, and go up into the country to look for their fellows. This was a great ²¹*disappointment* to us, for now we were ²²*at aloss what to do,* as our seizing those seven men on shore would be no advantage to us if we let the boat escape. They would row away to the ship, and then the rest of them would be sure ²³*to weigh* and ²⁴*set sail,* and so our recovering the ship would be lost. However, we had no ²⁵*remedy* but to wait and see what the ²⁶*issue* of things might present.

他們發出兩三聲大叫，拚命地喊着，試着他們能不能使同伴們聽見。但是毫無用處。他們於是立成環式，放了一排他們的小鎗。實在我們聽了那個，回音把樹林都震響起來。但是事亦徒然；那些在洞穴中的人，我們確定，不能夠聽見；在我們防守之下的那些，雖然聽得很清楚，然不敢向他們囘答。他們對於遣事，非常驚駭，他們以後曾經告訴我們；他們决心一齊再上船中去，使他們知道攏總的水手皆被殺了；長舢板被鑿穿了。他們立卽重駛行他們的小船，大家一齊上了船。

船主是非常地吃驚，甚至昏亂起來，對於遣事，相信他們要再上大船去，揚帆而行，以爲他們的同伴的生命必難保全，這樣他仍舊是把船失掉，他曾希望着我們能把牠復得的。但是他對於別一事上立刻又更驚嚇起來。

他們駛行未遠，我們便看見他們一齊重行來到岸上，但是取了新的步驟，看起來好像他們曾經會過了議；就是，留下三人在船上，其餘的上岸去，跑進曠野去找尋他們的人。這事對於我們是一種大的失望，因爲現在我們是不知所措，我們把那七人在岸上捉住，對於我們是沒有利益的，假使我們讓那只船逃走。他們將要把船搖向大船，其餘的人一定要起錨帆，這樣我們復得大船的希望便斷絕了。然而，我們沒有補救之法，除等候和觀望事之如何結果而外。

The seven men came on shore, and the three who
[1]*remained* in the boat put her off to a good distance from the
shore, and came to an [2]*anchor* to wait for them; so that
it was [3]*impossible* for us to come at them in the boat.
Those that came on shore [4]*kept close together*, marching
towards the top of the little hill under which my [5]*habitation*
lay; and we could see them plainly, though they could not
[6]*perceive* us. We should have been very glad if they would
have come nearer to us, so that we might have fired at
them, or that they would have gone farther off, that we
might come abroad. But when they were come to the
brow of the hill where they could see a great way into the
[7]*valleys* and woods, which lay towards the northeast part,
and where the island lay lowest, they shouted and [8]*hallooed*
till they were weary. Not [9]*caring*, it seems, to venture far
from the shore, nor far from one another, they sat down
together under a tree to consider it. Had they thought fit
to go to sleep there, as the other part of them had done,
they had done the job for us; but they were too full of
[10]*apprehensions* of danger to venture to go to sleep, though
they could not tell what the danger was they had to fear.

The captain made a very just [11]*proposal* to me upon this
[12]*consultation* of theirs; namely, that perhaps they would all
fire a [13]*volley* again, to [14]*endeavor* to make their fellows hear,
and that we should all sally upon them just at the [15]*juncture*
when their pieces were all [16]*discharged*, and they would
certainly yield, and we should have them without [17]*bloodshed*.
I liked this proposal, [18]*provided* it was done while we were
near enough to come up to them before they could load
their pieces again. But this event did not happen; and we
lay still a long time, very [19]*irresolute* what course to take.

七人上了岸，那三個留下在小船中的人把船駛行到離岸甚遠的地方去，下了錨，等候着他們；這樣我們是不能夠到船中他們身邊去。上了岸的人們，彼此緊隨着，向小山的頂上而行。在山的下面就是我的住所所在之處，我們明白地看見他們，雖然他們看不見我等。我們將要很快樂，假使他們靠近我們走來，那末我們可以射擊他們，或者假使他們走得遠些，那末我們可以到外面去。但是當他們到了山岡之時，在那裏，他們能夠看見山谷和樹林中老遠的地方，山谷和樹林是在東北的部份上，在那裏，島面是最低的，他們大叫和喊叫，直至於疲困始止。看起來，不願再冒險離岸遠去，也不願大家遠離，他們一齊在樹下坐下來商議着。假使他們想着合宜地在那裏睡覺，像他們另一部份人曾經做過的，那末他們便使我們完成大事了；但是他們是過於恐怕着危險，竟致不敢入睡，雖然他們不知道他們所恐怖的是那一種的危險。

船主向我提了一個正當提議，在會議處置他們的當中；就是，或者他們將要再放一排鎗，竭力使他們的人聽見，我們一齊突出而攻之，適當他們鎗彈放完之時，他們一定要屈服；我們可以不流血得着他們。我喜愛這個提議，倘若是做了當我們是很近的去到他們那裏，在他們再裝彈藥入鎗之前。但是這事未曾實現；我們靜靜地躺下很久，茫然不知何所適從。

1.留下。2.錨。3.不能。4.彼此緊隨。5.住所。6.見。7.山谷。8.喊叫。9.介意。願。10.恐怖。11.提議。12.會議。23.山谷。14.竭力。5.際。16.放畢。17.流血。18.設或。19.不知

At length, I told them there would be nothing to be done, in my opinion, till night. Then, if they did not return to the boat, perhaps we might find a way to get between them and the shore, and so might use some ¹*stratagem* with those in the boat to get them on shore. We waited a great while, though very ²*impatient* for their ³*removing*; and were very uneasy when, after long ⁴*consultation*, we saw them all start up, and march down towards the sea. It seems they had such dreadful ⁵*apprehensions* of the danger of the place that they ⁶*resolved* to go on board the ship again, give their companions over for lost, and so go on with their ⁷*intended* voyage with the ship.

CHAPTER XLIII

As soon as I ⁸*perceived* them go towards the shore, I imagined it to be, as it ⁹*really* was, that they had given over their ¹⁰*search*, and were going back again. The captain as soon as I told him my thoughts, ¹¹*was ready to sink at the apprehension of it.* But I presently thought of a stratagem ¹²*to fetch* them back again, which ¹³*answered my end to a tittle.*

I ordered Friday and the captain's mate to go over the little ¹⁴*creek* westward, towards the place where the savages came on shore when Friday was ¹⁵*rescued*, and so soon as they came to a little rising ground, at about half a mile distance I bade them ²⁹*halloo out,* as loud as they could, and wait till they found the seamen heard them. As soon as ever they heard the seamen answer them, they should return it again, and then, *keeping out of sight, take a round,* always answering when the other hallooed, to draw them as far into the island and among the woods as possible, and then ¹⁸*wheel about* again to me by such ways as I directed them

最後，我告訴他們，或者無事可做；按照我意，直至夜間。假使他們不同至小艇，或者我們找出方法來到他們和岸之中的地方去，這樣便可以設法，和在小船內的那些人，使他們上岸來。我們等了許久，雖然等候着他們的移動，是再不能忍耐了；到是狠不安的，在長久的會議之後，我們看見他們一齊站立起來，向海而行。好像是他們對於那個地方的危險是非常恐怖的，他們遂决心重上大船去，以為他們同伴必定失去生命了，這樣便去乘船繼續着他們立意的旅行。

一經我看見他們向海岸而去，我猜想將要是這樣，實係

第 四 十 三 章

一經我看見他們向海岸而去，我猜想將要是這樣，實係如此，他們不再尋找同伴，重行同去，船主，一經我告訴他我的思想，覺悟之餘，便心灰意喪起來。但是我立即想出一法，使他們重行同來，這事竟逢我目的了。

我命星期五和船主的同事到西面小溪那邊去，向那個地方，在那裏，野人們上了岸；當星期五是被救了，一經他們來到了一座小的聳高的地面，大約半英里的距離，我命他們大叫着，竭力地喊着，等着直至他們覺着那些水手聽見他們之時，一經他們聽見水手回答他們，他們須立即回答，不為他們所見，繞行一周，常常地答應着，當別人大叫之時，把他們竭力領得很遠，到島中和樹林中來，於是再轉同到我這裏來，從我指示他們的那條路走來。

They were just going into the boat when Friday and the mate hallooed. They presently heard them, and, answering, ran along the shore [1]*westward*, towards the voice they heard, when they were stopped by the creek, where the water being up, they could not get over, and called for the boat to come up and set them over; as, indeed, I expected.

When they had set themselves over, I [2]*observed* that, the boat being gone a good way into the creek, and, as it were, in a [3]*harbor* within the land, they took one of the three men out of her, to go along with them, and left only two in the boat, having [4]*fastened* her to the [5]*stump* of a little tree on the shore. This was what I wished for. [6]*Immediately* leaving Friday and the captain's mate to their business, I took the rest with me; and, [7]*crossing* the creek out of their sight, we [8]*surprised* the two man before they were [9]*aware*,—one of them lying of the shore, and the other being in the boat. The fellow on shore was between sleeping and waking and going to start up. The captain, who was [10]*foremost*, ran in upon him, and knocked him down, and then called out to him in the boat to yield, or he was a dead man.

There needed very few [11]*arguments* to [12]*persuade* a single man to yield, when he saw five men upon him and his [13]*comrade* knocked down, Besides, this was, it seems, one of the three who were [14]*not so hearty* in the [15]*mutiny* as the rest of the crew, and therefore he was easily persuaded not only to yield, but afterwards to join very [16]*sincerely* with us. In the mean time, Friday and the captain's mate so well managed their business with the rest that they drew them, by hallooing and answering, from one hill to another, and from one wood to another till they not only

他們剛進小船，星期五和那個船伙便大叫起來。他們立刻聽見，回答着，沿着岸向西方跑去，對着他們聽見的聲音的地方跑，他們陡然被小溪攔住了路，在那裏，水是高的，他們不能越過。叫小船來把們渡過去；寶在，我是希望着這樣。

當他們渡過了小溪之時，我注意着那只小船駛到小溪之中很遠的地方去了，就是這樣，駛到陸地之中的海口內去，他們把小船中三人中的一人帶着和他們偕行，僅留兩人在船中，把船繫在岸上一株小樹的幹上。這就是我所希望的事。立即留下了星期五和那船伙去做他們的事，我把其餘的人帶着走；橫過了小溪。不爲他們所見，乘彼二人之不意，加以襲擊，—— 一人躺在岸上，一人在船中。在岸上的人是在半醒半睡之中，要想立起身來。船主，他是最前的一人；衝到他的前面，把他打倒，於是向在船中的人叫着，叫他歸順，否則性命休矣。

無需多言來勸誘一人投降，當他看見五個人攻打他，而他的同伴又被打倒了。其外，看起來，這就是三人中的一人，他在叛變之中，不是狠熱心的人，如同其餘的水手一般，所以他是很容易地被勸誘，不但歸順，而且以後還很忠寶的和我們在一處。在其時，星期五和船長的同事把他們的事處理得這樣好，他們把那些人引了來，用了叫聲和回答的聲，從此山到那山，從此林到那林，直至他們不但令彼等疲倦異常，而且把他們留在那個地方，在那裏，他們是一定的，在天黑以前，他們決計不能重行回到小船中去。寶在，他們自已也非常的疲倦了，當他們回到我們面前之時。

[1]*heartily* tired them, but left them where they were very sure they could not reach back to the boat before it was dark. Indeed, they were heartily [2]*tired* themselves, also, by the time they came back to us.

We had nothing now to do but to watch for them in the dark, and to fall upon them so as to make sure work with them. It was several hours after Friday came back to me before they came back to their boat. We could hear the foremost of them, long before they came quite up, calling to those behind to come along; and could also hear them answer, and [3]*complain* how [4]*lame* and tired they were, and not able to come any faster; which was very [5]*welcome* news to us. At length they came up to the boat; but it is [6]*impossible* to express their [7]*confusion* when they found the boat fast aground in the creek, the [8]*tide* [9]*ebbed* out, and their two men gone. We could hear them call one to another in a most [10]*lamentable* manner, telling one another they were got into an [11]*enchanted* island; that either there were [12]*inhabitants* in it, and they should all be [13]*murdered,* or else there were [14]*devils* and [15]*spirits* in it, and they should be all carried away and [16]*devoured.*

They hallooed again, and called their two [17]*comrades* by their names a great many times; but no answer. After some time we could see them, by the little light there was, running about, [18]*wringing* their hands like men in [19]*despair.* Sometimes they would go and sit down in the boat to rest themselves; then come ashore again, and walk about again, and so the same thing over again. My men would fain have had me give them leave to fall upon them at once in the dark; but I was willing to take them at some [20]*advantage,* so as to spare them, and kill as few of them as I could.

當現在我們無事可做除卻在黑暗之中看守他們之時，我們要襲擊他們，俾得一戰而敗之。在星期五回來以後，在他們回轉他的小船之前，又過了幾個鐘點。我們能夠聽見他們之中最前的一人，在他們寂寂的上來很久以前，叫那些後隨的人前進；也能夠聽見他們回答，多訴着他們是怎樣地跛行而困倦，不能再向前走快；這是令我們可喜的信息。最後，他們到了小船那裏；但是這是不可能地去表明他們大亂的情形，當他們看見了小船固定着在地上，在小溪之中，潮退了：他們的二人走了。我們能夠聽見他們互相叫着，其情形至可哀憐，互相告訴他們是來到了一座被妖迷的島上了；就是或者有人住在上面，他們將要完全被殺，否則，在島中必有鬼神，他們都要被帶走而被吞吃了。

他們重行叫着，叫他們同伴二人的名字許多次；但是沒有回答。過了些時，我們能夠看見他們，趁了少許的亮光，跑來跑去，扭着手如同在失望之中的人一樣。有時，他們去坐下來，在船中去休息着；後來又來到岸上，重行散着步，反來復去地做同樣的事。我的人們極願我讓他們去在黑暗之中立刻攻擊他們，但是我情願占他們的上風，這樣去把他們分開來，竭力地去把他們人數稍加殺傷。

1. 異常. 2. 疲困. 3. 訴. 4. 跛行. 5. 令人可喜的. 6. 不能. 7. 大亂. 8. 潮. 9. 退潮. 10. 可哀的. 11. 被妖迷. 12. 居民. 13. 殺. 14. 鬼. 15. 神. 16. 吞吃. 17. 同伴. 17. 扭. 19. 失望. 20. 上風.

Especially I was unwilling to [1]*hazard* the killing of any of our men, knowing the others were very well armed. I resolved to wait, to see if they did not separate. Therefore, to make sure of them, I drew my [2]*ambuscade* nearer, and ordered Friday and the captain [3]*to creep upon* their hands and feet, as close to the ground as they could, that they might not be discovered, and get as near them as they possibly could, before they [4]*offered* to fire.

They had not been long in that [5]*posture* when the [6]*boatswain*, who was the [7]*principal ringleader* of the [8]*mutiny*, and had now shown himself the most [9]*dejected* and [10]*dispirited* of all the rest, came walking towards them, with two more of the crew. The captain was so eager at having this [11]*principal rogue* so much in his power, that he could hardly have [12]*patience* to let him come so near as to be sure of him, for they only heard his tongue before. But when they came nearer, the captain and Friday, [13]*starting up* on their feet, let fly at them. The boatswain was killed upon the spot; the next man was shot in the body and fell just by him, though he did not die till an hour or two after; and the third ran for it. At the noise of the fire I immediately advanced with my [14]*whole army.* which was now eight men ; namely, myself, [15]*generalissimo*; Friday, my [16]*lieutenant general*; the captain and his two men, and the three prisoners of war whom we had trusted with arms.

We came upon them, indeed, in the dark, so that they could not see our number; and I made the man they had left in the boat, who was now one of us. call to them by name, to try if I could bring them to a [17]*parley* and so perhaps might [18]*reduce* them to terms. This fell out just as we [19]*desired*; for, indeed, it was easy to think, as their

尤其是我不願冒險去使我之中任何人被殺傷，知道別的人是武裝齊備的。我決心等候，看看他們分別沒有分別。於是，使他們一定如此，我把埋伏所弄得靠近些，命令星期五和那船伙匍匐而行，竭力地貼着地面，那末他們不與爲人所見，竭力地去貼近他們，在他們開始放鎗之前。

　　他們在這種景況之中不甚長久，陡然地那個水手長，他是叛變中的領袖，現在較之其餘的人們格外顯示着憂愁沮喪，走向他們之前，和着其他兩個水手。船主是這樣的切望，他有這個罪魁在他手掌之中，他竟不能忍耐地讓他走得這樣近去確定是他，因爲他們以前僅僅聽見他的口音。但是當他們走得較近之時，船主和星期五，忽然起立，發槍射擊他們。水手長立卽被殺；第二人在身上被打中了，貼正倒在他的身邊，雖然他直至一二小時以後方纔死去；第三人急急逃去。聽見鎗聲，我立卽率全軍前進，軍中有八人；就是，我自已，大元帥；星期五，我的副都統；船主和他的兩個人，以及戰時所俘的三個俘虜，我們曾授彼等以軍器。

　　我們到了他們面前，實在，在黑暗之中，以致他們不能知道我們的人數；我使他們留下在小船中的那個人，他現在是我們中的一人了，叫他們的名字，試試看我能不能使他們開一談判，這樣或者能夠逼迫他們降順。此事結果正如我等所願；因爲，實在，這是很容易地去想：他們的景況現在旣然是如此，他們是很情願的降服了。

condition then was, they would be very willing to
¹*capitulate*. So he calls out as loud as he could to one of
them." Tom Smith! Tom Smith!" Tom Smith answered
immediately, "Is that Robinson?" for it seems he knew
the ²*voice*. The other answered,"Ay, ay; for God's sake,
Tom Smith, throw down your arms and yield, or you are
all dead man this moment."

"Who must we yield to? Where are they?" says Smith
again. "Here they are," says he ;"here's our captain
and fifty men with him, have been ³*hunting* you these two
hours. The boatswain is killed, Will Fry is ⁴*wounded*, and
I am a prisoner. If you do not yield, you are all lost,"
"Will they ⁵*give us quarter* then?" says Tom Smith, "and
we will yield." "I'll go and ask, if you ⁶*promise*, to yield,
says Robinson. So he asked the captain ; and the captain
himself then calls out,"You, Smith, you know my voice;
if you lay down your arms immediately, and ⁷*submit*, you
shall have your lives, all but Will Atkins."

Upon this, Will Atkins cried out, "For God's sake
captain, give me quarter! What have I done? They have
all been as bad as I ;" which, by the way, was not true ;
for, it seems, this Will Atkins was the first man that laid
hold of the captain when they first ⁸*mutinied*, and used him
⁹*barbarously* in tying his hands and giving him ¹⁰*injurious*
language. However, the captain told him he must lay
down his arms ¹¹*at discretion*, and ¹²*trust to the governor*'s
mercy,—by which he meant me, for they all called me
governor. In a word, they all laid down their arms, and
begged their lives. I sent the man that had ¹³*parleyed* with
them, and two more, who bound them all. Then my great
army of fifty men, which, with those three, were in all but

這樣地竭力地向他們其中一人叫道，"湯姆斯密斯！湯姆斯密斯！"湯姆斯密斯立卽回答，"是魯賓孫嗎？"因爲看起來像俙得那個聲音。別的一人答道，"是，是；爲上帝之故，湯姆斯密斯，把你的武器挪下來歸順罷，否則，你們立刻不免一死。

　　"我們必須向誰歸順呢？他們是誰？"湯密斯重行說。"他們是在這裏，"他說；這裏是我們的船主以及五十個水手和他在一處，這兩個鐘頭之中，他們是追逐你們。水手長被殺了，韋爾佛萊受傷了，我是被俘了。假使你不歸順，你們大家都要死去。""那末他們將恕我等以不死嗎？"湯姆斯密斯說，我們將情願歸順。""我去問，假使你們情願歸順，"魯賓孫說。他於是問船主；船主親自叫出來，'你，斯密斯，你懂得我的聲音；假使你們立刻挪下武器，歸順，你們可得生命，但韋爾阿特金斯不在其內。

　　因此之故，韋爾阿特金斯大叫道，"看上帝份上，船主，饒恕我罷！我做了什麼事？他們是和我一樣的壞；"閒說起來，那到不是實情；因爲，看起來，這個韋爾阿特金斯當水手們叛變之時是第一個捉住船長的人，虐待船主，把他手綁起來，咒罵着他。然而，船主告訴他他必須無條件挪下武器來，唯主宰之命是聽，——他是指我而言，因爲他們都叫我作主宰。總之，他們一齊把武器放下而乞命。我遣那個和他們開過談判的人，還有別的二人，去把他們綁起來。於是我的大軍五十人，加了那三人，攏總只有八人，去捉住他們和他們的小船；不過我使我自己和別的一人不在場，爲了身分之故。

eight, came up and ¹*seized* upon them and upon their boat; only that I kept myself and one more out of sight, for reasons of state.

Our next work was to ²*repair* the boat, and think of ³*seizing* the ship. As for the captain, now he had ⁴*leisure* to ⁵*parley* with them he ⁶*expostulated* with them upon the ⁷*villainy* of their ⁸*practices* with him, and upon the further ⁹*wickedness* of their ¹⁰*design*, and how certainly it must bring them ¹¹*to misery* and distress in the end, and perhaps to the ¹²*gallows*.

They all appeared very ¹³*penitent*, and ¹⁴*begged hard* for their lives. As for that, he told them they were not his prisoners, but those of the commander of the island; that they thought they had set him on shore in a barren, ¹⁵*uninhabited* island, but it had pleased God so to direct them that it was inhabited, and that the Governor was an Englishman; that he might ¹⁶*hang* them all there, if he pleased, but as he had given them all quarter, he ¹⁷*supposed* he would sent them to England, to be ¹⁸*dealt* with there as justice ¹⁹*required,* except Atkins, whom he was commanded by the governor to advise to prepare for death, for that he would be hanged in the morning.

Though this was all but a ²⁰*fiction* of his own, yet it had its desired ²¹*effect*. Atkins fell upon his knees, to beg the captain to ²²*intercede with* the governor for his life; and all the rest begged of him, for God's sake, that they might not be sent to England.

It now occurred to me that the time of our deliverance was come, and that it would be a most easy thing to bring these fellows in to be hearty ²³*in getting possession of* the ship. So I ²⁴*retired* in the dark from them, that they might

第二次我們的工作是修理那只小船，想去取那只大船。至於船主，現在他有工夫去和他們談判，他向他們理論他們對他行為的奸詐，以及後來他們思想的邪惡，怎樣後來他們一定要身遭不幸和苦痛，或者要上縊架。

他們都現出懺罪之狀，苦求饒恕生命。至於那事，他告訴他們，他們不是他的俘虜，但是是島中的主宰的；他們想他們是把他置在一所無生產無人居住的島上，但是上帝却願意把他們指示着到有人居住的島上，主宰還是一個英國人；他可以在那裏把他們一齊縊死，假使他願意，但是他旣然饒恕了他們；他猜想他要把他們送到英國去，秉公而處理他們的罪，除去韋爾阿特金斯以外，他被主宰命令着預備受死，因爲在早上他將要被絞殺。

雖然這不過他心中的設想而已，然而這事到達其所欲之效果。阿特金斯屈膝下跪，求船主向主宰代彼乞命；其餘的人向他哀求，看上帝份上，不要把他們送到英國去。

現在我偶想着我們被救之時已經來了，這是一椿極容易的事把這些人帶進去；很心願地去占有那只大船。這樣我從他們之中退到暗處，他們或者不曾看見他們的主宰是怎樣的一個人把船主叫到我面前來。

1.捉。2.修理。3.捉。4.閒暇。5.談判。6.理論。0.奸詐。8.行爲。9.邪惡。10.思想。11.不幸。12.縊架。13.海。14.苦求。15.無人住的。16.縊殺。17.猜想。18.處理。19.要。20.設想。21.達到。22.向……哀求。23.占有。24.退至暗處。

not see what kind of a governor they had, and called the
captain to me. When I called, as at a good distance, one
of the men was ordered to speak again, and say to the
captain, "Captain, the commander calls for you;" and
presently the captain replied, "Tell [1]*his Excellency* I am
just coming." This more perfectly [2]*amazed* them, and
they all believed that the commander [3]*was just by,* with his
fifty men.

Upon the captain's coming to me, I told him my [4]*proj-
ect* for seizing the ship, which he liked wonderfully well,
and resolved to put it in [5]*execution* the next morning. But,
in order to execute it [6]*with more art,* and to be [7]*secure* of
[8]*success,* I told him we must [9]*divide* the prisoners. and that
he should go and take Atkins, and two more of the worst
of them, and send them [10]*pinioned* to the cave where the
others lay. This was [11]*committed to* Friday and the two men
who came on shore with the captain. They [12]*conveyed* them
to the cave as to a prison, and it was, indeed, a [13]*dismal*
place. The others I ordered to my bower. As it was
fenced in, and they pinioned, the place was secure enough,
considering they were upon their [14]*behavior.*

To these in the morning I sent the captain, who was to
enter into a parley with them; in a word, to try them, and
tell me whether he thought they might be [15]*trusted* or not
to go on board and [16]*surprise* the ship. He talked to
them of the [17]*injury* done him, of the condition they were
[18]*brought to,* and that though the governor had given them
quarter for their lives as to the present action, yet that if
they were sent to England they would all be hanged in
[19]*chains*: but that if they would join in so just an [20]*attempt*
as to recover the ship, he would have the the governor's
[21]*engagement* for their [22]*pardon.*

當我呼叫之時，在很遠的距離之中，水手中的一人是被命令着再說話，向船長說，"船長，主宰喚你；"船主立刻囘答，"告訴大人，我就來了。"這事使他們更加吃驚，他們都相信主宰是適在近處，同他的五十個人。

船主來到我的面前之時，我把我要取那只大船的企謀告訴他，他對於這事非常贊成；決定第二天早晨去實行此事。但是，要把這事很機巧地實行起來，一定要使牠成功，我告訴他，我們須把俘虜分開，他將去看守阿特金斯和他們之中最壞的二人，把他們綁着送到別的人所在的洞穴中去。這事委託給星期五和那同船長一陣上岸的兩個人。他們把他們送到洞穴中，如同到囚中去一般，那裏是，實在如此，一所愁慘的地方。其餘的人我命人送到我的小亭中去。亭子旣然有籬笆圍住，他們是被綁着，這地方是安全的，注意着他們還被人看管着呢。

在早上，我遣船主到他們那裏去，他是和他們開談判去；總之，試試他們，告訴我他是否想着他們是否可信任的，到小船上去，攻打大船，他向他們談及他們受的傷害，他們所處的境地，雖然主宰是饒了他們的生命，依照現在的舉動，然而假使他們被送到英國去，他們一定要被練鎖住；但是假使他們情願加入重謨大船的正當的企謀，他將得主宰的許可而饒恕他們。

CHAPTER XLIV

ANY one may [1]*guess* how readily such a [2]*proposal* would be [3]*accepted* by men in their condition. They fell down on their knees to the captain, and promised, with the [4]*deepest* [5]*imprecations*, that they would be faithful to him to the last [6]*drop*. and that they should own their lives to him, and would go with him all over the world; that they would own him as a father to them as long as they lived. "Well," said the captain, "I must go and tell the governor what you say, and see what I can do to bring him to [7]*consent* to it." So he brought me an account of the [8]*temper* he found them in, and that he [9]*verily* believed they would be faithful.

However, that we might be very [10]*secure*, I told him he should go back again and [11]*choose* out five of them, and tell them that they might see he did not want men, but that he would take out those five to be his [12]*assistants*, and that the governor would keep the other two, and the three that were sent prisoners to the [13]*castle* (my cave), as [14]*hostages* for the [15]*fidelity* of those five; and that if they proved unfaithful in the [16]*execution*, the five hostages should be hanged in chains alive on the shore. This looked [17]*severe*, and [18]*convinced* them that the governor was [19]*in earnest*; however, they had no way left them but [20]*to accept* it; and it was now the business of the prisoners, as much as of the captain, to persuade the other five to do their [21]*duty*.

Our strength was now thus ordered for the [22]*expedition*: first, the captain, his mate, and [23]*passenger*; second, the two prisoners of the first [24]*gang*, to whom, having their character from the captain, I had given their [25]*liberty*

第 四 十 四 章

　　任何人可以猜想着這樣的一個提議當然是要被身處那種景况之中的人們所立卽採納的。他們向船長下跪，允許着，極力哀求，他們雖至於死必忠心服從着他，他們的生命由他而得，情願隨他遊行全世界；一經他們活着，他們將視他如生父一般。"好"船主說，"我必須去告訴主宰你們所說的話，看看我能不能得其許可。"這樣，他便給我他所覺着他們現在的性情的一個報告，他實在地相信他們將要是忠誠不二。

　　然而，我們可以一定，我告訴他將要重行同去，從他們之中選出五人來，告訴他們他們可以知道他不需要所有的人，但是他要選出五人來做他的助手，主宰將保着別的二人，三個人將要如俘虜一般送到堡中去（我的洞中），作爲那五個人的忠誠不二的質品；假使他們不忠誠實行其事，五個質品將要在岸上活活地用鍊條鎖住。這事瞧起來狠殘酷的，使他們覺悟着主宰是眞確的；然而他們除接受此事以外，別無他法；現在這是囚虜的事務，對於船主亦然，去勸導那另外的五人去做他們的本分內的事。

　　我們的力量現在是爲這個事業而派定了：第一，船主，他的同伴和搭客；第二，第一班的兩個囚虜從船主口中得知了他們的品格，我已經給了他們自由，並給他們式器；

and trusted them with arms ; third, the other two that I had kept till now in my bower pinioned, but, [1]*on the captain's motion*, had now [2]*released* ; fourth, these five, released at last ; so that they were twelve in all, besides five we kept prisoners in the cave for hostages.

I asked the captain if he was willing [3]*to venture* with these hands on board the ship. As for me and my man Friday, I did not think it was proper for us [4]*to stir* having seven men left behind ; and it was [5]*employment* enough for us to keep them [6]*asunder*, and supply them with [7]*victuals*. As to the five in the cave, I [8]*resolved* to keep them fast ; but Friday went in twice a day to them, to supply them with [9]*necessaries* ; and I made the other two carry [10]*provisions* to a certain distance, where Friday was to take them.

When I showed myself to the two hostages, it was with the captain, who told them I was the person the governor had ordered to look after them, and that it was the governor's [11]*pleasure* they should not stir anywhere but by my [12]*direction* ; that if they did, they would be [13]*fetched* into the castle, and be laid in irons. So, as we never [14]*suffered* them to see me as governor, I now appeared as another person, and spoke of the governor, the [15]*garrison*, the castle, and the like, [16]*upon all occasions*.

The captain now had no [17]*difficulty* before him but to furnish his two boats, [18]*stop the breach* of one, and man them, He made his passenger captain of one, with four of the men ; and himself, his mate, and five more, went in the other. They [19]*contrived* their business very well, for they came up to the ship about [20]*midnight*. As soon as they came [21]*within call of* the ship, he made Robinson [22]*hail* them, and tell them they had [23]*brought off* the men and the

574

第三,另外的二人,直至現在我把他們保留在小亭之內綁着,但是,承了船主之意,現在把他們釋放了;第四,這五人,後來釋放了;這樣他們一共是十二人,除去那五人我們拘留在洞穴之中作質品之外。

我問船主他願不願去冒險和那些人到大船上去。一於我和我的人星期五,我不想這是對我們合宜地去走動,有了七個人留在後面;這是我們的事務來把他們分開,用食物供給他們。至於在洞穴中的那五人,我決心不給他們食物;但是星期五每天到他們那裏去兩次,用必需品來供給他們;我使別的兩人把食品攜到某種距離以內的地方去,在那裏,星期五去拿牠們。

當我在二個質人的面前現身之時,還是和船主一同去的,他告訴他們說我是主宰命令着來看管他們的人,主宰是狠快樂的,假使他們除聽我指揮以外,不往他處而去;使他們去到他處,他們將被傾入洞穴,鎖以鐐鍊。這樣,既然我們終不令他們知道我是主宰,我現在現出身來好像是旁人一般,說及主宰,防守人,堡壘,其他等等常時這般地說。

現在船主沒有困艱當前,除要去裝置他的兩只小船以外;塞一只的破隙,而處置水手於其中。他使他的搭客作一只小船的船主,並有四個水手,他自己,他的同伴,再加五人,到另一只小船中去。他們把事務進行得甚好,因為他們將及午夜方到大船傍面。一經他們貼近大船,他使魯濱孫招呼着他們,吿訴他們他們曾經把水手們和小船帶走,

boat, but that it was a long time before they had found them, and the like, holding them in [1]*a chat* till they came to the ship's side. Then the captain and the mate, entering first with their arms, immediately knocked down the second mate and [2]*carpenter* with the [3]*butt end* of their [4]*muskets*, being very faithfully [5]*seconded* by their men. They [6]*secured* all the rest that were upon the [7]*main* and [8]*quarter decks*, and began to fasten the [9]*hatches* to keep them down that were below. The other boat and their man, entering at the fore [10]*chains'* secured the [11]*forecastle* of the ship, and the [12]*scuttle* which went down into the [13]*cookroom*, making three men they found there prisoners.

when this was done, and all safe upon deck, the captain ordered the [14]*mate*, with three men, [15]*to break into* the [16]*round-house*, where the new [17]*rebel* captain lay, who, having taken the [18]*alarm*, had gat up, and with two men and a boy had got [19]*firearms* in their hands. When the mate, with a [20]*crow*, [21]*split* open the door, the new captain and his men fired boldly among them, and wounded the mate with a [22]*musket ball*, which broke his arm and wounded two more of the men, but killed nobody. The mate, calling for help, [23]*rushed*, however, into the roundhouse, wounded as he was, and, with his pistol, shot the new captain through the head, the [24]*bullet* entering at his mouth, and coming out again behind one of his ears, so that he never spoke a word more. Upon this the rest yielded, and the ship was taken [25]*effectually*, without any more lives lost.

As soon as the ship was thus [26]*secured*, the captain ordered seven guns to be fired, which was the [27]*signal* agreed upon with me to give me notice of his [28]*success*, which, you may be sure, I was very glad to hear, having sat watching

但是過了許久，他們方纔尋着他們，其他等語，和他們談心，直至他們來到了船則方止。於是船主和他的同伴，帶了武器先進去，立卽把第二個伴伴和木匠用他們的槍柄把他們打倒，是被他們的人狠忠心地幫助着。在船面和在船後的所有的人都被他們捉住了，開始着繫那槍口門，使在下面的下去。另外一只小船和水手們，走進前面的鍊子裏去，捉住大船的前段和小槍口，牠直伸下去到廚室中爲止，把他們尋獲着的三人在那裏拘禁着。

當這事完了以後，和各人都安全地在甲板上以後，船主命令他的同伴，和三個人，闖入船長室內去，在那裏，新的反孩的船長藏着，他，得了警報，立了起來，同兩個人和一個小叛手中拿有火器。當那個伙伴，用了一根鐵艇，把門破開，新船長和他的人們很勇敢地在他們之中射擊起來，一粒槍彈把伙伴打傷了，把他的膀臂打中，又傷了二人，但是未曾把任何人打死。伙伴，呼着救，衝到船長室內，雖負着傷，用他的手槍，把新船主打了一槍，彈從頭內穿過，彈丸進了他的口中，又從他的一只耳朵後面出來，以至於他遂不再發言了。因此之故，其餘的人皆歸順了，大船是很有效果的被得着了，沒有別的生命再失去。

一經大船被獲，船主命人開了七槍，那就是和我約定的暗號，使我知道他的成功，你可以一定，我聽了那個是狠快樂的，我坐在岸上守待着，直到差不多早上兩點鐘光景。

1.談話.2.木匠.3.槍柄.4.槍.5.助.6.捉住.7.大船面.8.船後段.9.槍口門.10.鍊.11.船前段.12.小槍口 13.廚房.14.同伴.15.闖入.16.船長室.17.反叛.18.警報.19.火器.20.鐵艇.21.破開.22.槍彈.23.衝進.24.子彈.25.有效力.26.安全.27.記號.28.成功.

upon the shore for it till near two o'clock in the morning.
Having thus heard the signal *plainly*, I laid me down ; and
it having been a day of great *²fatigue* to me, I slept very
sound, till I was surprised with the *³noise* of a gun.
⁴Starting up, I heard a man call me by the name of
" Governor ! Governor !" and presently I knew the captain's voice ; when, *⁵climbing up* to the top of the hill,
there he stood, and, pointing to the ship, he *⁶embraced* me
in his arms. " My dear friend and *⁷deliverer*," says he,
" there's your ship ; for she is all yours, and so are we,
and all that belong to her." I *⁸cast my eyes* to the ship,
and there she *⁹rode*, within little more than half a mile of
the shore ; for they had *¹⁰weighed* her anchor as soon as
they were masters of her, and, the weather being fair, had
¹¹brought her to an anchor just against the mouth of the little
creek. The tide being up, the captain had brought the
¹²pinnace in near the place where I had first landed my
rafts, and so landed just at my door.

I was at first ready to sink down with the surprise ; for
I saw my deliverance, indeed, *¹³visibly* put into my hands,
all things easy, and a large ship just ready to carry me
away whither I pleased to go. At first, for some time, I
was not able to *¹⁴answer* him one word ; but as he had taken
me in his arms, I *¹⁵held fast* by him, or I should have fallen
to the ground. He perceived the surprise, and immediately *¹⁶pulled* a bottle out of his pocket and gave me a *¹⁷dram*
of cordial which he had brought on purpose for me.
After I had drunk it, I sat down upon the ground ; and
though it *¹⁸brought me to myself* yet it was a good while
before I could speak a word to him.

明白地聽見了暗號以後，我躺下來；這日對於我是狠疲倦的，我遂睡得很熟，直到我被槍聲驚醒始止。驚醒起來，我聽見一個人叫喚我"主宰！主宰！"立刻我知道是船長的聲音；爬上小山之頂，他立在那裏，指着大船，他把我攄抱在他的臂內，"我的親愛的友人和拯救者，"他說，"那邊是你的大船；因為牠全是你的，我們以及那些附屬的東西，也是你的。"我注視着那只大船，在那邊牠碇泊着，離岸不過半英里遠；因為他們起了錨—經他們得了牠之時，天氣是晴朗的，他們把牠停駛而拋錨碇泊了，貼正對那小溪的口上。潮是高的，船主把大舢板帶到貼近的那個地方去，在那裏，我曾經把木筏弄上岸去；這樣弄上了岸直到我的大門口。

　　起初我驚愕着預備跌下地去；因為我看見了我的拯救實在，很明顯地到了我的手中，各樣事情都易辦了，一只大船預備着把我帶到我所悅意去的地方。起先，有些時，我一字也不能囘答他；但是當他把我拖入臂中之時，我緊握着他，如其不然；我一定要跌下地去。他見了這個不意之事，立卽從他的口袋中取出一瓶酒來；給了我若干量的補血酒，那是他特意為我帶在身旁的。我喝了以後，坐在地上，雖然牠使我蘇醒，然而歇了許久；我方能和他說一句話。

1. 明白之狀. 2. 疲困. 3. 聲音. 4. 驚起. 5. 爬上. 6. 抱住. 7. 拯救人. 8. 注視. 9. 碇泊. 10. 起錨. 11. 拋錨碇泊. 12. 大舢板. 13. 可見之狀. 14. 答. 15. 執住. 16. 拿出. 17. 量名. 18. 令我蘇醒.

All this time the poor man was in as great an [1]*ecstasy* as I, only not under any surprise as I was. He said a thousand kind and tender things to me, [2]*to compose* and bring me to myself; but such was the [3]*flood of joy* in my [4]*breast* that it put all my [5]*spirits* into [6]*confusion*. At last it [7]*broke out into tears*; and, in a little while after, I recovered my speech. We [8]*rejoiced* together. I told him I looked upon him as a man sent by Heaven to deliver me, and that the whole [9]*transaction* seemed to be [10]*a chain of wonders*; that such things as these were the testimonies we [11]*had of a secret hand of* Providence governing the world, and an [12]*evidence* that the eye of an [13]*infinite power* could search into the [14]*remotest* [15]*cornor* of the world, and send help to the miserable whenever he pleased.

When we had talked awhile, the captain told me he had brought me some little [16]*refreshment*, such as the ship [17]*afforded*, and such as the [18]*wretches* that had been so long his masters had not [19]*plundered* him of. Upon this, he called aloud to the boat and bade his men bring the things ashore that were for the governor; and, indeed, it was a present as if I had been one that was not to be carried away with them, but as if I had been [20]*to dwell* upon the island still. First, he had brought me a case of bottles full of excellent [21]*cordial* waters, six large bottles of [22]*Madeira wine* (the bottles held two [23]*quarts* each), two pounds of excellent good [24]*tobacco*, twelve good pieces of the ship's beef, and six pieces of [25]*pork*, with a bag of peas, and about a hundred-weight of [26]*biscuit*. He also [27]*brought* me a box of sugar a box of flour, a bag full of [28]*lemons* two bottles of [29]*lime juice*, and [30]*abundance* of other things.

攏總這些時候，這個可憐的人和我是一般地狂喜，不過不像我是在驚愕之中。他對我說了許多仁愛和柔順的話，安慰我使我復原；但是我胸中是這樣地一陣一陣地快慰；却使我精神錯亂起來。最後，我忽然淚下；過了不久之時，我囘復了我的言語能力。我們一淘快活着。我告訴他我視他如同天上派下來救我的人一樣，各項的事務看起來宛如一串接連奇事；像這樣的事實是我們得着那管理全世界的上帝的祕密的助力的證據，眞是一個確證，無所不能的上帝的目光能夠搜尋到世界上最遠之處，碰着他喜歡之時，他就給不幸之人以扶助。

當我們說了半天的話，船主告訴我他爲我帶了些滋養的東西來，就大船所能供給者而言，這是那些壞坏子在克服他很長久時間之中尙未刼掠淨盡的東西。因此，他向小船大叫着，吩咐人們把這主宰的東西拿上岸來；實在，這是一件禮物，好像是一個他們不帶走的人，但是須要仍舊住在島上的一個人。起初，他帶給我一箱的酒瓶，裝滿了甘美的補血藥水，六大瓶馬得利酒（每瓶裝有兩參脫之量），兩磅極好的烟草，十二塊好的羊肉，六塊猪肉，一袋豆子，大約一百磅的餅干。他又帶給我一盒糖，一盒粉，一滿袋檸檬，兩瓶檸檬汁，以及多量的旁的物件。

But besides these, and what was a thousand times more useful to me, he brought me six new, clean ¹*shirts*, six very good ²*neckcloths*, two pairs of ³*gloves*, one pair of shoes, a hat, and one pair of ⁴*stockings*, with a very good suit of clothes of his own, which had been worn but very little. In a word, he clothed me from head to foot. It was a very kind and agreeable present, as any one may ⁵*imagine*, to one in my ⁶*cirumstances*, but never was anything in the world of that kind so unpleasant, ⁷*awkward*, and uneasy as it was to me to wear such clothes at first.

After these ⁸*ceremonies* were past, and after all his good things were brought into my little ⁹*apartment*, we began to ¹⁰*consult* what was to be done with the prisoners we had,—whether we might venture to take them away with us or no, ¹¹*especially* two of them, whom he knew to be ¹²*incorrigible* and ¹³*refractory* to the last ¹⁴*degree*. The captain said he knew they were such ¹⁵*rogues* that there was no ¹⁶*obliging* them, and if he did carry them away, it must be in irons, as ¹⁷*maiefoctors*, to be ¹⁸*delivered over to justice* at the first English ¹⁹*colony* he could come to. Upon this I told him that, if he desired it, I would undertake to bring the two men he spoke of to make it their own ²⁰*request* that he should leave them upon the island. "I should be very glad or that," says the captain, "with all my heart." Well," says I, "I will send for them up, and talk with them for you." So I ²¹*caused* Friday and the two ²²*hostages* to go to the cave and bring up the five men, pinioned as they were, to the ²³*bower* and keep them there till I came.

After some time I came thither, ²⁴*dressed in my new habit* Being all met, and the captain with me, I caused the men to be brought before me, and I told them I had got a full

但是在這些物件以外，那個是對我更加一千倍的有用，他帶給我六件新的，乾淨的襯衫，六條很好的頸巾，兩副手套，一雙鞋，一頂帽，一雙襪；以及他自己把我從頭至足穿着起來。這是一樣很好的和可愛的禮品，任何人皆可猜想得到的，對於一個人在我的環境之中，但是在世界上，永遠沒有像那種東西這樣的不好，醜怪，和不安，當我起初穿着這些衣衫之時。

這些禮式行過以後，把他所有的好東西帶到我的小室中以後，我們開始討論對於我們的俘虜將採取何種辦法，我們是否可以冒險帶他們同去，尤其是他們之中二人，他知道他們是不可改的，頑梗之至。船長說他是不可施恩的惡棍，假使他眞帶他們走，必須要鐐鍊着，像罪犯一般，送到他來到的第一個英國殖民地方，送交官吏究辦。因此，我告訴他，假使他願意這般做，我將去使他所說的二人自己請求着他把他們留在島上。"對於這事，我是很快樂的，"船主說，"極願如此。""好，"我說，"我將召他們來，代你和他們說。"我於是使星期五和兩個質人到洞穴中去把那五人領來，他們是被綁着，到小亭中去，把他們留在那邊，等候我來。

過了些時，我到那邊去，身衣新服。大家遇着了，船主和我，我叫着把那些人領到我面前來，我告訴他們我得了他們對於船主奸惡行爲的詳細報告，

account of their ¹*villainous* ²*behavior* to the captain, and how
they had run away with the ship, and were ³*preparing* to
⁴*commit* further ⁵*robberies*, but that Providence had ⁶*insnared*
them ⁷*in their own ways*, and that they were fallen into the
pit which they had ⁸*digged* for others. I let them know
that by my direction the ship had been ⁹*seized*; that she lay
now in the road; and that they might see by and by that
their new captain had received the ¹⁰*reward* of his ¹¹*villainy*,
and that they would see him hanging at the ¹²*yardarm*. As
to them, I wanted to know what they had to say why I
should not ¹³*execute* them as ¹⁴*pirates* taken in the fact, as they
could not doubt but I had ¹⁵*authority* so to do.

One of them answered, in the name of the rest, that they
had nothing to say but this, that when they were taken
the captain ¹⁶*promised* them their lives; and they ¹⁷*humble*
¹⁸*implored* my ¹⁹*mercy*, But I told them I knew not what
mercy to show them; for as for myself, I had ²⁰*resolved* to
quit the island with all my men, and had ²¹*taken passage* with
the captain to go to England; and as for the captain, he
could not carry them to England other than as prisoners in
irons, to be tried for ²²*mutiny* and running away with the
ship; the ²³*consequence* of which they must needs know,
would be the ²⁴*gallows*. I could not tell what was best for
them, unless they had a mind to take their fate in the island
If they desired that, as I had liberty to leave ⸱ the island. I
had some ²⁵*inclination* to give them their lives, if they
thought they could shift on shore. They seemed very
thankful for it, and said they would much rather venture
to stay there than be carried to England to be hanged. So
I left it on that ²⁶*issue.*

他們如何乘船而走，預備再犯刼掠之事，但是上天使他們入了羅網，卽以其人之道，還治其人之身，他們墜入他們所掘着陷人之阱中。我使他們知道，在我指揮之下，大船是獲得了；牠現在拋錨於碇泊之所；他們不久可以看見他們的新船主已經得了他的奸詐的酬報、他們將要看見他吊在帆桁端之上，至於他們，我願意知道他們要說些什麼，爲什麼我不把他們視同當場捕獲之海盜而殺之，他們是不懷疑地是我有着權力這樣做。

　　他們之中一人囘答，爲其餘的人作代表；說他們沒有別的話說，只有這個，當他們被捉之時，船主曾經允許他們以不死；他們伏求我的寬宥但是我告訴他們我不知道怎樣地向他們表示着寬宥；因爲致於我自巳，我決心帶我的人離開此島，和船主乘船同往英國；至於船主，他不能帶他們到英國去，除非把他們鎖着和囚犯一樣，因謀叛而受鞠訊，和大船同走；那個的結局，他們一定要知道，就是絞之刑。我不能向他們說出最好的話，假使他們不願在島上受死刑。倘若他們願意那樣做，我有自由權來離開島，我有饒他們生命的傾向，假使他們想他們能在岸上設法謀生。看起來他們對於這個很爲感謝，說他們寧願冒險逗留此處，不願同至英國受絞刑。因此我遂聽彼等所欲。

CHAPTER XLV

WHEN they had all [1]*declared* their [2]*willingness* to stay, I then told them I would let them into the story of my living there, and put them into the way of making it easy to them. Accordingly, I gave them the whole history of the place, and of my coming to it; showed them my [3]*fortifications*, the way I made my bread, [4]*planted* my corn, [5]*cured* my [6]*grapes*, and, in a word, all that was necessary to make them easy. I told them the story, also, of the fifteen Spaniards that were to be expected, for whom I left a letter, and made them [7]*promise* to treat them in common with themselves. Here it may be [8]*noted* that the captain, who had ink on board, was greatly surprised that I never [9]*hit upon* a way of making ink of [10]*charcoal* and water, or of something else, as I had done things much more difficult.

I left then my [11]*firearms*; namely, five muskets, three fowling-pieces, and three swords. I had above a [12]*barrel* and a half of powder left; for after the first year or two I used but little, and wasted none. I gave them a [13]*description* of the way I managed the goats, and directions to milk and fatten them, and to make both [14]*butter* and [15]*cheese*. In a word, I gave them every part of my own story, and told them I should [16]*prevail with* the captain to leave them two barrels of [17]*gunpowder* more, and some garden seeds which I told them I would have been very glad of. Also, I gave them the bag of peas which the captain had brought me to eat, and bade them be sure to sow and [18]*increase* them.

Having done all this, I left them the next day, and went on board the ship. We prepared immediately to sail, but did not [19]*weigh* that night. The next morning early, two

586

第 四 十 五 章

　當他們一齊宣示情願留而不去之後，我就告訴他們我將把我住在那裏的故事告知他們，敎導他們容易生活之法。我於是指示他們這地方的整個的故事，以及我來到此處的故事；指示他們我的堡壘，我做麵包，種穀，晾曬葡萄的方法，總之，以及攏總那些使他們生活容易的需要物。我也告訴他們十五個西班牙人的故事，我們期望着他們來，我留下一信給他們，使他們允許着和他們同樣待遇。這裏必須注意着，船主，他在船上有墨水，是很驚奇的我永遠未曾覓得用木炭和水製成墨水的方法，或者別的東西，旣然我曾造了許多很難製的物件。

　我留給他們我的火器，就是，五只槍，三只打鳥槍，三把刀。我有一桶有半以上的火藥留下；因爲在第一或第二年以後，我用得很少，一點也未曾損廢。我給他們我管理山羊方法的描寫，以及擠乳使牠們肥壯的方法，製造牛油和乳酪等事。總之，我給他們我的故事的各部份，告訴他們我將去說服船主再留給他們兩桶火藥，以及若干花園中的種子，我告訴他們我對於邦個是很欣喜的。我也給他們船主帶與我吃的那一袋豆子，吩咐他們一定要去種而使牠們增多。

　這些事完畢以後，第二天我離開他們，到大船上去。我們立卽預備起程，但是那天晚上卻未曾起錨。第二早晨很早的辰光，五人中的二人

of the five men came ¹*swimming* to the ship's side, **and,**
making the most ²*lamentable* com*plaint* of the other three,
begged to be taken into the ship for God's sake, for **they**
should be ³*murdered*, and begged the captain to take **them**
on board, though he hanged them immediately. Upon
this the captain ⁴*preteneded* to have no power without me.
After some difficulty, and after their ⁵*solemn* ⁶*promises* of
⁷*amendment*, they were taken on board, and were, some
time after, soundly ⁸*whipped*; after which they proved **very**
honest and quiet fellows.

Some time after this, the boat was ordered on shore, **the**
tide being up, with the things promised to the men; **to**
which the captain, at my ⁹*intercession*, caused their chests
and clothes to be added, which they took, and were very
thankful for. I also ¹⁰*encouraged* them by telling them that
if it lay in my power to send any ¹¹*vessel* to take them in,
I would not forget them.

When I took leave of this island, I carried on board, for
¹²*relics*, the great goat-skin cap I had made, my ¹³*umbrella*,
and my ¹⁴*parrot*. Also, I forget not to take the money I
formerly mentioned, which had lain by me so long useless
that it was grown rusty or ¹⁵*tarnished*, and could hardly pass
for silver till it had been a little ¹⁶*rubbed* and ¹⁷*handled*, as also
they money I found in the wreck of the Spanish ship.

And thus I left the island, the 19th of December, **as I**
found by the ship's account, in the year 16*86*, after I had
boon upon it eight and twenty years, two months, **and**
nineteen days; being delivered from this second ¹⁸*captivity*
the same day of the month that I first made my ¹⁹*eacape* **in**
the longboat from among the Moors of Sallee. In this

泅到大船的側面來，做出對於其他三人的最衰憐的怨訴來，要求看上帝分上許他們進船，因為他們將被謀殺，哀求船主帶他們入船否則他們將要立刻縊殺他們。因此之故，船主假裝着說，若未得我的許可，他無權力來答應他們的要求。經過了若干困難以後許，以及經過了他們允改前非以後，他們是被領上船來，過了些時，他們就重受鞭笞；此事以後，他們遂成為誠實和安靜的人了。

此後過了些時，小船是被搬上岸來，潮是高，以及那些允許給那些水手的東西；船主，以我之請求，使他們的箱子和衣衫加增上去，他們拿了那個，很感謝的。我也鼓勵他們，告訴他們說，假使是在我權力之內派些船來帶他們進去，我決不會忘記他們。

當我離島之時，我帶上船去，作為記念品，我所做的那頂山羊皮的小帽，傘和鸚鵡。我也不忘記拿我先前敍述過的錢幣，久存我處而未經用去，已生銹了，不能作銀子用了，直至略為摩擦而使用之以後，我也把我在那西班牙船的破毀中所尋獲的錢幣帶走。

這樣我離開了島，十二月十九日，我在大船的報告上尋着的日子，一千六百八十六年，在我在島上住了二十八年兩月和十九日之後；從第二次囚禁中被救了，同月的同一日，我第一次從薩里地方摩爾人手中在長艏板內逃走出來。

1. 泅。2. 可衰。3. 怨訴。4. 殺。5 假裝。6. 莊重的允許。7. 改過。8. 鞭笞。9. 請求。10. 鼓勵。11. 船。12. 記念品。13. 傘。14. 鸚鵡。15. 銹。16. 摩擦。17. 使用。18. 囚俘。19. 逃走。

vessel, after a long voyage, I [1]*arrived* in England the 11th of June, in the year 1687, having been thirty-five years [2]*absent*.

When I came to England, I was as perfect [3]*a stranger* to all the world as if I had never been known there. My [4]*benefactor* and faithful [5]*steward*, whom I had left my money in trust with, was alive, but was become a widow the second time, and very low in the world. But my father was dead, and my mother; and as I had been long ago given over for [6]*dead*, there had been no provision made for me; so that, in a word, I found nothing to relieve or [7]*assist* me. The little money I had would not do much for me as to settling in the world.

I met with one piece of [8]*gratitude*, indeed which I did not expect; and this was that the master of the ship, whom I had so happily delivered, and by the same means saved the ship and [9]*cargo*, having given a very handsome [10]*account* to the owners of the manner in which I had saved the lives of the men, and the ship, they [11]*invited* me to meet them and some other merchants [12]*concerned*, and all together made me a very [13]*handsome* [14]*compliment* upon the subject, and a present of almost £200 [15]*sterling*.

After making several [16]*reflections* upon the [17]*circumstances* of my life, and how little way this would go towards [18]*settling* me in the world, I resolved to go to Lisbon, and see if I might not come at some [19]*information* of the state of my [20]*plantation*, in Brazil, and of what was become of my [21]*partner*, who, I had reason to suppose, had some years past given me over for dead. With this view I took shipping for Lisbon, where I arrived in April following. My man Friday [22]*accompanied* me very honestly in all these [23]*ramblings*,

在這只船中；在一個久長的旅行以後，一千六百八十七年六月十一日我到了英國，離開牠有三十五年了。

當我到了英國以後，我變成一個完全不識世事的人；好像我永遠未曾到過那裏一般。我的恩人和忠心的管家，我曾以銀錢託彼管理，他尚活着，但是又做了寡婦，境況甚為蕭條。但是我的父親死了，我的母親亦然；人以為我已死久矣，沒有食物來為我預備着；總之，我找不出安慰或找助我的東西。我所有的些少的錢幣，對於我成家立業是不敷所用的。

遇着一陣的感激聲，實在我到未曾星望着那個；這就是那只船的主人；我很快樂地把他拯救出來，用了同一方法，救了船和船貨，在他的主人前面將彼事之始末和盤託出，他報告說我救了水手的生命，船，他們請我去見他們和其餘有關係的商人們，各人論及此事；向我道謝不置，送了我差不多值二百金磅的禮品。

對於我生活的環境稍加回想以後，關於我立身處世的一事，此款不甚有濟，我決心到里斯朋去，看看我能不能略得在巴勒喜爾種植情形和我的合股人的消息，他，我有理由去猜想，在數年前以為我死去了。因此，我乘舟向里斯朋去，在四月中我到了那邊。我的人星期五在這些漫遊之中很誠實地伴着我，不論何時他總是一個最忠心的僕人。

1.抵.2.不在.3.不識世事之人.4.恩人.5.管家.6.死.7.幫助.8.感恩 9.船貨.10.報告.11.請.12.有關係的.13.美好的.14.感謝.15.金幣.16.回想.17.環境.18.安置.19.消息.20.種植.21.合股人.22.件.23.漫遊.

and proved a most faithful servant upon all occassions. When I came to Lisbon, I found out, by [1]*inquiry*, and to my particular [2]*satisfaction*, my old friend. the captain of the sihp who first took me up at sea off the shore of Africa. He was now grown old, and had [3]*left off going to sea*, having put his son into his ship, who still used the Brazil trade. They old man did not know me. Indeed ,I hardly knew him; but I soon brought him to my [4]*remembrance*, and as soon brought myself to his remembrance, when I told him who I was.

After some [5]*passionate* [6]*expressions* of the old [7]*acquaintance* between us, I inquired, you may be sure, after my [8]*plantation* and my [9]*partner*. The old man told me he had not been in Brazil for about nine years, but that he could [10]*assure* me that when he came away my partner was living. He believed I would have a very good account of the [11]*improvement* of the plantation ; for that, upon the general belief of my being cast away and drowned, my [12]*trustees* had given in the account of the produce of my part of the plantation to the government.

He told me he could not tell exactly to what degree the plantation was [13]*improved*; but this he knew, that my partner was grown [14]*exceeding* rich upon the enjoying his part of it; that as to my being [15]*restored* to a quiet [16]*possession* of it, there was no [17]*question* to be made of that, my partner being alive [18]*to witness my title*, and my name being also [19]*enrolled* in the [20]*register* of the country .

After a few days' further [21]*conference* with this [22]*ancient* friend, he brought me an account of the first six years' income of my plantation, [22]*signed* by my partner and the merchant [24]*trustees*. I found by this account that every

592

當我到了里斯朋之後，用了詢問的方法，我找着了，使我心滿意起，我的老友，大船上的主人，他從前曾載我到非洲海岸去的。他現在老了，丟却航業了，把他的兒子放在他的船上，他仍舊從事勒喜爾的貿易。老人不認得我了。實在，我也狠難的辨認他了；但是我不久便使我回憶着他，也使他回憶到我，當我告訴他我是誰之後。

在我們知交有年，一往情深的交談以後，我詢問，你可以確定，我的種植地和我的合股人。老人告訴我他有八年不到勒喜爾去了，但是他能向我確定說，當他去的時候，我的合股人是活着。他相信我將得着種值的進步的報告；因為，我的船遇難而因以溺死的一說，人皆深信不疑，我的受託人把我名下所應得出產獲利之數，盡數呈入於政府了。

他告訴我他不能確切地說種植的發達到了那種地步；但是他知道這事，我的合股人發了大財，享受他名下所應得的一份而致富；至於復得我所有之財產而悄然收管着，為我所應有而為我恢復之者，必無疑義，我的合股人添差可為我作證，而且我的名字也在國中註冊處登記了。

和老友再行商議數日以後，他給我我的種植起頭六年的進款的報告，我的合股人和受託的商人都簽了字在上面。從這個報告上，我見每年入款皆加增得很多；但是，開銷很大，數目起初是很小的。

year the income considerably increased ; but, the [1]*disburse-ments* being large, the sum at first was small. However, the old man let me see that he was [2]*debtor to* me four hundred and seventy [3]*moidores* of gald, besides sixty [4]*chests* of sugar, and fifteen [5]*double rolls* of [6]*tobacco.*

Never was anything more honorable than the [7]*proceedings* which followed. In less than seven months I received a large [8]*packet* from the [9]*survivors* of my [10]*trustees,* the merchants, for whose account I went to sea. There was also a letter of my partner's [11]*congratulating* me very [12]*affectionately* upon my being alive, and concluding with a hearty tender of his [13]*friendship,* and that of his family. He sent me, as a present, seven fine [14]*leopards' skins,* which he had [15]*received* from Africa, by some other ship that he had sent thither, and which, it seems, had made a better voyage than I. He sent me also five chests of [16]*excellent* sweet-merts, and a hundred pieces of gold [17]*uncoined.* not quite so large as [18]*moidores.* By the same fleet, my two merchant trustees shipped me one thousand two hundred [19]*chests* of [20]*sugar,* eight hundred rolls of tobacco, and the rest of the whole account in gold.

I might well say now, indeed, that the latter end of Job was better than the beginning. It is [21]*impossible* to express the [22]*flutterings* of my very heart when I found all my wealth about me ; for as the Brazil ships come all in [23]*fleets,* the same ships which brought my letters brought my goods, and the [24]*effects* were safe in the river before the letters came to my hand. In a word, I [25]*turned pale,* and grew sick ; and, had not the old man run and [26]*fetched* me a [27]*cordial,* I believe the sudden surprise of joy had overset nature, and I had died upon the [28]*spot.* Nay, after that, I continued very [29]*ill,* and was so some hours.

然而，老人使我我明白他欠我四百七十金摩多，在六十箱糖和十五箱雙捲的烟葉以外。

永還沒有比到下面的事件更加可貴的。在不及七月的工夫，我從我的倘生存的受託人，那個商人那邊接到了一個包件，我到海中去是爲他的緣故。還有我的合股人的一封信，賀我的倘生存於世上，末了有着友誼上和他的家庭上的懸摯的致詞。他逞我，像禮物一般，七塊好的豹皮，那是他從美洲得著的，他派了別的船到那邊去，經過了比我好的一個航程。他又逞我五箱甘美的糖果，一百枚未鑄的金錢，不十分如同摩多一般大。乘了同樣的船，我的兩個商人委託者給我帶來了一千二百箱糖，八百捲烟草，其餘帳目的現金洋，

現在·我可以說，實在如此，晚境勝於當初了。這是不可能的去表示心中的紛亂，當我見了我的全部財產在我身旁之時；因爲既然巴勒喜爾船整隊而來，帶我的信的同樣的船又把我的貨帶來了，貨物在江中是平安的，在信未到我的手中以前。總而言之，我變成灰白色了，要害病了；假使沒有那老人跑去替我拿一些補藥來，我相信猝然驚喜必致變亂天性，在那裏我或者巳經死去了。豈止如此，在此事以後：我仍舊病得很厲害，幾個鐘頭都是如此。

I was now master ¹*all on a sudden*, of above five thou-sand pounds ²*sterling* in money, and had an ³*estate*, as I might well call it, in Brazil, of above a thousand pounds a year, as sure as an estate of lands in England, In a word, I was in a condition which I scarce knew how to understand, or how to ⁴*compose* myself for the enjoyment of it. The fiast thing I did was to ⁵*recompense* my original ⁶*benefactor*, my good old captain, who had been first ⁷*charitable* to me in my ⁸*distress*, kind to me in my beginning, and honest to me at the end. I showed him all that was sent to me; I told him that, next to the providence of Heaven, which ⁹*disposed* all things, it was owing to him, and that it now lay on me ¹⁰ *to reward* him, which I would do a ¹¹*hundredfold*. I first returned to him the hundred ¹²*moidores* I had received of him; then I ¹³*sent* for a ¹⁴*notary*, and caused him to ¹⁵*drow up* a general ¹⁶*release* or ¹⁷*discharge* from the four hundred and seventy moidores, which he had acknowledged he owed me, in the fullest manner possible; and by a ¹⁸*clause* in the end, I made a grant of one hundred moidores a year to him during his life, and fifty moidores a year to his son after him, for his life. Thus I ¹⁹*requited* my old man.

I had not a cave now to hide my money in, or a place where it mignt lie without look or key till it grew ²⁰*moldy* and ²¹*tarnished* before anybodyo would meddle with it. On the ²²*contrary*, I knew not where to put it, or whom to trust with it. My old patron, the captain, indeed, was honest, and that was the only ²³*refuge* I had. In the next place, my ²⁴*interest* in Baazil seemed to ²⁵*summon me thither*. But now I could not tell how to think of going thither till I had ²⁶*setted my* ²⁷*affairs*, and left my ²⁸*effects* in some safe hands behind me. At first I thought of my old friend the

　　突然之間，我現在是千磅現金的金幣以上的主人翁了，我還有一宗產業，我很可以這般地叫牠，在巴勒喜爾，每年在一千磅以上，其安全如在英國的地產一般。總而言之，我是在我自己不很明白的境況之中，或者我不知道怎樣地去安然享受牠。我第一次所做的事就是去報答我起初的恩人，我的好心的老船主，他從前當我遇難之時，對我很是仁慈，開始待我以寬仁，終則待我以誠實。我把入途有的東西一齊給他看；我告訴他，次於上天的意旨，牠處置世間萬物，先前欠了他，現在是我的本分來報答他，我將要百倍報之。第一步我把我從他那裏收到的一百摩多還給他；後來我召來了一位書記官，使他起一張免債憑單的的稿在四百七十摩多上面，他曾經承認著他欠我那個，備極詳細；末加一款．我於他的一生允許每年給他一百摩多，在他身死以後，我船他的兒子的一生，每年給他五十摩多。這樣我報答了我的老人。

　　現在我沒有洞穴來藏我的金錢，或者一座地方，在那裏，錢幣可以無需用鎖鑰來藏著，直至牠發霉生銹為止，在任何人過問牠以前。反之，我不知道把牠放在何處，或把牠交託於誰。我的主顧，船長，實在，是誠實的，那就是我所有的收藏之所。第二步，我在巴勒喜爾的利益看起來宛如要召我往那邊去。但是現在我不能說怎樣想到那邊去，直至我將各事安排妥貼為止，以及把我的財產留在可靠人的手頭以後，方能成行。起初我想到了我的老朋友，那個寡婦，我知道她是誠實的，可以待我公道；但是那時她是年邁了而且窮困，依我所見，她或者負了債。總之，除我自己回到英國去，把我的財產帶去之外，無他法了。

[1]*widow*, who I knew was honest, and would be just to me; but then she was in years and but poor, and, for aught I knew. might be [2]*in debt*. In a word, I had no way but to go back to England myself, and take my [3]*eflects* with me.

I landed safe at [4]*Dover* the 14th of January, after having had a [5]*severe cold season* to travel in. Poor Friday was really [6]*frightened* when he saw the mountains all covered with snow, and felt cold weather, which he had never seen or felt before in his life.

My principal [7]*guide* and [8]*privy* [9]*counsellor* was my good, ancient widow, who, [10]*in gratitude for* the money I had sent her, thought no pains too much nor care too great to [11]*employ* for me. I trusted her so entirely with everything that I was [12]*perfectly* easy as to the [13]*security* of my effects.

Any one would think that in this state of [14]*complicated* good fortune, I was past running any more [15]*hazards*,—and so, indeed, I had been, if other [16]*circumstances* had [17]*concurred* But I was [18]*inured* to a wandering life, and had no family; so I had a great mind to be upon the wing again. Especially I could not [19]*resist* the strong [20]*inclination* I had to see my island, and to know if the poor Spaniards were in being there. My true friend, the window, earnestly [21]*dissuaded* me from it, and so far [22]*prevailed* with me that for almost seven years she [23]*prevented* my running abroad, during which time I took my two [24]*nephews* into my care. The eldest, having some thing of his own, I [25]*bred up* as a gentleman, and gave him a [26]*settlement* of some addition to his estate after my [27]*decease*. The other I placed with the captain of a ship. After five years, finding him a [28]*sensible*, bold, [29]*enterprising* young fellow, I put him into a good ship, and sent him to sea.

正月十四日，我安全抵得夫爾海口，經過了嚴寒的季候的旅程。可憐的星期五是實在地吃驚了，當他看見山上蓋滿了雪，天氣寒冷，在他有生以來，他却永遠未曾看見這個和覺着這個。

我的主要的引路人和私人的顧問者就是那個好的，老的寡婦，她，因感謝着我送她錢之故，不以爲勞苦，不以爲煩悶，爲我盡力効勞。我把各事都委託她，至於貨物之安全與否，我心甚是寧貼。

任何人皆可想到，在佳運交集之時，我是不再去冒危險了，——這樣，實在，我是如此，假使他事相合而至。但是我習於游蕩之身世，沒有家屬；我於是亟欲出發而再作遠遊。尤其是我不能抵抗我想再去觀望那座島的強烈的傾向，我還想知道那些可憐的西班牙人是否已經到了那裏。我的誠實的朋友，那個寡婦，極力勸阻我勿作此舉；她說服了我，差不多七年了，她阻止我出外去，在那七年之中，我收留我的兩個姪子而撫養他們。最長我，稍有資產，我養育他成爲良善之人，在我死後，我將在他的財產之上再給他些產業。我把另外的一個姪子置在一隻船上船長的那邊。五年以後：我見他成爲一個易感動的，勇敢的，敢作敢爲的少年了，我把他置在一隻好船中，遣他入海。

In the mean time, I [1]*in part* settled myself. First of all, I married, and had three children, two sons and one [2]*daughter*, But my wife dying, and my nephew [3]*coming home with good success* from a voyage to Spain, my [4]*inclination* to go abroad, and his [5]*importunity*, [6]*prevailed*, and [7]*engaged* me to go in his ship as a private trader to the East Indies. This was in the year 1694.

In this voyage I [8]*visited* my new colony in the island, saw my [4]*successors* the Spaniards, and had the whole story of their lives, and of the [10]*villains* I left there,—how at first the [11]*insulted* the poor Spaniards, how they afterwards agreed, [12]*disagreed*, [13]*united*, [14]*separated*, and how at last the Spaniards were [15]*obliged* to use [16]*violence* with them ; how they were [17]*subjected to* the Spaniards, how honestly the Spaniards used them,—a history, if it were entered into, as full of *variety* and wonderful accidents as my own part ; particularly, also, as to their [19]*battles* with the Caribbeans, who landed several times upon the island, and as to the [20]*improvement* they made upon the island itself.

Here I [21]*staid* about twenty days, and left them [22]*supplies* of all [23]*necessary* things, and particularty of arms, powder, shot, clothes, tools, and two workmen whom I had brought from England with me—namely, a [24]*carpenter* and a *smith*.

Besides this, I [26]*shared* the lands into parts with them. I [27]*reserved* to myself the [28]*property* pf the whole. but gave them such parts, [29]*respectively*, as they agreed on ; and having [30]*settled* all things with them, and engaged them not to leave the place, I left them there.

在其時，我稍稍處置了我自己的事。第一步，我娶了親，有了三個孩子，兩個男孩，一個女孩。但是我的妻死了，我的姪子，旅行自西班牙歸來，大獲勝利而回，我要出外的傾向，以及他慫我，勸我和約我乘他的船去，像私人商人一般，到東印度去。這事是在一千六百九十四年。

在這次航程之中，我拜訪了島上的新殖民地，看見我的繼續人，西班牙人，得了他們生活的全部的故事，以及我留在那邊的幾個惡棍的故事，——怎樣起初他們陵辱西班牙人，怎樣以後他們相合，不相合，聯合，分開，以及最後西班牙人怎樣不得不用強力來對待他們；他們怎樣服順了西班牙人，西班牙人怎樣誠實地對待他們，——一個故事，假使遂及了牠，全篇滿載各種奇異之事像我的故事一般；尤其是，也是如此，至於他們攻打那些卡里冰人，他們幾次上岸到了島上來，以及至於他們在島上所做的進步的事業。

我在那裏留了大約二十天，留給他們日用必需之物，尤其是武器火藥，子彈，衣衫，器具，以及我從英國帶來的兩個工人，——就是一個木匠和個冶工。

其外，我為他們區分土地而公派之。我保守著全地，以為我一人的產業；但是給他們那些部份，照各自所屬者，而得他們同意；替他們安排了各事，勸他們不要離開那個地方，我就把他們留在那裏。

VERSES

SUPPOSED TO BE WRITTEN BY ALEXANDER SELKIRK, DURING HIS SOLITARY ABODE IN THE ISLAND OF JUAN FERNANDEZ

I am [1]*monarch* of all [2]*survey,*
  My right there is none to [3]*dispute ;*
From the center all round to the sea
  I am lord of the fowl and the brute.
O, [4]*Solitude !* where are the [5]*charms*
  That [6]*sages* have seen in thy face ?
Better dwell in [7]*the midst of alarms*
  Than [8]*reign* in this [9]*horrible* place.

I am out of [10]*humanity's reach,*
  I must finish my journey alone,
Never hear the sweet music of speech,
  I start at the sound of my own.
The [11]*beasts* that roam over the plain
  My form with [12]*indifference* see ;
They are so [13]*unacquainted* with men.
  Their [14]*tameness* is [15]*shocking* to me.

Society, friendship, and love,
  [16]*Divinely* [17]*bestow's* upon man,
Oh, had I the wings of a dove,
  How soon would I taste you again !
My sorrows I then might [18]*assuage*
  In the ways of [19]*religion* and truth,
Might learn from the [20]*wisdom of age,*
  And be cheer'd by the [21]*sallies* of youth.

詩

傳爲亞力山大塞可克在孤身居於玄鮫朗第島中時所作

我是一切臨視的君王，
　　無人能與我爭權利；
環繞大地而直至海的中央
　　我是禽鳥獸類的大帝。
哦，孤寂！悅樂在那邊
　　聖人發見在你的面上？
最好居住於驚慌恐怖之間
　　比得御宇在可怖的地方。
我之居處爲人類所不能蒞臨，
　　我必須獨自一人將旅程完畢，
永遠未聞人類言語的聲音，
　　每聞自己的聲音突然起立。
野獸遨遊乎平原之巔
　　雖見予形，毫無懼態；
他們素不和人類相周旋，
　　他們的馴服使我驚怪。
社交，友誼，以及情愛，
　　天帝所賜予吾人，
哦，假使我能有鴿之雙翅在，
　　頃刻我便復能和君等共苦辛！
我可以稍減憂愁和憔悴
　　論及宗教和眞誠，
我能學習因年老而加增之智慧，
　　而爲少年的暢樂所歡欣。

Religion ! what [1]*treasure* untold
 Resides in that heavenly word !
More [2]*precious* than silver or gold,
 Or all that this earth can [3]*afford*
But the sound of [4]*the church-going bell*
 These valleys and rocks never heard,
Ne'er sigh'd at the sound of a [5]*knell*,
 Or smiled when a [6]*sabbath* appear'd.

Ye winds, that have [7]*made me your sport*,
 Convey to this [8]*desolate* shore
Some cordiarl, [9]*endearing* [10]*report*
 Of a land I shall visit no more.
My friends, do they now and then [11]*send*
 A wish or a thought after me ?
Oh tell me I yet have a friend,
 Though a friend I am never to see.

How fleet is the glance of the mind !
 Compared with the speed of its flight,
The [12]*tempest* itself lags behind,
 And the [13]*swift-winged* arrows of light.
When I think of my own native land,
 In a moment I seem to be there ;
But alas ! [14]*recollection* at hand
 Soom hurries me back to [15]*despair.*

But the sea-fowl has gono to her nest,
 The beast is laid down in his [16]*lair* ;
Even here is a season of rest,
 And I to my [17]*cabin* [18]*repair.*
There's mercy in every place,
 And [19]*mercy* [20]*encouraging* thought !
Gives even [21]*affliction* a grace,
 And [22]*reconciles* man to his lot.

       —WILLIAM COWPER

宗教！何種未開發之寶藏
　　而居於上天言語的裏面！
尤可貴較之銀幣和金洋，
　　以及各物而爲地土所能供獻。
但是召人入禮拜堂祈禱之鐘聲
　　這些山谷和岩石永遠未曾聽見，
永遠未曾歇息當殯鐘之長鳴，
　　或者微笑當安息日之出現。
你，風，以我爲戲玩，
　　遣我至孤寂的岸上，
某種陸地的深愛親切的報傳，
　　我將不能最去拜望。
我的友人們，他們是否時時
　　向我致意問候？
哦，告訴我我仍有一個相知，
　　雖然我將永不能再見故舊。
思想是何等的急馳！
　　比較着彼速度之如電，
颶風自身亦退後遲遲，
　　以及迅速如光之輕翼之箭。
當我思及爭之故郊，
　　在一時之間，我覺身在彼處；
但是可歎！在目前之思潮
　　立卽驅我入於失望之路。
但是海島向巢中飛行，
　　野獸在穴中過宿；
穴此處便是休息之時辰，
　　我於是歸向我之茅屋。
四面八方皆有恩惠，
　　恩惠，鼓勵着思潮！
給痛苦以撫慰，
　　使人順天知命，毋庸曉曉。

　　　　　威廉哥潑爾

全　　書　　完

1．寶藏．2．可貴．3．給．4．入禮拜堂之鐘聲．5．葬鐘之聲．6．安息日．7．以我爲汝玩具．8．孤寂．9．親愛．10．報告．11．問候．2．颶風．13．快翅的．14．囘憶．15．失望．16．獸穴．17．茅屋．18．囘至．19．惻隱．20．鼓勵．21．苦痛．22．順命而行。

書名：魯濱孫飄流記（英漢對照附註釋）
系列：漢英對照經典英文文學文庫
主編：潘國森、陳劍聰
原作者：狄孚旦尼爾(笛福)
漢譯：奚識之等

出版：心一堂有限公司
地址：香港九龍旺角彌敦道610號
　　　荷李活商業中心18樓1805-06室
電話號碼：(852) 6715-0840
網址：www.sunyata.cc
　　　publish.sunyata.cc
電郵：sunyatabook@gmail.com
心一堂讀者論壇：http://bbs.sunyata.cc
網上書店：http://book.sunyata.cc

香港發行：香港聯合書刊物流有限公司
香港新界大埔汀麗路36號中華商務印刷
大廈3樓
電話號碼：(852)2150-2100
傳真號碼：(852)2407-3062
電郵：info@suplogistics.com.hk

台灣發行：秀威資訊科技股份有限公司
地址：台灣台北市內湖區瑞光路七十六巷
　　　六十五號一樓
電話號碼：+886-2-2796-3638
傳真號碼：+886-2-2796-1377
網絡書店：www.bodbooks.com.tw
心一堂台灣國家書店讀者服務中心：
地址：台灣台北市中山區松江路二0九號1樓
電話號碼：+886-2-2518-0207
傳真號碼：+886-2-2518-0778
網址：www.govbooks.com.tw

中國大陸發行 零售：
　　　深圳心一堂文化传播有限公司
深圳：中國深圳羅湖立新路六號東門
　　　博雅負一層零零八號
電話號碼：(86)0755-82224934
北京：中國北京東城區雍和宮大街四十號
心一堂官方淘寶流通處：
http://sunyatacc.taobao.com/

版次：2019年4月初版

　　　HKD 248
定價：NT　980

國際書號　978-988-8582-62-4

Title: The Life and Adventures of Robinson Crusoe
 (with Chinese translation)
Series: Classic English Literature
Collections with Chinese Translation
Editor: POON, Kwok-Sum(MCIoL,
DipTranCIoL), CHEN, Kim
by Daniel Defoe
Translated and Annotated (in Chinese)
by Richard S.C.HSI

Published in Hong Kong by Sunyata Ltd
Address: Unit 1805-06, 18/F, Hollywood Plaza,610
Nathan Road, Mong Kok, Kowloon, Hong Kong
Tel: (852) 6715-0840
Website: publish.sunyata.cc
Email: sunyatabook@fmail.com
Online bookstore: http://book.sunyata.cc

Distributed in Hong Kong by:
SUP PUBLISHING LOGISTICS(HK)
LIMITED
Address：3/F, C & C Buliding,
36 Ting Lai Road, Tai Po, N.T.,
Hong Kong
Tel：(852) 2150-2100
Fax：(852) 2407-3062
E-mail：info@suplogistics.com.hk

Distributed in Taiwan by:
Showwe Information Co. Ltd.
Address: 1/F, No.65, Lane 76, Rueiguang
Road, Neihu District, Taipei, Taiwan
Website: www.bodbooks.com.tw

First Edition April 2019
HKD 248
NT 980

ISBN: 978-988-8582-62-4